A dozen plans surged through the fisherman's mind . . .

Flee? They would have to travel on foot. They had no horses. They would be caught.

Take the boat and sail away? Perhaps, but the *Arathé* was built for fishing, not speed. Any Neherian rake would run her down, and any Neherian captain would be only too keen to chase a Fossan vessel—particularly his. Hide somewhere in the village? They would be found. Resist? His skills with the sword were as rusty as his blade, and even at their best would barely match what he had seen this morning.

They were given no chance to implement any plan.

Boom, boom, boom came a series of heavy blows on the door. Opuntia shrieked, then put a hand across her mouth. Noetos knew nobody who knocked like that.

Boom, boom, boom.

Arathé knew who it was. She'd got it horribly wrong, had taken far too long to tell her story, and had clearly not been as effective with the Voice as she'd hoped.

The Recruiters had come for her.

By Russell Kirkpatrick

The Fire of Heaven Trilogy

Across the Face of the World

In the Earth Abides the Flame

The Right Hand of God

The Broken Man Trilogy

Path of Revenge

Dark Heart

Beyond the Wall of Time

RUSSELL KIRKPATRICK

PATH *of* REVENGE

www.orbitbooks.net

New York London

Copyright © 2007 by Russell Kirkpatrick
Excerpt from *Dark Heart* copyright © 2008 by Russell Kirkpatrick
All rights reserved. Except as permitted under the U.S. Copyright Act of 1976, no part of this publication may be reproduced, distributed, or transmitted in any form or by any means, or stored in a data base or retrieval system, without the prior written permission of the publisher.

Maps by Russell Kirkpatrick

Orbit
Hachette Book Group USA
237 Park Avenue
New York, NY 10017
Visit our Web site at www.orbitbooks.net

Orbit is an imprint of Hachette Book Group USA, Inc.
The Orbit name and logo is a trademark of Little, Brown Book Group Ltd.

Printed in the United States of America

Originally published by Voyager, Australia: 2007
First Orbit edition: August 2008

10 9 8 7 6 5 4 3 2 1

*To the Down-under
speculative fiction
community*

CONTENTS

OCEANA

70°

Ice Circle

Plutobaran.

60°

Issanes.
The Vollervei.
Iaebone
Stormwave Lake.
Iskelse
SNA
Vapmalak.
VAZTHA.
FIRANES. *PLONIA.*
Imennost.
50°
R. Iglufo
R. Fenbok.
R. Glufo
Ramm. *Ciennan.* *Stantone.*
TREIKA. *R. Lavat.*
R. Sagon.
Lavaeck.
Remparer Mtns.
40° *F A L T H A*
DEUVERRE.
Plafond. *R. Lanus.*
R. Aleinus. *Instruire.* *Kaskyne.* *PISKASIA.*
Wodhaitic Sea. *Mercium.* *REDANA'A.*
Brunhaven. *Vindicare.*
S T R A U X.
30° *DERUIS.* *Tammanoussa.*
Bay of Betwixt *Bi'r Bukhat.* *R. Lifeblood.* *R. Sagssa.* *Desieca.*
Beremy. *Dhauria.*
Northern Tropic *NEMOHAIM.* *Ghadir Massuh.*
20° *SARISTA.*
VERTENSIA. *Kauma.*
Corrigia. *Jardin.* *Dhau Bid.*
10°
Idehan Kahal.

Sea of Kahal.

Equator
Punta Kahal. *J N*
Golfo Muerte. *The* *Bon Muerte*
Maia. *Impenetrab*
10° *OCEANA*
CRYNON *NOMANS*
PROFUNDIA.
Momoa. *Banibaal.*
20° *ANEHRA.* *Anse*
Southern Tropic *QUEDA.*
Tahreyn. *Ette* *Marasmos.*
Desert.
30° *L. Ponna.* *E L A M A Q*
Neve Elama. *The*
40° *STEPE.* *Stone Plain*
Punta
Ogalla.
IDEHAN
Vardingai. *BENAR.*
50° *Mariano.*
·Omen
Turfum·
Plateaux
60° *Lul.* *MOUNTAINS*

Ice Circle
70° *· Ilixa*
Island.

LEGEND.

▨	Woodland	▨	Cropland
▨	Grassland	☐	Barren
▨	Desert		
	Wasteland (Pattern)		
▨	Swamp	▨	Tundra

Nestor's Cylindrical Projection.
Caution: Scale is accurate only along the Equator.

30° 20° 10° 0° 10° 20°

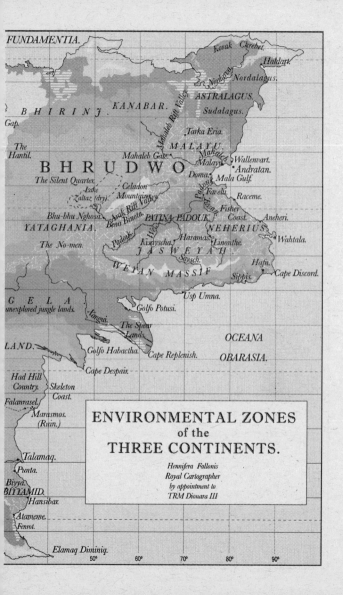

ENVIRONMENTAL ZONES
of the
THREE CONTINENTS.

Hennifera Fallonis
Royal Cartographer
by appointment to
TRM Dionara III

BRONZE MAP

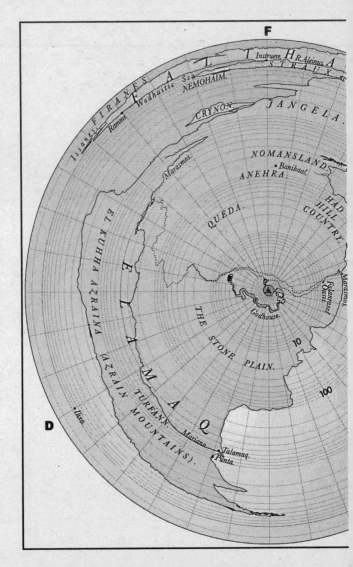

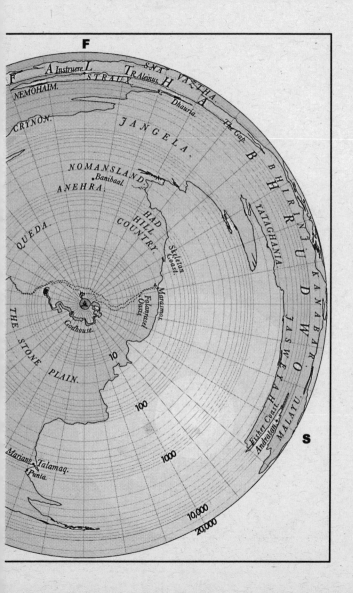

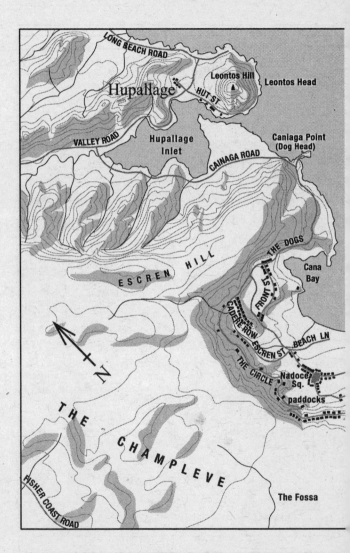

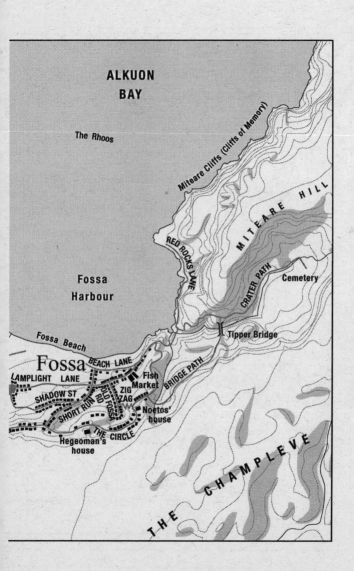

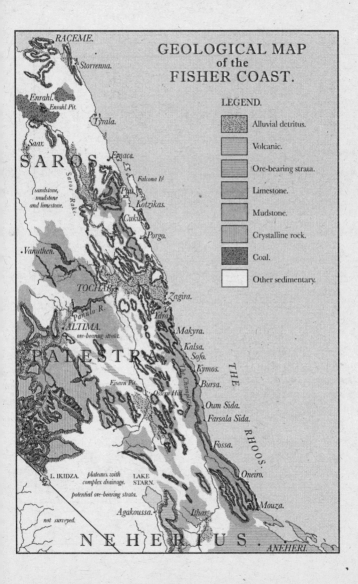

GEOLOGICAL MAP
of the
FISHER COAST.

LEGEND.

Alluvial detritus.

Volcanic.

Ore-bearing strata.

Limestone.

Mudstone.

Crystalline rock.

Coal.

Other sedimentary.

RACEME.

Storrenna.

Enrahl.
Enrahl Pit.

Tyrala.

Saar.

SAROS

Engaca.

Falcona Id

Pux.
Kotzikas.

Cuku.

Porgo.

sandstone,
mudstone
and limestone.

Saros Rake.

Varuthen.

TOCHAR.

Zagira.

Ponalo R.

Tara.

ALTIMA.
ore-bearing strata.

Makyra.

PALESTRA

Kalsa.
Sofo.

Kymos.

THE

Bursa.

Eisarn Pit.

Osten Hill

The Champ.

Oum Sida.

Farsala Sida.

RHOOS

Fossa.

Oneiro.

L. IKIDZA.

plateaux with
complex drainage.

LAKE
STARN.

potential ore-bearing strata.

not surveyed.

Agakoussa.

Ilhar.

Mouza.

NEHERIUS.

ANEHERI.

TALAMAQ

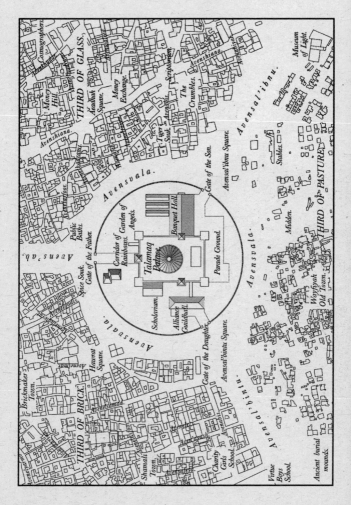

PROLOGUE

HOW TO KILL AN IMMORTAL?

The question whispers along the cold stone walls. It has a life of its own, this question. Husk imagines the words have found a path through the maze of corridors deep beneath Andratan, a route to freedom, so many times has he whispered them over the last seventy years.

Perhaps they have, he thinks. *Perhaps they have*. But freedom, however tempting, is not the path he intends to take. A far more dangerous route invites him onward.

Breathe in.

Searing pain as sweet air mixes with the wreckage of blood-fouled lungs. Agony. Torment. *Must stay strong, must not be sidetracked. Concentrate . . .*

Ah, there!

A fleeting mind-touch, anticipated, expected. Someone walks the corridor. Two people. Warders on their regular rounds. They will expect him to be in his cell, not at large in the corridor. Draw a little from them both, just a little from their memories. There, and there. One of the men stumbles and utters a curse. The mind-touch tells Husk this, who has no ears to hear. He has drawn too much—still careless—but the bright power, so necessary, how can it be resisted? It supplies the strength for thought, for the rational part of his mind to function. For another breath.

Breathe out.

One jailer, new to the task, says something to the other. Husk can feel it, faint currents of air brushing against his open wounds like the promise of healing. He hears the question in the jailer's mind: *what is that dreadful smell?* Husk knows, but he cannot tell. Husk is ashamed, but he is powerless to alter what he is.

Breathe in.

He suppresses the cough reflex. Coughing would set him back days, would consume too much of his carefully pieced-together strength. So much strength required to stave off the pain, to keep the broken body working; so little left to maintain mind contact with those in his thrall. The captain, the priest and the girl. One cough, one spasm such as those he suffered in the early years, and he could lose contact. He worries especially about the girl, the most recent, the most vulnerable of his acquisitions. Lose her, lose the Stone, lose everything.

Breathe out.

In the few moments of clarity he has been able to fashion during seventy years of suffering, Husk has often thought on the impossibility of the task he has set himself. It is all he focuses on. All that matters. Seventy dreadful years. He should have let go in the beginning, should have fallen into the death that hovered so close, but he did not. He has held his betrayal clenched tightly in his hand for so long now he cannot release it, cannot choose death even if he wanted it.

Breathe in.

A known smell nearby. A rat. Plenty of them down

here. They learn to stay away from him. He can draw them to him, kill them with his mind, send his will spiking into their tiny brains. Without the fat, juicy rats he would never have survived. This one scuttles nervously past him on the other side of the corridor. He can sense it, though his eyeless sockets cannot see it. The rat knows about Husk, oh yes.

Breathe out.

How to kill an immortal?

Again and again he asked the darkness, and after so many long and painful years of silence the darkness delivered him an answer.

Breathe in.

Less than two years ago she was sent down here, his answer, his sweet answer. Strongly gifted, she saw through his mask, found him lying on the floor of his cell. Pitied him. *Oh, angel!* He remembers the caress of the cloth she applied to the worst of his wounds, unimaginable balm in the midst of raging pain. He repaid her by driving a small spike of himself into her vulnerable young mind, and there he found her secret.

It was hidden in a sealed-off corner of her memory, too painful to examine until he rooted it out and lanced it with his magic. She was aware of the existence of a Stone, though she did not know what it was or what it could do. Husk knows what it can do. He needs it. With the Stone he can undo the magic of an immortal. With the Stone he can bring his enemy down.

Breathe out.

He lets the breath out slowly, lest excitement overwhelm good sense. His little spike is secure but he checks it just the same, seeing through her eyes, hearing through her ears, though she is many weeks' journey from his prison, part of an expedition he arranged for her to join. They are using her again, but what is that to one such as he who has experienced the horror of being unmade?

Breathe in.

He reviews his plan. The Stone she will bring him is the key to everything. But it will not be sufficient on its own. Just as well, then, that he has set two other opportunistic spikes. The first he drove into the self-deluded mind of a priest from the west, a foolish Falthan spy. The lies Husk taught him will certainly draw forth the Falthan queen, she with the Blood he so desperately needs. The second he set in the naïve mind of a young, brash captain, an explorer from Elamaq, the great southern empire. The temptation he placed there will bring north the Emperor to wield the Stone and take the Blood.

Breathe out.

Husk is in the perfect place to gnaw on his dreams of revenge. The master of this terrible prison can pick the very thoughts out of one's mind, but down here, in the crawling depths of the Undying Man's dungeon, everyone harbours such dreams. Their futile hungers mask Husk's far more powerful desire. He disguises himself, cloaks his continued existence with the rotted hopelessness and petty anger of his cellmates. Here, only here, can he safely put together a plan to destroy his destroyer.

How to kill an immortal?

Using the Stone, the Blood and the Emperor, that is how. Husk will have them all in his hands very soon. And then revenge.

Breathe in. And savour.

FISHERMAN

CHAPTER 1

THE RECRUITERS

THE NORTHERN SUN, tinged with a tired orange at day's end, ebbed slowly towards the dark sea-cliffs. Small white clouds scuttled out of her way like lambs fleeing a farmer's dog. The air remained warm even as the sun weakened, unusual in early spring, especially under a clearing sky. A black-beaked gull hung for a moment against the darkening firmament, then wheeled and, with a cry, plunged into the eggshell-blue water in search of the day's last catch.

Other fishermen wended their way home, their tasks done. Trousers rolled up to their knees, three men talked animatedly together as they walked barefooted across the warm sand. The nets had been full today, the work demanding enough to prevent the men sharing their gossip until now. Of course, such a plentiful catch meant a hard row home, then two hours of hauling nets to the fish market followed by tedious cleaning and repair work; but now, with the sun setting over their shoulders, their nets hung out and their boat beached, the fishermen forgot the stiffness in their backs and began to think about the excitement to come.

"Warm wind tonight," one of them said, an older man with thinning hair and the beginnings of a paunch. "Good for the celebrations."

"Good for the dancing, you mean," said the young man beside him, poking an elbow into his ribs. "You think the warm air will bring out the widow Nellas." All three men laughed.

"Well it might, well it might," the older man agreed. "But I know who else it'll bring out. All of young Mustar's admirers, that's who. Half the cliff-girls will stand there sighing at his magnificent body. None of the dandies who live on The Circle have bodies like that." He leaned over and wagged a finger in Mustar's handsome face. "You keep your shirt on tonight, you hear, or I'll crack your head."

Mustar smiled. "Tonight I oil myself up and leave my shirt at home," he announced. "The cliff-girls can look all they want, but they can't touch. I'm saving myself for the widow Nellas!"

"You're not!" cried the old man, then reddened at their laughter.

"No one will be able to dance," he said, trying to recover his poise. "Not once I take my shirt off. The cobbles will be covered in drool from all the panting tongues."

"Once the Recruiters get a sight of your flabby gut, Sautea, they'll pack up and head straight for Neherius," Mustar said. "Maybe you'd better stay home tonight. I shall go up and suggest it to the Hegeoman." More laughter accompanied the absurd idea that a fisherman could be on speaking terms with the village leader.

"You speak more wisdom than my son," the third man said to Mustar. His voice, though rich and good-natured, was unmistakably one of authority. The prudent man would step lightly around its owner, even when he indulged in gentle mockery, as he did now. "Are you sure you won't be applying for recruitment?"

"Noetos, you know me better than that. I'm far better off working for the Fisher of Fossa than risking my fate up north." Mustar frowned. "Not that there's anything to risk. Arathé, now, she made the right choice."

Noetos laughed and ruffled the young man's hair. "I understand you, lad. Don't think it hasn't been hard for us with my girl in the service of Andratan. But it was all for the best." Unquestioningly for the best. He remembered how the boys of Fossa, Mustar at their head, had lusted after her. Arathé had done well to escape this village and the mean life it promised her.

A position in the service of Andratan. It was what most of them wanted, the young people growing up without prospects below the dark cliffs of Fossa. A chance to be tutored in the arts of magic, to live a useful, meaningful life. Noetos could understand their motivation. There was little for them here.

The three men negotiated the ruts and bumps of Beach Lane as they talked, and off to the west the orange sun touched the cliffs more in surrender than triumph. "Aye, another season like this one and I'll be able to afford the down payment on a boat of my own," the youth continued, then stopped. Embarrassment spread over his features, as though he'd been shamed by speaking his dream aloud, and he rubbed his thin moustache nervously.

"Will you now?" Noetos growled, his brows lowering in mock anger. "A boat of your own! And what will I do for a spotter once you've gone?"

The young man looked around uneasily but found no support from Sautea, who hid behind a poker face. He turned back to Noetos.

"Aaah, Mustar, you think I didn't know about your plans?" the big man boomed. "I've already put the word out amongst the other boats. I'll have no problem finding a spotter when you move on. Maybe I'll get one who can find some fish for me!" he said, and clapped the youngster on the shoulder.

"Four nets' worth of spotting isn't so bad," Mustar said. "I'll do all right on my own. My Pa always said I should aim for my own boat."

"Halieutes would have said that, wouldn't he? It's not as simple as that, of course, not by a long cast. And now he's no longer here to guide you, I suppose you'll be coming to me for advice." The big man's voice was mild.

"Fishing advice, maybe," the handsome youth answered, a sly smile on his lips. "But not dancing advice. I've seen you dance. Have you ever seen a stranded whale flop about on a beach? Kindest thing I could say about your dancing. Perhaps I could trade you advice?"

"I don't need advice," Fisher Noetos said, smiling in turn. "Unlike you, lad, I am married, and so no longer need to dance." He spun around and pointed a finger at Sautea, whose mouth was open. "And don't you say anything!"

The older man grinned. "Wouldn't dream of it, my friend," he said, merriment wrapped around the words. "You may not care to dance, but we Old Fossans would love to see you at the gathering tonight. No one cares that you are a cliff-man now. Will you come?"

A frown creased Noetos's brow. "I doubt Opuntia will

wish to go. She will want to remain home to prepare my son for the Recruiters. Sorry, Sautea. Pass on my regards to the widow Nellas, and if she chooses to dance with you, tell her to wear her heaviest boots." The jest was forced, but Sautea laughed regardless.

They reached the junction of Beach Lane and Short Run. Normally the three men would share the road up the gentle slope of Short Run, turn left onto Lamplight Lane, Fossa's main road, then right into Old Fossa Road, where the fishermen lived with their families. Noetos would leave them there, as he had each day for the past two years, and climb the steep Zig Zag up the side of the cliff to The Circle, the road that wound its way around the cliff that enfolded Fossa, holding her close to the sea. Today, however, pleading a stiffness in his joints, he bade them farewell at the bottom of Short Run and continued south along Beach Lane towards the place where The Circle descended towards the sea along a spur of rock. The two men, the old and the young, watched their master walk slowly away, rubbing his shoulder as he went.

"I'll always live in Old Fossa, just like Pa did, even when I'm rich enough to own four boats," the youth declared fervently.

"Then don't marry for beauty alone," his companion replied.

Noetos kept massaging his shoulder until he was sure his friends had vanished up Short Run, then relaxed and lengthened his stride. The deception was necessary, though he couldn't identify the impulse that sent him the longer way home. *Am I so ashamed of my choice to live on the cliff that I will no longer walk through Old Fossa?*

Or is it my choice not to attend the celebrations tonight that sees me behaving like a cliff-man?

He looked inward, despising himself, *Never a cliff-man*, he vowed, as he always did, though he knew the vow was hollow. He lived on the cliff, right on The Circle in a place of honour, and had done since everything had changed two years ago this very night, the last time the Recruiters had come to Fossa. Opuntia had been beside herself with happiness when their daughter had been chosen.

Dusk settled around his shoulders like a cloak of guilt as Noetos reached the beginning of The Circle. He began the climb he had promised himself never to take—another vow broken—then turned and looked out angrily over Fossa and the small world that had smothered him every day of his adult life.

For a hundred leagues north and south of here the Fisher Coast was the same: a land of rolling hills and waving grasses, fertile and forest-sprinkled, ended abruptly to the east by a cliff plunging hundreds of paces to the blue-green ocean. Here and there the waves had taken bites out of the land, and long ago fisher-folk had fashioned cliff-dwellings in these deep, protective embayments from which they could raid the sea. People had been living in places like Fossa for thousands of years, long before nations like Rhoudhos came into existence, long before the Undying Man welded those nations together into one mighty land called Bhrudwo.

Other fishing villages grew, became great ports, centres of trade and commerce, places of renown; but Fossa remained small, hedged in by tall cliffs, pinched against the ocean. Noetos looked up, his eye tracing the cliff-top arcing away ahead and to his right. He turned his head further to where the dark walls enclosed Fossa Harbour, separating it from the wider expanse of Alkuon Bay and the reefs on the edge of sight. *The cliffs*, he thought wearily, *the damn cliffs that dominate us all, shaping our very lives*.

As always when prey to such moods his mind filled with images from his father's stories. The wide plains and beautiful cities of Rhoudhos, lost forever. His grandfather burning at the stake, flames in his grey hair, stubbornly defying the Undying Man. The great decline following his death. Rhoudhos thrown to the Neherian wolves, who almost swallowed it whole, leaving Saros and Palestra to absorb the remnants. Fields fired, stately buildings torn down, books and artwork burned, bodies left in piles to rot. A time for savages.

Nothing but pain ever came of such reminiscence.

He was now high enough that he could look down into Old Fossa, a collection of huts and lean-tos, the place he had lived until two years ago. A few lights indicated that some still had not left for the celebrations. His gaze rested fondly on the roof of the small house he had purchased with the last of his father's money. The house where he and Opuntia had brought up two children. He tried not to wish things had remained the way they were. He tried to imagine things were better now with a child a thousand leagues to the north, a wife who cared only that she had finally climbed out of Old Fossa to her new house on the cliff, a boat named after the beautiful girl whom they had sent away, and a son who seemed determined to follow in her footsteps. He tried hard, but he had never possessed a good imagination.

The Circle finally brought him up to the first cliffhouses.

Made of cliff-stones, individually selected and carefully
mortared together, these houses were far more substantial
than those in Old Fossa below. Up here on the cliff lived
the rich farmers, merchants and members of the town
council, including the Hegeoman who ruled them all. The
cliff-folk grudgingly allowed space for one fisher-family
to live on the heights, by agreement the most able (the
wealthiest, in their eyes). The house Noetos now occupied had been lived in by fishermen for hundreds of
years—until the time of Halieutes, Mustar's renowned
father.

Halieutes, the greatest Fisher Fossa had ever known.
He who had taken his one-man boat out through The
Rhoos and into the open sea that now belonged to the Neherian fleet, not once but many times. He stole the fish
from under their long, pointed noses, becoming a legend
to all in Fossa and the first fisherman in centuries to be a
genuine cliff-hero.

But Halieutes, despising the honour offered by the
Hegeoman, never lived in the cliff-house set aside for
him.

The cobbled road beneath Noetos's feet bent momentarily to the right, then around to the left as the spur
joined the cliffs proper. Here sat the cliff-house allocated
to the Fisher of Fossa, positioned directly above Old
Fossa as though the cliff-men wanted him to remember
his elevation from the despised huts and shanties—and
to think on how swift might be the fall back down. Living in the cliff-house had been such heady pleasure in
those first few weeks, the title of fisher giving as much
satisfaction as the house itself and the glorious views
over the harbour. But the excitement had faded in the two

years since, and he had begun to doubt that the price he had paid was worth it.

Up the narrow path he went and, with a sigh, opened the front door.

Anomer stood in the centre of the gathering room, hands clasped behind his back, answering rapid-fire questions from his mother. She concentrated on the history of the Fisher Coast, with emphasis on the time since it had been drawn into the Bhrudwan ambit. The Recruiters asked those questions when working in these parts, knowing as they did the legacy of resistance to Bhrudwan rule along the coast. Few Fossans were accepted for service, partly because such history was usually suppressed, but Noetos and Opuntia believed in a wide education and taught their children far more than what was offered in the school. Eyes bright, the tall, thin youth answered with confidence, the words forcing their way past his Adam's apple even before his mother had finished asking the question.

"We're so proud of you!" she said in the breathless voice Noetos hated so much. The boy was nearly a man, not a six-year-old child. "Surely you will be chosen to join your sister!"

The fisherman half-turned to his wife, then thought better of it. She simply would not hear his criticism. Time and again he had told her that the odds were stacked against their son's selection, but she had convinced herself otherwise. Instead he looked his son in the eye.

"Have you practised the sword today?" This was Anomer's weakest skill. He would understand the point of the question. *Don't hope for too much, son.*

"I have," he said confidently, though he did offer a

small nod to his father in acknowledgment of the unspoken caution.

Noetos quirked a shaggy eyebrow: *do you really understand your chances?*

"Don't worry," the boy said solemnly. "I will endeavour to do my best to please you both." So proper.

Noetos smiled at his son. "You already have, Anomer. Now I suggest you soon seek out your bed and wrestle from it what sleep you can. Tiredness will take the edge off your skills."

Anomer nodded and strode off towards his room, his willowy limbs impossibly graceful, just like his sister, just like his mother. *Unlike his father.* Turning to his wife, Noetos marvelled again at her beauty: her high cheekbones, her clear, bronzed skin, her dark eyes. *Hollow, all hollow*, the fisherman reflected. He held his admiration largely at arm's length these days. It seemed Opuntia had everything she wanted, an everything that no longer included him.

Of late a question had been growing in the fisherman's mind. How could his wife's desires not have included watching her girl grow into womanhood? Noetos had not realised just how much he would miss his sparkly-eyed daughter, and he cast a glance over to the far corner of the room where stood a small bust of his daughter's head, carved from a pale green sea-stone he'd found a few years ago, a pretty thing shot through with white swirls.

Five gold pieces it had cost him to have it carved, a full twentieth part of what he had sold her for; a foolish extravagance that had bought him fat less peace of mind than he'd hoped at the time. He'd never told Opuntia about the expense, inflating the price of the boat to hide the cost.

He'd dismissed his crew on the afternoon his daughter had been accepted by the Recruiters, then taken the boat himself around Dog Head to Hupallage, where a master carver plied his trade. There the carving had been swiftly completed, the old man working from charcoal drawings Noetos made from memory.

That night Noetos showed his daughter the sculpture he'd paid so much for. She had been flattered but puzzled, and asked him why he had done something so sentimental when it was so unnecessary. "Do not fear, I will return to you," she'd said, her voice filled with excitement. "Then you can put the carving aside." He'd smiled at her, and in the weeks following her departure his eyes had returned often to the smiling face sitting atop its plain whitestone plinth.

Now all he had left of the money paid him by the Recruiters were memories in charcoal and stone. Why, then, was he allowing his only remaining child to try for recruitment?

"Now that Anomer has retired, I'm thinking of taking a walk down to the beach," Noetos said casually, an eye on Opuntia as he spoke. She stiffened, and he could read everything she was about to say from the set of her shoulders.

"I'll convey your apologies to your friends," he said before she could respond. The remark was calculated to hurt her. "Saphis and Hudora are certain to be there, and Sautea is going to drag Nellas along. Not that she'll take much dragging." He kept his voice light, carefully goading her. "Must be ages since you last saw Nellas. You did hear that her husband died? What was his name again?"

She turned and drew herself up, her mouth the thinnest

of lines. "Very well, Fisher," she said icily, her eyes boring into his own. "Go down to the beach and play with your friends. I will make up a pallet in the hallway for you, so that when you return, stumbling and stinking, you do not disturb those of us who wish to keep civilised hours."

"Are you sure you will not come with me?" he asked her, putting all of himself in the question. Her eyes widened momentarily, but then narrowed again.

"One of us must remain responsible, Noetos. Go ahead, creep down the lane to another night of coarse talk and drunkenness, but do not expect me to be party to your childishness."

"I'm not creeping, I'm letting you know—"

"I have been invited to the house of our Hegeoman for drinks and conversation," she said, a slight smile at one corner of her mouth the only betrayal of her excitement. "There we will meet the Recruiters. I may be able to speak on Anomer's behalf."

"So be it. You go and fawn all over your betters. Do whatever you can to sell our son off like a slave, just as you did our daughter. See if you can earn us another boat! Shall we call this one the *Anomer*?" He took a deep, steadying breath, but it did nothing to curb his anger. "How many fish is our son worth? How far up The Circle do we have to climb, Opuntia? Go on, go and see if you can win further favours from the Hegeoman and all his cursed cliff-born friends. Just don't go giving them any favours of your own!"

He stood there, breathing heavily, in a kind of shock, having with that last sally broken yet another vow. He had intended never voicing his suspicions, but it was too late now, far too late.

The blood drained from her face, leaving a pasty mask limned with hatred. "You stupid, thick-headed man," she hissed, reaching him in a stride and striking him across the face. "You know nothing. You are the anchor that would drag us back down to our old hut. The fools of Old Fossa call you a hero just because you are too idiotic to stay inside the harbour. But when I go fishing for far more important things, I get nothing but anger in return."

"That's the first time you've touched me in months," Noetos said quietly. "The last time was almost as abrupt, as I recall."

She stepped away from him, contempt on her face and in the way she held herself. "You had promise once," she whispered, and to his surprise she wiped a tear from her eye. "I remember loving you so much. I loved your daring, your spark, your intelligence. I loved the way you gave up everything for me. But somewhere along the way you took it all back. Now you love only your friends and your fish. Is it any wonder our love died? Is it any wonder I—" She clamped her mouth shut, but could not prevent the flush spreading across her neck.

"You what, Opuntia? No, don't tell me; I don't want to hear it." Noetos felt suddenly tired. "Keep your sordid life to yourself, and I'll keep my selfish life to mine." He turned away from her, and only then noticed the white face of his son staring at them both from the half-opened halfway door.

Slamming the door had been an unnecessary gesture, Noetos acknowledged to himself as he hurried down the Zig Zag. He knew he had precipitated the argument, and was prepared to admit that he'd used his words like barbs, callously setting them in Opuntia's ready mouth. He shouldn't have been surprised, then, when she'd struggled on his hook. What had hurt him far more than her words, her near-admission, was the look on Anomer's face. It was the face of his son that hung accusingly in his mind, and from which he sought to flee by rushing to the beachside celebrations.

A four-fifths moon, more yellow than white, hung just above the water as he found the sand at the end of Beach Lane. The tide was on the wane, an hour past full. At the touch of the wet sand on his feet Noetos ceased being a father and a husband. His shoulders loosened, his pace slowed and the heavy weight disappeared from the pit of his stomach.

A few hundred paces to his left the celebrations had already spilled out onto the beach. A bonfire flickered fitfully, having not long been lit, and fire-blurred silhouettes ran back and forth across the dark sand. Good-natured shrieks drifted along the beach towards the fisherman and in response a great hunger rose within him for the earnest discussion of friends, dancing, good food and laughter. Above all, laughter. Ah, how his weary soul needed laughter.

Not yet. He slowed himself still further, searching within for the control he had so spectacularly lost back at his house. Hitching up his robe, he walked out into the gentle surf as though he traversed a bridge of light towards the moon. Sand and water hissed around his feet, his ankles and then his knees. Fifty paces from the shore he stopped, allowing the push and pull of the sea to wash away what it could.

By the time he turned back towards the beach the moon

had risen well above the distant reefs, shrinking and whitening as it always did on spring nights like this. He'd tried night fishing but it held no enjoyment and little profit for him. The Rhoos could not be navigated at night, and in the darkness it felt to Noetos as though the cliffs surrounded him on all sides. Only beyond the reefs, out past the huge breakers in the deep Neherian fishing grounds, could he feel free of them.

Now he allowed himself to walk more quickly along the beach, drawn with longing towards the lights and sounds of friendship. He splashed in the shallows like the child he once had been. By the time he reached the celebrations his robe was wet all the way to his waist, and tears glistened on his cheeks.

His fragile mood did not last. Noetos had never been a sociable drunk: alcohol made him argumentative and poor company. He had a couple of dances, sang along with the fiddlers and sampled the seared fish from the braziers near the beach, but tonight nothing could keep him from noticing what he had always tried to deny. His Old Fossan friends wanted little to do with him. The bitter knowledge sent him back to the beer-barrels, where he handed over a few coppers for two mugs of ale.

Just how pathetic am I? He drew down the beer and waited for someone to join him.

Mustar had already lost his shirt. Just as Sautea had anticipated, a group of cliff-girls had gathered around him, dressed in their finery and with far too much flesh showing. The fool had begun boasting, exaggerating his deeds on the fishing grounds, not realising that none of them would take him seriously, that every word he spoke emphasised what a poor catch he'd make for a cliff-girl, no matter how his muscles glowed in the firelight. They'd play him on their line, one after the other, but eventually they'd throw him back. When Noetos wandered over towards the group, a mug in each hand, Mustar was talking about the new boat he was going to purchase. Fool boy.

"Took me twenty years to get my own boat," Noetos interrupted in a thick voice. "That's because I wanted one that could navigate The Rhoos. I couldn't have afforded *Arathé* without the money the Recruiters paid. Not just the boat. The equipment costs near as much as the boat itself, and you have to lay plenty aside to pay your men's wages in the lean times." He gestured as he spoke, spilling ale on the sand. "Have to earn enough to buy pretty things for your wife."

Mustar had clearly not listened. "My own boat!" he said fiercely, the smiles of the cliff-girls egging him on. "Then maybe I could fish outside the reef, and drive those cursed Neherians away from our beds!"

Noetos turned on the youth. "Forget about the Neherians. They own the Fisher Coast, have done for generations. They tolerate me for now; I'm no real threat to them. Halieutes was another matter."

Another voice intruded into his argument. "Noetos, friend, not tonight." Sautea put a warning hand on his captain's shoulder, but the red-haired man shook it off.

"If not tonight, then when? Mustar announces he's leaving us, if not this year then the next, for his own boat. Going out beyond the reef, he says. Wants to chase the Neherians away. Does anyone think this has nothing to do with Halieutes?"

"No, Noetos—"

"Yes, Noetos! Here's a question for you! Why does the child always have to be sacrificed for the dreams of the parent? Halieutes lay for months in his cot before he died. His own stupidity put him there, not the tortures of the Neherians, barbarians though they are. Even on his back he learned no wisdom. He should have kept his mouth shut rather than encouraging his son to emulate his legendary feats. What will satisfy the shade of your father, Mustar? When you become Fisher of Fossa in my place, go out beyond The Rhoos once too often in your new boat and watch as they carve away the skin of your crew with their knives? When they are staked out on the rocks for the tide, screaming for release, will it be praise you hear your father's voice speak? Will you look kindly on his advice as you sink, netwrapped, to the bottom of the sea, waiting for your breath to give out or for the sharks to find you?"

He stopped, sour-stomached and out of breath, and realised he had been shouting. The cliff-girls had drawn back into the shadows beyond the bonfire, back towards Lamplight Lane where the fiddlers played their shanties. Mustar looked at his master, stony-faced.

"My father spoke highly of you," the youth said, his voice stretched as though he was reluctant to let go of the words. "He said you were a man of courage. But he never told me you were blind."

"Blind? I see more clearly than anyone in this circle of death!" Noetos shouted, waving his arms around and spilling ale everywhere. "Would that it were I for sale in the Recruiters' meat market on the morrow rather than my own son! Then perhaps I could go somewhere that has some meaning!"

Without warning a strong arm took his hand and forced

it up his back. "Then go home, Noetos, and find your
meaning there," said Sautea. "I know you could break my
grip, friend, but don't try, for your own sake."

Noetos decided not to resist, and was propelled gently
up the beach towards Lamplight Lane. There, under a
brightly burning lamp, stood half a dozen robed and
cowled figures. The Recruiters. Not at the Hegeoman's
house after all. That set Noetos laughing, a sour laugh that
burned in his gut.

The hoods of the Recruiters turned away from the
sight; all but one, which followed the progress of the cursing drunk until he vanished into the shrouded distance.

The tension in the cliff-house was unbearable the following morning, the absence of healing words far more hurtful than the sharp words spoken the previous night; and it
was with considerable relief that the family of Noetos the
fisherman made their way along The Circle to Short Run,
then down Shadow Street to Nadoce Square on Lamplight
Lane. There the candidates for selection presented themselves to the Recruiters, and a large crowd gathered to
watch.

Noetos and Opuntia sat on the benches provided for
relatives of the candidates. The fisherman couldn't help
noticing that his wife sat as far from him as she could
without occasioning comment. She had been waiting up
for him when he returned the previous night, an unpleasant surprise as he had expected her to remain late at the
Hegeoman's house. No doubt the party had broken up
when the Recruiters had left for the beach. She'd said
nothing, even after he had vomited on the clean white tiles
of their kitchen. *If I'd taken out a knife and gutted myself,*

she still would have said nothing, Noetos reflected bitterly. I am *blind. How could I not have seen what was going on?*

Six Recruiters had come to Fossa this time. All six were robed in grey with deep cowls that covered their heads, making it difficult to discern much about them apart from their sex. Five men, one woman. Usually only four came on their biennial sweep through the Fisher Coast, though as Noetos watched he saw that four of the six were true Recruiters, responsible for testing the candidates. The other two were servants.

It was said that the Recruiters were failed aspirants to the rank of *Maghdi Dasht*. These *Maghdi Dasht*, an ancient term meaning "Heart of the Desert", were the most powerful of the Undying Man's servants, skilled in magic and warcraft, and reported directly to him. The Recruiters, hardly less powerful, also answered only to Andratan. This meant they were above the laws of any country they passed through. Truly a law unto themselves.

A young lad from Escren Street fenced with one of the figures, both using training swords. The lad's movements were small, tight, as though he was not prepared to risk being hit—or, more likely, simply too scared to move freely. He'd never be selected.

The Recruiters sought soldiers, minstrels, scholars and leaders. They favoured candidates who were outstanding in one skill over those merely competent in all four, but inadequacy in any of the four skills would disqualify an aspirant. The Recruiters did not have to choose a candidate from any particular village, though they did, apparently, have a quota to fill from the Fisher Coast. The chosen ones were taken to Andratan, where Bhrudwo's best tutors would teach them magical arts designed to enhance their natural talents, whatever was necessary for a lifetime's service to the Undying Man. The rewards were immense. Power, wealth, meaning, everything a dead-end place like Fossa lacked. A hundred gold coins were paid immediately to the family of the one chosen, and another hundred to the village Hegeoman or City Factor. With such an incentive the Hegeoman traditionally paid for a beachfront celebration the night before the Testing, and actively encouraged the youth of the village to present themselves as candidates. Not that their parents needed persuading. A hundred gold coins was sufficient for a family to live on for years; enough to bribe the Hegeoman into opening the cliff-house to Noetos the fisherman, with enough remaining to purchase the *Arathé*. "Something for you, something for me," Opuntia had said, ever practical. *But she never realised that I hate being a fisherman.* Both the house and the boat were parting gifts from the daughter to her mother, and everyone but Opuntia knew it.

The Escren Street lad finally decided to strike out with his blade, throwing himself towards the cowled Recruiter with a lack of balance that would have seen him killed in a battle or duel. The hooded shape drifted half a pace back, then twisted sideways and dealt the ill-prepared youth a nasty blow on the shins and another between the shoulders before he could react. Noetos raised his eyebrows. The cloth-draped arm had been blindingly quick. The lad's eyes watered and he dropped his sword.

One of the two servants, clearly a scribe, made a strike across a piece of parchment. The other servant gazed at the dwindling line of candidates, not shifting her gaze even when hailed by one of the Recruiters.

The scribe called out, "Anomer tal Noetos!" Opuntia stiffened beside him, and their son walked slowly, elegantly, out into the cobbled square. The first test. Noetos gripped the bench.

A Recruiter tossed a practice sword to Anomer, who caught it by the hilt. Noetos nodded. He'd taught the boy the importance of confidence at the beginning of swordplay. Knowledge not expected of a fisherman, certainly, but Noetos had told his family he'd learned his bladecraft in border skirmishes as a young man. Not so far from the truth. "Make the first move," he had instructed Anomer. "Take the game to your opponent. Don't sit back. You'll not be able to move when the time comes otherwise."

Anomer made the first move: a clumsy thrust that he somehow turned into a feint. It drew the cloaked figure in close, only to find that the tall, thin boy had leapt to the left and now drove in with a much crisper thrust. The Recruiter leaned back and dealt with the blow, though with difficulty, deflecting it along the length of his own blade.

"Good move," Noetos muttered. The little rascal had cooked that one up on his own.

The Recruiter took the initiative, grasping his sword in both hands and launching a furious series of strokes. Anomer barely countered them. Noetos could not tell whether the cloaked man held himself in reserve.

A series of strokes later—as quick as Anomer could deliver, quick enough to make the Recruiter work—his son was ordered to put up his sword.

"Very good balance," came a composed, high-pitched northern accent from within the cowl. "You show promise. Is the sword your best skill, youngster?"

"No, lord." Anomer's voice was clear and undaunted. No sign of exertion. "I believe it the least of my skills."

"And your best?" The voice was piqued with interest.

"Intelligence, lord."

"Is that so? Ataphaxus!" the cowled figure snapped. Another of the Recruiters sprang forward, a question already on his lips.

"Tell me, youth, why will the Neherians always dominate the Fisher Coast?"

Noetos drew a startled breath, and the gathered crowd murmured uneasily. What sort of question was that?

As if in answer, Ataphaxus the Recruiter turned to the benches. "It is not enough to know the things that are. True intelligence seeks to understand the reasons *why* these things are." The undercurrent of whispering grew louder among the benches. What were his words if not designed to provoke?

Anomer shrugged his shoulders. "If I was truly wise I would not try to answer this question in such a public place, here in front of my friends and family. However, I can offer you this thought, my lord. It is a matter of population. The Neherians are a numerous people, and they have a wide view of the world from their favoured harbours. We Fossans are few, and see no further than our own sheltered bay. The Neherians dominate the Fisher Coast because they look beyond it. We are contained by our harbour because we see all we need within it."

"And with this in mind, which Fisher country supplies the most recruits for Andratan?"

"Palestra, my lord," Anomer answered promptly. "Neherius would, all other things being equal, but their lords do not allow the very best of their youth to be examined by the Recruiters. Thus they extend their advantage over their neighbours because they see humans as more valuable than the gold they are exchanged for."

Dangerous! Noetos gripped the bench until his knuckles whitened. Anomer had succeeded in offending everyone present. He offended Fossa and all the other fishing villages by saying they were not as clever as the Neherians, who owed their advantage to the strategy of avoiding the Recruiters. He offended the Recruiters by claiming they were being duped by Neherius. *Could this be true? And, if so, how could Anomer possibly know it?*

His son was left standing in the middle of the square, sword still in his hand, while all four Recruiters huddled together. Before Noetos could do more than worry, they turned to face the boy.

"You, Anomer tal Noetos, have finished here. You will return to your home with your family and await our pleasure. In the meantime, we call Siela tar Follia."

Within moments the bewildered boy and his parents found themselves outside Nadoce Square and on Lamplight Lane, walking home along an empty street.

"What are they going to do to us?" Opuntia moaned. "What are they going to do?"

Noetos ignored her and placed an arm around his son. He had no answer for the question his wife posed, and wondered how long they would have to wait.

A cool afternoon sea breeze had dragged in pale clouds by the time a sharp rap echoed in the living room of the Fisher house. For quick raps, then even before Noetos could rouse himself from his couch, four more. Rushed, insistent, not like the self-assured deliberateness the

Recruiters had shown this morning. He hurried to the door.

Behind him Opuntia drew her arms tight around Anomer, whose grim face hadn't changed for hours, no matter what foolish things his mother had said. They would be slain on the spot, she'd exclaimed, or taken out to Nadoce Square and publicly executed as an example to all who dared criticise Bhrudwan policy. Later she had rallied and spent an hour trying to convince herself that they would be commended for their son's brave words, and he would be appointed as the Hegeoman's adviser. Both scenarios were nonsense, Noetos thought, but he was not prepared to admit how closely some of her thoughts mirrored his own.

The fisherman took a settling breath and pulled open the door just as the cloaked and cowled figure made to rap on it again. The figure jerked back, then rushed past in a rustle of cloth. Before Noetos knew it he found himself seated on his couch beside his wife and son, with the Recruiter standing before him, sword out, tip resting on the tiles.

Only one? Where were the others? Could they fight this one off if he went to strike at them? Why had he not thought to fetch his sword down from its place in the roof?

The figure standing there was not a Recruiter. It was the female servant. Her wide-hipped, full-breasted shape had been obscured by her grey robe.

"What do you want with us?" Noetos asked, struggling to keep the fear out of his voice. "What have we done to offend your masters?"

Still the figure said nothing. Then, in a smoth gesture that Noetos jerked away from, she let the sword fall to the floor and swept her cowl back, revealing a swollen face, deep, ravaged eyes and a shockingly bald head. Opuntia gave a cry of fright, then held her tongue.

"I repeat: what do you want with us?" the fisherman asked again. Something was not right here, his soldier's sense told him, and an air of deadly danger settled on the room.

The servant opened her mouth and made a sound like a baby crying. Some sort of foreign language? No, not a language. The woman made the noise again, waving her arms in what was undoubtedly frustration, tears leaking out of her eyes. What was going on here?

"Ahhh . . . waay! Ahh . . . WAAAY!" said the woman, then opened her mouth and pointed to it.

"She has no tongue," said Anomer, horrified. "She can't talk."

"What are you trying to say to us?" Noetos stood, as though there was something he could do to help her. The woman shook with something like rage, waved her arms again and pointed to them, then to herself.

"I don't know what she's saying," the fisherman said, pity in his voice. "Perhaps we should go and get the Recruiters."

"Nnnn! Nnnnnn!" the servant cried, shaking her head vigorously. She swept a desperate glance around the room, then cried in triumph and strode over to the plinth holding the bust of Arathé. Before any of them could stop her she took the plinth in one hand, held it up, pointed to herself and then to the carving.

"Ahhway!" she said.

Opuntia jerked to her feet, screamed as though taken by a sword, then fell to the floor.

The truth eluded Noetos a moment longer. He turned from his unconscious wife to look again at . . . at . . .

His daughter.

No, no, not his daughter, not his sweet Arathé. Not her, please Alkuon, not her. But he looked at the bust on the plinth and looked again at the raddled servant of the Recruiters, and the dreadful truth hooked him.

Oh, no. God of the sea, please, no.

Everything blurred. His feet didn't seem to move, but somehow he found himself holding his daughter, crying into her robe, then pulling his weeping wife to her feet, and none of it was true, but here stood his daughter, sobbing; face buried in his shoulder. Anomer still as death on the couch . . . *Oh, Arathé, what have they done to you?*

Gradually things began to come back into focus, but his eyes beheld a different world. A world in which someone could do dreadful things to his daughter without his knowledge, a world in which he was powerless to undo the damage that had been done. *Her tongue!* She had been such an eloquent, passionate speaker, shaming him again and again with her zeal and her forthright views, and it had been this passion two years ago that attracted the notice of the Recruiters. A leader, they announced, and took her . . . but in truth he had offered her up to them. Sold her. Now he witnessed the result of the transaction.

What else had been done to her? He looked on his daughter and forced himself to smile, and was rewarded with a wan smile in return, breaking his heart. She had been willow-thin two years ago, but now she was large, possibly twice the size she had been. Her eyes, once so clear, were dark holes in her face. Lines, folds and open sores covered her skin, which seemed

that of an old woman. Her hair was gone completely:
eyebrows as well as scalp-hair.

What was left? Oh mercy, Arathé was still there, buried
somewhere within that awful disguise, he could feel it.
Alkuon be thanked, something remained.

"What happened to you, Arathé?" Anomer stood beside
him, his first movement since the truth had been revealed.
"Can you tell us what happened?" His voice was clear,
calm, soothing.

"Aaa . . . waaah . . . ahhhn," said the tongueless mouth.
Eyes begging for understanding. Noetos had no idea what
she meant.

"Andratan?" Anomer hazarded, and was rewarded by a
quick smile, a faint echo of the sister she'd once been.
"They did this to you in Andratan? Why?"

"Nnooh . . . obaay," she replied, every sound an effort,
her mouth moving in exaggerated fashion to form the
words.

"You wouldn't obey them?" The boy's eyes were
bright, as though solving one of the wooden puzzles he'd
loved as a child. His sister nodded again.

Then she raised her hands and began to speak further,
using her palms and fingers to make the sibilant and frica-
tive sounds she could not manage with her mouth. Noetos
was drawn into the puzzle, his mind whirring to learn the
keys to this new language of mouth-vowels and hand-
consonants, while behind them on the couch his wife
sobbed unconsolably.

"Maay (clap) me (hand signal) eernnh mah (two-finger
flick on thumb) (clap)."

"Make me learn . . ." Noetos shrugged. His daughter
nodded.

"Maah (finger flick) (clap)."

"Magic!" cried Anomer. His sister nodded, tears running down her cheeks.

"Fff . . . eww (tap on cheek) baaah (fist into palm)."

"It felt bad. The magic made you feel bad?" She nodded again to her brother.

"(Fist into palm) aaaynn (two-finger flick on thumb)," she said, pointing behind her to the door.

"Danger!" Anomer said. "Danger? Someone comes?"

"(Rub hands together) Oon!" Soon!

"The Recruiters? You have escaped from the Recruiters?" She nodded again, soberly this time.

"They made me their slave," she told them, in a series of halting sounds and hand signals. "They brought me south with them, not knowing this is where I come from."

"Why did they take out your tongue?" Anomer asked her. To Noetos it seemed as though the years had peeled away like scales, and his son and daughter once again played the word games they had delighted in as children.

Oh, if only.

"Not them. I refused to learn magic, even though I had the best Voice they had heard in Andratan for years. It felt foul. It kept making me sick. I told them I would not learn it, so they cut out my tongue and made me a slave for anyone on Andratan to use."

The fisherman's mind went white for a moment, then cooled again. Unspeakable cruelty in the place they had been taught was an island of grandeur, of greatness.

"We don't have time for this." Noetos tried to work out how long his daughter had been here. Minutes, just minutes. "Surely they will be coming after you?"

No, she explained. Not yet. She had tried what she believed she'd never be able to do again, and forced her clumsy mouth to shape the magical Voice she had learned in Andratan. To her astonishment she had been partially successful, turning the Recruiters' early afternoon sleep into something more substantial, but still a long way short of the deep unconsciousness she had willed. She had taken up one of their swords, ready to slay them all; but they had been kind to her, after a fashion, kinder at least than the tutors of Andratan, and so she had not been able to strike any of them with it. In the end she had settled for cloaking them with deep layers of sleep, enough to keep them immobile until evening.

Though reassured, Noetos moved around the room as his daughter spoke, gathering things they would need if they had to leave. Opuntia saw what he was doing and followed suit.

Hurrying, always hurrying, but still pitifully slow, Arathé told them her story, while Anomer translated. She had been taken to Andratan in honour, one with the Voice, capable of harnessing the wild Water magic. She would serve the Undying Man himself. Such honour! The first few weeks were marvellous, even though the cold fortress made her uncomfortable, as she learned from her masters how to manipulate the flows of Water magic bound within her. So easily, so powerfully, could she wield it her teachers speculated that as the daughter of a fisherman she must have been exposed to a source of Water magic as a child.

But soon she baulked at the demands the magic put on her—and, she noticed, on those around her. It seemed that the more she used the Voice, the more she drew . . . something . . . from those nearby. Her tutors began to bring servants and criminals to sit in the corner of the room where she trained, and at the end of each session they lay unconscious where they had fallen. She asked her teachers why this was so, and was not above shaping the questions with her Voice to draw out the answers she sought. Eventually she pieced together what no one would tell her: the magic of the Voice used the strength of others to operate.

Arathé rejected her gift then, gentle child, and nothing her tutors said could change her mind. She had expected at worst to be put off the island, and had been shocked beyond belief when the hooded men came for her and took her deep beneath the fortress to the most dreadful place. She had cried out her tutors' names at first, then when the men guided the knife towards her mouth she had shouted for her father, the last clear words she would ever utter.

They had kept her there for an indeterminate time, then had taken her back up to the teaching rooms where her former tutors used her cruelly. They force-fed her to make her gain weight, and every day would place her in the corner of the room while some young acolyte or other learned how to harness the Voice. Drawing from her. None of the acolytes were as good as she had been, but she took little comfort from that.

Six months ago she had become too weak even for such use, so had been put out of the castle and taken to a city called Malayu on the mainland. There the Recruiters had received her and pressed her into less onerous service, still draining her when the Voice or other magic was required, but far less often than on Andratan. Her periods of consciousness lasted much longer now, and she began to fight her new masters in ways they would not notice; at first a series of small defiances, then by teaching herself a language of sorts in case she ever had a chance to communicate. How she had wished she could speak to the eager youths of the Fisher Coast during her journey southwards, to warn them of what awaited them in Andratan, but she was never given a chance.

She had wondered why they brought her southwards along the coast. Surely they could have assigned her to another Recruiting Cabal? Or did they know nothing of her history? Gradually it dawned on her that they saw her as completely powerless and had not bothered to ask her Andratan tutors anything about her past. There was little about her current appearance that marked her as one from the Fisher Coast, and so when the Cabal finally arrived in Fossa her masters truly had no idea that they had brought her home.

Arathé had seen her father the previous night, dancing and drinking at the Fossan celebrations. Even though she'd hoped to meet her family, she had been shocked to see him, her first link to any sort of life in nearly two years, and in that moment a desperate plan came to her. Her resolve was strengthened beyond measure the next morning when she discovered her younger brother was one of the candidates for recruitment. She knew with a dreadful certainty that he would be chosen. He had been equally Voice-gifted as a child. They would not miss it.

She watched him fight, heard his answer to their two-edged question and revised her opinion. He had the greater gift. With all her being she knew she had to warn him of his likely fate, so she used the Voice to put the Recruiters to sleep, then left them in their tent near Nadoce Square and used the back streets to find her family at their house in Old Fossa Road.

There her plan came closet to foundering, for the house

she had been brought up in was now home to another, and she could not ask the new occupants what had become of her family without risking everything. So she had gone down to the beach in despair, hoping that her father might be there mending nets, even though he had been commanded home. There her luck had turned, for she found the boat named after her and, knowing her mother, guessed the rest. She knew where the Fisher's cliff-house was, and made her way as swiftly as her abused frame allowed.

And now, she asked them, what were they to do?

A dozen plans surged through the fisherman's mind like a king tide through The Rhoos. Flee? They would have to travel on foot. They had no horses. They would be caught. Take the boat and sail away? Perhaps, but the *Arathé* was built for fishing, not speed. Any Neherian rake would run her down, and any Neherian captain would be only too keen to chase a Fossan vessel—particularly his. Hide somewhere in the village? They would be found. Resist? His skills with the sword were as rusty as his blade, and even at their best would barely match what he had seen this morning.

They were given no chance to implement any plan.

Boom, boom, boom came a series of heavy blows on the door. Opuntia shrieked, then put a hand across her mouth. Noetos knew nobody who knocked like that.

Boom, boom, boom.

Arathé knew who it was. She'd got it horribly wrong, had taken far too long to tell her story, and had clearly not been as effective with the Voice as she'd hoped.

The Recruiters had come for her.

CHAPTER 2

BURNING HIS BOATS

"DON'T MAKE THEM WAIT," Anomer said to his father. "Go and answer the door. They may be here only to speak to me. I will take Mother and Arathé into the kitchen."

Noetos stood in the centre of the great room, composing himself.

"Go on!" his son urged, shoving him in the small of the back. The fisherman stumbled over to the stout wooden door of his magnificent home and opened it a hand's-width.

"Who is this disturbing our sleep?" he grumbled, blinking as though roused from early afternoon torpor, running a careless hand through his dishevelled hair while observing every detail with sharp eyes. He needed to walk through this carefully. His son had acted quickly, shaming him, and it might be that the lives of everyone he loved depended on how he behaved in the next few minutes.

Two grey-cloaked figures stood on his portico, one behind the other. The closer of the two seemed relaxed, his head cocked to one side under his cowl, a non-threatening posture designed to put him at ease; but the other Recruiter stood in a slight crouch, coiled for action, hand on his sword-hilt, head moving slightly from side to side as he watched carefully for danger. *Not a friendly visit, then. They want more than just Anomer. They know.*

"Your son answered our question this morning so wondrously well," the nearer figure said in his high-pitched, singsong voice. "We have a few more questions for him. And some for his father as well," he added with the barest hint of menace. "May we come in?"

"I'm sorry, sirs, but my wife is unwell, and I have summoned the village physician to her bedside. We are in no position to entertain visitors this afternoon. Perhaps you might return tomorrow. Or maybe Anomer could accompany you to your own accommodation?"

"Ah, then our arrival is indeed providential, for my companion here is a physician. A good one, undoubtedly superior to any hedge-doctor that might have washed up on the coarse sand of this village. Open your door and let him attend her."

Noetos began to sweat, and wished he could wipe away the betraying sheen that had sprung up on his brow. "My lords, I thank you for your offer. But our physician is well versed in the needs of my wife, and brings with him the unguent she needs—"

"What she needs, if she wishes to retain any semblance of good health," the second Recruiter said, his mellifluous voice all the more intimidating because of its mildness, "is for her foolish husband to open the door to this house. Do it now." He drew his sword a few inches out of its scabbard, and its sharp edge glittered in the harsh Fossan sunlight.

In answer Noetos slammed the door shut and drew

down the bar. Beside him Anomer drove a wedge under the jamb. "Have your mother and sister escaped?" Noetos asked him.

"Two more Recruiters wait outside the back door. I listened to them talk: they tracked Arathé by the sword she took from them, and know she is here. We cannot get past them."

"Yet we must. We *must*. I have my family back, son. I would not lose you now."

The Recruiters did not try to force open the front door by strength. What they were doing became clear as a shimmer of blue fire spread over the wooden surface of the door. Noetos sprang back: it was cold to the touch. He'd never seen magic before, aside from the battlefield, and that only in the distance. Illusion, he'd been told. This, however, looked disturbingly real.

The door began to splinter.

"Go back to the others!" Noetos cried, then grabbed a chair, stood on it and stretched up towards the translucent cupola that served to let light into their living room. Feeling around the joint where the glass dome met the stone ceiling, he found his old scabbard, then his sword, along with a few cockroach husks. Ignoring the latter, he belted the scabbard around his waist, where it hung comfortably, as it had always done. Years since he'd worn it, years since he'd used anything but training blades with Arathé and Anomer. Once learned, never forgotten. He hoped.

Sudden shouts erupted behind him, somewhere down the end of the hallway that led to the kitchen and bedrooms. Fear gripped his heart then, and he leaped down from the chair just in time to watch his front door collapse in a sheet of flame that washed outwards, then vanished.

Behind the magic flame the two Recruiters, swords drawn, strode into his house. The might of Andratan.

It was nearly twenty years since Noetos had fought in the Neherian war. He'd been a teenager when he last drew a killing sword, fighting beside his father. He slew Neherians, took wounds, but the fields of battle lost their lustre well before the time he found himself sitting on a rocky Neherian field, his father's head in his lap, sightless eyes staring into his own.

Twenty years, but it seemed his arm remembered the sword all too well. He threw himself backwards across the room to the hallway, then took a position at the entrance. Behind him the sounds of fighting continued, blade on blade. Anomer must have retrieved his short sword from his bedroom, or perhaps he'd picked up his sister's blade. *Good. If it has gone on this long, Anomer must have secured some kind of advantage.*

Within seconds the Recruiters were upon him. There was no cry, no challenge, no quarter. Just blows swifter than he could imagine, heavier than anything the Neherians had brought to bear on him. His arm remembered the sword, but he had never been accounted a good defensive swordsman. His years of training had not prepared him for this.

He backed further into the hallway, defending grimly but bleeding from a nick to his sword arm, and drew the two swordsmen in. Now they were constricted, and could not make the swings necessary for their fearsome blows. It became a contest of thrust and parry, rapier-like, with swords ill suited for the purpose. The fisherman expected more magic from the Recruiters at any moment, but none came: perhaps they had over-extended themselves with the door? He could only hope.

Risking the briefest glance over his shoulder, Noetos caught a pale flash—Anomer, he thought—fighting off two swordsmen identical to those in front of him. *This can end only one way*, the fisherman admitted, and tried out an idea just forming in his mind. Slashing upwards, he brought down the night curtain separating the hallway from the gathering room. The falling cloth took the Recruiters by surprise, fouling their blades.

"Now, Anomer!" he cried, hoping that the boy remained sharp-witted. As he turned he was relieved to see his son slipping through the kitchen door. Noetos made it through moments before the Recruiters came storming down the hallway. Not a substantial door. He grabbed at the kitchen table, tipped the remains of the midday meal onto the floor with a clatter, and wedged it across the door. A few more seconds bought.

Arathé stood there, still looking nothing like the daughter he knew, with a bloody sword in her hands. "She got one of them, father," Anomer said. "She said something and he just froze . . ."

"Scullery window!" Noetos whispered urgently. "Now!" Behind him the Recruiters did not bother with magic this time. Instead they beat at the door with their sword-hilts, blows that rattled the bar and loosened the hinges. "Hurry!"

Noetos flung himself at the narrow window, bruising his shoulders in an attempt to clamber through. A hand reached out and pulled him forward. For a moment the fisherman stuck, his hips wedged fast, but he twisted back and forth until he came free, accompanied by a ripping sound. He had thought the hand was his son's, but as he emerged into the shadows under the cliff he found himself looking into the grim face of his wife.

After nodding his thanks, he spun around and reached back through the window, clasping his daughter's cold hands in his. She struggled up onto the bench, gritted her teeth and tried to squeeze through, but it was immediately apparent that she would never make it. Half in, half out, she hissed in frustration, looked into her father's eyes and slipped her hand from his.

"Nngo!" she said, twisting her mouth to shape the words. "Ngo!"

She still had the Voice. Noetos found himself scrambling with his wife and son down the narrow gully behind the house, under the cliff, at her command. He could not resist her even though her words cut against his deepest desire. The Voice relaxed its hold on him, however, and instantly he turned and headed back up the gully—just in time to hear a woman scream, then to witness some sort of detonation accompanied by a blue flash. The ground rocked beneath them.

"Arathé!" he cried, as two more explosions followed, caving in the rear of the Fisher House and bringing rocks cascading down from the cliff above them. "Arathé!"

A hand took him by the shoulder; he struck at it half-heartedly, eyes still on the spot where the kitchen had been, now a place of blue fire and rising smoke and dust. "They will kill us if they catch us," Anomer said. "Fetch help from the village. Hurry!"

Finally his son's urgency reached him, and within moments Noetos and what remained of his family stood on The Circle.

"I will get help from the Hegeoman," Opuntia said

huskily, her first words since the Recruiters had invaded their home. "Anomer will protect me."

"And I will raise Old Fossa," said the big fisherman grimly, nodding towards the ruins of his house. "Then nothing will protect them."

His wife and son ran along The Circle, disappearing around a curve in the road, safe for the moment. He had to check. She might be lying there, wounded or dying. But he could not leave. He'd run away before, twenty years ago, had abandoned his family, leaving them in a Neherian clearing on a terrible day of ambush, betrayal and torture. He had lived then, when everyone else had died.

He'd hated himself ever since.

Noetos turned from the top of the Zig Zag and crept back towards the Fisher House. This was madness. The Recruiters would be waiting with their swords and their magic. Suicidal madness, a special sort of insanity born of the irreconcilable clash of guilt and love. But a worse insanity waited to seize him if he chose to flee. He had abandoned her once; he could not do it again.

He made it to the front door without glimpsing his attackers. A quick glance inside: still no sign of them. He eased through the remains of the door, picked his way past scattered furniture and ventured carefully towards the hallway. Faint scuffling sounds came from ahead of him; blue smoke drifted out of the darkened entrance, clearing enough for him to see a robed figure lying face down in the hallway. Bald-headed, limbs splayed brokenly, kitchen knife protruding from her back, unmoving. He froze.

Two cowled figures glided out of the blue mist, swords raised. Noetos, shouting in grief and frustration, backed away from them. One of the Recruiters barked a word of command, and from their swords came two bright blue flashes. The crack of magical power lifted Noetos off his feet, throwing him back against the wall, knocking his sword from his hand.

His foot bumped against something—the sculpture of his daughter—and he snatched it from its plinth, ready to throw it if the Recruiters came closer. They did not need to. The fisherman did not see what happened then, as he closed his eyes against the killing magic. There was a rumble, a blue flare against his eyelids, then shouts of chagrin from the Recruiters. When Noetos opened his eyes all that remained was a momentary blue crackling around the bust in his hand, then nothing. His two foes looked at each other, astonished.

Noetos jerked himself upright, tucking the carving into his belt. He could not leave it. His daughter was beyond saving, his sword was beyond reach, and clearly he could not defeat two wielders of such magic. In a swift motion he leapt high into the air, his hands awkwardly grasping the base of the cupola, then swung himself up into the light-filled space. Safe from swords for a moment, but exposed even so. As the Recruiters ran towards the spot where he had been, he snatched the carving from his belt and smashed at a pane of glass with it. He heaved himself through the hole he had made.

Rapid as thought he picked himself up, then ran across the roof and hurled himself over the edge, across the three-pace gap to the flat roof of his bathhouse. Encumbered by the carving, he barely gained purchase on the small flat roof. He considered throwing the object away, but found he could not. It was all he had left of her.

*　　*　　*

First one, then the other of the Recruiters emerged onto the roof of the Fisher House and looked around in bewilderment, which grew into incomprehension and shouts of anger when a thorough search of the roof and grounds failed to reveal any sign of the man.

There were mysteries tied up in riddles here in this village. A boy who handled a sword like a warrior, who had answered Ataphaxus in a Voice so pure it could, with training, shape anything its owner put his mind to, and who had intelligence to go with his skill. What could he become once he discovered his power? His father was a bluff fisherman who wielded with real skill a sword marked with the device of the legendary Duke of Rhoudhos, and who, to pile wonder on wonder, carried a carving made of pure huanu stone, surely the largest piece in existence. And their own tongueless servant who had unerringly found her way to these extraordinary people, who had then risked their lives to protect her. These people had to be found. Questions had to be asked, connections made. And the huanu stone had, at all costs, to be recovered.

Noetos heard the shouting. It encouraged him to run even faster along The Circle towards the spur that led down to the shore. A quick glance behind him revealed nothing. He saw the entrance to the little-used Bridge Path, ducked to his right and set off along the stony track. *Along here, down to the beach, then back up to Old Fossa.*

Bridge Path led from The Circle into a small embayment in the cliffs known as The Crater, where the dead of Fossa enjoyed their final rest. Open only to the east, and that a narrow entrance surrounded by bluffs, The Crater was shrouded in almost perpetual shadow. Near Tipper

Bridge the fisherman stopped for a moment, undecided about his route, and heard the rattle of stones behind him.

They had not given up.

The village must surely have been roused by now. Opuntia and Anomer would have enlisted the aid of their Hegeoman, who would have gathered dozens of villagers. The explosions must have echoed around the cliffs, and the smoke would draw a crowd. Surely there was little even four such as the Recruiters could do against a whole village.

Around the bluff and into the entrance to The Crater came his two pursuers, then a third, running hard. Noetos waited where he was a moment longer, expecting to see villagers sprinting after them, but the path behind them remained stubbornly empty.

Across the bridge or a scramble up the slope? He chose the bridge, then remembered the mechanism and blessed his choice. There was a pin as long as a man's arm at either end, serving to tie the Tipper Bridge firmly to its supports. Removed, the bridge would sway either side of its one central pivot. These pins had been part of the bridge for centuries, the bridge itself one element of an elaborate defence the ancient Fossans had devised against their enemies. The Hegeoman had recently reinstituted the yearly task of taking the pins out and cleaning them. *Just as well*, the fisherman thought as he bent down to pull out the first pin.

Sweat plastering his hair to his scalp and flicking into his eyes, Noetos dashed across the bridge in a few heartbeats, stopping to draw the second pin out of its sleeve. Tipper Bridge creaked, but made no other sound.

His pursuers approached. He willed them onto the

bridge, but the three of them stood in plain view on the far side, perhaps twenty paces from him, and made no move to hazard the narrow structure.

"Don't you want me?" the fisherman asked them, hoping the sneer in his voice masked the fear underneath. "Isn't that why you've come this far?" Then a more frightening thought struck him. Could they hurl that blue fire across the rocky gully? Instantly he regretted his provocative words.

"Want you? What would we want with a worn-out fisherman from a village scared of its own shadow?" The smooth voice of the lead Recruiter floated across the space between them, echoing around the cliffs above the bridge.

"I was wondering that myself," Noetos said conversationally. Why, indeed, were they still pursuing him? "Perhaps you have heard of my prowess with a net, and wish to learn my secrets? If so, you have not been civil enough in your asking. I will keep my fish-lore to myself." His eyes flicked over their shoulders, but still he could see no villagers coming to his aid. *Delay, delay*.

"You wonder where your townsmen are, why they have not yet come to help you," the voice continued, and Noetos felt the stirrings of real fear at the words. "You sent your wife and son to your village leader in the belief that he would be sympathetic to your predicament, that he would raise the village to defend you against the Recruiters who threatened you. The problem with this course of action should become clear to you if you take a moment to reflect. Tell me, fisherman, would the Hegeoman of this puerile village give you or your family a moment's thought if threatened with the loss of the hundred gold coins we offer for your son? Would he not be much more likely to hand your family over to the two Recruiters who followed them to his house?"

"Betrayer!" Noetos cried, consumed by fury, and leapt at his tormentors. The bridge gave way under his left foot.

Yawing crazily, it threw him towards the gully twenty paces below. His right foot snagged in the sleeve that housed the pin. His ankle twisted painfully, but held. For a moment he hung out over the gully, and the dry, rocky watercourse below him spiralled as he swung; then the bridge tilted back and he dragged himself up to the path. Improbably, the stone carving still remained nestled in his belt.

The leader of the Recruiters hissed his annoyance — his reaction telling the fisherman they wished him dead — and signalled his fellows to scramble across the gully as best they could. Noetos turned and ran.

Despair rose to smother his fear. Undoubtedly the beast told the truth. He had lost everything in one dreadful afternoon except his own life, and that now appeared forfeit. He sprinted away from The Crater, down towards Red Rocks Lane and the sea, working feeling into his ankle as he ran.

They were fifty paces behind him when he reached Red Rocks Lane, and he knew by the time he reached Beach Lane he had come to the end of his endurance. He was a strong man, he knew that, a strength born of twenty years on the boats, but that strength was concentrated in his upper body. His lungs still had air, but his calves felt like tree stumps.

There was only one place he could make use of his advantages. To his right lay the boats of the village. At the far end of the row, the largest. The *Arathé*.

Now for it. Using the last of his strength, he stumbled across the dry mid-tide sands. *Curse the tide!* He would have to drag the boat across the beach to the water. *Impossible. Give up now.*

Still he tried. *Stubborn!* The *Arathé* was slim and light-weight but it was a large boat, easily holding a crew of three, and usually it took all of them to launch her. The nets alone weighed as much as any one of them could carry, but there were no nets in her today. Noetos grabbed her stern and pulled hard, but she did nothing but squirm around on the sand.

One last refuge, then. Kicking off his sandals, the fisherman ran a hundred paces out into the surf, then threw himself into the water where the deep channel flowed. With relief he saw the tide was still going out, and the current surged along with him. Burdened as he was by the stone carving, he employed his powerful frame to swim out towards the reef, away from his pursuers.

"We have most of what really matters," the head Recruiter remarked to his two companions as they watched their quarry swim away. "With patience, we will obtain it all. Bilitharn has the mother and the boy, and the father seems resourceful enough to mount some sort of rescue attempt."

"Perhaps we could exchange the woman for the stone?" one of his companions suggested.

"It will not be necessary. He will come to us, and we will deal with him when he does. We will leave now, cutting short the rest of our journey. I feel certain that when we arrive at the Great Keep with the golden-voiced boy and the huanu stone, we will be able to name our own reward."

"Could the father cause us any problems?" the second Recruiter asked.

The head Recruiter gazed out into the harbour, where a faint splashing and flat wake marked the progress of the surprising fisherman. "No," he said after a pause. "No man is dangerous when what he holds dear is in the hands of his enemies." He cupped his hand in an unmistakable gesture. "Such a man moves with caution, lest he harm that which he wishes to redeem. We have nothing to fear from him."

It took Noetos an hour to swim out to the reef. Once, more than twenty years ago now, he had swum there in half the time to win a wager, but he had been younger then and had not already run himself to a standstill. There were no fishermen on the harbour today, though the weather promised a good catch. Noetos wondered at that. Most of the fishermen he'd met at the celebration last night had told him they would be staying ashore to watch the candidates being tested, but he had expected one or two of the Cadere Row mob to be on the water, Testing or no Testing. But there were no boats, no one to give him a ride back to shore.

He dragged himself out of the water and onto the rough rocks of the reef, the dark line that might as well have been another cliff to the Fossans, and lay there, completely exhausted.

It was only then, stretched out on the rock above the booming surf, clothes drying in the late afternoon sun, that shock set in. For a long time he shook uncontrollably, his thoughts indistinguishable from nightmares. His daughter returned to him hideously changed, maimed and pallid as a ghost, to unfold a story of suffering and torture. The touch of her cold hand on his still remained, and he curled his hand into his chest as though nursing a burn. Anomer and Opuntia betrayed by the Hegeoman, the man to whom his wife believed they owed their good fortune—her lover, he admitted—and now in the hands of the Recruiters. Soon the reason why Arathé had sought out a certain fisher-family would be known to them. He imagined their questioning, could see his wife and son suffering torment at their cruel hands. Swords, knives, blue fire. But one vision more than all the others dominated his mind. A robed shape, limbs splayed, a knife in her back. He could not begin to encompass the sorrow welling up within him, and behind that treacherous sea of grief, making ready to spring on him, the dark storm-clouds of anger and guilt gathered.

Spray from the breakers began to spatter his tunic. The tide had risen, the sun hovered close to the cliffs, and soon the rocks would be covered by swirling green water. Nothing short of the tide could have washed the deadness from his limbs and the torpor from his mind. He raised himself to his elbows and looked back at the familiar view: the Cliffs of Memory to his left—*how aptly named*, he thought bitterly—and the embayment in which Fossa huddled, more like a spider in a knothole than ever, a blackness in front of him. He would not swim towards that hated place. Instead, he would break into a certain storage shed at Cana Bay and see what he could find.

Diving from his rocky perch, Noetos the fisherman swam away from the reef and, under a sky darkening with gathering clouds, began the slow strokes towards Dog Head.

Much later that evening a damp figure came walking cautiously down The Dog, the path that led from Cana Bay to

Fossa. There was a more polite name for it—and another far less polite—but the Fossans had called it. The Dog for generations, after the low promontory that could be seen from the path. For a time the darkness seemed on the brink of rain, but the clouds had lowered and now the cool air swirled with fog. *Late in the season for fog*, Noetos thought, wondering if the unusual weather would make his task easier or more difficult. He shrugged his shoulders, telling himself it didn't matter. What could be more difficult than the already impossible?

A moment later he fell into a crouch, then scurried towards the deeper shadows as the muffled sounds of human speech came from the lane ahead of him. Four villagers emerged from the grey blankness, wrapped up against the thick mist, silhouettes with smoky breath, voices fading in and out with the mysterious thickening and thinning fog always brought. They each carried a stick of some kind. *Fishing pole? Not a night for the flatfish.* No, they carried gaffs from their boats.

Intent on his own hunt, the man in the deeper shadows realised that the villagers—Cadere Row men, by the sound of them—were also hunting. It had to be so. Their slow walk was now revealed as a search, heads swivelling to the left and right, sticks forward. Looking for someone.

"Done flipped 'is pate," one of them said. "Killed 'is wife and boy."

"But why?" Noetos recognised the whiny voice as that of Domoss, the boy who had fouled lines with the *Arathé* last year when a week of bad weather had confined them to harbour. "Why? Nobody in his right mind would take a knife to his kin."

"That's just it. Not in his right mind, see?"

"Go on!" A third voice joined in. "If I was hitched to that squawker, I'd take a knife to her. How could a man stand it?"

"You'd take som'thin' to her, but it wouldn't be your knife." The speaker barked a laugh, and the others joined in.

"Maybe that's why his head went funny," Domoss speculated. "Driven mad by his wife!"

A darker voice cut across the chatter. "Enough talk! There's a reward, remember? Maybe large enough to afford better company than you lot, I'm hoping." Noetos was almost sure the voice belonged to Arnessan. A bully and a coward. Typical Cadere Rower.

"Bastard thinks 'e's smarter than us, that's for sure, living up on the cliff like a noble. I want the reward of seeing the big fool's arrogant face when we catch 'im." Thin laughter drifted back from the group, as they gradually faded into the mist.

Improbably, in view of all that had happened to Noetos that day, it was this last exchange that finally broke through his defences and touched off his carefully guarded anger. So much of this had been his fault, he was ready to admit. He should have fought harder against the wishes of his wife and daughter, should have found some way of preventing Arathé from putting herself forward, even though it had been he who had delighted in filling her head with stories of the world beyond the claustrophobic cliffs of Fossa. Should have married the girl he loved, not the girl he desired. But he was surely not to blame for the fact that he lived in Fisher House and not in Old Fossa.

Come now, fisherman, he told himself mockingly,

placing a stress on the last word, *harness your anger with the intelligence you were once so famous for. Do this right, or run away and leave your loved ones in the hands of your enemies, as you have done before*. He knew he lashed himself unfairly, but he needed the sting to action.

A huge figure materialised from nowhere and stood, arms wide, in front of the frightened Cadere Row men. Domoss cried out, and they all took a step backwards.

"Not the weather for fishing tonight, lads!" a voice boomed at them. "What is it you're trying to catch?" The words were edged with something close to madness, the arms remained spread wide, and none of them missed the fishing spear in his hand.

Perhaps three seconds passed before the fishermen realised who addressed them. "Noetos! We were looking for—" one of them began, but a swift kick to the ankle silenced him.

"We were going to check out the fishing on the other side of Dog Head," Domoss said, craftiness in his voice. "Mayn't be any fog there."

"No fish either, not tonight, boys, take my word for it." The big man drew closer; the Cadere Row mob took a step back. "I've been for a swim over by Dog Head, and the fish are in their beds, where all good fishermen should be. But you would know that, lads, since it's your favourite spot, being dogs yourselves."

No doubt about it, the man had gone mad. Nervous eyes imagined they could see blood running down the upraised pike, and all heard the insanity in his voice. No telling what an insane man could do, especially one with this man's size and strength.

"Tell me, friends, what are you really hunting? Could it be the Recruiters want me stopped before I hack the rest of Fossa to death?" And he laughed then, a crazed giggle that sent tendrils of fear shooting down their spines, dissolving the little resolve they had for their task.

The Cadere Row mob found themselves "escorting" the Fisher of Fossa along Front Street and into Lamplight Lane towards Nadoce Square. They passed other villagers, foolhardy individuals and circumspect groups busy searching the misty streets for the murderer among them, and each time Domoss gave them a nervous greeting. He did not attempt to draw close to them, or to cry out, clearly aware of the pike in the fisherman's hand.

Truly it had not been difficult to intimidate the men of Cadere Row. If they had so chosen, the four men could have subdued him with their gaffs, but Noetos had counted on them not being prepared to risk a madman's wrath.

The whole village, it seemed, was out in the fog searching for him. Why? The Cadere Row mob knew nothing other than the story they had been told. But he'd heard their words of jealousy and hatred. He had never guessed the depth of feeling against him. How little he had fitted into the place he'd chosen to hide in all these years.

Nadoce Square glowed fitfully under an eerie fog-shrouded light from the tall tapers normally raised for special occasions. With a little prompting Domoss explained that each group had been instructed to report to the Square once their area had been searched. *That explains the lights.* But having spread the story of his family's deaths, the Recruiters would not be holding them in Nadoce

Square for everyone to see; though there must be at least one of the hooded figures here, coordinating the search.

Two of them, he decided, after straining his eyes to see through the flame-lit fog. Two Recruiters surrounded by twenty or so villagers reporting their findings, or lack of them, and receiving new instructions. The Hegeoman stood beside them, hands clasped nervously behind his back.

Beside Noetos the Cadere Row boys knelt, their heads touching the cobbles. He'd promised a swift death for the first to make noise, a slow death for the rest. Clearly they believed him.

He began measuring times and distances in his mind. Thirty paces—twenty seconds—to the nearest hooded figure. Would he be able to overpower the Recruiter before the villagers intervened? Would they intervene at all?

The mist swirled. The Recruiter turned to face the shadows where Noetos hid.

There was something unnerving in that hooded gaze: pale grey robes surrounding a black oval. A sudden blue light flared within the cowl, an echo of the magic the Recruiters had used against him.

"Welcome, Fisher," said the high-pitched voice, and the raw power within it nearly jerked him out into the Square. The robe took on a bluish tinge. Power shimmered within the cowl, growing more intense by the second, reaching out, compelling him. He fought it with increasing desperation.

"I feel you there," the voice continued, a voice set with hooks. "I feel your anger." The villagers fell away from the terrifying figure, some making warding signs. At least one staggered as though burned by the fire. "I can sense

your weakness, your guilt." The last word was clearly
savoured, the speaker elongating it, drawing it out, casting
it like a spell, like a net, looking for purchase within
Noetos's soul. It seemed to the frightened fisherman that
a blue tentacle reached across the Square, searching,
probing, coming for him. Down into the shadows it
came, pulsing with baleful energy; and as it hovered
over his head, he knew he should have fled this place,
that there were more dreadful powers in this world than
he imagined.

The tentacle struck, crackled like a log too wet to burn,
and vanished with a pop. From the Square came a cry of
anguish, then silence.

"Still has his little secret with him, then," the second
Recruiter said. "Are you all right?"

The mist came down more heavily. Noetos thought he
could make out a robed figure sprawled on the cobbles,
slowly getting to his feet. Beside him the Cadere Row
men kept their heads down. The fisherman didn't have to
renew his threats, which was fortunate, as he doubted he
had the strength left to carry them out.

"Noetos tal Upanas, we have learned a great deal about
you this afternoon," the second voice said calmly. "We enjoyed our discussions with our guests, though initially
they were somewhat reluctant to share their knowledge
with us."

They are trying to fan the flames of my anger.

"We now know why our servant sought you out.
Arathé, that was her name, was it not?"

*Baiting me. Somehow their magic depends on my
response.*

"Truly, we did not know her name until today. She was

a very biddable servant. She did anything we told her to do." Noetos fought his rage as the Recruiter began to shimmer with power. "Now you have lost a son as well as a daughter. Perhaps you will be more fortunate this time, and we will decide to fashion him into one of us. Maybe this one will get to keep his tongue."

"Listen to them!" Noetos shouted across the Square, unable to resist their goading. "They lied to you! They killed my daughter, and have taken my wife and son!"

Another thread of blue power flowed towards him, thicker and faster than before. "I am one of you!" the fisherman cried desperately. "Help me!"

As the thread approached, a blue finger of obscenity in the mist, the Hegeoman turned to face him. "You are one of us no longer," he said in his unctuous voice. "The Recruiters may exact upon your body any justice they see fit to take. This is my judgment." Turning his back, he folded his arms.

Noetos could feel the power of the Recruiter taking a grasp of him. In some fashion the magic-wielder had the ability to seek out his emotions; yet, knowing this, the fisherman could not contain his anger and despair. He knew he had no defence against such an attack. As the blue filament hovered above him, Noetos turned and ran.

There were no roads connecting Fossa with the outside world. In ancient times, it was said, the village had been on the major north route taken by southern raiding parties, and had regularly suffered at the hands of invaders. The Fossans were never numerous enough to defend themselves effectively, and time and again those left alive were forced to begin anew. Finally a group of survivors decided that hiding would be more sensible than fighting, so erased any evidence of the cliff-side village from the farmlands above. From that time onward all that could be seen from the Fisher Coast Road were waving grasses and wheat fields. Strategically placed belts of trees kept anyone travelling the road from seeing the cliff-line. The maxim "out of sight, out of mind" was adopted by the Fossans, whose farmers took a different route to their fields every day so as not to leave any permanent track. However, there were a number of narrow paths down to The Circle from the cliff-top, and it was one of these, much later that night, the Recruiters used to make their way out.

Noetos crouched behind a rocky outcrop and watched them leave. In the hours since the confrontation in Nadoce Square the bewildered fisherman had wandered the murky streets of Fossa, trying to understand what had happened to him; lurking in the shadows of the village that had been his home all his adult life, avoiding people he knew, some of whom he had called friends.

The fog lifted during his wanderings, rolling away towards the sea. Out beyond the reef it hung, waiting for a chance to creep in again should the night breeze relax. Noetos had found himself walking along the cliff-top with no thought beyond the overwhelming sorrow gripping him; at one point he stood right at the edge of the cliff looking down on the remains of Fisher House, and spent some time wondering if it should become his tomb. That the scene of his daughter's betrayal and death could become his own resting place seemed fit, but he knew he would not let himself fall. The Recruiters had set him a puzzle, with his wife and son as the prize, and he would attempt to solve it.

Now he watched a party of seven slowly climb the stony path behind the house of the Hegeoman. They walked in single file, moving in and out of shadow, the last limping even though he used a stick. *Hah, Arathé had wounded one.* Two bound figures staggered along in the middle of the line. Noetos was sure his enemies would not be able to sense him from his rocky perch fifty paces away, but the last of the Recruiters turned as he reached the path's summit, threw his cowl back and called across the cool spring night.

"You are marked, fisherman! Wherever you go, we will know you. And think on this. Any attempt to prise your family from our grasp will end in something far worse than mere failure. We have revealed but a small part of our power. If you are a more foolish man than you have yet demonstrated, you will pursue us; and if you do, you will feel the full extent of our magic on some lonely road, far from help, far from home. Go and gnaw the bones of your grief in some other village, and try to forget you ever had a family. And pray that we do not one day decide to return for you!"

One by one the Recruiters and their captives disappeared over the top of the cliff. Within a few moments Noetos was left on his own, truly alone.

The eastern sky took on the pearly glow of dawn before the fisherman stirred from his perch. Like a monk of Hagga Rock considering his vows, Noetos had allowed his thoughts to range wide through the night, trying to hold on to his sanity, trying to force his emotions into more comfortable channels. How he hated magic! Such a filthy way of ruining the lives of innocent people. What had drawn it here, to a small fishing village? Was there knowledge he was missing, some pattern he did not see? Was this his past returning to bedevil him, as he feared? Or did it all revolve around Arathé? He thought about his daughter and her suffering, the moment when they took her tongue, her degradation since then, her body lying pierced by a kitchen knife, one he'd purchased and sharpened himself. But most of all he thought of his own past: a battlefield, a cooling body and the way a man could lose courage—not in the face of death, but in the face of futility.

He would leave the village and follow the Recruiters, as they no doubt expected he would. *Futile*. But first he had one further task to perform.

The Hegeoman awoke with a hand across his mouth and a sword held against his side. His struggling earned him a bleeding lip, and the ferocious face of his attacker promised more. His wife lay snoring, undisturbed by the stirring beside her. Shivering with more than the cold, the village leader eased himself out of bed and donned his nightshirt while the fisherman waited, arms folded. With this madman on the loose, why had he thought it safe to leave his house undefended?

Because he is not a madman, the frightened man acknowledged. *Because he did not kill his family; because I betrayed them to the devious Recruiters who did not tell me all the truth*. The village leader was nothing if not a pragmatic man, and as he searched his larder for food and drink to fill the sacks from his own kitchen, he knew he might very well die today.

He's not mad, but he is a hothead, a man with a splinter

in his soul, prickly and obstinate at best. Not a man to offend. Aside from yesterday's events the Hegeoman knew other reasons why he might have made an enemy of the fisherman. With these reasons in mind he had handed Opuntia and her son to the Recruiters when they came to his house with their wild story—which, except for the nonsense of Arathé being transformed into some monster, turned out not to have been wild at all. He hoped Noetos did not know those reasons, or the possibility of his imminent death would become a certainty.

Relax. He knows nothing. Opuntia is a clever woman with a boor for a husband. Even if he suspects our dalliance it will serve only to distract him from the real issue.

The fisherman forced him to dress, then take up a sack bulging with provisions and walk across the cool tiles of his atrium at the point of a sword. Once the door closed behind them and they stood in the gentle early morning breeze, the Hegeoman allowed himself a little hope. Surely if he was to be killed, it would not be here, out in the open.

"Quickly, now!" the fisherman growled in his ear, and the two of them hurried down The Circle, past Fisher House—his captor did not spare it a glance—all the way down to Beach Lane and the sea.

"A captive for a captive," said a voice behind him conversationally as they came to the beach. "A death for a death. You betrayed my family. Tell me why I shouldn't kill you."

The Hegeoman turned. "Because I don't want to die," he said.

The laughter that followed this statement echoed around the cliffs. *Surely someone will hear? Surely some-*

one will save me! But he knew how unlikely this was. He himself had ordered his villagers out of their homes last night, making them stay out in the dark to search for the man beside him. They would not be rising early this morning.

"Ah, my friend, you are as sorry a man as I have met," the fisherman said. They reached the place of the boats, not a place the Hegeoman visited often. *An escape by boat?* Hope soared, then died. *We'd never get past the Neherian fleet.*

"This is what I wish to do to you in answer to what you did to me. I wish to truss you up, put you into my boat, set fire to it and then launch you into the harbour. It would do me good to listen to your screams."

The Hegeoman's hope strengthened further. No one talked of what they intended to do before they did it. He'd heard that somewhere. "But you won't," he said, "because you would never burn your precious boat. You are here to collect the goods you need, and then you will use me to help you escape the village."

More laughter. "Half-right, Hegeoman. True, I won't kill you today, as long as you are very careful to obey me. And I am going to use you, and not just to escape the village. We are going a lot further than that, you and I."

"By boat? I can't sail."

"Oh, I know. What use is the leader of a fishing village who knows nothing of the sea? But we are not going by boat." They arrived at the Fisher's boats as he spoke. The Hegeoman knew of them: the first, a small dory not unlike that used by the other fishermen of Fossa, paint peeling, showing signs of neglect. The second, the largest fishing craft ever to put out from Fossa, bought from the

Neherians by surreptitious means—in which he himself
had taken a part—and skilfully guided out of the harbour
into the rich but forbidden coastal waters. One strip of
colour under the gunwale, altered at irregular intervals to
aid in disguise. Already a legend.

And the name of the vessel? Yes, he knew the name.
After the events of yesterday, a dangerous name. He
would have to be careful here, very careful, despite the
fisherman's promise to stay his hand. Death and destruction lurked behind the big man's dark eyes.

"This is the *Arathé*," Noetos said, his voice tight with
emotion. "Purchased along with the right to live in Fisher
House, using the gold-price earned by the sale of my daughter. Arathé is now dead. Fisher House is destroyed. It only
remains for me to complete the transaction."

He made the Hegeoman clamber over the side and into
the *Arathé*. "Under the seat you will find three rucksacks.
Pull out all three, then take one, roll it up tightly and put
it in one of the others. When you've done that, toss them
to me."

The village leader hurried to do what he'd been bidden,
while the fisherman gathered driftwood and made a pile
beside the boat. Dawn had spread itself over the silver sky,
and soon the sun would flood the village with its harsh
light. The Hegeoman thought of slowing his swift movements in the hope of delaying the fisherman, but feared
the sword too much to risk it.

"Now take my tinderbox—you'll find it under the bow
seat, that's at the other end of the boat to the stern—and
light the fire I've set." He complied.

"There is a bucket near the stern, the end of the boat
facing the sea. In it you will find a sticky black substance.

We will heat it, then I want you to spread it around the bottom of the boat. Don't get any on yourself. Hurry!"

Tar. What would a fisherman want with tar?

"Do it now, then jump out of the boat quickly if you value your skin."

Oh.

Still the Hegeoman hesitated. This threatened his secret, the deepest secret of all. Would the Neherians, waiting these past weeks out to sea, take this fire to be the signal they were expecting?

He had no choice. The fool Fisher set flame to his boats himself. At least he could truthfully claim it had not been by his hand should the Neherians be angered by the false alarm.

The two of them backed away from the *Arathé*. Within moments the flames caught, and black smoke began to pour from her. They were halfway along the beach when the flames became visible. As they walked the fisherman constantly turned to watch his boats dying, his face hard. As though he had executed an enemy. The Hegeoman imagined himself lying in that boat, trussed up, while the flames ate at his skin.

They took the steepest of the paths out of Fossa, the one from Front Street up Escren Hill. Behind them they could hear faint shouts as people saw the fire; small figures poured out of Old Fossa Road as fishermen sought to prevent their own boats being claimed by the conflagration.

At the top of the cliff Noetos paused to watch the death of the *Arathé*. This was an ending, he knew. The last time he would look across the hated harbour, the grey-green sea, the pale beach, the shadowed cliffs. Smoke billowed from his boat, drifting out past the reef as though escorting her soul out to sea.

The transaction was complete. All that remained of Arathé now was a small sculpture tucked away in his belt.

Noetos gave his captive a slap across his legs with the flat of his father's blade, rescued from the wreck of his home, and they plunged into the deep grass of Escren Hill. Behind them Fossa disappeared from view. No paths up here; he would have to make a path of his own.

A path of revenge.

COSMOGRAPHER

CHAPTER 3

GARDEN OF ANGELS

IT WAS SAID IN THE Great Houses, where some
people knew, and echoed in the souks, where they definitely did not, that early morning was the best time to
view the Garden of Angels. Certainly a visitor to the Emperor's Talamaq Palace would not see the garden at its
best in the afternoon, when the sea breeze stirred the
desert dust from the streets and middens of the city and interfered with the play of light on the celebrated golden
fountains of Talamaq. Needless to say, Jau Maranaya,
scion of a lesser Amaqi Alliance, had not been given an
early morning appointment.

Nevertheless, to be given any appointment at the Emperor's Palace was an honour, even one at midafternoon
when the broiling air addled the wits and made even a
grateful man impatient. Jau stood for a moment before
the great Gate of the Father, composing himself, and
once again ran through in his mind what this meeting
would mean. He had it down like a mantra. Preferment,
patronage, prestige, profit. Especially profit. His cus-
tomers and competitors knew about his appointment

with the Emperor, he'd made sure of that. They would come to his emporium to ask him questions, and would buy his goods without the customary haggling. He would move up the city's hierarchy of traders, and his fortune would surely grow. And if he was fortunate he might be invited to join one of the greater Alliances. He was young yet, and clever. Who knew how high he might aspire?

Two Omeran guards stood before the massive wooden gate, arms folded, scowls on their broad, dark, inhuman faces. "Health to the Emperor!" Jau said companionably to the nearer of them, and made to approach the gate.

"Wait, ma sor," the Omeran said in a soft voice, stepping a pace forward. *A gelding, then.* The Emperor was rumoured to have a number of them in his employ, and here stood the evidence. Two legs they had, and two arms, but no Amaqi would mistake an Omeran for human. This one had soft features to match the voice, but was menacing enough to keep Jau from questioning the order.

"And that is *good* health to the Emperor," said the other guard, and his voice was definitely not soft.

"Good health, yes, that is what I mean," Jau said, more politely than he felt. Where had they learned to speak like this? He had put Omerans to death for lesser slights, but these were the Emperor's trained guards. Who knew what latitude they were allowed? He wanted to ask how long he must wait, but the guards seemed ready to turn aside any question he might ask. He would not lower himself to be refused by an Omeran, even one in the Emperor's employ.

They were mind readers too, it appeared. "Until the shadow of the stick touches the gate, ma sor," the first guard said, pointing to a slender pole stuck in the ground to his left. "You wait." The words sounded as much threat as command.

Jau judged he had about a sunwidth to endure. Frankly, he was unsure why he should wait at all. Appointments with the Emperor were by necessity punctual affairs, involving as they did the Corridor of Rainbows, and the timing of his arrival was important. The functionary who delivered his summons explained all this to him, though he knew much of it anyway; it appeared members of the lesser Alliances knew more than the Emperor suspected.

The Emperor's Palace, the functionary had told him, the Talamaq after which the city was named, was one of the world's wonders, with pillars of gold and glass fingering the sky. Well, everyone knew that. Prisms and mirrors took the sun's light and shepherded it into the Corridor of Rainbows, where those Amaqi graced by an appointment with the Emperor approached the throne. The colours displayed in the corridor depended on one's status and the level of regard in which one was held. This was also widely known. Subject to constant rumour and gossip, in fact. The corridor reflected the ineffable will of the Emperor, the court official told him, but Jau was aware how it really worked: the path of the sun was known for every day of the year, charted by cosmographers, and cunning machinery altered the mirrors and prisms to break up the light into the colours of the rainbow. The operators, Omerans painstakingly trained for the task, could flood the Corridor of Rainbows with any combination of colours the Emperor dictated, depending only on the weather—though clouds seldom obscured the sun above Talamaq—and the time of day. A triumph of Amaqi science, and a powerful political tool.

The functionary had left Jau in no doubt about the honour being done him. In fact, the tedious man had coached
him for the better part of an afternoon on how he was to
behave. What he was to say, where he was to stand, where
he was—and was not—to look. Jau listened attentively,
his nervousness increasing with every word, but comforted himself with the knowledge that this was exactly
the effect the instructions were designed to produce.

Jau Maranaya expected the green, perhaps, or maybe
even the yellow. He dreamed of the red, glorious red, of
course; everyone did. Red meant the highest favour of the
throne. Indigo and violet were not to be countenanced:
these seldom-used colours usually heralded some form of
punishment. And there were rumours of an eighth colour.
Black, the sentence of death. No one in the lesser Alliances knew about the black. It was something Jau heard
once, no more, from a street-seller. He assigned it no
credibility.

Clearly, then, punctuality was critical to the colour of
the corridor. So why the wait? His time had been speci-
fied. Would not this delay ruin the Emperor's visible
sign of favour to him? Or—and the thought settled on
him like a benison—had the Emperor heard about his
latest gift to the city? He had culled some of his Omerans and gifted the land they'd grazed for a small hunting
preserve. Perhaps the August One himself might desire
to hunt? Did this so-precise delay herald the red? Jau
would think of some gracious way to issue an invitation
to his Emperor should this prove to be the case.

He could well afford the gift, he reflected as he waited
in the stifling heat. Years of petty graft had filled his cof-
fers with good Amaqi gold. He knew people all over the

city in positions of influence and trust; people with secrets he had made it his business to uncover. They were only too happy to put a little aside from taxes or profits in order to buy his discretion. And if they refused, he had them taken care of. It was expensive, this care-taking, but paying to rid himself of people with scruples cost him but a small part of the profit he made from those who had none.

"It is time, ma sor," said one of the Omerans, pulling the pole from the ground and breaking it across his knee. This action disquieted the visitor, but he was allowed no time to reflect. "You must come now."

The Gate of the Father swung open like his own father's welcoming arms, and Jau Maranaya gasped in astonishment at the scene spread before him. Though it shamed him before the Omeran guards, he could not help crying out. The Garden of Angels was everything he had been told.

He assembled his words, his descriptions, even as he walked through the garden. He imagined returning to his family and telling them of the stately fountains, spreading lawns, sculpted bushes and exotic plants of every imaginable shape and size. The Emperor treated water as a plaything, he would tell them. He spent it on fancies. On colours and shapes. On the play of light, on the texture of grass scissors short or left knee-high and waving in the afternoon breeze. He heard water splashing, trickling, gushing, tinkling, pouring. It sent a frisson of desire through him. This was the deliberate exercise of power through profligacy. Such power, to waste water in the pursuit of beauty! He would tell his family that his honouring by the Emperor was perhaps the first step to taking all this power for himself.

A gardener, a small, wizened woman with a fork in her hand, emerged from behind a hedge and smiled an improbable smile full of gleaming white teeth. "Very good, very good," the woman said, eyeing him like a particularly interesting botanical specimen. Before Jau could respond, the gardener disappeared behind her hedge. His unease grew, partly masked by a faint disappointment. He'd hoped for more time in the fabled garden—indeed, he ought to have insisted on waiting here for his delayed summons rather than out on the dusty street—but the Omeran guards bustled him through the sparkling grounds and towards a small, unadorned door.

He had to kneel to enter the Corridor of Rainbows. A little heavy-handed, surely. *If I become Emperor I will not insist on such things*. He saw himself as more openhearted than that. But as he scrabbled on his knees through the door, his body felt as small as did his soul. Small and vulnerable.

This, then, was the famed Corridor of Rainbows.

He was early, even though the guards had held him back until this moment, and no light yet penetrated the corridor. He walked some distance, unsure of where he should position himself. Somewhere to his left, he'd been told, lay an open space, a gallery in which the Emperor himself sat, hidden behind the golden mask he always wore, surrounded by his court. At the moment it was in darkness. He'd not heard that the Emperor sat in the dark before his subjects were honoured, but this gesture of humility only made his reward greater. Once the prisms and mirrors took effect he'd be able to see them, bathed in the colour of the Emperor's choosing. The reality, of course, was that the colour would bathe him. He, not the Emperor, will soon be the centre of attention. Was it too much to hope for red?

"Hea, Jau Maranaya." A voice spoke in greeting, rumbling through the corridor, filling the darkness around him. "Hea!" The voice of the Emperor.

Jau's great moment was irredeemably spoiled by the malfunction of the corridor. Where was his colour? What had happened that the Emperor himself continued to sit in the dark? No matter the honour intended, Jau's enemies would make capital out of his discomfiture once they heard of it.

"Hea, ma great sor," Jau began, as protocol dictated. "Despite the corridor not functioning as it should, I acknowledge the . . . honour . . . done me . . ."

His voice died away to silence as the truth took hold of his mind. He could hear them breathing in the darkness, the intentional darkness chosen for him.

"The hidden eighth colour of the rainbow," said the voice, "a colour suited to your perfidy. We choose not to look upon you, and invoke instead the darkness to cover your many sins. Let your accusers now speak."

And they spoke, oh they spoke, one after another, each voice a knife paring away the frightened man's illusions. "I paid you to keep silent about my theft," said one, invisible in the darkness yet so present to Jau's terrified mind's eye. "My confession absolves me of my crime." "You bribed me to overlook customs due on your goods," said another, "and my confession absolves me of my crime." Jau's head swam at the depth of the betrayal, the completeness of official knowledge of his crimes. Long before the last accuser finished speaking he had become a hollow man, all illusions scooped out by the words of these once-bought men and women. Facing himself in the dark he began to shake and whimper in fear, and the Emperor and his court listened in silence to the sound of guilt.

Later, after the sentence was pronounced and he was removed to the dungeons beneath the Palace, his whimpers turned to screams. An Omeran went to work on him, first prodding and scraping, then cutting and burning, until his spirit seemed ready to separate from his tortured body. Methodically they destroyed his beloved flesh past any healing, and the pain took him into a world beyond his most dreaded nightmare. Then a man wearing a hood came and asked him questions, not about his offending—he had confessed his crimes and begged forgiveness until something in his throat had broken—but about what impending death felt like. Like a little child in an earthquake, lost and bewildered, running towards shelter of any kind, Jau begged the man in the hood for help. But the hooded man just asked his gentle questions, coaxing answers out of the captive's ruined throat as the Omeran thinned out the fragile connection between Jau Maranaya and this world.

Despite his extremely he saw the hooded man turn to the Omeran and heard him speak. "This I have learned today. Being born is a violence akin to being thrown from a cliff." His words carried the solemn weight of a newly learned truth. "Only it takes a lifetime to strike the rocks below."

And, wonder of wonders, the Omeran replied thoughtfully, as though he was an equal.

"No, ma great sor, we fall from a cliff of unknowable height, hoping it will take seventy years at least to get to the bottom, but fearing it might be much less—might be now, or *now*—all the while trying to forget we are falling."

The man in the hood laughed at this, as though a sly joke had been made at the expense of the universe. "We are learning, my friend, from one whose fall is almost over. Let us see what else this unfortunate has to teach us before we give him his landing."

Before the end the hooded man removed his covering, and Jau received his last and greatest shock of the day. And at dawn, when the shrieking and pleading were over, and all the lessons learned and recorded, Jau Maranaya was taken to the Garden of Angels and laid to rest in the bed prepared for him.

Lenares shifted her aching buttocks, trying to ease the cramps hurting her. This was her first time in the Talamaq Palace, and she knew she had to behave. She did not want people to notice her until the right time, but sitting on a hard wooden bench for (calculate) seven and eight-fifteenth hours had made her afraid that if she did not find relief soon she would cry out with the pain.

"Why must we put up with this, ma dama?" she whispered irritably to Mahudia, the head of her order. "Why could we not have stayed home? We could have been summoned when it was our turn to meet the Emperor. I want to go home."

The Chief Cosmographer turned to her young charge, patience puckering her kindly, open face. "The Emperor has his reasons," she answered primly. "Be still, girl. If my bones can bear this waiting, so can yours. Be thankful you are not the one about to face *his* crimes." She waved a slim wrist towards the Corridor of Rainbows and, as she did, the light began to fade.

The day's entertainment had made Lenares angry. She knew it was wrong to think such thoughts—"treasonous," Mahudia called her words when she'd whispered them in her ear—but to Lenares their beloved Emperor acted like a bully. Earlier in the day she had watched a man praised for squeezing extra rental money from poor stallholders in Avensvala (she listened to the long list of figures and calculated seventeen thousand, five hundred and sixty-three mola total profit at thirty-six point three per cent, a figure eleven point three per cent over the odds). He was honoured with yellow-green light and some flattering praise. Another man had been told off because he'd been kind to tenants in the Third of Glass, and as a result hadn't collected as much rent as the Emperor demanded. The Emperor hadn't raised his voice from behind his big yellow mask, but the man had been scared and, in between stuttering and grovelling, promised to do much better. Lenares couldn't understand what was wrong with being kind. Wasn't that what they were all taught to be? Hadn't Mahudia told them the Emperor was the kindest of all men?

Following this a tall, thin woman had been bathed in orange light, and rewarded with one thousand mola (two point four five eight eight three five times the average annual cosmographer's salary, Lenares calculated to six decimal places) for her part in uncovering an assassination attempt. Apparently the woman had overheard some discussion among her fellow seamstresses and reported it to her seniors—at considerable risk to herself, she said. Lenares did not believe the woman's story, though she could not say why. According to Mahudia, who called it intuition, Lenares was seldom wrong. *Never* wrong, according to herself.

Of much more interest was an army captain's lengthy report on a journey of exploration to the little-known lands fatherwards of Elamaq. The report listed the value of items received through judicious trading (the captain emphasised this repeatedly) but was silent on the shape of the land, the beliefs and customs of the people and other things of interest to a cosmographer. This frustrated Lenares. *Why are the important things always ignored?* The man was awarded a generous annual stipend of one percent of the value of his plunder (she calculated the stipend as thirty-one thousand, one hundred and seventy-eight point nine mola, seventy-six point six six six nine one two six times the average annual cosmographer's salary, to seven decimal places this time). The Emperor would meet with him again soon, the herald said.

Cramped and bored, Lenares had little to occupy her mind as she waited for Mahudia to present her to the Emperor and his court. She was special, everybody said so, even the jealous ones who continued to tease her. Lenares was about to become the latest fully commissioned cosmographer, a rare thing in these secular days, bringing the total to sixteen women and two men. This total was the lowest since the establishment of the Elamaq Empire three thousand, one hundred and seventeen years ago (one million, one hundred and thirty-eight thousand, six hundred and seventy-two days ago, including leap years and other adjustments, she calculated absently). She should be treated with reverence and honour, but after watching the day's tawdry display of greed she doubted the Emperor would recognise her value.

The Emperor knew something about value, however. This was clear from the wonder of Lenares' surroundings. Mahudia, who said she had been here many times before, had spent some time this morning explaining this to her, warning her not to touch anything. Lenares liked to touch things. She enjoyed the sensations texture created on her fingers. She wanted to run her hands over the thick red and blue rugs arranged on the pale stone floor. If only she was allowed to touch the tapestries hanging on the walls, each depicting a scene of importance in the empire's glorious past, she would be happy. She imagined how they would smell. The information they might yield to her! Yet the effect of the rich carpets, the detailed tapestries, the paintings framed in gold, the bronze statues, the intricate mosaics—colours, textures, scents—was to frustrate her still further. Why display these things only to deny her the opportunity to look at them? Perhaps when she was raised a true cosmographer she would be granted permission. She would ask the Emperor.

Now the corridor was readied to reward yet another revenue-gatherer or informer. Lenares prepared to sink her mind back into distance-and-bearing calculations for the Third of Pasture, the fatherback sector of the city, just for the fun of playing with the numbers. Around her the light dimmed, and dimmed further, through blue and indigo and violet. Her head jerked up, calculations forgotten, as the Emperor addressed the invisible figure in the dark corridor.

What followed made her feel ill. The crooked stallholder was undoubtedly a bad man, she could hear it in his thin voice quivering in the darkness, but the way the Emperor dealt with him seemed unfair to her. His crime was behaving like a bully, just like the Emperor, only smaller. Her all-loving ruler forced frightened citizens to testify against this man. "I sold Jau Maranaya many secrets from my employer's factory," said one man, smelling of terror as he spoke, his voice hesitating as though he had been forced to learn his speech. She could hear his fear; it frightened her. "He threatened to tell my wife and employer about my perverted liaisons with Omeran females if I didn't." A silence: Lenares imagined him glancing around the chamber, shame and misery in his eyes. "My confession absolves my crime." But the man's frightened voice made it clear that his crime was not absolved. Something awful would be done to him. Why else would he be so scared?

And what would happen to the stallholder in the corridor? He deserved some punishment, but not this humiliation. How many other people would die for imitating their Emperor? *We have lost our way*, Lenares realised, using a phrase her teacher often employed. The thought made her feel sick, especially in the light of what she knew. *We cannot afford to lose our way, not now.*

Two Omeran guards bundled the man out. Hauled him away like refuse. Gentle pale light flooded the audience hall through the Corridor of Rainbows, and around Lenares people took deep breaths and began to stretch aching muscles. It seemed the Emperor had had enough of audiences: he instructed his herald to dip the royal standard, signalling the end of the day's court.

Beside Lenares, Mahudia bit her lip, concern etched on her pale patrician face. "He has forgotten us," she said, and to the young cosmographer's literal mind the comment seemed to sum up everything she had seen.

They filed unregarded from the vast audience hall, and passed quickly through the Garden of Angels. The garden's delicate beauty touched her far less than it had this morning. Perhaps it was her black mood, or the cramps still causing her pain. She paused to stare interestedly for a few moments at an elderly gardener standing in a deep, narrow hole, then left the woman to get on with her digging. Her tables of figures called to her.

"I am so ashamed, Lenares. You ought not to have been brushed aside in this manner." Mahudia followed her words with a hug.

"I don't care," the girl replied, her mouth half-full of bread. "I don't need the Emperor's blessing to be what I am."

"But we do." Worry rippled through the Chief Cosmographer's voice. "Thanks to your calculations we know that something has changed in the world, and we need the Emperor's help to combat it."

"Soon I will know what it is and where to find it," Lenares said, seizing the moment.

"You will?" Mahudia smiled warmly. "That's wonderful news. But it will mean nothing unless we can persuade the Emperor to listen."

Back to this again. The young cosmographer didn't care overmuch about the Emperor and his doings. She couldn't see how he could do much about the growing change she could sense in the world around her. The change fascinated her, consumed her, forcing her to check all her calculations again and again for error, even though she never made mistakes. *What is the change like?* Mahudia asked her regularly. Impossible to answer. Lenares' world was different to that experienced by others. Hers was made up not of people and events, but of nodes, each node a number, with threads between the nodes giving them meaning. She was not good with words, Lenares knew this, but no one saw numbers as she saw them. Numbers were places, real places in the landscape of her mind, each place connected to thousands of other places by a network of threads like lines on a map. Except this map was not fixed on paper; it was constantly on the move, with herself at the centre. She had a highly developed spatial sense, Mahudia always said by way of explanation. Lenares shrugged. Unimportant.

Much more important was the widening hole in the threads of her world, a jagged tear as though someone had taken a knife to her mind. It terrified her.

Lenares suspected the hole had always been there. Something had always lurked just beyond her best efforts to bring it into focus, a shape with no shape—a nothingness, she had no words for it—that interfered with her perception of an ordered world. When she first tried putting it into words Mahudia named it randomness, said it was a metaphor for the changing world Lenares had always been afraid of. Part of her specialness. Lenares always shrugged when her teachers said things like that. The words sounded right because they were clever, but they didn't fit into the nodes and threads, so they were wrong. She could not demonstrate this to the third degree of proof needed for cosmography, not yet, so she was not believed by anyone but Mahudia.

But soon she would be. Soon they would all believe

her. The hole in the world was large now, hundreds of bright threads hanging loose in the devouring blackness, and every time she checked her calculations a few more threads separated and another node fell out of the pattern. It was not natural, whatever Mahudia said. Lenares now had the means to locate the circumference of this hole, using strange numbers she had invented to give shape to the shapeless. To fight the nothingness that was destroying her ordered world. This knowledge was to be her gift to the Emperor, the father of the Amaqi, the wise, great man whom Mahudia had taught her to love.

The Emperor, however, was not a great man. He did not deserve to be loved. He behaved more like the bullies she'd been tormented by throughout her miserable childhood. She hated bullies. Why should she share her great discovery with such a person?

Lenares nibbled at a strand of her hair, then pushed it up between her lips and her nose. She always did this when she was thinking. *We have lost our way*. What if the threads they were travelling ended at the hole? What if the next node was unreachable? What if their nodes were the next to be engulfed? She needed time to do more calculations, but all people wanted to do was talk. Even Mahudia, who was so nice to her, talked far too much. Sometimes she could not stand it.

"The Emperor will not listen to us," Lenares said. "I think he is part of the problem. He is a weakness in the pattern. When I do my calculations I will find his node, and the hole will be nearby." As she said this, she knew it to be true. She could always tell whether or not words fitted the pattern. No one could lie to her.

Mahudia looked troubled by this. "We must try," she

said, then plucked at her bottom lip in a characteristic gesture. Lenares knew exactly how many times she had seen Mahudia do this. It was a thread, giving meaning to the node that was the Chief Cosmographer.

"When I work out where the hole is, I want to go and look at it," Lenares announced.

"I thought you might." Mahudia's face was stern. "I won't let you. It would be dangerous. Wouldn't you rather calculate some way we can put a stop to it, heal the gash, put the world back together?"

"I'm going to my room," Lenares said, unable to bear her mentor's face. She didn't like Mahudia when she wore her angry face.

"Find out how much time we have left," Mahudia called to the retreating figure, and received the usual shrug in response.

The summons came early the next morning. The day was already hot and promised to grow much hotter—in more ways than one, Mahudia reflected. All seventeen cosmographers, and the one who was to be raised, had been invited to attend upon the Emperor within the hour. They were to present themselves at the Gate of the Father, and would be received in the Garden of Angels. Such honour. They were to be properly grateful. They were not to be late.

Mahudia sent young Galla around the rooms to wake her charges. "Swiftly, girl; one hour is not long." The cosmographers were not a presentable lot. Obsessives never were, and one could not be a true cosmographer without having such a nature. They would need the full hour to stumble out of their beds and into their unfamiliar best clothes, such as they were. Only the Blessed Three knew how they were to travel across the city to Talamaq Palace in time for their appointment.

"My lady!" It was Galla, returned from her errand, her whining voice like rhubarb on the tongue. "Lenares won't come out of her room."

Not today, please the Son, let her not be taken by one of her humours. Mahudia rushed down the cold stone corridor, which was unadorned by painting, cloth or art—meaningless irrelevancies—but still managed to trip on a flagstone and bruise both her palms and her left knee. She was in poor humour herself by the time she arrived at Lenares' room.

The Chief Cosmographer found the girl sitting at her desk, wide-eyed and crying. She had clearly been upset for hours, by the state of her. All the rubbish on her desk—insect husks, pieces of paper, feathers, a myriad of incongruous objects—had been moved about, as happened whenever Lenares was agitated. *Something in her world has changed, and she has rebuilt it all over again.* Mahudia sighed, dismayed. So powerfully gifted, so difficult to love, so impossible to control.

"Lenares?" she hazarded. "Our new cosmographer?"

A pasty-white face turned to her, and Mahudia took an involuntary step backwards. All expression had been stripped from the girl's features. Her enormous eyes were dull, her pale cheeks hollow and her honey-coloured hair hung lankly over her face. All the gains of the last eight years appeared to have been wiped away.

It was the face of a violated young girl, a face Mahudia had not seen for a decade, since a certain alley one late summer afternoon when she and Palaman had driven the last of the youths away. The day they found Lenares, saw her for the first time, naked, dirty and unresponsive, answering only to her inner voices, perhaps unaware—they had never been sure—of what the youths had been doing to her. Of how they had ruined her.

Years passed before they found a way through the seemingly impervious casing around the girl. They had no intention of training her as a cosmographer, not then. She was clearly subnormal, a thin, troubled waif who spent her uncommunicative days collecting plants and making piles of them in her room. Leaves, roots, stems, petals, branches everywhere. Palaman had hoped, though, to use her as a servant. Money was tight; the Emperor seemed to have forgotten about the cosmographers, and their stipend was reduced every year by some court functionary. But Lenares proved little use as a servant. Even when she understood what was required of her, she was apt to wander off on errands of her own devising, offering no apology and indifferent to the beatings that followed.

Palaman, the head of their order, died without seeing Lenares bloom. Mahudia tried to look after the difficult girl, but without Palaman there seemed little point. One day, no different to any other day, she had taken the girl with her when she taught the acolytes' class. They were studying *ilm al-raml* geomancy, the ancient technique of discerning the nature and activities of the gods from the shape of the physical landscape, and as usual the new recruits struggled with the simplest locational task. Mahudia turned away from them as she did every year, affecting disgust, and made to point at the map of Elamaq spread across the wall.

To her astonishment, one of the girls piped up. "Marasmos."

The newly-appointed Chief Cosmographer spun around. "Marasmos, ma dama," she corrected testily, trying to cover her shock with brusqueness while raking the class with her stare. Who had spoken? Nobody ever got the answer right. Was this a lucky guess?

"Marasmos, ma dama," came the voice again. She jerked her head around but could not locate the speaker. Which of her pupils . . .

"It was Lenares, ma dama," one of the girls—she had forgotten which one, all the faces blurred after a while—said to her.

"Lenares Lackbrain," another girl muttered, and a few of the class laughed. Their laughter stopped short at the look on their teacher's face.

"Lenares, did you speak to me?" Shock gave way to a heady exhilaration. *Could it be possible?*

"You asked what project could only be undertaken because of the expanding influence of the Son," the blessed girl said in an animated voice, startlingly different to her usual monotone. "The Amaqi under Emperor Pouna III diverted the Marasmos River to deprive the Marasmian people of their major water source. The river was harnessed to allow the city of Talamaq to grow, and now waters the Third of Pasture. A year later an Amaqi army led by Pouna the Great destroyed the weakened Marasmian kingdom, eliminating the last resistance to Amaqi domination of Elamaq. *Ilm al-raml* geomancy was crucial in this success. I think cosmographers calculated the movement of the Son closer to Talamaq, and moved the river to follow Him. Am I right? Can I see the calculations? Have they been kept?"

Complete, stunned silence met this discourse. Mahudia

could not have been more shocked if the cosmographers' pet goat had spoken to her. Less, actually, as there was at least historical precedent for talking goats, if the legends were to be believed.

"You have the date of the river damming wrong," the girl continued. "It was a year later than you told us. It must have been. Check your notes. The Son could not have come closer to Talamaq on the date you said."

Having finished her revelation, Lenares turned back to her battered desk and continued to arrange the small collection of leaves she carried with her at all times. A deeply troubled Mahudia had checked her notes that afternoon and discovered a transcribing error she had perpetuated for at least fifteen years.

From that day on the girl blossomed, learning to interact with others in at least a limited fashion, showing a talent for cosmography so rare as to have been thought extinct in this secular age. She grew taller than the other girls, adding to her otherworldly appearance. Her plain, sorrowful face had changed with her personality, becoming progressively more expressive.

Until today.

"Oh, Lenares, what has happened?"

An almost imperceptible shake of the head was the only reply.

The tears did not stop, even after Mahudia washed and dressed her new cosmographer, just as she had done every day for two years after they'd first found her. Until the day Lenares had spoken in that acolytes' class. The hour allowed them by the Emperor had long passed before the cosmographers made their way from their quarters to the Talamaq Palace. Lenares wept the whole journey, almost unconsciously it seemed, a picture of desolation. Mahudia worried more about her protégé's state of mind than about how the Emperor, notoriously capricious, would respond to their lateness. After all, the Emperor was most likely to censure them at worst. Hopefully. The world would be deprived of far more if Lenares' talents were lost.

A thick heat haze squeezed down upon the city, making the spires and minarets appear out of the gloom as though from the sleeve of a trickster. Were the cosmographers merely standing in the morning heat they would sweat; hustling daughterwards across the Third of Glass the perspiration poured from them. To their right the plastered houses on Money Hill, above the worst of the haze, shimmered in the heat. The usual crush around Gold Souk and the money exchange forced them through two dark, noisome alleyways, the second of which brought them back to Hadrami Avenue. Another five minutes and they reached the cobbled Avensvala, the wide avenue encircling the Talamaq Palace, panting and puffing like blown horses, irretrievably late. The three golden rizen-stone towers of Talamaq loomed out of the haze like impatient sentries, ready to rebuff their excuses.

As they were admitted by unsmiling guards to the Garden of Angels, the girl muttered something. Mahudia heard it as much through her skin, holding the girl's cold, thin hand in hers, as through her ears. Patience. Lenares often repeated herself.

When the words came again, the Chief Cosmographer had to bend to catch them, delivered as they were without inflection, on the edge of hearing.

"The hole in the world. It is coming. To the garden."

*   *   *

The self-styled Philosopher-King, the Emperor of the Amaqi, ruler of the known world, remained motionless on his bench despite his burgeoning impatience. He refused to rub his aching buttocks. His favourite spot in the entire garden, the place he visited to forget the troubles associated with ruling an empire, would not be sullied by his anger.

His two Omeran bodyguards matched him for stillness, though only because they did not have the intelligence to be distracted. The perfect guards.

Torve, his beloved companion, hovered discreetly a few paces away, bent over a rose.

"What do you think I should see planted in the new bed, Torve?" The Emperor prided himself on his green fingers.

"Given the poor quality of the fertiliser, ma great sor, we should think carefully about which specimens might grow." Torve lifted his dark, inhuman face from the pure white rose he cupped tenderly in his hand. "Perhaps some kind of spikegrass?"

The Emperor laughed. "Excellent choice. Fool's Felt, then?"

"Ma great sor, Fool's Felt is too long-lived for that bed."

The sally drew a smile from the Emperor. Clever beast, clever indeed. An Omeran with the ability to think, to read, to discuss philosophical texts. Ought to have been crushed under chariot wheels, of course, as soon as its freakish intelligence showed itself. Instead it was given to him as a pet when he was but the young heir, and he indulged it shamelessly. And now the result: a life-long companion. Totally loyal, completely discreet. The product of generations of Omerans bred for obedience.

"Something insignificant. Nondescript. We will think more on it." The Emperor scratched at his beard under his mask.

His Omeran companion returned to contemplating the roses. Strange species, Omerans, the Emperor reflected, not for the first time. Some scholars even claimed a common ancestry with humans some time in the distant past. Possible, he supposed, but unlikely. The Amaqi valued intelligence above all things, and the Omerans were clearly deficient in this regard, Torve notwithstanding. All speculation was moot, regardless, as Emperor after Emperor down through the centuries declared Omerans emphatically non-human. Self-serving, of course, but something could be both self-serving and true.

Today the Emperor had his Omeran dressed in pale lavender, an echo of his own royal purple. Torve's tunic was threaded with lemon, intricate designs of hummingbirds and flowers set off by bright yellow button work. The message—that the Omeran supped constantly from the Emperor's largesse—could not be mistaken. The pantaloons were a plainer cut, lest the courtiers and Alliance members took offence. The feet were clad in soft white leather shoes, not very practical in the Garden of Angels but certainly comfortable in this heat.

No matter how the Omeran was dressed, its heritage could not be disguised. Dark brown skin, much darker than the golden Amaqi tone. A high forehead above a broad face, the eyes wide apart, square-jawed and thick-necked, distinctly simian features that were echoed in hairy knuckles and exaggerated musculature. Brutish physical features that appeared inexpertly carved from some hardwood tree.

He himself wore purple, of course, threaded with gold. His jacket depicted summer showers, the bounty of the Emperor falling on his subjects from golden clouds, and the subject of a private joke between himself and Torve. Pantaloons of overlapping cloth created a rippling effect when he walked, something his seamstresses had come up with recently and which was already becoming something of a sensation at his court. The golden mask he always wore in public sat easily on his face, the weight borne by the bridge of his nose. He had a permanent callus there. His shoes were gilded leather, his hat fashionably square with a tassel of gold thread, and he wore kid-leather gloves. He was very pleased with the effect, and refused to spoil it by rubbing at his sore buttocks.

The Gate of the Father opened inwards, and the wretched cosmographers filed into the Garden of Angels. Relics of a religious past, an anachronism in the secular world with its emphasis on the ever-present Now, the cosmographers were hated by the Amaqi precisely because they reminded everyone of their history. In a culture that chose to focus on the present, this was a major failing.

The Emperor doubted they were aware of this.

He watched them as they filed slowly across the lawn towards his bench. The Chief Cosmographer, Son sear her soul, held hands with a young woman who looked none too happy at the fact. Was this why she—the Emperor searched his mind for her name, appended to countless petitions for audiences, how could he have forgotten?—was this why Mahudia joined with the cosmographers? To dally with the acolytes? The daughter of Hudan, leader of the Elborans, one of the most important Alliances, could live in luxury if she chose. Late thirties, if he remembered correctly. Fine features, full-breasted, and with a fortune in trust from her father, she could pick and choose from the noblemen of the city. Had she chosen perversion instead?

The cosmographers were an unkempt group. He looked on their attire: dishevelled, unfashionable clothing, purple bibs faded from repeated washing. What fool Emperor had granted them the right to wear purple? Why were they once held in such honour? Dishevelled bodies, dishevelled minds. What was the woman running? A shelter for undesirable girls? And what was she doing with the generous stipend he granted them? Clearly not using it to purchase cloth! The Emperor suspected the Chief Cosmographer lined her own pockets. There were questions to be asked.

The young woman accompanying Mahudia looked unwell, in point of fact. Pale face, red eyes, weeping. Puffy lips moving as though cursing someone. She had been punished, then. For what transgression? Resisting the attentions of her mistress?

The cosmographers made their obeisance, prostrating themselves thrice as required. The Emperor observed Mahudia drag the young woman to the ground for the first obeisance, directing her unmistakably vacant stare to the grass. A half-wit, no doubt of it. Half-wits in normal society were ritually strangled to death when so assessed, preserving the clear distinction between humans and Omerans. The cosmographers were supposed to be intellectually gifted, yet they sheltered such a one among them.

Not for much longer.

"Arise," he commanded them. "You may kneel on the

grass before us." The cosmographers had been checked for weapons at the gate, and his guards were capable of overpowering any treasonous attack from the men and women before him.

"We trust you found yesterday's court instructive." He spoke to Mahudia; the others listened. He had cultivated a compelling voice, had trained it for years, and used it ruthlessly. "The black is not often seen by ordinary citizenry. You have been privileged. And you are further privileged today."

Mahudia nodded her head in acknowledgment, as was proper. "We thank you, ma great sor, for this unexpected invitation. We seek your blessing on our new cosmographer, and would ask you a boon."

A boon? What could the woman possibly want that she had not asked for a hundred times in her interminable missives? *Deal with this one issue at a time. Blessing, then boon.*

Mahudia stood, dragging the half-wit with her.

The Emperor stood in turn, almost knocking over the bench in his haste to put some distance between himself and the distasteful girl. He forced himself to relax his tense muscles. He would not allow the girl to unsettle him.

"*This* is your latest cosmographer?" he asked, and watched the colour drain from Mahudia's face in response to his tone. How could she think he would not be affronted by this?

"Ma great sor, she is—"

"A lackwit," he finished. "A charity or something worse. Your plaything, perhaps."

Now her colour returned, but she dared not speak. Well-trained daughter of a prominent Alliance member.

The Emperor adopted a conciliatory tone. "How can we bless a half-wit? You know what must be done with her." He knew he should speak more harshly, but did not want the ambience of his garden disturbed.

"She is no half-wit, ma great sor!" His ear picked up a note of pleading in her voice, piquing his interest. "Sometimes those carrying the greatest gifts also bear unusual burdens. She sees . . . she sees—"

"I see the hole in the world," said the half-wit in a droning voice, her wet eyes unfocused in the manner of a third-rate carnival-ground seer. "Here, in this garden. We should not be here. We must leave."

The Emperor turned to the abomination. "We decide when—or if—you leave. Torve, we shall keep this one for further examination. If she can show us she is worthy of our blessing, she will receive it."

Mahudia showed the good sense to bow her head in helpless submission, but then jerked it up again, against all protocol, as a deep rumble came from the ground directly beneath them. There was a pause, a soundless moment, the birds silent—as they had been for some time, the Emperor realised, only the gentle sound of water from fountains around the garden, patter patter patter—followed by a roar and a powerful jerk that knocked the cosmographers to the ground. The Garden of Angels was instantly transformed into a heaving sea of green, ponderous earth-waves carrying with them bursting pipes, reeling fountains, bushes and trees. Branches whipped and cracked all around them, falling across rippling lawns. People cried out in terror. The world itself seemed to roar at them, a voice filled with agony.

In the midst of this crashing and grinding the Emperor stood unmoving, legs apart, hands braced against the bench. He willed himself not to fall. Refused the terror clawing at him. He mastered his fear and watched wide-eyed as the earth ripped asunder across the width of the garden, a wet brown mouth opening as if to swallow whatever it could. Trees fell into the maw. People crawled desperately away from the gash— gardeners, cosmographers, guards. An elderly gardener stumbled, lost her footing and pitched backwards into the darkness with a thin cry. Tree roots flicked up like serpent tongues. A foul breath came from the gaping mouth, choking the Emperor who imagined he smelled the decay and corruption underneath his garden. As if all the dead bodies conspired revenge against him.

He must not die. This was what he was afraid of, above all. He had built an entire empire as a bulwark against death, something to take shelter within, to keep him safe. And yet, in spite of all his planning, his careful investigations into death and the circumstances surrounding it, the countless people he'd observed as they died, death now reached out a palsied hand to take him. The gods would have him, would punish him for his blasphemy. Paralysed now, he could only watch as a tree root snaked towards him, tip quivering, searching, grasping, winding itself around his leg.

The roaring stopped, the earth ceased shuddering. There was a crash as a last tree toppled to the ground, then another as a wall of the glorious Talamaq Palace belatedly collapsed in a dusty heap. The Emperor's ears rang, but despite this he heard the inarticulate groaning of his subjects as they pulled themselves to their feet. Avoiding the water pooling in new-formed depressions, stepping around the overturned hedges and the diagonal slash of the sundered earth, his people came from wherever in or around the Palace they'd been and slowly gathered around him, their Emperor, the only one to remain standing throughout the shaking. He realised how he must appear to them; a god amongst mere mortals. One who could stand against the power of the earth. Immortal in bearing, in wisdom, in countenance, in courage. In everything but fact.

Might that one day be changed?

He watched one of his Omeran guards, uniform plastered with mud, draw his sword and cut the tree root away from his Emperor's leg. *Legends will grow around this*, the great man realised. *I will be worshipped*.

Events had driven all memory of the half-wit's words from his head until he was reminded by Torve's whispers in his ear. The Emperor turned to his companion.

"She did say that, did she not. Set her apart. We have questions for her."

He clicked his tongue in annoyance. His first words after this event would be remembered. They ought not to have been about a half-wit.

Taking a deep, steadying breath, he addressed his subjects, who continued to gather, coming from the Palace and grounds. "Seemingly the gods are displeased with our garden," he said dryly. His courtiers laughed: none believed in the gods, at least openly. "We in turn are displeased by their response. The Garden of Angels will be rebuilt, and all marks of the intervention of the Three will be expunged. In the meantime, we will journey through our beloved city to survey the extent of the damage and offer assistance to our subjects. Then we will ascertain why we continue to sponsor cosmographers who cannot predict the actions of their gods, or even prove their existence."

His subjects bowed before him; he dismissed them with a gesture. Let others see to the dead and the wounded. For now he needed a stiff drink—more than one, in fact—and then he had some questions to ask.

CHAPTER 4

QUESTIONS AND ANSWERS

THE AIR FELT DRY AND STALE in the room far below the Emperor's Palace. Though she knew the room to be a dungeon, a dangerous place where terrible things happened, Lenares felt safe here. The thick stone walls hid her, no longer exposing her to the bright questing mind she had briefly glimpsed earlier that day through the hole in the world. The dreadful fear had relaxed its grip, though Mahudia was clearly still terrified, holding Lenares' chained hand with annoying tightness.

Lenares tried to talk with her, to comfort her, but Mahudia appeared beyond comfort. "Hush," she replied to anything Lenares said. "Hush." And once: "We are in the Emperor's domain now. We should not speak."

So Lenares remained silent, sitting on a wooden bench, calculating furiously, her free hand moving small piles of dust back and forth. The hole had revealed itself, and by doing so had given her an absolute value upon which to hang her strange numbers. She had numerous adjustments to make. Her mind worked without her conscious volition: she sat back as a spectator and watched the patterns select themselves, watched the equations emerge and resolve. Watched expectantly, with mounting excitement, as the conclusion began to take shape.

She was special. None of the other cosmographers could think like her. The trouble was, this conclusion was so big, so important, that they would not believe her even when she explained it to them using her strange numbers. She was not sure she believed it herself. She would have to find out for herself. She would have to go to the place—

The rusty metal door swung open and two people walked in. Lenares remembered seeing one of them in the Garden of Angels, over by the white roses. Not a tall man, he looked different from the people she was used to seeing in the Third of Glass. He had very dark skin, a wide face, a broad nose, and crinkly lines around his eyes. She studied him for a moment, assigning him a node, calculating his position relative to the tear in the garden, her new absolute. The numbers declared him trustworthy, a relief. He had a nice face. Soft, open.

The other person wore a hood. Mahudia whimpered in fear and tried to spider-walk away from the hooded figure. Her head cracked against the stone wall behind her. She shrieked once and then fell silent.

"What are you afraid of, cosmographer?" The hooded person approached Mahudia's cowering body. The voice was muffled, distorted somehow, but Lenares couldn't be fooled. Voice tricks could not disguise the numbers. She knew who this man was. Her instincts told her not to reveal this knowledge, not yet. He must have a reason for his disguise.

"Don't—please, don't touch her," Mahudia pleaded.

Lenares started in surprise, and tears came to her eyes. *Mahudia is not frightened for herself alone. She is frightened for me!*

"Touch her? We will do a lot more than touch her, cosmographer, if we choose to. I see from your face you know what we can do here, in our domain. Let me ask you, then, why you think we have you and your companion here?"

Mahudia levered herself onto her elbows and drew her knees close to her body. "The Emperor wants to know about the warning Lenares offered."

The hooded man turned to his colleague. "See? I told you she is no simpleton. Mahudia comes from some of our purest bloodlines. This is no puzzle to her."

His companion nodded. "She is courageous as well as intelligent."

Mahudia spoke. "If you know who my father is, you must know he will object to my mistreatment. He will seek audience with the Emperor, and will find some way to secure our release." Her raised chin was a brave attempt at defiance, but Lenares could see her whole body shaking. Mahudia was scared.

The reply was swift and brutal. "We know who your father is. In fact, the Emperor has already dispatched a messenger to sor Hudan to tell him of the tragic death of his daughter today in the Garden of Angels. It appears she was swallowed by the earth, so unfortunately no body will made available for burial."

Lenares watched as the words punctured Mahudia's pretend defiance, her head dropping until her chin rested on her chest.

"We must question the girl, and question her hard. You

know this, Mahudia. The less you cooperate, the harder
we will question. Look at it." The man in the hood gestured towards Lenares as though pointing to a cow or a
pig. "Look. There's not much there to begin with. How
much do you think will remain of your pet when we have
finished?"

"Cruel," Mahudia whispered. "So cruel." She gathered
herself. "I will cooperate."

"Of course you will," said the hooded man, and
nodded.

At the nod the Omeran sprang forward and grabbed a
pair of shears from a low bench. Mahudia gasped and
Lenares squealed in surprise as he hacked off a hank of
Lenares' hair. He let her go, then strode over to a brazier
and cast the hair into the embers. A scorched smell drifted
over them. Mahudia began to weep.

Lenares ran her free hand over the spot on her head
where her hair had been taken. No one was supposed to
touch her without asking; Mahudia made that rule to stop
the others picking on her. *But the rules don't hold in here.*

"I know who you are," she said to the hooded man, fix-
ing him with her most direct stare. The man flinched, just
like the Emperor had when Mahudia introduced her to
him in the garden. "Your hood and your clever voice trick
fool everyone, but not me. I don't believe my eyes or my
ears. I see the real world, and you look the same to me
whether you wear a hood or a mask. *I know your secret.*"

She expected the man to he shocked and angry, but he
threw back his head and laughed. "Ah, Mahudia, you have
chosen your pet well. I hope she gives you as much pleasure as Torve gives me!"

A word, a name spoken, the mention of the mask

perhaps, gave the secret to Mahudia. She said nothing, but Lenares could read the shock clearly on her face. The man in the hood saw she knew.

"So you know why you cannot leave this place, my dear," said the Emperor, pushing back his hood to reveal a golden mask. "We will make it clean, though, out of respect for your father. That is, if your pet does what we want."

"Don't hurt her." The words were weak, the only defence Mahudia had left.

This had gone far enough. Lenares knew how to deal with bullies. "Hurt me and you will never know what I have learned. Without the things I know, you will never get what you want."

"And what do I want?" Mockery in the voice.

"You want to live forever," she said simply, throwing the words at him as though tossing him a poisonous spider. "You're afraid to die."

"Who told you that?"

"No one. The numbers are clear. I can see what you are by looking at the numbers in my head. They make a pattern and the pattern tells me all about you. That's how I know you are frightened. That's what makes you mean and cruel. Your fear draws the hole—"

"Enough!" the Emperor roared, and backhanded Lenares across her face, knocking her to the stone floor.

It was much later, in the depths of the night, though Mahudia could not be certain of the time. Lenares lectured them. It marked her difference that she would instruct her captors in a dungeon rather than bemoan her fate or plead for her life. The Emperor listened and said little. The Omeran took notes.

"Everything is made up of numbers," Lenares explained, her voice more animated than earlier, thickened somewhat by her bruised nose. "Mahudia is made up of numbers. The numbers describe how she looks, how she smells, whether she's nice or mean. If I look at the numbers connected to her I can tell things about her past and even some things about her future."

The Emperor leaned over to whisper in the ear of his pet, who muttered an inaudible answer. They were still clearly uncertain, but perhaps not as sceptical as they had been an hour ago. Lenares continued to wear them down with her remorseless arguments.

"What number tells you how Mahudia smells?" asked the Emperor.

"Not just one number. The numbers change all the time. But her nicest smell is usually linked to eighty-three."

"Why eighty-three?" the Omeran asked.

"Eighty-three has a sliced-apple smell. It smells of sweetness, of goodness, of health."

Lenares spoke slowly, as though explaining to a child. Mahudia felt like a child listening to her. No cosmographer in history had had such a profound understanding of numbers, she was certain, not even the Emperor who founded the art three millennia ago. What they dreamed of, aspired to, this child had.

"What other numbers are smells?"

"Eighty-three is sometimes not a smell," Lenares continued, as though the Omeran had not spoken. She became like this when explaining something. She possessed an uncanny intensity about her, as though a powerful candle had been lit within her body. She had the supreme gift of being able to focus fully on one thing. Mahudia lost the thread for a moment, and backtracked.

"What are my numbers?" the Emperor had asked.

"Ninety-one and one hundred and twenty-one are your most obvious numbers," Lenares was saying. "There are more, but I haven't known you very long so I can't see them yet. Ninety-one means lots of things, but one of the things it means is the scent of roses, while one hundred and twenty-one can mean the smell of dead rats in a larder." She said this matter-of-factly, despite whom she was talking to; she was, Mahudia knew, incapable of the subtlety required to dissemble, especially when talking about her numbers. "Put ninety-one and one hundred and twenty-one together and you have two hundred and twelve, a palindrome, another of your numbers, meaning death hidden by the pretence of health whichever way you look. Palindromes are numbers that hide the truth."

"I am a palindrome, then?" The Emperor had a sharp mind, very sharp. Mahudia hoped Lenares would not forget this.

"You are made up of palindromes," the girl replied. "They are special numbers."

Mahudia couldn't work out if this constituted a naïve attempt at flattery. Lenares generally argued that all numbers were special. She also did not flatter.

"What happens if you multiply the numbers?" the Omeran asked.

Lenares beamed at him, as though he was slightly less dim-witted than her other pupils. "Addition is flat, like a table-top. Multiplication has a shape like a box. There are even more complicated ways of putting numbers together, and these ways have shapes with more . . ." she searched for the word, "more surfaces. More dimensions."

"Eleven thousand and eleven," the Omeran announced, obviously proud of himself.

"Good." Lenares nodded to the Omeran. "But very slow. Eleven thousand and eleven, one digit short of perfect oneness, a very special number and another palindrome."

But with a hole in the middle, Lenares did not say. She was showing unaccustomed caution. A man with a void inside him, perhaps, Mahudia speculated. Or a rent?

"This is fascinating," the Emperor said, addressing Mahudia. "You have taught it to mouth meaningless philosophies and attach homilies to numbers. Of what use is this to anyone?"

"As much use as your Omeran is to you, ma great sor," she ventured; and immediately regretting her words, turned her gaze away so she didn't have to see her fate written in her Emperor's eyes. No matter what the Emperor decided to do with Lenares, Mahudia feared she would not leave the room alive. She glanced in his direction: his dark eyes were on her, hot and furious, shining through his mask. She was lost. All that remained was to fight for the girl.

Lenares scowled, unaware of the by-play. "Numbers define the universe," she said impatiently. "Even the gods leave traces when they act on the world. Reading the numbers correctly enables the cosmographers to know where the gods are and what they are doing."

"We haven't had a cosmographer capable of reading the numbers correctly for five hundred years or more," Mahudia added.

"I can read them correctly." Lenares snapped out her assertion. "But lately my calculations have been going wrong."

"Forgetting your tricks?" the Emperor mocked.

Lenares gave him a rude stare. "No. Something very important in the world is changing, affecting all the numbers around it. Things are being destroyed, and it is going to get worse. I see it as a great and growing gap in my mind, a hole in the world. I was going to tell the Emperor when he granted me an audience to raise me as a cosmographer, but he was rude and put me aside. I don't have to tell him now, though, do I?"

"Are we in danger from this hole?"

"It nearly killed you today."

"Ah. And you say you can tell us where it is?"

"And what it is, I think."

The Emperor clicked his tongue in impatience. "What is it, then?"

"I think the hole in the world is a missing god."

The silence following this pronouncement lasted just a little too long. *The Emperor is taking this seriously*, Mahudia realised, and her heart warmed. Her precious child held the power in this room now. They would not dare kill Lenares until she told them what she knew, and once they fully understood her value they would not harm her. They would exalt her and the cosmographers with her. The secularisation of Elamaq would be reversed. She was sure of it.

One fear eased; another rose in its place. *A missing god?* A cold finger touched Mahudia's spine as she considered her protégé's words.

Elamaq was the latest incarnation of the Amaqi people's desire to rule. How was it taught to infants? Elamaq the empire, Amaqi the people, Talamaq the city and the Palace of the Emperor, who ruled by the authority of the Three. At least, that was how she had been taught.

Mahudia's mind swept across the Great Land. The Elamaq Empire stretched more than a thousand leagues across the central and sonwards parts of the great continent, and as far from fatherwards to fatherback.

She chastised herself silently. The Emperor, in his quest to rid the empire of references to the gods, had forbidden the use of the old directional labels. Fatherwards was now "north" by decree; fatherback, the opposite direction, "south." Sonwards, daughterwards and their opposites had no direct counterpart in the new system. "East" and "west" were to be used instead. Mahudia sighed. The Emperor could not read her mind. She would continue to use the old notation, as would the rest of the cosmographers.

Her thoughts, sidetracked for a moment, returned to the missing god. Continuously occupied for over thirty thousand years, the lands of the empire were old and tired by comparison to the young lands said to lie fatherwards. Elamaq was a land of stone and sand, of pale deserts, of arthritic hills, of ephemeral rivers and mist-bound coasts. It was also a land of ancient enmity.

Long before people learned of their existence, three gods ruled the Great Land. The Omerans said that the Daughter dominated the gods, and the troubles had begun when the Father and the Son united together to usurp her. The views of the Omerans would not have been considered credible in Elamaq had they been known to any but the cosmographers and a few other scholars.

The Amaqi told stories about the harlotry of the

Daughter, base acts she committed with the ancestors of men, from which the Omerans were brought forth. This explained the need for her unnatural offspring to be kept in servitude, they said. The Son ruled the other two gods, the feeble Father and his Daughter the whore, and the Emperor reigned under the Son, the lord of a vigorous, dynamic empire, contaminated neither by womanish ways nor by the tired morals of the old.

Or the Son *would* rule the gods, had he not been declared nonexistent by the latest Emperor. The epoch of the Three was over by decree. The Amaqi would make their way in the world, would conquer the world, without any supernatural encumbrances.

The followers of the Father no longer told any stories. They had been obliterated from the earth thousands of years ago, so the story went, victims of revenge for some atrocity or other. The cosmographers collected any scroll mentioning the Father's worshippers: in three thousand years they had assembled half a dozen. No one remembered them.

Father, Son and Daughter. Few of the many formerly independent kingdoms that now made up Elamaq could agree on the relationship between the Three, but all agreed on the number of the gods and the name of each. And everyone—everyone but the Amaqi, it seemed—remembered what had happened to the Mother.

It was possible even for gods to die. But the legends associated with the Mother all talked of the catastrophic loss of life resulting from her death, of the destruction and remaking of the earth, of centuries of suffering and desolation.

When gods died, they did not die alone.

*   *   *

A fevered excitement gripped the Emperor of the Amaqi when he heard the half-wit make her pronouncement. He had been truly worried that the girl had been taught merely to perform tricks, that her "numbers" behaved in the same way as did the most credulous form of star-reading: the things she had said about him, for example, were the sort of things anyone might say about a king or emperor, though not normally to his face. He had feared she was a fake.

This evening the Emperor had for a time convinced himself that the half-wit possessed the ability to read faces. It wasn't unknown. Ambassadors were often chosen for the skill. Faces behaved differently depending on whether their wearers spoke truth or lied. He himself had witnessed hundreds of desperate people who in their extremity had tried to convince him that lies were truth. He knew what to look for in his search for the truth behind death, had learned what the eye and muscle movements meant. Perhaps the half-wit had a natural gift.

However, this line of thinking didn't explain how she could read a face perpetually hidden behind a golden mask. He could not be read. Torve, then? Even more obviously, such a talent could not account for her eerie prediction in the Garden of Angels. Could it have been coincidence, or had the gods found an unlikely mouthpiece?

No. The gods would not use one such as she to speak forth their truth. Therefore any predictive quality to her words must be coincidental.

A missing god? The thought made him nervous. He had been defying the gods for years, and would continue to do so for as long as he could. Forever. They had never openly opposed him. Dead, or alive but weakened: it made no difference. Of course they were missing. He had banished them! They might as well not exist. They did not exist. He was the power now.

As a result, the cosmographers were missing something. A central purpose, a reason for continued existence. Perhaps the half-wit sensed the lack as a "hole" in the world—or, more likely, it was this lack she had been instructed by Mahudia to emphasise. A political campaign, a quest for power. This he could understand.

In fact, this was how he would use her. She would become his political tool. With her insight he could strip the bark of lies and deceit away from the Alliances and expose their rotten wood. And, if she proved as talented as he hoped, she would be introduced to his quest, his lifelong battle to wrest immortality from the gods.

Ah, he was arguing in circles, contradicting himself at every turn. The only possible explanation was also the least palatable. The girl really could see things hidden from others.

Torve was talking to him.

"She knew about the earth tremor," his pet said quietly, echoing his own thoughts. "I'd like to learn how she knew."

Ah. So his pet wanted a pet of his own. For what purpose?

"We will sleep now," he told Torve. "In the morning we will bring this girl with us when we speak to our brave explorer-captain. Maybe she can tell us how much of the man's story is true and how much is lies for the sake of reward. As for the other . . ." He glanced at the undeniably attractive face of the noblewoman. "We will see what she can teach us about death. She may be instructive."

Emperor and servant left the questing room and locked their prisoners in. Servant turned to Emperor and resumed the conversation as they climbed the stone steps towards their rooms. "I see your scepticism, ma great sor," he said. "Yet to me her thinking opens doors I never even knew existed. Please do not lightly dismiss her ramblings."

"You believe her tale of a missing god?"

"Ma great sor, you allow me to speak my mind, to take liberties forbidden to humans. In this fashion I serve you like none other can."

"So you always preface remarks you believe I will not like. You need not be concerned. How can the noises of an animal offend its master?"

"Yet may an owner take a whip to his donkey to stop it braying in the streets."

"You are no donkey. You may speak."

"Then, my lord, I would say the girl offers evidence attesting to the existence of the gods we declared extinct. It is up to us whether we find that evidence compelling. But we will not know unless we hear it all."

"You *like* the half-wit?" As always, the Emperor could read his pet.

No embarrassment clouded Torve's honest face; further proof that, for all his cleverness, he was not human—for what human would not be affronted to be associated with a half-wit? "Ma great sor, she excites my mind in ways I have never imagined."

"You cannot have her. Not in that way, not in any way. You are my one indulgence. Torve: though I am the Emperor of all Elamaq, were I to favour a half-wit as well as an Omeran all the Alliances would turn on me."

Torve smiled. "My lord, I will enjoy the excitement her words offer me until such time as they cease. I will learn everything I can from her. When the time comes I will help you search out her dying thoughts. And perhaps something she says might touch upon our deepest matter. Has she not already hinted as much?"

The Emperor of Elamaq acknowledged the point. He would forgo a chance to further his research into death if the half-wit's ways with numbers proved effective. And if she could provide even a hint to aid his elusive quest, he would keep her alive, however much he despised her.

Torve rose before dawn. He tidied his pallet, donned a simple white robe and padded across the small room to his chamberpot. After relieving himself, he unrolled his carpet and performed his Defiance.

The Defiance was known by all Omerans. It had been instituted thousands of years ago by the first Omerans taken as slaves, and refined into an elaborate ritual by Capixaba of long-lost Queda. The Amaqi knew of the ritual, having seen Omerans practise it wherever they could find an open space, and assumed it was part of the Omeran obsession with fitness, albeit with cultural overtones. Torve fostered this belief, keeping the real meaning hidden. He saw it as a secret rebellion, a hidden heart of disobedience, a ritualised disorder. Torve practised Defiance every morning, and knew it to be the core of his identity.

The Omeran stood motionless in the centre of the room, feet shoulder-width apart, hands lightly clasped behind his back, in a state of readiness. Suddenly he dropped from this standing position onto his back, arms spread wide, his hands barely cushioning his fall, then with a flick of his shoulders raised his legs and torso into the air. In the same movement he sent his body spinning, rotating on his shoulder blades, first one way, then the other. He feinted a kick, as though at an imaginary opponent, but today his opponent was not very skilful so he did not follow through with his attack. Capixaba taught that attacks should be shown but not completed if the outcome was certain: true defiance asserted superiority without enforcing it. In this way the Omerans had survived as slaves while all other races had been killed or absorbed by the rapacious Amaqi.

With another shrug of his shoulders Torve regained his feet, completely balanced. His imaginary opponent struck, an acrobatic swivel and high kick. Torve waited just long enough to draw the complete movement from his opponent, then bent at the waist in time to avoid the attack. He could almost feel the swish of the bare foot passing over his head. The Defiance was not a weapon to destroy an opponent; it was a tool to humiliate him—or her. Women were equally adept. So Torve practised his deceptions, feinting here, hinting at his full ability there, drawing the best out of his opponent, showing her that her most potent attacks were ineffective against him. Then, when his imaginary opponent acknowledge Torve's mastery by leaving the pala, the playing field, the Omeran executed a dizzying sequence of spins and kicks from all positions: on his feet, his back, standing on his head. He then circled the room three times and bowed to his opponent, his Defiance over for the morning.

He laved his cooling body with water from a small china bowl, cleansing the sweat from his matted body

hair, dried himself slowly, then opened his door and retrieved the clothes left for him by the Palace steward.
These clothes were always selected by the Emperor. He
was not allowed to choose his own attire, for what interest would an animal have in clothing? Today his master
had decided on matching pink jacket and pantaloons. He
was the Emperor's fashion accessory. Torve said nothing,
he thought nothing, despite the humiliating knowledge.
He put on the clothes.

He left his room without a backward glance: apart from
his small carpet, there was nothing of himself in it. He was
self-contained in the most literal sense. Where others in-
vested parts of themselves in their possessions and in
other people, everything Torve was he held secretly within
his skin. He had been bred for service and for loyalty. It
was impossible for him to harbour notions of disobedience against his enslaver. He did not need to. His Defiance
was over for the morning.

Torve walked briskly but with an unconscious grace
down the marble corridor to the Emperor's suite. There he
would await his master's pleasure. His days and his years
had regularly been filled with the indescribable, for his
master was a sadist and a torturer, determined to uncover
the secret of eternal life by studying death, the enemy.
Torve had watched impassively as Amaqi and Omerans
alike were taken apart in experiments. He had kept notes.
Participated. Not to do so would be unthinkable. For three
thousand years his forebears had been bred to slavery, and
his inherited emotional insulation against the horror of his
service ensured he remained unscarred. The girl, though:
she had seen into him, had used her unique vision to penetrate the three-thousand-year thickness of his soul. For

the first time in his life Torve found himself profoundly
unsettled.

This morning the girl named Lenares had been his imaginary opponent. He had defied her, tricked her, humili-
ated her, triumphed over her, but his uneasiness remained.
He arrived at his master's oakpanelled door, nodded to the
Amaqi servants waiting there, and stood motionless in the
corridor, feet shoulder-width apart, hands lightly clasped
behind his back, in a state of readiness.

The Emperor emerged, mask already in place as always, today clad in a full red robe lined in purple. He
often favoured full-length robes as it allowed him to wear
elevated shoes. Without a word Torve swung in behind
him as they made their way towards the throne room.

"Did you dream about the girl last night?" the Emperor
asked casually. His face would have worn a leer, had it been
visible.

Torve forced himself to smile. "I thought about her
claims, ma great sor," he answered carefully. "I thought
about her way of seeing. I am still convinced we should
try to learn everything we can from her."

"I can guess what you want to learn from her. It was
only to be expected: you have grown up. I may have to
speak to the surgeon about this. We can't have you on heat
the whole time."

Torve turned a bland stare towards his master. "However I may best serve you, my lord," he responded, containing his fear, knowing that to avoid the surgeon's knife
he must be careful what he said about the unusual girl. "I
think of your great quest above all else. Perhaps you wish
to have someone else help you with her questioning?"

This occasioned a sharp bark of laughter. "Of course

not. We are a team. It would take me years to train another to your level of skill. Just be careful, that is all."

Palace guards opened the double doors into the throne room. This vast domed chamber was on a far different scale to the small annex to the Corridor of Rainbows. The throne, directly under the huge cap to the great gold dome above, was surrounded by a marble floor decorated with mosaics representing the races conquered by the Amaqi, in turn flanked by a double row of crystal columns, a triumph of forgotten engineers executing the will of some ancient chancellor. They, not the vaulted dome with its painting of the three gods, nor the acclaimed mosaics on the marble floor, were the true glory of this space. The crystal columns reflected and amplified the colours worn by the court, already in attendance on their Emperor; blues, greens, reds, golds, yellows, every exotic shade and hue their tailors could purchase from the caravans that came through the city, all to be found shifting and swirling in the crystal separating the court from the throne.

Down went a hundred courtiers and as many other functionaries as the doors opened, foreheads to the floor, the faint rustle of fabric the only sound as the court abased itself before the Emperor. Alone, he walked slowly to his throne; lately he had been taking longer and longer to make the eighty paces to the platform. A message to his advisers. Torve believed, warning them that their expansionist plans would not be rushed. The courtiers were obliged to wait, listening to the sound of their sovereign's feet—step, pause, pause, step, pause, pause—as he kept them in their uncomfortable position. The Omeran imagined he could hear corsets straining, but was careful to keep his amusement private. This room held danger for him. He was tolerated as an eccentricity, but knew he may one day be traded by his master for some political concession or other.

The slow stepping ceased. Trumpets sounded a fanfare—newly composed each day, though Torve wondered if he had heard this one before—and the court representing the great Alliances rose to stand before their Emperor. The Omeran took his accustomed stance by the double doors, now closed.

"Bring the exalted Captain Duon," the herald cried from his place beside the glittering throne, and the double doors opened again to admit a guard clad in ceremonial silver armour, carrying a staff with the Emperor's banner affixed to it. "Captain Duon at the Emperor's pleasure," the silver guard announced, and gave way to the captain himself.

Torve had seen the captain two days previously, when he had first reported the results of his expedition to the Emperor, and was surprised at the change in the man. Not forty-eight hours ago Captain Duon had looked more scarecrow than human, wild hair and a shaggy beard disguising what, now he had shaved, were clearly patrician features. A man who had seemed uncouth now appeared urbane, cultured, worthy of the rewards the Emperor had granted him. Undoubtedly those rewards had already borne their first fruit: the hero now looked the part. Tall, smooth-skinned, golden-haired, with a wide mouth and full lips. Gasps of admiration and delight came from many of the women—and some of the men—of the court.

"Ma great sor," the man said in a melodious voice after walking to the platform and performing his obeisance, "you requested a full accounting of my adventures. I have brought an inventory to aid in this task." He pulled a thick notebook from his breast pocket.

"You misunderstand our purpose," the Emperor interrupted. "We will not require an inventory. We wish a different kind of accounting. This morning we seek to uncover truths which together may give the Amaqi the key to all the world's riches."

The Emperor was not given to overstatement, so an excited murmur of conversation filled the silence following these words. The court—and Torve, his intimate—were caught off balance, as nothing of the Emperor's purpose in this matter had come to their attention, bribes, spies and confidences notwithstanding.

"Bring the cosmographer," cried the herald, and Torve jerked his head around at the word. Again the double doors swung wide, this time to admit . . .

"Lenares the Cosmographer," boomed the banner-bearer, "at the Emperor's pleasure."

In she walked, his opponent, clad in a beautiful white dress edged in purple as was the cosmographers' gift, her pale hair exquisitely coiffured, swept back from her face: Lenares. Lenares! How had this been accomplished? What wiles had his master employed to get her to present so well? She had certainly not spent the night in the questioning room. She had been perfumed, rouge applied to her face, and she walked as though born to the court. The Emperor had organised this without consulting him.

She turned to Torve and oh, she smiled, and he was sure he was dreaming. And as she turned away and walked towards the throne he realised there were some attacks against which defiance was useless.

*   *   *

"Lenares the Cosmographer at the Emperor's pleasure," the man in shining armour said. Lenares recognised her cue to walk to the throne as she had been taught. Left, right, small steps, chin raised. Easy. They had explained it to her as a ritual, and she had grasped the concept. She had always loved order and ceremony. She saw the clever Omeran and smiled at him, wanting to greet him or wave but knowing that as part of the ritual she was not permitted to speak in this room until she was spoken to.

They had come for her not long after the Emperor and the Omeran left her and Mahudia alone. Six women took her from the cold room and brought her to a wonderful room of silks and mirrors. There they talked to her about what would be required of her. At first Lenares was angry, but gradually they had captured her interest. A bath, water laboriously borne by servants from the kitchens—she made them all leave the room when the time came to immerse herself in the steaming water—had been followed by sleep amongst scented pillows, then an early awakening. She didn't mind. She'd never needed much sleep. The women spoke softly, respectfully to her: can we wash your hair? Can we make you beautiful? She said yes, as it was part of the ritual, and allowed them to touch her even though it was against her rules. So many new experiences, so much new information to take in. She watched them as they worked, listened as they chatted, absorbed it all with her single-minded concentration. She surprised them, as she knew she would, by how rapidly she learned to do what they wanted. She was special. Why should she not do better than they expected?

And if the looks she received from the crowd were anything to go by, she still did better than they expected.

Lenares felt a thrill of pride. This was what she had thought would happen two days ago when the Emperor had disappointed her so badly. Now she exulted in the glory of it.

Ninety-seven, ninety-eight, ninety-nine, one hundred paces. A good number to end on. She knelt, then lowered her forehead to the cool marble floor. She was not happy about this part, but she knew all eyes were on her even now, so she endured it. Counted to five, then climbed back to her knees and repeated the exercise twice more. Finally she raised her head, got to her feet and looked into the masked face of the man who had hurt her, who had said he didn't believe her but who really did, who was using her as part of some complicated plan.

He nodded, a false thing, and welcomed her to the court. She turned and acknowledged the crowd, just as she had been instructed, adding a little twirl of her own before turning back to the Emperor. They admired her; she took note of the frank stares of the courtiers, and it affected her like strong wine to a child.

Torve stood eighty paces away from the throne, having as usual to strain to hear what was being said. Bored courtiers held their own discussions, and there were other noises arising from the assembly of a hundred people. He was accustomed to this, however, as his master insisted on reviewing the day's proceedings every evening. As a consequence he had developed a sharp and comprehensive memory.

The Emperor introduced his two subjects to each other, then offered a précis of each to the court. Captain Taleth Duon he described as an adventurer from the Anaphil Alliance, a minor Alliance represented at court by an elderly matriarch and her grandson. The family was well respected but, because they were originally from Punta, a coastal city fifty leagues to fatherback, they were at a disadvantage in the Talamaq Palace. His master did not say this directly, of course, but it was there to be heard in his words.

"Captain Duon has risen rapidly through the ranks by hard work and obedience." Not by the usual method of patronage or purchase of a commission. "He came to our attention as a result of his activities coordinating drought relief in Punta province, and gained promotion to captain after supervising the cleansing of the Third of Brick." Enthusiastic but poorly connected, doing the dirty work shunned by the aristocracy.

"We rewarded him by granting him an explorer's licence. He chose to travel fatherwards and brave the dangers of Nomansland; you will recall we sent him on his journey with much celebration four years ago last summer."

Already his master was losing the court's attention. Bored courtiers stifled yawns, picked at their nails with elegant knives or their noses with equally elegant fingers, and pretended to listen. The Emperor must have some plan. Given his expressed loathing for the cosmographer girl, and the minor status of the explorer, there must be something important ahead.

"Our courageous explorer has returned! And as you are about to hear, he brings with him knowledge that may well make the fortunes of everyone in this room, and bring vast new lands under our control."

Torve watched the court's reaction to this carefully phrased statement. The less wealthy courtiers leaned forward, nails or nostrils forgotten, while the richest men frowned and scratched their beards as they considered the prospect of losing their privileged positions. The Emperor would be interested in these reactions. Clever, very clever.

"Now, our dear Captain. We have some questions for you. Our fair cosmographer here will judge their worth, as will this court, so speak you true."

Captain Duon nodded his head enthusiastically, his adam's apple bobbing up and down. "I will, ma great sor."

Torve pursed his lips. *Don't overdo it, Captain. This is a cynical court.*

"Very well. You passed through Nomansland without incident?"

"Yes, ma great sor. We engaged an excellent guide from among the Nehra and as a result lost only three of our porters, which is accounted an excellent passage."

"And then?"

"We were warned that unseasonal storms had made hazardous the coast road fatherwards, so we wintered in the highlands of a country called Jasweyah. This allowed the sick and the weary among us to recover from the crossing of Nomansland, and gave me the opportunity to pick up a smattering of their tongue. In Jasweyah we first heard tales of the Undying Man, the ruler of Bhrudwo, the name they give to the fatherwards lands."

The Emperor leaned forward, his lips parted. Torve sensed his excitement. "What tales, my Captain?"

"Ma great sor, the inhabitants of Bhrudwo are diverse. Some are cultured and knowledgeable about civilised things, such that they may perhaps rival our more backward provinces. Others are uncouth mountain tribesmen or illiterate fishermen scrabbling for a living among bird-raddled seacliffs. Nevertheless, they all speak of their lord with fear and respect. He has turned Bhrudwo into a king-dom almost to be compared to Elamaq."

"And how long has it taken him?"

"My lord, they say he has ruled this kingdom for two thousand years. Hence the epithet."

Barks and titters of laughter drifted across the chamber.

"Come now, man. Surely you mean his ancestors have ruled the kingdom for two millennia?" The Emperor enjoyed scenes like this. He had already heard the report, but made a show of extracting the information. *Why, though, is Lenares here?* Torve wondered.

"No, ma great sor. The people were adamant. The man who rules them now is the same man who ruled their fathers, grandfathers and so on back through time."

"It's a trick, of course. A simple trick." An astonishingly deep voice rumbled through the chamber, right on cue. So predictable. The leader of the Grandaran Alliance, perhaps the richest man in the empire aside from the Emperor himself, clever and dynamic in his youth, but now a self-important man who could see little further than his belly. His Alliance had fallen apart around him in the last few years and he failed to mark it. "All disguises and misinformation, ma great sor. Why are y' wasting our time with this nonsense?"

Ever-dependable Lord Tumille, a valuable if unwitting servant of the Emperor. Almost worth the trouble he caused. Torve smiled.

"Do you not think that thought has occurred to the citizens of this Bhrudwo, Tumille?" The Emperor spoke softly, with artistry, steering the court deftly towards some as-yet-unguessable conclusion. "Why would they believe this tale without evidence?"

"Credulous and uncivilised, clearly, ma great sor," rumbled the reply. "What else can be expected from barbarians?"

The Emperor turned to Captain Duon. "Well?"

"Ma great sor, we thought the same, but it was we who were considered barbarians for not knowing the story of the Undying Man. Time and again the story was told to us, and while there were regional differences the storytellers agreed on all important points. It seems that two thousand years ago a man challenged the gods and defeated them, forcing them to surrender the secret of immortality. Rather than sharing the knowledge with humanity, this man selfishly kept it to himself. The gods drove him away and he took the fatherwards lands as his own kingdom. From there he has waged war on the gods ever since."

Lord Tumille laughed his heavy laugh. "Does everyone live happily ever after?" His allies in the court laughed with him.

"That was the story we were told, ma sor," the captain replied, his face impassive, though surely he must have been feeling uncertainty at this questioning. "From what I was told, the Undying Man is not happy, though he does live ever after. He has conducted two wars against his enemy—a land to the west that remains outside his control, in which live a people said to be favoured by the gods—and has lost both times, even though he is the strongest wizard in the fatherwards lands. The latter war was only seventy years ago, and the Undying Man was badly beaten, suffering severely. He has spent his time since then regaining his wizardly strength. This tale is spread all over the lands we visited, and has not been suppressed by the Undying Man or his agents. Everyone knows it. Yet his hold on the fatherwards lands is secure."

"Very well, but what matters this talk of wars and wizards to us?" This from a pasty-faced young man with a thin beard standing beside Lord Tumille. An ally, a son perhaps, but new to the court. Torve had not seen him before. Vacuous, if his first public comment was typical of the man.

"Perhaps it will help, ma sor, if I describe the fatherwards lands to you." Duon turned and raised an eyebrow to his Emperor, who nodded. Lenares stood nearby, her whole attention on the explorer, as though she sought to absorb his words through her flesh. Torve shuddered. *How could one defy such a gaze?*

The captain screwed his eyes shut. "I remember my first sight of the coast," he said, opening his eyes again and massaging his temple with long fingers. "We came over a ridge some time after dawn just as the mist cleared. Below us lay a patchwork of fields, some planted, some ploughed, some fallow, surrounded by tall trees, all glistening in golden sunlight. Such colours! A crystal stream flowed through the fields." He closed his eyes again and waved his hand in front of him as he spoke, shaping the folds and valleys, perhaps, or the rippling of the water. "The stream runs all year round, our guide told us. We didn't believe him. He laughed and pointed to the ocean. The water was not bronze like our oceans, but cool and blue. As we watched, a squall swept across the water and up the coastal cliffs towards us. The guide grumbled, but we lifted our faces to the soft rain. Water, everything is water, the whole of the fatherwards lands is defined by it." He opened his eyes. "My lords, the land is rich beyond belief. While we suffer drought after drought and our children die, Bhrudwo offers mead and honey for us and for our children. And, my lords, there are few there to stop us taking it."

"Do you speak of trade or of conquest?" Tumille got the question out just ahead of a dozen other lords.

The Emperor smiled at his court. "Does anyone here think there is a difference?"

Ah. Here was the plan, then. A campaign of conquest, the first of the reign. Destabilising the mounting opposition to his restrictive policies, undermining the positioning of the major factions, just as Torve and his master had often discussed.

The cleverer ones grasped it straightaway. Heads turned to neighbours, and for a moment the chamber was filled with whispered speculation. Torve diligently noted which courtiers appeared confused and which looked satisfied.

"Are a few exotic luxuries really worth the attention of my court?" The Emperor was being disingenuous, even the slowest among them knew it. The nuance seemed to have escaped Captain Duon, however.

"Ma great sor, there are treasures beyond the telling in Bhrudwo!" he said anxiously. "Permit me to read to the court from this list—"

"We have already indicated that an inventory is not necessary. Be silent, Captain, or risk doing your cause further harm."

Captain Duon's face turned pale. He replaced the notebook he had been fingering inside his tailored jacket. He wanted to lead the next expedition, Torve guessed, and had just clumsily shown his hand to a number of powerful potential rivals. The next venture would be far better equipped, with the capacity to bring much wealth back to Talamaq. There would be many candidates for such a position.

Torve's mind raced ahead. His master must already have decided: there would be another expedition, and Captain Duon would lead it. The Emperor could not risk giving such a prize to anyone in the court with true power.

"Now, we invite our cosmographer to comment on the veracity of Captain Duon's assessment." The Emperor turned to face Lenares.

The girl's face coloured in response. Clearly she knew she was being asked a question, but just as clearly she did not understand it. Torve watched her. *If the silence continues much longer, the Emperor may damage his own cause . . .*

"Is Captain Duon telling the truth?" A few titters of laughter accompanied the Emperor's clarification.

"Everything he says is true, but none of it is accurate." Lenares snapped out the words. Clearly she knew she was being mocked.

"What do you mean?"

"He believes what he says. He is not lying. But he has exaggerated some of what he says because he wants us to feel how strange things are in the fatherwards lands."

"Oh? Captain, is the cosmographer correct?"

Such a dilemma.

"Ma great sor, I have tried to help you and the court understand the wonder of the fatherwards lands. If you had wanted only the bare facts, my inventory would have sufficed."

Oh dear. A clever answer, but not a wise one. The Emperor would use his dark voice.

"Captain, is the cosmographer correct?"

Torve felt his stomach flutter. His chest constricted as though some great weight had settled on it. So much of his life's effort had gone into ensuring the dark voice was not used.

"She is, ma great sor."

"Hah! Anyone who knows these explorer types could have guessed that." Tumille again, taking a risk by inter-jecting so soon after the Emperor had used the dark voice. "Stands to reason. The boy wants to tell a good story."

Lenares lifted her chin and turned her blazing eyes on the lord. "Why are you still sleeping with your daughter?" she asked.

A collective indrawn breath followed the words, then a dozen things happened at once. Torve found himself hard pressed to keep up. Lord Tumille roared an angry denial, and beside him his wife turned and slapped his red face, her own face pinched and white. To Tumille's left a slim girl, new to the court, fell to the floor in a faint. The thin-bearded man bent to help her to her feet, then recoiled from her in obvious disgust. A babble of voices erupted across the chamber, ripples from the stone Lenares had thrown amongst them. The cacophony was completed by the sound of the Emperor laughing.

"Ah, Lenares," he said as Tumille's friends led the dis-graced man out, arms under his slumped shoulders, while the slim girl lay on the mosaic floor unregarded. "I am convinced. You have a dangerous gift."

His master was right, Torve acknowledged. Lenares was dangerous. She had no social grace, no sense of situ-ational awareness, to keep her from speaking the truth she saw. An opponent with no understanding of the rules. Someone to be avoided no matter the cost.

Someone to be pursued with all he possessed.

CHAPTER 5

EXPEDITION

ALL HEADS TURNED TOWARDS Lenares the moment she walked through the door into the cosmographers' house. People filled the wide hallway leading to the living quarters: sixteen cosmographers, twenty acolytes, all the servants, even the cleaners, clucking at the dirty sandals treading on their polished stone floor. Including herself, ninety-six feet dirtying the flagstones.

She was beseiged with questions. Where had she been? Where was Mahudia? What did the Emperor want? Where did she get that dress? On and on they went, jabbering at her, leaning towards her, touching her, not respecting her need for space, for silence, ignoring what she was trying to tell them.

Lenares found it unbearable. She put her hands to her head and screamed.

The babble ceased. The silence eased her like scented oil, the kind the women of the Palace had poured over her after the scratching of the pumice loofah. Lenares wanted to tell all the people to go away, but that would only make them angry.

"I'll answer your questions, one at a time, please," she said primly, and sat down on the nearest bench. "Can someone bring me something to eat? A spiced sausage would be nice." One of the acolytes—she didn't see who—scampered off towards the kitchen. That felt good. Lenares the Cosmographer, favoured of the Emperor, whom people obeyed.

"I saw the Emperor," she said, unable to help herself. "He invited me to speak at his court."

Two girls rolled their eyes at each other. Lenares knew what that meant.

"I don't care if you believe me or not. I'm just telling you where I've been. That's where I got this dress; the Emperor gave it to me. If I didn't go to his court, where else would I have got it from?"

"Never mind the dress," said Nehane. The older of the two male cosmographers and the highest ranked behind Mahudia herself, Nehane was a nice man, short and round, bald except for a funny tuft of white hair behind each ear. He was very clever, but there was something sad in his past. Lenares had never learned exactly what it was, but it concerned his mother. "Where is Mahudia? Why did she not return with you?"

"Mahudia is in the dungeons," Lenares replied. Her words were received with a chorus of anxious groans.

Nehane knelt down in front of Lenares, his brown eyes wide open, fixed on her. "The dungeons? What has she done wrong? What are they doing with her?"

"They asked us questions. About the earthquake, about the hole in the world and the missing god. They believed me, even if none of you do." She looked past Nehane's concerned face, trying to catch the eye of Rouza or Palain.

Neither paid her any attention: Palain was in Rouza's ear, no doubt gossiping.

"Asked you questions? You were both in the dungeons?" Nehane scratched his head, then puffed out an annoyed breath. "You had better tell us the whole story. And we had better listen carefully," he said, raising his voice at this last. He turned and got to his feet. "I'll tolerate no fun-making. Lenares is a cosmographer now, and is to be accorded the respect you others hope one day to receive. Am I clear?"

"Yes, Cosmographer Nehane," the acolytes chorused.

Lenares tried, but she could not keep a satisfied grin from settling on her face as she told them her story. Many of these acolytes, and even some of the cosmographers, had *hurt* her in the past. Palain and Rouza were the worst, always making trouble for her, blaming her for things she hadn't done, telling Mahudia when she went through a phase of bed-wetting, and always playing tricks, silly practical jokes to make her look a fool. The worst was the time they broke into her room and shifted everything slightly, just enough to put all her thinking out. She'd had a headache for days until they'd told her what they had done. Everyone had thought it a great joke. Even Mahudia had laughed.

Gradually Rouza and Palain faded from her mind as she warmed to her story. Twice now in one day she had found herself the focus of attention, and the feeling of belonging, of wellbeing, wrapped itself around her like an embrace. This was what being a cosmographer was supposed to be like.

Some of her listeners did not believe her story, she could tell. More accurately, they thought she was muddling things up again. *Acolytes, mostly, but they no longer count. I only have to convince the cosmographers.* She told them how she predicted the earthquake, and of the questioning the Emperor and his pet Omeran had subjected them to. This last detail convinced a number of the cosmographers she was telling the truth. Torve the Omeran was known to all who had been raised cosmographers in the last decade. He and his master had become inseparable, Nehane told her. It was something of a scandal.

"I'm inclined to believe you, strange as it sounds," he said when her tale had come to an end. "Thank you, Lenares; you have done well."

Lenares bowed her head, as was proper, and covered her mouth to hide her smile. Rouza didn't like it when she smiled, and would make trouble for her if she saw it. But Rouza remained an acolyte, while Lenares was a cosmographer, and the acolyte couldn't hurt her now, could she?

"The question is, what do we do?" Nehane hitched his robe a little higher. "Lenares assures us that, apart from a few threats, the Emperor inflicted no harm on Mahudia. But we cannot be certain she will remain unharmed in that terrible place. We all know the rumours regarding what happens there. Lyanal, take Pettera and go to the guildhall of the Elboran Alliance." He gestured to one of the younger cosmographers, a quiet, studious woman—a bit of a dullard, Lenares had always thought—and a female acolyte Lenares spent little time with. "There you are to make enquiries of sor Hudan, Mahudia's father. We must find out what he knows, if anything. I will go to the Palace and seek an audience with an official regarding Mahudia's disposition."

"I will accompany you," said Arazma, Rouza's mother

and the oldest of the cosmographers. She had suffered a wasting sickness ten years ago, but unlike most who contracted it she had regained at least a semblance of health, though she was partially palsied down one side. Lenares did not like her.

Nehane frowned. "Then Rouza will assist us."

"Ma sor, I have much studying to do," the girl said in her piping voice. "I am already compromised because of yesterday's events. Please don't let me fall further behind."

Why could they not see how false she was? Such a liar, always twisting the truth, as now. Sympathy for her mother, the other girls had decided, meant she was indulged. Nobody except Palain liked her.

"Very well. Archenna? Fetch ma dama Arazma's walking stick. We will leave immediately. Lenares, you look exhausted. Go and get some sleep. The rest of you, follow Rouza's excellent example and study hard. Make Mahudia proud of you when she returns."

Acolytes ran off down the corridor, while cosmographers made a more dignified exit. Lenares stretched and yawned; she was tired, though at the same time she brimmed with energy. Yesterday she would have rushed away with her fellow acolytes. Today she tried walking in a more sedate fashion, though she could not help skipping a few steps.

Along the corridor, counting her steps, careful not to step on the cracks between the flagstones, past the servants' quarters to her left, then—deep breath—straight on where she would ordinarily turn right into the acolytes' quarters. Directly ahead of her stood the double doors into the cosmographers' common room. Another deep breath, then she pushed them open and walked through.

Disappointment. The cosmographers were supposed to line either side of the common room while the Chief Cosmographer issued the newly raised cosmographer a welcome and showed her to her new quarters. However, the only person in the room sat in a couch with her back to Lenares and didn't even turn her head when she entered the room. Where was the welcome? The speech? It was tradition!

But the Emperor held Mahudia in his dungeon, and Nehane had gone to see about her. Perhaps the welcome would be conducted when they returned. Lenares walked over to the cosmographer.

"Vinaru, do you know which room is mine?"

The middle-aged woman peered at her with heavy-lidded eyes, making her seem half-asleep, just as she always looked when teaching advanced numeracy to the acolytes. "Lenares, isn't it?" She knew full well who it was. "Our new cosmographer. I opposed your elevation, you know. Still do. Oh yes, your work is adequate, sometimes brilliant. But you're fragile, girl. Unstable. No spine to you. You'll need constant management. You drive Mahudia to distraction, that you do. More trouble than you're worth, in my opinion. Time you knew what I thought."

Lenares stood there, her mouth open in shock. How could her teacher say such things?

Vinaru's eyes narrowed. "My word, have I surprised you? And to think you claim you can read everyone's minds with those numbers of yours! A pity your ability does not match your conceit!"

"You don't understand." Lenares tried to keep her voice from wailing. "I can't read all the numbers I see. I'd never be able to move from one spot if I did. You don't want to understand, Vinaru, you're just jealous that I'm better at numeracy than you."

The lidded eyes sprang open. "Oh? Better, are you? You are a fool. And you will call me ma dama Vinaru, that you will. I intend to have respect from you, if nothing else."

"But I am a cosmographer newly raised! I do not have to add the honorific. Mahudia said!"

"Until I see some proof that you deserve the title, you will address me properly, girl. Now leave me in peace. Go back to your room and study. Son knows you need it."

"But . . . but what about my room?" Lenares pointed towards the corridor leading to the cosmographers' quarters. "I don't know which room I've been given."

The woman laughed. "Poor Lenares. Mahudia's vain pet has missed out on her welcome, and now she labours under the impression that a room has been prepared for her in the cosmographers' quarters. How disappointed she will be when she finds out that no such room exists. Who did you think was going to prepare it for you, stupid girl? Mahudia lies captive in a dungeon, injured or dead for all we know, and you are so selfish you expected someone else to make ready a room for you! You want the Chief Cosmographer to break out of her cell so she can tuck in your blankets? Pah! Go back to your room in the acolytes' quarters and thank the Son on your knees you have accommodation of any sort."

"A fog of despair descended on Lenares' mind, blurring her thoughts. "Yes, ma dama Vinaru," she said meekly, then turned and left the common room.

So deeply immersed in her misery was she by the time she reached the acolytes' quarters, she failed to notice the suspiciously half-open door to the common room. She pushed at the door, heard a rattle, and glanced up in time to receive a face full of water.

Her mind broke into several functioning parts, one part registering the shock of the cold, dirty water from a cleaner's bucket, another assessing and then becoming angry at the damage to her dress, a third playing with numbers, figuring probabilities but knowing there was no need as a fourth part of her mind heard the laughter she had grown to hate, and until a few minutes ago had thought to have put behind her forever.

A fifth and surprising thought came to her. *I am a cosmographer*, it said. *Nothing Vinaru thinks can change that. I have been raised because of what I do with numbers, not because people like me.* It was as though the bucket of water dispersed the fog Vinaru had brought down upon her.

She turned her face to the laughter. Rouza and Palain laughed the loudest, of course, but even the girls who hated Rouza laughed along with her. They meant to be hurtful, but Lenares could not feel the hurt. She was no longer who they thought she was. She had never been able to see her own numbers, but knew that if she could, there would be a change in them.

"Oh dear," Rouza said in her squeaky voice. "You're all wet, ma dama Lenares." Dutiful laughter followed the words.

"Let us help you out of that dress, ma dama Lenares," Palain said sweetly. She turned to the others. "We have to look after our newraised cosmographer. We don't want her to catch a cold." More laughter. A few of the girls rose from their chairs, ready to pluck at her clothes.

Lenares registered this with only a fraction of her mind. Something different seemed to be happening to her. Usually one loud emotion dominated all the others, and faced with a practical joke like this she would scream or fight or run, or do something equally embarrassing. But today all the parts of her mind seemed to have found a balance. She could choose how to react.

"Thank you, Palain and Rouza," she said, forcing herself to smile. "I know you wanted to hurt me, but instead you have reminded me I am no longer a child. I'm not like you. I'm wet to the skin, but at least I'm not stupid to the bone."

She raised her skirts, then turned her gaze to the door to the sleeping quarters and began to count like the ladies-in-waiting had taught her. A stunned silence followed her slow steps across the common room and down the hall. She reached twenty-five before she stood in front of her door. Five fives. Five parts of her mind in balance. She opened her door and went in, closed it behind her without looking back, then collapsed on her bed, wet dress and all, and cried herself to sleep.

The Emperor raised a white-gloved hand, calling Torve to a halt. The kid gloves were a recent affectation, a statement of purity in an increasingly corrupt court. Of course, such statements could be deceiving, as his master had just finished proving. Torve could still smell the remnants of his master's excitement, bloodlust born of an obsessive cruelty that left the Omeran continually amazed. The old woman hadn't known much: her only mistake having been to be found in the wrong place. Despite the questioning she had not been able to explain how she had penetrated Palace security to find herself in the Garden of Angels. Nor could she explain how she had located her foolish son's resting place. This despite the brutal and inventive nature of her questioning.

His master had used the new toxins acquired recently from a barbarian caravan, experimenting with them while Torve chronicled their effects. The Emperor's excitement spiralled down to disappointment when no final insight was forthcoming from his subject. For all his efforts, his master's explorations of the realm of death seemed to have stalled.

Torve spent some time after that trying to scour away what he had seen, to little effect. Water on the skin, however vigorously applied, could not remove the growing horror taking shape within him. Even his Defiance no longer kept the memories at bay.

He followed his master into a small meeting chamber, accompanied by two Omeran guards who looked on him with pity in their eyes. *We grieve for you*, their flat gazes said. *We know how you serve your master.*

"When the Lords Hudan and Tumille arrive, show them in directly," the Emperor said to his guards, waving them away. One guard nodded, then followed his fellow from the room. They would stand watch at a door some way down the hall, Torve knew, one of many strategies to foil assassins, though close enough to intervene should something go amiss.

"We are tired of being kept waiting," the Emperor said, more to himself than to Torve, after some minutes had elapsed. "We do believe it is time to show these Alliances something of the Emperor's true power."

The door opened as if in response to his words. Hudan

entered with his customary economy of movement, made his obeisance and took a seat. He was followed not by Tumille but by a young man with a wispy beard unsuccessfully disguising a weak chin. Mila, Tumille's oldest son. *Ah.*

As always, his Emperor was there ahead of him, the question asked before the obeisance could begin. "How did he die?"

The boy did not answer until his obeisance was complete. "Ma great sor, my father took his own life. He could not live with his shame, he said." The bitterness in the young man's gaze betrayed the truth: suicide had been offered, and chosen, as an alternative to a painful death delivered by his family.

The Emperor clicked his tongue at the news, as though deprived of an opportunity. A *waste*, Torve thought. *The dying reflections of one such as Tumille would have been worth much.* A loyal but troubling thought.

"You have the right of primogeniture to be here, boy, but you'll be of little use to us for many years." The Emperor shifted to his low, compelling voice, and the young man paled. "Go back to your mother and your sister."

The boy's feet jerked and he half-turned towards the door; but then he screwed up his face and stood firm. "My place is here, representing one of the larger Alliances in Elamaq. I owe them, and my family, my allegiance." Brave or foolish—or possibly both. Torve winced and prepared himself.

The Emperor's eyebrows flew up, visible above his mask. "You defy a direct order?"

A ghastly weight settled on the room with the words, a presence so deep and heavy it seemed to bend reality

around itself. Shadows gathered, pressing down upon
them with their own gravity. The Emperor's mask seemed
to puff out, as though moulded to the skin of another, the
face of a younger man. Below him, floorboards groaned.
Tumille's son sank to his knees. The breath caught in
Torve's throat. Surely his master would not . . .

He did not. The moment passed, the weight withdrew,
the shadows receded.

"You surprise us. We would not have expected any
spawn of Tumille's to show such teeth." The Emperor
paused in apparent thought. "We will support your bid to
lead your Alliance, though it will cost you. A discussion
for later. Remain, then, and learn what we had planned for
your father and his ally, ma sor Hudan."

Torve calmed his breathing as he half-listened to his
master explain to an incredulous boy the reality behind
yesterday's pronouncements from the throne. Hudan
said little, mostly nodding to support his Emperor when
required. The Omeran knew his master withheld much:
he himself knew far more than Hudan and Tumille's
son were told, and had divined still more; but that there
were further plans as yet hidden was a certainty. The
Emperor of Elamaq was an obsessive man who planned
with meticulous detail, attending to every possibility,
yet was also capable of thinking while on the move, a
rare skill. Obsessive. The perfect word to describe the
man at the dark heart of the empire.

So. The expedition fatherwards was to be an army of
conquest, a grand and expensive undertaking to enlarge
the land of the Amaqi, to claim rich lands and their
bounty. Something to satisfy everyone, even the gods people no longer believed in. Certainly the Alliances would

compete to be represented in this venture, so great would
be the financial rewards. The Emperor stood to gain territory and the power associated with new subjects. Torve
read two further reasons his master would sponsor such an
expedition. It would keep the Alliances quiet, depriving
them of much of their power here in Talamaq, allowing
the Emperor to consolidate his hold on the throne. He
would remain behind, of course. The expedition could
have no negative outcome for him, whether it succeeded
or failed. In fact, the loss of the entire army at the hands
of the Bhrudwans, while unlikely, might actually be
preferable to a victory, so severely would it weaken the
Alliances. Preferable but for the second reason: the whispers of immortality Captain Duon had brought back with
him. These rumours, above all else, had drawn his master's eyes fatherwards to where a supposedly immortal
man ruled. Open a vein, collect the blood, drink it down
and live forever, or some such thing. No more need for
torture. No more questions for the dying. An end to his
master's obsession.

Torve hoped the legends of immortality were true. He
hoped it with all his heart.

Hudan stirred in his seat. "A word, ma great sor?"

The royal hand waved, the mask inclined slightly.

"I understand you have my daughter in custody. She is,
of course, your subject, to do with as you wish." No expression on the man's face, no betrayal of feeling. An example of why this man led thousands. "I would humbly
request, however, that in its dealings with her the Empire
would be mindful of the delicate balance between the Elboran and Pasmaran Alliances. I feel we will be of more use
to you if the present stalemate continues."

"*Had* your daughter," the Emperor said. "Had. We have come to an understanding with her. The cosmographers are about to make themselves useful."

"Ma great sor," Hudan acknowledged.

"You are the wisest man in the empire," the Emperor continued, the comment dragging a slight reaction from the normally imperturbable man. "As such, you will understand when we suggest it would be best if you found yourself confined to your bed for the next few weeks. Food poisoning, perhaps? We, too, are concerned about balance. You weigh heavily on our scales."

Only the raised eyebrows gave away Hudan's surprise. He did not ask the questions that must have been consuming him. Why? How could he profit from remaining behind? Would this not upset the balance between the Alliances? Torve marvelled at the man's composure.

"The empire needs leaders such as yourself," the Emperor said to Hudan as the men rose from their seats. And that, Torve reflected, was tantamount to inviting Hudan to take the throne should anything happen to the man currently sitting on it.

Plans within plans.

Lenares was lying on her bed, blanket under her arm, face pressed into her pillow, when her door opened.

"Ma dama Mahudia!" The pillow went one way, the blanket another as she scrambled to her feet. About to open her arms for a hug, she remembered herself just in time.

"Just Mahudia. You are raised, so no longer need to use the honorific." Mahudia's voice settled like a blanket over her, soothing, calming. "I hear you've been having adventures."

"Ma da—Mahudia, if only you could have seen me! Everybody staring at me, amazed at what I said to them. Did you hear about my dress? It took three seamstresses most of the night to sew. Look! Well, it's dirty now, but everyone thought I looked wonderful!"

"Was this when you returned to speak to Nehane?"

"No, silly, when the Emperor introduced me to his court!" She put her knuckles to her mouth as she realised what she had said, but Mahudia didn't seem to have noticed. "I wish you had been there."

"So do I, Lenares. Spending a day in the dungeons was undoubtedly less entertaining than your experiences, I'm sure." Just a little tartness in the voice, but Lenares heard it.

"I . . . Forgive me, Mahudia, I should have worried more about you, but so many good things happened to distract me. The Emperor threatened you, I remember. He said your father would be told you had been killed in the Garden of Angels. What happened?"

Lenares was annoyed with herself. Ever since she'd been old enough to understand, people had been telling her how selfish she was, how little she thought about the needs of others. She tried so hard, but such thoughts did not stick in her head if they were not associated with numbers and patterns. Social skills, Mahudia called this kind of remembering.

"I came to an understanding with the Emperor, who realised the risk of my father finding out the truth was too great, particularly since he'd seen fit to release you." Mahudia smiled fondly. "Part of the understanding was that neither you nor I would repeat anything the Emperor said. That won't be too hard, will it?"

"No," said Lenares, faintly disturbed. There was something in what Mahudia had just said . . . She reached for her numbers, but then put them aside. *She always tells me the truth—or, at least, when she lies, it is for my own benefit. "Come on, Lenares, it tastes nice." "They didn't mean to hurt you." Other such white lies.* Too hard? What would prove too hard for her to hear would be losing Mahudia's trust.

Mahudia peered at her, as though she could read the conflict on her face.

"Lenares, child, the Emperor and his Omeran friend had a long discussion with me today. I can't tell you all of it. I'm not allowed to. If I hadn't agreed to keep silent, they wouldn't have let me go. That's all right, isn't it?"

She nodded. "They didn't hurt you at all?"

"Not once I persuaded them of your worth, Cosmographer Lenares." A smile, a hint of pride. "You have saved the cosmographers, you know."

"Saved them?"

"The Emperor thought to disband us, to put aside three thousand years of accumulated knowledge. Your actions convinced him otherwise."

Again, a hint of evasion, of something not quite right. Some truth Mahudia insisted on shielding her from, no doubt. She shook off the suspicion.

"I am about to call a meeting," Mahudia said. "But I will tell you first, since it concerns you. The Emperor has announced an expedition to the fatherwards lands, beyond Nomansland, and he wants the cosmographers to be an integral part of the expedition. He specifically named you, Lenares."

No! How could she leave now? What was the Emperor

thinking? The tear in the world grew bigger every day. Now she was a cosmographer she could choose her task, and she had already decided to find the tear and what was causing it. *And you will not be able to go to court*, whispered another, deeper voice. Her face crumpled.

"It is a great honour," Mahudia whispered close to her ear. "I thought you'd be pleased."

No, no, no! She had never once been out of the city. The prospect of open desert, of wide rocky nothingness, frightened her. How could she read the numbers when there was nothing to read? She would have no point of reference, no reality to which she could secure herself.

"It has been decided," Mahudia said, arms folded.

No, a hundred times no! The Omeran servant of the Emperor had disturbed her. Everyone knew Omerans were dumb animals. So how could this one reason? How could it do calculations in its head? Another mystery to resolve. She could not, could not possibly leave Talamaq without knowing more about the Omeran.

Lenares found herself on her bed, curling into a ball, with Mahudia standing over her, pleading, coercing, demanding. The voice washed over her: just Mahudia's anxious sounds, irrelevant, meaningless.

"No," she said into her mattress. "No. No. No." Again and again she said it, in time with the beating of her heart; a hundred times she said it, then another hundred, then a third. When she finally turned her gaze towards the door, Mahudia had gone.

The golden mask turned towards him. "You know why you have to go, Torve. If you do not acquiesce I will make it a command."

"Ma great sor, my place is by your side."

"Words that must never be uttered in the hearing of the Alliances. 'No one stands beside the Emperor of Elamaq,' they would say as they dragged you to the block. 'All must kneel before him.' Your place, my friend, is wherever I say it is."

"But how can I be of service if I am separated from you?" Torve tried to contain his panic.

"Do you really need to ask me that question? Tell me, who else could I trust to collect the great prize and not use it for themselves?"

The Omeran bowed his head. The Emperor's command had been inevitable from the moment Captain Duon mentioned the legends from Bhrudwo. He'd marshalled many arguments against his master's wishes, from the sophisticated to the desperate, but despite his fear he found himself reluctant to use them. The expedition would see him isolated and powerless, vulnerable to those opposed to the Emperor. He would be separated from his master for the first time since he'd been given as a gift, so long ago he could not remember it. Separated from the man he hated, the man he loved, his constant companion, a twisted torturer. *Ah.* A part of him actually welcomed the Emperor's plan. *The part of me sickened by what he does in the dungeons. If I can bring back the immortal blood, the killing will stop.* And there was something else, a kernel of curiosity seeded within his fear: a desire to see how he would behave, what he would do without the golden mask always by his side.

"No, ma great sor, the question need not have been asked. I am yours, body and heart, and I cannot disobey you."

This last he knew as a certainty. Bred for obedience, all Omerans knew it. *Obedience at the very core of what we are. Our curse and our salvation.*

"I have left instructions with Duon," the Emperor continued. "The Lord of Bhrudwo is to be captured alive if possible. We do not know how efficacious the blood will be if taken from a dead man."

Torve raised his head. "Of course, the very idea of killing an immortal must be at the least an uncertain one, ma great sor. How can someone claim immortality if they can be killed?"

The mask nodded. "Ah, Torve, your thoughts and mine travel ever on the same path. I have spoken at length with our philosophers and wise men on this subject. They are, of course, of many opinions. Frata the Logician claims, rightly in my view, that an immortal must by definition live forever. The corollary is that immortals can never die, even if they themselves wish it, no more than a man can fly or a camel live under the sea."

"Yet, my master, how might an immortal live if his head is separated from his body? If his bones are ground to dust? If the very blood preserving his life is drained from his veins?"

"And so argued Pragmatist Sybil and her cadre, with some force. She and Frata nearly came to blows. You can see, my friend, why I want this immortal alive. It is not enough to become an immortal; I must understand the limits of immortality, if there are any such, and prepare for them." He leaned forward on his throne. "The experiments might take some time."

Torve kept his features impassive, while inside he reeled from the blow. *Fool.* Would he forever underestimate the depths of the one he served? *There will be no end to his experiments*. The promise of blood filled his future.

Unaware of the effect of his words, the Emperor went on to discuss various aspects of the arrangements for the expedition, though without Torve's full attention. Preparations would take at least a month, apparently. Investment would be solicited from those Alliances most likely to benefit. The Emperor himself would contribute a large sum. He mooted recalling his older son from exile in Nobe to act as political officer, proposing that if the foolish boy performed well his sentence would be commuted or even waived. The idea was sound but not without risk, Torve commented, though in truth the words flowed from his tongue without any real consideration. In the same fashion he mouthed further meaningless responses to his master, who in his preoccupation clearly did not notice his servant's misery—nor would it have merited sympathy if it had been noticed, Torve reflected.

The day wore on. Heralds and pages ran to and fro with instructions, their bright cloaks registering as little more than flashes before Torve's eyes. The Emperor's court convened later in the day, after the afternoon's heat had died down, and the Omeran resumed his usual position near the doors. Even a full-fledged argument between two of the minor Alliances was not sufficient to capture his attention: some disagreement over rank on the expedition saw two young fools cast their hats to the floor in the traditional gesture, though the Emperor overruled the duel.

While a small part of his mind monitored the tensions between the factions in the court, Torve began to question whether slavery was better than death. The Omerans existed only because their forebears surrendered to the

Amaqi rather than suffer the genocide meted out to many of the other races of the great continent. Had they made the right choice? Would the Omerans have been better to go the way of the Galantha or the Poppy-eaters or the First Men, harried and hounded to extinction? Three thousand years of Amaqi domination had led to this: their reduction to *animals*, a designation not wholly inaccurate for the unthinkingly obedient house servants and farm workers who made up the majority of what the Amaqi called the Omeran "stock," and perhaps too generous for the lives endured by those who satisfied the Amaqi in secret rooms throughout the city. How could extinction be worse than this? How could it be worse than washing someone's entrails from his forearms?

Despair is the great enemy. The thought rose from its deeply ingrained place, the Omeran answer to such thinking. Torve supposed it had been placed there by his mother and father, though he would never know: like all young Omerans he had been taken from his parents when very young, and could not remember their names or faces. *Learn your Defiance. Do not struggle against what others make you into. Despair is the great enemy.* A litany to keep a race alive in the face of a ruthless foe.

Torve watched the argument between the Syrenian and Anaphil Alliances gradually subside into bickering and snide comments. The two would-be duellists angrily pulled their hats back down onto their heads, then turned to their parents for more instructions. The Amaqi had succeeded in making slaves out of their own children. Look at those two: had the Emperor permitted them they would have fought to the blood, or perhaps to the death, over some point of pride, a minuscule tilt in the ongoing balancing between all the Alliances. Was it really their choice? *Do they really have more freedom than me?* Was the Emperor the only free man in the empire?

The Emperor, free? A man enslaved by obsession, a man terrorised by the fear of death, bent into cruelty by it. A man so free he had not ventured from the city in more than a decade, and never left his Palace without a full complement of guards. A man whose uncovered face it was death to see. Who would be alone, without counsel, when Torve left with the expedition. Whose only consolation had been the Garden of Angels, a place of restful beauty and of searing evil. Oh, and the friendship of an animal.

Torve's heart ached for him.

Trumpets blew, their fanfare billowing across Avensal'ibnu Square towards the golden Talamaq Palace. Soldiers and spectators alike waited, immobile. The male choirs, arranged on temporary scaffolding around three sides of the open space, began their deep humming. The sound from a thousand throats worked its stirring magic, as it always did. Certainly Captain Duon felt himself stirred, his own throat vibrating, the hairs on his arms and neck rising in response. Glorious. The word seemed to have a deeper meaning today. His skin prickled as a hundred sweet female voices joined the sound—glorious!—and the trumpets sounded again, this time taking the theme hummed by the choir and making of it a victorious paean to the empire.

At precisely the right moment the shimmering silver curtain behind the balcony of the Talamaq Palace parted, and the man in the golden mask came through. With deliberate steps he walked to the balcony's railing, paused a moment, then lifted his hands to the heavens. The music ceased.

Glorious.

A cathartic silence settled upon them all.

It seemed every citizen of Talamaq, and many from the surrounding towns, had come to see off the fatherwards expedition. The Emperor's great gambit. Twenty thousand men: a compact fighting force augmented by a hundred unstoppable chariots that would cut a bloody swathe through any enemy foolish enough to stand against them. Duon knew only a small proportion of Talamaq's half-million residents could fit into the broad square before the Palace, but the knowledge did nothing to diminish his awe at the public display of power and glory.

The Emperor lowered his arms to his sides, and it seemed as though a grinding weight settled on the square. An enormous presence, said to be the legacy of a hundred emperors, the Spirit of Empire itself. Only the truly dedicated Amaqi could sense the Spirit. Duon knew himself to be gifted, a legacy from some mixed-blood ancestor, so his mother always said: but today his heart thrilled as he not only felt the weight, but also heard a descending note, a groaning akin to the fall of a mighty tree.

The citizenry knelt, while the soldiers remained standing. Duon wished he could prostrate himself on the ground and cry out his love for the Emperor.

In that moment of silence, just before the man in the golden mask began to speak, Captain Duon heard the faintest sound of mocking laughter.

It seemed to be coming from behind him. His right arm twitched, the beginning of a movement towards his belt knife, but he arrested the motion. He dared not turn his head, not in this sacred moment. To answer the laughter with death would be its own blasphemy. But he expected the crowd to descend on the one who laughed and tear him apart.

No one moved. Perhaps no one else heard the mockery. Nevertheless, it was a stain on the glory of the moment, and it filled Duon with anger.

The Emperor spoke.

"Amaqi, welcome," he said.

"Welcome, ma great sor!" boomed the reply. Duon shouted with the rest, drowning out the dry chuckling.

"We share with you today your great joy. The Elamaq Empire is to expand fatherwards into lands rich with bounty. Our expedition is our mighty hand reaching forth to take these riches. From now on we will be greater and more glorious than any people ever known."

The crowd cheered madly, many throwing streamers carefully wound for the occasion into the air.

"Foolishness," said a voice behind Duon.

This time he could not help himself. He spun around, hand on knife hilt, to meet the eyes of a dozen startled commanders. None of them had spoken, he could see it on their faces.

"Let us honour those risking their lives for us," said the Emperor. "Captain Taleth Salmadi Duon leads our great army. Step forward, Captain, that our Amaqi may see the face of their hopes and dreams."

A thousand subtle sounds of people shifting, standing on tiptoes, craning their necks for a better view. Duon knew he had been caught with his back to the Emperor, and turned to the man in the mask with as much dignity as he could raise. Deep breath, hands picking at the hem of his cloak as the silence deepened, another deep breath and a step forward into the open space below the balcony. A second step, then a third. He made obeisance to the Emperor, then stepped forward again. A second obeisance, then a third. Utter silence. He remained motionless, forehead to the burning cobbles, sweat running uncomfortably up his back and across his neck to drip on the ground. Then onto his feet, face up to the balcony, where the Emperor nodded. Finally Duon turned to the gathered citizenry.

A single trumpeter blew a fanfare, and the crowd cheered again. Such an honour! Captain Duon found himself filling with pride in the face of such sustained spontaneous adoration.

"Spontaneous?" came the voice from behind him. "Professional cheerleaders have been practising this for days."

This time Duon's muscles did not even twitch. There was no one behind him save the Emperor. And how could the speaker, wherever he was, have known what he was thinking?

It is a jiran, he told himself in desperation as the Emperor continued to explain the purpose of the expedition to his citizens. *A sprite of the desert seeking to torment me, to bring humiliation to the Emperor.* But Captain Duon knew it wasn't a *jiran*. The voice came from within his own mind.

The glorious day crumbled to dust.

The man on the balcony droned on for a long time. Lenares fidgeted in her palanquin, counting the number of stitches visible on the pillow beside her, then slid back the door still further for a better view of the square. She had resigned herself to the journey and was anxious to get it over with. She'd asked Mahudia and Nehane how long they would be away, how many days before she could return to resume her study of the hole in the world, but they had answered her evasively. She persisted with her questions, receiving a scolding from Mahudia for nagging. When Nehane admitted the expedition could take more than a week, anger had given way to despair.

Over the previous weeks the hole had become much larger, heading off in some unexpected directions. Vectors, she corrected herself, savouring the new word. She had hoped her calculations would have been predictive, but aside from the earthquake in the Garden of Angels and its many aftershocks, so frequent she had given up warning people about them, she seemed powerless to deduce the shape or intention of the hole in the world. Yes, intention was a good word. It acted like it was seeking something or someone, reminding her of the stray kitten taken in by the cosmographers last year. Sneak, sneak, sneak, pause . . . *pounce*. Looking for her? No, looking for a number of people, she had decided, as it tore at the world in at least three different directions. Worse, it no longer expanded at a steady rate. Another week might see the damage increase until it was beyond repair. And now this fool wittered about the need for caution in all their dealings. Caution? They needed haste, not caution! Hadn't she told the Emperor how serious the hole had become? Why did no one truly believe her?

On and on squawked the man on the balcony, like a demented bird standing on its perch. She took a moment to set herself, to establish her centre, in preparation for leaving the city. A deep breath, then a clearing of her mind save for the imprint of the Palace before her, the three rizen towers lining up with the three great avenues, each signalling a cardinal direction. Sonwards, the direction the sun rose on the longest day of the year. Fatherwards, the sun's zenith. And daughterwards, the place of the setting midsummer sun. Superior to the graticular systems once used by the subjugated races of Elamaq. Left, right, forward and back, four directions only. With their counters, fatherback, sonback and daughterback, the Amaqi system offered six directions at sixty-degree intervals, not four at ninety.

Here I am, in the centre of the universe. See the three directions streaming out from me. As I count the steps I take and refer to the stars, I will retain contact with Talamaq. I will be centred. My calculations will retain their context.

As long as nothing happens to interfere.

Finally the man stopped his useless barking and withdrew from the balcony. The moment he disappeared, his strange numbers gone from her vision, signalled the beginning of yet another rumbling aftershock. The scaffold underneath the balcony creaked, then something snapped and a cloud of plaster dust rose to obscure her view. When it cleared the structure sagged forwards, and on the ground below it two people lay unmoving amidst a scattering of rubble and scaffolding. An official poked her head out between the silver curtains, then withdrew it rapidly.

Lenares didn't believe in omens, but knew that such beliefs, though outlawed by the Emperor, were still held among the Amaqi. However, aftershocks were now so common in the city that few if any citizens seemed to be making a fuss. Certainly they were leaving the square very quickly, but there was no evidence of panic.

They would make a fuss if they knew what she knew.

Ahead of her the expedition filed out of the square and along the Avensvala, led by the foot soldiers, ten abreast, flanked each side by camel riders. Rank after rank moved away, raising dust as they marched: she would count them as soon as she had an opportunity, but there were many thousands. She ran her eye down the ranks: an estimate flashed through her mind. Twenty thousand. Far too many for the sort of expedition she'd thought was being conducted.

In front of her the charioteers waited, their precious horses standing perfectly still despite the provocation of dust and noise. Watching the horsemasters train these exotic beasts had been a favourite pastime before the numbers had taken over her life.

"Ugly brutes, aren't they," said Mahudia from the other end of the sumptuous palanquin.

"I love the sound they make when you feed them grass," said Lenares dreamily. "They used to blow into my hand and make me laugh."

"I never understood your fascination for them. Camels are far nobler, far more intelligent. A proper beast for an Amaqi."

"Camels are stupid," Lenares said. "Little piggy eyes—"

The planquin shook, then rose at the front end, tipping a squealing Lenares back against Mahudia. The ornate door slid shut with a snap, nearly crushing her fingers. Up came the back end, flinging Lenares into the pillows. Something crashed into her head, and wetness ran down her face. She shrieked.

Shouting came from outside. The palanquin was lowered to the ground, the doors were slid open and concerned faces peered inside. Lenares hissed at them.

"My ladies, I am so sorry for what happened." A courteous voice, a soft fatherback accent, a beautiful face, deep brown eyes, long lashes, features almost too fine for a man. "Your bearers, they are untrained, they do not know how to treat their passengers with care." The man leaned into the palanquin, pulling silken sheets and pillows away from the cosmographers. "We will teach them, yes?"

"Thank you," Mahudia said, and brushed her hair back with her hand. "You are very kind."

The man smiled, all white teeth and dimples. "To me has been given the task of looking after the cosmographers. I have made a poor start, have I not? The Omerans assigned to your palanquin, they will be punished. I myself and three of the soldiers will carry you until your bearers recover from this punishment."

"Our sincerest thanks," Mahudia offered, and Lenares was surprised to see she blushed as she spoke.

"Ah, this, this is the wonder of the Emperor's court," the courteous man said, leaning further into the palanquin. Lenares looked around, then realised she was the object of his attention. She smiled nervously at him, an effort he repaid with a dazzling smile of his own, quickly replaced by a frown.

"But you have taken hurt!" he said, and took her face in his soft hands. "Struck by a cup of water, or something of the sort. You are wet, and you have a nasty bruise. I will attend to it myself." He made to draw something from his pocket.

"No need," said Mahudia briskly. "I can deal with the girl. We will require fresh water and a cloth bandage to bring down the swelling."

"You guard her well, as all precious things should be guarded. Is she not to be approached?" The man's frank gaze swept over Lenares, making her flush despite herself.

Mahudia smiled encouragingly. "Lenares may not be approached, though you might have more success with her guardian."

The man's plucked eyebrows rose. "I will remember this should our journey afford the opportunity. Be assured I will offer you both the best of care." He smiled again, such a pretty smile, as shallow and calculating as one from Rouza, then withdrew from the palanquin. Lenares knew from the numbers she'd assigned to the man that he would present himself to them again and again, seeking their favours. Disgusting.

Orders were shouted, their litter rose above the dust, and the journey began.

Lenares took the ends of her hair, nibbled at them and wedged them under her nose. She suspected they would be gone for much longer than a week.

QUEEN

CHAPTER 6

DEATH OF A KING

THE FALTHAN QUEEN CONSIDERED it far too hot up here in the tower. Stifling, in fact. But the king loved to look out over his beloved city, its towers and tenements, its walls and bridges, its swirling crowds of people, and she saw no reason to argue with him about the heat, especially now.

Not now.

She stood at the east window and wished for a cool breeze. She wished for a lot of things, actually, but a cool breeze would have been something, at least. A sign, perhaps. The air stayed stubbornly humid, so unlike the lands in which she and the king had grown up together. The whole of Instruere, its half a million inhabitants, slumbered under an autumn haze. She lifted her eyes further but could see nothing beyond the Aleinus River. Not just the city. Faltha itself slumbered, rocked in the arms of lassitude.

The sound of ragged breathing ceased. She pushed herself away from the window and was at the king's side in a moment. He shuddered, took a great gulping breath and opened his eyes.

"Oh," he said. "I'm . . . still here."

The queen found she could not reply. A Halite priest had once spoken to her of the joy associated with passing to the Most High, both for the departing one and for those left behind, but she could see nothing to rejoice about. All very well for him, young and idealistic, immersed in the fervour of his cult, to say such things with the seeming immortality of decades stretching in front of him. She could have told him a thing or two about immortality—would have, had he shown any inclination to listen to what she said. Well, that was unfair. He'd kept out of the tower as she'd commanded. Mostly, she supposed, because she'd barred the door. The Halites had been very upset by that. King Leith was, after all, the younger brother of their god.

"Stella," the king whispered, and the love in his voice made her heart clench as tight as a fist.

"Leith?"

No answer. He'd sunk back into unconsciousness. She fussed with his bedclothes a little, then bent over and kissed his papery cheek.

He looked so old. *Was* so old; the Sixteen Kingdoms of Faltha had celebrated his seventieth year of rule in an extravagant ceremony a bare six weeks ago. Even then, the signs of Leith's terminal illness could not be hidden. He had been carried to his throne by servants before the ceremonies began, and there feted for far too long, until tears of pain rolled down his mottled face. In the end she'd called a premature halt to the evening. The kings, priests and ambassadors had understood, they'd said, but the necessity of retiring with the king meant she could no longer listen to their gossip and their arguments. So frustrating. She had to know what was being discussed. There would be a struggle for power in Faltha once Leith died, and Stella saw it as her duty to make that struggle as painless for Faltha as possible. She'd regretted having to leave, but it was proper, and the Falthans insisted on propriety.

Seventy years. Even now she was not convinced Leith had made the correct decision in accepting the throne. Barely seventeen years as a person, followed by seventy years as a king. Ripped out of his—their—village in the far north when Bhrudwan warriors kidnapped his parents, and dragged reluctantly into the Falthan War, the great conflict of their age. He had recovered the Jugom Ark, the flaming arrow of the Most High, then led the Falthan army east to counter the might of Bhrudwo, and in the end faced the Destroyer in single combat. How could anyone live a normal life after such events? And how could becoming the Lord of Faltha have helped the boy Leith once was become the man he should have been?

No. She shook her head; memory was so fickle. It had been Hal, Leith's brother. Hal had faced the Destroyer in single combat, not Leith. He had taken Leith's place, the foster brother assuming the role of the natural-born son. Had been struck down, seemingly slain, only to return—from the dead, the Halites claimed, the central tenet of their doctrine—to defeat the Destroyer at the moment of his triumph.

So much confusion that day in the Hall of Meeting: the end of an age, the beginning of another. The Bhrudwan army had swept into Instruere, led by their cruel lord, while the remnants of the Falthan army were held outside the gates under a sorcerous geas. Hal had failed in his bid to bind the Bhrudwans by his own magic and had fallen to the Destroyer, who had bound the Falthan armies in return, his Truthspell rendering them unable to fight. All their hopes gone. The Destroyer had only to witness their surrender and sign the secession document himself, and his lordship would extend across the whole of the northern world.

In a few turbulent moments everything had changed. From her own vantage point beside the Destroyer, just a pace from the events that saved Faltha, Stella saw little. Leith believed that the majestic carving of the Most High on the ceiling of the Hall of Meeting came to life. The carving wore his brother Hal's face, Leith insisted, and it loosed an arrow—the Jugom Ark—at the Destroyer, severing his remaining hand, breaking the Truthspell by rendering him incapable of signing the document.

So Leith said. But Leith had been responsible, at least in part, for Hal's death. As leader of the Falthan army, Leith had been the one challenged by the Destroyer to single combat, but Hal had taken it upon himself, saving his brother. What would be more natural, then, than for Leith to imagine his brother coming back to life to save them all? Then to go further and interpret Hal's death as a deliberate sacrifice?

The more the Halites preached the doctrine, the less Stella believed it. It smacked of sophistry, of stretching a truth to fit the facts. And the few discernible facts were ambiguous: the Destroyer certainly lost his hand—she more than anyone else alive could attest to that—but whether it was before or during the melee that erupted in the Hall of Meeting she could not say. It was also true that the carved figure of the Most High now most certainly wore Hal's face. Though even this was disputed: some of the old Company—those who had set out from Firanes in search of Leith and Hal's parents—argued that people now remembered Hal from the carving. Both Farr of Withwestwa Wood, and their own Haufuth, their village leader, maintained this until they died.

Slim evidence upon which to build a religion. But well-meaning people—zealots—had arisen in the months immediately following the Destroyer's defeat, claiming special insight into the "meaning behind events" and proclaiming their belief in Hal. Some were telling the truth, or as much of it as they knew: the Company from Firanes had built quite a following during their stay in Instruere, and Hal had been a part of that. However, his wizardly powers had not at that time been widely known; most of the magic exercised by the Company had been attributed to Leith and the Jugon Ark. Conveniently forgotten now, or at least glossed over. It pleased people to exaggerate the truth, or more often mix it with hearsay, until it became difficult to remember what had actually happened.

Leith could have broken the Halites' rising power with a few words. It was entirely on his testimony, after all, that their beliefs were built. This was the largest barrier between him and Stella, and they had never successfully breached it.

Well, perhaps not the largest.

Stella wandered over to the east window again and leaned out, her face catching the beginnings of a breeze. Leith never understood what had happened to her after she had given herself to Deorc. That was the real reason why their long marriage had proved difficult. None of the Company had understood. She was honestly not sure that she understood herself.

The king moaned a name. Hers? She was too far gone in her reminiscence to turn.

While the Company were raising an army from Instruere and the surrounding Falthan lands to oppose the Destroyer, she had fallen for a man named Tanghin. Foolishly she left the Company and sought him out, only to find he had been assuming a disguise to ensnare her. He revealed himself to her as Deorc, the Destroyer's lieutenant, who had infiltrated Instruere and intended to rule in his master's name. He had been commanded by his master to capture one of the Company, but had desired her for himself. When the Destroyer learned of his servant's treachery he destroyed Deorc, but not before pulling Stella through his blue fire into his terrible presence. The memories of that day, filled with fear and pain, were still too tender to examine closely, even after seventy years. From then on she had been forced to assume the role of the Undying Man's consort. He inflicted agony on her, shared with her . . . gave her the gift of immortality, the curse placed on him for denying the Most High two thousand years ago. Now his eternal pain ran through her veins, a barrier between her and every other human. The cruelty of it was beyond her comprehension.

Yet he had loved her. A monstrous love, a love born of hunger, of loneliness and a desperate need, but love nonetheless. For the first time in her life she had been needed, not just desired.

The Halites had one thing right. She had been the one to assist the Destroyer in his escape from Instruere. Handless, powerless, unable even to harness the manifold powers of his servants, the *Maghdi Dasht*, he had relied on her to guide him to safety. The priests named it a betrayal of Faltha, proof of her complicity with Bhrudwo. She could not deny it.

How could she have refused him? He needed her.

Leith had risked his life to attempt her rescue. She supposed the Halites also had that right. But Leith had not rescued her. She had refused him, unwilling to leave her care of another of the Destroyer's servants, a eunuch whose tongue had been cut out for showing kindness to her. She knew what the Halites would make of that if they ever found out. Now that Leith lay dying, the secret would remain in her mind alone.

She had made her own escape months later. Exhausted, starved, at the far edge of despair, she had hallucinated a vision of the tongueless man speaking in Hal's voice. He bade her flee. In her weakened state she had taken his advice, and had lived with the guilt ever since. She arrived back in Instruere on the day Leith ascended the newly created Falthan throne. Leith, dear Leith, took her in when everyone else vilified her; made her his wife and elevated her to his queen.

Queen? In name only. The Halites' pernicious doctrine labelled her as the Destroyer's Consort. She had seen their reaching for herself, all through the Seven Scrolls they held sacred. Such teachings engendered widespread mistrust; a mistrust grown worse over the years as the Halites strengthened their hold on the populace. Faltha would never be hers to rule. Whoever took power here would make it his first action to hand her over to the Koinobia, the Halite "common-life" church—that is, if they did not simply seize her in the interim. The most likely scenario was that the Council of Faltha would take power here in Instruere, the Sixteen Kingdoms would once again act with true independence and she would be lost in the scramble for power, a minor consideration, mourned by a literal handful of people. And so Faltha would begin the long spiral down into defencelessness, and would one day once again be vulnerable to Bhrudwo's immortal lord. Yes, it would take hundreds of years for the Destroyer to recover, and as long for the Falthans to weaken. But when that happened, she alone of those alive today would be there to see it.

The Halites would not be able to kill her. Even after seventy years she did not fully understand what immortality meant, but she doubted anything short of brutal dismemberment would end her suffering. Perhaps not even that.

There were millions of sets of eyes open right at this moment. A thousand years from now all those eyes would be closed but for two sets. Hers and his. Reflections in agony. And one precious set of eyes would be closed forever by the end of this day.

She turned away from the window, her heart cold in her chest. Here she was, seventy years on, committing the same selfish sin that had entrapped her back then. Thinking of herself when someone else had the greater need. She drew closer to the bed: an unnatural pallor suffused the king's face, and he breathed shallowly and unevenly. Not long, then.

She thought of the years she had spent with this kind, generous, unselfish man. It had never been her intention to marry a man from her own isolated village: to her, Leith and the other village boys represented a safe life, a small life, a meaningless, inconsequential life like those her parents had lived. As a girl her consuming ambition had been to escape to somewhere interesting, exciting, important. Instead, excitement came to her village, sweeping her up in the most important events in Faltha for a thousand years. Despite this she had ended up with Leith, as the so-called Queen of Faltha. She had helped Leith make decisions involving thousands of people. Had lived a life unimaginable to her parents. Had been loved, truly loved.

Yet . . .

Yet, it had been a life made for her by others. Defined by the pain of the Destroyer's blood, the cruelty of the Halite doctrine, the mercy of the Falthan king. Such a full life, such a privileged life, such a constrained life; she was not ungrateful, not exactly. *The man who loves me, whom I . . . love—allow yourself to think it—is dying.* And yet her overriding feeling was one of freedom.

Perhaps the Halites were right to condemn her. Perhaps they understated the depths of her selfishness. They would be shocked at what she planned to do next.

The afternoon wore on. Though Stella had specifically instructed all three of the royal physicians to keep the gravity of the king's condition secret, such things did not escape others who worked in the Hall, and a crowd of curious onlookers began to gather on the grassy space below the tower. Individual citizens, families with food baskets, stallholders, one or two russet-cloaked Halite priests. Their clamour filtered up to her.

She ignored them. Let them wonder, let them speculate, let them treat as a holiday the day the world was losing a wonderful man. They did not know, they had forgotten. The Destroyer was already half a myth; scholars wrote revisionist histories explaining real events as metaphorical. Even the presence of the Jugom Ark, glittering on the altar in the Hall of Meeting in Instruere, failed to dampen their foolish philandering with the facts. No different to the priests, really, serving their own god. Phemanderac had been commissioned to write an official history of the Falthan War, but in sixty years had not finished it. Afraid to insult or belittle any of his friends, he'd spent far too long on the maps.

It didn't matter. None of it did. Her eyes lifted beyond the city, where the haze had given way to the afternoon breeze. Out past the ever-wide Central Plains towards the gates of Aleinus, where Hal had laid down his life for his brother. And for Faltha, she added, remembering Halite orthodoxy. She could not see the Gates; their bluff slopes and enormous cliffs were well over the horizon. Thousands of leagues further lay Bhrudwo and the island of Andratan, on which Kannwar, the Destroyer, Lord of Bhrudwo, the Undying Man, was said by Dhaurian spies to be hiding, recuperating from his great defeat and loss of power. She narrowed her eyes, as if by squinting she could somehow make out the Tower of Farsight, highest bulwark on Andratan, from where he might be looking, searching the western sky.

A knock at the door, a servant offering refreshment. Without bothering to unbar the door, Stella peered through the grille and waved her away. Behind the woman two physicians hovered. She waved them away also. Turned back to her window.

She could feel him, that was the problem. His blood burned in her veins. Those first years had been pure agony, a chronic pain no palliative could suppress, wearing away at her sanity just as she knew it wore away at his. Then, over the last five decades, it had gradually eased— as she slowly healed and as, no doubt, he recovered. Did he feel her pain? She thought so. And recently he had begun to feel different somehow, less caustic, more desperate, as though taken by some affliction. Powerful, most certainly, more powerful than ever. Yet something had changed, and not for the better.

Stella did not love him. She did not doubt her self-judgment on this matter, having been brutally honest with herself, knowing what *being needed* could do to a woman's soul. Particularly one who had not been able to have children. No, she carried no love for their great enemy. She hated him. His desire for revenge on the Most High had cost thousands of lives, among them some she had counted as friends. His actions had been, at times, nothing short of deeply evil. She remembered a village, a pile of hands and feet, the cries of children. His ravaged face as he made his escape from Instruere, drawing on her, reckless of her life.

Yet . . .

Yet, he could not hide from her, nor she from him. He and she: the only two of a different species.

No sound from behind her. She turned, fearing she had missed Leith's last moment.

He was sitting up in bed, his face glowing, healthier-seeming by far than at any time in the last month. His eyes bright, focused on her, alive with knowledge. She had seen enough prolonged death to know what this was. The false bloom before the final blight.

He breathed deeply, then spoke in the voice of a hurt child.

"You're going to him."

A dozen answers flashed through her mind. *No, Leith, how could you think such a thing? I was just looking at the crowds below. I would never dishonour your memory by travelling to Bhrudwo. You're tired; why don't you close your eyes and rest? I was just gazing out of the window. The east window. It could have been any window. Any direction.*

"Yes."

The word surprised her, shocked her, ripped a ragged breath from her. Leith simply nodded.

"Should have gone long ago. Nothing but persecution and imprisonment for you here. Tried to warn you; too pig-headed to listen. Listen now. Go. Go now."

Stella stood there, facing the knowing regard of the man she was hurting one last time, and wept until her chest and stomach hurt.

"Leith, oh Leith, I . . ." She could not finish. No lies, no shadings of the truth, no manufacturing of more lifelong guilt, not when she would carry it for eternity without hope of absolution. No falsehood to wrap Leith in, smoothing his final journey. She took his hand, hoping it would be enough. She had no words for him.

"Go," he said. "Something not right in what happened all those years ago. We missed something. He knows. Something coming, a terrible thing, greater far than Kannwar. He knows. You go. Get . . . answers to your questions." He paused for breath: the effort of speaking told on him.

"Leith, you must rest."

"Stella," he said, and her heart broke anew at the way he said it, the layers of meaning in his thin voice. "Stella, thank you. But you must go. Save yourself, save him, save them all."

His eyes opened further, as though he experienced

some private hallucination. "My brother . . . thanks you too. Wants you to leave." Opened still further. "And now I must . . . must also go." Closed.

A last breath, a last whisper.

"Goodbye, my love," he said, and left her.

His hand was cold when finally she forced herself to let it go. Cold and empty. She stood up, easing bones supposedly near ninety years old that insisted on behaving as though she was still a young woman. At this moment she felt no kinship with the man in the bed, with the people in the city, with anyone at all. They could die; she could not. She was different. Thoroughly other. Completely alone.

She wolfed down the cold gruel and emptied the water jug ignored this past day. Even the act of taking food and drink seemed pointless: forty years ago she had experimented with fasting, testing the limits of her immortality. The results were debilitating but not fatal; her muscles wasted somewhat in those weeks, but whatever had been set within her sustained her in any extremity. She'd resumed eating and drinking out of habit. Something to remind her of her humanity.

She threw the jug across the room. It shattered on the wall near the north window.

A few minutes' rummaging in the drawers by the bed secured several tiny but valuable pieces of jewellery, which she placed in a small bag looped around her neck. She looked as long as she dared for something to help disguise her from those down below who awaited news of the king, those she needed to avoid, but found nothing. She would be walking into their hateful hands. She sighed. Better walking than being dragged.

Face the bed one last time. A bow, a touch to the cheek, a kiss. A deep breath. Then a slow turn, so hard to do, a hand to the door, ease up the bar, open, close the door behind her, eyes blurry, not looking back.

Stella had no idea how long ago the servant had last checked on the king. Perhaps she ascended the stairs even now, physicians in tow, seeking an update on the king's condition. Or perhaps they enjoyed a meal together, or had taken themselves home for the evening.

One foot in front of the other. A grey haze seemed to have descended on her: blinking away the tears helped her see a little better. A lock of her grey hair, dyed to help conceal her impossible youth, flicked an eye, a stinging sharpness. She fought back a cry of anguish. Not here, not now, not yet.

She came to herself enough to wonder where the guards were. There was, of course, no tradition for this, as Faltha had never before had a king, but she had expected some sort of Death Watch, as practised by many of Faltha's kingdoms. She had spoken to Elast, Captain of the Guard, about this. Ten guards at least, including Elast himself. Where were they? Why had no guardsmen come to check on their king?

She turned left at the base of the stairs, head up, walking briskly. Over the years she had adopted the gait of an old woman as part of an attempt to disguise her lack of aging. She had to hope her youthful figure would not be recognised as that of the queen.

Finally, at the arched wooden door to the street, she came across a guard. One, and not senior. He looked her over, his eyes narrowing with what she initially thought was suspicion, but then recognised as lust. Obviously tak-

ing her for a servant he made a series of lewd suggestions
to her, each more inventive than the last. She forced herself to smile, though inwardly heartsick. She would take
the chance he offered her.

"Is that all you can do?" she said roughly. "Talk?"

"More than talk," he replied heavily, licking his lips.
"Won't talk at all if that's how you like it. Make you talk,
though."

Stella caught a glimpse over his shoulder, and her skin
chilled. The servant approached, accompanied by four people: two of the royal physicians and two Halite priests. She
recognised both the priests. One was the Archpriest himself, a tall man with an artificial dignity she despised. A
very powerful man. Not a man she wanted to meet today.

"You're still talking," she said desperately.

"In here, then." He grabbed at her arm; she brushed
him off with a flick of her hand and a coquettish grin,
then followed him into the small annexe serving as a
guardroom.

The man had his sword off and jerkin open even before
she closed the door behind her. She picked up his weapon
and smiled again. "It's a big sword," she said, sliding it
suggestively out of its scabbard.

"I have a bigger," the guard said, leering at her.

"Not big enough," she replied, and levelled the blade
at him.

"You bitch, what—" He stared into her eyes, and belated recognition spread across his face. He sank to the
floor on his knees, mouth so wide open Stella struggled to
suppress hysterical laughter.

"My queen," he said boarsely, and stopped to clear his
throat. "I thought . . . I am new here." He closed his eyes.

"Clearly."

"How could I?" He began to tremble.

"I led you on. Sit up; you look ridiculous."

He regained some self-possession, wiped his palms on his jerkin and laced himself up, then sat on his haunches. "The king?"

"Is dead."

A sharp, indrawn breath. "Dead? But . . . but we were told, your majesty . . . The priests told us the king was in no danger!" The light went out of his eyes.

"And do you take your orders from the priests?"

"No, of course not. But Captain Elast confirmed it for us. Out of his own mouth I heard it. The senior officers are off discussing it now. Next week, they said, the Death Watch would begin. Your majesty," he added.

"A play for power, then, already begun. Do you understand? The priests and physicians have colluded to remove the Instruian Guard, a preface to their bid for control of Instruere and, ultimately, Faltha. I wonder what they offered Elast. Or what they threatened him with. Either way, you are betrayed."

"I understand, my queen." All too well, by the sick look on his face.

Stella continued. "If you have been here more than a few days, you will know what the king's death means for me. What they will do to me."

He nodded. "They won't, though, will they? Your majesty," he added after a moment, still clearly yet to come to terms with what was happening.

"I do not care to find out. I know you will not ask, but what the priests say about me is not true. Well, it *is* true, but not in the fashion the priests have taught you. I do not, however, wish to discuss it with them. I doubt they have the wit to understand how truth can be turned into something else."

"Your majesty?" Colour gradually returned to the man's face. Good.

"What is your name?"

"Robal, my lady. Robal Anders of Austrau, that is."

"Austrau? Excellent. Well then, Robal Anders, how would you like to do your queen a great service?"

The guard fought an obvious battle to keep his face perfectly still.

"Oh dear, you are going to be a difficult man, aren't you. Just do as I say for now. And don't worry. They may hate me, they may want to get rid of me, but when I write a letter explaining that I have taken you into my service, they will provide for your wife and children."

The man looked shocked. "No family, my queen. Do you think I would have . . . that I would . . . if I . . . I wouldn't!"

"No family? Better and better. Nevertheless, your sergeant and paymaster will need to know. Still, that will have to wait for later. For now, Robal Anders of Austrau, can you get me out of Instruere without attracting attention?"

"Blessed King Leith is not likely to survive the night," one of the physicians was saying, the eldest one—Pyrus or Palus, something like that—in between panting for breath. What was wrong with the man? There were fewer than three hundred steps.

"We are surprised he has remained with us this long," said a second physician. *Lamayan.* The young priest dragged the name from his memory. Conal prided himself on knowing such details. His master, the Archpriest, hadn't bothered to learn the physicians' names. Hadn't even asked. He barely tolerated them, he often said, with their smug belief in their own curative powers. In the coming Kingdom of the Most High, doctors would take their orders from priests, who would tell them when to intervene and when to leave well alone.

The Archpriest grunted something the physicians would take for assent, and followed them upwards, dragging Conal along in his wake.

The queen had baulked the priesthood long enough. Doctors might have a place in the kingdom, but she did not, not as things currently stood. As it said in the Mahnumsen Scrolls, "Stella Pellwen knelt before the Destroyer and did as he commanded," scroll six, line one hundred and eighteen. There was no doubt about this, no other way the words could be interpreted. Further, it said, "His consort brought forth the Declaration and placed it in his hand," scroll seven, line thirty-one. And, most damning, "She led him, handless and bleeding, through the lanes and alleyways of Instruere, giving him succour from her very spirit," scroll seven, line two hundred and twelve. King Leith had provided her with a chance of redemption, as was proper for the brother of Hal, but according to the Archpriest the woman had never shown the humility that accompanied true repentance. When the king passed on, the Koinobia would offer her counselling for as long as was necessary. Her repentance was much to be desired. The eighth scroll was unfinished still, after all. The name of the priest who brought her to repentance would be central to bringing the Mahnusmen Scrolls to a fitting conclusion.

It was Conal's recurring vision: the queen receiving the essentials of faith from his hand, the devout priest of Hal. He knew his desire for this was partly selfish, and he repented of it. But he honestly wished for her redemption for her own sake, and for the sake of the thousands of Halite followers. If Stella Pellwen could be persuaded to receive the Fire of the Most High, who among men was truly beyond the Koinobia?

"Our fervent hope is that the king does not suffer overlong," said the Archpriest, his words drawing careful glances from the physicians. *They do not understand*, Conal realised; *they think death is the end, and so fight it with their meagre resources*. Had Hal not shown the way beyond death?

"Here we are, my lords," the servant woman said, knocking on the door. There was no response, not an uncommon thing, apparently, since the queen had taken over the king's care.

The Archpriest gestured, and Conal stepped forward. "Allow me," he said, and stooped to look through the small, grilled aperture in the door. He could see most of the room. There lay the king, eyes open and sightless, face drained of blood. Dead, clearly dead. And where was the queen? He craned his neck left and right, but there were one or two crannies he could not see into. A little further forward, perhaps . . . His head knocked against the grille, and the door unlatched.

"Ah." Not barred, then. *Either she has accepted the inevitable, or* . . . He pushed the door open and stepped into the king's high chamber.

"The king is dead," the Archpriest announced.

At his solemn words the physicians rushed to the

bedside, pulling their now-useless instruments from their bags.

"Aye, the sainted brother of Hal has passed into the realm of fire," the Archpriest continued in his gentle, dangerous voice. "We will grieve for him, and the kingdom he leaves behind, at the appropriate time. Sadly, his queen has abandoned him." His voice dripped with feigned disappointment. The man had never taken the queen's redemption seriously, in Conal's opinion. "She has avoided those charged with setting watch on her."

The servant woman turned to him and curtseyed nervously. "My lord, I came up to the door only an hour ago. The doctors came with me. They will tell you she commanded me to leave." She turned to them, an imploring look on her face.

The senior of the two physicians raised his head from whatever he was doing with the body. "We will say no such thing. We saw nothing, heard nothing but this woman bidding us return down the stairs, saying that the queen had waved us away."

"But . . ." The woman seemed to shrink under their regard.

"I will testify that I did not hear the queen speak. The Koinobia may draw any conclusion it sees fit."

Fat tears rolled down the woman's cheeks. "My lords, I want the witch to pay for her crimes just as you do." Her voice shook. "I would not . . . would never help her escape. On my life!"

"As it shall be," intoned the Archpriest solemnly. "The Koinobia will determine the truth of this. You, woman, will accompany Conal here to his sanctum and answer his questions truthfully. We will know if you lie."

"I will say what you want me to say," the servant said in a flat voice.

"The truth, no matter how much more might be achieved by falsehood."

"Yes, lord." This on the edge of hearing.

"Are you sending me away, your eminence?" Conal controlled his anger. World-changing moments were by definition rare, and he did not want to be excluded from this one.

"You are a stubborn reed, for all you feign obedience." Dark, cold eyes held him effortlessly. "How far must I bend you before you become truly pliant, I wonder? You shall take the woman for questioning, but you may not question her yourself. Give her to Narl, with instructions to show more restraint this time. While he is busy you will retire to your sanctum and copy out the seventh scroll in its entirety, then burn your copy. You have many lessons to learn."

"Yes, my lord." His anger drenched in fear, Conal supposed he made a show of humility, but his lord would not be fooled. He made to leave the chamber.

"On further thought, you will wait a moment longer. Search this room for any clue as to the queen's whereabouts. Thoroughly, with a single mind. Am I clear?"

"My lord." Singlemindedness, the Archpriest's lodestone. *Let nothing else distract from the task at hand, and the task will be completed successfully.* Conal began his search, feeling more like a servant than a senior figure in the Koinobia.

His lord turned to the physicians. "There remains much to be done. One of you must go to the Pinion and report King Leith's death. The bell must be rung, the citizens must be told. A great man has left us today, and your services are of no use now." *If they ever were*, Conal almost heard him add.

The two physicians looked at each other. The older of the two nodded, then packed up his bag and left without another word.

The younger man turned to the Archpriest, a knowing look in his eye. "I know what you will ask," he said.

"Oh?"

The physician's confidence surprised Conal, causing him to look up from his search. Was the man really that clever?

"Say on." The Archpriest wore an inscrutable look.

"The answer is no, there is no evidence the king's death has been hastened. We cannot be certain, of course, but none of the telltale signs are in evidence."

A clever man indeed, knowing what his master sought and not making him ask for it. The Archpriest obviously thought so too. "Do you believe?" he asked the physician.

"I believe . . . a number of things, my lord. Not all of them are compatible with Halite teaching, but I do honour to the deeds and memory of the Mahnumsens, older and younger."

Clever and brave. Talents wasted on a physician. Despite his anger, Conal found himself intrigued by the young man, surely no more than his own age. He continued his search of the chamber, half an ear on the conversation.

"Then you will know how important it is that we locate the queen as soon as possible. Not just for her sake, but for all those who might otherwise become your patients, or even end up beyond the reach of your arts, in this time of uncertainty. You are a physician. Do you see how you might save many lives in the next few hours?"

Conal watched the man rise slowly, saw comprehension spread across his pinched features.

"I do, though I do not do the bidding of the Koinobia unless I believe it to be sound." Brave indeed.

"I *bid* you to do nothing. I *ask* in humility. Please, sir physician, find the queen. Accept any aid the Koinobia can offer. Keep her safe from the mob, those who would take our teachings to the extreme and find themselves tempted to exact vengeance upon her body. And when you consider what should be done with her, keep the safety of my personal sanctum in mind."

The man said nothing, just nodded intermittently as though working through the Archpriest's words in search of fishhooks. No need for such hooks: men of principle were more likely to be lured and held by the truth spoken without guile. As this man had been lured and held.

"You may hear from me," the physician said, and took his leave. Conal followed the man, pulling the frightened servant woman along by the hand. Of such business, distasteful as it was, the Kingdom of Hal was made.

A single bell began to toll as Robal led Stella through the Dock Gate and out of Onstruere's warren of lanes and alleys. Six heartbeats between each peal. All around them dock workers, sailors, warehouse workers and other citizens of Instruere put down their tools and burdens and turned and faced towards the source of the sound, the Pinion's great bell. The Pinion had once been a a dungeon, but was now used as the city's guardhouse, and stood a good half-hour's eastward walk from where they stood.

The silence and stillness increased between each tolling, until the only other sound was the faint murmuring of the Aleinus River surrounding the city.

"We have to wait," Stella said as the guard made to move on. Though she knew how many times the bell would toll, she found herself counting. Thirty-one, thirty-two, thirty-three. On and on it rang, silence and sound intermingled, tolling out the sum of a man's life. Eighty-five, eighty-six, eighty-seven. The last peal hung in the air long after it should have faded. A deep silence fell, stretching on as Instruere honoured its king, people all around Stella wiping tears from their eyes, holding each other, standing unnaturally still. The queen found she had reason to regret her uncharitable thoughts up in the tower chamber.

A touch to the shoulder freed Robal from the stasis. Stella nodded to the nearest dock, where a dark-skinned woman stood with three boys, their hats held over their hearts. They had the look of the Wodrani: leathery, outdoor faces, braided hair, narrow eyes. The queen decided to try her luck.

"Madam?" she called as she drew closer to the dock. "Would you accept a commission?"

"Hush'm," the woman replied, speaking from the corner of her mouth. "Cain't you b'seein' and a'hearin' respeck we b'payin' the king?"

"I'm sorry?" Stella had no idea what she'd been told, but guessed the words had contained censure of some sort, given the look on the woman's face.

"My ma says for you to shut up until she's finished paying respect to King Leith," said the youngest of the three boys, no older than ten. "So shut up."

Stella closed her mouth on the ready retort she had fashioned, and signalled for Robal to do likewise. They waited patiently beside the Wodrani.

After a few moments Robal rose up on his toes, stared intently at something in the distance, then bent down to whisper in Stella's ear. "Beg pardon, your majesty, but there are guards pouring through the Dock Gate." *Looking for you*, he didn't have to add. They both turned to the Wodrani woman.

"Bester king ever of all," the woman said, and slapped her rumpled hat back on her head. "We river traders ha' never had years like'n these, allpraise to the king." She spat something she had been chewing onto the ground, turned to the boys, nodded, then walked towards the end of the dock and the barge waiting there.

Stella tried again, panic edging her voice. "Please, madam, we would like passage on your vessel."

"Ma steers, and you'll find none better on the river 'tween here and the Gates." It was the youngest boy: the older two scurried after the woman. "But she don't do the deals. Deals are man's work. I do the deals." He fixed them with an intense stare, one eye screwed shut. "The hold's full, but we could take a couple'a people upriver. That is, if they weren't an Instruian Guard and the blessed Queen o' Faltha."

"Oh," Stella said. She glanced over her shoulder: the guards had begun a systematic search of the docks and warehouses. She turned back to the boy, who winked at her.

"O'course, what I know and what m'brothers and Ma know are different things. Where to, and what're you offering?"

"Upriver, as far as you'll take us," Stella replied urgently, "and we're offering this." She tipped the contents of her small bag into her hand, then held up a diamond brooch between finger and thumb. "Far too much for the passage, as you can see, but I have nothing of lesser value."

The boy shook his head slowly. "Ma will know something's up if I show her that. Never mind. Come on board while I figger something out." He wiped his nose with his hand, then held it out. "Deal?"

Stella did not hesitate. "Deal." Relief coursed through her body as she shook the boy's dirty hand.

The three boys untied the ropes, shifted the cargo and poled the barge into the Great River. Ma stood in the stern, hand on the riller, a constant eye searching for anything amiss. Stella and Robal found a place amidships, hunkering down between bulky crates.

"Always ready, slow and steady," the youngest boy cried as they eased the barge out into the tidal river. "Sun and moon, get there soon," the other boys replied as they poled.

Four pairs of Wodrani eyes swept the river ahead, while two pairs of Instruian eyes closed in grateful relief. So it was that six pairs of eyes did not see the small boat drifting up-tide behind them. Nor did they see the veteran guard finish his turn at the oars and hand them over to the young priest.

CHAPTER 7

THE MAREMMA

"THIS IS EXQUISITE. A theological argument in the middle of a river. Are all the guardsmen in Instruere like you, or am I just particularly unlucky?"

"Unlucky? Your majesty, had you chosen to seduce any other guardsman, you would be hearing a great deal about weaponry and the state of the Instruian walls."

"Seduce you? *Seduce* you? *You* were the one who made the suggestions. Since the moment you realised your mistake I've kept you at arm's length, and you will not be getting any closer."

"And do you think by avoiding my question you will also avoid thinking about the issue?"

"Why were you not appointed to the Council of Faltha by the King of Straux? You could have kept them amused for months." She smiled at him to take the sting from her words. "We're only three days upriver from Instruere. I could always get this boat turned around, go back and exchange you for someone who makes sense."

"Avoiding the issue, my mother always said, is a sure sign the issue needs to be discussed. So answer my question, your majesty, if it please you. Whose son was Hal?"

"All right. Hal was brought up by Mahnum and Indrett, my father- and mother-in-law. They found him abandoned as a child. After Hal's death we uncovered the identity of his mother. Tinei was a local woman who fell pregnant because of a particularly vicious abduction and rape. The father is unknown. How does this aid us in our discussion?"

"Unknown, my Queen? That's not what the Halites say. They say that Hal is the child of the Most High."

"Really? Do they really think that the Most High caused Tinei to be with child? I hope not, because she suffered abominably. The attack left her a cripple. She died before we ever left Loulea."

"Hal's father is the Most High," Robal said stubbornly.

"And what proof do they have of that?" Stella snapped. "I've never been able to understand why Hal's parentage matters so much. Actually, I do. It ties up all the truth into a neat package for consumption by the believers. Black and white, good and evil, us and them. They don't know what to do with me, though, which is why they want to hold endless and undoubtedly painful 'talks' with me. Who cares who Hal's father was? Surely what he did is more important than who he was?"

He peered at her suspiciously from under his wild fringe. "You are not telling me everything you know."

"And this surprises you? You know how I feel about the Halite doctrine. I'm the nearest thing to the Destroyer in their eyes. They refuse to listen to what really happened to me. Every grain of sand they uncover is turned into a mountain of solid rock. You would be no different. If I told you what I really think about Hal and his origins you would put me to death yourself."

"If I could, I would not," murmured the guard.

"If you could? What do you mean by that?" Stella stared at him, trying to read his intent, but the day's gloaming defeated her.

All trace of humour left his voice. "If you will allow me to be candid, your majesty, I think you would be hard to kill. Should anyone want to, that is."

"Oh?" His words chilled her. "What makes you say that?" She spoke with more intensity than intended.

"You want me to tell you everything I know, yet you keep secrets from me? Believe me, your majesty, now we have fled Instruere we are no longer queen and guard. We are simply Stella and Robal, trying to escape those who seek us. We will remain together only by trusting each other."

"And who will be the first to take the risk?" Stella raised her chin and glared in the man's direction. He did not reply, but she heard him exhale slowly. *Not as calm as he appears, then.*

"A great man died three days ago," she said, her voice gentler. "A man whom I loved. He was the only protection I had against those who sought to bring me down. It will be a long time before I can think seriously about trusting anyone else."

No sound for a while save the chirping of crickets and the slop of water against the gunwale.

"I am sorry, my lady," he said eventually. "You seem so strong, so self-possessed. It is hard putting myself in your place."

Stella did not feel inclined to answer him.

After a while Robal spoke again. "You are right. He was a great king, a great man." He breathed out heavily. "My grandfather practically worshipped him. Do you know King Leith came out to Austrau and personally dealt with the maesters at the height of the grain wars? My gran said he had them looking for their arses in their earholes, if you'll pardon the expression."

"I remember." She smiled wistfully to herself. "I told him to be more careful with his words, but he was right. The maesters needed setting down."

"You were there?"

"Of course. You must have . . . No, of course not, you had not yet been born. Oh, Most High, Robal, I can't live with this, and I can't die. I am going to go mad."

She had fought so hard for so long, she was not yet ready for this to overwhelm her, was certainly not ready to reveal so much to a stranger. She dug her nails into the palms of her hands, resisting the urge to scream, to lash out, to throw herself into the river, or into the arms of the bluff guard opposite her.

"You won't go mad, my queen. But where *are* you going to go?"

"I don't know." A true answer, if not the whole truth. "Upriver somewhere. A place where I won't be recognised." She snorted, thinking of the portraits depicting the royal couple, liberally scattered across the Sixteen Kingdoms. "It'll be a long journey."

"The river's a good place, your majesty. Upriver is even better. The guards will search downriver, along the coast and the roads leading west, back to Firances and Loulea, thinking you will try to go home. It's what I would have done." A pause. Stella could see no more than his shadowy outline, but could imagine the grimace on his normally cheeky face. "Why didn't you, your majesty? Why didn't you head for home?"

"Home? I've just left home."

Home was most certainly not Loulea, the small Firanese village far to the west where she had been born and raised. Stella had left her village, her parents and her drunkard of a brother with few regrets. Newly crowned after the Falthan War, Leith had persuaded her to accompany him on a journey to Firanes—their duty, he told her—including the trek north to Loulea in the cool autumn. She had forgotten how cold the coastlands of Firanes could be, but was reminded by the early snowfall that delayed them a week. Eventually they had taken lodgings in Vapnatak, the nearest large town, left their entourage there and walked the last few miles alone to their small village.

A mistake. The villagers turned out to cheer the king and queen, but were disappointed not to see the horses and the soldiers and the other trappings of glory. Leith tried to explain who they were, but had been met with incredulity and disbelief. Leith and Stella died years ago, they said. The same year the old village headman went missing. A bad year, that. But what were the affairs of Loulea to the King and Queen of Faltha? Why were they asking such questions, saying such things, stirring up such grief? The gulf between villager and royalty seemed too broad for their direct, practical minds to cross.

The village council eventually gathered the gist of the tale, and were offered sufficient proofs by the king that they could no longer deny the true identity of their royal guests. They were shocked, but there were none of the celebrations

Stella had expected. Instead, Leith and Stella were taken to her father's grave, fresh-dug, next to that of her brother, who had apparently not lasted more than a few months after their supposed deaths. Stella's mother, a broken figure, did not recognise them. Had recognised none but her husband for two years.

That evening, during the festivities celebrating the visit of the king and queen, Stella begged Leith to take them home to Instruere. Their welcome had left Leith feeling uncomfortable, she could tell, but he was a man of duty and would not listen to her. After the feast the young village headman spoke quietly to them both, advising them to leave. "I know who you are, but many of the villagers do not. The way you talk of Loulea as if it was your home is confusing them. Please, your majesties, we have enjoyed and have been honoured by your visit, but we would respectfully ask you to depart at your earliest opportunity."

"But how could Loulea have forgotten us? It is less than ten years since we lived among them." The queen who asked that question had been young; despite all she had suffered during the Falthan War, she had yet to learn that indifference wounded deeper than hatred.

"How could they have forgotten?" the headman repeated. "Stella, take a good look at me and answer your own question."

Druin. The boy she had almost been betrothed to, whose boorish behaviour had driven her to leave Loulea. A boy grown into a young man, a changed man, with a responsibility taken no less seriously than that of the man she had married. Surely too young to be a village leader, though, as Stella reminded herself, older than his queen.

"You did not recognise Hermesa either, your majesty."

The epithet sounded like a curse from his lips. "Or if you did, you chose not to acknowledge her." He presented his wife to the royal pair, and patiently answered their awkward, embarrassed questions about the fortunes of their other childhood friends.

It seemed that Druin had not been the village's first choice for their leader, but Malos and Rauth had moved to the south, down Oln way, to farm together, leaving Loulea needing new blood. He'd fought in the rebellion to oust the corrupt Firanese regent, one of those who had betrayed Faltha to the Destroyer, and won renown for himself and his village. Now Druin and Hermesa ran their village with at least as much integrity and common sense as Leith and Stella ruled Faltha, and with a great deal less bureaucratic interference.

The King and Queen of Faltha left Loulea early the next morning. Only a few children lined the Westway to see them go. It had been a valuable, if hard, lesson for them both.

"I will not go back to that village," Stella told the guardsman sitting quietly in the dark. "If the Halites waste their effort searching the West, it will be because they never bothered to learn anything of me. I find this a pleasing thought."

"They will check upriver, too," Robal said. "My role in your escape will already be known. This will mean the Instruian Guard will offer every assistance to the Koinobia. Nowhere in Faltha will be safe."

"Nowhere? Faltha is a very large place."

"Not large enough, with respect, your majesty."

"You may be right." She sighed. "As it happens, I do not intend to hide anywhere in Faltha."

"Ah then, you will be wanting to go further east."

"Am I to be forever cursed with clever men?" she asked, exasperated. "If my plans and motives are so transparent, why are the agents of the Koinobia not upon us even now?"

"Because no one wants to travel the Maremma," said a young voice from near the rail to their left. Gren, the youngest of the Wodrani boys, called Mite by his brothers. "Three weeks of stink and bugs, following the river through the swamps. Takes a deal of experience not to get lost. They'll be waitin' for you at Vindicare on the far side."

"You're taking a risk having us as passengers," Stella commented.

"Part of our life on the river," Gren said airily. "'Tis risky just travellin' through the Maremma. People die here all the time. Washed away by floods, taken by diseases and simply gettin' lost in all the dead-end waterpaths. Not so bad during autumn, though. Especially not with Ma at the tiller."

"You should address the queen more formally," Robal said testily. "It wouldn't hurt to say 'your majesty'."

"Ain't my queen," Gren answered. "Queen of Faltha, not Queen of the Wodrani. We're not one of the Sixteen. We were here long before the First Men came traipsin' over the desert. I'm not sayin' we ain't grateful, though," he added swiftly, as the guardsman made to stand. "The Falthan army did keep the Bhrudwans away from the Wodranian Mountains, and King Leith hasn't interfered with us since."

"As to that, why didn't the Wodrani send troops to help the Falthan army?"

"Peace, Robal; these are old questions, and we are beholden to these people."

"It's all right, your majesty," said the boy, and grinned his mischievous grin. "I don't rightly know what the answer is to that. Ma might know, being as how she's what we call a *scalla*, nobility in your language. Don't know how you'll ask her, though, without making her suspicious of you. She's sharp, is Ma."

Involuntarily Stella turned her head to the stern, where Ma no doubt sat hunched over the tiller, muttering to herself. *Nobility?*

"Nah, Philla has taken over the tiller." The boy clicked his tongue. "Always meant to make a song about that. Sounds much better in your language, o'course. Anyway, Ma caught some flatfish, and she wants a hand gettin' 'em ready for cooking, she says. Would your majesty and her handsome guard like to help her with supper?"

He ducked Robal's genial clip about the ear and ran away towards the stern, cackling like a demented hen. "Philla has the tiller," he sang. "Ain't that a killer!" Various other improvisations floated back to them on the breeze.

"Flatfish." Robal sounded disgusted.

"I'm sure they'll be nicer than the flatfish we had last night."

"Ah, but will they compare to the flatfish of the night before?"

"Only one way to find out," Stella said with a theatrical sigh. "On your feet, guard, you have a fish to gut."

The guard squeezed past her, taking a fraction longer than necessary, and preceded her into the barge's small cabin.

*   *   *

A near-full moon rose above the Maremma, silvering the night mist and bringing the giant kingfrogs out in search of caddis flies, swamp snakes or anything else foolish enough to come within leaping range. The early autumn heat lay heavy on the many winding branches of the Aleinus River, on the hundreds of oxbow lakes, old loops of the river abandoned as the Aleinus tried in vain to find a less puzzling way through the mire; on the thousands of animals hiding from the kingfrogs; on the millions of insects flitting back and forth across the stagnant water; and on the rowboat making its way stealthily towards the barge moored to one of countless islands.

Cloth wrapped around the oars dampened the worst of the splashes, and helped mitigate against the formation of blisters. Even after two weeks manning the oars of this rowboat, Conal remained uncomfortable with every aspect of watercraft, and as a consequence Dribna the guard manoeuvred the boat as they tried to get close to the barge without being discovered. The cacophony generated by the frightening kingfrogs helped, but to the young Halite priest the noises Dribna made sounded absurdly loud.

"Take the oars," Dribna whispered.

"What?" They had spent an hour working out a plan, and this wasn't part of it.

"Just take the oars, priest. Hold the boat steady."

Conal took them with reluctance, easing his sore muscles back into the hated position. The guard released them, eased himself forward and carefully raised himself to a standing position in the bow.

"What are you doing?" Conal tried to pitch his voice not to carry, and obviously succeeded too well as Dribna made no reply.

They drew close to the barge. A small dark shape sat in the stern, gnawing on something. The priest thought of his own empty belly. They'd taken on provisions at Barathea, when it became clear that the Wodrani were taking the Destroyer's Consort into the Maremma, but Conal's coin had not stretched as far as his normally well-fed belly demanded. It was so hard to concentrate on one's task when hunger ate away at one's mind.

What was the guardsman doing now? He reached down into the boat, setting the craft slopping in the turbid water, and seized one of the oars from the priest's hand. "What?" Conal repeated, more forcefully.

With one vigorous movement Dribna raised the oar above his head and brought it down—hard—on top of the dark shape. "Dribna! No!" the priest whispered, much too late. The shape slumped to one side, then dropped like a rock into the river.

"What have you done?" Conal said. "Get in there and rescue him!"

"Couldn't have him alerting the others," the guard said, seemingly unconcerned. "Now, let's board the barge and get what we came for."

"I can't swim," said the priest, more to himself than to Dribna. "And I'm not letting whoever it is drown. How do you know it's not the queen herself?"

"Too small, I think," came the reply, but his tone was uncertain. "Ah, you're right, I should have checked."

Conal could wait no longer. He stood up with a jerk, his unexpected motion tipping the guard into the water on the other side. An inexpert jump landed him belly-first in the river, and he was immediately swallowed by an impossible inky blackness. Opening his mouth to call for help proved as foolish as his initial leap. The small shape was forgotten as his mouth filled with water and panic froze his veins.

Down, down like a stone. Weeds wrapped themselves around his flailing arms. Spots grew before his eyes. The man of light, drowning in the darkness.

Something jerked his legs. *A fish, a big fish!* he thought, overcome with fear. The fish dragged his legs upwards: he would be eaten while he drowned. A small part of his mind prepared to give an account of his deeds to the Most High.

"I gottim, Ma!" he heard someone call, just as he emerged from the water. He wriggled his body in a desultory effort to break free of the grip on his ankles, but his mind had already given up. He hung in the air a moment, then landed with a thump on a wooden floor of some kind. The grip relented; he found himself on his side, retching, bringing up muddy water in a series of explosive convulsions.

"Lookit," said another voice. "Is this what banged Philla?"

"Musta been." The first voice. "I'll bang *him*."

Actions were suited to the angry words: Conal received a series of thumps on his back, loosening the remaining water in his lungs which he puked weakly onto the floor in front of him.

"Is the . . . is the boy, whoever, all right?" the priest got out before being overcome by another convulsive retch.

"Yeh, perfec'ly fine, being smacked on the head an' all, nearly drowned, thanks for askin'. Finer than you will be if he don't get better." A second, younger voice.

"I'm a priest. I mean you no harm." Conal tried to reassure them.

"Well, we mean you some harm, so shut yer whinin'."

"Look, lady, we fished a priest out of the swamp. Wonder what he tastes like?"

A finely crafted shoe slid into his vision, working its way under his chin.

"A priest?" said the shoe's owner. A woman. A voice he knew. "He would be right at home in the swamp, I would have thought. Let's see if we know him." The foot jerked upwards, encouraging him to turn onto his back. He lay there gasping, looking up into the angry eyes of his queen.

"Oh yes, we know this one, all right. The Archpriest's favourite little boy. I'm accustomed to seeing him dressed in more finery than this, though. Dear oh dear, look what's happened to your cloak! So he sent his catamite to do his distasteful work, did he? Afraid of getting his hands dirty? Or are the guards waiting for your signal to attack? You had best find your tongue, sir, or you might have another chance to perfect your swimming technique."

"Did you get—" he coughed "—did you find the guard? He might still be in the boat, but I think I tipped him in the water. His was the blow that knocked the boy from your boat."

"No one else gone swimmin' tonight, my lady," a small boy said. "Not that I seen."

"There was another with you?" the queen asked sharply. "You're not trying to deflect blame?"

"I tell you the truth. There are only the two of us. He told me we wouldn't hurt anyone. Your majesty, he changed the plan without any discussion, and knocked the boy into the river. I jumped in to rescue the boy, and I suppose I tipped the guard out of the boat. Or perhaps he swam to safety. Please believe me."

"Jarner?" The queen addressed an older boy.

"Nuh. No sign of nobody else."

Something thumped onto the deck behind them. Frightened and somewhat disorientated, Conal raised himself onto his hands and turned his head. He could make out a dark bundle, soaking wet, an arm's length away. It was covered by what looked like the guard's cloak. He reached towards it.

"Keep your hands to yourself," growled a new voice, and a booted foot came down hard on his fingers. He yelped and jerked his hand back.

"Found this knocking against the side of the barge," the new voice said. "The kingfrogs hadn't got to it yet. Can't tell how long it's been in the water." The man, wearing the uniform of an Instruian Guardsman, peeled the cloak away from the shape.

"The guard?" the queen asked Conal.

Conal had to draw close in the faint light. "Yes," he said, moments before heaving himself to the side of the barge and vomiting into the river.

"Now what?" he heard the queen say. "What do we do with a dead guard and a live priest?"

"Better if it had been a live guard and a dead priest," Robal said, poking Conal in the ribs with his foot. "We could have used another guard."

"Not this one, I think," said the queen, eyeing the body with distaste spread across her handsome face. "If the priest is telling the truth we might as well have kept swamp snakes in our cloaks."

"All I'm saying is it would be easier if we had two bundles to throw into the river instead of one."

"No killing."

"Ah, I suppose not. The swamp is foul enough as it is, without adding this to it." The guard nudged Conal again, this time a little harder. "Get up, son."

"It's our barge," said the youngest boy. "We decide 'bout killin'. This dead one c'n go back to the water, and the live 'un can join him soon as we truss up his arms."

The guard spread his arms helplessly. "It's their barge," he said. "Can't go against their wishes."

The queen stepped over to the young boy. "Oh yes we can. The stone I gave you in payment will more than cover passage to Vindicare for all three of us. But, just to make sure, I have another stone here, an emerald, which should be more than enough to purchase this barge and the hire of a steerswoman and three competent sailors to bring her through the Maremma." She held out her hand. Conal could not see what lay in her palm, but the boy's eyes opened wide.

"Where was you hidin' that?"

"You didn't find it when you went through our things, did you, Gren," said the queen, and the boy took a step back. "Are you going to take it or not?"

"What are ya gonna do with the barge once we get to Vindicare? We'd buy it back at a fair price."

The Falthan queen laughed, a very human sound from the woman the priests knew as the Destroyer's Consort. "A fair price? I'm sure. Are we agreed, then? And don't wipe your hand on your nose this time."

The boy lowered his own hand from his face, grimaced shamefacedly and placed it in hers, shook it and deftly pocketed whatever she had offered him.

"Robal, bring the priest to the cabin. Let's see if we can't get rid of some of his stink. If we succeed, perhaps we can permit him to dine with us. I have some questions for him."

"And while he's answering them, perhaps he'll eat my flatfish," Robal muttered.

Stella asked the young priest to accompany her up to the deck, leaving Robal to pick over the remains of the fish meal. Despite his protests, the guardsman ate everything set in front of him with evident relish. She smiled. A strong, resourceful, impressive man, more intelligent than he cared to appear, who treated her with a strange but warming mixture of deference and familiarity. A man whom she hoped to persuade to accompany her on the journey ahead.

Unlike the man who knelt before her now. She could think of no one she would like less as a travelling companion. Physically small, with a white, puffy face dominated by a flat nose and thick red lips sitting uneasily under thinning hair, the priest looked up at her but managed to avoid her eyes. Untrustworthy. Venal. Stella knew better than to judge a man by his appearance, but when that appearance confirmed her prejudices, it was a difficult tendency to counter. This man would bring trouble.

A soft rain began to fall. The priest pulled his wrap closer around him, but did not complain. *I have him cowed for the moment.* The trick was to make the moment last as long as possible.

"My name is Stella. It is the name you must always use when talking to me or about me. Since it appears in the Mahnumsen Scrolls only once I do not expect others to identify me when you use it. I will not tolerate being re-

ferred to as 'the Destroyer's Consort' or any similar epithet.
Now, what is your name?"

"I . . . Conal of Yosse, your m—Stella." A surprisingly
deep voice for such a small man.

"Yosse? The village an hour's ride north of Longbridge?" Stella was surprised: most of the Halite priests
lived in Instruere. As the city was built on an island in the
middle of the Aleinus River, it could only be approached
by bridge or by boat. The northern bridge, Longbridge,
was always crowded with people, making the journey a
time-consuming one. Besides, living in the city gave a citizen more prestige, a higher standing in the community.
There was more wealth to be had in Instruere than in the
Kingdom of Deuverre to the north or Straux to the south.

Perhaps she had wrongly assessed the man.

"You serve the Archpriest directly?"

"The . . . the Archpriest?" The man certainly could not
mask his emotions. This was a subject he wanted to avoid.

"Don't think to deceive me. I have seen you in his company regularly." She thinned her mouth to show her displeasure. "Or, at least, walking respectfully behind him.
Are you a scribe designated to record his every word,
working diligently to fill the eighth scroll?"

"Something like that." He smiled wanly. "Though I
have been promised advancement. Do I look so much like
a scribe?"

"A guess, no more," she said, though something about
the man had begun to disturb her. She hoped it had been a
guess, because the image of him bent over a desk, laboriously copying an old scroll, still sat strongly in her mind.
She felt some sort of connection with the priest; something resonated within her, something familiar. Faint but

familiar. Maybe she had met him at some function, or perhaps run across his parents. *Be patient, let it settle, it will become clear.* "An important task. Oh, and do stand up."

He nodded a careful agreement as he got to his feet. Out to the north distant thunder rumbled, a lazy autumn storm stalking the plains.

"Why did the Archpriest send you and your late companion after me?" Stella kept her voice pleasant. "Was it just to advise me as to the date of the royal funeral?"

"No, my queen . . . er, Stella." He spoke with a growing confidence. "I'm sure you are aware that the Koinobia wishes to speak with you in detail concerning the events surrounding the Ascension of Hal Mahnumsen and the defeat of the Destroyer. You offer us a . . . *unique* perspective, and in return we offer you a chance to influence the way you have been represented in our sacred writings."

"Very well, I'll speak with you."

"If you will not agree to share your story with us, how can you expect . . . I beg your pardon?"

"I said I'll speak with you. Not with the Archpriest, not in his sanctum, not where a questioner can do his foul work on me. I'll speak with *you*. Here, now, over the next few days. You'll take notes and report the conversation fairly and without alteration to your Archpriest. He will decide whether to accept or reject it. But if he rejects it, you will know he is interested in something other than the truth."

"I couldn't."

"Can you swim?" she asked casually, casting a glance at the dark waters below.

"You did not have me thrown overboard when doing so would have served your interests," the young man said, licking his lips, "and I cannot imagine you would do so now. Very well, I will listen to and record your views, though unless we have a witness I doubt the Archpriest will give them any credence. Perhaps your guardsman will verify our discussions?"

"I am sure he will. But why would your word not be believed?"

"Because the Archpriest does not know I am here," the small man admitted. "I was talked into this by the senior royal physician, whom the Archpriest asked to track you. I suspect he'll think I'm trying to make a name for myself."

"And are you?" She held his gaze.

He grimaced, clearly unused to such directness. "Yes, I am," he admitted. "But I'm not here only for myself. I want to explain something to you . . ."

His voice tailed off. In the silence the rain pattered down on the deck and the tarpaulin covering the Wodrani family's upriver goods.

"You want to offer me redemption," Stella said flatly. "You care about my moral condition. That's lovely. The only problems are the assumptions you make. Two in particular anger me: that I am fallen far enough to need redemption, and that you are upright enough to deliver it to me. Frankly, I doubt both."

The priest mumbled something.

"You'll have to speak up." It had become harder to hear, due to a persistent and growing rumble from the north. The storm? No, this was not the sound of thunder, and there were no lightning flashes to be seen. What would make such a noise?

"My lady, I said that perhaps we could suspend judgment until we have heard—"

"Be quiet," Stella said, interrupting him. "Listen! What do you hear?"

The rumble grew louder, then louder still. She could not tell whether what caused it was growing larger or moving closer, or both. The mist had gone but the darkness defeated her gaze. A deeper blackness ... from which came an ear-splitting growling, accompanied by something that sounded like the tearing and cracking of trees. The situation went from interesting to frightening in an instant. Robal burst up onto the deck, followed by the four Wodrani. It was now impossible to hold a conversation. They could barely hear each other shout.

Something was not right about this. Stella could feel a dreadful unease boiling in her immortal blood. A *presence* lurked in the storm, a knowing intelligence, enormous and inimical, and it was *searching*. In the back of her mind another presence, normally dull and quiescent, unfolded to full awareness.

Him.

Waiting for permission.

She vacillated for a fraught moment. There were no words between them, never had been; just a tenuous link through their shared blood. What was she being asked to give her assent to?

The thing, storm, whatever it was, bore straight for them, chewing up the swamp as it came. A depthless fear, far beyond any concern for her own death, lowered itself upon her. A howling hunger, a giant maw, gateway to an endless gullet in which waited ... something terrible beyond imagining. The presence inside her head waited, patient but anxious, for her response.

Yes.

Something like lightning surged down from her head, along her arms, out from her fingers and up into the roaring darkness. She could feel it but not see it as it discharged from her. There was a great crack and thump, and a searing flash of light. The dark thing above her vanished, and the presence in her mind settled back to the edge of her awareness.

Utter silence fell on the swamp, save for Ma's perpetual muttering. Then other things started falling, many things, crashing through the foliage some distance from the boat then splashing into the river somewhat nearer. The sounds stopped.

"What was that?" the priest, Conal, asked. "I've never heard anything like that."

"Sounded like a—" the oldest Wodrani boy began, but was interrupted by a series of thumps and splashes all around them. On the deck, in the water, then falling on them were hundreds, thousands of solid objects.

Stella cried out with pain as something hit the back of her neck. She fell to the deck, her hands covering her head. "What is it? What is this?" she screamed. The rain continued.

"Kingfrogs!" one of the boys shouted. "It's raining kingfrogs!"

The things were enormous, at least a foot long, though with the splatter they made on the deck and the lack of light it was difficult to tell.

"Get y' 'lowdecks!" Ma bellowed. "Be more'm froggies next!"

Stella half-crawled, half-scrambled over a slimy deck to the hatch, suffering more painful blows to her back and legs. Behind her Robal waited patiently, hands above his head, until the hatchway cleared. He closed it behind him, then moved into the crowded cabin and held out his hand.

"You were right, Ma," he said. "Flatfish."

The thumping continued intermittently above them for a few minutes longer, slowly dying away into silence.

"Ma says she's seen this afore," the youngest boy explained. "On Espumere, not far fr'm here, 'bout this time a year. Big whirlwind over the lake, she saw, then a rain o' fish. Whirlwind sucks 'em up and drops 'em."

"I've never heard of it," said Robal, a nervous look on his face. "I know many who would consider such an event ominous."

"They would, were they not of the Koinobia," the priest said with a superior air. "The Kingdom of Hal will replace such superstition with fact."

Despite herself, Stella rose to the bait. "And respect for others?"

"Not if they're wrong."

She grimaced: *the priest has teeth.*

The hatch opened and another of the Wodrani boys—the middle one, Philla—poked his bandaged head into the cabin.

"Kingfrogs, catfish, swamp snakes, flatfish, pout and eel. Anything livin' in the swamp now collected on th' barge. All dead, all squished. Good eating, 'cept for the frogs."

Stella made a face as the lad's brothers climbed up through the hatchway and into the night.

"I don't see how the frogs could be any worse than the flatfish," Robal said. "Everything we eat tastes of swamp. How much longer until we reach Vindicare?"

"I have no idea," she replied. "Philla said it can take two or three weeks to navigate the Maremma."

The burly guardsman put his head in his hands. "May Philla be proved wrong, if it please Hal," he groaned.

Philla was proved wrong, though Robal was not happy about it. Conal heard him say so many times every day. A full month after they had entered the Maremma the Wodrani barge finally emerged from the swamplands to make the relatively straightforward journey to Vindicare. The river ran lower than Ma, who had travelled the Aleinus for thirty years, had ever seen, making travel extremely hard work. Apart from that one freakish night of thunderstorms, whirlwinds and raining frogs, the days were relentlessly humid and rainless, the nights sultry and almost unbearable. The swamp seemed to dry up around them: large-leaved lilies browning around the edges, the multicoloured, delicate orchids withering, dead fish littering the stagnant pools cut off from their water source, and the Great River Aleinus shrivelling until the travellers could see her bones. And the stink! Rot and decay made the close, stale air of the tiny cabin infinitely preferable to spending time abovedecks, and no one looked forward to the two shifts of poling everyone was required to do daily. Only the cicadas seemed to thrive, if the racket they set up day and night was any guide. The heat was incredible.

"Never seen weather like it, and I bin up 'n' down the river fer twelve years," the oldest boy, Jarner, told them time and again. "Ma disremembers weather like it too, and she's bin . . ."

Conal tuned the words out. He had a great deal to think about, having spent at least two hours every day poling the boat in the company of the Destroyer's Consort. He asked questions, he listened to her answers, and gradually a story emerged worryingly different to Holy Writ. Not necessarily more favourable to the queen, surprisingly. The picture Stella painted of herself was of a self-absorbed girl, one with courage bordering on foolhardiness mixed with contempt for her family and her village. So many details flatly contradicted the scrolls. "She sought to leave the village with them, looking for adventure and to seek her fortune, and none of the Company could stand against her will." So read the Second Scroll, line ninety-two. Not so, Stella said. She had thought the Mahnumsen brothers were dead, as did the rest of the village, killed by the Bhrudwan raiders along with their parents. After all, she had been to their funeral. Why would she have sought them out deliberately if she thought they were dead? No, she had stumbled across them and they had forced her to accompany them, fearing she would expose their plan to the village.

The young priest had no answer to this. The queen—Stella—could be deceiving him, but she sounded truthful to his ears. She told him of her attraction to Wira, the formidable young mountain man the Company met along the Westway; and, the way she described it, she had virtually thrown herself at him. Why would she have told him that, knowing it reflected badly on her later behaviour with Deorc, the Destroyer's lieutenant, and the Destroyer himself, unless it was true? The truth of it counted against her, but her willingness to share it counted in her favour. So confusing. "And the girl, the snake among them, bided her time until she could snare a man of power through whom to rule." That from the Fourth Scroll, line two hundred and twelve. Again, close to the truth but inside out, Stella responded when he quoted this to her. She had wanted a man of significance, she told him, but only because she felt so insignificant herself.

It made sense, the way she told it.

Day after day of discussion, sometimes tense, often slow and fragmentary, as she made herself relive the events of seventy years ago, and still the story was but a third complete. He knew she intended to part company with him at Vindicare, but he would think of some way to remain with her until her story was told.

She asked him about his own background. He would not tell her his big secret, of course; there was no knowing what she would make of it, but it was certain that if she found out about his own journey to Andratan her openness would end. Instead he told her of his upbringing, of his large family and elderly parents, of staying at home in Yosse to look after his ailing mother while his siblings found employment in far-flung parts of Faltha. Of the contentment he found in the Koinobia, particularly in the discipline and insight scholarship offered. Of the pride he felt when the Archpriest himself had sought him out. He told her of the day the holy man sat cross-legged on the flaxen floor of their house and asked him to serve the Koinobia as a Halite priest.

She was surprised and somewhat embarrassed when Conal told her that she, Stella Pellwen, had been his specialty. He had studied the Mahnumsen Scrolls and could recite them word for word. Had spoken to anyone he could find who had memories of that time and, though most of the Company were now dead, learned that people held memories at odds with the Writ. The senior clerics were pleased with his progress, and for the last three years he, Conal of Yosse, had been considered the foremost authority on the Destroyer's Consort—"begging your pardon," he hastily added. That was why, he supposed, the Archpriest had asked Conal to accompany him to the bedside of the dying King Leith.

– The woman opposite him—the subject of a decade or more of his most careful research—was clearly uncomfortable with this knowledge. "You're crazy," she'd said with her characteristic and strangely endearing bluntness. "How can such an obsession possibly be a healthy thing? And if you wanted to find out what really happened, why did you not simply ask me?"

Conal had shaken his head. "It is not simple to ask her majesty anything," he had replied. "Even with the influence of the Koinobia and a letter written personally by the Archpriest himself I could not secure an interview with you. I was fobbed off with every manner of excuse."

"Oh," she'd said. "It was *you* with the letter. Well, I must apologise. I'm afraid your letter—more specifically, the hand it was written in—ensured you would never be granted an audience." She seemed genuinely sorry.

Conal found himself . . . Well, if he was honest, he found himself developing feelings for her. His studies and interviews had led him to expect a cold, scheming woman, haggard, crippled, full of bitterness and hate. Instead he had found a warm and sensitive person, clearly grieving for the loss of her husband and king. She treated him with respect, which was little short of astonishing given the way she was regarded by the Halites.

She was eighty-eight years old, for Hal's sake, but it was impossible to remember this when talking with her.

Her clear skin and fine-boned elfin features were those of a northern woman in her thirties, certainly no older, though a closer look revealed an old scar across her left cheek, starting from beside her eye and extending down to her neck, perhaps a burn of some kind. Interestingly, her right hand seemed not to function properly: at rest it made a claw. She seemed to have adapted to it, however. She certainly shirked none of her duties. Her hair, silver-edged a month ago, now appeared uniformly black: she must have previously dyed it to look older. Obviously she no longer had access to the dye. And there was something about her eyes, something knowing, something patient, understanding. Day after day he looked into her dark eyes, weighing her words, and felt himself drawn towards her.

The young priest worried about this. He lay awake on those unbearably hot nights as the barge rocked gently against its mooring, trying to work out whether she had woven a glamour around him. Conal knew himself to be a lonely man, having devoted himself to the priesthood and to his scholarship. While Halites were encouraged to marry, he had never made the time; nor, frankly, had the opportunity ever presented itself. Oh, there had been a shy, plain girl in Yosse, serious and sensible, but her parents sent her away when they realised a priest without prospects courted her interest. So of course he was susceptible to the emotions encouraged by continued intimacy, and grew angry at the thought, the realistic thought, that he might be so desperate for affection he would fall in love with a woman older than his grandmother. So many contradictory thoughts: pleasure that such a famous, formidable figure might confide in him; respect for her courage; excitement at the gradual unfolding of her story; fear that she might be manipulating him for her own ends; apprehension at what the Archpriest would say about his escapades; and self-loathing in the face of his own wilful emotions. Sometimes he thought he could hear cruel laughter in the back of his head. *Please, Most High, don't let me make a fool of myself.*

But the queen was a perceptive woman, and Conal was afraid he already had.

CHAPTER 8

LOSS OF A QUEEN

"WHAT DO YOU WANT WITH THE MAN, anyway?" Robal said. "I don't like him. Windy, opinion-ated, full of himself. He'll cause you trouble, that he will."

Stella sighed. Her guardsman grew more headstrong by the day as awe faded and responsibility increased. She needed a protector, a companion, not a father figure less than half her age. He ought to be set down, but how?

The two of them stood in the stern, Robal to starboard, Stella to port, using their long poles to push the barge for-ward against the current. They were positioned either side of Ma who had the tiller, and who never participated in their conversations nor gave any indication she under-stood them. The youngest Wodrani boy scurried about amidships, checking their cargo, shifting tradable items to more accessible locations and securing their own supplies, while the two older boys poled either side of the cabin. The river, now one wide channel, flowed somewhat more powerfully than in either the multi-channelled Maremma or the tidal range near Instruere, and even four polers earned them only grudging progress. Conal stood alone in the bow, most of his body hidden from Stella behind the cabin, though every now and again she caught sight of his cloak whipping about in the rising southerly breeze. And ahead of them, visible to all even in the heat haze of late morning, Vindicare sprawled on the southern side of the river, to the right as they looked, like a drunkard sleeping off a bender.

"You think *he'll* cause me trouble?" Stella said. "The milksop priest? Does he nag me constantly about other members of the crew? Is he full of admonitions about the Koinobia and the priesthood of Hal? Has he spent most of the morning warning me of the dangers we are likely to encounter in Vindicare? I do not believe he has."

Robal's lips thinned, but he forbore from comment.

She found it so hard to rebuke him, drat the man. After all, he was much less attractive with a frown than with a smile. She liked his smile, and often found herself bantering with him just to watch the upward curve of his lips at her witticisms. His was a strong, generous face, broad and full-featured, with laughter lines and wide-set eyes characteristic of Austrau, the province from where he came. An outdoorsman's face set atop an outdoorsman's body: tanned, muscled and well-proportioned. She had not looked on a man, including her husband, in this fashion for quite some time: after all, Leith had been old for twenty years and more, while she remained young. Not that they had ever . . . She sighed. Yet another of the many curses of her blood.

"You forget yourself. By your own account you have survived fire and water, and have seen more death than any cussin' soldier I know. You have been betrayed by those you loved and by those who ought to love you."

Robal took one hand from his pole and gestured widely, as though to encompass all of Faltha. "The priest is an unknown. Or worse, what we know of him is not promising. I do not understand your lack of prudence, really I don't. It makes you easy to talk to, but very hard to guard."

She had actually made him angry. Moreover, he had some justification. He thrashed at the water with his pole, forcing her to match his furious strokes.

"For the sake of the Most High, slow down! How am I supposed to keep up?" she said, beginning to breathe heavily. "Conal should be given at least one chance to prove himself. I cannot believe he means to betray me, nor that we remain in any real danger. It has been over a month since we left Instruere. Surely the Halites will have given up the search by now. All I need is a barber for my hair, some henna and tea leaves to add a reddish tinge, and some new clothes—or perhaps I'll continue with these rags." She indicated the sleeveless, rough-edged tunic and knee-length breeches she had been wearing for over a week. The Wodrani had traded for them, along with fresh provisions and replacements for Robal's guardsman uniform and Conal's priestly clothes—now very much the worse for wear—from an isolated farmhouse at the western edge of the swamplands. "A month of sun on my skin, a month of poling this stupid hunk of wood upriver—" she nodded towards her muscled arms—"who would recognise their sovereign?"

Robal smiled despite his obvious intention to remain stern. "I certainly see a young woman and not a queen. But if I was placed in Vindicare to watch for a woman coming from the west who had spent a month in the sun and who would most likely he wearing something other than royal robes, I might want to take a closer look at you." He laid a faint stress on the last phrase, making Stella laugh despite herself.

"You are a bad man," she said, biting her lip as she shook her head in mock sorrow. "And what makes it worse is that you are right. About the warning, that is," she added hastily, damping down his cheeky grin before it emerged. "I am worried about what has happened in Instruere, whether the Council of Faltha succeeded in taking power, whether another king has been raised or some other faction has assumed the rulership of the city, and the best people to talk to are the traders in the markets. I doubt either you or Conal could gain the information I require. Nevertheless, I will remain on the barge while we are alongside the docks, as you suggest. Conal will go into the city to search for news of Instruere, and yes, you may follow him. Should he seek to make contact with the Koinobia," she said slowly, "you may take the minimum action required to keep him from doing so."

"Very sensible. And if I may add—"

"You may not. If I should learn that you have precipitated violent action in a misguided attempt to protect me, you may discover that there is at least limited justification for the Koinobia's fear of me. I want the priest alive and in good health. He may be the only chance I have to correct the written record of the Falthan War." *And maybe erase the people's hatred and distrust of the Destroyer's Consort so central to the Mahnumsen Scrolls.*

"You don't trust me?" His handsome, lopsided smile dimpled at her. *Oh dear.* She took a deep breath.

"Not yet. I enjoy your company, and am learning to respect your judgment. But trust is earned, not given, unless one is a fool, and I hope my foolish days are over. Go now and earn it."

A shout came from the bow: the barge drew near the docks. They had previously been told that fare-paying passengers would only get in the way and were to go belowdecks. Robal shook his head at her reproachfully, shipped and secured his pole, then offered her his hand. Conal made way for them at the hatch.

Stella glanced towards the stern just before the hatch closed. Ma looked up for a moment, her eyes clear and far too knowing, then hunched back down and continued her muttering.

Vindicare, the second city of the Kingdom of Straux and the administrative capital of Austrau, suffered badly in the autumn drought. An ugly city at the best of times, it was beset by the traditional problems of second cities everywhere, having been used by a series of rulers to line the pockets of rich nobles and merchants in Mercium, the chief city of Straux. There were no notable public buildings, few of the streets were cobbled, and to Conal the people seemed shabbier and duller than those in Instruere. The authorities clearly had no idea about the need for an efficient waste management system, he noted as he made his way between the market stalls. He imagined writing a treatise on the subject. *Drains: The Key to Civilisation*. Not a promising title for a scholarly paper, but certainly one Vindicare's leaders ought to read. Perhaps they had, and the overpowering stench of the city was due to the lack of water. The place could certainly do with a good downpour. He took another breath. Several good downpours.

The instructions given him by the Destroyer's Consort

had been specific. He was not to draw attention to himself, was not to ask any leading questions that would identify him as having been away from news sources for a month. Instead he was to listen while bargaining for essential supplies. She had drawn him up a list. There had been nothing on the barge with which to write other than charcoal and poor-quality parchment, but her hand was neat and precise, with none of the ornate affectations common among the women who served the Koinobia. Not that the medium allowed affectation, he allowed.

The priest was having difficulty keeping his mind on his task. The first day in a month he had not spent time with her and already he found himself pining for her company like some pathetic cur. He actually felt physically ill. Could she have cast a glamour over him? Would he really be able to sense magic, as the Archpriest had assured him he would? He had certainly sensed unearthly powers during his few terrifying days on Andratan as a spy for the Koinobia. But nothing he experienced there felt like this. That power had been cold, this feeling was warm.

He shook his head at his own folly.

"Sir? Sir? Are you well?"

"Eh? What? Ah . . . no, I am feeling a little unwell, in fact," he said. A friendly-faced girl smiled at him from her side of the stall.

"You've been looking at our wares for a long time," she said. "Can't decide what to buy your love?"

He looked down at the display. He appeared to have stopped in front of a jeweller's stall, guided there by his unconscious mind while he mooned over the Destroyer's Consort. The Archpriest would be scandalised if he could read minds. Was there any hope for him?

"It's just that Gor over there gets twitchy when people spend too long staring and not buying," she continued, still smiling. Her head nodded to one side, indicating a tall, broad-shouldered man standing six paces away. "Gor the Mite," she added helpfully.

"Oh. No, I don't want to buy, I want to sell. Would you be interested in this?" He flipped the queen's leather pouch out from his borrowed jerkin, upended it into his hand and held out the four stones, small but undoubtedly valuable even bereft of their settings.

The girl's demeanour changed, the false smile put away for the next customer. "Gor," she barked.

"Mistress," the man said as he strode over to them.

"The list, please."

The exchange, the sudden change in attitude, made Conal uneasy. List? What could have gone wrong?

"Two rubies, an emerald and a singstone," Gor the Mite read carefully from a crumpled note. "Singstone flecked with gold. Should have two small grooves if removed from its setting."

"Like this, do you think?" She picked the deep blue singstone from Conal's hand before he was able to close his fingers over it.

"Just like that," the broad-shouldered man rumbled.

The girl took the note. "Apprehend and detain anyone with stones of this description, then notify the guards," she read, then looked up. "Why doesn't it say anything about a reward?"

Belatedly Conal realised the trouble he was in. "I don't have all the stones on that list. It's just a coincidence." He found himself breathing shallowly, but could not clamp down on the panic he felt.

The girl stared at him disbelievingly. "Singstones are rare. And this one matches perfectly the description we were given. Where did you get it from?"

"The stones are my mother's, well, from her estate really. You see, she died recently, and—"

He stopped. Neither one believed him, he could see it on their faces. He wasn't very good at lying. At that moment a grey-clad guard emerged from a side road, and the brute Gor beckoned him over.

"Bathania, we have a problem—"

Conal chose that moment, while the guard was still a few steps away, to try his escape. Gor made a lunge for him, missing his collar by a finger-width. The guard cried out and gave chase: at least Conal thought it was the guard, for he caught a glimpse of grey close behind him as he pelted down the busy cobbled street. Bitter thoughts lanced through his head. Failure, whether or not he was captured. He'd not heard a thing about the political situation in Instruere, had not purchased anything on the queen's list, had not even sold the jewels. She would not be happy . . .

Within fifty or sixty strides he was gasping for air, sucking at it as though he breathed through wool. *Unfit. Must find a hiding place. Turn this into a contest of brains rather than stamina.* A glance over his shoulder revealed the guard close behind him, and gaining, while further behind two figures picked themselves up off the road. The guard shouted at him to stop. He looked for something, anything, to throw at his pursuer. The stalls were all behind him; he'd run the wrong way. Nothing here but people. He could use them. Groups of citizens who were angered by someone jostling his way through them were more likely to hinder than help a second person. There had to be an open door, an alley, somewhere to hide . . .

A loose cobble gave way under his left foot, sending both him and his pursuer to the ground in a mass of uncoordinated arms and legs. A loud crack, like the smack a heavy scroll made when hitting a stone floor, came from somewhere underneath him. He wriggled clear of the guard's struggling weight, then screwed his eyes tightly shut as agony washed over him. The cracking sound had come from him, from his left arm. He got unsteadily to his feet, cradling his left forearm with his right.

The guard twitched, stirred and raised bleary eyes in his direction. Conal took a few steps and whimpered with each one. He tried, but the pain was horrendous. All his energy drained from him, obliterated by shock. *I failed her, and it hurts*.

"Now, Mister Running Man," the guard said, panting out the words, "tell me why you refused to stop for a Guardsman of Vindicare."

"I . . . I thought you were a thief," Conal replied before his tongue could recall the lie. "I thought you wanted to hurt me." That was true, at least. "My arm hurts. Can you take me somewhere to get it fixed?"

"You could see I was wearing the grey, so why did you run? You know only Koinobia-appointed guards wear the grey. You've had a three-week to get used to us. And why did the jeweller want to speak to me?"

"She thought I had stones like those written on a piece of paper," Conal answered.

"Emerald, rubies and singstone?" The guard placed a hand on Conal's shoulder, sending a shockwave of pain through the priest's frame.

"I . . . I have a singstone and a ruby," he answered, licking his too-dry lips. "At least I *had* a singstone. The jeweller has it now." Something the guard had said tried to get his attention, but could not compete with the incessant throbbing of his forearm.

"And are these stones the ones we're looking for?" asked the guard.

Why would you ask so directly? Do you expect criminals to tell you the truth? His thoughts must have revealed themselves on his face, because the guard stooped a little and looked into his eyes.

"You didn't know about the grey, and you have the stones. You're not from 'round here, are you? Otherwise you'd know that the grey Koinobia guards of Vindicare always give citizens a chance to tell the truth." His eyes narrowed. "She's here, isn't she. The Consort bitch. Here in Vindicare."

Look into my eyes, Conal willed desperately. *See my truthfulness.* "No, she's not in Vindicare."

"Too careful an answer, Running Man, and not careful enough," the guard said, smiling grimly. "To know she's not here means you know where she is. You will take me to her, so the Koinobia's justice can be executed upon her."

No need to lie. No need to run. No need to think. He hoped he would be better at defiance.

"No," he said.

Stella sat on a wooden bench in the barge's cabin and stared at the backs of her hands. A queen no longer, her nails were cracked and split, her skin rough from poling. A disguise of sorts, half-completed but hopefully al-

ready efficacious. She had few regrets at leaving Instruere and seventy years of power behind. Even had the
Halites not wanted to harm her, she would not have remained long in the Falthan capital, having become
heartily sick of the trappings that, despite the king's best
efforts, snarled everything they tried to do. *Let someone
else carry the burden. Time to find another life.*

Above her the scraping and thumping of cargo being
transferred finally ceased. The Wodrani family would
make a tidy profit from their month on the Aleinus: court
fashions required silk and colourful cloth imported from
Sarista, and while a certain amount made it over the Veridian Borders, it was limited in quantity and therefore expensive, beyond the reach of all but the most wealthy. The
nobility of Vindicare, such as they were, would have their
seamstresses purchase bolt after bolt of the cloth Ma and
her sons had brought upriver from Instruere. Good. Such
families deserved their share of Faltha's prosperity.

The silence left her alone with her thoughts, truly alone
for the first time since Leith's passing. She shook her head
angrily: already she found herself applying euphemisms
to his death, as though he were a wagon now disappeared
from view around a corner. *Call it death; that's what it is.*

In seventy years she had never succeeded in telling
Leith the true complexity of her feelings for him. She
had loved him, but not with the deep passion of a lover.
More that of a grateful, close friend; latterly, as he grew
older and she did not, that of a daughter for a father. A
great comfort, a generosity beyond what she deserved,
but not the love sung of by midsummer bards. Not what
she had felt for Wira, or even, Most High forgive her,
for Tanghin. Leith knew—he must have known—she

did not return his feelings in quite the same fashion he offered them. Must have known.

Eventually she could stand the silence no longer. She left the bench and made her way topside. Robal had warned her to keep out of sight, but she was destroying herself down in the cabin, the windowless walls mirroring the inside of her head. She would not be recognised sitting here in the lee of the cabin, sheltering from the desiccating simoom wind tormenting the city.

The docks and slipways were largely empty. Had been since they were greatly enlarged during the barge-building period of the Falthan War, when fifty thousand troops had been poled upriver, from Vindicare to the Aleinus Gates, on massive rafts built here. The forests had been stripped for leagues around, and would take centuries to recover. Another adventure she had missed out on while enjoying the delights of being the Destroyer's Consort. One other barge, two masted fishing boats and a half-dozen or so small dinghies were made fast to the nearest wharf; she could see other wharfs beyond, stretching hundreds of paces into the river, with only the odd mast visible.

She sighed. Vindicare had never been a prosperous city, despite the pressure Leith had brought to bear on the King of Straux to spread the kingdom's wealth. So many failures, so few successes.

Suddenly uneasy, Stella swung around to face the tiller. No sign of Ma: where had she gone? Jarner had remarked that she would have Ma for company, so it was reasonable to expect the woman to have remained on board. How long had she been gone?

She tried to relax. Couldn't the Wodrani woman be allowed to go ashore to stretch her legs? Must she insist on seeing danger everywhere? She was becoming like Robal, seeing threats in every situation. Truth to tell, she had been unsettled since the night of the storm—whatever it was—on the Maremma. It had been as though she'd seen through a window into another world, where ravenous beasts prowled the skies looking for her. The fabric of her nightmares.

The sound of footfalls on the wharf pulled her attention ashore. Peering around the side of the cabin, into the grit-laden simoom, she could not at first identify the source. *There.* Ma had company. She led two men in odd grey uniforms along the wharf towards the barge.

No time to consider. With all the warnings Robal had given her echoing in her ears, Stella dived into the river. The water was surprisingly warm, though somewhat cloudy. She held her breath for as long as she could, then came to the surface and dog-paddled her way under the wharf. There might be some sensible explanation, probably was, for Ma bringing two uniformed men to the barge, but her mind screamed betrayal and she did not want to be found by the men making the heavy-booted sounds above her.

Three shapes flickered in the narrow spaces between the boards, stopping directly overhead. *Were they friends they would have proceeded straight on to the barge.*

"She'm not here, missirs." Ma's voice floated down to her.

"Can't be far away," an angry male voice said. "We'd've seen her if she came along the wharf. Look in the cabin and among the cargo. I'm gonna check the wharf, see if she's hiding anywhere."

Time to move. The thought echoed strangely in her

ears, as though spoken by someone else. There was something sorcerous at work here. But she had no time to consider the problem. She stroked her way to the other barge, using it as cover to get closer to the next wharf. Perhaps she could escape to the city, find Robal and Conal . . .

No. The sight of a dinghy tethered to the barge gave her a better idea. She struggled her way into the boat, slipped the mooring, eased the oars into the painters and began to row. Even pressure on both oars, smooth strokes, pull the blades through the water, don't splash . . .

"There! On the river! In a boat!"

She looked up to see both men staring across a growing expanse of water at her.

"You! Stop!" cried one of the men. A cry guaranteed to encourage her continued flight, Stella thought.

"No, you fool. Get us a boat. Quick!" the other man said, and they sprinted down the wharf and disappeared from view. Within moments a dinghy emerged around the end of the wharf, one man on each oar, making good progress towards her amid a shower of sparkling spray.

Stella stroked on, pointing her dinghy upstream, searching for the current. A plan dropped into her mind, fully formed, no doubt concocted from her memories of rowing races on the lake near Loulea. *Tempt them to spend their energy, draw them closer, make them sprint, use them up. They'll think they will catch me easily. I'm an old woman.* She laughed, then settled to her work. Easy, rhythmical strokes.

The two guards gained rapidly. At least one of them had experience in rowboats, as it was not easy to pursue a craft when facing the other way. One of the guards shouted repeatedly for her to give herself up, his head half-turned towards her. His shouts became more breath-less as they drew closer. Finally Stella felt the current begin to buffet her craft, and she angled the dinghy directly into it. She slowed noticeably, but did not try to overpower the water. The month spent poling in the Maremma had served her well. She felt tired but not exhausted.

The men were two boat-lengths from her when the current took them unprepared. She watched them panic, both flailing at the water with their oars, taking faster rather than deeper strokes, their blades actually spending less time in the water. It was working.

Robal groaned as he watched the fool priestling trip over his own feet and fall hard on the cobbles, the grey fellow on top of him. A dry snap indicated a broken bone, a sound familiar to him from the parade ground. Why had Stella trusted this man?

The grey man lay sprawled on the cobbles. *Run, priest, you useless lard-lump, run! Get up, at least! Run, that's it!* A couple of steps and the priest dissolved into whimpers. Robal fingered his sword-hilt. Not his favourite blade; he'd been wearing a three-quarter broadblade when he'd left the city with Stella. Still, it would most likely do. The grey man wore a longsword but would hardly be adept, not in a provincial town like Vindicare. The Austrau were farmers, not swordsmen; he'd nearly become one himself, after all.

He began to make his way carefully towards the two men, around whom the curious but nervous crowd had cleared a space. By the time he'd positioned himself at the head of the crowd the two men had begun talking. *Good, not a robbery at least. But that grey coat looks like a uniform.* Robal listened more closely.

Koinobia-appointed guards? *Koinobia*-appointed? Where were the Straux soldiers who normally served as guards? Bully-boys they had been in the main, but at least they were loyal to the King of Straux. What had happened to them? He listened further.

It could not be. The Koinobia taking power in Faltha? He didn't believe it. But a churning feeling began to sour his stomach all the same.

The two exchanged more words, then the grey guard smiled a smile Robal recognised, that of someone intending harm. *Time to move.* The words doubled in his head, as though Stella said them at the same time. Was she in trouble?

"No," said the priest; for a moment Robal hesitated, thinking the denial directed at him.

"Perhaps truth can be won from blade's edge," the grey guard said, and drew his sword. The crowd groaned, took three hurried steps back and then one forward, leaving Robal in an expanded circle with the priest and the guard. So much for surprise.

"You there," said the grey guard, "step back. I require witnesses, but I do not want anyone else to get hurt." His eyes flicked between Robal and the priest as he spoke. They must have seen something soldierly in Robal's stance, or perhaps the bulge of his sword. "Hold this man for me," he said to two men in the crowd, thrusting the priest towards them. "We have an oaf who thinks he can disobey the rules."

"And what rules are these?" Robal said in his best parade-ground growl. *Watch the man, see how he holds*

*his sword. Keep him talking and learn his habits, his
weaknesses. Well trained, this one, having likely swapped
his king's livery for that of the Koinobia. Of course, he
will be watching me, assessing what sort of fighter he
faces.* Robal kept his stance at ease, his hand away from
his hilt, showing nothing.

"Another stranger? This one with a sword, which
makes you Robal Anders, a . . . let me see . . ." He pan-
tomimed unrolling a scroll, playing to the crowd. "A
'middle-aged carouser and troublemaker of the former Instruian Guard. Last seen with the Destroyer's Consort.
Take alive if possible.' Well, old man, let's see if we can
take you alive."

Middle-aged? Carouser? Well, there had been a few parties, more than a few in the old days, but he was no habitual drunkard. Though he'd spotted an inn on the waterfront
he was looking forward to visiting. No matter. The grey
guard adopted a fighting crouch and moved slowly towards
him, balanced nicely on the balls of his feet, sword in the
left hand but room on the hilt for a two-handed grip.
Greaves loosely laced. He could use that if he had to.

"Will you not defend yourself, Robal the Carouser?"

He smiled, and the grey guard took a step back. Whoever had penned his brief and disparaging description had
neglected to mention his years of training under Achtal,
the renegade Bhrudwan Lord of Fear.

Troublemaker? Definitely.

He waited until he saw the man's left arm steady, the
prelude to a sweeping stroke, then drew his three-quarter
sword and was ready with the parry before the stroke arrived. A clash and skitter and the crowd drew back. The
fighters disengaged.

"I know what you're thinking, and you are right: I am better than you," Robal said conversationally, eyeing the growing unease on the grey guard's face. "I've lost count of the number of left-handed Straux soldiers I've sparred with. Predictable to a man. Comes from a chronic lack of imagination. Of course, I could make a mistake. But how likely is that in comparison to the blunder you've already made? Come now, lad, use your head. Put your sticker away. If you strike at me again with it, I will kill you."

The guard glanced around the crowd as though trying to summon courage from something he saw there. Perhaps he wanted them to shame him into continuing with the duel. No one would meet his eye. The tip of his blade wavered, then dropped; he spun and, with a curse, shouldered his way through the crowd. For a moment the only sound in the street was that of the man's boots slapping the cobbles.

"Out of here, now," Robal commanded, grabbing the priest's collar. "He'll be back with more of the grey-coated fools. Besides, now they know she's here we'll have to take her somewhere safe."

"My arm, it hurts," the priest whined. "Can't we get it seen to?"

Robal gave the collar a sharp tug. "You wouldn't like how I'd see to it," he growled as he sheathed his sword. "Now come on. This Koinobia takeover smells foul to me."

They stumbled their way back up the street, in the opposite direction to which the guard had disappeared. "What did he mean, the guard?" asked the priest, between gasps. "How could the Koinobia have taken control of the city? Why would we? We're not a political organisation."

"You are now," Robal said. "And, by the look of the people back there, not a very popular one."

"So that is what the Archpriest meant about the King-dom of Hal," the priest said, mostly to himself. "We—I—thought he referred to a spiritual kingdom. What has he done?" To his credit, the man carried a concerned look on his face all the way from the central city to the docks, the pain of his arm seemingly forgotten.

Something odd was happening at the docks. A crowd stood on the riverbank—surely not the same people they had just left behind in the street, though that man with the green jerkin looked familiar—all staring out to the water beyond the docks. They were shouting. *At what?* Robal squinted against the rippled brightness of the water.

"Stella! It's the queen!" the fool priest shouted, tugging at Robal's arm. "Look!"

"Quiet, you bloated bookworm! No one's supposed to know!" But he looked all the same. It was her, or some-one dressed like her, in a small boat, leading—being chased by—a second boat rowed by two greycoats. He groaned. They gained on her by the second: she had come to a standstill, clearly at the end of her strength.

But no. Both boats had come to a halt in the rippling current. *Clever girl*, he acknowledged as he grabbed the priest by his good arm and ran along the nearest wharf, followed by the watching Vindicari.

And so begins the strangest pursuit in history, Robal thought, helpless to intervene. The two boats were now ac-tually losing ground to the current, a pace every few sec-onds. Stella seemed to be shouting at the men, taunting them perhaps. She was certainly expending much less effort than they were. Abruptly her boat found a calmer spot and she shot forward, now a dozen boat-lengths ahead—but then slowed down, almost allowing them to draw closer. Conserving her energy while encouraging them to use their remaining reserves. *Very clever girl.*

"We could grab a boat and row out there," the priest said quietly.

"Oh yes? Ever rowed a boat before?" He did not disguise the scorn in his voice. Useless fellow. "It takes a special technique, I'm told. And what will you use for a left arm?"

"We need to do something."

"You are right. We need to be somewhere else when the grey guards turn up in force. We'll be no use to her in prison. And I, for one, don't want to face a certain greycoat without a sword in my hand."

With a roar the two rowers redoubled their efforts, but it proved their undoing. Robal watched as one of them accidentally elbowed the other, forcing one of his hands off his oar. In an instant the river plucked the oar from his remaining hand, sending it spiralling lazily downstream.

"Fool!" came a shout across the water, accompanied by laughter from the crowd. Robal watched as Stella pulled firmly at her oars, turning her boat athwart the current, heading for the far side of the river, which was barely visible in the dust-filled distance. The guards' boat followed their oar downstream, both men paddling with their hands, trying to manoeuvre closer to shore. Within minutes they had disappeared around a bend.

Robal led the priest through the festive crowd, many of whom were exchanging coins as though paying out wagers. "We have to get across the river," he said.

"They hate the greycoats, don't they," the priest said

sadly. "I suppose not one wager was placed on the guards to win the race." He sighed. "What has the Archpriest done?"

"There have to be two sides to every wager, priest," Robal said, shaking his head. "Even if one person covers all the bets. Now, did you mark where Stella beached her boat?"

"Er, no. Didn't you?"

"I did, and just as well. You must stop relying on others to do the work and start to contribute yourself. Now, follow me. We have to find a boat."

Stella bent over her oars, completely exhausted. She had seen Conal and Robal on the wharf—at least, it had looked like them—and so had forced herself to row as hard as possible straight for the far bank, in the hope they would be sensible enough to notice the place she landed. In retrospect it wasn't the cleverest thing she could have done, but it seemed of a piece with the plan she'd come up with. Unpredictability sometimes worked as well as cleverness, and the idea of hiding in the rushes had captured her mind like a compulsion. Though she ought not to remain in the dinghy overlong; there may have been more guards keeping an eye on her progress. She would wait here just long enough to regain her breath. Just a little longer. She backed the boat into a thick section of rushes, shipped her oars and curled up lengthways on the seat. Relief and bone-weariness overwhelmed her like birds of prey descending on a carcass. She would wait here. Only for a moment . . .

She awoke to a sore head and the sound of the rushes swishing in the wind. What a fool she had been! The hot middle-day sun had burned one side of her face, her lips were dry and cracked, her muscles stiff, the leg that had been curled up underneath her numb.

The rushes continued to swish all around her. But the clouds ... the clouds hung in the air like limp flags. The simoom had died while she slept. Then what had made the rushes rustle?

Shouts erupted to her left and to her right. Startled, but not yet truly fearful, she took up an oar as defence as two men waded through the rushes towards her. Robal and Conal? Guards?

Neither.

Two unkempt, bearded men stood by the stern of her little boat, staring down at her with dangerous smiles. "This is she, sure, sure," one said to the other.

"Just where Da said," the other man replied.

"Don't see what's so special 'bout her. We've had plenty prettier."

"Right, missa, you come with us," the second man said to her. He reached for the gunwale.

"What—" She cleared her throat. "What if I don't want to come?" As quick as she could, muscles still paralysingly slow, head thick with sun and tiredness, she half-stood and swung the oar at the closer of the two men. It hit his shoulder with a resounding *thud* and jolted free of her grasp.

"You'll regret that, missa," the man hissed. He hefted the oar, then swung it, handle first, towards her. She made to duck; her leg collapsed under her and she fell into the path of the oar, which took her behind the ear with a blow far harder than anything she could have imagined. She shrieked, her head exploded with pain, and a blurry white light swallowed everything.

Just before the light went out she heard a voice say, "Ramzy, you fool, you've killed her."

The next she knew she was leaning over the bow, vomiting into the water, then some time later lying in the dinghy, staring into the sun, her head afire with pain, and later again lapping bilge water from the bottom of the boat.

"She's coming to."

"She should be dead, you dolt. Look at that oar. Five fingers thick and snapped in half. You hit me like that, I'd be dead."

"She fell into it. She's witchy, like Da, no need to worry about her. Anyway, she got me a good one. Still can't move my arm."

"Pah. You'll move it quickly enough when the work's over and the fun begins."

"Look at her, drinking her own blood."

"*Oh*. Stella eased her eyes open: the water in which she lay was cloudy and red, as though someone had poured a half-fermented Trenstane wine into the boat.

"You hear us, missa?"

She did, but her body gave out again and she faded away into the light.

Her final awakening found her draped over a shoulder, presumably not that of the man she had hit with the oar. He walked slowly, but she felt every step. Her left ear buzzed loudly, damaged, no doubt, from the blow the brute had landed behind it. She could barely raise the energy to be worried about it.

She could see very little from her disorienting vantage. A few long-leafed plants, a gravel path, an almost-dry stream, a wooden doorstep. The man stood up straight: the sudden movement went to her stomach and she vomited over his back. Growls from him, laughter from his companion. He threw her onto a mattress of rushes and stripped off his filthy shirt. For a moment she feared . . . but no, he bent over and picked up the shirt, bundled it up carefully and threw it into a corner.

"Here she is, Da. Ramzy bashed her head in but she's all right, look."

"Silence, boy." So a snake would sound were it given voice. "Let me look at her."

A grey-cloaked figure shuffled into her field of vision, then tossed back its hood. Stella's breath caught in her throat. *Oh no, no.*

Depthless hollows for eyes, a nose cauterised by fire, skin cracked and weeping like a lake bed in a drought. So like her first vision of the Destroyer, when she had seen him unmasked at the extremity of his power. This was not he. The presence in her head remained remote, but she felt a stirring, as though someone ventured to look through her eyes.

The lipless mouth opened on a bright red throat. "It is she. The one who abandoned our lord. I have felt her drawing closer for a week or more, and here she is in my house." A pale tongue flicked out, flicked back in. "It took the best part of my power to draw her here. Ramzy, Tunza, you have done well."

"Our reward?" one of the bearded men—Tunza— asked carefully, submission in his voice.

"Very well. One prisoner each. Take them outside, but keep the noise down. There may be those seeking this one out."

The two men left the room.

"I would welcome your friends," the snake-man said, his eye-slits narrowing. His first words to her. "They would provide entertainment. Though not the sort I will derive from you." His ruined face hungered.

"You know what I am, do you not?" he said.

And she did, the bitter knowledge descending on her as he spoke, as the sorcery keeping him alive caked her with its familiar foul aroma.

A *Maghdi Dasht*, a Lord of Fear.

Like his fellow lords he had been used up in the service of his master, one of a hundred or more *Maghdi Dasht* who sacrificed their lives aiding the Destroyer to escape Instruere seventy years ago. The greatest magicians of their time, they had been drained of power by their master and reduced to empty shells. The Falthans had assumed them dead—such a dangerous, erroneous assumption. Now proved false.

"Yes, I know what you are," she said, terror and repugnance fighting for mastery of her voice.

"But you do not know how much power I expended to place my thoughts in your head. On the river you followed my plan and thought it your own. So here you are."

She stared at him, unable to speak.

"And do you know what I want from you?"

The truth descended on her like a cage. The Lords of Fear had been a cadre of magicians high in the Destroyer's service, familiar with the workings of power. Achtal, the renegade Bhrudwan who chose to serve Hal, had been merely an acolyte, not a fully trained Lord of Fear. Nevertheless he had served Faltha well, playing his part in bringing his former master down, and had served out his days training the guardsmen of Instruere in the battle

techniques of the *Maghdi Dasht*. Achtal had never quite
shed his strangeness, but Stella had forgotten the dread accompanying the Lords of Fear. Thirteen thirteens had
been their number, and all had accompanied their master
westwards on his journey of conquest. This one knew who
she was, which meant he *knew* what ran through her veins.
Could sense it, undoubtedly; it would smell like a sweet
fragrance to him.

Wanted it.

Yes, she tried to say, *I know what you want*, but dark
dread robbed her of her voice.

"I see you do. I have waited ten and three score years
in this hateful land. I will wait no longer."

Reaching into the folds of his dirty grey robe, the monster drew out a dagger with a twisted blade. Stella tried to
back away, but her body refused to cooperate. He raised
the blade in front of his face, both hands on the hilt, point
to the ceiling, and spoke a series of arcane words. The
blade seemed to glow in his hands. He moved the dagger
towards her throat, and his dreadful gaze, intense and ravenous, settled on her.

"She came through the rushes here, I'm sure of it! Look,
can't you see the broken stems?" Robal said angrily; unreasonably, in Conal's opinion. "She must have pulled the
boat along the riverbank."

"I see the stems," Conal replied, "but how can you tell
what caused them to break? Couldn't the wind have done
it?" He used his voice of reason, so difficult to find on this
dreadful day, but it sounded like whining in his own ears
and served only to inflame the guardsman.

"The wind? A gust a pace wide beat a winding path

through the rushes, beginning just where Stella came ashore? As likely as the wind blowing you over and breaking your arm. Stella thinks you intelligent: prove her right by using your brain, man! What else could it be but Stella pulling her boat?"

"I don't know, I don't know," said the miserable priest. "But she's in peril of her life, wherever she is."

Since his arm had been broken Conal had inhabited an unreal world. He had never experienced any serious pain before, and the continued grinding agony of his left forearm had done something to his mind. It seemed all his priestly morality was a façade, a veneer quickly abraded by the constant ache. Unpriestly thoughts flowed through his mind like a flood: deep angers, towering resentments, fears fit to paralyse him, and a stream of curse-words in a language he had never thought to hear again. The language of Andratan.

Madness.

Was he so weak that insanity could come from a broken arm? He had barely been able to prevent himself saying some of the things he had been thinking, and at one point while rowing across the river he had actually begun to tip the hateful guardsman out of the boat. Thankfully he had come to his senses before the man noticed, or Conal would be the one in the water, he knew it.

But no matter how much he fought them, the delusions grew worse. Perhaps *because* he fought, his callow mind told him. A voice had begun to speak to him, sounding for all the world like the voice that laughed at him whenever he entertained private thoughts about the queen. No, no, he could not let this happen! Voices, delusions, everything in his head would see him kicked out of the Koinobia.

Here was the voice again, hoarse, breathless: *she's being held in a cottage, follow the broken reeds, you'll find the boat soon, then a path to your left.* The words came from a white place behind his eyes, like a nail driven through the back of his head into his brain, pulsing brightly, flowing through all his senses.

"How do you know? What are you saying, priest?"

"I'm sorry?" He could barely see what lay in front of him. Another image—Stella on the floor of a hut, her face ashen-white—superimposed itself on his sight. He could barely hear the guardsman, his ears instead full of a hissing voice.

"What is wrong with you? You just told me to follow the broken reeds until we find a path to a cottage, something like that. How do you know?"

I don't know, I don't know, please help me, his mind shrieked, but his voice said, "Do you think the Most High wishes the queen dead? If not, follow my lead."

"I wouldn't follow you if you had the keys to a Sna Vazthan harem," the guard said, then added, as if to himself: "First sign of trouble and he goes to pieces."

You're right, I have, help me. "If you will not follow, I must go ahead alone." *No, no, let me rest.* "Keep up with me if you are able."

As soon as the words were uttered the white spike burst into incandescence. Strength surged through his body. *What, what is this?* His arms and legs began pumping, propelling his reluctant body through the rushes. He closed his eyes, willed his muscles to stop, but he might as well have willed his heart to cease its staccato beating.

"Hey, wait! What . . . where are you going?" The voice came from a long way behind him.

Time became a confused smear of sound, vision and fear. His true sight disappeared, to be replaced by visions of grey cloaks, frightened faces and the cruel blade of a dagger held high. He heard nothing but cold words, the intoning of an incantation, overlaid with a woman's pleading voice. And fear, above all fear, fear of plans ruined, of power lost, of revenge unsatisfied.

Robal staggered on, unable to keep up with the feral madman his companion had become. Despite his very best efforts, the ungainly, timid priest outpaced him, thrashing through the reeds and river shallows with absolutely no sense of self-preservation. Surely a man possessed, a thought that frightened him mightily. Had he heard the voice of the Most High speaking through the priest? Until a few moments ago he would have bet his life that the priest, with all his foolishness, was further from the Most High than he, a simple soldier.

But here was the boat, and there the path, just as he had said. And there the mad priest was, some way down the path, a berserker from the scrolls of legend, a huge branch in his left hand—the hand affixed to a broken arm, he reminded himself—making ready to deliver a blow. There it went! It lifted the recipient off his feet. He drew his sword, knowing somehow it would not be necessary.

Now he could hear the priest. The madman uttered a cry of rage, of pain, a tortured howl surely not from the Most High; and continued to scream long after his breath must have run out. Longer, longer. And still he screamed, as though all the agony in the world funnelled through one mouth.

Robal could barely speak, so exhausted was he when

finally he reached the man, who howled still. "Conal! Priest!" No response. He banged him on the back, once, twice, and jerked his hand away. The man *burned*! But at least the scream stopped.

"Sword," the priest said in a voice like a falling mountain, and grabbed the hilt of Robal's blade. Instinctively Robal grasped Conal's hand, ignoring the heat pouring from him, but despite using all his strength could not prevent Conal twisting the sword from his grasp. The priest strode forward over the shattered head of the man he had struck with the branch, making for a small cottage a few dozen paces away. Sword in the left hand, the guardsman noted, though the priest wrote with his right.

Robal followed, badly frightened. For a moment there was no sound save the reluctant tramp of his own boots, then a woman's shrill cry came from somewhere ahead of him. Two thumps, then another cry, a third thump and the cry cut off.

"Stella!" Conal bellowed, and rushed forward, blade outstretched as though it were a pike. As the priest disappeared through the door to the cottage, shrieking like a lunatic, Robal was sure he saw smoke coming from his hair.

INTERLUDE

In his extremity, Husk is forced to abandon prudence and draw power from anything he can find. All around the lower levels of Andratan rats drop dead, and outside the fortress birds fall from the sky. Prisoners drift into comas; guards find themselves on their knees, struggling for breath. It is far too late to worry if the Lord of Andratan will sense the disturbance; there is no possibility of disguising what is happening in his keep. The raw magic coursing through Husk and out to his three spikes is unmixed agony to him, his blood having turned to something like acid. His already maimed body begins to steam. He chuffs out a breath, fouler than a crypt.

Something is desperately wrong with the world outside Andratan. He has known this for weeks now, has bent his thoughts towards puzzling it out. *Why now?* he asks himself. Such cursed coincidence, this interference to the fabric of intersecting wills that lesser men know as magic. If coincidence it is. Have his actions, small as they are, drawn something opportunistic to nibble at his carefully laid plans like a rat at poisoned bait?

More, I need more.

In one of the cells a prisoner's brain bursts. Blood dribbles from the woman's mouth.

More.

A torturer collapses in the larger of the two chambers, falling across a brazier filled with glowing coals. He shrieks as his flesh begins to melt, but cannot roll away. Husk has stolen everything he has.

Could it be the Destroyer? Husk wonders. Is he even now manipulating events, aligning them in opposition to Husk's own plans? It defies all logic. All the Undying Man has to do in order to snuff out Husk's cleverness is to descend from his precious tower and come down to the dungeon. Husk has no real defence against a physical attack. *Stealth, all must be done with stealth.* But the strength of the one opposing him, whoever it is, leaves no room for stealth.

Another breath. His body, such as it is, begins to fail him. He will have to withdraw from one of his spikes, leave a third of his plan exposed to chance. If this is what his opponent intends, Husk is about to lose everything. But he *cannot* . . .

He hangs onto his sweet angel by the merest thread. She is in danger, yes, but not under the remorseless assault his captain and his priest are suffering. She has a degree of magic herself; perhaps she will draw upon it and keep herself alive until Husk can once again attend to her. He is left with nothing but hope.

He lets her go, hoping he can find her again.

The Most High himself, perhaps? Husk can imagine no other being capable of the immense power he has seen through the unwitting eyes of those he has spiked. Puissance so intense it has burned out some of the threads of the world's tapestry. Who is capable of that but an immortal? And, as far as Husk knows, there are only three immortals. *Soon to be four*, he promises himself. But he has been in a dungeon for seventy years. Might the blessed contagion have spread?

No. He cannot imagine either the Destroyer or his one-time consort sharing their immortality. One is too jealous of his power, the other too caring to risk infecting others. Might then the Most High have begun a third kingdom? Dona Mihst and Faltha have both failed to a degree; it is possible, unknowable.

He curses his state, then counsels himself to patience. He has no energy to waste on anything other than preserving the Falthan queen. With a hiss he resumes his battle.

FISHERMAN

CHAPTER 9

THE NEHERIAN FLEET

THE COUNTRYSIDE NORTH OF Fossa glittered in the clear noonday sunlight, which played on the beaded remnants of a gentle midmorning rain. Grassy fields spotted with sheep and goats alternated with orchards, ploughed ground and newly planted fields to the west of the narrow, stony Fisher Coast Road, creating a pleasant tapestry spread over rumpled hill country. Here and there tree-fringed outcrops of bare grey rock poked obstinately through the fertile soil, the only land not harnessed in some way for agricultural use. This kind of landscape was widely known as Palestra Country, a reference to the nation nominally ruling over this section of the Fisher Coast.

Tall oak stands and groves of squat fruit trees filled The Champleve, the Palestran name for the narrow strip of land between the road and the eastern cliff-top. A gentle sea breeze ruffled the oaks' budding crowns in the same fashion a genial father might tousle a favourite son's head, shaking out sparkling drops of water. Certainly as Noetos watched the trees he could feel his own father's hand in his hair, triggering an unexpected pang of loss.

He made his way north along the road, The Champleve to the right, Palestra Country to the left, and the Hegeoman stumbling reluctantly ahead of him. Noetos wasted a great deal of his breath ordering his captive to hurry, barking commands, even pushing him in the back; despite this, progress was far slower than he was comfortable with.

Perhaps the journey, slow as it was, would have been more tolerable had it been conducted in silence. Instead, the Hegeoman insisted on using whatever wind he had on haranguing the fisherman with arguments as to how blind fools rushed into trouble, what dreadful things might be happening in Fossa, and the nature of the pursuit the villagers would send. Certainly the man often turned his head, peering behind him as though expecting to see something coming up the road. Noetos kept his eyes firmly focused on the road ahead: likely the villagers would fail to notice the man's absence, and when finally they realised he was missing they would probably celebrate, led no doubt by the man's poor wife. Well, no, in fairness he was a popular leader, for all that he had not a brain in his head; but there were many more likely places to be searched, such as the base of the cliffs or in the burnt-out shells of the boats, before parties were sent north and south along the Fisher Coast Road. No, Noetos's troubles lay before him, not behind him.

"No smoke to be seen," the Hegeoman reported with satisfaction. "Not since we crossed the last ridge."

"You said that half an hour ago. The boats won't burn forever. You expecting someone to set them alight again?"

The Hegeoman hunched his shoulders in response, and turned back to the road. "No, no, just curious. You can't expect me to be happy about being forced to accompany you on your mad journey."

Noetos drew his sword in answer. The sound of it sliding from its scabbard sent the Hegeoman lurching forward until separated from his captor by a few paces. "I don't understand this," the man said plaintively. "What have I done to warrant your anger?"

"What have you done?" Noetos repeated. "Bregor, you may be the village leader, but I despair of you. My son and my wife are somewhere ahead of us, held captive by magicians, and you claim you do not understand why I am angry at you? You turned my family over to the Recruiters and made me an enemy of my village. Anomer and Opuntia sought safety at your house, but you denied it to them. I would have thought you would at least have granted Opuntia sanctuary."

"You don't understand. These are government officials, Noetos. Anomer offended the Recruiters, we all saw that. You were sent home in disgrace. I was surprised, certainly, when your wife and son turned up at my door, but what grounds did I have to withhold them when the Recruiters requested custody? They were in no danger."

"No danger? I saw my own daughter dead on the floor of my house, a knife in her back, and you tell me there was no danger?"

Both men increased their pace, the Hegeoman in response to the fisherman.

"But . . . this tale of your daughter makes no sense," the Hegeoman said, puffing heavily. "Opuntia said nothing of this to me. Her concern was for her own safety and that of her son."

Noetos heard the familiarity in the way the man said

his wife's name. He had been hearing it all morning, whenever the conversation took this turn, and had found it difficult to resist making an issue of it. Impossible to resist.

"I'm surprised Opuntia failed to find shelter in your house," he said evenly. "My understanding is she has found shelter there many times before."

"What do you mean?" The Hegeoman's sweaty face turned to face him, eyes wide: he knew exactly what was meant.

"Adultery." The word burned on the fisherman's tongue. Such a sweeping euphemism for lying with another man's wife, with the wrestling and grunting it entailed, the shocking intimacy of it. Or another woman's husband: there was another injured party in this, he acknowledged. "Bregor, you were sleeping with Opuntia."

"Sleeping with her?" The man puffed up with anger. "Yes, she came to my house, but not to see me, not at the start anyway. She actually came to speak to Merle, looking for advice as to how to deal with a drunkard husband, as it happens. When Merle explained the situation to me I spoke with her also."

"Alone?"

"Sometimes, yes. Think what you like, Fisher, your problem is not that I paid your wife too much attention; it is that you did not pay her enough."

Noetos jerked his head back as though from a blow. He was so certain—Opuntia had behaved like someone with a guilty secret—but the Hegeoman's words cut him like truth. He had no proof, no confession; and their marriage had been a broken thing for so long now he was just as likely to have misinterpreted her guilt. Perhaps she was simply ashamed of seeking help from others. Scared of his reaction when he heard of it.

With good reason, Noetos admitted to himself grimly.

"We could be of little help to her with regard to her marriage," the Hegeoman continued, his words cutting at Noetos like the blade of a boning knife. "So we offered her the things she lacked at home: interesting and stimulating conversation, news of the world beyond the cliffs, even philosophical discussion. Noetos, I am frightened of you, I won't pretend otherwise, but you made the accusation, so you should not resent the explanation. Come back with me to Fossa and talk with Merle. She will explain it better than I can."

"So you did not sleep with her?"

"Opuntia is a beautiful and clever woman. She aspires to far more than a simple headman of a fishing village. For some reason she thought you had promised her more than she could find in Fossa. What promises you made to her, and why she should have believed them, I do not know. But once married you delivered on none of them. She often talked of feeling trapped, as though the cliffs were a cage. *She* couldn't put out to sea in a boat and escape."

The fisherman winced as his own nightmare came back to him. "You've said enough," he admitted.

The Hegeoman continued relentlessly. "She saw her time with Merle and myself, and with the other cliff-dwellers, as freedom from her cage; yet she never ran from her obligations, never shirked her duties to her husband and family. And now, after years trapped in Fossa, she is out on the road. Spending time as a guest of the Recruiters, who surely cannot mean her harm, may be the best thing that could have happened to her."

No, it is not as simple as that. I would have let her go had she asked. But not in the company of these magicians, not with the ones who killed my daughter. The magic, the swordplay, the body in the hall: these things gave the lie to the Hegeoman's reassurances. Anomer and Opuntia were in real danger, and Noetos knew himself to be their only hope. He would press on, seeking to overtake them; then, by argument or by force, attempt to take his family from them. After that . . . After that, they could talk together about their future. Find somewhere he could continue to hide, somewhere Opuntia's ambition could be satisfied. Clearly they could no longer live in Fossa. But where would they go?

It was only later, as the afternoon sea-clouds lowered and a faint drizzle dampened the two travellers, that Noetos had another thought. *I asked Bregor twice, but he did not answer my question.* But by then he was too tired and heartsore to repeat it.

Over the next few days the fisherman forced the pace, his gnawing anxiety driving him on, but his captive could muster nothing more than a walk, no matter how he was chivvied. By the afternoon of the fourth day since he had left Fossa, Noetos was willing to concede he had made a mistake.

"Face it, you took me with you out of anger," the Hegeoman said equably as they took a late lunch amid the clods and mud of a freshly turned field, hidden from the road by a small rise. "What use was I ever going to be?"

Noetos set aside the cheese he was eating and scowled at the man. "I can think of a dozen uses," he said. "An exchange of hostages, an admittedly poor packhorse, a glib tongue should we get into trouble, a guide on the road north . . ." The fisherman paused, trying to think of more items to add to his list.

The Hegeoman counted them off as they were listed. "Four uses," he summarised, holding four fingers in the air. "As for a guide, should we go past Kymos, which we most certainly will this afternoon if you insist on keeping up this ridiculous pace, we will be beyond my knowledge. Time to let me go home."

"I'm right about the glib tongue, though."

"And I'm right about your anger," the Hegeoman returned. "You think with your fists."

"I hit with them too," Noetos rumbled. "You're here and that is that. The Recruiters have my family, and you are partly responsible. So you can help get them back."

"How?"

Not the question he wanted asked; not one he had an answer to. Yet the infuriating man asked it a dozen or more times a day. How indeed? Two men—no, realistically *one* man with a sword against four magicians. *Sounds like the plot of a bard's tale.* An ambush might work, if he ever caught up to his quarry. He was no tracker, and had no idea whether the Recruiters had even come this way. It was the direction they had taken when they left Fossa, but there were inland villages they might have gone to. Every time he came to a crossroad he would stand there, sick at heart, until the Hegeoman made some sarcastic comment.

"I don't know," he said, as he always did. "But I must try. You cannot imagine what it was like, seeing your beloved daughter ruined by those men."

"Forgive me, Fisher, but that is the part I fail to

understand," the Hegeoman said, obviously choosing his words with care. "Why would Andratan hurt its servants? We have been sending our sons and daughters north for generations, and this is the first we have heard of it. Surely if evil of the kind this woman—"

"My daughter," Noetos growled.

"—this *woman* described, whoever she was, actually happened, we would have learned of it, and the, er, trade would have been compromised throughout the Fisher country. They can't risk it, therefore they don't do it. It didn't happen. The girl was not your daughter. She was someone playing a trick on you; or perhaps, in your grief, you tricked yourself."

Reasonable, so reasonable. And so wrong. "You were there in Nadoce Square when the Recruiter attacked me," Noetos said stubbornly. "You cast me out of the village. You must have seen their magic at work."

"The blue snakes you insist they used against you? I've told you, I saw nothing. They exchanged words with you, that is all; and they were much more reasonable than you were." The man sighed, and patted his greasy hands on his shirt with some delicacy. "Fisher, I have to say this. Ever since you sent your daughter north and claimed Fisher House, you have been an unhappy man. A sour old bear shambling about the village looking for something to sink his teeth into. People avoid you, my friend. Surely you know this? Did you really expect Old Fossa to love you for climbing the despised cliffs and living above them? Even if you hadn't become unbearable company?"

Noetos struggled with and overcame the urge to shut the man up. *Face the truth, however unpleasant.*

"So now the Recruiters return, and your sensible wife

wants to send Anomer north. Most families would see this as an honour, but no, all you can see is your loss. Why, Fisher? You always said you did not intend Anomer to inherit your boats. You never took him fishing, not once. What other life did you have planned for him? None of us in The Circle can understand your thinking. We were proud of your son, the way he sparred with Pantella, the courage he showed when answering Ataphaxus' question, rash though that answer was. He could have been trained to be a diplomat, a governor, perhaps even served in Andratan itself. But instead, the next thing we know you are threatening villagers and our guests, and objecting when the Recruiters take your family into safe custody. Noetos, most people think you have gone mad. Have you?"

Was this how he appeared to others? Had he really been so visibly unhappy? He could sense himself losing control, feels his eyes beginning to sting. *You have your proof*, he acknowledged silently to his village leader.

He did not know how long he sat there, his chin on his chest, before he felt a hand grip his shoulder.

"Put out the fire," the Hegeoman said in a low voice. "Put it out, put it out!"

"What?" Noetos snapped back to reality. "Why?"

His companion snatched up handfuls of dirt and threw them on the low flame, splashing into the simmering soup and knocking the pot over. The fire hissed and went out.

"What are you doing?"

In answer the Hegeoman pointed over Noetos's shoulder, then began scrambling amongst their gear. The fisherman turned to see threads of smoke drifting towards them.

"Field fire?" he said. "The wrong time of year, surely?"

The Hegeoman shrugged. "Do you want to stay here and argue with the flames?" He strapped on his pack and stood up, the now empty soup pot in his hand.

"We will be safe in this field," said Noetos. "The fire will not burn bare earth."

"Spoken with all the knowledge of a fisherman. In a bad fire sparks jump right across open spaces such as this. And we have to worry about smoke as much as flame: we've lost farmers before, dead in a field fire without ever being touched by the flames. The smoke will smother you. Do you want to wait here and learn this for yourself?"

By the end of the explanation Noetos was on his feet, hurriedly packing away the remainder of their possessions. "Where do we go?"

"Safest place is the sea. The fires don't come down the cliffs."

They ran across the field, clods spraying up behind them. *But it rained last night, as it has every night since we left Fossa*, Noetos found himself thinking. *How could the fields catch fire? And surely it is too early in the growing season for there to be anything much in the fields to burn?*

Over the Fisher Coast Road they crossed, then through a copse of fir trees and across another bare field. They had escaped the smoke; the fire seemed to be seated somewhere to their left and ahead. Fingers of grey stretched above them, borne on some higher breeze. Ahead the ground rose sharply.

"Slow down," the Hegeoman gasped, "we're near the cliff . . ."

They crested the rise and found themselves standing at the cliff-edge, the rise commanding a wide view of the coast to north and south. Bays, promontories, wide sandy beaches, the reef in the distance, rich blue sea. Their heads turned towards the source of the smoke.

"Oh," the Hegeoman said.

"What is it?" Noetos, confounded by the smoke, did not have the Hegeoman's keen eyes. "What do you see?"

"I, ah, nothing, the fire is further away than I thought, it looks like a few trees burning down below the cliffs. We're safe, we can go."

A pall of smoke drifted across them, further obscuring their vision and setting them both to coughing. Then the sea breeze gusted, clearing the smoke away.

Noetos grabbed the Hegeoman by the shirt while keeping his gaze focused on the harbour below and to their left. "A few trees?" He dragged his captive around in front of him, perilously close to the crumbling cliff-edge. "And the entire Neherian fleet has come to watch them burn?"

Thirty or more ships there were, hove to in deep water perhaps five hundred swimming strokes offshore, all wearing the red Neherian stripe just above the waterline. An enormous tri-masted carrack, clearly the flagship, rigged in a way Noetos had never seen or heard of, sur-rounded by five elderly but impressive cogs and perhaps a dozen dromonds of varying sizes. The rest were fishing boats, including a gaff-rigged ketch he recognised as one that frequented the Fossan fishing beds beyond The Rhoos.

He dragged the reluctant Hegeoman along the cliff-top until they stood directly above the source of the fire, then drew his sword. "Now," he said. "You are going to tell me what this means. And don't waste your breath pretending you know nothing about it."

A fishing village lay below them. Or, more accurately, what remained of a fishing village. Blackened skeletons instead of simple wooden fishing huts; stone houses collapsed into piles of rock. Most of the fires were already dying down, though flames had but recently begun their work on half a dozen dwellings. The destruction was by no means universal, however. A number of buildings remained untouched, whether because they were scheduled for firing or were to be left alone, Noetos could not tell.

Most of the activity was focused on the beach. A dozen or so longboats had been drawn up to the south of the village, and planks had been thrown across them so one could walk from the first to the last. Figures—women and children, the Fisher realised as he looked more closely, most likely villagers—were being marched along the planks. They had filled the first three boats, and began filling the fourth as he watched.

A faint sound of shouting reached their ears. It came from the rightmost of the longboats, though it was hard to . . . Yes, their attention seemed to be focused on a small knot of people on the beach. Neherians and captives. The shouting came from relatives of the captives, then.

With a sinking heart Noetos knew what was to come. He had been in a war with these people; he understood their brutal capabilities, their methods. *They are pacifying the village. Their remaining captives are the holdouts, the leaders who will not agree to serve them, even though their families are held.* That there were so many surprised him. A brave leadership.

More smoke drifted towards the two men watching from the cliff-top, momentarily blurring their view. When it cleared, the captives had been secured somehow to the walls and doors of a group of buildings, almost certainly a market of some kind. Two figures with burning sticks approached the buildings. The Neherian way: control the body by severing the head. Always by force, never by negotiation.

"What are they doing?" the Hegeoman asked in a small voice. His tone of voice made it clear he understood what he witnessed, knew what was going to happen. Perhaps he hoped Noetos might supply him with a plausible alternative explanation.

"Killing," Noetos replied tonelessly. "They are good at that."

"But . . . the village leaders?"

"Death is death. If someone has to die, better the leaders responsible for the village than some other sacrifice." *Why does their identity bother you so much?*

"But by surrendering, they have surely saved the lives of their villagers," said the Hegeoman. "They should be rewarded, not punished. It is not fair that they should die!"

The shouting below grew louder, coming both from the captives and from the longboats. The two Neherians set flame to the buildings to the accompaniment of shrieks from the boats.

"Never surrender to a Neherian, Bregor," Noetos said, his head aching with memory. "If you do, he will take your mother and torture her in front of your eyes. He will take your brothers and hamstring them one by one, then set his dogs on them. He will rape your sisters while shouting vileness at you, before cutting their throats. He will take your father and behead him with his own sword, taking care to spatter you with his lifeblood. Then he will let you live, though you beg him to kill you." The fisherman clamped his mouth shut, too late to stop his memories spilling out.

The Hegeoman's mouth opened wide enough for both of them.

One of the buildings was a fish-processing house, it seemed, for the fire caught at once and burned ferociously, sending thick black smoke billowing into the sky. Noetos had smelled burning fish oil before, but never mixed with the smell of charred human flesh. He found himself dry-retching, the Hegeoman's unsteady hand on his back.

"You've never seen death like this before, have you," Noetos said, spitting bitter saliva from his mouth. "It should be you throwing up."

The white-faced man gave no answer. Noetos took a closer look at the Hegeoman's features: his eyes did not see the desperate scene below them, but gazed inward on some dreadful private vision. Alarm bells rang inside the fisherman's mind.

He was about to press Bregor for answers, but was distracted by the two Neherian figures throwing down their firebrands and rushing to the beach. There they signalled to their fellows, a few of whom came ashore, beaching their boats in a hurry, uncaring of keel damage. So unlike the Neherians, normally fastidious about such things. What had them so worried? The newly arrived Neherians took pails from their boats, dipped them hurriedly in the water and ran with them to the burning market. *Ah, I see.* They were worried about the black smoke, which could only mean one thing.

A further thought occurred to him. As a result, several seemingly unrelated things the Hegeoman had said came together, sending a chill through his body.

"This is not an isolated raid." He turned to the man kneeling beside him.

"No." A voice thinned by shock.

"Which way are they working? North or south?" He held his breath.

"North." Little more than a whisper.

"*What have you done?*"

"I—"

"Three things. First, you were nervous when I burned the *Arathé*, but I assumed it was because I threatened to tie you up and burn you with it. Second, you are distressed because the village leadership has just been put to death. And third, the Neherians don't want their burning to get out of control. You know what these three things say to me? They say the Neherians are razing the coast one village at a time, and because they don't want the next village to know what is coming they've launched their raids in the spring, when the prevailing winds are nor-easterly, and are working their way north. It says to me you knew this was coming, you stinking cut, and you sold us out on the promise of gentle treatment. How were you going to signal them? Smoke, perhaps? Did you think I'd called them down when I fired my vessel? And now you've seen what happens to village leaders who surrender to the raiders, you are rightly filled with fear. You look down at this village—Kymos I assume—and see Fossa. Don't you? *Don't you?*"

He grabbed the man by the throat with one burly hand, with no thought other than to crush his windpipe.

"Why shouldn't I take you down for a closer look? A discussion, perhaps, with your allies? What do you think they would do with you?" Saliva spat from his lips; he barely noticed it. The Hegeoman's hands opened and closed convulsively. "How much did they pay you? What did they offer you? Your own worthless life? Or—or, dear Alkuon, did you honestly think you were doing the right thing? Did they tell you this was inevitable? Did they impress you with their sophistication and wealth? Did they guarantee no deaths? Alkuon drown you, have you never listened to the tales of the Neherian Wars? How many men, women and children have died because of you, you worthless cliff-scum?"

The hands twitched closed one last time, then slowly uncurled. Noetos's vision cleared, though a red mist remained: the face above his throttling hand had turned blue and the mouth lolled open.

"Ah, you were never any good," the fisherman declared, near to sobbing, and dropped the Hegeoman to the ground.

Shouting drew his attention away from the body at his feet. A handful of the Neherians gestured up at the cliffs, in his direction, at him. The wind carried the sound of their excited jabbering to him, though he could not make out words; how loudly must he have been shouting? *We're no threat, leave us alone*. But he knew they would not. The meaning of their signals, the heads bent together, the searching for a cliff path, left no doubt.

He had not killed the Hegeoman. Part of him burned to finish the task; another part knew it for the action of a frustrated, powerless man, an action he would regret should he complete it. Behind his words and actions a great grief began building up, like water behind a dam of sticks.

Noetos swore fervently. If only he had the courage to

leave the Hegeoman where he had fallen; if only he was prepared to face the voice already crying in his mind. *Don't leave me, son,* it cried; *stay with me, bury your family, avenge our deaths . . .*

He could not refuse. He picked up the unconscious Bregor and slung him over his shoulder, grunting at the weight of the man and his backpack. Running was easiest bent well forward, with the weight working to his advantage, but the hot tears in his eyes made the dash to the road a dangerous one. In his mind he ran from a clearing twenty years ago, and from the gruesome scattering of mutilated bodies lying there, but this time he carried his dead father who whispered to him, "Avenge us, avenge us." His whispering was overlaid by the Neherians laughing and fingering their swords as they debated how much of a head-start they would grant him. Noetos cried and cried as the bitter memories possessed him, the memories he had tried to escape by hiding in the fishing village, memories now emerging from their hiding places with their sounds and their smells and their begging and pleading and cruel laughter, goading him on along the road, directing him to a copse of privet and bramble, the darkness beckoning him in, offering him a shadowy place to hide, ringed by cliffs, where no one knew who he was or what he had done—*avenge us, avenge us, avenge us . . .*

Groaning, sounds of distress, tugs at his shoulder. Noetos jerked awake, snatching at and missing the hand resting on his arm. The burden of his memories crashed in on him, catching him without his usual preparedness, and the breath caught in his throat, making him retch. A hand entered his vision, offering him a container filled with water.

He took it and up-ended it down his throat, trying to wash out the constriction there, but the dam held. Memories lodged in his gullet. His hand began to shake, and the container fell to the shadowed ground with a soft thump.

A moment later, he followed.

Fossa's village leader knelt next to the unconscious form of the fisherman, by turns pinching his nose and covering his mouth, trying to silence the man's snoring. Somewhere near their hiding place, outside the copse, the Neherians searched for the people who had spied on them. In the confines of the hideaway, the snorting, blowing sounds the fisherman made sounded outrageously loud. Bregor had to hope they would not attract attention.

At least the snoring was better than the talking. The fisherman had an annoying habit of talking in his sleep. In fact, on the second night north of Fossa Noetos had held a long discussion with himself. It would have been funny had Bregor not been trying to sleep. With the Neherians nearby it might well be fatal.

He tried to swallow and cringed with the pain. Fisher the Madman had done him some sort of damage; he could not speak at all, able only to make harsh honking sounds which hurt dreadfully, and he frequently spat up blood. In the evening and night since, he had been able to swallow water only with extreme determination. He had not tried to eat.

Yet he knew he had been fortunate. His mind kept painting lurid pictures of Fossa; of the burning houses, the members of the Village Council wriggling and screaming amid the flames, the rest of the villagers chained in the longboats, heading out through The Rhoos for the last time. He saw himself surrounded by Neherians, their sincere smiles replaced by hungry looks as they prepared to . . . to . . .

That night he did not sleep. He found himself starting at every rustle in the copse, and doubted his ruined throat would allow him to settle in any case. At some point he went to make water, and in the distance he saw at least three separate glows from fires near the road. Parties of Neherians searching for them, perhaps; or maybe placed to intercept anyone who might see the destruction they had wrought and rush ahead to warn villages to the north. Their presence denied him what would otherwise have been the ideal opportunity to escape Noetos's clutches.

The night gave him plenty of time to reflect on what he ought to do. *I have been played for a fool*. The betrayer betrayed. Yet his intention had been pure, had been in the village's best interest. The promises he'd received that first night when approached by the Neherian agent had been signed by the Duke of Neherius himself, inviolable, watertight. Surely the village would have understood. The Neherians were determined to have the coast; they were the only ones who made use of it, after all. The coastal villages would be suffered to remain, would fall under Neherian protection, were guaranteed buying rights for Neherian produce, including fish, at very favourable prices. The agent had spoken in such a gentle, reasonable voice. The Neherians did not want the farmland, and wasn't that where the Fossan men of substance earned their living? Palestran possession of the lands above the cliff-top would remain undisturbed, while the lands below the cliff-top would be ceded to Neherius. Some villages would resist, their leaders mired in outdated concepts of ownership, the agent said sorrowfully. They would be cleansed. Now, make your mark here.

The Recruiters had been a complication. The Hegeoman had received a message a few days before they arrived, advising him to send a signal immediately they left. A small fire at the top of the cliff would suffice, the unsigned note said. He had decided to delay matters long enough to alert a few people, giving them time to relocate themselves and their possessions inland. His family, of course, and some of those on The Circle. Simple prudence. But Noetos had interfered, burning his boat and no doubt inadvertently signalling the Neherian fleet with the smoke it had made.

At least he could deny signalling them himself.

His thoughts had only just softened on the borders of sleep when the fisherman awoke, tried to stand and fell against him, sending them both rolling into the brambles. The man's absurdly large hands fumbled unsuccessfully for his sword.

"Well, my friend, welcome to a bitter day," he said in an altogether too loud voice. Bregor assumed the man spoke to him, but he could not be sure. He couldn't answer in any case.

A meaty hand pulled him out into the sunlight. The fisherman's red-bearded face stared directly into his own.

"You're quiet. Does your throat hurt?"

The Hegeoman nodded, his throat working to make a whine not unlike a cur under a boot. It summed up his feelings precisely.

"I have done some damage, haven't I? Good. You'll not be making any traitorous promises with that mouth for some time." Noetos smiled bitterly.

"We have a decision to make," he continued after a pause. "Do we maintain our pursuit of the Recruiters, try to warn the next village to the north of the Neherian fleet, or return to Fossa and aid any survivors? Any preference? I'll talk the three options through. You indicate if any of them make sense."

You forgot the fourth option, the Hegeoman wanted to say. *Flee. Flee inland as far from the Neherian death fleet as we can. Call into the Palestran capital and warn them if we must; at least it will make our cowardice seem sensible, if not noble. Though no one in Tochar would credit us, and they do not have the soldiery or sea-craft to defend themselves against the fleet even if they did believe.* The Neherians had recently signed a series of non-aggression treaties; the false comfort offered by such documents would far outweigh the garbled reports of two provincials.

"First, we could leave the Neherians to their month or more of slaughter—I assume they will work their way north through Palestra to Saros, reuniting Greater Rhoudhos under their own banner—and carry on our pursuit of the Recruiters. The chaos ahead might even work in our favour, though I admit I have yet to think of any sane way of rescuing my family and taking my revenge."

Bregor raised an eyebrow, trying to indicate ambivalence. *It has always been a mad plan, fool fisherman*, he wanted to say. *If you had remained in Fossa the Recruiters would have released your family. Though you would be dead by now, of course: knowing you, you would have taken on the entire Neherian fleet in your boat, screaming defiance as you rammed their flagship.*

"When I first saw the fleet at Kymos and worked out the extent of your treachery I wanted to return to Fossa.

Any chance they have been left alone until the fleet returns south?"

A shake of the head disposed of that hope. The Hegeoman watched the shutters draw over Noetos's eyes.

"I doubt, then, there will be anyone left in Fossa to benefit from our aid," he continued. "So that leaves the third option. How fast can you run?"

Bregor shook his head, indicating his damaged throat.

"That fast? Excellent. I would hate to leave you on your own, with nothing but burned villages and angry Neherians for company. My time of leaving people behind is over."

The Hegeoman sighed. *And how will two men, one injured and both on foot, keep pace with a sailing fleet?* Not a question he could ask with hands and eyebrows, but Noetos seemed to understand the objection nevertheless.

"The Neherians will take a day, at least, to pacify each fishing village and move on to the next," he said, musing. "We may not be able to pass them today or tomorrow but, if we bypass the next few villages, we should be able to get ahead of them. I don't wish to leave anyone to the Neherians, but there are at least thirty settlements between Fossa and Raceme. The more we save, the happier I'll be. And you, weasel man, have a chance to redeem yourself."

He drew his sword, looked sourly at the naked blade, and slapped the Hegeoman lightly on his rump with the flat. "As long as you hold nothing back this time, that is. Every minute we save could mean another village kept out of Neherian hands. If we leave now and make use of the road . . . Ach!" He swore. "We cannot use the road; the Neherians will undoubtedly have set watch on it north and south of their fleet, to prevent word getting out. Weak fool! We should have made our escape north last night, using the darkness as our cover. How will we avoid them today? I don't want to sacrifice another village by waiting for nightfall!"

He turned and spat on the ground. "I should have been gentler with you," he conceded. "I could benefit from your ideas. How long . . . Can you . . ."

The Hegeoman shook his head. He had tried shaping speech, but no matter how careful he was, the wreck of his larynx responded only with pain. Likely a depressingly long recovery period.

"Very well, then." The big fisherman shrugged his broad shoulders. "We will look for an inland path, or think of something else while on our feet. Come on, my friend, gather up our belongings. The one thing we cannot do is remain here."

No, Bregor thought. *The one thing we cannot do is rescue your family, if they need rescuing. Or have you forgotten?*

Neither Noetos nor the Hegeoman could recall the name of the fishing village immediately north of Kymos. Neherian control of offshore fishing denied Fossans easy access outside their bay and the chance to meet other fishermen, so Noetos had very little idea of how far north the village was, or even how large it might be. Of course, had the Hegeoman known the name, he would not have been able to speak it. The fisherman knew he would regret his attack of rage, even though he felt it justified.

Any time in the previous four days since they had left Fossa, Noetos would have welcomed the resulting silence. The man had spouted a constant flow of babble, as though he was fuelled by words. Politicians worked with speech, but fishermen understood the need for silence. Out on the dangerous, inscrutable water every sense had to be focused on the task and, until the catch was made, talk was kept to a minimum. Today, however, the silence resulting from the Hegeoman's injury meant Noetos had no relief from his spiralling thoughts.

He had always been a deep thinker. His mother said it whenever visitors came to the estate, mostly to explain his tendency as a child to answer every query with a monosyllable. But it was true: as a youngster he seldom indulged in what his father called "chitchat." Saw no point in it. Who benefited from his dutiful rendition of the expected answer? As a sort of rebellion agaisnt his family's expectations he went through a phase of answering every question honestly, until his father beat him for responding to a simple query about his health by describing in lurid detail the effects of a recent bout of chickenpox. He understood why his father punished him, knew just how insolent his inappropriate honesty had been, but judged the problem to be with the flippant question, not the detailed, overlong answer. *If they don't want to know, they shouldn't ask.*

His tendency to contemplation and solitude had led him to the written word. Recognising this, his father, despairing for a time of imparting more important skills such as swordplay and accountancy, gave the young boy access to the family library. *Noetos is a third son*, his father said to his mother: *let him be a scholar.* There, once the huge oaken doors were closed, sealing his world away from that of others, his self-imposed studies absorbed him completely. He had never been happier than during the sum-

mers spent in the library, lying on the floor with maps and
scrolls spread out all around him. A musty smell, the
sound of a fly buzzing against a shutter, a discreet whisper
as someone sought not to interrupt him: all could cause his
heart to turn over in sweet memory. Alone with his
thoughts, he could travel around the world and back in
time to when . . .

Such a deep thinker, so everyone said. But now, when
he most needed his thinking skills, nothing came to him.
Slow and composed, no need to panic, he repeated to himself, but these words circled each other in his head, making their own distracting noise. He had no better idea than
to leave the road and strike inland, hoping to pass the Neherians, though he knew travel would be much slower in
the hills. Better than thrusting himself into Neherian jaws.

The two men made good time along the northern road,
much better time than before they discovered the Neherian fleet, confirming Noetos's belief that Bregor had
been deliberately holding him back. The first path they
came to, an hour or so after they set out, looked promising, but the Hegeoman shook his head vigorously and
seemed to be indicating that the track bent to the south,
taking them away from where they needed to go. A second path petered out a few hundred paces from the road,
forcing them to turn back. Noetos cursed his memory:
years looking at maps and charts, yet not one useful fragment remained. Then, before they could find either a third
path or a better solution, they came across the Neherian
watchers.

Cleverly, the Neherians had positioned themselves atop
a rise in the road, giving them a long view to the south.
Only the prudence of keeping to the edge of the road when

approaching the crest of a hill kept Noetos and his captive
from being seen. At least, he hoped they had not been
seen. The fisherman observed the sentries for a minute or
so: they kept a desultory watch, but there was no likelihood of overcoming them with a surprise attack. Though
as he continued to examine them, he did notice they paid
little or no attention to the road north of them. Would it be
as simple as sneaking past them, then rejoining the road?
Noetos thought not. Why would they not watch the north,
unless another group lay in wait, watching the northern
approaches? It seemed much more likely that the Neherians would position multiple watchers on the Fisher Coast
Road, as their raids depended so heavily on surprise. Any
inquisitive traveller, shepherd or farmer would be taken,
questioned and likely thrown from the nearby cliff.

"Come on, you feckless dissolute," Noetos said with
false cheer as he hauled the Hegeoman, who had puffed
and blown his way up the last three hills, away from the
road and over a low stone fence. "Time to get some
exercise."

Bregor beckoned him close. "Slow ... across ...
fields," he got out of his throat in barely more than a whisper. Observation or complaint? Probably the latter, the
fisherman decided.

"This is our only way forward," he replied as he
walked determinedly across the grassy field.

*Think. The Recruiters have either already encountered
the Neherians or they have done what we are doing.* He
doubted the magicians would want to tangle with the main
force of Neherius, as their policy of non-interference in
local politics was well known, but they would not suffer
being baulked in their desire to travel north. Perhaps they

had made an agreement with the fleet? Even now they
might be sailing for Andratan. Certainly when they realised a full-scale raid was taking place the Recruiters
would not be stopping at the villages. Or would they?
Would they conduct their tests at a village and leave the
villagers unwarned, staying just ahead of the invading
fleet? Or would they abandon the idea of testing the
coastal villages and perhaps travel inland? It would add a
week or two to their journey, but a stop at Tochar would
surely yield many young men and women willing to sell
their futures. But perhaps the Recruiters had already
passed through inland Palestra on their way south.

Impossible to know, yet so much depended on it. The
only sensible thing to do was to find a local and ask. And
for that they must travel further inland, away from the
coast road.

The land about them sloped gradually upwards, higher
to their left and lower to their right. Three more fields, the
last one containing a bull (asleep, fortunately), led them to
their first real climb, up and over a knuckled ridge. On the
far side they were forced to beat through a stand of gorse,
made worse by a deep but hidden stream at the bottom
into which they both stumbled. Noetos fell into a gorse
bush and the heavy landing somehow caused his buckle to
loosen: his sword and scabbard fell into the water. For a
few worrying minutes they sloshed around the stream, the
fisherman sucking at his bleeding hand, until the Hegeoman stood on the hilt.

They walked downstream for a time, between weed-
trammelled banks and through stagnant, fly-blown pools.
Judging the gorse to have thinned, the two men scrambled
up the left bank and through a narrow belt of trees, to find

themselves in an olive orchard. Again, the land tried to force them to the right and north. Noetos began to lose his sense of direction. The sun, directly overhead, gave him no assistance, leaving him afraid he had been turned around. Eventually he decided to make for the highest point of land, a bare, flat-topped hill some distance to their right. From there he would see a house, a road, a village, something. Surely someone had to tend these fields.

They made better time by following winding animal tracks than by beating directly across the ridges. The sheep knew best. Though fit, Noetos felt a growing ache in his leg muscles as they pushed up the broad hill: a gut-line tightness in his left calf twinged every step. Behind him the Hegeoman panted like an old man, mouth opening and closing so like a puffer fish the fisherman almost let slip a laugh, until he considered what this effort would be costing the man and held back his mirth. He'd not done Bregor any permanent damage, had he? *Not the sort of damage the Neherians would have done him had I not taken him captive.* And he was not like the Neherians, cruel for no good reason.

The last thirty feet of the hill was an almost vertical band of rock, around the base of which the sheep trails went left and right. Following the more heavily used rightmost path—judging by the droppings, anyway—they came to a narrow, steeply-sloping gulch which cut down through the vertical rock, evidently used by the sheep as access to the summit. The Hegeoman stood bent over, hands on knees, shaking his head.

"Come on, Bregor, not far to go," Noetos said, and stretched out a hand to him. The Hegeoman took it in his own, an odd look in his eye. Slowly, with a care for their footing on the loose rock on the floor of the gulch, they manoeuvred their way towards the top of the hill.

At the summit they both fell to their knees, exhausted.

Noetos recovered first. "Let's see where we are, then," he said, pushing himself to his feet.

A broad vista presented itself. To the east the land they had traversed that morning spread out its patchwork to the darker line of The Champleve, beyond which sparkled the ocean.

Despite knowing their search for help would be better served to the west, Noetos found himself drawn to the sea. He had never seen it from such an elevation. From left to right across the blue waters were sprinkled the islets, reefs and atolls that made up The Roudhosa—known by villagers as The Rhoos—the enormous island chain that once bracketed the lands of the Dukedom of Roudhos. At least, the lands as they were before the Neherians destroyed them nearly fifty years ago. Now the Neherians—the rump of Roudhos—held sway from the coast to the outer reefs and beyond. Palestra and Saros had footholds on the seashore, no more; and, if the Neherian raids succeeded, not even that. How long before the Neherians drove inland like a tidal wave, swamping the small countries to their north and west, until Roudhos was made anew in their cruel image?

If I keep staring at the sea, not very long, he thought, and forced himself to turn away. He strode with purpose past the Hegeoman, still slumped on the ground, and across the hundred paces of short grass that made up the crown of the hill, until he could see to the west.

Ah. Ah, yes. Familiar landmarks unrolled themselves in front of him like a scroll. There, that town in the middle

distance would be Altima, Palestra's third city. Perhaps
two days' walk from where he stood, the town sat astride
the Panulo River, which glinted here and there amid the
fields on either side of the town wall. Down dropped his
gaze, following a dark groove in the landscape which
originated at Altima and aimed itself directly at the hill on
which he stood: the Palestran Line, along which the ore
that provided Palestra's wealth was carted. As he stared at
it he could hear his tutor's voice: *Palestra supplies iron to
much of southern Bhrudwo, and the best deposits, from
the Eisarn seam, are traded across the world.* Which
meant that the large pit perhaps a league away was Eisarn
itself, and this knowledge supplied the name of the hill
under his feet. Ossern. *The same name as the pit, just an
older form*, his tutor had explained as his young charge
pored over the map of northern Roudhos. Or what had
once been northern Roudhos. Fragments of his suppressed
past threatened to pour through his mind, history lessons,
geographical facts . . . He clamped down hard on them.

"There! People!" Bregor's outstretched arm pointed
down at Eisarn Pit, his exclamation more breath than
voice. He had come up beside Noetos unheard. Without a
glance towards his captor, the Hegeoman turned towards
the gulch and a way down, leaving the fisherman nothing
to do but hurry to catch him up.

CHAPTER 10

THE ALCHEMIST

A LIGHT SHOWER OF RAIN greeted the two Fossans as they slipped and stumbled their way to the base of Ossern Hill. Within minutes the sheep track turned to mud, caking Noetos's boots and grabbing at Bregor's lighter shoes.

"Put your hand on my shoulder," said Noetos, "otherwise we'll never get there."

The Hegeoman did as he was asked, then peered past the fisherman's substantial frame, trying to orient himself. He felt much better since their rest on the summit. Though his throat still hurt to swallow, the weight on his shoulders seemed to have lessened and the pain in his legs had reduced to a deadened ache. Perhaps he could endure this madness after all . . . if not for the thought of Merle, his wife, likely in the faithless hands of the Neherians.

"Go right," he said hoarsely in Noetos' ear, the effort of speaking tugging mercilessly on his throat.

"You sure? I thought the pit was off to the left, according to the sun."

"Moving," Bregor said, pointing to the hazy yellow glow in the swirling clouds.

"Oh. Yes." To his credit the fisherman nodded, though visibly embarrassed. "Thank you," he said. They left the sticky path and made their way through a belt of pine trees towards a grassy meadow.

Halfway across the meadow Bregor turned to look back at Ossern Hill, trying to measure their progress so he could guess how far they had to go until they reached the pit. The moment he set eyes on the hill he realised with a sinking feeling he had left his pack, containing much of the food Noetos had taken from his house, sitting on the summit.

"Are you coming? The Neherians won't wait forever." The fisherman's voice, to Bregor's ear at least, sounded stretched with lack of patience.

Bregor considered not telling the man. If the loss went unnoticed until they stopped to make camp, then perhaps he could pick up the pack Noetos carried and pretend he'd just taken it from his own shoulders. Confuse Noetos into thinking he had made the mistake. It would shave some of the pig-headed pride from the fisherman; maybe even convince him to abandon this futile chase after his family, and seek their return through the proper channels. Or something.

He *considered* it for a moment, and discarded it. *This is not a man to anger unnecessarily*, he reminded himself, fingering his throat. *Nor is he a fool*.

"Fisher," he said, squeezing Noetos's shoulder. "Pack."

"Eh?"

He mimed the pack sitting on his shoulders, then pointed at the hill over his right shoulder.

Noetos needed no more hints. His face darkened and his brows lowered, creating exactly the effect dear Opuntia hated so much.

"Bregor, you stumbling imbecile, what do you do instead of thinking? How did you make it to adulthood? Ah, what's the use? Go on, go find your way back and retrieve it. I'll wait here."

And you accuse me of not thinking? Bregor kept this thought unsaid. He nodded to his captor, head bent obsequiously, and backed away. *Don't change your mind, don't think it through . . .*

"Wait," Noetos said. "The moment you put the pack on your shoulders you will be off back to Fossa. In fact, knowing you, you probably won't even wait to pick up the pack, forgetting that it's four or five days' march back home." He put his hands to his head and shook it in disgust.

"We will abandon it, and get by with what remains in my pack. We can exist on short rations until we get to a village. I'm sure they'll be grateful enough to give us something to eat when they hear our warning."

So close . . . Bregor couldn't help himself. *Fossa first,* he thought as the image of Merle's face hung in his mind. Before he could consider it further he spun on his heel and ran, legs and arms pumping in every direction. *He must be tired, he'll give me up like he gave up the pack.*

He found himself sprinting towards a rainbow: the shower had passed to the north, and in the east a small bow hung over Ossern Hill. The scene jerked from side to side as he threw himself into his escape. Small ruts and hollows threatened to trip him; the grass slapped wetly against his legs, making running difficult. Fifty paces, a hundred, and his calves felt like tree trunks trying to take root every time he planted one on the ground. Trying to breathe was like attempting to suck meat through a reed.

He didn't make it to the end of the field. His legs went from under him, defeated by the slippery grass and uneven ground, and he ploughed hard into the earth. Something cracked underneath him as he landed. He groaned, spat out a broadweed stalk, levered himself up on his elbows and pulled a dry stick, now in two pieces, from under his hips. The fisherman stared down at him.

"Thought . . . you wanted . . . pack . . . quickly," Bregor said weakly between sobbing gasps, knowing how ridiculous the excuse sounded even as he said it; then spat out fresh blood. He braced himself for what was to come.

"Don't speak," Noetos said, in a surprisingly gentle voice. "You've reinjured your throat. Stay where you are; I'll be back in a minute with water."

Bregor lowered his head to the wet earth, thoroughly exhausted in body and mind. Within moments he found a halfway place between unconsciousness and sleep, a place where he could ignore the voice that told him he was an ineffectual, cowardly, man. *I try to do what is right*, was his last thought. *If only I didn't get it so wrong.*

Some time later he drifted away from his place of pity and came to himself, awakening to the sound of Noetos talking with someone. No, talking with *himself. Not again. Every night since they had left Fossa, and now under the afternoon sun. What must he be like to live with?* Well, Bregor didn't have to imagine. Opuntia had not exaggerated.

". . . is worried about Merle. Must be. But why didn't he mention her before now? I could have understood it had he begged to go back, to see if he could save her somehow. It's what I'd do. What I'm doing."

A pause, then he spoke again in a more thoughtful voice. "But such a fool. An alliance with the Neherians? Might as well have skinned himself on the beach and invited the sharks to feast on his flesh."

"Noetos," the Hegeoman rasped, his mouth close to the fisherman's ear. "Wake up. You're dreaming." Even the effort of whispering sent him into a coughing fit.

"Father? Upanas? Be easy, father." Noetos's voice, thick with sleep, sounded uncertain.

Is he hearing me? Bregor wondered. "There were reasons, fisherman," he said, using his breath and mouth to shape his words, protecting his throat. "It didn't seem foolish at the time."

"It was foolish," Noetos said, his eyes still closed. "Bregor is a frightened fool. He knows nothing. But I have done many foolish things myself out of fear. Particularly when I ought to have defended my family. So courageous. I fled when faced with the duty to avenge my family and, with great valour, I hid in that fish-stinking Alkuon-forsaken village filled with fools."

What is this? What family is he referring to? "There is still hope," Bregor whispered.

"There was never any hope. Blame Grandfather if you must blame anyone. He defied the Destroyer's command and had his dukedom ripped from him along with his life. Now *there* was a fool. And what good did his defiance do? Cost him Roudhos, which is what his enemies wanted."

"Your *grandfather*?" the Hegeoman said, and in his surprise he voiced the words, further damaging his throat. "The last Duke of Roudhos was your grandfather?"

"So you always told us," said the sleeping fisherman. "You were angry that the dukedom you stood to inherit was reduced to a fraction of the Fisher Coast. A bitter man. Bitterness make people do foolish things, doesn't it, father; such as trying to make deals with rival Neherian factions. Leads them and their families to forest glades where their lives are ended badly, while I could only cower and watch."

"You saw me die?" Transfixed by the revelation, Bregor found himself unable to resist playing along.

"I saw them take your head," came the reply. "But you were dead already. I watched you die as they butchered your children."

"You hate him, don't you?"

"Hate . . . who? Father? Is that you?" Noetos began to stir, clearly anxious. "Father?"

The Hegeoman pulled away from him. No matter how much more he might find out by playing along with the fisherman's dream, it was not worth the risk of being found out.

It proved to be a wise decision. Noetos continued to stir, rolled over onto his stomach, then awoke and rubbed his eyes. After a few moments Noetos stood and came over to him.

"How are you feeling, Bregor?"

He began to answer, but thought better of it, shrugging instead.

"It's all right, it's all right," Noetos soothed, as if he was a fractious infant. "I gave you some water while you were unconscious. You swallowed some of it, so that should see you right for a time."

"Sorry," Bregor whispered, all breath and mouth. "So sorry."

He meant it. Grandson to the infamous last Duke of Roudhos? His family tortured and slain before his eyes? Opuntia had revealed none of this during her visits with him and Merle. *Perhaps she doesn't know.*

"So am I, my friend." Noetos turned his head away, though not before Bregor caught the edge of shame on the fisherman's face.

The Hegeoman continued to think things through that afternoon as they walked. The behaviour of the Recruiters suddenly seemed more sinister. How much did they know about Noetos and his family? The fisherman—the *pretend* fisherman, Bregor reminded himself—had obviously chosen Fossa as a hiding place. Now he was being drawn out by agents of Andratan. Could this really be co-incidence? What plans had they all been caught up in? And what role did the Neherian fleet play in all this?

"I give you a choice," Noetos said eventually. "You can leave, now, in any direction you like, though you'll have to go and fetch the pack from Ossern Hill. Or we can rest here today and camp overnight." He sat down on the damp ground and indicated for Bregor to do likewise.

The Hegeoman shook his head sharply at both suggestions, but sat anyway. His useless sprint had taken a great deal out of him.

"What, then? Are you well enough to resume our journey immediately? Is this what you choose?"

Bregor nodded solemnly. What he had heard—what he had coaxed from his oblivious companion—needed to be thought about. Investigated. A need for answers settled on him, along with a conviction that the quickest way back to Fossa was onwards.

"I'll make no secret of it," Noetos said. "I wish to get to the first northern village as soon as I can. Every day we lose is another village fallen to the Neherians, with who knows how many deaths. And my family grows further and further out of my reach. Are you able to come with me?"

Another nod, more emphatic than he felt.

Noetos hauled him to his feet, and they were on their way.

Noetos sensed he had broken something in the Hegeoman. Not just in his throat, but in his spirit. The man, who had been so obviously straining at the bit to return to Fossa, had instead given in to Noetos's purpose, with no clue as to why. Shamed into it, perhaps, or uncertain of his ability to survive the walk home. Neither reason sufficed. He thought it unlikely Bregor had suffered an attack of virtue.

Whatever the reason, Noetos felt the lift in his own spirits. The man was useless, but any company on the road was surely better than none.

They found their way into a wide, shallow basin, drained by a stream running counter to the direction they needed to go. Two paces across, the stream looked diseased, with a verdigris stain at either edge. After carefully wading through the water, they climbed the far slope of the basin. Noetos expected to see evidence of the Eisarn diggings at any moment. It was hours since they had left the summit of Ossern Hill; they ought to have come across some sign of the mine or the Palestran Line by now . . .

Some subtle sign gave him a bare moment's warning.

A glimpse of a wider vista, perhaps, an instinctual feel of space, or a small change in the flow of air. He made a lunge at Bregor's arm, catching his sleeve and jerking him back from the sudden emptiness at their feet. He fought to arrest his own momentum, and caught a whirling vision of the ground—huts, piles of stones, layers of orange rock, the tops of trees—far below. Bregor sprang back, sending them both tumbling to the ground at the edge of the chasm.

"We have found Eisarn," Noetos said, unnecessarily, after a long silence, and crawled forward.

Stones dislodged by their scrambling were only now clattering to the pit floor, hundreds of feet below. The fisherman watched, hands on knees, as three tiny figures emerged from a nearby hut, cast their eyes over the area, then shouted something up to him. The fractured cliffs of the pit garbled the words. Something angry, no doubt. More men joined the group.

Noetos replied by gesticulating left and right. *Work it out*, he willed them. *Which way down?*

Eventually one of the men understood, and waved to the fisherman's right. Noetos waved back in acknowledgment. "Come on, Bregor," he said wearily, and plucked at the man's collar.

They found a path a few minutes' walk along the edge of the pit, marked by a collection of rusting shovels and picks. No more than a pace wide, it plunged over the lip, then wound off to the right, notched into the side of the enormous quarry. Knowing the likelihood of the Hegeoman tripping over his own feet at any opportunity, Noetos kept a hand on his shoulder.

The immensity of the pit began to affect his nerves,

making his feet tingle and filling his head with mad ideas of falling. He could hear his tutor's voice in his head: *If one man can dig a rectangular hole five paces wide and two paces deep in a day, how many men would it take . . .* He shook his head in annoyance. *Far too many.* The tiny-seeming trees at the far edge gave him some idea of scale, as did the collection of huts, the minuscule figures beside them still pointing in their direction. Beyond the huts he could see machinery of some sort, wheels and gears, from which came a nerve-abrading grinding. Further away still, horses and donkeys grazed on bales of hay. Sensing the beginnings of dizziness, he jerked his head away from the unsettling view, studying instead the near-vertical rock-face to his right. Layers of crumbling dirt alternated with rust-coloured rock, as though some giant—presumably the same giant who had later dug the hole—had spread lard and honey over bread again and again. The clearly defined boundaries of each layer sloped down towards him, making the path seem steeper than it was.

"Dangerous," came the hoarse understatement from in front of him.

As they wound around the northern wall of the great pit, a clearer sense of the space began to emerge. A thousand paces wide, a thousand long, two hundred paces deep, Noetos estimated; then, acknowledging his tutor, he added: *It would take a thousand men four thousand days, master.* Over ten years! Unless the hole had already been here, and men had simply enlarged it. The side of the pit nearest to the Palestran Line sloped much more gently and, as they approached, he noted it was made of a different type of rock. Crushed rock, darker, mainly grey with some brown. A mixture of the lard and the honey?

Halfway to the bottom of the pit they came to the Palestran Line, which climbed the shallow gradient out of the quarry. A man drove a two-mule cart up the Line towards them; the small tray was laden with the brown rock, and neither the drover nor his mules looked in any hurry. Another cart, this one empty, drew towards them from a distant notch in the rim. Noetos waved it down.

The drover, clearly used to giving rides, indicated the tray without comment. Minutes later Noetos and Bregor found themselves walking towards a small group of ragged men.

"Who're you an' whaddiya want?" one asked, a tall fellow with heavy brows.

"No threat to you," Noetos replied. "We are two fishermen from Fossa village, a week's walk to the southeast."

"Heard of it," another man acknowledged. Thin and tousle-haired, with pale, dirty skin and black hair growing from his ears, he was not a prepossessing sight.

"So that's who you are. Who you *say* you are." This from a third man, stockier but just as dirty. "What's it you're wanting?"

"Help," Noetos said bluntly. It wouldn't do to try to win these fellows with clever words; it would be the facts or nothing. He knew the type, had sailed with them every day. Until recently. "Help, not for us, but for the fishing villages north and east of here. The Neherians are raiding. Their whole fleet is out there."

"They raiding mines in their ships, then?" one wag asked, a youngster, clearly not old enough to remember the ever-present threat from the south. His comment did not bring the laughter he had been expecting.

"No. But when they have burned all the towns and villages on the coast, where will they look next? Where does the real wealth of Palestra lie?"

"Something in that," the first man said, rubbing the stubble on his jaw. "Need to go up to Altima fer that, fetch enough men to drive off the longboats. Presume they still usin' longboats?"

The man's words heartened Noetos: he sounded like one who had dealt with the Neherians before. "Or we could hurry north," he said, "and warn the villages in their path. They could choose to fight or flee. Someone could be sent to Altima and to Tochar to raise the army, but the villages come first."

"Risky, that. Like as the salties have men posted on the roads t' warn 'em."

"We'll have to go around them, approach the villages from the north," Noetos conceded.

"Why? Let the fishermen take care o' their own," the youth said. "We should stay here, git ready to face 'em. 'Sides, we got the mine to run. We're due a bonus, and I ain't missin' it. An' Duke Eltos ain't gonna be that happy if we bust off t'play heroes."

A few men voiced assent to this argument.

"H'aint you bin lisnin?" said a smaller, older man who looked as though he'd just been taken from a pickle jar. "We let these buzzards get themsel's the coast, we'll be next, and you c'n bet they'll come down on us like a tunna slag. You want that, you're more a fool than Ma named you." He clipped the youth hard over the ear.

"What about Eltos?" the ear-hair man asked plaintively. "He'll be sore if we run off 'n' leave his mine to run down."

"Be sorer if we let the Neherians wreck it, or take it fer 'emselves," said the first man. "Time we had a vote."

"Besen't we wait 'til dayshift come out?" asked the stocky man. "Maybe some o' them'll be wanting t'bash Neherians too."

The first man, clearly some sort of overseer or foreman by his words, addressed Noetos. "Y'reckon we can wait 'til rimdown?"

"Rimdown?" the fisherman echoed, puzzled.

"Shift changes when the sun kisses the rim o' the pit. We go down, they go up. Good for us in the summer, good for them in the winter. About an hour from now."

Noetos sighed. "We would be better to wait for morning, I think. I certainly couldn't imagine trying to find my way east in the dark, though I'm loath to give another village away."

"Ah, but we miners see well in the dark," the overseer said. "Though you might be right. It'll give us time to find our weapons, sharpen 'em up good." He leaned closer to the two villagers. "I lived in a fishin' village on a time. Used t' go fish-stickin' with a fearsome gaff. You use gaffs? Ah well, no matter. Kymos, that's the name of the place where I lived. Got chased out by a woman I angered. Had a gaff in her hand, as I remember." He rubbed his chin.

"You tellin' fishin' stories?" one of the men called.

"Just tellin' 'em about my gaff."

"Gaff? That what you call it? Where you been stickin' it lately?"

"Kymos?" Noetos interrupted. "The Neherians have already visited Kymos. I'm sorry."

"Have they now." The overseer scratched his face.

"Best I find me a good sharp gaff, then, and see if Neherians wriggle like fishes."

Shouts of encouragement followed this avowal.

"Don't need a vote," the stocky man said. "Plenty a'
volunteers."

"Maybe we can conscript some farmers on our way,"
Noetos added.

"Maybe. We'll be better at warning than fighting, I'm
thinking," the overseer said. "We'll take the mules.
They'll get us there quicker."

"And maybe you might help me recover my wife and
son," Noetos said carefully, wondering how far he could
push these men. "They're being held captive, as are many
villagers." No need to mention by whom, not yet. "My
daughter . . . My daughter Arathè was murdered." Half-
truth, but it would serve. "This is all I have left of her," he
said as he pulled the carving out from his pack and held it
up for them to see.

Immediately he knew he had done something wrong.
Silence worked its way back through the group of miners,
the men holding themselves absolutely still, focused on
the object in his hand. Somewhere behind him a mule
walked endlessly around a grinding machine, the only
sound in the otherwise sepulchral pit. Noetos looked more
closely at the bust of his daughter, wondering if it had
transformed into something strange, capable of bringing
so complete a silence to the voluble miners. A religious
silence.

"Er," said a man near the back of the group. "Excuse
me, fellow, oh my, yes. Could I . . . could I come and have
a closer look?"

Increasingly nervous, Noetos took a step backwards.

"Why? Have you seen her? Did she come this way? What did she do?" He imagined her, pawn of the Recruiters, casting Voice-spells on the miners, killing some, sparing others. "What is wrong?"

"The stone," said the man at the back, forcing his way forward. "Oh my, the stone. I promise I won't touch it, but could you just hold it out so I can look?"

Bemused, Noetos did as he was requested. The man came close, then stepped back and with a cry of "Just a moment!" went dashing off into one of the huts, only to emerge a minute or so later with a curved glass.

"Hold it out, sir, if you would," the man said.

As he did so, the fisherman took note of the difference between this man and the others: he was clean, untouched by the dirt and dust that begrimed the rest of the miners.

"I am an alchemist, and I should be able to tell . . . yes . . . oh my, oh my." He looked up from his glass, the full intensity of his gaze boring its way into Noetos's eyes. "You don't know what this is, do you?" he whispered.

"I would have said it was a carving of my daughter, but I am guessing that is not what you mean."

"Oh dear, dear me, no. This is huanu, that's what it is," the alchemist said, and fifty people behind him exhaled as one.

Noetos sat on a rough wooden bench in the alchemist's untidy and crowded hut, his head whirling like the change of tide through The Rhoos, and listened as the nature of his carving was explained to him.

"Oh my," the alchemist said, running his hand through his sandy hair. "What you have here is a piece of huanu stone. You haven't heard of huanu, right?"

Noetos shook his head slightly, though the word did tickle a buried memory. Beside him the Hegeoman nodded, eyes alight.

"Understandable; most people consider it a fairy tale, if they've heard of it at all. Looks like your mute friend knows something."

"Not mute," Noetos admitted. "Just injured. He said something I didn't like," he added, with a meaningful look at the alchemist.

"Oh. Oh my. Well, if you must employ violence, please leave my hands alone, if you would. I need them for my work. Most important work, yes; though now you are here, perhaps not as important as I thought. Hmm." Another glare from the fisherman cut him short.

"Hm. My, well, we mine here for iron ore, so everyone thinks, and they are right, of course. Except in reality we seek the huanu on behalf of Duke Eltos. In every seam of ore one can find—if one is very patient, very skilled, very fortunate perhaps—a small amount of huanu stone. By small, this is what I mean."

He pulled a set of keys from his pocket, took one and opened a heavy-looking safe set in the stone floor. After a moment of careful exploration, he pulled out a tiny glass vial filled with water, brought it over to Noetos and Bregor, and held it under their noses.

"Huanu," he said, gently shaking the vial.

"I can't see it," Noetos said. "There are too many little gritty bits of sand . . . oh."

"My, yes, oh indeed. Let me explain. Eisarn Pit as you see it now is on the move. A thousand years ago it was just outside Altima, not as wide or deep as now, just an exploratory pit, testing the viability of the seam. We dig, following the ore, and fill the hole behind us with spoil, thus moving Eisarn gradually southeastwards. Even back then, at the northwestern edge of the deposit, it was clear that a minuscule amount of huanu was mixed with the ore. We test it, you see; perhaps we can show you." His face lit up, as though he were a parent on All-Gift Night.

"Later, later," Noetos said, intrigued and frustrated. "Tell me about the huanu."

"Very well, yes. Well. Somewhere in the seam the huanu stone is concentrated; it is this way with every seam ever mined, though the amounts involved are still very small. Very small," he repeated, casting a covert glance at Noetos's carving sitting on a small table in front of him. "We mine the ore, yes, and Palestra becomes rich, but we look for the huanu."

"Yes, oh my, yes," Noetos said mockingly, his patience at an end. "But why, Alkuon be begged, why? What is so special about huanu?" Beside him, Bregor sighed and shook his head.

"Why? You ask why? Did I not say? Oh dear. Huanu is the most valuable substance known. I'm sure I said that. Your carving there is worth all of Palestra, with plenty left over."

What? "But, but," Noetos spluttered, his hand reflexively grasping at the bust of Arathé, "but why? What makes it so valuable, and why haven't I heard of it? What does it do?"

"What does it do? Oh my. Actually, you should know, if my guess is right. May I?" The alchemist held out a quivering hand.

Noetos fought his reluctance to surrender the carving. *Is it more valuable now than when it was just a likeness of my daughter?* "Of course." He placed his daughter into the alchemist's hand.

"Now, look closely. The stone is pale green, with swirls of white. But look here and here. Two tiny flecks of blue." The spots he indicated were so small as to be barely visible. "Well, this is the thing. The value of huanu comes from its ability to resist magic. Absorb it, defeat it. When magic is used near huanu, the stone draws the power in and neutralises it. Oh my, yes. Am I right in thinking you have been close to a wielder of magic in recent times?"

A shimmer of blue fire spreads over the door to his house, which collapses in a sheet of flame. The Recruiters loose their power upon him; it flares brightly against his closed eyelids. A momentary blue crackling around the carving in his hand, then nothing. Shouts of anger. A tentacle of dreadful power reaches across Nadoce Square, searching for him, striking him, crackling and vanishing, leaving him unharmed.

"Yes, I have." Noetos sighed and wiped his hands on his trousers. Beside him Bregor voiced the word in a breathy echo. "Yes."

"My oh my, then I do not have to explain why this substance is so valuable, do I."

Not a question, but Noetos shook his head anyway. A substance that repelled magic would keep a kingdom safe from the sort of sorcery regularly employed in the struggles for power in Bhrudwo. And oh, had he only known its power, he could have used the stone to help save his family. Could have attacked the Recruiters without fear of their magic. *Still could.*

"It's my job, you know. My career," the alchemist continued, leaving Noetos to work through all the implications of what he had just heard. "Finding the huanu, that is. No one knows why the stone is found in the ore, or why it is deposited in such characteristic leads. Gantha of the Timon guild says the seams are made of the detritus of ancient seas, and that the huanu stone is the petrified remnants of a magician, or magicians, or perhaps a magical animal. Wrote a paper on it, he did, and gained the favour and financial backing of the pretender to the Palestran throne. Oh my, it didn't do him much good when his patron was assassinated. Me, I think he was wrong. What sea have you heard of that is many leagues long and only a few hundred paces wide? And why would a magician be found in every one of these unnaturally narrow seas? No, most certainly not. I've even heard philosophers seriously postulate that huanu is the by-product of conflicts between the gods. Bah!" He shook his head at the foolishness of academics.

"My theory is that the seams are the result of stars crashing to earth. Happens, you know," he said defensively, as if expecting Noetos and Bregor to laugh at him. Their impassive faces left him puzzled. "Well, it would explain the shape of the ore deposits, that it would," he continued. "And the huanu, of course, is the remnant of the star itself, so is not of this world, according to my theory, and so contradicts the natural order. See, a perfect explanation." He sighed. "It can never be proved correct, sadly, unless I'm present when a star falls. One always hopes," he finished wistfully.

"Alkuon forbid," Noetos said.

"Yes, Alkuon indeed. I know he is just a curse word to you seamen," the alchemist said, his words rattling in the fisherman's brain, "but did you know Alkuon was originally a stone god? Oh yes, worshipped by miners everywhere. Now, I have a question for you, yes, just one."

Noetos raised his eyebrows, not exactly an encouragement to continue, but the alchemist seemed unable to pick up such cues and proceeded to ask his question regardless. "Where did you find it? Can you tell me?" He leaned forward, curiosity all over his face.

"On a small island in the midst of The Rhoos," Noetos answered, ignoring the Hegeoman's exasperated head-shake and hiss. "There are a thousand islands in The Rhoos," he added, "so I protect my village's interests, if there is any village remaining after the Neherians have finished with it. The Rhoos is a series of reefs beginning a mile or so offshore from the village of Fossa. Extends many miles out to sea, and hundreds of miles north and south."

"Fossa, ah!" A broad grin split the alchemist's pale, round face. He dived to the floor, grabbed a scroll—for a moment Noetos thought he sought a weapon, and flinched—and unrolled it there on the cool stone. "Come, come and look." He smiled at the fisherman's hunched, defensive posture. "It's all right, it's only a map, maps can't hurt."

The two men from Fossa gathered around the enthusi-astic, obsessive man. *Geological Map of the Fisher Coast* the map was labelled.

"This line here, this is the Palestran Line, running from Altima southeast towards Ossern. The brown wash is the extent of the seam; see how the road has been built on the slag from the mine. We fill up the hole as we go, oh my, indeed. Here is Eisarn, close to Ossern Hill. We've long suspected that Ossern might be the heart of the seam, the motherlode, where we would find the huanu. Now, here's the interesting part, oh my, yes. If I rule a line here, look, an extension of the Palestran Line in the same direction, where does it cross the coast?"

"Fossa," whispered the Hegeoman.

"Not conclusive proof, oh no, but excellent circumstantial evidence. Yes, yes. One enormous seam with Fossa at the centre. No wonder you recovered such a large huanu fragment. We may have to shift our operation there, you understand. Was there . . . was there much more of it, did you notice?"

Hah, thought Noetos. *They'd have to bring dirt into Fossa to make it a hole*. The image of hundreds of men completing the cliffs so they encircled the village absorbed his attention for a moment.

"Sir? Did you see more huanu stone on this island?"

"Not as I remember. I only picked the stone up by chance; it dug into my back when I sat to eat my midday meal. I was curious; I'd never seen rock like it. Thought it might make a good sinker for one of our nets, but I changed my mind when I came ashore. Opuntia—my wife—liked the look of it."

"How did it end up as a carving?"

"I took it to Diphona of Hupallage, a master carver. He shaped the stone, though it defeated all but his sharpest blade. Cost me five gold coins."

"Oh my, oh my. What did he do with the splinters and shards?"

"I have no idea. Look—I don't know your name— could this not wait until we see to the task at hand?"

"Olifa is my name, yes, though they all call me Omiy here. Their little joke, ha ha. Oh yes, this can wait. Ignore me, I'm forever curious, always have one more question. Like to drive people mad, they tell me. Oh my. It's just that the cast-off fragments alone would be worth a kingdom. Think of how long Palestrans have been digging along the Ossern seam. We have a few dozen jars such as the one I showed you, and ten tiny nuggets. I found one of them—the smallest of the ten, half the size of a fingernail—but many alchemists working at Eisarn over the centuries can't even claim that, oh no. Fifty-one jars, ten nuggets. Rewards for a thousand years of labour."

The door of the hut banged open and a bald head poked inside. "Is it true?" enquired its owner in a deep voice. From the hungry look in his eyes Noetos had no doubt he referred to the stone, not to the Neherian fleet.

"Patience, Papunas, we are almost finished. The day shift will get their chance to look, oh my, yes. Tell Seren we will be out in a minute."

The minute was more like ten; but eventually the three men emerged from the hut to face a hundred or more miners gathered around in a semicircle. The alchemist opened his mouth to speak, but before he could make a sound Noetos moved in front of him.

"I'll show you the stone because I know it is important to you," he said. "But let no one forget our main business. The Neherians are destroying the fishing villages north of here, and we can save lives if we can warn their inhabitants. Now," he growled, turning to Omiy, "conduct your test and be done with this."

"Aye, we'll see the test," the overseer of the night shift said.

A small, shy lad stepped forward from the mass of miners. *Young to be a miner*, Noetos thought, surprised.

"Put the stone down on the ground over here, if you please," he said in a squeaky boy's voice.

Far too young. Nevertheless, Noetos did as he was bid.

With no warning conjuration the boy flicked a finger at the grass growing by one of the huts. Instantly a few blades caught fire, accompanied by a hissing noise. Noetos jumped back, startled.

"Looks like fire magic, but it's water magic right enough," the boy said. "'S my job here, testing rock for huanu. Any huanu here, I find it."

He turned to the bust of Arathé, nestled on the stone floor of the pit, and gestured with his hand. Noetos saw something, a faint blue flash, a pale imitation of the power of the Recruiters. Effective, nonetheless: the flame sizzled against the stone, then vanished, and the boy jerked his hand back with a cry of pain.

"Have a look at the stone," the overseer demanded.

Noetos bent over the carving. "Yes, there is a third blue mark," he said eventually.

He expected cheering, perhaps, or chatter at the least, not this awed silence. Had he just taken away their livelihoods as effectively as if someone had dumped a lifetime's supply of fish on Fossa market? Or was the mining profession to become much more important in the future? Neither, Noetos reasoned. It would be more like seeing the Undying Man in the flesh after serving him for a lifetime. Awe and terror mixed in together.

"We all see the proof," said the night-shift overseer, iron in his voice. "Anyone who tries t' take the stone from its keeper gets thrown from the south rim, are you hearing me? Now, there'll be a shy moon tonight, so we wait 'til first light 'fore we go off to warn the villages. Get plenty of sleep. We'll be goin' fast and light, and we won't be hangin' 'round for stragglers."

"Shy moon?" Noetos enquired of the alchemist, in whose cabin he and the Hegeoman were apparently to be billeted.

"Hiding behind clouds; yes, clouds and rain tonight. Not our friend, the weather, but consider how much more difficult the villages will be to burn tomorrow. Oh yes, friend enough. Now, to bed and to sleep."

"I hope so," Noetos said. A thought struck him. "You don't talk in your sleep as well, do you?"

"Oh my, no. What a waste that would be!"

The fisherman turned to his silent companion. "At last, something in our favour," he said as they reached the alchemist's hut, and was rewarded with a smile.

If Noetos had thought the alchemist an odd fish before, it was nothing to his behaviour once they entered his hut. Without a word the man began to gather up his possessions, including his maps, scrolls and clothes, assembled them on the floor and then wrapped them in a large sack. He followed this by taking the precious vial from his safe and placing it in a pocket of his shirt.

"Right, clearly we cannot sleep here tonight, indeed no. I will commandeer one of the empty huts nearer the Palestran Line and we will sleep there. Come, then; gather your things and make a pile by the door. We'll make our move as soon as darkness falls, oh yes."

"What move? Why can't we sleep here?" Noetos asked.

"Observation, oh my, yes. The key to survival, it is. Did you not observe the faces surrounding you? Some of their owners are, I am sure, right now thinking about your stone, yes indeed, and soon they will be plotting how to relieve you of it, yes, oh my, yes. Who wants to be here when they come to get it? Not I, for one, undeniably not. Seren and Papunas will be pressed hard to control them, that is if Papunas himself is not leading one of the groups to take it from you. And they will not bring magic to bear against you, oh no; they will use axes and picks wielded by their ore-toughened arms, that they will. Axes and picks. Do you want to observe that?"

"You've made your point," Noetos said wearily. "We'll sit here and eat something from our packs, since no one has offered to feed us, and then we'll follow you. Just find us somewhere safe."

"Not fed you? Oh my, of course, you are missing out on the evening meal. Well then, go and eat, by all means. I will remain behind until it is dark enough to move my possessions. Go on! Follow the others; they'll all be going to the dining hall."

Omiy explained that in the hall there would be safety in numbers: none would dare move against him yet, lest they be attacked by those of like mind but greater prudence. Later, in the midst of night, it would be a different tale.

"Go and eat," he repeated. "But keep the stone hidden, oh my, so as few as necessary are tempted."

Noetos and the Hegeoman, more of a ghost than a person without his voice, found their way to the large but sparsely furnished dining hall, and were given food—reconstituted meat and turnip, barely palatable, but welcome nonetheless—and, wonder of wonders, warm beer. Beer was served thrice a week to the miners, but apparently every night to the possessor of a huanu stone.

The fisherman supped his drink while listening to the chatter, grunting a cautious, barely civil reply to anyone who tried to engage him in conversation, avoiding the covetous stares of men Omiy would doubtless accuse of plotting to take Arathé away from him. The Hegeoman had trouble eating, and Noetos was forced to batter the food into a paste before his companion could force it down. Even then it clearly gave him pain.

Halfway back to the hut they were accosted. Noetos turned, already swinging an arm to strike the man emerging from the shadows, but held the punch when Omiy whispered his name. His name, the start of a sentence, or perhaps an expostulation. Who knew?

He took them to a run-down hut fifty paces from his own. Inside, the two cots were dilapidated and covered in spiders' webs, but the alchemist ignored this, dropping himself into the closer of the cots.

"What of my companion? Where will he sleep?" Noetos asked, but Omiy merely put a finger to his lips.

"Ah, I've slept on boards before," said the fisherman. "Go on, Bregor, take the bed. No telling when you'll next have the chance to sleep in such luxury."

The Hegeoman snorted in repy, his mouth quirking upwards at the corners. *Good. The man recovers his humour*, Noetos thought. *Perhaps he will soon recover his voice, and we can go about recovering our families*.

There was straw enough on the floor to cushion Noetos's bulk. He turned on one side, cradled Arathé close to his chest, and fell at once into a deep sleep.

CHAPTER 11

MAKYRA BAY

STAMPING ABOUT, TRYING TO keep warm in the cold pre-dawn air lying thick in Eisarn Pit, was not Noetos's idea of preparation for a rescue mission, especially given the number of times he had been woken during the night.

The first time, innocent enough, had been to the sound of Omiy's snores. The man did not talk in his sleep; he would not have had the breath for it, given the prodigious sounds he made. For a while the fisherman had lain awake worrying that others, knowing of this nocturnal excess, would locate them by the simple expedient of listening at the door.

The second, third and fourth times were disturbances outside, all from the same direction. The second involved a great deal of crashing about, accompanied by the breaking of timber, while the third and fourth sounded like fistfights of some magnitude. *Real Cadere Row stuff*, Noetos thought dreamily.

They emerged from their hut some time before dawn to see the entire day shift standing in a circle around the alchemist's hut, or what remained of it.

Noetos had missed the fire, or perhaps the crashing and banging he had heard during the night had been alchemical explosions. A few rough-looking fellows sat on the rocky ground apart from the others, having various bruises attended to.

"Truss these lads up," said Papunas, the day-shift overseer, grimacing from the pain of a purpling bruise to his right cheek. He gestured, and two men set to with ropes. "Truss 'em tight."

He turned to the ruffians, presenting them with a face like a winter storm. "I warned you boys. Did y' think I was bluffin'? That I'd go back on my word, 'spite speakin' in front of a hundred men who'll despise me if I do? Dupes if you did. You'll be flying at rimfall."

One of the five captives, the youngest in appearance, began to blubber. Three of the others stared defiantly at their overseer; the fourth lay unconscious on the ground. Eventually one of the captives kicked the crying boy in the leg. "Ah, shuddup, Dagla. We took us chances an' we lost. Coulda bin us goosin' outa here with th' magic stone under us arms. Instead we get t' see how deep this pit really is."

"I didn't wanna do it," the younger man snuffled. "But Gawl here said we all had t' stick together. It's all right fer him, he's old 'n' not much use. But why d'y'wanna throw a good pair o' arms like mine off the rim?" His red eyes pleaded with his overseer.

"Did you hear my warning?" Papunas enunciated each word carefully. The young man hung his head.

Noetos could stand it no longer. He knew what it was like to plead for his life. "Overseer," he said, walking over to the knot of captives and onlookers, "I have a suggestion. Will you allow me to present it to you?"

"Go on," the man said warily, taking a fig from a sticky mass in his pocket and sticking it in his mouth.

"We will be sending miners west to Altima and north to Tochar to warn the Palestrans about the Neherian fleet," said Noetos. "The rest of the volunteers are coming east with me to warn the coastal villages. But what about the village the Neherians are about to attack? We should be able to warn those villages to the north of the fleet with little trouble, but there are lives to be saved today if we start now and make haste. I didn't consider it before, because we will likely lose men in any confrontation with the Neherians. But these men here, they are lost anyway. Wouldn't it be better for their deaths to mean something? Or, if they survive, to have redeemed themselves? Put weapons in their hands and let them try to save a village."

Three of the five men raised their heads, hope replacing resignation on their faces. Far better to die in battle than be executed. Better still to live.

Papunas pursed his lips. "How do you know which village the ship-boys will be plunderin'?"

"We don't. But we'll be able to work it out when we see where the Neherians place their lookouts on the Fisher Coast Road. Then all we need to do is follow the smoke."

"An' what's t' stop these lads agreein' to this, then scarperin' t' save their own stinkin' skins?"

Noetos took a steadying breath. "I'll command them," he said.

Papunas spat out the fig. "You? Fishin' man? Who's going t' prevent these friendly boys from jumping you and carvin' out yer tripes?"

The fisherman took a step forward and drew his sword. "Perhaps these friendly boys," he said as his blade flashed once, "recognise competent swordsmanship,"—another flash, and again—"when they see it." Two more flicks and five sets of wrists were free of their restraining ropes, their owners rubbing their raw skin. He'd nicked one, but the man had the sense to hide the blood from his overseer. The youngest lad's eyes bulged with fright.

"Huh. Not bad, fishin' man. Good enough t' take care of this lot. If they'll swear to you, you can have 'em."

He drew close to Noetos. "Watch that Gawl," he whispered. "He's mean and full of tricks. He'll have you soon as look."

Noetos acknowledged the advice, then accepted dubious promises from four of the men. The fifth, still unconscious, could be of no use and so would likely not escape the rim.

"Starting . . . an army," Bregor said approvingly in his hoarse whisper. "Use them . . . after."

"If I can."

The thin, ear-haired miner led a white-muzzled mule towards him. Noetos eyed it more warily than he did his newly sworn men; he had last sat astride any kind of mount over twenty years ago. No chance for practice, however. A series of whistles and shouts were followed by a few frustrating minutes watching one of the miners trying to get his mule to stand still so he could mount it. The embarrassed miner finally asked for help, while all around him the others laughed.

Finally they were on their way. Though these mules were docile, unlike the highly strung thoroughbreds Noetos had become familiar with in his youth, his poise and deftness were slow to come back. The pain associated with sitting on a moving beast returned quickly, however:

before they reached the rim his legs were beginning to
spasm, attributable to his clenching his mount's sides with
his thighs, a useless added protection against falling into
the mine. At the rim he took a last glance down into Eisarn Pit, wondering as he did so how long it would take to
reach the bottom if he were thrown from the rim, and what
thoughts would occupy his mind before he reached it.

Noetos and Bregor were accompanied by ten miners,
five from each shift, as well as the alchemist, a wrangler
carrying extra mule shoes and tack, and his four sworn
men. Seren, the night-shift overseer, commanded the miners, each of whom rode a mule. Noetos's sworn men
shared two mules, all that could be spared; riders had been
sent to Altima and Tochar, taking mounts Noetos now be-
grudged. The animals moved painfully slowly, not much
faster than walking pace, but they were remarkably sure-
footed, negotiating open country without the stumbling
and backtracking he and Bregor had encountered when on
their own. The miners all seemed experienced with mules:
perhaps they took turns driving the carts along the
Palestran Line. Even the Hegeoman coped with the animal he rode.

As dawn broke in a riot of red they passed Ossern
Hill well off to their right, then turned further left,
heading north away from the rising sun, and wound
their way through a series of limestone bluffs, old rock-
bones draped in soft grass. This was familiar country;
not that the fisherman had travelled this road before,
but he had spent many hours riding among similar hills
in the land of his birth. Though the hills stirred unwelcome memories, Noetos found himself comforted by
their velvety ruggedness, as if he were returning home

after a long absence. He would probably be comforted by anything other than the stark bleakness of the cliffs around Fossa, he acknowledged wryly.

By midafternoon they had covered ten leagues, but it was apparent to everyone that they would not make the coast before nightfall.

"We c'n ride some in the darkness," Seren said, "but the moon'll be shy agin tonight, and we don't want t' ride into them Neherian patrols. Best we go on a little way 'n' make camp well short o' the road."

They walked their mounts for three or four hours after the sun went down, the exercise allowing Noetos the chance to work some feeling back into his legs. "Hungry?" a husky voice asked from beside him. Bregor's recovery continued, thankfully. The man was a fool, no doubt, a misguided fool, but his intentions had been honest. He had believed he was doing the best for Fossa, and perhaps he hadn't deserved the treatment Noetos had given him. "Thank you," the fisherman said, and smiled as he took the piece of leathery salted beef his fellow Fossan offered.

Camp turned out to be three canvas lean-tos put together by Noetos's men, whom the other miners had already begun treating as little more than slaves. Following a word from Seren they sited the openings to the west, as the night mist came from the sea; but some time during the night a stiff breeze from the east blew up and woke the entire camp. Two of the lean-tos were blown over, their stick-frames scattered. The miners hastily took the third down before it could collapse. There seemed no point in trying to get any more sleep.

Unusual to get seaward winds before midsummer,

Noetos thought as he helped the others clear up what they could of their hapless camp. *That is, if by unusual I mean never.* As a fisherman he'd become familiar with the rhythms of the land and the sea, the different ways they behaved. The land did not cool down enough to produce seaward night winds until late in the autumn, when the land cooled much faster than the sea. *And this breeze is warm, not cold.*

A flickering off to his right caught his eye, in the direction of the sea. A fire? No, more than one. And the light was the wrong colour. He ran hard up the ridge behind which they had set up camp, careless of his footing, knowing what he would see when he reached the summit.

There was a fire, right enough, much further away than he'd expected, a tiny flicker in the distance to his left, to the north. Not the cause of the lights he had seen. They came again, confirming his guess. Lightning flashed from cloud to cloud at the eastern edge of sight, the flickering enlivening the blackness, silhouetting the billowing edges of what Noetos knew would be huge storm-clouds. They were far too far away to hear the thunder, especially with this wind blowing towards the storm . . . *Ah.* Storms like this one sucked wind towards themselves; by the velocity of this breeze and the distance to the lightning flashes— almost constant flashing now—the storm must be enormous. He could imagine the swirling black rain-skirts, the giant anvil-shaped thunderheads, rearing into the sky. *A boat-killer. I hope no one is out there tonight.*

A moment later he modified his thought. *I hope the entire Neherian fleet is out there tonight.*

No one could tell for certain just how far away dawn might be, so they ate a cold breakfast of oat cakes and salted beef, took water from a nearby stream, tended to the mules and began a slow and careful walk northeastwards, leading the mules by their halters. Before long they crested a ridge and saw the first of the Neherian fires, much closer now. After some debate they pulled back to the near side of the ridge and made their way until they judged themselves as close to the Neherians as cover would allow them. After tethering the mules to thorn bushes and leaving them in the care of the wrangler, the party climbed the ridge and hid themselves just short of the summit.

"I want to know what village they plan to attack today," Noetos said. "That way my sworn men can get there as early as possible. Perhaps we may not even have to fight."

"We'll have to fight to gain that knowledge," Bregor said, rubbing his throat.

"Not if I can help it," Noetos replied.

All plans should be simple, his favourite tutor had taught him in the days when he'd had hopes the young Noetos would become a warrior. This plan certainly was. Of course, Cyclamere always followed this admonition with another: *all plans should be adaptable*. Well, he was not the warrior his tutor had hoped for. Simple would have to suffice.

His spy, the youngest of his sworn men, returned and held up first six fingers, then one. More men than he'd expected, but not so many that they need abandon their plan. He waved the miners forward.

Divested of their belt buckles, coins and anything else that might make a sound, they covered the ground quietly enough. Noetos had counselled them not to look directly at the fire. "Should it come to fighting, we need to preserve our night vision," he explained. "They will be blinded by their own flames."

The men halted just out of the firelight. One guard awake, his spy had that part right, but there were seven others, not six, wrapped up in bedrolls. Sixteen against eight, seven of whom were asleep. Noetos and his friends would win this skirmish, but the fisherman wanted victory with no losses—on either side, if possible. This was not the real fight.

Noetos eased his way around the fire, staying well beyond the reach of the light, until he crouched behind the drowsy guard. One of the miners began making noises like a snuffling pig—quite a talent, really—and the guard's head jerked up. His attention taken by the sound, he did not notice Noetos come up behind him.

The fisherman seized the guard by the throat and placed a hand over his mouth. "No noise," he whispered in the man's ear. A half-nod indicated the man's wide-eyed acquiescence. Slowly and with care the fisherman undid his prisoner's belt, eased it free and placed the scabbarded sword on the ground.

Seeing the guard secured, the miners came forward, clubs and pikes at the ready.

"How do you wake the men in the morning?" Noetos asked softly.

The man licked his lips. "I . . . I whistle."

"Do you? And how do you warn them if enemies approach?" Noetos watched the man's eyes, a trick his father had taught him.

"Ah . . . I would call out," he said. His eyes, easily visible in the firelight, went up and to the right.

Liar.

"Here's my quandary. I do not want you all to die, but if I let you whistle, your men will wake with their hands on their swords, expecting to encounter an enemy, and my friends here will have to kill them. So tell me again, how do you wake the men?" All this delivered in a crisp monotone, the clear diction of soldierly efficiency. *Act how you would have them believe.* Ten years of attendance to hated lessons finally rewarded.

The man's eyes widened. "I shake them by the shoulders," he said, and his own shoulders slumped.

Noetos mimed the action, and his men spread out, one to a bedroll, the others waiting beyond the firelight. Seven pairs of eyes watched him, and when he nodded they shook the shoulders of each sleeping man, while holding their weapon at the ready. Seven men jerked awake to the sight of a club, a pike or a rusty blade hovering over them; six sighed at the inevitable and lay still, but the seventh erupted to his feet with a scream, scattering blankets everywhere. His captor hesitated a moment too long: his feeble strike missed, and the Neherian was able to stumble backwards and draw his sword.

"Good work, Dagla," Gawl murmured. "Shoulda left the boy at home with 'is ma."

"Take my man!" Noetos commanded Dagla, and the boy, anxious to redeem himself, thrust forward with his pike, resting the point between the lax guard's shoulder blades.

Noetos drew his blade and strode forward to engage the Neherian. *So much for the plan. Now for luck.*

"Why are you behaving like this?" the man protested. "We're just travellers on the road!"

Noetos breathed his relief. A confident bladesman would not stop to complain. The fisherman offered no answer to the Neherian's question. Let the man wonder about him.

His opponent was a smaller man, as were most people he'd fought. Shorter reach, but probably fast. Had the look of a well-trained soldier. As it proved the man led with his sword foot and launched a sequence of long-range thrusts.

Noetos had never been a scientific swordsman, despite his tutors' best efforts. No expense had been spared in teaching him the turn of the wrist, the angle of the blade, the movements of large and small muscles, the importance of the back and neck. He knew the theory, and could spar in this fashion if it was demanded of him, had done so when teaching Anomer; but whenever it came to a fight the young Noetos had always reverted to his superior strength.

As he did now. He backed out of reach, then charged forward, as if trying to impale himself on his opponent's blade, blocking the next thrust with a scything sweep that nearly freed the blade from the man's hand. The Neherian grunted and responded by taking a two-handed grip. Stupidity. The man's advantage was gone in a moment as Noetos eased in closer to exploit his strength. A series of heavy strokes had the Neherian scrambling to block him.

"I'm looking to disarm you, not kill you," Noetos panted. His opponent took two steps back to give himself time to catch his breath. "But we are out of time." Noetos followed an overhand blow with a slashing left-to-right cut, angling upwards. The Neherian barely parried the second stroke. He must know he was bare moments from defeat.

But Noetos had another goal. His blows had manouevred the Neherian close to the miners waiting beyond the firelight. One more slash. His opponent was now entirely defensive. As the man readied himself for perhaps his final parry, a dark figure stepped out from the shadows and struck him on the back of the head with a club. The soldier collapsed to the ground with a groan.

"I have no idea whether you are honourable or not," Noetos said to the unconscious man. "Involved as you are with this enterprise, I doubt it. Nevertheless, that was no way for swordplay to end and I apologise to you for it." He paused to wipe the sweat from his eyes.

"And, Seren, I thank you." The overseer nodded, still holding his club at the ready should the man wake. Noetos smiled. "Take their swords. Even if you don't want them, they are better out of Neherian hands. In any case, a sword is an extremely valuable item."

"What d' we do with the N'herians, my lord?" one of his sworn men asked. "Kinda stupid to let 'em go so they can go blabbin' to the other salties."

"Our immediate task is to persuade one of these men to tell us where the fleet is. We will decide what to do with them based on how quickly they tell us what we need to know."

The Neherians heard this, as he'd intended. The faces he could see in the firelight closed to the same determined expression. Not what he'd hoped but, knowing their history and training, about what he had expected.

"Gawl, bring your pig-sticker over here," he said.

The unsavoury miner pulled out his knife from under his jacket, a grin on his thick-lipped mouth, anticipating the next command.

"Noetos, no, I beg of you," the Hegeoman cried, then succumbed to a coughing fit.

"Which one, my lord?" the miner asked, licking his lips. The Neherians pushed their shoulders back into their bedrolls, trying to make themselves smaller.

"Why don't you choose?" Noetos stepped back beyond the fire, leaving the thoroughly unpleasant Gawl to deliberate.

"That one," the miner said, pointing at the most terrified of the Neherians. The youngest, Noetos noted. Good. The young man's face went white. Gawl bent over him. "Hold 'm down, Pril. Tumar, take his legs, but be careful with 'em, I'll be wantin' 'em later. Dagla, come 'n' hold his arms. Come on! You'll learn somethin'."

The youth moved reluctantly, but did as he was told.

"Leave the boy alone, you barbarians," growled a grey-bearded man in the characteristic Neherian flat-vowelled speech. "The fleet is scheduled to be at Makyra today. You will never get there in time, which is the only reason I tell you this. Now, put all thought of torture aside and slay us with honour, as is our right as soldiers. I will die happy as I picture your frustration."

"Honour?" Noetos felt his face heat with rage. "*Honour?* The sort of honour you extend to blameless villagers? Are you asking to be burned alive? What sort of honour does a *Neherian* believe himself to have?"

"I would not expect a witless brute to understand the concept."

The fisherman turned to Gawl. "Give me the knife."

Gawl hesitated, no doubt taken aback by the sudden burst of fury.

"*Give me the knife!*" Noetos roared, and struck Gawl a

blow with an open hand. "Do what I say when I say it, or throw yourself from the nearest cliff!"

The Hegeoman spoke. "Noetos, my friend, we don't have the time for this—"

"Shut your face, you coward. I—*need* this." He picked up the notched knife from where Gawl had dropped it, and leaned over the Neherian.

The Hegeoman felt powerless. Opuntia had often talked of Noetos's infamous rages, but this was the first time he had seen one for himself—*well, not the first time*, he corrected himself, fingering his aching throat. The figure bending over the frightened Neherian was no longer the truculent fisherman but, if he understood correctly, a much younger man who finally had the power to strike back at his hated persecutors, half a life later. *Choose your words carefully.*

"This will not bring back your family!" Bregor rasped, coughing as he spoke.

Noetos froze at his words.

Dare he? He put out a hand and rested it on the Fisher's rigid shoulders.

There was a long moment of balance: he could feel it in the twitching of muscles in Noetos's back. Then the shoulders slumped, and a long breath came from the lungs under his palm.

"Ah, Bregor, you are right, and so utterly wrong," Noetos said, turning towards him with a broken look on his face.

"Come, friend, we have lives to save." Bregor tried to keep his voice level, but it resisted his control. The fisherman's words invited a moment of revelation; the words rested on his tongue. *Neither the time nor the place to tell him you know his secret.* He bit them back, saying instead: "Bind these men, leave them some water in a bowl, and let us make haste to Makyra."

"Aye, that would be best," Noetos said, bitterness thickening his voice. "But *he* comes with us." The fisherman indicated the Neherian greybeard. "A surety against any surprises."

"He will slow us down," Seren growled.

"He may save our lives. He comes. Now make yourselves ready. Dawn is not far away."

Bregor watched the miners move about with surprising efficiency, though when he thought more on it he realised such efficiency would be required in order for the men to work underground together. Noetos wandered away from the firelight, gave Gawl back his knife, then slumped forward, hands on knees. Alarmed, Bregor took a few steps towards the man, then thought better of it. Not a battle he could help with.

They headed north along the Fisher Coast Road as the sun rose behind them and to their right. The road here ran wide and straight, offering little cover should they come across another Neherian patrol. Noetos's captive remained tight-lipped when questioned about this, no doubt believing that Noetos would not torture him. *Not a belief I would trust to*, Bregor thought with a shudder.

"Time to leave the road," Noetos announced, and tried to pull his reluctant mount to his left, where rough country stretched to a foreshortened horizon. Bregor kept a smile from his face as he watched the struggle: clearly the animal enjoyed the ease of travel offered by the road. Though it wouldn't do to have Noetos lose his temper again. Sighing, he eased forward and waited while the fisherman tugged uselessly at the reins, then slapped the mule hard on its croup. The animal jerked forwards, nearly unseating its rider.

"Oh my, can anyone else smell smoke?" the alchemist asked in his irritating voice.

Noetos answered with a cry of anger, and dug his heels into his mount's flanks. "Come on, you foolish animal!" he yelled. The mule laid its ears flat and trotted forward a few paces. The fisherman looked around wildly.

"Seren! Take your men and ride north! Stay off the road. Omiy has the map; you must warn the villages. We will deal with Makyra. Go!"

"Just so's you know, we ain't happy about this," Seren said. "You marchin' off to the Neherians with th' huanu stone in your pocket. Anything could happen. Nothin' worse than the salties gettin' hold of it."

Bregor had been wondering when it might come to this. He was surprised the miners had left it this late to express their concerns. "They might already have their own supply," Noetos said. "After all, they fish in and around The Rhoos."

"Oh my, there's no call to take the stone into battle," the alchemist said. "You could—"

"Don't even think of suggesting I leave the stone with any of you," Noetos said. "I'm taking my sworn men to help the people of Makyra Bay. You are riding north to warn the coastal villages of what is coming. No further arguments! Off with you!"

Still they hesitated, then Seren echoed the command and the miners trotted off across the Palestra Country, disappearing from sight beyond a ridge.

No further commands were needed. Bregor gave Noetos's mule another slap of encouragement, and the seven men were off across The Champleve at what passed for a gallop, heading for the Neherian fleet.

The sure-footed beasts took them across the grassy ground with a surprising economy of effort. Even Noetos's mule gave no further trouble. *Inquisitive animals; perhaps they want to investigate the source of the smoke? No telling with mules.* Bregor was more worried about their companions: the captive Neherian, head jerking from side to side as he rode with Gawl, less dangerous than Noetos's sworn men. Should the miners decide to oppose the fisherman they would surely overwhelm him. They would have no mercy on his companion, Bregor knew. His bowels rumbled at the thought of being cast from the sea-cliff.

Which suddenly opened wide before them. Makyra Bay described a wide curve in the Fisher Coast, island-studded, sun-caressed, hemmed in by The Rhoos. The Neherian fleet lay at anchor off the bay, sails furled. Something looked odd about one or two of the ships . . .

"Damaged rigging, hah!" Noetos crowed. "Caught up in last night's storm, praise Alkuon!"

Bregor watched the man's gaze move to Makyra's wide beach, his pleasure evaporating as he saw the flames. The same pattern as at Kymos: longboats drawn up, villagers in a large group on the beach, being led to the boats, while a smaller group were held apart at sword-point. Flames, not long set to houses, crackled and spat, their burning sending increasingly tall columns of smoke into the sky.

"Find the nearest path," Noetos said urgently.

"No need," the Hegeoman replied. "These mounts will

pick their way down all but the steepest cliff. This way might be best." He indicated a narrow gut to their right, hidden from the beach by bushes.

"Follow Bregor!" Noetos commanded his sworn men, and just like that the Hegeoman rode at the head of an invading army.

Of seven—no, six—men, he reminded himself. The utter absurdity of it finally penetrated his brain. *Noetos seems careless of his own life, with some reason. His sworn men are dead should they refuse to fight. What is my excuse for this suicide?*

Too cowardly to stand up and be a coward, he decided, and giggled to himself at his own crowning foolishness.

Amid a clattering of stones they reached level ground, still some distance from the beach. The strip of coast was much wider than it had seemed from the cliff-top.

Now what?

Bregor prayed fervently for Noetos to have an attack of cowardice, or even common sense, but his prayers were wasted.

"We can do nothing for the villagers being herded into the longboats," Noetos said. "Not yet. But we might be able to prevent any burnings today. Bregor, stay here with our mules and the Neherian. Take Gawl's knife and back the prisoner to death if he moves or makes a sound. The rest of us will sneak our way into the village. If the Neherians repeat the pattern we saw at Kymos, we will be ideally placed to rescue the village leaders."

The Hegeoman wanted to protest. Two pleas formulated themselves in his mind: one begging to be taken with Noetos and his sworn men, to avoid the shame of being thought craven; the other not wanting to be left alone with this trained soldier. Hack him to death? He even entertained momentarily the idea of leaving the Neherian and simply fleeing. In the end his mouth remained closed and he nodded what he hoped was the appearance of brave agreement, while closing his hand tightly on the knife.

He withdrew a little way up the narrow culvert, giving him a wide view of the bay. By the time he had secured the mules and his prisoner, he could see Noetos and his men running between buildings, drawing close to the smaller, more heavily guarded group of villagers. He found it difficult not to shout instructions to them, especially as he could see men walking purposefully through the village, going in and out of homes, most likely searching for villagers who had hidden themselves. *They must be forcing someone to give them a complete list of all who live in the village*; Bregor wondered what form the "forcing" would take.

He adjusted his position for a better view, and heard a rustling sound from close behind. He barely had time to turn before a black shape landed on him, driving the wind from his chest. He tried to voice a cry for help, but could not summon the air he needed. The shape drew back. A man—no, a woman. Did women sail with the Neherians? Her freckled face was screwed up with fierce hatred.

"Scum!" she hissed, and raised a weapon. "You'll not take me prisoner!"

"No, lady, you are mistaken—"

Down came the weapon, cracking against the side of his head, and Bregor's world dissolved into rising white light followed by descending darkness.

One of Noetos's men lay stretched on the ground, writhing in pain, and they had not yet confronted a single Neherian. The lad Dagla had twisted his ankle on a loose cobble, crashing to the ground with such a noise Noetos had been sure the Neherians would be drawn to the spot. Cursing the boy's carelessness, while knowing he was being unfair, Noetos carried him to one of the houses, with help from Gawl.

"You'll have to take your chances here," he said to the boy, who bit his lip in an attempt to make no noise. "For Alkuon's sake, stay out of sight."

Noetos set no store by omens, but this was not a promising beginning. Though perhaps they might do better without Dagla; the lad did seem to deserve the scorn Gawl heaped on him.

"Swords out," he said as they came to a cobbled road. "We will get as close as we can to the villagers. If we are seen by Neherians, we are to run. That is a command. If you get caught, there will be no rescue. If events fall out badly, make your death mean something."

"I'm here t' kill, not t' die." Gawl smirked evilly as he fingered his Neherian sword, which undoubtedly he would use as a club. Nevertheless, his miner's strength and unpredictability would make him a difficult opponent.

A shout from behind. Noetos spun around to see a Neherian staring at them, twenty paces away. Just one. With a curse he sprinted towards the man, ignoring the startled cries from his men. *If I can just get this one before he warns his fellows, nothing will be lost . . .*

His quarry ducked into a alley. A moment later Noetos swung around the corner into the sandy lane and crashed unseeing into a group of Neherians, knocking them to the ground. The advantage of surprise saw him up on his feet a fraction before his enemies.

No chance to run.

No desire to run.

He held his sword tip-high, waiting for the trigger. They were Neherians, they would provide him with one. Six of them; one at least was bound to be a fool.

"Well, finally something of interest in this puerile village. A man who can hold a sword." This from a bony man with a pencil-thin moustache.

"But behold, brothers, how he grips it! Does he look to club us with it, or has he just returned from beating his wife's washing?" General laughter.

"Perhaps his wife was one of those we had earlier. Most of them were ugly enough to be married to this fellow."

Trigger enough.

No backswing, no warning, just pure strength, he pushed the blade down and to the left, and threw himself after it. He struck the bony man just above his knee-guard, felt the reassuring pull of the sword biting into the flesh of the man's thigh. He jerked the blade after him, rolled once and fetched up against the side of the lane. The bony man had only just begun to wail when Noetos let out a roar and charged them all from their right.

The first rule of effective swordplay is to take your opponent's space away from him. The calm, measured voice of Cycalamere, the best of his arms tutors. With his manoeuvre he now owned the lane; his enemies were backed against the opposite wall. No space to swing their blades unless he backed away. Which he was not going to do.

Madness, one part of his mind cried, but the fear was drowned in twenty years of exaltation. He brought to bear every scrap of knowledge, every remembered trick, and all of his physical presence. High cut to the right, a stab-and-twist, then a flurry of defence as three swords drove at him. Two blows he parried; the third found a way through and sliced a flap of skin from his forearm.

The blow drew something up from where it lurked, buried deep within him. He screamed with rage, then began to beat at the dumbfounded Neherians with his blade, in precisely the fashion they had mocked him about. But they had no inkling of his strength, and the years of guilt that stiffened his arm.

Blow after blow, a dervish dance of carnage, careless of his own defence. A blade, lifted in a futile attempt to block the madman's blows, was driven down into its owner's helm. The fisherman's next stroke took the helm and the head inside from the man's shoulders. One man tried to crawl away; Noetos kicked out at him, his boot taking the man in the ribs with a loud crunch. He felt a prick in his right shoulder, swung blindly and took the fingers from another man.

Time to run.

He spun, leaped over a body and ran for the entrance to the lane.

"Y' didn't run," said a voice. Noetos wiped the sweat and blood from his eyes, and acknowledged the accusing glare on Gawl's face.

"Neither did you," he replied. "But we run now!"

"No need," said the gap-toothed man. "Not bein' chased." They ran nonetheless.

"Then we run a little slower, but we still run. The Neherians know we're here."

"Best y' tell that to Pril and Tumar. They saw you was occupyin' them Neherians, so they went after the villagers."

Noetos groaned, but he had, after all, set the example. "The small group?" Even as he asked, he knew what the answer would be.

"Nope. They went to set free the wimmin' 'n' babes."

"Oh, Alkuon," Noetos breathed. Dead men indeed, they'd chosen to take only one part of his instructions seriously. The wrong part.

"Come on then, Gawl. Let us go and bleed for Makyra."

"You're doin' that already, my lord. Nasty gash, that." The fellow managed to sound glad to be witnessing it.

Don't look at it. Don't give yourself an excuse.

"Why didn't you go with the others, Gawl?"

"Someone had to look after you, my lord. Seein' as you attacked when you was suppos't to run."

There was logic buried somewhere in that, Noetos guessed, but he was too tired to look for it. "Lead on, Gawl," he said, and settled into a steady run.

Bregor awoke to double vision and stabbing pains in his forehead. A youngish woman in a low-cut black dress bent over him, mopping his brow. He felt too ill to react with either surprise or anger, though he knew he ought to be angry that this woman had hit him and surprised that she now tended his wounds. Instead he felt a mild curiosity that she should be attired as though going to a ball.

"I'm not going to ask if you are all right," she said, her voice a staccato salvo of words. "Clearly you are not. Now, how many fingers am I holding up?"

Bregor tried to see her hand, or hands. "Some," he said eventually.

"That is not a good sign. Oh dear, I hit you too hard,

and I ought not to have hit you at all. You are a Palestran, are you not?"

"I am. The Hegeoman of Fossa village, actually."

"Oh! I have a sister there—never mind that. I thought you were one of those Neherians and you had one of ours captive. It wasn't until after I freed him that I realised my mistake. He laughed at me. I thought he would make me his prisoner, but he left."

"Something more urgent to do, m'lady. Like warn the Neherians that a mission had arrived to attempt a rescue."

The woman swore, a vile oath Bregor had heard only on the lips of Cadere Row men, and that only when they didn't think he was listening. "I have made a mess, haven't I."

"How long since he made off?"

"No more than a few minutes, sir. Time enough to warn the others. If you have superior numbers, perhaps it will not matter," she ended hopefully.

"How many Neherians are down on the beach?" Bregor asked, trying to stand.

She put out a pale-skinned arm to support him. "At least fifty, perhaps more. Though some have gone back to their ship with the first of the longboats."

Bregor took a deep, settling breath. He really did feel unwell, but there had to be something he could do to retrieve the situation. "No, we most definitely do not have superior numbers," he said. "Did any of your leaders escape?"

"Only one," the woman said, with a peculiar emphasis on the latter word.

"Where is he? Take me to him!" He took a closer look at her: his right eye was still fuzzy, lending her a strangely incomplete image, but she had stiffened at his words, her face a mask. He thought carefully about what he had said.

"Or her." He closed his eyes and cursed his slowness of mind. "Don't bother; I deduce she is not far away."

"Permit me to introduce myself," she said, and sat down beside him. "I am Consina, the Hegeoma of Makyra Bay. A number of my friends are in deep trouble because I have eluded the Neherians. They do not want anyone escaping their net; if I were to warn the villages north of here, their raid would be at an end. Their anxiety to have me in their custody might soon cost my friends their lives. When I came across you I thought you might be a bargaining piece. I struck you before I thought. I apologise."

"It's all right. Well, that is, it isn't, but . . ." His words tailed off and a horrible thought entered his mind.

"Did they offer you bribes to betray your village?" he asked before he could rein in his words.

Her eyes narrowed. "Of course not! This was a complete surprise, otherwise . . . Bribes? They offered you bribes? You *knew* this was coming?"

"Ah, it can all be explained," he said hastily, his words now coming as fast as hers, despite his sore throat. "But not now. I don't like the idea of the Neherians killing people. That's what they did at Kymos; we saw them burn the village leaders alive." Again he snapped his mouth shut, far too late.

She moaned, and tears leaked from her eyes. "I knew it," she said, her voice aquiver. "They took us by surprise, gathered us all on the beach and divided us into two groups, leaders and the rest. I knocked down a guard and ran, hoping others would follow. When I looked back two guards were in pursuit, but none of my people had tried to escape. They didn't catch me; I'm the fastest in the village, man or woman. I thought the division into two groups spoke of something sinister."

He patted her on the arm, glad he had diverted her attention from his inadvertent confession. "I feel well enough to take a look at the beach. There might yet be something we can do."

He stood, then pulled her to her feet, and they began to pick their way down the narrow valley towards the village.

"What happened at Fossa? Were the leaders killed there also? How did you escape? What did they do with the other villagers?" Her questions tumbled over one another like anxious kittens at meal time.

"Later, later. The Neherians place the villagers in longboats and paddle them out to the ships waiting in the bay. Noetos, our leader, thinks they might be taken south for slaves."

"Oh, oh, the children! This cannot be allowed to happen!" She tugged on his arm, urging him to walk faster.

His head hurt, he felt the beginnings of nausea, but also an odd pride that, at the least, he was not running away.

Noetos peered around the corner of the last house before the beach, then fingered the impromptu bandage on his arm. His vantage point gave him a wide view: the houses fronting the beach swept around in a semicircle, mimicking the curve of the shore. He studied the disposition of the invaders, who had now split into three groups. Nearest were those guarding the massed group of villagers, perhaps thirty men armed with swords and pikes. Fifty paces to their left as he saw it was a smaller group, half a dozen

Neherians with drawn swords pointing at two men lying face down in the sand. His two sworn men. *Not dead; they would not be guarded if they were dead.* He couldn't even remember their names. The third group, ten or so Neherians surrounding as many villagers, stood much further away, near the far end of the row of houses.

The fisherman ran through the list of impossibilities. Attack the third group, two against ten, with one minute to overwhelm them before their reinforcements arrived. Attack the second group, two against six, rescue his sworn men, then attack the third group, four against ten. Or assault the first group, two against thirty. Even if he could guarantee there were no real swordsmen among them—which he could not—the beach offered no tactical advantages. It was not a narrow lane, where one man could dominate a space. No matter which group he and Gawl assailed, within moments they would be taking on practically the entire invading force.

When confronted by overwhelmingly superior numbers, Cyclamere said in that dispassionate voice of his, *disengage. If you must continue the battle, withdraw and wait for the strategic moment. Look to surprise or deceive your opponent. If nothing presents itself, and no reinforcements are due, flee.*

Withdraw and wait. They could not remain in such an exposed position. Nor could they hide inside one of the houses, as they might well become trapped. Up, then. Like all dwellings on the Fisher Coast these beachfront homes had flat roofs, with parapets to shelter behind. A few words with Gawl, followed by a leg boost, saw Noetos on the roof. He pulled the miner up after him, grunting at the pain in his arms and shoulders.

The withdrawal component completed successfully, Noetos settled down to wait. As he stretched his legs to find a comfortable position, Gawl tapped him on the shoulder and pointed—not down at the beach, but along the row of roofs to their left. There, perhaps a dozen houses away, another figure hauled himself onto a roof, then hobbled forward and ducked down behind a parapet.

"Don't any of you people know how to obey orders?" Noetos growled, secretly pleased at the boy's courage.

"Nuh. We go by us instincts in the mine, 'wise the smothergas or the creepin' water gets us," Gawl muttered. "What's that lameborn fool up to?"

The boy limped back the way he had come, then disappeared. A minute or so he re-emerged, this time on a roof further away.

"Ah. Something is happening with the captive village leaders," Noetos observed. They were being herded towards the houses—towards the house upon which roof Dagla lay hidden. "The boy must have anticipated this."

Two of the Neherians detached themselves from those guarding the village leaders and strode purposefully between the houses. A number of dwellings behind them were still ablaze; they approached one and, with care, each selected a burning timber from the wreckage.

"We are out of time," Noetos breathed.

Shouts of rage and fear erupted from their right, jerking their attention in that direction. Something was happening near the longboats, three of which had already been loaded with human cargo. People were spilling out of the vessels, falling into the water. One of the longboats had been holed; one end beached, the other submerged in three feet of water.

The worst scenario for a commander, murmured Cyclamere, *is when unplanned engagement occurs on multiple fronts*. As he tried to divide his attention between the three groups, Noetos wished the remembered voice would shut up.

From his elevated vantage point the fisherman watched, amazed, as two black shapes—seals?—moved slowly through the water beyond the longboats, popped their heads above the surface for a moment—people, not seals—resubmerged and headed for the second longboat. The two heads emerged again, hidden from the Neherians by the bulk of the longboat, and one began to attack the boat with something sharp. A shocked Noetos realised he recognised the face of his village Hegeoman.

Lacking the view Noetos enjoyed, it took the Neherian commander, wherever he was, some time to work out what was happening. In the noise and confusion caused by sixty or more villagers crying out in fear as boats sank beneath them, his orders were obviously lost. Noetos had been trying to identify the commanding officer since he had taken position on the roof, and had narrowed his choice down to perhaps four men, but none of them seemed to be effective in sorting out the mess.

Unplanned engagements do, however, provide an opportunity for a decisive commander to take the initiative.

"Come on," Noetos whispered to Gawl. "Time to go by our instincts."

The man replied with a gap-toothed grin.

They were forced to wait an unnervingly long time—although probably no longer than sixty heartbeats—while the soldiers searching houses or otherwise engaged in the village rushed back to the beach. When the cobbled street

had cleared, Gawl and Noetos scrambled down from the
roof and ran swiftly towards the house on whose roof
Dagla hid; the house, if Noetos understood the situation,
in which the Makyra village elders would be burned alive.

Cries of pain and anger greeted their arrival. Signalling
Gawl to remain at street level, Noetos climbed an external
ladder to the roof. Dagla started when Noetos appeared at
his side, then offered him an enthusiastic grin.

"Well, m' lord," he said, "I'm makin' my death mean
somethin' as you told us." So saying, he took up a stone
from a pile at his feet and hurled it over the parapet. A
thunk, not unlike the sound a fish made when it hit the
deck, and a cry of pain. "I'm a good shot," he added unnecessarily. "Lotsa stones at Eisarn Pit, lotsa time to
practise."

Eyes wide, Noetos peered over the parapet. Five men
already down, including both the Neherians carrying the
burning timbers, which smouldered on the sand. One of
the men was a villager, blood pouring from a wound to his
back. From sword, not stone. Two pairs of figures struggled; the other village elders sat docilely on the ground,
too old or afraid to fight or flee, though no one guarded
them.

"Noetos!" Gawl cried, appearing at the top of the ladder. "Ware!"

He was followed onto the roof by three, no four, Neherians armed with swords. One of them Noetos recognised
from the battle in the lane; from the look on the man's face
it was clear the recognition was mutual.

Noetos smiled. "Keep throwing those stones, son," he
said, patting Dagla on the shoulder. "We'll keep the Neherians off your back."

The boy laughed, a joyful sound.

He didn't need Cyclamere's comment, though it was given anyway. *Should your enemy, by some foolishness on their part, offer you the tactical advantage, take it immediately.*

"Come, Gawl," he said in a voice intended to carry, "you are the better swordsman. I yield the floor to you."

The fools should have set fire to the house as soon as Dagla started throwing his stones. Too late for them now.

Gawl smiled his wicked smile, and drew his sword in his ham-fisted grip.

The Neherian from the lane blanched. "We need re-inforcements," he said, and ran for the ladder, just as Noetos had gambled he would. As one, the three other Neherians turned to see the man disappear from sight. "Hey—" one of them began.

"Now," Noetos said. The three guards flinched at the sound of his voice.

The fight was brief, and ended when Gawl muscled the only real swordsman of the three off the roof. The unfortunate man caught his foot in the ladder as he fell, snapping his leg like a dry stick and leaving him hanging upside down, whimpering in pain.

By the time Noetos and Gawl reached the village elders—stopping only to assist the Neherian swordsman to complete his fall to the street—the beach was in chaos. His two sworn men were still under guard, but only by a single swordsman, whose cries for assistance went unanswered until Noetos ended them.

The situation at the longboats was beyond comprehension. A number of bodies floated in the water, a few more lay sprawled on the beach. The Neherians were divided

into two groups. One fought the villagers, cutting them
down ruthlessly, sticks and poles proving no match for
swords. The second group fled in a longboat—by order or
through cowardice, Noetos could not tell. He could see no
sign of the two "seals."

"Come on, men," he said when Dagla rejoined them.
"Time to risk everything."

"Again?" one of them said, and they all laughed.

Noetos sat on the sand amongst his sworn men, chewing on a hunk of bread. All around him the villagers of
Makyra Bay worked to erase the devastation wrought
by the Neherians. Fourteen villagers slain, the village
Hegeoma had told him, and a number of wounded to
care for. Two would not survive the day. Twice that
many Neherians to bury. A third of the houses burned to
the ground. Boats sunk, livelihoods lost. Celebrations
and grief mixed together in a bittersweet potion.

The remnant of the Neherian soldiers, fought to a
standstill by Noetos's men and the courageous villagers,
had taken the only seaworthy longboat and rowed for their
lives. "You have ensured your own deaths," their commander had snarled at the villagers as he made his retreat.
"We will return, and none of you will be left alive."

Noetos had wanted to wade out into the bay to cross
swords with the man, so consumed was he with battle-
lust, but Bregor had placed a wet hand on his shoulder, restraining him. "He'll not be back," the man said,
satisfaction in his voice. "Just watch."

Halfway between the beach and the anchored fleet, the
longboat stopped dead in the water and shouts of terror
drifted back towards the village. The boat went down

slowly, giving the Neherians enough time to save their lives, had they known how to swim.

"Fancy sending non-swimmers on a ship-borne raid," Noetos said reflectively. "Do I have to ask how you knew?"

Bregor smiled. "You would think a man who cannot swim would take the time to check the seaworthiness of his vessel, would you not? Though I do not remember them having the opportunity. Someone's private army was pressing them hard, as I recall."

"As for swimmers, I did not know Bregor the Hegeoman possessed the ability. Frankly, I'm astonished. The Hegeoman I knew from Fossa wanted nothing to do with the sea."

"You know little of my life, fisherman," Bregor said, an edge in his voice not accounted for by the damage to his throat. "I was thirty years old when you sought admittance to Fossa. What could you know of how those years were spent?"

"That's why I was surprised," Noetos replied equably. "What other talents does Bregor the Seal possess?"

The Hegeoman of Fossa looked Noetos the fisherman in the eye. "I have no doubt we will find out in the days to come," he said, "as we attempt to rescue your family."

Noetos nodded, content, and relaxed for the first time in days. Should the Neherians decide to invest the village he would have plenty of warning. There would be little the salties—he liked the word, it described them well—could do if the Makyrans were prepared to abandon the remaining houses and take the unassailable cliff-top. He asked someone if they could arrange a bath and a change of clothes, then allowed a harried village doctor to tend his wounds before closing his eyes.

COSMOGRAPHER

CHAPTER 12

EMPEROR OF THE DESERT

LENARES SPENT MOST OF each day gazing out of the opening in the palanquin, curtain pulled back, no matter how much Mahudia grumbled about sand in the silks, sun in her eyes or damage to her skin. The pure, un-cluttered beauty of the desert eased the young cosmographer's heart anew every time she looked upon it. Fine gravel, red-grey on brown, crunched beneath their bearers' feet, part of a random yet orderly landscape stretching to the horizon. The others found it tedious. They used words like *sterile* and *boring* and *inhospitable*. For Lenares, the subtle shades of stone and sand acted as an anodyne to the gaudy colours and party-like atmosphere of the expedition, while the gentle whispering of the desert breeze helped mask the brazen shouting and braying of man and beast, and the never-changing horizon of the stone plain they crawled across stood in restful contrast to the constant motion of her sterile, boring, inhospitable fellow travellers.

So sick of their constant complaining did she become that, after the first day out of Talamaq, Lenares ordered the bearers to walk at the daughterward edge of the expedition's wide column. This gave her the best views of the desert. She could look out at the play of light and shadow in the morning, with the low sun casting every stone into sharp relief, perfectly suited to her clear morning mind; while in the afternoon the westering sun blended the gravel carpet into a soothing pattern, easing her towards a blissful state of half-wakefulness. During the latter hours she nodded near the borders of sleep, letting her constant calculation slow and simplify until they almost stopped. Like this afternoon. So peaceful, so perfect.

But no matter how restful the days became, she ensured she continued to count the steps her bearers took, an almost unconscious record of the distance from Talamaq. She had been fearful of this journey, but her counting and the peacefulness left her feeling centred and relaxed. It was almost enough to make her forget the hole that threatened the world. Almost.

"Draw the curtain, girl, and come out of the sun. Look at what it's doing to your skin! You'll be complaining if you get burned again."

Lenares thought the pink tinge to her pale skin looked nice, but she knew ma dama was right, so she pulled the curtain across a little.

"Ah, girl," Mahudia said, exasperation in her voice, "you will dry up like a raisin in the sun."

Lenares laughed at the image: a shrivelled little wide-eyed girl with its wrinkled hand in Mahudia's.

But she was a little girl no more, she reminded herself. She was now a cosmographer, one who didn't have to do everything she was told, who could stick her head out of the opening if she wanted to. One who knew things, important things. Things no one else knew. One who was special.

Her numbers told her many things. For example, she was certainly the only one who noticed that the gravel they crunched their way across day after day was slowly growing larger. It was a trick, of course, she knew that; the stones weren't actually growing, but the further father-wards they went, the larger the stones became. They had been thumbnail-sized on the first day of their journey. Now, a week later, they were the size of her fist. It was as though some giant had stood in a random spot in the desert and scattered millions of stones in every direction, the smaller ones going further. Another image to make her laugh; she chuckled about the giant and the rocks all through the afternoon, until Mahudia told her to be quiet.

So, the numbers whispered to her, *you draw closer to larger things. To where the giant stands with his pile of rocks.* The idea made her a little nervous, so she put it out of her mind.

She tried not to think of the hole in the world either. Whenever the numbers steered her thoughts in that di-rection she would resort to counting the stones. Know-ing something of her mind, Mahudia had warned her not to count the stones. She'd said Lenares might go mad try-ing to count them all. But Mahudia didn't know as much as she thought. Counting the stones was restful. So much of her time in Talamaq was consumed by measuring the relationships between unique things: people, buildings, streets, behaviours; all different, a multi-hued palette that taxed her to her limits. Out here in the stony desert things remained where they were put, and the relation-ships between the stones were not important. Her simple stone-counting allowed her to slip into a soothing one-dimensionality.

Despite the gnawing worry at the back of her mind, Lenares had never been happier.

Torve was deeply unhappy. He found himself in an invidious position. The Emperor had packed him off on this expedition as his eyes and ears, yet his august lord had surely known how little authority or even freedom he would have. When he hesitantly reminded Captain Duon and the other senior staff of the Emperor's commands, he was laughed at. Laughed at, then ordered to serve the captain, and anyone else who bid him, in the same fashion he had served the Emperor.

Not in exactly the same fashion, of course. Captain Duon did not experiment on the living bodies of his subjects, nor did he engage in philosophical discussions with Omerans. When he did notice Torve it was to correct something he had done, such correction given in a bored voice. As though Torve did not matter. After the intimacy the Emperor had offered him, he found this behaviour demeaning, but knew it was what every other Omeran in the empire experienced.

Worse, much worse, was to follow. Some of the lords and scions of various Alliances, having witnessed the Emperor's favour to this Omeran at court, sought to flatter and indulge him at every opportunity. Still more of them sought to bring him low. Jeering, physical contact such as pushes and elbows to the stomach, contradictory or impossible orders and suchlike became his lot. Not a moment to himself from sunrise to sunset. He began to realise he had never known what it meant to be Omeran.

And they, the Omerans themselves, were the worst. They knew of him too, and struck out at him repeatedly for no real reason he could discern. The behaviour of the Amaqi lords and ladies he could understand: he was being used by people to position themselves relative to each other and to the throne. But what motivated his fellow Omerans to spit on him, strike him and shower him with scorn? It distressed him deeply, but he could get no answer from them.

Given all this, which surely his master must have anticipated, why had Torve been sent on this journey? Nothing his lord ever did was ill-conceived, therefore there must be a plan; if so, what was it? His commission was clear: to recover the Bhrudwan, or at least a sample of his blood. But the Emperor had deliberately withheld the power to carry through with it. Was he simply not powerful enough to protect his servant from this distance? Had he miscalculated? Or—and this riddled Torve with worry—had he ceased being useful, and was this a sophisticated way of divesting the Emperor of an increasingly embarrassing companion?

He found his only moments of freedom before dawn and after sunset. Free from the demands of the dust-ridden procession, Torve would take himself off into the darkness, looking to lose himself in the solitude, to create a quiet place some distance away from the tents and the fires and animals and palanquins where he would try to reason out the Emperor's plan. He was usually able to exercise at least part of his Defiance amidst the gravel. He imagined others of the Omerans finding places to practise the ancient discipline, though he had not seen evidence of this at any stage along their journey.

On one such evening he evaded the last of the petty demands from haughty lordlings, hid from the gang of Omerans looking to avenge themselves for some imagined insult, and walked quietly beyond the tethered camels. A group of travel-hardened veterans sat around a fire, drinking *ti* from small cups and playing counters; they looked up as he passed, smiled at him—probably mistaking him for a fellow veteran, dressed as he was in his voluminous burnous, a kind of desert cloak—and went on with their game. He nodded politely to them, then walked out into the silent twilight like a lone ship leaving the safety of a busy port.

The horizon turned turquoise, and then closed in around him as it faded to black. Torve shivered as the sterile heat of day bled away, to be replaced by a creeping coolness that, by dawn, would turn to real cold. He stood still as an owl hooted softly somewhere ahead of him, to be answered by a second owl close by, giving him the sense he'd interrupted an ongoing debate over territory. From the distance came the snarl of a fox. Desert survivors.

He inhaled the night air and blew out a long, sighing breath, as though he could expel the anger and bitterness his treatment had sown within him. Tonight he would make his bed out here, away from the others, alone in the land he had been told when young—by his parents, perhaps—had once belonged to his mother's ancestors. The Amaqi had come fatherwards and crushed the gentle people living here, leaving nothing, not even a name to remember them by.

Torve settled down to his supper: a heel of bread, lightly seasoned with cinnamon, followed by a small pouch of tepid water. The moon rose as he ate, a fragile silver disc imparting a ghostly sheen to the stone plain around him. A few paces to his left lay a small area of sand, piled against a stony ridge. It would do. He laid down his bread and shrugged off his burnous. His Defiance was a morning practice, but the stony ground had prevented him conducting the full ritual. He would take the opportunity now.

For the first time in his life his opponent was an Omeran. No specific person, just a mélange of all those he had encountered in the last week. They sought to reject him, to push him into a state of non-being, he realised as he defended himself against random, uneven strikes. They did not want him to be Omeran. He occupied some middle place, neither Omeran nor Amaqi, and they found this threatening. A foot whistled past his ear: more than one opponent, then. He would be tested.

Defiance had never been so difficult. They were right, they were right: he had betrayed his race by allowing the Emperor to use him; it would be better to find a way of killing himself, better to wander out into the desert until he died of thirst. He dropped onto his back, his legs whirring out in the direction of the expedition camp. Nothing held back, no attempt to establish dominance and withdraw; his kicks were aimed at chests, throats, faces twisted with hatred.

With no warning his opponents melted away like the ghosts they were, leaving him alone, panting as he lay on the sand. *No, not alone.* Three small, dark-skinned children sat huddled together on the gravel, their wide eyes watching him, heads turning in unison to follow him as he levered himself from his back to his knees. Each was dressed in an identical strip of black cloth with a hole in the centre through which to put one's head, allowing the fabric to hang down in front and behind. It was tied at the waist by a cord of rope, leaving their limbs free. Their hair lay in tight curls, uniformly short, and the moon silvered their black limbs. Two boys, leaning forward as though drinking him in with their eyes; one girl, sitting shyly back on her heels.

One of the boys, the taller and so probably the elder, stood and took a step forward onto the sand. He raised his narrow eyebrows and stretched out a hand, palm up. *Asking permission.* Torve nodded, both hands pushing forward, fingers crooked. *Go ahead. Show me.*

The boy glided forward, amazingly light on his feet, and beckoned the other two children to his side; then— Torve's skin chilled as he watched—the three of them mimicked exactly the Defiance he had just completed.

Well, not exactly. Where he had been jerky, they were smooth; where he had overbalanced, they retained their poise. Where he performed a ritual, they danced. An immensely sweet sorrow settled upon him as he watched them measure his worth in their fluid movements.

These are not children of camp followers. Who would let these ones run about practically unclothed in the darkness, prey to wild animals? And he had not seen such faces before, wider even than his own, with the barest of turned-up snub noses, unaffected smiles playing across their lips. And the way they moved, like nothing he had ever seen.

The three children finished their—*his*—dance, and smiled timidly at him. Hoping for his approval. Approval? He wanted to fall at their feet, beg them to explain to him how they turned defiance into dance.

Or perhaps we turned dance into defiance?

He tried to mask his shock at this thought, making his smile as welcoming as he could, concerned he might appear to them like a lynxcat or some other predator. "Here," he said, reaching behind himself, not daring to take his eyes from them, to bring out the remainder of his bread.

The otherworldly children stared at his offering; he put it down carefully on the sand and backed away a few paces. A slender hand darted out, snaring the bread. In a moment the children were nibbling at it, laughing with sparkling dark eyes at the unfamiliar flavour, a language of sibilants flowing between them like the hiss of a fountain in the Garden of Angels. No, an unfortunate metaphor; the thought of that terrible place, of the Emperor and his victims, the children buried there, shadowed the night with ugliness. He closed his eyes and passed his hand across his face.

When he opened his eyes the children were gone.

They must be close by, I only closed my eyes for a moment. There was enough light to enable him to see, but absolutely no movement anywhere around him.

His heart plummeted. *A dream, a desert vision.* Yet there were scuff marks in the sand, too light to have been his, his bread was gone, and a faint, strange scent hung in the air. He did not know what was possible here in the desert. While his logical mind told him to believe the evidence of his eyes, he wondered if his thoughts about ancestors had led to the dream. Perhaps he had noted the marks in the sand before his Defiance, his mind providing a fanciful interpretation.

He lay himself down to sleep, careful not to erase the scuff marks, and dreamed of dancing limbs.

*   *   *

When Torve awoke near dawn the three children had returned. They were kneeling beside what Torve first took to be a weathered rock, but was in fact an old woman in robes of black. All four faces, the three smooth and the one wrinkled, gazed at him with ardent curiosity.

He gazed at them in turn. He found himself unable to give a name to the glow behind their eyes, the light that danced across their faces. Mischief, perhaps; a joyful enchantment, a shining innocence—no, all descriptions were inadequate. Totally bewitching. When the old woman held out a wooden bowl and beckoned for him to drink, he did not think of refusing. Goat's milk mixed with something narcotic; it went down smoothly and lingered on his tongue.

His grin widened as the effects of the drink whirled in his head. The woman stood and indicated he should follow. He gave the expedition and his duties no thought, and slipped away after the four dream-figures, placing his feet in their footprints, stepping on the stones they had used. Five figures bearing away from the camp, even their walk a dance to some desert rhythm.

Torve had no idea how long the journey took, nor which direction they went; at times the sun shone from over his left shoulder, and later over his right. They left the stone plain behind and weaved a path among a dune sea. Finally they arrived at a camp. Seven low leather tents, in the process of being struck. Men, women and children robed in blue or black, the older with black head coverings, moving with efficiency and purpose in almost complete silence, as though they feared discovery. Goats and camels and donkeys, loaded up with everything these people owned, waited patiently for the order to move out.

One of the men welcomed him, offering a hand, palm out. Torve reciprocated, and the man let his palm touch that of the Omeran, drawing it slowly back so that his callused fingers ran across Torve's palm, then pulled his hand away and touched his chest. Words of greeting were spoken, but Torve understood nothing. It did not seem to matter. The others left their packing and gathered around him in a circle. At the man's signal everyone sank to the sand. Torve followed suit.

The people told him a story. The younger children, of which there were nine, walked gracefully back and forth in front of him, as though travelling from place to place. Nomadic, bearing their burdens on their backs. Then the adults and youths, numbering about twenty, stood up and accosted the children. Their movements were jerky, awkward, a pointed caricature of the businesslike Amaqi gait. Dancing around the bemused adults, the children continued on their way, only to be confronted again at the next pass. This time one of the adults knocked a child to the ground as if using a club or a spear. The other children, wearing confusion on their faces like a mourning veil, mimed the burial of their fallen sister; while they mourned, the adults attacked them from behind. Two of the children escaped, hand in hand, darting away from the camp, while the others were beaten to the ground, where they lay still.

Perhaps it was the effect of the narcotic, or that Torve's imagination had been augmented by the simplicity and power of the story, but he believed he heard the thump of sword on bone and the bewildered cries of the people as they were erased from the desert by the callous Amaqi. Though the story was told in complete silence, he imagined he heard weeping, a sound of distress that pulled at him at such a fundamental level he searched in vain for something he could do to help.

The story ended, the man—the leader of the clan, it appeared—bowed to him, every member of the clan filed past him and touched his cheek with the palm of their right hand, and the three children led him away from the camp. Through and over dunes they went, the sand scorching beneath their feet, the relentless sun hammering down on them in waves of oppressive heat; they kept to the shadows where possible, and wound long black cloths around their heads when it was not. Ahead of them the horizon danced, a lake-like shimmer. *Mirage. I've heard of mirages*, he thought woozily, his lack of head covering beginning to tell. *When you see things that are not there. Like that long line of camels and people hovering well above the glittering horizon.* No, that was real. *The expedition.* Somehow not as real as the children accompanying him—

—who were gone.

This day, Lenares considered, had rapidly become the hottest yet. The whole sonward third of the sky was difficult to look at; the sun blazed at them, a small, fierce white circle angry that city-dwellers in colourful clothes would dare intrude into its dominion.

Near noon the palanquin halted. Their chatelain, the man with the fatherback accent, poked his pretty head through the curtains. "Ma dama Mahudia, ma dama Lenares, Captain Duon has judged the weather too hot for afternoon travel. We are resting here for two or three hours until the afternoon cool comes. Can I offer either of you some water?"

Lenares hated the man. Saying one thing and meaning another was behaviour bound to unsettle her; and when this was a man's only mode of behaviour, it set her teeth on edge. He might as well be saying: "I'm doing you a favour, one of many; why not grant me a favour in return?" She knew what sort of favour he would want.

Mahudia, though, was almost as bad. She spoke politely with the chatelain, but Lenares suspected she had granted him at least one favour in the past week. How else to explain the proprietorial smugness on his face, or the eagerness in her voice? Twice now, when Lenares walked through the camp on some errand of Mahudia's, the man had cornered her, his clove-cloaked breath in her face, his hands twitching. Both times she had kicked him on the knee. Next time she would aim higher.

"Water would be wonderful, thank you, Chasico," Mahudia trilled.

"I will fetch a jug for you immediately. Would ma dama Lenares care to come with me? She must be careful to stretch her legs. It would not do for her to be carried all the way to the land of the barbarians. She would arrive there the consistency of a giant dumpling." He laughed genially, his mouth contorting in its lying shape under his predator eyes.

"She will not be going anywhere with you, Sico the Letch," said a gruff voice, and a bearded man appeared at the opposite curtain. "Ma dama Lenares is required to attend upon ma sor Duon at the instant. She is to bring any documents or papers in her possession."

"Well then, we must make ready," Mahudia said, and began to smooth down her robe.

"I am sorry, ma dama, but the invitation specifies ma

dama Lenares and no other. We will return her to you in time for the caravan to resume its journey later this afternoon."

Mahudia frowned but forbore further comment. The chatelain snapped the curtain closed in what seemed like disgust, while Duon's messenger waited patiently.

"I have no documents or papers," Lenares said.

"Oh? You are Lenares the Cosmographer?" The man appeared surprised.

"I'm a special cosmographer," she told him. "I don't need parchment to hold my ideas. They are all stored here," and she tapped her forehead.

"Very well, special cosmographer," the man said. "Come with me, and bring your head full of ideas with you. Captain Duon has others to meet, and does not take kindly to waiting."

The day outside the palanquin was intolerably hot. The intense heat made every step an effort, as though the air pressed against her limbs. Above her the bronzed sky appeared to draw closer. She knew it for a trick of the light, but the sky and the sun reminded her uncomfortably of the skin of the world and the hole in it, growing larger, nearer. There was no one specific set of numbers, no one calculation that offered her warning, but rather a combination of probabilities. How likely was this, given that, that and that? The strange numbers she had invented to summarise these ever-shifting probabilities ticked away constantly at the back of her head, their overall shape bearing a summary colour she had come to regard as predictive. When enough unlikely things intersected in the environment around her, the shape attenuated and changed colour.

As it did now.

A surge of red filled her mind. The shape changed to a funnel, with the narrow end pointing towards her. At the same time a sharp pain seized her temples and squeezed. She stumbled and fell to her hands and knees, cutting her left palm on an unusually sharp stone.

"Are you all right, ma dama?" the messenger enquired, a hand on her shoulder.

"Don't touch me," she said, her words partly mangled by a suddenly thick tongue. Could the hole reach into her mind, or was this shock due to the swiftness of the change?

"Very well," the man said, and withdrew his hand.

She clambered to her feet and sucked at her bleeding palm. The pain in her head died away somewhat, but the redness continued to pulse in time with her rapid heartbeat. She could see nothing nearby to account for the sudden change, even though she knew the hole was drawing closer.

"Take me to Captain Duon, quickly," she gasped out. "He has to warn . . ." *Who? About what?* Her numbers were not yet specific enough to be of any use.

"That's where we're going," said the messenger. "If you would care to follow me?"

They approached a small knot of angry men. "Slaves come and go," said one man, a gourd in his hand. "We buried our Omeran last night. That's why we want to use the Emperor's pet."

The last two words pulsed bright red in Lenares' mind. She halted just outside the circle of men, who were gathered around a well.

"Ma dama, we do not have time—"

"No!" she snapped, slapping at the messenger. "Be quiet!"

"You can't have him because we cannot find him," said a man in the blue robe of the Elboran Alliance. "We have men searching the camp for him, and when he is found he is likely to be incapacitated for a few days. So find another to carry your water."

"It pleases you to humble the Emperor in his absence?" the man with the gourd asked.

"As it would you. A small piece in an elaborate game, to be sure, but we have made the Emperor's pet ours to use."

Something significant was being said, Lenares sensed, but she was slow to work out what it was.

"Or would be, if you could find him!" The men around the well laughed.

"Excuse me, ma sor," Lenares said, her tongue still unwieldy. "Excuse me!" The men moved aside, thinking she had come for water.

Lenares faced the man from the Elboran Alliance. He was a big man, dark-faced and with a well-trimmed beard. She cleared her throat. "You are looking for the Omeran called Torve?"

"We are, girl. What of it?"

"Ma dama Lenares, the Emperor's cosmographer, not 'girl', if you please," she said, her tone occasioning a lift in the Elboran's eyebrows.

"The numbers girl," someone muttered. "The one who put the wind up old Tumille."

"Doesn't look so pretty without that dress," said a voice behind her. Lenares did not turn around.

"As you will, ma dama Lenares," the Elboran said with exaggerated courtesy. "What is this about the Emperor's Omeran?"

"He is currently serving the cosmographers, ma sor," Lenares said, the lie coming from her swollen tongue with difficulty; but immediately it was spoken, the pulsing red light in her head halved in intensity.

"Oh? And when will he be returned? Ma dama?"

"Ma sor, there is no one to return him to." She hoped she had read the conversation correctly. "He is here to serve the Emperor, not any particular group."

"Then what claim do the cosmographers have on him?"

Trapped by her lies, Lenares tried not to panic. "None, ma sor. He wanted us to help him with some calculations. Have we done something wrong?"

The man pursed his lips, and made a small gesture with his hand. A smaller man next to him, attired as a soldier, bowed fractionally and left the group.

He's going to search the cosmographers' tents for Torve. What will happen when he is not to be found?

"No, you cosmographers have done nothing wrong, ma dama Lenares. The status of this Omeran is still unclear. We know the Emperor sent him on this expedition for some purpose, and we are uncomfortable not knowing what it is. Without the Emperor's protection, the Omeran suffers all manner of degradation. It is our mind to protect it. No one likes seeing animals suffer, particularly if by keeping it safe we can serve the Emperor's interests."

Lies mixed with truth. Why did people persist in thinking they could deceive her? As for that, why had she thought she could deceive anyone?

Because she did not want to see Torve hurt.

"Ma dama, excuse me but Captain Duon is waiting . . ." The messenger tugged at her robe, then looked up as the gaze of every man around the well fastened on him.

"Are you on your way to Duon?" the Elboran asked Lenares.

The messenger answered. "Ma sor, this woman has a most important meeting with Captain Duon, and I will be in trouble if she is late."

"Trouble?" crooned the Elboran. "My, my. Are you under the misapprehension that Dandy Duon is in charge of this expedition?" There was a dangerous undercurrent in his voice. The messenger heard it, and took a step backwards. "If there is anything of importance to be discussed, we will hear about it first."

The unfortunate messenger cleared his throat. "With the greatest of respect, ma sor, neither the girl nor I know what the meeting is to be about."

As the Elboran prepared to reply, the red shape in Lenares' mind developed a second and third funnel, accompanied by a roaring sound like nothing she had ever heard. For a moment she thought everyone must be able to hear it, but since no one else reacted, she realised it was wholly within her head. It was the first time any of her visions had been accompanied by such a sound. A dry part of her mind catalogued the occasion for further study.

The noise made the next few minutes' conversation inaudible, though fortunately none of the men appeared to speak directly to her. She began to back her way slowly through the crowd; as she did so the roaring began to fade.

How much longer until the hole in the world manifests itself here? Minutes? Hours? It had been most of a night and part of the next morning between the time she had first noticed the hole grow larger and the arrival of the earthquake in the Garden of Angels. Would she have as much time now?

She was frightened that the hole in the world might be searching for her. She did not know what would happen if it found her.

The soldier sent to look for Torve returned before she could escape the gathering and flee to Captain Duon with her warnings. There was something Lenares recognised about the soldier, though she had never before seen his face. She dreaded what he was about to say.

"I spoke with the cosmographers, ma sor Enui, and though I did not get to see the Omeran, they assured me it was at work in one of their tents." The man delivered his report in the crisp diction of a professional, yet Lenares was certain she had heard him speak prior to this. His pale, watery eyes transfixed her, and the colour in her mind reddened further. *Why is he lying?* "They assured me it would be available for the needs of the expedition later this afternoon. I will fetch it for you then, ma sor."

Lenares kept her silence with difficulty. The soldier surely served the Elboran. Why had he lied? At his word she should have been exposed as a liar herself, and the hunt for Torve would continue. And why was the man familiar?

She raised her eyes to his. A face she did not know, of that she was certain. *Accept my gift to you*, it seemed to say.

A short nod from the Elboran dismissed the conversation, and Lenares turned away from the enigmatic soldier to face the messenger.

"We must go, quickly," she whispered.

The Elboran was not finished, however. "Dryman, accompany the esteemed cosmographer to her meeting with Duon, would you, and report to me on what transpires."

"Very well, ma sor," the soldier replied.

"But you are not invited—" The sentence ended in a squawk as the point of the soldier's knife tickled the messenger's throat.

"Take us to Duon," he said, with all the authority of an emperor.

Dryman the soldier continued to puzzle Lenares as they made their way along the rows between tents. In fact, he defeated her. None of her numbers were of any use; it was almost as though he was a negative, an inverse of a person. Even with the crushing pain in her mind growing ever stronger, she tried as hard as she could to penetrate his mystery as they walked briskly to Captain Duon's tent.

The soldier was slightly below average height, with short limbs and neck. Unremarkable features capped off a forgettable physique. He carried his head high, though, giving an impression of . . . not authority, exactly, but of competence. He seemed equal to anything. The perfect soldier, it appeared.

She had progressed no further in her surreptitious examination of the man when they arrived at the open space in front of Captain Duon's tent. The captain himself stood and began to welcome her formally to the expedition.

Lenares fidgeted through the first few sentences. There was no time for this.

"Captain Duon," she said, her voice cutting across his greeting. "There is a hole in the world. It is approaching the expedition right now. You should warn everyone."

"What? Hole in where? Warn them about what? Is this another of your witchy predictions?"

"No, ma sor. Cosmography, not witchery. The world is

made of numbers, and I can see the patterns they make. Something terrible is breaking through from outside the world. It has made a hole in the patterns. I can prove it to anyone trained in mathematics."

"Yes, I did want to talk with you about your cosmography. They say you are the best of your generation, so I suppose I should expect some . . . er, eccentricity along with the brilliance. I wish to consult you about the expedition; in particular, which route we should take to Marasmos and the supply ship waiting there. There is a debate, you see, among the Alliances as to which of the three main paths is best for our purposes."

He stopped speaking. The cosmographer was bent over, hands over her ears, panting as if she were about to give birth.

"It is too late," she said weakly, and sank to the ground.

She did not fully lose consciousness, though she wished she could. Her head was crammed with intense pain, her ears filled with roaring. When after a minute or so she was able to stand, the roaring continued. It seemed to come from two, no three, parts of the camp. She turned towards the nearest sound: something golden flashed across a row between tents. An animal? Whatever it was, it was the source of the roaring sound.

Or one of the sources. Behind her a second roar rose up. All fear fled in the face of the chance to put a shape, a name perhaps, to the hole. She turned and dashed in the direction of the roar.

A hand clamped on her arm. "Do you think that's wise?" the soldier said.

"Don't care," she answered. "Let me go, I have to see."

"Then come with me," he said, and drew his sword.

Somewhere behind them Duon was shouting orders, but no one appeared to be listening. Thousands of soldiers in the camp, yet none seemed to be organising a defence against . . . whatever it was, whatever they were. Duon forgotten, Lenares and the soldier raced down the path between two rows of tents, pushing past screaming people running the other way.

They arrived at an open space near the edge of the camp—close to her own palanquin, a suddenly nervous Lenares realised. As she turned to look for it, a cry of agony and fear rang out, closely followed by the sound of splintering wood. Her palanquin burst asunder and from it emerged . . . a golden and white shape. No. A woman screaming, her legs held fast in the mouth of a . . . of a *lion*.

Mahudia.

A second figure, this one red, stumbled out of the remains of the palanquin. A man covered in blood. Chasico. He collapsed as they watched.

The lion was a male. Lenares had seen drawings showing the flowing mane, powerful haunches, large jaws. They had not prepared her for the magnificence and terror of the animal.

Lenares had been afraid for herself many times, and had always been able to respond with anger and aggression. This was the first time she had been really afraid for someone else, and it paralysed her.

Mahudia! M—mother!

Mahudia screamed again, pleading for help as the lion dragged her across the stony ground. No one rushed to her aid, though a number of men shouted, attempting to scare the animal away. The lion dropped its prey, placed a paw on her leg, and looked around, confused.

"This is not the way lions behave," said Dryman the soldier in a thoughtful voice. Lenares jumped, having forgotten he was there. "They avoid people. Never would they attack a caravan of any size, let alone one like ours. Something is wrong."

I could have told you that.

"Please," Mahudia said, her voice surprisingly small. "Please, someone."

A phalanx of soldiers marched into the open space from Lenares' left. Four men pulled spears from a barrel, stepped forward and threw, one after another. The first two spears bracketed the lion, the third glanced off its head, and the fourth took Mahudia in the thigh. She shrieked.

The lion snarled, then lifted its head and roared. Every soldier took a step backwards; a few drew their swords. A second phalanx arrived.

"Why won't someone do something?" Lenares moaned.

"Nothing to be done," said the soldier, his eyes strangely avid as he took in the scene. "The woman is dead."

"No, no, she is still—"

The lion dipped its head and took Mahudia's shoulder in its jaws. The snap and crunch of bones would echo in Lenares' mind forever, along with the despairing cry of her only true mother. Up came the animal's head, its prey hanging from its mouth. Another volley of spears, one lodging in the lion's flank. Powerful muscles contracted, then released: the predator leaped forward and loped

swiftly away from the caravan, Mahudia flopping awkwardly in its jaws like a tailor's dummy and making no
sound.

Torve bit his lip, unnerved. Twice now the odd children
had vanished. Both times could perhaps be explained by
his lack of attention, though how did the children know
when to make their leave? Could they have predicted his
distraction, or had they caused it? He could not accept
they were either hallucinations or magical beings, though
both explanations crossed his mind more than once on his
walk back to the caravan. Fabrications born of his desire
to discover his own past? Romantic notions of hidden resistance to the Amaqi? Or the remnants of a culture that
had survived the Amaqi assault, and might one day reclaim lands and power? Too many questions and no way
to find the answers.

Another issue began to intrude on his thoughts. How
was he to explain his absence? No answers to this question either. He stilled himself, preparing for the beatings.
They would come from a number of Alliances, as power
was up for grabs and he had become a symbol. He would
endure their words, their blows. What had the Emperor
been thinking?

As he drew closer to the expedition he became aware
of commotion in the camp. At two or three places along
the strung-out line he could see movement, surprising in
the debilitating early afternoon heat. A blurred shape detached from the caravan and came rapidly towards him,
moving with unnatural speed.

If he had been unnerved before, he was terrified now.
A lifetime of serving the Emperor had taught him much

about the power and cruelty of men but nothing about the supernatural. He peered at the shape, trying to penetrate the desert haze. An animal, a large animal, no, an *enormous* animal, broke to the left of him, bounding on powerful legs, a spear hanging from its flank, something in its mouth.

Torve made no effort to conceal himself, but the creature didn't see him, passing some distance to his left, slowing as it went. *What is it?* The animal disappeared into a shallow basin. Cautiously, Torve followed, flattening himself to the ground at the edge of the slight depression.

The monstrous shape, some sort of demonic cat—*a lion?*—pawed at a ragged shape on the ground. *Oh no*. The shape scrabbled weakly with one arm, dragging itself a few feet away from the cat's claws. It made a thin wailing sound as it struggled. The golden eyes watched with interest, playing with its prey, letting it believe it could escape; then a heavy paw came down on the blood-smeared body. The breath huffed out of it.

The animal padded forward until it stood directly over the body, its face a golden mask. Emperor of the desert. The cat lowered its face and, with a jerk, snapped its victim's neck. Then it settled down to feed.

CHAPTER 13

THE PLACE OF THE GIANT

THE EXPEDITION ARRIVED at the centre of the stone plain three frantic days later. Captain Duon had ordered extreme haste, careless of the welfare of the animals, bearers and soldiers, forcing the caravan to travel even in the heat of the day. No more lions had been seen, but few disagreed with the order. A rumour suggesting people had gone missing spread throughout the camp, increasing the general level of anxiety. No one was spared the extra work their haste entailed. Torve was allowed no more than four hours' sleep a night, though scarcely more put upon than the minor members of various Alliances, who were pressed into bearing palanquins, drawing water from the wells, serving meals and even latrine duty.

The caravan suffered dreadfully from this forced march. The fatherwards trail was not used regularly—no desert trail saw regular traffic—and broke up under the wheels, hoofs and feet of the expedition. Stone chips bruised feet and ankles, crippled horses and camels and shook wagons until there wasn't one in the caravan that did not require repair. Dust found its way into every crack and crevice, affecting everything mechanical and causing discomfort to anything organic. The camp followers, poorly equipped and plodding along at the rear of the caravan, suffered most.

A broad watercourse marked the centre of the stone plain. Incised from sonback to sonwards deep into the regolith, the valley was perhaps a mile wide, and Torve could see abundant evidence that during the rare floods water filled the valley from side to side, many feet deep. The caravan made its sinuous way down into the valley, which at least offered shelter from the hot fatherwards desert wind. There Captain Duon's glorious expedition shuddered to a halt, allowed the dust to settle and drew a collective breath.

Along with a few of the more articulate Omerans, Torve was employed by Captain Duon to notify Alliance leaders of a conference to be held in the late morning. No invitation had been issued to the cosmographers, but one of the Elboran soldiers suggested Torve advise them of Duon's intent. So it was that the Omeran encountered Lenares for the first time since the expedition had left Talamaq.

"Hello," she said, her wan face peeking shyly out from her repaired palanquin. "I heard you were part of this expedition. It is good to see you."

"And you, ma dama cosmographer," he replied, suddenly finding it difficult to breathe. "I was sorry to hear about what happened to your . . . to Mahudia. I'm sure the Emperor, were he here, would add his condolences to mine."

Her face fell. "I am sorry too," she said in a small voice. "The soldiers said you found her body." A single tear leaked from her right eye.

Torve nodded. He had avoided a potentially dangerous moment by telling the soldiers he had pursued the lion from the camp. Eyebrows were raised but, as he had hoped, they were not interested in the doings of an Omeran—unless those doings cast him in a bad light.

Lenares leaned forward. Torve held his breath, hoping she wouldn't ask her next question.

She asked it. "Was she . . . did she suffer, my Mahudia?"

This was a woman to whom it was useless to offer lies, no matter how well intentioned. "She suffered, ma dama Lenares. But she was brave. Even at the end she had not given up hope of escape."

The girl smiled tightly, her hollow eyes glittering. "Did they catch the lion? The soldiers didn't say."

"Oh yes, they caught it. Surrounded it with spear-wielding soldiers and filled it with holes. I mean no insult when I say it was a shame, ma dama Mahudia's death notwithstanding." Torve had learned a great deal about lions from camp gossip in the last three days, though he had no way of knowing what was true. Lions were predators, though, everyone agreed on that. One might just as well kill a cat for catching a mouse. "It was only doing what lions do."

"No, it wasn't," Lenares said in her characteristically abrupt manner. "It was sent, along with two others."

This woman raised so many questions. "Sent? How can a lion be sent? And what do you mean by saying there were two others?"

"Nehane said I was not to talk about it. He says that if I contradict Captain Duon for no good cause I will bring shame and hardship upon the cosmographers. But I don't see how the truth can bring shame."

"The truth can bring shame if people don't want to believe it," Torve said carefully. Talking with Lenares was like negotiating one's way through quicksand.

"No!" she countered angrily. "Shame is something you feel. I refuse to feel shame for telling the truth."

He nodded, acknowledging the point. "And what truth do the cosmographers want you to withhold?"

"The hole in the world struck at us three days ago. Whoever is making the hole sent three things to target three people. I think the other two things were also lions, because so many people claim to have seen one."

"Everyone claims to have seen the lion because they all want to be part of the excitement," Torve said.

"The people I spoke to told the truth," said Lenares with her disarming intensity. Her words made people not only acknowledge her, Torve reflected, but also forced them to choose whether to believe her. Almost like the few remaining priests of the three gods. As though she herself were a god. *Was a god just someone who made outrageous, unprovable claims?* The Emperor would enjoy debating that thought—but, of course, he was not here.

"Then I believe you." He was rewarded with a smile.

"I warned Captain Duon that the hole was approaching," she said, the smile changing to a grimace. "But it does no good to warn people unless I can predict what form the attack will take and who it is directed at."

"Who was this attack aimed at?" Torve asked.

"Me," she answered, without any modesty. The word sounded outrageous. "And two others. I don't know who, and I can't even guess until the numbers become clearer."

"So the lion—I'm sorry, lions—were sent. By whom?"

Lenares looked at him. Such a direct stare. She licked

her lips and answered, "I don't know. But I know *what* the hole is. I need to speak to Captain Duon; we are all in danger."

"Then I will take you to him," Torve responded. "He has called a meeting."

"To talk about the hole?" she asked eagerly.

"Well, I don't know. But you should be there, I think. We will have to hurry; he may have already started by now."

"Are any of the other cosmographers coming? Does Nehane know?"

"I do not think so. Should he?"

A long pause. "No."

He offered her his hand, but she ignored it and clambered out of the palanquin unaided. Someone still looked after her, Torve noted with relief, as she wore a clean, serviceable dress and was as tidy as anyone could be after three hard days' travel. Her beautiful hair had been tied back with ribbons, creating an unfortunate child-like effect. He wished he could untie the ribbons and let her hair loose.

He cleared his throat. "We need to go quickly," he said, and took her elbow.

"Don't touch—" she began, then smiled hesitantly at him. "You can touch me. But only my hand."

He took her hand and tried to will his soul into his newly roughened palm and fingers. Could she sense his . . . his regard for her?

"Your skin is prickly," she said, but did not let go, allowing him to guide her through the camp.

Confusion overwhelmed Torve. Lenares was a girl child, a woman, a mystic, a half-wit, a genius, a goddess. Simple, complex, naïve, vulnerable, all-knowing. He had no right to touch her; the Emperor would send him to the surgeon should he find out. *A half-wit and an animal*, he would say. What could come of this but condemnation? In fact, any Alliance member who saw them together would likely take offence. He dropped her hand, and she made a small noise he thought sounded like disappointment, but could equally have been relief.

From elation to despair in a moment. Torve could not remember feeling so bewildered.

The meeting had indeed begun by the time Lenares and her guide neared Captain Duon's tent. A large awning sheltered the thirty or so invitees, all Alliance members, who sat or squatted on cushions according to preference. There was no place for her.

She directed an angry glare at the Emperor's Omeran. "You lied to me," she said under her breath.

"No, I did not," he replied. "You would have detected a lie. I merely said you should be at the meeting. Not a lie; of course you should be."

Her eyes widened. "That is so," she admitted. "You are clever."

He gave her a little shrug that could have meant anything, but she had the measure of his numbers now. Her comment had pleased him. Silly, when the Omeran was really only an animal, but she felt warmed inside by his pleasure.

She stood at the corner of the tent, behind and to the left of the captain, in the shadows. Torve prudently hid himself around the corner, where he could hear but not be seen. If they saw him, he had told her, they would give him work to do.

Captain Duon was speaking. She dismissed Torve from her mind.

"I wonder how long these lions have been trailing the expedition," he said in a precise voice, every consonant clearly enunciated. "We have found bodies near the camp on two of the last three mornings."

"Bodies? Whose? How were they killed?" By his head covering, Lenares could tell the speaker belonged to the Pasmaran Alliance, possibly a senior member.

"Who they were is not presently known. No one has been reported missing. It has been suggested they came from the camp followers, which seems more likely if the one I saw is anything to go by. As for how they died, each body was covered in cuts and puncture wounds. Very messy." He shuddered.

"Lions, then."

Captain Duon wiped his hand across his long fringe of hair, a characteristic gesture. "No sign of feeding, though, not like the unfortunate cosmographer woman. Why would—"

A blue-robed Elboran lord interjected. "We won't outrun them. We would be better, my lord, to make camp and hunt them down. Then we can move on at a proper pace."

"It is another week to Marasmos," Captain Duon snapped at him, perhaps angry at having been interrupted. "If we stop to hunt lions we may provide some entertainment for your young men, but their—most likely futile—efforts will be watched by increasingly hungry soldiers. We have a bare week's supplies remaining in the wagons."

"Are you sure the supply ship will arrive in time?"

asked an older man wearing the green sleeve-stripe of the Grandaran Alliance. "I always thought that was the weak point of this venture. Never had much faith in ships."

"I'm sure it will," Duon said, clearly searching for patience.

"The animals are on short rations already," one of the minor lords grumbled.

"Not the horses, I hope," said another, obviously alarmed. "We won't win any battles without the chariots."

"If we do not make Marasmos in a timely manner, the horses may *be* our rations," Duon replied flatly.

"What does lion meat taste like?" a minor Syrenian lord asked the fellow next to him, in a voice louder than he'd doubtless intended.

"Not as appetising as human meat, so have a care," Duon said, but spoiled the effect by sniffing delicately as though the thought of eating any kind of meat disturbed him. "We are here to select a route to Marasmos, not to argue about lions. If I am to be forced to hold a meeting when the choice of route is obvious, I do not want it complicated by irrelevancies."

"Three dead bodies—five, if you count the cosmographer woman and her lover—can hardly be considered an irrelevancy." The Elboran lord leaned back, satisfied his words had scored a hit.

"That 'cosmographer woman' was the daughter of your stay-at-home leader," said the senior Pasmaran. "Show some respect."

"Why? She was just a woman. Hudan's a cold-hearted prick, he won't care. Probably busy making more as we speak."

"How many people are on this expedition?" Captain

Duon's face had darkened; he seemed about to lose his temper. "Officially?"

"You would know better than I," the Elboran replied warily. "Ma sor Captain."

"You must have some idea. A large number of them are yours, after all."

"Four thousand or so. There must be twenty thousand soldiers here. What of it?" The Elboran dropped any pretence of civility.

"And another ten thousand camp followers," Duon said. "Cooks, strappers, armourers, blacksmiths, musicians, whores, moneylenders—and a lion or two, perhaps." His witticism raised a polite laugh. "Thirty thousand in total. Of those, we lose at least twenty people every day. Fifty people yesterday. Fights, fevers, fluxes, the three banes of every expedition. Accidents too. Did Aromant here tell you," he pointed at one of the Pasmarans, "that his second cook tipped yesterday's stew over himself and scalded himself to death?"

"Explains the lumps," the senior Pasmaran said, an old man with a grey beard and pitiless eyes. "Make your point."

Lenares could hear the captain's teeth grind together. "My point is that we can deal most efficiently with the lions by adding them to the list of things that cull any expedition. We will, of course, keep a lookout for them, issuing warnings when and if necessary. Each Alliance may detail as many soldiers as they see fit for this purpose. But no chasing after shadows, make that clear to your men. We shall wait for no one."

Lenares stepped out from the shadows before Torve could stop her. "You are wasting your time," she said in a clear, steady voice.

Every head swung in her direction. She knew her words would make them angry, but what point was there in knowing things no one else knew if she had to keep them to herself?

"And you are?" The senior Elboran got to his feet, making ready to dismiss her.

"Ask ma sor Enui," she said, pointing to the big man sitting next to him, the man with the well-trimmed beard she had spoken with at the well just before the lion attack. "Or ask Captain Duon. I am Lenares the Cosmographer, and I have come to tell you not to waste your time looking for lions. They are gone and they will not return."

"Why ever not?" The senior Pasmaran stood in turn, one hand stroking his long white beard. "Once they have fed on human flesh, they will not go back to the gazelle or the camel. They will have to be killed."

"Have a care arguing with this woman," Duon said. "She is the cosmographer introduced to the court by the Emperor. You were not there, ma sor Losanda, but I am sure you were told about her."

"And I, for one, believed not a word of it." The Elboran named Farouq leaned forward, his wide-set eyes taking her in. She stared at him in turn. Her numbers, gathered from the man's expression, his posture and the regard of the men around him, as well as from the little he had said, spoke to Lenares of an iron will, of deep cruelty, an unbreakable pride.

He curled his lip. "Do you know how unlikely it is that a child such as yourself knows anything of value, or can offer even a half-coherent opinion on any subject? I am now into my third thirty years, and I have never seen it. You are no exception, I will wager the entire wealth of the

Elboran Alliance on it. A foil, perhaps unwitting, for the Emperor to dispose of Tumille, and not before time. You who speak of time-wasting, you will waste no more of *our* time. Enui, take your soldiers and arrest this child."

So many numbers cascading from his words, from the ripple of his facial muscles, the flicker of his eyes and of those surrounding him, reactions to key words in his speech. Raw data, processed into shapes and insights. More than enough to stay his unbelief.

Lenares chose her words with care. "You think the Emperor told me about ma sor Tumille? Then did he also tell me that ma sor Enui knows more than he has so far told you about the money missing from your Alliance?"

The three soldiers, including the one called Dryman, hesitated at this.

"How could you . . ." Even the Emperor could not have . . . Enui, have you spoken to this young woman of Elboran finances?" Farouq's fierce eyes, clouded now by doubt, transfixed his subordinate. Around the gathering, men from rival Alliances leaned forward unconsciously.

"No, ma sor," the man said, licking his lips. "She is a witch, seeking to divide the Elboran Alliance. A trickster! She should not be listened to!"

"Makhara, Suweya, hold the man Enui in your custody until I can speak with him more closely. Child, you have won yourself a few moments' reprieve."

"I have done no such thing," she bit back at him. "Captain Duon commands the cosmographers; the Emperor said so."

"Ah, the Emperor," said the Elboran. "Such a powerful man. And yet—do you see him here?" He waved a hand at his soldiers. "What matters outside Talamaq is *effective* power. Duon here commands none of the Alliances. The Alliances command the soldiers. If we choose not to acknowledge the Emperor, then we hold effective power." His dangerous eyes glinted. "Duon relies on us, don't you, Captain?"

"You will only have power over traitors like yourself," Lenares said. "We cosmographers will serve the Emperor through Captain Duon." She clenched her fists and took a step towards the Elboran leader. "And if you prevent the captain from commanding the expedition, you will lose my help and everyone here will die."

"I don't know what you are," Farouq said. "Some sort of unnatural creature, perhaps, a desert *jiran* who emptied out a little girl's mind and took possession of her soul. Whatever you are, I will not allow—"

"Don't you understand?" she shouted at him, spraying those nearby with saliva. "One of the three gods is missing, and I think I know which one! He went missing many years ago, but no one noticed. Why should they? Elamaq hasn't had a true cosmographer in three thousand years! Now one of the remaining two gods feels strong enough to enlarge the hole the Father left behind. The earthquake in Talamaq last moon was caused by the hole getting larger, and the lions were sent to waylay us because we— because *I*—know what is happening! Do you think the attacks will stop? They won't! They will become worse and worse. The desert itself will rise up against us, unless we can stop it!"

Thirty blank faces looked intently at her, each wearing an identical bemused expression.

I am just a puppet show for them. They see me as a . . . a crazed lackwit. They will destroy me before they ever listen to my words. They are all going to die. She began to cry. *Ma dama Mahudia, come and make it better!*

The millions of numbers, the thousands of calculations that sustained the shapes and colours of her inner vision, spiralled up through her being. Out of control. Needing to be expressed. Doubted, disbelieved. Deadly.

"How many times must I prove myself?" Her arm stabbed out. "You! Betrayer!" she screamed at one startled man. "Murderer!" at another. An irresistible cascade. Eyes closed, she no longer saw whom she pointed at. "Thief! Emperor! Lia*rrrr! Oh Mahudia, please help me!*"

The numbers rose to a crescendo, eroding her consciousness like a wind whipping over a dune, then petered out into an empty, forsaken darkness.

This is where the giant stood. He cast his rocks from here and created the stone plain, crushed chunks of granite plucked from the barren mountains around him. From the dust caused by the crashing rocks he made the sand seas. He beckoned the winds to sculpt pleasing patterns in the sand. Here and there he plunged a giant finger into the ground, forming oases of green amid the russet purity. He took form in the desert he had made, and for thousands of turnings of the sun he dwelt there alone.

Numbers, numbers, falling through her mind like rain in a parched place.

This is where the people lived. Spun from the sand, weaned by the wind, the children of the desert gathered together by the pools of water. Lions and hyenas, insects and birds, deer and humans shoulder to shoulder, lapping from the pools. Looking around themselves, wondering where they came from, the children begin searching for their god.

Numbers, numbers, forming calm pools in the seared sands of her mind.

This is where the giant hid. Like a dung beetle he burrowed into the sand, hoping to avoid the people and their demands. But they saw his unchanging shape amongst the shifting sands, and worshipped him. He had created the desert from which they had sprung, and he could not gainsay them.

Numbers, numbers, shaping themselves around the jagged breaks in her head.

This is where the giant became a god. Bowing to necessity, he lived with the people who had chosen him. The god became more like his people as he lived with them, and they became more like him. They, too, began to shape the place they lived in, while he began searching for someone to love. For a long time they lived together, the people and their god, until the Time of Quarrels.

Numbers, sweet numbers, identifying all the broken and scattered parts of her consciousness.

This is where the people fought. Under the weeping eye of their god some ran and some chased, some became predators, others prey. Some made traps and others became snared in them. The quiet pools ran red with blood, and mercy in those times was a rare and precious thing. The god tried to help, but the people were wilful and, apart from two, a man and a woman, none would listen to his advice.

Numbers, numbers, shaping a story to fuse her shattered mind into something workable.

This is where two new gods were born. The god took the woman and made her his Daughter, and took the man and made him his Son. All the other people found their own places to dwell, but the god lived in the desert with his Son and his Daughter, and there they dwelled together for turnings of the sun beyond knowledge.

Numbers, numbers, her reality, her sustenance and betrayal, her blessing and her curse.

This is where the god was betrayed. In a battle of armies without number, the Son and the Daughter defeated their Father and drove him out of the desert. From here, from the centre of the stone plain in the midst of the desert, the god left Elamaq with his few faithful followers. The Son and the Daughter did not kill their father, though they could have. Instead they began an argument that became a fight lasting three thousand years, ending only when one was forced into exile, all her people finally enslaved.

Numbers, numbers, offering cruel revelation that no one else will believe.

This is where the one remaining god began experimenting with the hole in the world left by his Father. Using it to touch the world, to influence events and outcomes, to disrupt and destroy. To enlarge the hole so that he can once again step into the world. He remembers what it is like to be human and wishes to repeat the experience, while retaining the power granted him by his Father, the giant of the desert.

She will remember none of the numbers when she awakens. Pity her.

Torve laid Lenares out on the cooling sand. He had found for them a shadowed place under a red-rimmed overhang at the fatherback side of the valley; safe for now, though later in the afternoon they would be left without shade. He fussed with the sticks he had found under the overhang until he had made a frame he could hang the blanket from. If she had not regained consciousness by the time the sun found its way under the overhang, the makeshift shelter would keep the sun from damaging her.

If she had not regained consciousness by then, she might never.

She had collapsed while screaming incoherently at the most important men of the expedition. Foaming at the mouth like a rabid animal. Some kind of seizure, it appeared, most likely triggered by the frustration of finding herself disbelieved. Cushions scattered everywhere, senior members of various Alliances scattered along with them. Noise and confusion. Lenares convulsing unregarded in their midst. Captain Duon calling for order, no one calling for assistance. Torve forced to watch, unable to help, as the important men dusted themselves off and sought somewhere else to reconvene their meeting.

By the time everyone bar a few guards had left, and Torve could go to her without fear of being seen, Lenares was in a bad state. Tongue bitten, blood and foam all over her face, limbs contorted and still twitching, bruised from where she had crashed against people. He picked her up and draped her carefully over his shoulder. So light, so insubstantial, as though most of her was somewhere else. She did not stir.

There was only one place he could take her. He tried to act as though he had a right to be carrying an obviously ill woman, but despite his efforts his progress attracted stares and comments. The cosmographers had their own tented area near the more informal tents of the camp followers. He made his way towards it.

"Goodness, what happened to her?" a male cosmographer said when Torve found their tents at last; but it was not a question, because the man turned his back when the Omeran began to explain. "Arazma, Vinaru!" the man called. "Come quickly, you are needed. Lenares has had some kind of accident."

Two women, one old, the other of middle age, emerged from the nearest tent and together took Lenares from Torve's shoulder and carried her inside. Through the tent flap Torve glimpsed many curious faces. The man followed the two women into the tent, drew the flap closed behind him and said, just before he went beyond Torve's hearing, "There is no one to tell us what happened . . ."

Abandoned outside the cosmographers' tents, barred from Lenares' side, Torve found he could not leave. Someone from one Alliance or another would scoop him up and put him to work, and he might not get back to Lenares until well after dark, if at all. He would have to hide. Thought translated into action: he found a half-empty hay wagon perhaps twenty paces from the tent, let the nearer side down and squeezed underneath the shelter it afforded.

Barely in time. One of the soldiers from Captain Duon's gathering made his way towards the tent. No doubt a belated thought from Captain Duon—or, more likely, ma sor Farouq. Gather her up if she is still alive. Question her, empty her out, dispose of her.

Short for a soldier, the man walked without that rolling gait they all seemed to adopt. More of a swagger. Definitely one of Farouq's men.

His calls drew the male Torve had seen before. "You are the senior cosmographer?" the soldier asked. An answer in the affirmative encouraged the soldier to deliver his message.

"I am a mercenary newly taken into the service of the Elboran Alliance. Should you see the cosmographer Lenares, my new master, ma sor Farouq, would consider it a personal favour if you were to let him know. He is concerned for her wellbeing, having witnessed her experience a seizure, and believes one of his physicians, skilled in fatherback medicines, can aid her. Be assured that Cosmographer Lenares is not in any kind of trouble, and she will be delivered safely to you when my master has finished with her. Her care is my master's primary concern. After all," he added with a straight face, "none of us would like the cosmographers to experience more tragedy, would we?"

Without waiting for a reply the soldier turned on his heel and strode away. When he was out of earshot a head—the middle-aged woman Torve had seen previously—appeared through the tent flap. "Was that a threat?" she asked the male cosmographer.

"Oh yes," he replied. "Most definitely. Instruct the others: no one is to tell anyone that we have Lenares here. The fool girl has done something to offend the Elborans. We need to find out what it is, while keeping her out of the grasp of that soldier and his master."

"Do we?" A calculating look spread over the woman's narrow face. "Let them have her. Mahudia should never have insisted we go on this expedition, and if anyone ought to have remained behind, it is Lenares Lackwit."

The man winced. "I don't know why Mahudia was so enthusiastic about this journey," he said, sighing. "But I do know the Emperor ordered Lenares to accompany

Captain Duon, and Mahudia convinced him that we should all come. Whether her decision was ill-advised or not, it cost her everything, Vinaru. I think we have an obligation to . . . to her adopted daughter."

"Bah. The lackwit is a disturbance, and undermines the discipline necessary to produce good cosmographers." This last was said as though it were the worst crime the speaker could think of. "The moment I think we are in danger by sheltering her I'll shove her out of the tent myself, and they can do what they like to her."

Torve watched the two cosmographers withdraw into their tent, disturbed by what he had heard. These were the people Lenares had grown up with, yet at least one of them would have no misgivings about betraying her. How could Torve abandon her to her friends, if her friends proved to be her enemies? And what could he do to protect her, if her friends refused even to acknowledge his existence?

All he could do was wait and watch.

He stretched, trying to find a comfortable position on the riverbed gravel. No breeze penetrated under the wagon; the air, intensely hot, was stupefying, and the last three days had seen him worked extremely hard. So what happened next was inevitable. Despite his concern for her vulnerability and the awkward discomfort of his position under the wagon, Torve fell asleep.

He awoke with a headache. He always did after short naps. Four pairs of feet, two shod with boots, two with sturdy walking shoes, stood directly in front of his wagon; the discussion going on above him had pulled him out of a restless sleep.

"Are you sure?" The voice of an authoritative male.

"We *saw* her." A young girl's voice, pleading to be believed.

Another girl added, "Nehane tried to keep her secret, but the rest of the cosmographers abide by the law."

"You are good citizens," said a second man. Torve cringed at the insincerity in his voice. "Once we have the girl, you may come to our quarters for your . . . reward."

Both girls giggled, obviously unconscious of the menace in the man's inflection. "Don't forget our names," one said. "Rouza and Palain, faithful to the Emperor and his brave, bold soldiers."

"Are any of your people armed?" asked the authoritative voice.

Don't answer, Torve willed. *You will ensure the death of anyone you name.*

"Only Nehane," said one of the girls airily. "He has a sword thing, but he doesn't know how to use it."

Torve willed the last of the muddy pain gone from his head. How could someone training for a position requiring a keen intelligence be so simple-minded? He slid out backwards from under the wagon, away from the four pairs of feet, grimacing as the stones rattled under his body.

The second man spoke. "You two wait. No matter what you hear or see, don't move from beside this wagon. You will be safe here."

If that is not warning enough of what you have unleashed, then you are both truly ignorant young women.

Torve forced himself to wait. The thought of Lenares in the hands of the Elborans ate at him, but any foolish action on his part would be seen and dealt with by the soldiers. The two men approached the tent: not until their

attention became fully absorbed by talking to whoever answered their summons did he stand up and walk briskly
away from the cosmographers' area. As soon as he was
out of sight he broke into a run, circling around behind
the tent.

A moment's effort saw him under the side of the tent
and up on his feet. He found himself in a small space, a
partition curtained off from the main room, filled with
three small pallets. He sprang towards the only one occupied, to discover someone hovered there already. A cosmographer, not a doctor. The woman he recognised from
the tent flap earlier, the one who wanted to hand Lenares
over to the Elborans.

"Who are you?" she asked, squinting as though struggling with imperfect eyesight. "You're the Emperor's
Omeran. How dare you intrude on our quarters!"

"Be silent," Torve said, trying to inject emperor-like
strength of command into his voice. "In the name of the
Emperor I claim this woman."

"You are taking her?" She drew a knife from her robe.
"I can't allow that. The girl's lived too long on sufferance;
I'll not have her causing the cosmographers continual
trouble. She draws attention to us at a time when we'd be
best to remain forgotten."

The blade was for Lenares, not him, Torve realised.

"Put the knife down," he growled. Unless she was
blind, she could no doubt see the shock and anger on his
face. *To do this to one of your own . . .*

"It would be a kindness," she hissed.

"Not to her," Torve said. "Now, do as I say and be
silent."

"You're too late," the cosmographer said, malicious

glee ruling her voice. "I sent for the soldiers. They will be here in a moment."

Torve brushed past the woman, gambling that she would not use the knife on him. He lifted Lenares up from the pallet, along with a blanket, and cradled her in his arms. He was aware that his life would be forfeit for this action, but some indeterminate time ago he had stepped over a line he hadn't even noticed, and his current actions seemed fated, driven by some external source. Or perhaps the Emperor was right: each person had but a few real moments of life, comprising the vital choices they made, and the rest was merely filling.

Raised voices came through the curtain. Torve spoke to the cosmographer: "Say nothing, woman, or the two girls you sent will die." Her face confirmed his guess and she held her tongue. She could not know his threat was hollow.

It took longer than he'd hoped to lift the canvas side of the tent, roll Lenares out and follow her, but the argument in the main room showed no sign of ending. He took Lenares up and, even with the threat of discovery, snatched a moment to look on her face. By no means beautiful even by Amaqi standards, let alone Omeran, her features were further spoiled by the absence of consciousness; whatever beauty she possessed came from her animated, almost frenetic liveliness. He looked more closely. She breathed still, but seemed little more than a shell.

He swung his head left and right. Nowhere to go. No ally in the camp to whom he could take her. His only friend lay insensible on his shoulder. Bred for obedience, the Omeran found himself with no one to tell him what to do. Thirty thousand people nearby to tell him what not to

do. He would not listen to them. He would nurse Lenares
back to health and listen to her.

In the meantime, however, she remained unconscious
and could not give him guidance. Choosing what to do,
making decisions that could differentiate between life and
death for the woman in his arms, did not come naturally.
He found it hard to force his mind along unfamiliar path-
ways. *Freedom. They call it freedom*, he told himself.
Then why did it feel like another kind of servitude?

Eventually he chose to take Lenares in a fatherbackly
direction. His decision was made not through any rational
thought process, but because they would be discovered
should they remain where they were. There were good reasons for his choice, though he thought of them only after
the fact: the passage through the camp followers' disor-
ganised tent city took him away from any searching soldiers and made him less conspicuous. He was unknown
here. Certainly, fewer heads turned. Indeed, he saw far
stranger sights than a man carrying an unconscious
woman: a little laughing boy riding a pink pig; two women
wrestling on the stones, hands in each other's hair, being
cheered by a crowd of onlookers; and a desperate knife
fight taking place in the shadows between two tents.

His shoulder ached. Insubstantial she might be, but
Lenares, unconscious, had become a burden disproportion-
ate to her size. Eventually he passed the last tent, worked
his way through the pickets and stumbled out into the desert
solitude. Found a place in the shadows hidden from sun and
soldiers both. And now he sat beside the unconscious
cosmographer, totally helpless, waiting for her to awaken.

Not knowing what he would do if she did not.

*   *   *

He cleaned her face with a cloth strip torn from his shirt and as much spit as he could muster. Waited. Shifted her slightly to keep her out of the sun, arranging her limbs to give her the least discomfort. Waited. Wished he had water to give her, and contemplated going back to the camp to get some, but imagined her awakening on her own out in the desert and decided not to leave her, not yet.

Waited.

The sun caught up with the two of them as it fell towards the daughterwards horizon. He tried to move his makeshift shelter, but it collapsed in a clatter of sticks. Lenares made no response. She was alive, but damaged inside her head. She reminded him of some of those the Emperor had experimented on, looking to capture the moment between life and death, searching for any way to hold life in a dead vessel. They would gaze blankly, free from pain and from every intelligent thought, and die eventually anyway.

No. There was only one thing he could do, so he did it. He performed his Defiance in the face of the sun, in the face of death; and this time he tried to dance it, holding an image of the desert dream-children in his mind as he moved against his impossible, inexorable opponents. Flowing from stance to stance as he had seen the children do, the stances themselves disappearing until everything he did was one movement, and the sun could not trap him, and death could not hold him, and he towered like a giant above the world and everything in it, achieving for the very first time that state of exaltation others had told him about.

The moment lasted forever.

"That was beautiful," Lenares said.

Her voice pulled him back into the world of heat and death. His eyes flew open. Impossibly, there she was, kneeling on the sand, smiling sunnily, her heart in her eyes.

She should be dead, or at least suffering a brain-sick agony. He knew how people who'd had seizures behaved when they awoke. Instead, she crawled on her knees towards him, concern growing on her face, as though he were the sick one and she the rescuer.

Could it have been his Defiance? Had he pushed death back for her? Relief, shaded with awe, flooded through him.

"Oh, Lenares, I was so worried about you," he said, and burst into tears.

Her deep eyes widened. "Don't cry, Torve," she said. "Don't cry."

"I'm sorry. I thought you were dead."

She frowned. "I don't remember what happened. There was a meeting, you were there, we were hiding, and then . . . and then, nothing. Is the meeting over? Why are we out here in the desert? Where is the camp?"

"Lenares, you fell sick—"

"I can't remember! But I always remember. What happened to me? Torve, you were there. What happened?"

Her face, so beautiful a moment ago, now looked drawn.

"Shh now, let me tell you." He described the conversation at the meeting as best he could, then told her about her seizure and subsequent events, remembering that she could see through lies. *What a dreadful gift*, he thought as he explained why they had ended up out in the desert. *No buffer between oneself and reality. A gift—or a lack?* Was the buffer something humans had made to protect themselves? Another thought, as his mind raced: was this part of what separated humans from gods? Did gods truly have no illusions to limit them? The Emperor would say—he put what the Emperor might say out of his mind. The Emperor, a man with few illusions of his own, was not here.

Lenares nodded as he told her about the seizure, and did not become upset. She hissed when he explained the treachery of the cosmographers, and smiled when he described how he had cleaned her up.

"I've had seizures before, when I was a child," she said. "Mahudia called them fits. I had them when people wanted me to do impossible things, like say something wasn't true when it was. I don't remember what I said to Captain Duon and the others, but if they tried to stop me telling the truth it might have made me have another fit."

Torve thought carefully before asking his question. "And did you . . . did you recover quickly after your fits?"

"No, I spent days in bed, mostly asleep, before I—oh." She ran her hands over her face. "Perhaps I have recovered more quickly because I am older." She shook her head. "No, I don't see . . . The numbers only start again after I woke up, and I was already better."

Torve licked his lips. "You were unconscious all afternoon, with cuts and bruises over your face and arms. You bled from your mouth where you bit your tongue during the seizure. When I started my Defiance, the dance you saw me doing, you were unconscious still. But when I finished, you were awake and . . . and healed." *Impossible*.

"Show me," Lenares said. "Show me your dance." She settled back expectantly, as though a mystery was about to be solved.

"Lenares, I cannot. The Defiance is a secret dance. I can't defy my enemies when—" he was about to say *when one of them is present*, but bit back on his words just in time "—when I am not alone. At least, when I believe I am not alone."

She caught his shading of the truth, he could tell, but did not press him. His own thoughts wandered: he had been watched twice recently, once by Lenares and once by the desert children, both times unknowing. But the dream-children had danced the Defiance with him as an audience. Perhaps they had not seen him as an enemy. Or would the Defiance work even when observed by his enemies? If the desert children were indeed of his imagination, perhaps none of the rules held.

Lenares seemed preoccupied with something else. Various expressions chased each other across her expressive face: calculation, thoughtfulness, frustration.

"I have counted the number of steps we have taken since the expedition left the Avensfather Gate," she said. "My own steps and those of our bearers, adding those that went fatherwards, subtracting those that went in other directions. It is automatic, it goes on in my head without me thinking about it." She looked at him as though she expected him to understand. "I have calculations for the angles," she explained. "Even if we travel on a line in a sonback direction, I can work out how far fatherwards we have come. Distance and bearing. I use the sun and the stars too. It is important to me. I need to know where I am for all my other numbers to work. All my other numbers are relative to each other, but I need an absolute. Since my seizure, my counting has stopped. How many steps did you carry me, and in what direction?"

His eyes widened in fear. A trivial thing, but he could understand that she needed a centre, something to base herself on. So similar to his Defiance. He was about to fail her.

"I don't know," he said.

"Then I will have to go back to where I had my fit," she said. "Mahudia knew not to move me after a fit. I suppose you are not to blame." She sighed. "We will need food and water if we are to survive in the desert. We can take some from the expedition. It's not really stealing. We would have used the food and water anyway had we remained with them."

"Go back? Steal? Lenares, they will catch us and put us to death." He didn't know if they would be killed, but they would be imprisoned of a certainty. "What of the hole in the world? If we are killed, who will defend Elamaq against it?"

"We have to go back," Lenares said stubbornly. "Otherwise I will have to start every calculation again. It has taken me years, and we don't have the time. The hole will come back, and if I don't know when it is coming it will get me."

Torve closed his eyes, then had an idea. "What if we wait until the expedition leaves, then I take you to the place where you had your seizure? In the meantime, I could fetch food and water from the camp followers. Wouldn't that be just as good, and a lot less risky?"

She nodded slowly. "It would depend on how accurate you were. Do you think you could tell exactly where Captain Duon's tent had been once the expedition leaves?"

No. How to avoid answering? He would do anything rather than risk her back at the camp.

He turned away, so she would not see his face as he formulated his lie. A small dust-cloud in the direction of the camp caught his eye. Was the expedition moving already? Surely they would rest at least one night? No, the cloud was much closer than the camp . . .

"Lenares, someone is coming," he hissed.

They scattered the sticks, smoothed out the sand and carried the blanket with them as they fled. Torve could not be sure if the cloud meant pursuit, or if whoever came towards them had some other purpose, but he could not wait to find out.

Lenares travelled in a strange world. All her life she had been surrounded by shapes, colours and sounds that threatened to overwhelm her with their reality, their immediacy. She had worked it out eventually: other people had a filter that told them what was important and what was not. They trusted these filters, called them *experience* or *common sense* or, in others, *prejudice*. But to her everything was important. She trusted no filter. How could she ignore anything? When she was young her mind came dangerously close to burning out, overloaded by life.

What had saved her was her developing ability to see the links between everything, and turn those relationships into numbers. Her mind ignored nothing, cataloguing everything, weighing, balancing, selecting.

However, since her seizure she had lost her inner scales. She could no longer weigh and balance the sensations coming through her eyes, ears, nose, mouth and skin. The world pressed in on her, beating at her fragile defences. She tried not to panic, but she needed to get back to the place where she had been afflicted with the seizure.

And now they were fleeing in the wrong direction, it was all she could do to stifle a scream.

The Omeran led her along the base of the cliff; the fatherback side of the valley, he had said, but she couldn't tell. She stumbled along after him, throat dry, legs aching, aches and pains surfacing all over her body as though she were being beaten by an invisible man. They were definitely being pursued, Torve said: the dust-cloud had stopped at the cliff-edge where they had rested, and was now moving in their direction. Perhaps one of the camp followers had told the soldiers about them. Though her body hurt, there was no time to stop and rest.

Darkness came upon them quickly, as it always did in the desert. Behind and to their left a sprinkling of lights sprang up where the expedition had camped, while their pursuers lit torches, illuminating the valley walls. Torve cursed, then reached out and clasped her hand in his.

"Why don't they let us go?" he asked. "If they want us dead, the desert will take care of killing us. Has Captain Duon finally realised how important you are?"

"Do you mean he might take me back? He might listen to me?"

"Lenares, I don't know. It could be the Elborans looking to capture you. We can't take that risk."

He doesn't even consider the risk to himself, Lenares realised. Whether those following had been sent by the captain or the Elborans, Torve would be punished at best, slain at worst. She could not expose him to that, not when he had saved her from the cosmographers' betrayal.

"They are drawing closer," Torve said, panic in his voice. "Quick! In here!"

He pulled her to his left, towards a dark shadow in the

valley wall. *A cave of some sort*, Lenares thought as he jerked her roughly through the narrow opening. She stifled a cry as her elbow cracked against the rock.

It was not a cave. The stars still shone above them in a narrow, crooked slot of diamond-studded purple. She stared at the sky, entranced, and lost her footing. With her hand still clasped firmly in that of the Omeran, she slid then tumbled down a steep sandy slope. Abruptly everything turned icy cold and dark. They had fallen into water.

CHAPTER 14

HOUSE OF THE GODS

SPLUTTERING AND COUGHING, Torve pulled Lenares from the black pool and laid her on the cool sand. Her head had barely been submerged, yet she lay unmoving. She breathed still, her heart beat strongly, her skin was warm and it was unlikely she had swallowed any water. He could not understand what was wrong. Another seizure? Surely not. But full darkness was upon them, and he could see very little by the sliver of starlight above him.

Thunderous voices erupted all around him: ". . . came this way. I saw . . ." ". . . getting too dark to see where they . . ." ". . . don't understand why Duon wants to . . ." A series of male voices, rising and falling, echoing as though the words reverberated around an enclosed space. ". . . uncanny girl, no wonder Captain Duon wants . . ." ". . . don't expect to be out here all night . . ." After a few startled minutes, he realised he was hearing a series of speakers walking past the opening to this place, their words caught and amplified unnervingly by the cavern. At least a dozen snippets of conversation played out before the footfalls faded and silence fell.

The silence was almost complete. Not only were the constant clankings, mutterings and clatter of a normal evening camp missing, the random susurrations of the desert also seemed to be suppressed here, wherever *here* was. An aid to thinking, this lack of distraction, if only he had any sort of sensible decision to make. Lenares had presented him with a cruel dilemma: to serve Captain Duon but stay out of his hands. Clearly he could not leave this sheltered place until Lenares revived, and even then he would have to be certain the searching soldiers had returned to the camp.

Torve let out a deep breath he hadn't known he'd been holding. Safe; after a fashion, at least. The damp air, cooled by the nearby water, washed over him soothingly, chilling his skin. He draped an arm around Lenares' shoulder, nuzzled his face into the back of her neck, and fell asleep.

His bladder woke him not long before dawn. The dark sliver above him shaded towards blue, giving enough light for him to see the face of the girl lying in his arms. She appeared merely asleep; exhausted, not unconscious. He disentangled himself from her, found a private spot and relieved himself, then performed his Defiance.

This time the dance felt natural. A Defiance that worked with his imaginary enemies rather than directly opposing them, using the strength of their attacks to spin him from one stance to the next. Again he reached above the mundane world, his Defiance elevating him to something other than a frightened, confused Omeran. Was this joyous feeling, he wondered, the state in which the Amaqi normally lived?

No, you fool, came a voice from the depths of his mind. *You are in love*.

Love? His Defiance tailed off, undermined by the unsettling thought. He supposed Omerans fell in love, though from what little he had heard, usually in brief discussions between tasks with others of his kind, Omerans were paired and mated by their owners. His own parents he knew nothing about, having been separated from them as an infant, given to the young Emperor by his master. Had his parents loved each other? Or had they been forcibly paired, compelled to forsake their real loves?

Sudden anxiety took hold of him. Lenares was as crippled as he; how could a pair such as they deal with love? That was—his anxiety increased—*if* she loved him, if she was even capable of love.

Most importantly, he wondered, ought he to treat love itself as an enemy? Something to be defied? Anything that might affect his obedience to the Emperor should surely be classified as an enemy; no matter his own wishes, he could not override his breeding. Obedience to hs master was at the core of his being. If the Emperor learned of his pet's feelings, he would order him neutered. And obedience to his master might well demand he not do or feel anything he knew would bring the Emperor's displeasure.

No. He slammed down shutters in his mind. *Best not to think such thoughts*. He could obey his Emperor and still harbour feelings for Lenares—and would do so, until his master ordered otherwise.

He turned and gazed at her. She slept on, breathing evenly, and he felt confident she would wake when her body had recovered.

Dawn had well and truly arrived by the time Torve

finished his morning ablutions. Light—though not direct sunlight—filtered down from the narrow sky over his head, illuminating a wonderland. The walls of the canyon were sheer, though not smooth, coloured a deep red not unlike the houses in Talamaq's Third of Brick. The pool was in fact a lake, filling most of the floor of the ravine, surrounded on both sides by a short strip of sand. Untouched by any breeze the waters acted as a perfect mirror, and in their depths he watched the last of the stars wink out.

The bright morning sunlight crept slowly down the daughterwards face of the canyon. It touched the highest section of red rock, and a flicker of multicoloured light came from a point in the rock and flashed across the narrow gap to the sonwards wall, accompanied by a faint pinging sound. Lenares jerked awake as a second, then a third flicker sent beams of light in random directions, also attended by soft sounds. Down the sunlight marched, and the daughterwards wall exploded in a wild burst of sound and radiance. Beams of light reflected off thousands of sparkling glass-like rock splinters embedded in the red walls, bouncing from one fragment to another, bathing the watchers in every colour of the rainbow, each beam emitting a unique sound so that, in combination, a gentle solar choir sang to them in voices beyond the world.

"Oh," Lenares said, all the sleep gone from her face. "Oh, oh, oh." Her eyes shone with their own glorious light as she watched.

For all its splendour, nothing in the Talamaq Palace had prepared Torve for such an overwhelming dance of light and colour. Subtle rather than brazen, the display continued to change as the sun worked its way down the wall, firing new rock fragments as it came. Then the light began slowly to die, as the sun's angle steepened and it could not reach the deeper-set rock flakes. Like an exhalation of breath the song faltered, the colours faded, and light and sound diminished at last, dying into a bittersweet silence.

This was the reality, then, the Corridor of Rainbows in the Talamaq Palace had been designed to copy. Because the sun took a different path across the sky, every day would bring a new song to anyone dwelling here. And Torve was suddenly certain that someone had indeed dwelled here; that this canyon had been home to some privileged and powerful being; and that the display Lenares and he had witnessed was nothing more than a daily wake-up call, just like the Emperor received every morning, though infinitely more impressive than old Pycunda's feeble knock.

Bewitched, Torve looked about the ravine, searching for other devices and delights. He quickly discovered the slope down which he and Lenares had fallen; climbing back up would be a difficult task. He could barely make out a vertical slit in the rock at the top of the sandy slope, a turn in the canyon beyond which must be the entrance they had stumbled through the previous evening.

In the opposite direction the ravine bent and twisted, then disappeared to the left with a promise of unexplored wonders. They would have to swim if they wished to look further, as the sandy beach did not extend all the way around the lake on either side.

His attention returned to the place through which they had stumbled into this wonderland. The canyon in which they stood was situated not half an hour's walk from the fatherwards path from Talamaq to Marasmos. How could this place not be the marvel of the empire? Why was there not a city built nearby, servicing visitors who paid gold and silver to gaze in awe at the display?

"Torve, please," Lenares said, touching him on his arm. "I must return to Captain Duon's tent. Even now I feel . . . broken. Take me back there, please." Her voice was raw.

He nodded. Once Lenares had recovered her numbers they could return here. "Come, then," he said, extending a hand to her.

The two of them began to work their way up the sandy slope, no more than thirty paces high. A third of the way up, sand began cascading past them, covering their feet and ankles. They eased their feet free and took another step, triggering more sand. With a hiss the whole slope moved, sending them sliding, still upright, back to the beach beside the pool.

Lenares laughed and flicked a tangle of hair out of her eyes. "Again?"

After the third time they found themselves at the base of the slope, this time in a painful snarl of limbs, neither of them laughed. Their efforts had succeeded only in steepening the slope; every movement now sent sand sloughing down in sheets. Torve pulled Lenares to her feet, and shook himself in an attempt to free his clothing of loose sand. Another avalanche hissed past them, much of it finishing in the pool.

Increasingly worried, Torve searched for handholds in the sheer walls either side of the sandy slope. Higher up the wall, well beyond his reach, the rocks were clearly jointed, but lower down they had been worn smooth by water. After a number of futile attempts to force a hand-hold in the wall, he gave up, sucking at a bruised hand and growling in frustration. Lenares began to cry.

An hour later Torve himself was ready to cry. They had fallen in easily enough, but could not climb out. Trapped like insects under glass. Was the canyon simply a snare for inquisitive people? If they dug under the sand, would they find a forlorn scattering of skeletons?

"We must follow the canyon in order to discover another way out." He tried to sound optimistic. There *would* be another way back to the dry riverbed.

"But the expedition may be gone by then. What happens if there is a sandstorm? We may never find where Captain Duon pitched his tent. Then I would have to travel all the way back to Talamaq."

Privately Torve wondered if this might, in fact, be the plan of the intelligence behind the hole in the world. He dared not voice the thought aloud.

"I don't think we have a choice," he said. "We get no nearer to the expedition by remaining here."

As soon as Lenares had refreshed herself and attended to her woman's matters, they left the deep, dark pool behind them. Holding hands, they waded through the cool shallows between one slender, pale beach and the next, drawn on by a growing excitement at what they might find.

The feeling that they walked from room to room in someone's house grew stronger in Torve's mind, enhanced further when the canyon curved left and opened into a circular basin at least fifty paces across.

Ferns and grasses softened the base of the canyon walls on both sides, and framed a small jewel-like lake of seemingly infinite depth. Surrounding the lake were three large rock outcrops, far too regular to be natural, shaped like enormous low-backed seats. Torve scrambled up the nearest of the three and noted the signs of wear, the softening of the angular grey rock where a giant figure might have sat. The basin seemed like nothing other than a reception room, a place for intimate conversation, three large heads bent together.

"Do you think," he asked Lenares breathlessly, "do you think this might be a place where the three gods meet?"

The cosmographer scowled at him. "I don't know," she said. "They can't still meet here, because one of them is missing. I remember that. But without my numbers nothing is clear to me, not even you. Especially not you. Something is different about you today. What is it?"

So direct, as always. He dropped down to the floor of the basin and walked over to her, then took her hand in his and looked intently into her troubled eyes. Perhaps she would understand directness. He took a deep breath, drew her closer, bent forward and kissed her softly on the lips.

"That," he murmured, "is what is different."

"Oh," she said, a gentle exhalation of air against his cheek. "I've known *that* since before we left Talamaq. But I thought Omerans weren't allowed . . . weren't allowed to . . . Mahudia told me it is dirty with Omerans, since they are animals."

He pushed himself away from her, something deep within him wounded by her careless—no, her *direct* speech. "It is true," he said, not looking at her. "True that the Amaqi and Omerans both consider relations between their species dirt—distasteful. But not true that Omerans are animals. I am not an animal, Lenares. Look, there are birds here in this place. Are they filled with awe because they dwell in the house of the gods? They are not, but I am. How can I be called an animal? Compared to a bird or a beast?"

Her gaze was at once tender and confused. "But the birds fall in love here, like we have," she said, and with her words Torve's traitorous heart leaped. "They . . . they mate and have chicks. Are we not just like them?"

"You are no animal," he said.

"Lenares Lackwit," she said in a singsong voice, as though mimicking the voice of another. "Fit for living with the pigs, a smelly, silly swine." Her face screwed up in misery and silent tears ran down her cheeks. "Don't touch me."

"Why not?" Torve asked, though he let her hand go. "Because I am an animal, or because you are?"

"Because everyone thinks we are. The cosmographers would shun me if they found out. The Emperor . . ."

"He would send me to the surgeon. He doesn't want to breed from me. But, Lenares, why do you care what the cosmographers think? They were willing to hand you over to the Elborans. And how can the Emperor command me to forsake you when he is hundreds of leagues away? Until we are once again in the place where our betters command us, can't we do as we please?"

She bit her lip and sniffed, her tears drying on her face. "Mahudia put up with me because of what I could do. The others, even Nehane, didn't really like me. Rouza and Palain and Vinaru hated me. Everyone, even Mahudia, treated me like a pet with a poisonous sting. But you . . ." She choked back a sob. "From the first you liked me, loved me, for what I am. And I . . ."

"Yes?" he prompted.

"I am in love with an Omeran," she said, and buried herself in his arms and wept.

*   *   *

In the course of the next few days Torve and Lenares walked through the many rooms of the house of the gods. They drank liberally from the numerous pools and were harmed by none; partook of the bright red berries from small trees growing in crevices in the rock, and felt no need for other sustenance. They wandered into a beautiful play-room one evening, a bowl of shining blue stone surrounding an orange pool, water-sculpted shelves arranged like seating for an audience. As the sun set they watched a chill mist rise from the lake, to be formed by a gentle breeze into an endless variety of fantastic shapes. Torve imagined he could hear children's laughter echo faintly around the bowl as the misty grotesqueries cavorted before them.

The next morning they bathed in a warm, steamy pool with a faint rotten-egg smell and watched the play of rippled light on the red rock walls above them, then went on to discover a long hall in which both walls towered over them like breaking waves, smooth-sided curves with vertical fissures completing the illusion. A reminder, perhaps, that there was a more mundane world beyond the beautiful desert. Torve and Lenares walked through the hall quietly, hand in hand, so as not to shatter the illusion and cause the waves to break over them.

Whenever they walked together they held hands, but seldom did they kiss. It was as though they teetered on the brink of a depthless precipice, and the merest step forward would plunge them both into a chasm of cascading events neither could escape. Battered and broken by those who should have loved them, it was no surprise they were themselves cautious, Torve reflected. Their constant touching seemed as much for reassurance as anything: was she still there? Did he still feel the same?

They spent a frustrating morning clambering through and over an enormous tangle of odd-shaped rocks, which Torve eventually concluded was a nursery for a colossal child. An evening's camp was made at the base of a gossamer waterfall trickling from a spring high in the sonwards wall, the late sunlight creating the illusion of blood seeping from a wound. Another spring, this one emerging from a slot at ground level, they found to be icy cold and provided them a great deal of splashing and dunking fun. A hall between rooms featured a series of visually jarring carvings, most of which were beyond their comprehension. The occasional animal was recognisable, as were two desert scenes, but was that an enormous snake winding between the dunes, or perhaps an improbable river in the desert? A final room, truly unearthly, featured no less than nine perfectly circular pools arranged in three rows, each pool shaded by a tall plant with broad leaves. Neither Torve nor Lenares could work out what the room might have been used for, but he guessed from the foot-polished stone floor that this chamber had seen more use than all of the others.

In all this time there had been no side corridors, no alternative routes, no lessening of the steepness of the canyon walls. So it came as a distinctly unpleasant surprise when the final room came to a dead end, a vertical cliff-face surrounding it on all sides except the narrow notch through which they had entered it. Torve sat on a rock with his head in his hands, while beside him Lenares whimpered in frustration.

A frenzied desperation took hold of Torve, forcing him to his feet. He ran to the nearest wall and grabbed at the

rock, looking for handholds. Abandoning his usual caution he threw himself against the rock and worked his way
up from the rocky floor.

What use is this? a voice in his mind asked tartly. *Even
if you scale the wall, Lenares can't. Do you plan to leave
her here?*

Never!

The rocks in this wall were compressed, squat, brick-
like shapes, some sticking out further than others, providing plenty of handholds. He managed to climb past the
smoother outcrops, rounded by the action of water over
centuries, and to reach the more angular rocks, which
gave him an easier passage. But the wall tilted above his
head, and he found himself climbing under and then
across an overhang. The rocks were more angular, yes, but
were also much more brittle and began breaking off in his
hands. Somewhere below him—he would not look
down—came a splash from one of the pools, and a concerned cry from Lenares. *Perhaps I can steal a rope from
the expedition, or plead with someone for help, if I make
it up this wall.*

He came to the end of his desperate energy, and found
himself hanging from the cliff, toes and hands dug in just
to hold him in place. He reached for another handhold,
tested it, put his weight on it—and it came loose in his
hand. He clutched at the rock-face, failed to find a hand-
hold, and a foot slipped. He closed his eyes in defeated
acquiescence as the rock in his other hand came away
from the cliff.

He landed in one of the pools, though from the agony
searing up and down his back as he sank into the pool's
depths, he might as well have landed on the stone floor. A

rock bubbled past him, disappearing into the blackness below. He tried to move his arms and legs, to swim back to the surface, but they would not respond.

A new agony seized him, a fire across the top of his head. He could not even struggle as his scalp seemed to lift off; then, as Lenares pulled him to the surface and to the edge of the pool by his hair, he gave thanks that he had not been able to fight her.

Despite Lenares' increasingly manic anxiety they stayed in the last room the rest of the day, allowing Torve to recover feeling in his arms and legs. His back was a mass of bruises, and the cold water Lenares continually applied to it eased the growing pain as feeling returned. He had heard of people crippled by similar falls—had seen one, the result of one of the Emperor's more spectacular experiments—and acknowledged his good fortune.

Although Lenares lay beside him that night, sleeping deeply, Torve could find no rest. Too many actions contrary to his nature combined to trouble him. The realisation that finding their way out of this enchanted place might be difficult—or impossible, if the enchantment was real—fought with his desire to have Lenares here to himself for as long as possible. *We could live here forever, feasting on berries and drinking the magical water of this place. What need do either of us have for masters if we have each other?*

But Lenares was compelled. He understood such compulsions. She had to find the hole in the world, had to confront the being she sensed behind it. It was what she believed she was made to do. And the only way to the hole was out of this place and back to the tent of Captain Duon.

He worried at it until dawn, then groaned as Lenares pushed away from him. "Torve," she said, excitement edging her voice, "was that light there yesterday?"

He squinted in the direction she pointed, into a narrow shaft of sunlight that came from the base of the cliff directly opposite the notch that had admitted them to this last room. A shiny stone? He scrambled after her, clutching his lower back. No—a way out. The smallest of holes, almost completely covered by sand; it would have been—was—invisible except when the dawn light shone through it.

They both dug at the sand with frantic hands, and for a time their hopes were dented as more and more sand came cascading in through the hole. But gradually the flow lessened, and at last they managed to uncover a threadlike tunnel under the cliff, stretching straight towards the sun. Torve took a last regretful look at the room of the gods, then plunged into the tunnel, Lenares at his heels.

The Omeran and the cosmographer found the expedition's campsite easily enough. The tunnel leading from the house of the gods brought them back to the wide river valley, a day's journey upvalley from the fatherwards path on which the expedition had camped. They did not know this, of course, when they chose the direction they would walk, and argued for both choices before deciding to head sonwards down the valley. It seemed the logical decision, given it was the opposite direction to the canyon they had just spent four days in, but Torve felt uneasy trusting his perceptions and memories of that place. He even scaled the cliff at a low point and walked half an hour fatherback across the stone plain, but did not find the canyon. This did nothing to ease his concerns, though Lenares seemed undisturbed when he returned with the puzzling news. He breathed a relieved sigh when familiar landmarks came into view, edged by the afternoon sun.

Lenares, however, was distraught. The expedition had moved on and there was no sign of where Captain Duon's tent might have been.

There remained plenty of evidence to fix the boundaries of the vast camp: the informal paths that had been beaten down by hundreds of boots, the latrines, dumps and burial grounds that defined any temporary site. But neither Torve nor Lenares could identify anything amongst the sand and stone that looked like a clearing in front of a tent site—or, more accurately, they could identify many such sites.

Torve trailed his foot through another site, marking it as having been examined. Endless days of similar inspections loomed ahead, an impossibility given their lack of food. Water they had in plenty from the well, the reason the camp had been located here in the first place; but for food they would have to find the expedition or go back to the house of the gods. For a moment he let his mind dwell on that cheerful thought, while something nagged at him . . .

The well.

"Lenares, you told me you spoke to the Elborans by the well. Is that right?"

"Why would I lie to you about it?" Lack of food and the loss of the expedition had made her somewhat bad-tempered.

"No, I'm asking to refresh my own memory. We know where the well is. Can you remember the number of steps you had counted when you stopped at the well?"

"Oh!" She clapped her hands together. "Of course I can!"

She hitched up her dress and ran in the direction of the well, heels kicking high like a little girl. When Torve arrived at the well, having walked at a more sedate pace—in truth, because he was exhausted—she hailed him with "Clever Torve!" He tried not to feel as though he were a dog being patted for an especially smart trick.

He could see a clear difference in her face. Some of the hard lines around her cheekbones had softened, a relaxation of the tension that had developed since her seizure. Her eyes burned with their familiar intensity, and when she spoke her words rattled out as though she needed to make room for more.

Had a mask come off, or had one just been put on?

He went to touch her—seeking reassurance her feelings had not changed, that they were part of her centre—but she held up a hand. He froze.

"I need time," she said, breathing heavily. "So many things—I have to fit everything into . . . Please, I cannot deal with distractions."

Torve understood what she meant, he *knew* she was not calling him a distraction, but the comment hurt him unbearably. "I will go and wait on the other side of the well," he said. "While you fit things together, I will think about how we might find food to survive."

He looked at Lenares hopefully, but her eyes were half-closed and she waved him away.

He busied himself, finding a discarded gourd amongst the detritus scattered around the camp, then some cloth to stuff in the cracks. The sun was touching the desert's rim when Torve successfully raised his water pouch from the well, detached the ancient rope and offered it to his cosmographer. She took it from him and downed the contents with a murmur of thanks; wearily he returned to the well and drew himself water.

"It worked," she said, immense satisfaction suffusing her words.

"You have recovered your numbers?"

"Oh yes, and much more. Please, Torve, we need to go back to the place in the canyon with the chairs. With what I know now, I think I could solve the whole mystery."

"Lenares, we cannot go back. Our only hope of survival is to make contact with the expedition. Where else can we get food? And how can we do anything about the hole you see if we remain on our own?"

"Oh, we don't have to worry about the expedition any longer," Lenares said, and gave a strange giggle. "They are all going to die."

"What? They are all going to *what*?" Torve staggered a step backwards; he had come to believe Lenares' pronouncements, accept them, make plans based on them. "Are you sure?"

She cocked her head at him. "The hole in the world has returned. Last time it sent the lions to kill three people; this time it sends something else to swallow the whole expedition."

"But why? What has been sent this time? Can't we warn them?"

"Why?" She thought a moment. "Because it thinks we are with the expedition, and wants to be certain of being rid of us. And no, we can't warn anyone. They've been gone for a long time; whatever was going to happen to them probably has already. I don't know what it is. I can't imagine what would be large enough to devour so many people."

Torve was appalled. Her callousness reminded him of the Emperor. "Lenares, how can you talk of thirty thousand deaths as though they are of no account? What of the cosmographers? I know they've not been good to you lately, but you grew up with many of them. Will you just abandon your friends?"

"But if I cannot do anything, what good does it do me to worry?"

"It makes you human!" he snapped, regretting the words even as they came out of his mouth. Lenares seemed to take no offence. "Anyway, I intend to follow the expedition and warn them."

Lenares stared at him. "And I want to go back to the canyon and learn as much as I can about the missing god," she said. "I remember . . . I am sure I had a dream about the three gods, just after my fit. If I can explore the circular room again, perhaps sit on one of the chairs, I'm sure I will understand much more—"

"But for what purpose? What is the point of understanding the hole in the world if by the time you have finished studying it, everyone else has been consumed by it? Surely we should alert the expedition first, then conduct our studies?"

The two of them began talking at each other, faster and faster, their words crashing together, until Lenares put her hands to her ears and screamed. The sound echoed from the valley sides, startling a large carrion bird some distance away, which rose lazily into the rapidly darkening sky. Torve put his hands over his own ears, blocking out the inhuman sound.

"Lenares, you are stubborn, I know that," he said in answer to her distressed look. "But I cannot follow you. I am bound by breeding to return to Captain Duon and warn him of the hole in the world, or, if I am too late, to bury his body and take news of him back to the Emperor."

"I thought . . . You said . . ." She stopped in obvious confusion.

"I did say," he replied in a gentle voice. "But I am what I am, Lenares. I am an Omeran, the Emperor's pet, and I must serve the Emperor. Your task is much more important than mine, but I cannot help you. Please believe me: I can no more turn aside from the Emperor's will than stop breathing."

Her face crumpled into tears. "Wouldn't the Emperor's will be to find out everything about the hole in the world?" she asked between sobs.

Torve sighed. "I rather think the Emperor would order me to try to save the expedition, but it does not matter. He has given me orders, the last of which was to keep secret the orders he has given me. I am required to obey him."

There being nothing more to say, no way to break the impasse, Torve and Lenares made themselves comfortable against the coming night chill and watched the swift desert sunset.

Just another sunset, but to Torve it seemed to signal the end of much more than merely another day.

Dawn came, waking a reluctant Torve from a dream in which he discovered further rooms in the house of the gods. With upturned faces he and Lenares dream-walked through a room filled with gentle rain, soft and warm. In the manner of dreams the room changed around them,

narrowing and deepening, and the water turned to a bur-
bling cascade. Running water, an extravagance worthy of
the Garden of Angels. With the thought, Torve saw the
Emperor standing on a rock near the head of the cascade,
looking down on them. *I know my duty*, Torve said to the
golden mask, which twitched up and down in response.
Dazzling sunlight filled a third open area, and the Emperor stood in the centre of the room and turned his mask
to face Lenares and Torve, their hands still guiltily clasped
together. The sun streamed from the golden face in blazing admonition . . .

Completely awake, the sun full in his face, the Omeran
found himself fervently wishing himself back into his
dream. Yesterday already seemed like a dream-country,
the harsh, angry words as yet unsaid, her smile a reality
rather than an ache in his heart. He turned, scanned her
sleeping place, but she was not there. Nor, he noted with
increasing concern, was she at the well, twenty or so paces
away.

He stood, stretching up on his toes, and saw nothing
but the featureless stony riverbed stretching away in every
direction.

She had taken the choice, if choice there ever was, out
of his hands.

CHAPTER 15

VALLEY OF THE DAMNED

TORVE KNELT AT THE FATHERWARD end of the expedition's old campsite, poring over footprints in a small sandy hollow. Gentle night breezes had softened the many once-sharp ridges made by soldiers' boots. In one place, however, the fresher prints of bare feet overlaid the blurred ridges.

A number of explanations came to mind. *Lenares may have wandered here during the night.* In a hopeful rather than realistic gesture he turned and looked in the direction of the well, out of sight over a gentle rise. His shoulders slumped. She would have gone directly fatherback towards the house of the gods; he doubted, in her obsession with that place, she would even have stopped by the well on her way, let alone come further in this direction. Besides, these footprints were too large for her delicate feet. And she had not left her shoes behind. He sighed. Equally unlikely was the possibility that one or more of the camp followers had returned to pick over the abandoned campsite. So little of value remained, which could be an indication either of successful scavengers or rigorous tidiness. Torve, knowing Captain Duon, suspected the latter.

Which left a further possibility. *Spies*. Of anyone in the expedition, Torve had the most reason to know that the desert was not empty. His dream-children wandered the desert freely, and he knew that, no matter what else they were, they left footprints behind. And they were surely not the only inhabitants of these harsh lands. Might his dream-children have shadowed the expedition father-wards through the stone plain, trying to satisfy their strange, unexplained curiosity about him?

Another thought came to him, and as he let it fill his mind he cursed his foolishness; his foolishness and Lenares', and especially that of Captain Duon. How could they all have forgotten? The Emperor had often discussed the geography and history of Elamaq with his pet Omeran; why had Torve not thought to review that knowledge as he travelled fatherwards? *Because you sought another kind of knowledge* came an unwelcome voice in his mind, one with the ring of truth about it. *You thought of yourself and your desires before those of your Emperor. And as a result the expedition may already be lost.*

Belatedly he considered what he knew. It was a favourite Amaqi tale, standard fare for the travelling players. Many years ago the twenty-third Emperor of Elamaq, the bookish but rightly feared Pouna III, sent a team of engineers into the mountains far to the sonback of the desert, with an Omeran labour force numbering in the thousands. There, over a period of twenty-four years, they constructed a great earth dam and diversion race, thereby capturing the headwaters of the Marasmos River. The purpose of this vast expenditure, which came close to bankrupting the empire—the Emperor had shown Torve copies of the original accounts—was twofold. First, to capture the water as part of the development of Talamaq as the Emperor's capital; and second, to consequently deprive the Marasmians, the last remaining sovereign opponents of the empire, of the water source upon which they depended.

The first the unfortunate Marasmians knew of the Emperor Pouna's engineering coup was when their ever-dependable river dried up. Foolishly they spent a season sacrificing to their gods in an attempt to encourage their river to relent, before finally sending an expedition sonback. That expedition did not return, though the Marasmians never found out why as by that time they had been surrounded by the Emperor's well-provisioned army. In the ensuing siege the weakened Marasmians were wiped out, their city of delicate spires and colleges of learning torn apart. Not one stone was left on top of another, and the ground was salted against any chance of future habitation.

It was said that Emperor Pouna III himself came fatherwards to witness the death of the last Marasmian, a symbolic act. The unfortunate woman, a nameless scholar, was captured early in the siege, forced to watch the death and destruction of everything she loved, then impaled, encased with salt and left on a hill overlooking the sterile plain.

It was said that Emperor Pouna remained with her until she died in great agony. Said by Torve's master, anyway, with great relish. Emperor Pouna III, forever after known as Pouna the Great, had been everything the current Emperor of Elamaq aspired to: intelligent, ruthless and, above all, long-lived. *But not eternal.*

How much of this was exaggeration or hearsay Torve could not know. His master had often speculated about the degree to which the story of Pouna the Great's life was the fanciful invention of subsequent storytellers, though the dry scrolls of the accountants and clerks alluded to even more horrific and ruthless events: revolts and repressions, cullings of the aristocracy, fratricide and worse. All of interest to his master. Whatever the reality, Torve now stood in the dry bed of what had once been the Marasmos River.

In the centuries since the sack of Marasmos there had been no attempt to resettle the area, so the Emperor's advisers had said. There were a few impoverished fishing villages on the Skeleton Coast, fatherwards and fatherback of the mouth of the former Marasmos River, but these were of little consequence to the empire. Tax collectors had long ago given up visiting the area, as the haggard fishermen accumulated no wealth. Torve wondered when last any accurate census or economic data had been collected from coastal regions. Captain Duon had seen no sign of inhabitants on his previous journey through the area, though this observation had little real value as the fatherward paths avoided the Skeleton Coast, taking routes many leagues inland of the desolate former city. Duon had reported nothing unusual, though there had been a mention of a man vanishing on the return journey. He had wandered from his tent one night, people said, his tracks leading into the heart of the stone plain.

A suspicion began to form in Torve's mind.

Lenares brushed the sand from her grubby dress, then stood and surveyed the result of her efforts. The sandy slope was spread out around the edges of the pool, and the stone stair she had been certain existed now rose before her: granite-grey, steps far too large for human feet, but climbable nonetheless. She had simply continued the process she and Torve had begun, undermining the slope until the sand had slumped in one final cascade. *If the gods sat on chairs, they also used stairs*. It had been a recurring mantra in her mind, one of the things that had driven her back here despite Torve's timid insistence on obedience to the bully-Emperor.

How much else did the sand cover?

Unable to contain the thrill rising within her, she ran, swam and waded her way from room to room. Oddly, the rooms were not exactly as she remembered them, nor were they in the same sequence, a fact she put down to having been without her fixed centre and her numbers on her earlier visit. Perhaps the shapes and colours and patterns and meanings pulsing and singing through her enlivened mind had laid bare things that had previously been hidden from her.

Here was the room with the chairs. Much larger than Lenares recalled, and much further from the first room, but last time they had backtracked in their explorations, perhaps explaining the discrepancy. To her surprise the jewel-like lake was still there, the focal point of the three chairs. She had expected . . . *Patience*, she told herself. Easy to ask of one self was patience, but impossible to exercise. By the time the sun stood overhead, shining directly down on the still water, she had paced around the room over a hundred times. *One hundred and seven times; twenty-one thousand, five hundred and seven steps*, her mind said. She brushed the thought aside impatiently. *Two hundred and one steps per circuit*, her inner voice prattled on. *Sixty-seven steps for a god*. And then a strange thought: *three gods equals one human*. Surely it was the other way around?

She closed her eyes and gritted her teeth. Sometimes she was prepared to admit that her numbers annoyed even her. So it was she missed the moment when the pool cleared and the image she knew had to be there revealed itself.

It was a map like none she had ever seen. Perfectly circular, it appeared to consist of a series of concentric circles designed to draw the eye to the centre. Asymmetrical detail lay underneath the circular grid; she ascended one of the chairs to get a better view of the image.

The map appeared to lie just beneath the surface of the pool, though she was not fool enough to test this theory. In the house of the gods her numbers took on shapes and patterns too complex for simple reflection; she laughed at the double meaning, her mind aflame with insight. The image seemed to have been carved from, or etched into, a burnished sheet of bronze, though that might have been the effect of the sun. Three great continents dominated the image, the largest centred on the map's own centre.

As she stared at the unsettling combination of symmetrical grid and random coastline, the pattern shifted in her head and she was suddenly able to see it for what it was. *Oh, so simple, so elegant*.

No one else would be able to understand it, she crowed. No matter how many others came to stare at this map of the world, none of them would appreciate the singularity of vision that had created it. In the middle of the map, drawn at a scale out of all proportion to the rest, was a detailed plan of the very room she occupied. Three chairs

surrounded a small pool, a minute mimicry of the real
pool it lay at the centre of. Thinking about it threatened to
turn Lenares' mind inside out. The other rooms were visible on the map, but the ones further from the Map Room,
as she already called it, were smaller. Not in reality, but a
trick of scale. *Scale is everything on this map. Things get
smaller the further they are from the centre. The further
they are from this pool.* Just like in real life, where objects were foreshortened, appearing smaller the further
they lay from her viewpoint. So at the margins of the map
she could see jagged coastlines, mountain ranges and
rivers, whole countries shown smaller than the Map
Room. *Elamaq may not be bigger than the other two continents, after all; it just seems so because it surrounds the
centre of the map.*

Such an odd scale . . . *a logarithmic scale!* She exulted
in her further discovery. Working from the centre outwards, each concentric circle was slightly closer to the
next larger one that enclosed it, until at the outer edge they
blurred into invisibility. The decreasing gap between the
circles reflected the progression of logarithmic numbers.
The effect was to create a constant foreshortening of scale
from the centre in every direction; the result, a map that at
once showed the detail of one room and the spread of the
whole world around it.

Now she had unlocked the secret, the name of any fea-
ture she concentrated on began to appear, floating above
the map as though on the surface of the water. Elamaq,
Bhrudwo, Faltha. Three continents, one central, two pe-
ripheral. Three chairs, three gods, three continents.

She wondered on whose chair she sat. What if she were
to climb up and sit on one of the two remaining chairs?

Would she see with the eyes of another god? Would the centre of the map shift? Would she see the plan of a second god-house, with another continent enlarged at the expense of its fellows?

More thoughts followed, racing through her mind like starving wolves behind their pack leader. What would it be like to see oneself as the very centre of the world, and know it for truth? Was this a reflection of her own desire, her own need for a centre? Had the pool merely made real the patterns of her mind? Or was she seeing as the gods saw? She was not sure whether the answers mattered, but knew she hungered for them with all her soul.

A sort of glory settled on her. Here, expressed on one elegant map, was the very essence and sum of a cosmographer's life's work. Staring down at the world, with herself at the secret, sacred heart, she found herself imbued with . . . with the very presence of a god. Goddess. Her skin prickled with power; she seemed about to burst. As though the ability to see as the gods saw, to see oneself at the centre, conferred . . .

Daughter, a rich contralto whispered, moving tenderly through the rooms of her mind, *you should not be here. This is too much even for you. In your pursuit of knowledge you have left wisdom behind. You must leave this place*—a hesitation, a catching of divine breath, a new urgency—*I must take you from here. My brother knows. He comes.*

Torve found Lenares on her haunches beside the well, eyes wide and wild, rocking back and forth as though in the throes of pain or ecstasy. For some time she could say nothing, unable to respond to his frantic questions. *Where*

*have you been? How did you get back to the well without
me seeing you?* He picked her up; she shivered in his
arms.

"I, I, I," she said, then repeated the sound in brackets of
three. "Eye, eye, eye." Torve could not tell whether she referred to herself or her vision; certainly her eyes were
glazed, her face puffy. She took three deep breaths,
gulped, then retched weakly. He lowered her to the
ground.

"Lenares?" he asked gently.

She looked up at him and smiled; then her face
changed and an unearthly look came into her eyes.

"I . . . I need parchment," she said incongruously.

"Parchment?" Torve's weak echo reflected the confusion he felt. "Lenares, where have you been?"

"Don't talk to me. Don't—I can't hold it in." She
pressed her hands against her temples.

"Lenares, am I not to talk to you? Is that what you ask
of me?"

"Please, please, leave me, let me—come with me. We
have to find the expedition." Her eyes filled with desperate hunger.

What has she seen?

So many things he could say; so much frustration and
heartache to deal with as she demanded he do what she
had refused to do up until now. Yet she wanted his silence.

He took her hand; she gripped his compulsively. "We
must hurry," she said.

"At least let me draw more water," said Torve. She
nodded, but her mind was somewhere other than on such
mundane concerns.

Later that day they made camp under a lone acacia tree.

Lenares had led him down the Marasmos riverbed, making no comment as to her choice of direction. Torve knew the expedition had followed the valley for a league or so and then turned fatherwards—the desert stone and sand offered ample evidence of this, as did items discarded intermittently—but did not ask her why she persisted sonwards. Events had moved beyond his comprehension, and he was forced to take Lenares on faith.

The sun set, enormous and oval in a bronze sky, as they made their pitiful camp. It wavered in the heat as it neared the horizon, the land seeming to clutch at it as though grasping for warmth in preparation for the coming cold of the desert night. Torve shared his water gourd with Lenares, then handed her a filthy blanket he had scavenged from the remains of the expedition. She took it without comment and found herself a spot on the far side of the tree, giving the appearance of avoiding him, which no doubt she was.

Later that night Torve gave up trying to sleep and, by the light of a pale yellow half-moon, crept over to where Lenares lay. She was clearly asleep, but next to her a strange pattern had been drawn in the sand. As he looked more closely he saw her right arm lay outstretched across the pattern, as though sleep had claimed her before she could finish it. It was a circular shape, filled with squiggles, blurred somewhat by the cool night breeze. He stared at it until his eyelids drooped, and when it was clear understanding would not come, he returned to his own patch of sand.

Hunger and its attendant weakness were their main adversaries over the next two days. Torve continued to hope they would find a grove of the red-berried bushes that had so nourished them in the canyon; on occasion he left Lenares' side and searched promising side valleys, but found nothing. No sign of animals and no means of hunting them. Lenares said nothing, preoccupied with whatever had driven her back to the well, and now drove her towards the expedition that had shunned them both. He had no idea whether she suffered hunger pangs, though she drank from the gourd whenever he offered it.

At the end of the third day sonwards of the well she reached for the gourd, forcing him to tip it upside down to indicate it was empty.

They would not last long if they continued without food and water.

The next morning Torve awoke to find himself alone. A glance sunwards was enough to locate Lenares a few hundred paces downvalley, her walk almost a totter. His eyes prickled with tears; licking dry lips, he hauled himself up on weak legs and made off after her.

Much of the day was forever blanked from Torve's memory. Whenever he came to himself he saw Lenares still some distance in front; his best efforts failed to make up any ground. Some time in the afternoon he stopped sweating and was still lucid enough to know what this meant. How was Lenares able to maintain her pace? The next time he regained awareness the cosmographer was a small speck in the hazy distance.

"Lenares," he croaked, forgetting he was not supposed to be speaking to her. "Lenares . . ." But his plea was swallowed by the desert.

A fifth day followed, the substance of an Amaqi nightmare. To be caught in the desert unprepared, drained by the sun, emptied of fluid and left as a desiccated husk,

was an ever-present possibility to anyone whose business
took them beyond the city wall. One that was meticu-
lously planned for or carefully avoided. Torve's skin reddened, then blistered, drawing even more precious fluid
away from his body. He learned to keep his swelling
tongue in his dry mouth, as his thick, salty saliva stung
his cracked lips whenever he licked them. His only salvation was Lenares' blanket, which shaded his head in the
afternoons. If they had been walking daughterwards,
Torve would have been dead by now.

He awoke from a standing doze to find himself surrounded by gnats. *I'm not dead*, he growled at them, but
he wasn't certain. Tap, tap, tap, the insects blundered into
him, always on his left side; they were flying from his left
to his right in a large cloud.

Something about this stirred his interest. *Where are the
insects going?* He let it go: it seemed too much effort to
think about it. Much easier to lie down and let them pass
overhead, on their way to . . . to wherever insects went in
the evening.

To water.

"Drink this," said a voice, startling him, distracting him
from thoughts of hope.

"Leave me alone," he rasped, his voice more puff than
words. "There is water—insects—must follow . . ." His
swollen tongue failed him, and his limbs flailed uselessly
in his urgency.

When he next awoke it was night. Lenares hovered
above him, the half-moon a halo about her hair, her
face in shadow. She dabbed at his mouth with a wet
cloth—a rag torn from her dress, Torve noted, as he
forced his eyes to focus—then trickled living sweet-

ness from the water pouch onto his tongue. He put out
a hand and snatched awkwardly at the pouch, but she
pulled it away.

Consciousness returned with roaring pain. It was dawn,
their fiery enemy already looking above the sonwards
horizon, and his neck and head boomed with every small
sound. Surprisingly he did not feel thirsty. He pushed his
tongue around his mouth: his gums hurt, and at least one
tooth had come loose.

"Lenares?" he called. In answer a hand came from behind him and caressed his face. *Cool.* He sat up, his limbs
screaming with pain, and sweat broke out all over his
body. He almost collapsed with relief.

Lenares leaned over him, her drawn face close to his.
Her skin was blackened on both cheeks, and her nose
seemed to have shrunk a little. "Can you stand?" she
asked him.

"You look terrible," he said as he struggled to his feet.
"Was it worth it? Have we caught up with the expedition?"

"I don't know," Lenares said, weariness lacing her
voice. "I think we may be ahead of them. It depends on
whether they stopped to rest in the afternoons. We could
search for evidence here of their passing when the sun is
a little higher."

"Where is here?" he asked, his eyes settling on a grove
of date palms.

"An oasis. I knew it was here. I saw it on a map." Her
face closed, as though she relived a memory too painful or
beautiful to bear.

The oasis was a beautiful sight. Situated in a sandy
basin a little lower than the rest of the riverbed, it had been
scoured out when the Marasmos ran between the cliffs,

perhaps; the site of some powerful current. Since then sand had drifted into the basin, lining the gently sloping sides down to a barely rippling pool surrounded by date palms. The dates were not ripe, unfortunately, but the sight was a welcome one, comparable in style if not in grandeur to the house of the gods they had left behind.

With that thought an ache sprang up within him, the remembrance of a place at once entrancing and forbidding; a place in which humans were not meant to dwell, yet somewhere they might long for if they knew of its existence. He wondered if the time they had spent there, the sense of being in a high place beyond mortal insight, might ultimately prove more curse than blessing. *Cursed is he who leaves the house of the gods; doubly cursed is he who remains . . .*

Torve could see a small piece of broken ground leading off to the left, most likely an animal track. They would have to be careful if they remained near the oasis: danger of a different, more prosaic kind awaited them if they were careless.

Something about Lenares' explanation made him uneasy. "But how did you know which route fatherwards they planned to take?" he asked her. "Even Captain Duon wasn't sure. Was that not why he called the meeting with the senior Alliance figures?"

Lenares looked away. "I guessed," she said. "I don't know. All I know is that if they went directly fatherwards like Captain Duon wanted, we would never have caught them. I thought our only chance was to travel as long as we could along the riverbed, then cut across the edge of the stone plain, reaching the coastal hill country before the expedition. I hoped that might be the route they chose."

"There is another reason, isn't there?" Torve knew Lenares would never have based any decision on mere guesswork. "I don't believe your analysis. Fatherwards of here is the rest of the stone plain, and if the expedition went that way we could have caught them in three days, provided they rested in the afternoons. You know something."

She looked directly at him. "You won't believe me," she said.

He shrugged. "Does it matter? I'll follow you whether I believe you or not."

"I am being pulled," she said. "The hole in the world has returned. I have felt it, have seen evidence of it, for the last week. It has enlarged much faster than I thought it would. Something is wrong with one of my calculations, or one of my strange numbers is wrong. The hole is here, all around us, and will reveal itself soon. I followed it as it moved sonwards, because I believed it thought I was part of the expedition. So, wherever the hole is, there the expedition will soon appear."

Torve grunted. His head, already thick with pain, seemed to turn itself inside out in an effort to follow her words. Who followed whom? He could not get the sequence straight: hole, expedition, Lenares, all chasing each other and being chased sonwards towards the Skeleton Coast . . .

Oh. Something he had reasoned out for himself, which he had subsequently forgotten in the trial of the desert, returned to the forefront of his mind with a crash.

He licked his lips. "Lenares, I know what the mind behind the hole in the world is unleashing on Captain Duon." Cold fear settled on him. Fear of what was to come, fear that Lenares would not believe him.

He needn't have worried. She stared at him with a burning avidity, as though she sought to drain his mind of everything he knew. "What? Tell me! If we know, we can warn the expedition!"

Torve arranged his thoughts carefully. "Captain Duon told the Emperor he lost a man on the stone plain on his way home from the first expedition. I think that man was captured by those who live here. You know what this riverbed was, don't you?" An unnecessary question for a cosmographer.

"Oh, yes. The old Marasmos River," she said, her face taking on her puzzle-solving look. "Are you saying that there are Marasmians alive still? After all these years?"

"Their descendants. They will have learned that Captain Duon intended to return this way with a far larger force. Whoever—whatever—is behind the hole in the world could have intervened, assisted the coastal peoples to raise an army. That is why the hole seems much larger."

He caught a movement out of the corner of his eye, jerked his head up in involuntary surprise. "That—that is why," he continued, lowering his voice, "that is why it surrounds us." He motioned discreetly left and right. "Don't turn to your right, Lenares—don't!"

She paused halfway through the act of spinning around. "What do you see?" she mouthed at him.

He turned slowly. "On the rim of the bluff to our right is a scout. He is still now, but he moved a few moments ago."

"What can we do?" Lenares asked, sinking to her knees. "You are right, I can feel it—the hole is getting smaller."

"Then the expedition cannot be far away. All we can do is wait. I'm sure the Marasmians, or whoever they are, know we are here. Although they may not; we haven't moved since sunrise." He thought carefully. "If we move now they will see us and take us for scouts. They would likely capture us, or at the least prevent us from leaving. We will have to wait for Captain Duon to come to us. And," he said, looking over his left shoulder, "we will not have long to wait."

The bright colours of the Amaqi expedition, dimmed somewhat by their passage through the desert, came streaming down through a gap in the fatherwards wall of the riverbed.

"The Marasmians will be some way behind them, remaining out of sight in the expedition's dust-cloud, closing the ring of this ambush," he said. "There will be slaughter."

Lenares nodded, her face pale. Torve touched her blackened cheek with his fingers. "Does this hurt?"

"I can only feel the hole in the world," she said, gasping out the words as though she were being crushed. He pulled his fingers away.

"Lenares, I don't understand. Why didn't the expedition just travel sonwards down the riverbed if the riverbed route is more direct?"

"Because it is not," she corrected, a trace of asperity in her voice. "The riverbed curves sonwards and then daughterback. In the last five days we have travelled almost as much between fatherwards and fatherback as we have sonwards. The expedition took the shorter but more exposed route."

"And now they are here," Torve said. "I only hope we can inform Captain Duon before the Marasmians strike."

*   *   *

The expedition made an impressive sight as it wound down to the riverbed. A hundred horsemen led an equal number of chariots, the Amaqi weapon that over the last thousand years had made them invincible in battle. Behind them came the foot soldiers, choking on the dust of the chariots. Drovers led the remaining animals, most of which drew food wagons. The horsemen approached the oasis where Torve and Lenares waited, while most of the foot soldiers continued to make their way down into the valley. The camp followers were nowhere to be seen, but undoubtedly trailed somewhere behind. They would suffer sorely in any battle, Torve realised, no matter the outcome.

He willed the riders on into the shadows, waiting until the first of them had dismounted and led their horses to the pool shadowed under the fatherback wall of the valley. He stepped forward, arms out and palms down, a gesture of calm.

"Please, ma sorra, listen to me. I have urgent news," he croaked.

Two of the horsemen went for their swords.

"Please!" Torve cried. "We are being watched. Do not give any indication that you know this, or the expedition is lost."

"By the Son," one of the men said, wonder in his voice, "it's that Omeran, the Emperor's pet. We thought it was lost."

"Farouq will pay a coin or two for its return," said another. "Here," the man drawled, holding out a water pouch, "draw me some water from the middle of the pool. Not the edge, mind. I want my water clean."

"Then don't get it to draw water for you," a third man

said, to general laughter. "It looks like it's been wandering lost in the desert sands."

The men sheathed their swords, satisfied there was no danger.

"That's because he has," said Lenares, stepping out of the shadows. "So have I. Think what you like about him and about me, but you have stepped into an ambush. Keep looking at the bluff above us, ma sor, and tell us what you see. The rest of you, continue to water your horses."

"It's the cosmographer. The runaway."

"Please," Lenares repeated, almost begging them. "Just look!" Her tone of voice, as much as the content of her information, caused a few of the soldiers to raise their heads.

"She is right," one of the men hissed. "There are *men* up above us."

Faces that had been relaxed, anticipating the relief offered by the oasis, swiftly assumed a soldierly mien. The first man to whom Torve had spoken bent and whispered into the ear of another man, who remounted a watered horse. "Ride slowly, so as not to arouse suspicion," he ordered. "We must spring this ambush, or at least be ready for it."

"Is he going to tell Captain Duon?" Torve asked, but was ignored as the horsemen, under the guise of setting up camp, spread the word.

"We must leave," Lenares said to Torve. "We must not get caught in the fighting. The god knows who I am, and will send someone to kill me."

Torve nodded, and began walking back towards the oasis.

"Stay where you are, Omeran," the first man

commanded. "And you, witch. My master will want to find out all about you."

"But Captain Duon already knows about us!" Lenares said, panic in her voice.

"Ah, then you are not aware of the little change in this expedition. Surprising, witch; I thought you knew everything. Duon no longer commands anyone. Sit down and ready yourself to meet the new commander of the Emperor's glorious army of conquest. If anyone can break the ambush—if ambush it is, and not some scheme of Duon's to reclaim power—he can."

"But—" Lenares began to wail.

"Be silent!" He put his hand on his sword-hilt.

Bewildered and exhausted, with no choice but to obey, Torve and Lenares sat on a rock next to the oasis and waited to see how the expedition's new leader would respond to their news.

Captain Taleth Salmadi Duon found his humiliation easier to bear if he avoided eye contact. For days now he had been a curiosity for the soldiers and the camp followers; it seemed that every member of the expedition had taken the opportunity to take a look at the man deposed as leader. Some were not polite in their comments, nor did they trouble to keep their voices lowered. The women took delight in making disparaging remarks about his golden hair, as did many of the men. One of the older women, a snarl-toothed farrier who had attended his horse on two occasions, rushed at him and, before his guards could prevent her, tore a handful of hair from his head. His scalp bled for hours. The guards kept the onlookers a good distance away after that, but he could still hear what they said about him.

He supposed the humiliation was necessary. Farouq wanted the expedition to reject their former leader as a part of cementing his own leadership. This exercise left no one in any doubt.

His hands were bound behind him, but he was otherwise unfettered. The six Elboran guards allocated to prevent his escape ensured that. Their purpose, he decided, was more a deterrent to anyone misguided enough to attempt to rescue him. The Pasmarans in particular might have had a vested interest in seeing him released, though if they were to return him to leadership it would be as a figurehead only. And now that Duon was deposed, the Anaphil Alliance had no power, so they would benefit most from his reinstatement. Farouq kept the few Anaphil representatives under close observation.

Duon's head ached uncomfortably. An odd feeling: a cold lump at the back of his neck, unlike anything in his experience. He found it unsettling. How could an illness make one cold in the midst of all this heat? And in only one place? Perhaps it was the cumulative effect of his disgrace. His neck and scalp were particularly uncomfortable today, and had been since dawn.

Farouq had come to see him as the sun crested the horizon. Not content with usurping his place as leader of the expedition, the Elboran Elder continued to pump him for information. Where was the next well? How long should they camp in the afternoon? How many more days until they reached Nomansland? Ironic, really, as the argument that led to Duon's foolish ultimatum and the calling of his bluff had been about the choice of route. He had been deposed for trying to impose his views on those too proud to take orders from a social inferior, yet his views were necessary, and were being actioned. He was leader in all but name.

Well, and in all but comfort. Farouq and his associates—he could think of less flattering descriptions, but he would remain a gentleman, in his mind at least—rode in sumptuously appointed palanquins, while he stumbled along in their dust.

His career was over. Even if the Emperor somehow appeared and confirmed his leadership, none would now follow him. *Those who desire to lead need to be worthy of leadership* was a widely held Amaqi dictum, and he had proved himself deficient. His plans for the future had shrivelled in his mind like a desert bloom at the end of the rainy season. He could see himself returning to Punta to live with his unendurable mother. Unless, of course, the Empero, or the leader of the Anaphil Alliance, of which he was a recently promoted senior member, simply took his head.

As for his head, it ached to distraction. For the last two days there had been a buzzing in his ears, almost forming words, at its worst when his head ached the most. It had taken a day for him to recall that dreadful voice in his head during the Leaving Ceremony at Talamaq. Was it possible? Could a man have a separate voice in his head, one with its own volition, with views and manners entirely the opposite of its host? Or was he insane? He had once seen a man bitten by a rabid bat while exploring the Caves of Turfann a week's trek daughterwards of Punta. Cuevarra felt ill for a few days on the journey home, but was then taken by hallucinations, believing himself to be the Son. His neighbours had stoned him to death rather than risk infection.

Try as he might, Duon could not remember being bitten by any animal. Nor, he thought, was his delusion on the day of the Leaving Ceremony anything like that suffered by poor Cuevarra. He had not felt unwell during his fatherwards journey. And it had been many weeks since they had left Talamaq. Rabies acted more quickly on its unfortunate victims—comfort of a sort.

Yzz . . . izza . . . foool went the sound in the back of his head. He ignored it.

He remembered the times travelling players had performed in Punta. As a child he sang along to the songs, thinking he knew the lyrics, but had discovered when he was a little older that much of what he thought he knew was wrong. One of the players had laughed at him. *Son, the human mind always tries to make sense out of whatever it hears. You thought we were singing about a sunset in a field of horses? What we sang was a nonsense verse, just sounds put to music, not words at all. No sunset, no horses.*

And now his mind heard words where there were none. An illness of some sort, a trick of the mind, nothing more. Not a voice.

Azz . . . blinzz . . . fool!

Random sounds.

His guards guided him down the steep slope to the Marasmos riverbed. He had argued that if the Alliances were determined to detour closer to the coast, the riverbed would be a much more sensible—if slightly longer—route. But all the Elders were interested in was haste. This was partly his own fault: had he not increased the pace after the lion attack, the Elders would probably not have realised just how fast a caravan could travel.

Though they complained while under forced march conditions, once they reached the Marasmos riverbed they
refused to believe such efforts could not be sustained.
*Curse that foolish cosmographer and her lover, falling
victim to a lion!* Even as the thought rippled through his
mind, he knew it was uncharitable.

But that other cosmographer, Lenares, the uncanny
one—her seizure had been the finish of his leadership. He
had given her credibility, so when hers was undermined,
his went with it. His last act as leader had been to argue
that she should be left alone, a course of inaction none had
agreed with. Farouq—ma sor Farouq, he corrected himself bitterly—sent one of his, Duon's, own soldiers after
her. Duon's remonstrations were laughed at. The real
struggle for power that afternoon had been between Pasmaran and Elboran, with the latter, more numerous,
emerging victorious. The other Alliances had rushed to
position themselves profitably with respect to the victor.
Captain Duon was no more use to anyone.

No . . . morrzzz . . . uzze . . . to mee . . . zzz.

Behind him the caravan continued to enter the valley.
Duon and his guards were now equidistant between the
fatherwards and fatherback bluffs, in the middle of what
was once, if the legends were to be believed, the bed of
a river that ran night and day every day of the year, even
in the heat of summer. He had seen streams sustained by
ice in the knotted peaks of the Maranon, but could not
imagine the water needed to fill this valley.

There was some evidence of recent river activity,
though. Duon could not prevent his explorer's mind from
cataloguing the small clues. Driftwood, mostly ash and
cypress, no doubt from the forests he had never seen, hun-

dreds of leagues to the sonback. Scour marks between the larger stones. Sand ridges perpendicular to the likely flow—probably pressure ridges left by a flood, or perhaps small dunes shaped by the downvalley wind. Their path took them between and parallel to the sand ridges.

A rider cantered past him, travelling in the opposite direction. Duon caught a glimpse of the man's tense face, observed the way he restrained himself and his horse, and knew something untoward had happened.

Good.

Not his thought. Or perhaps it was, and he was simply unwilling to admit his ungentlemanly conduct.

No time to consider. Farouq, who had been visiting the camp followers, rode past him in the direction of the vanguard, his face a brittle mask. Dryman, Duon's turncoat soldier, followed, jogging in his new leader's dust, more excitement than usual evident on his features. At a gesture from Farouq he halted and spoke to Duon's guard. The Elboran Elder continued on.

"Ambush ahead," Dryman said, breathing heavily. "Farouq thinks it trivial, but good soldiers ought to be prepared for anything. Divide the caravan into two units of equal size. Include the camp followers in the second unit, but send wagons forward to the first. Should the ambush be larger than our leader thinks, one of the two units should be able to disengage and escape."

What sort of idiotic advice was this? And on whose authority? Duon opened his mouth.

"Keep thizzz expedizzion togezzer," he said; then, horrified, snapped his mouth shut.

Dryman ignored him. "Go," he told the guards. "I am more than sufficient to guard one powerless man. As always, I am answerable to Farouq, so have no fear of being called to account."

The guards looked at each other warily, but left as he commanded.

"Something is about to happen, ma sor Duon," Dryman remarked, and winked at him. "Can you not feel it?" Truly the man was insufferable, a wide smile creasing his plain, pale face. Insufferable, or mad.

He izz mad? And you are the judgzz of thizz?

Duon froze.

The soldier seemed unperturbed by Duon's lack of response. "Come, then," he said. "The first thing to do is get you untied and find you a sword. I have a feeling you will need it."

With that, he drew plain-looking knife—plain, that was, unless one knew the value of the oft-tempered steel—and cut Duon's bonds. "Take the knife," Dryman said, handing it to him handle first. "We'll find you a longer blade shortly."

Duon glanced behind him. The last of the camp followers had finally set foot on the riverbed, and to him it seemed like a trap closing on his expedition. He turned to Dryman, eyes wide.

"Ah, you sense it too," the soldier said. "I had begun to wonder if my faith in you was misplaced."

Hizz faith? Who izz thizz man?

Duon clutched at his head in horror. None of the rationalisations he'd dredged up would suffice to explain this voice. "There is someone talking in my head. I am unfit for command." He hadn't meant to say it out loud.

"A voice?" Dryman said, tilting his head quizzically. "Really? I hope it encourages you to act sensibly. For example, we are approaching Farouq and his Elboran mob. Perhaps your voice might advise you to conceal your knife and put your hands behind your back?"

Duon nodded, badly frightened.

Dryman pushed through a ring of soldiers and stood, arms folded, at the edge of a large pool, two hundred paces wide. Duon followed him. This was the Falanrasel oasis, the largest spring between Talamaq and Nomansland, a crucial link in any fatherwards journey.

Unsure what was expected of him, Duon positioned himself immediately behind the soldier. Farouq stood on his right, facing a bedraggled woman with enormous eyes. The fey cosmographer. Her arms were held by a bluff-faced soldier. Dryman hissed, a sound echoed by the voice in Duon's head.

"A few spies don't make an ambush," Faroqu said. "We are grateful that you and your Omeran stumbled across them, but we are in no danger." The Elboran Elder was posturing for the benefit of his soldiers, trying to defuse panic. "The no-accounts above us no doubt wish to shepherd us out of their lands as swiftly as poss—"

A flash passed in front of Duon's eyes, followed by a meaty thwack and a scream from Farouq. A long wooden spear had penetrated his thigh and driven deep into the sand beneath him. A second spear barely missed his head, taking a soldier behind him in the stomach.

"Get this thing out of me!" roared Farouq as soldiers scattered, assumed defensive crouches or took cover behind their horses. Two brave men ran towards him; the third spear knocked one off his feet. Farouq's head jerked up, his eyes went wide and he thrust his bloody hands protectively in front of his face, but the next spear went through his hands and his head with a sound like a cracking jar.

A chorus of shouts came from the ridge above them, followed by a lethal rain of spears. Hundreds of them, turning the sky black, whistling through the air, clattering against each other in flight, splashing into the pool, burying themselves indiscriminately in sand, in horses and in soldiers. The oasis turned to a field of horror, transformed by the screams of men and animals, by dreadful wounds, merciful death and merciless agony, blood on the sand and in the water.

While most of the soldiers ran away from the cliff, seeking to get beyond the range of the spear-throwers, Torve snatched at Lenares' hand and dragged her through the oasis and towards the steep bluffs. A spear thumped into the ground just in front of them, throwing sand into their faces, but no others came close. They climbed a little way up the cliff, found a niche in the shadowed rockface and turned to watch the butchery below.

"They wouldn't listen, they wouldn't listen!" Lenares sobbed, her hands scrubbing at her face. "What use is it to be special if no one believes me?" She winced as her salty tears soaked into the broken skin of her cheeks.

"Some of the soldiers believed you," Torve said. "But their leaders will not accept anything we say as true. Lenares, forgive me, but we are not believable."

"Then what use am I?" she wailed.

From their vantage point the two observers saw the expedition pull back from both cliffs—the one they were on and the other on the far side of the valley—pouring into a boiling mass in the centre of the valley. The hail of whistling spears slowed, then ceased, as no targets remained within range. From under the thin-trunked spear forest that had sprung up around the oasis came the groans and cries of the wounded, accompanied by the muffled wriggling of men and horses trying to free themselves from ashwood spears that pinned them to the ground. Torve wished the spears would begin again; anything to silence the grinding cacophony assaulting his ears.

A shout from above heralded scrabbling sounds and the rattling of rocks, then after a few minutes the first of the desert savages clambered down the cliff on narrow paths. *If just one of them looks back in our direction* . . . Intent on the scene below, readying their curved knives, none of the attackers spared a glance behind them. In their thousands they came, dark-skinned, pale-skinned, men, women, a dozen different races, all wearing similar fierce expressions. Torve had not imagined that this many non-Amaqi remained in the world.

Reaching the valley floor, the warriors separated into two groups. The larger set out in pursuit of the remnants of the expedition. The remainder turned their attention to the wounded. Despite the severity of their wounds a few of the Amaqi fought their killers with the same desperation they would use to fight the Herald of Death herself; others welcomed the release of the spear or the knife as though greeting a lover. Boys barely old enough to handle a sword lay side by side with hardened veterans of campaigns in the daughterwards parts of Elamaq; young and old died together. The Marasmians left none alive.

We can do nothing, Torve repeated to himself. *We can do nothing*.

The slaughter of the wounded over, the warriors put their knives between their teeth, gathered up as many spears as they could carry and ran with enthusiasm towards the bulk of their enemy. For the briefest moment Torve imagined himself leading his Omeran people across the valley, swords and pikes in hands and hot anger in their hearts, ready to extract the full measure of revenge on the Amaqi for all the terrible things they had done to them. Except the Omerans would be more likely to turn on him than on their masters.

Out in the middle of the valley the Amaqi expedition appeared to be regrouping. Though they had lost many of their horses in the initial ambush, there remained enough to hitch to the formidable chariots. Horse-handlers disengaged the mules that had served to pull the chariots during the journey and rushed through the complicated set-up procedure. Other soldiers stood in the armoury wagons, passing out armour. There was nowhere near enough.

Looking more closely, Torve noticed pale lines either side of the massed Amaqi army, as though a giant had scored a series of grooves across the stony riverbed and filled them with sand. *They are too straight, those lines. Not natural.*

"Oh," Lenares said. "Oh. It is going to get very bad."

For a moment Torve imagined he could see the hole Lenares talked about. Or perhaps it was a trick of the light, an artefact of the sun glinting on the swords and armour of the Amaqi soldiers. Directly above the expedition the sky paled; a hard edge appeared, encompassing a circle within which could be seen a different sky. Wheeling gulls, whitecap waves.

He was distracted by sudden movement to the left and

right of the expedition. Figures emerged from behind the sand ridges, springing directly out of the ground. Thousands of Marasmians hidden in trenches, bursting out unseen by the disoriented, shocked, leaderless expedition. Torve found it hard to tell at this distance, but it looked like the warriors had drawn throwing knives. Right hand overhand, left hand underhand, thrown with deadly force into the melee, calculated to wreak maximum damage. Wails of surprise, fear and pain came their way, borne on the hot breeze.

Torve could not hold himself back. "Lenares, we have to try to help them!"

She glanced at him. "Would the Emperor send you into battle?"

The Omeran ignored her. *What I require now is courage, not wise counsel.* He began a rapid descent. "Wait here!" he tossed off behind him.

The smell of blood and faeces threatened to unman him as he worked his way through the forest of spears. Many of the bodies looked chewed up, as though forced through a monster's maw. *An apt description.* He pulled a spear free of the sand, hefted and discarded it, then thought carefully about his own abilities and picked it up again.

"What are you going to do with that?" Lenares said.

He turned on her. "I asked you to wait!"

"The hole is narrowing," she said, avoiding his gaze. "I want to see what happens."

"You could see perfectly well from the cliff! The hole has you as a target. Why put yourself in its eye?"

She snarled angrily at him. "All right, I'm coming so you don't get killed, and I want you to live because I . . . because I want you to live and not die." Her face threatened to crumple. "I don't think I like you when you won't let me lie to you."

"I like you when you tell the truth," he replied. "Everyone else is dishonest."

They left the sandy oasis and ran across the sun-hot stones towards the battle. The circle of Amaqi had shrunk considerably in the few minutes it took them to reach the encircling Marasmian warriors. Torve guided Lenares up a small hill to partial shelter behind a large rock. "There is nothing we can do; we cannot break through the encirclement. We can only wait. Something may present itself." Lenares bit her lip, but allowed Torve to guide her to the hiding place.

The battle was the most complex thing, the most beautiful and terrible thing, Lenares had ever seen. She found herself able to separate out her fears, her tiredness and the sun-inflicted pain from her perception of the events surrounding her. The shapes, sounds and colours that made up her objective reality poured into her mind so swiftly she was not able to convert them to numbers. All the better to see the underlying patterns, evidence of the godly hands that directed—and interfered with— the battle.

The hole in the world swirled above the valley. Still drawing inwards, like a knot being tightened, it screamed at her, a roiling mass of purple with jagged, bleeding edges. The Marasmians, standing in a circle of their own directly below the hole, drew strength from it somehow; Lenares could see the linkages, but could not understand how they had been established or how they worked.

A greedy, hungry presence radiated from the hole. By a

simple process of elimination Lenares knew now who he was. She had sat on the Daughter's seat in the house of the gods, and had heard her voice; this was not her. The Father was the missing god, driven out of Elamaq by his two ungrateful children, so it could not be him. That left the Son, the most respected by the Amaqi of the three gods, at least until the Emperor had spoken against god-worship. *Her enemy was the Son.* What she did not yet know was why the Son would lend strength to the enemies of the Amaqi.

But lend it he did, and at the same time the hole drew strength from the Amaqi army. Lenares watched as armoured soldiers cast down their swords in despair, to be slain by knife-wielding Marasmians who ought not to have stood a chance against them. The camp followers put up a more spirited defence—the god did not oppose them—but were being killed in their hundreds. In places brave Amaqi commanders rallied soldiers behind a few chariots or a defensive formation, and there had the upper hand against the desert warriors.

Another presence flowed through both armies, confounding much of what the Son tried to accomplish. The Daughter, her presence as sweet as a spring bloom, lent her courage to the pockets of Amaqi resistance, and sowed confusion in the Marasmian ranks. Yet she could not counteract the strategic—and supernatural—advantage owned by the attacking warriors. Nor could she, seemingly, confront the hole or the god within it directly. A delaying tactic at best.

Two other people registered as important nodes in the ever-changing tapestry Lenares beheld. One, a tall, blond-haired soldier, she recognised as Captain Duon. To her senses he glowed, a conduit for magical power: certainly none could stand before his sword. The captain wore a surprised look on his face, as though he could not believe the prowess he exhibited with the blade.

Beside him stood a soldier, shorter in stature, but, if anything, more of a lodestone of power in the battlefield. So much magic poured into the man that Lenares could not recognise him. Most disturbing was that both the Son and the Daughter were attempting to infuse their will into him; he coruscated with a swirling blend of purple and gold, masking his face and wrapping him like a shroud. So much seemed to depend on him, so much effort being expended, and yet Lenares knew nothing of him.

As she watched, one of the warriors, a chieftain with braided hair, burst through the Amaqi defences and threw a knife at the unknown soldier. Captain Duon knocked it out of the air with his sword, then turned and engaged the warrior, who used his spear as a staff. The exchange was a brief one. The captain parried the spear and thrust the man through before he could recover.

"It's time!" the unknown soldier called, his voice supernaturally amplified by one of the gods, Lenares could not distinguish which. "Abandon the field!"

Captain Duon bent his head to speak to the fellow, but received only a shake of the head in reply. The captain waved his arms in remonstration, which brought a further shake. The remnant of Amaqi soldiers formed around the two men, then began marching towards where Lenares and Torve had hidden. Before they realised what was happening, the Marasmians had given way before the Amaqis and the two observers had been enveloped by the army they were observing.

"I will not abandon the larger part of my expedition!" the captain roared as he passed the rock that hid Lenares and Torve. "They will be killed!"

"They are dead already, Captain," said a voice Lenares recognised. "Unless we disengage now we will join them in a graveless death."

"But all we have left are a few hundred soldiers! What of our chariots?"

"Toys for the Marasmians to amuse themselves with, ma sor," said the soldier.

Dryman, that was the man's name. Lenares risked a peek from behind the rock, but to her annoyance the gods had withdrawn their power from both men. Were they no longer relevant? Or had their escape been offered and accepted, somehow conceded? She suspected that Dryman had been the one the gods had contended for.

Torve pulled her up by her arm, and they fell in with the soldiers.

Behind them the Marasmians formed up again, closing their circle on the thousands of soldiers and camp followers still alive. Lenares knew what was about to happen, but did not want to watch. *But I have to. I might learn something more about the hole in the world. The more I study it, the more I can analyse its patterns.* So she observed when she could as they hurried fatherbackwards towards the oasis and freedom.

Many of the soldiers had not managed to arm themselves—weapons and armour were carried in wagons for ease of walking in desert conditions—and so sued for mercy on their knees. Others knew more about their adversaries and could guess what was in store for them; they fought on, but they were few and soon overwhelmed.

The camp followers stood in a daze and watched the
Marasmians advance, not understanding the depth of hatred that would soon burst over them, but sensing that
their time had come.

The day ended as a blood-red sun sank behind evening
cloud, sending rays of red-gold light across the desert towards the former valley of the Marasmos River. The few
hundred survivors of the Emperor's great expedition set
themselves watchfires on the fatherback bluffs, but the
flames could not keep the chill from their hearts as they
listened to the screams of the tortured, the raped and the
torn. They were forced to endure the travails of their countrymen, on whom the full revenge for the destruction of
Marasmos all those years ago was exacted. Taunts and
shouts from the victors, along with descriptions of what
they were doing to their captives, echoed across the valley. Duon wept, heartbroken at what he had done. Beside
him, Dryman watched and listened with an impassive
face.

Lenares could hear only two voices. Of course, she
knew she could not really hear them, but they haunted her
mind anyway. There, in the dark heart of her imagination,
Rouza and Palain huddled together as around them the
cosmographers were taken, one by one, cruelly tortured
and fed to the flames. Nehane, Vinaru, Lyanal, Pettera,
Arazma. The two girls, aware of the particular shape the
warriors' vengeance would take upon them, begged and
cried until rough hands pulled them apart and took them
to separate places where the shadows descended on them
and destroyed their worlds. Eventually, as dawn drew
near, they were carried to the fire, broken and bleeding,
and cast upon it to shriek their last minutes away.

Slow tears leaked down Lenares' cheeks. She had wanted to hurt them, they deserved it, but this . . . No one deserved this. What made it unbearable was the knowledge that the reality would be worse than her imagination. Much worse. And had the cosmographers accepted her, she would be suffering along with them.

No one slept that night, either in the valley of the damned or on the cliff-top above, save the silent dead.

INTERLUDE

The bright images of battle burn hot into Husk's mind, flickering through the spike set in the captain's brain. Anonymous faces snarling, grimacing, shouting. Bodies running, falling, tumbling. Blood underfoot, blood smeared across his captain's vision, dripping from his forehead, a shallow cut from a stray thrown knife. Heavy breathing as Duon leans on his sword for a brief moment. Husk sends further power through the spike, strengthening his host's tired muscles, allowing him to think clearly. Clear thinking is not a luxury Husk can afford.

Husk's carefully engineered plans are in danger of destruction. His manipulations have drawn the attention of some unholy power, which appears to be trying to bend his tools to its own use. Someone is working against him, he is sure of it now. Attacks against all three of his tools at the same time cannot be coincidence. Someone with an immensity of magic at their command, more than Husk can imagine, let alone encompass. Yet lacking in intelligence and finesse, trying to achieve their as-yet-unclear goals with brute force.

His protection is holding. He will protect his captain,

his priest and his angel by any means he can. If only he could have a moment free from this constant struggle; a period of calm to reflect on what is happening, to plan a new strategy, to somehow take the offensive instead of constantly reacting to events.

He sighs, a wheeze of hot, tortured air released into the cold air of the corridor. Husk has moved perhaps twenty paces in the last week, his slug-like body propelled forward in a wriggling motion that leaves skin, gristle and hair behind. His goal, the Tower of Farsight, is the highest place in Andratan castle and, at his present rate of progress, months away. He must move more rapidly, yet while his spikes are being assaulted, he cannot move at all.

A critical moment approaches. The captain has survived the worst of the battle: while a stray spear or sword could still kill him, the risk has decreased. His angel lives yet, though she is under siege. He can spare her no power. *Hold on, sweet one!* Husk turns his attention to the priest. His need is paramount. With an effort that sets himself back months, Husk overlays his adamant will on the weak-minded priest. Feeds him images, words, instructions, strength.

The fool resists. Has an abhorrence of such forceful possession. Fights against it with a manic energy.

Let go! Husk screams in white-throated agony as the depth of the struggle burns him. The priest has a will after all, and it is a strong one. It takes precious seconds to suppress.

The priest surrenders to Husk's will, takes up a sword and runs, the power of a master magician impelling him. Cries out the consort's name.

Too late, too late, Husk croons in misery.

Too late.

QUEEN

CHAPTER 16

THE CAGE

THE LORD OF FEAR NARROWED his eyes to slits. The woman made no move to defend herself, though she held within her an unguessable depth of power. He remained alert for any deception: she had, after all, been the consort of the Undying Man, and might be capable of anything. What his master had done for her had been the talk of the Bhrudwan army. The Lords of Fear had been able to sense the gift he had given her, but he had never told them the reason why it had been given. Galling, when every *Maghdi Dasht* longed to possess the gift for themselves. Yet, for all this, the only thing he could sense from her now was her fear.

Does she not know what she has? Bah, she does not deserve to retain it.

"I need only a small amount of your blood," he hissed. "But because I will brook no rival, you must die. To complete your death I must drain you. Do not struggle, or I will make your dying rich with agony."

"Please," she croaked, holding a hand out in front of

her. "Please!" Her screams sent a shiver through the Lord of Fear, feeding him.

Her eyes flickered, as if she listened to an inner voice, then rolled back in her head. She crumpled.

The *Maghdi Dasht* knelt beside her, lifted her chin and went to work with his knife.

Shouting from outside, a man bellowing his pain. The *Maghdi Dasht* turned, distracted in the act of lifting a pewter chalice to his lips. He put the cup, brimming with thick red liquid, down on the table.

The two fools he called sons would receive severe punishment for jeopardising the success of the ritual. "I told you both, no noise!" he growled, moving towards the door.

His eyes widened, then he pitched backwards with an animal cry, narrowly missing the table and landing with a thump on the wooden floor. A sword stood out from his chest. A wild figure, hair giving off smoke, had come through the doorway in a rush.

"Stella! Are you all right? Has he—"

The figure shrieked at what he saw.

The *Maghdi Dasht* dragged himself to his feet. One hand reached down and pulled out the sword. His mouth opened to emit a guttural cry of rage, and bright red blood gushed out, spattering the feet of the man who had struck him. The wounded magician slumped to his knees.

A second wild-eyed man burst into the room. "Conal, have you found her?" he said, out of breath.

He, too, cried out when he saw what had been done to the woman.

In his extremity the Lord of Fear reached deep within

himself, searching, summoning, drawing—*not enough power*—and was forced to reach outwards. Two strong men should suffice. Healing; then the chalice and immortality.

He drew from the first man, the one who had run him through with his blade. Shockingly, he encountered a deep well of raw magic. He immediately tried to withdraw, but the white presence in the man's head leaped forward eagerly and seized him.

And began to drink him dry.

Whichever direction Robal looked, horrors presented themselves to his shocked mind. The priest moaned, the lorn cry of a man who sounded as though he was in the throes of losing everything. Just beyond him the figure whom the priest had stabbed was . . . was *drying out*, skin flaking away, eyes popping, blood turning to a crimson powder. The transformation was accompanied by dreadful cracking sounds, like dry timber being broken over someone's knee.

And the worst sight of all . . . The guardsman's heart was not large enough to encompass what had been done to her. He closed his eyes, retched and forced himself to look. Nothing he had ever done was as difficult as opening his eyes again.

Her throat had been cut. Her wrists slashed. She hung from a butcher's hook embedded in a roof beam. Blood still dripped from her wounds, pooling on the wooden floor. Her chest had stilled; she was not breathing. Her empty eyes stared at him without expression.

Stella was dead.

And at that moment, Most High forgive him, all he

could think about was his own failure. His whole life lived under an illusion. His father and grandfather had stuffed his young head full of tales of what he might do for Faltha: golden summer stories of war and renown, of service and reward. None of them had involved leading the Falthan queen to her death.

The golden summer had just ended. He would walk out of this cabin into a bleak winter.

His eyes alighted on the small table and the chalice resting upon it. *Oh. Her blood.* Drained and prepared, ready to drink. *As though it is the key ingredient in some ritual.* He took a step back, appalled. *Her blood, is it magical? What does it confer on the one who drinks it?* Something dark and selfish rose up in his breast with the realisation. *Long life.* The reason she appeared so young when she should be in the twilight of her years.

Immortal.

The chance opened to him like a reluctant flower. Something good could come of this tragedy after all. With her blood he could make things right, could devote lifetimes to ridding Faltha of the priests, could lead an army eastwards and defeat the Destroyer, could ... *I could make something of myself after all, Granda; you'd be proud of me.*

Whimpering sounds came from somewhere in the cabin. He ignored them.

Visions boiled up in his head. Bold Robal Anders taking wound after wound in battle, slaying Lords of Fear with his two-handed blade. Robal the Wise, beloved counsellor, offering subtle correction to a grateful Council of Faltha. King Robal the Eternal at the head of a numberless army, calling defiance against Andratan. All possible—no, *inevitable*—if he were to take a sip. A life without limits.

He stepped over the desiccated remains of the magician and drew close to the table. His hand hung by his side a moment, wavered, and then reached towards the chalice.

"Don't drink it, Robal," said a woman's voice.

Robal Anders' spine turned to ice at the words; at his recognition of the voice that spoke them and the infinite weariness behind them. He did not want to, could not make himself, turn and face the speaker, so frightened was he at what he might see.

Even at this moment his hand continued until it had grasped the chalice's slim stem. But now the visions in his head were edged with blood, offering an eternity of dealing in death and darkness. Dark armies, darker dungeons. Robal Anders, the new Undying Man. A second Destroyer.

He put the chalice down, careful not to spill a drop, then turned to face her.

"I would not curse my worst enemy with such a fate," Stella said. She drew a shuddering breath. "And you are not my worst enemy."

She still hung from the beam, the meat hook buried in her back. Her feet dangled some distance above the floor. Her sallow face was new-lined with the marks of pain. The scar on her neck grew less visible even as he watched. A last drop of blood fell from her wrists, then they, too, began to heal.

Directly below her feet the priest knelt, his forehead pressed to the floor in what looked like worship.

"Robal," she said, licking her pale lips with an even paler tongue, "bring me the chalice."

Taking the chalice, cupping its bowl in his two hands,

then reaching up and placing it against her cold lips, turned him inside out. Blatant confirmation that this woman whom he admired was uncanny, sustained by something intrinsically evil. Her courage, warmth and humanity, all the virtues that had earned his respect, were underlain by this darkness and pain. He watched the liquid disappear as she drank. He watched the expression of loathing on her face.

He placed the empty chalice, now no more than a pretty object, on the table, then took her in his arms and lifted her away from the cruel barb.

"I cannot stand," she whispered in his ear.

"I will lay you down on the pallet here," he said.

"No! Not there. Take me outside and let me lie in the sun." She gasped another breath.

"You are hurt. You will catch a chill."

She tried to smile. "I have no secrets from you. I have survived a magician's knife; do you not think I will survive an afternoon breeze?"

He smiled at her courage and carried her outside, handling her as though she were made of crystal. He found a grassy place next to the path and laid her there. At once she closed her eyes; her features relaxed somewhat and her laboured breathing settled into a regular pattern.

Robal collapsed onto the path and began to weep.

Some time later Conal the priest rescued him from his spiralling thoughts. "Robal," the man said, tugging at his cloak. "Robal, what happened here?" He groaned then, clutching at his left arm.

The guardsman wiped his face with his hand and turned his gaze on the priest. "What do you mean? You know what happened. You saved Stella."

Conal's pinched features remained puzzled. "Saved Stella?" he echoed in his irritating fashion. "I didn't. I remember . . . I don't remember. Why does my arm hurt so much?"

"Priest, this mummery is not worthy even of you. Yes, you slew the magician who tried to kill the queen. Showed the speed, strength and courage her guardsman lacked. What else do you want me to say?"

"But, Robal, I don't recall any of it. We were standing in the reeds, arguing about where the queen might have gone; then I found myself in a room, on my knees, and she was just *hanging there*." His voice broke on the last two words.

"There is something we don't yet see," Robal said, easing himself to his feet. "I don't understand what happened to you; you say you don't remember it, but you acted like a man possessed. For a moment I thought the Most High himself had taken command of your body. How else would you have been able to charge like a bull through the rushes, bash the brains out of a man who opposed you, and stab a powerful magician to death?"

"I did all that?"

"Someone did, but it certainly wasn't you. Nor the Most High, not unless he is completely unlike what you priests tell us about him. You behaved more like Achtal the renegade Bhrudwan did in battle training." He realised that the priest might well have no idea who he was talking about. "Powerful, unstoppable, like a bear on a rampage. Does that sound like you?"

"No. Robal, the man cut her up!" Conal's voice was pitched higher every time he spoke. "There was blood all over the floor. He was about to drink it! Is she going to be all right?"

"Priest, I don't know the answer to that question. I don't have answers to any of this. But here are my best guesses. She stumbled on a magician, or she was drawn here by him, one or the other. I don't know how he found out about her secret, but he knew she was immortal and sought to gain that prize for himself. And either you are a hero with special powers who saved her with great courage and skill, or you were used by something or someone who cares about the queen. Or has plans for her. Ah, I cannot figure it out. There are too many unknowns!"

Conal's eyes grew as big as saucers. "Immortal?" he whispered. "When was she going to tell me about that?"

The guardsman clapped a meaty hand to his forehead. Foolish runaway mouth. *He didn't know. Nor did I, really, until today, not for certain, anyway. But he would have reasoned it out, surely. Eventually.*

"The magician was a Lord of Fear," said Stella, her weak voice barely audible. The two men turned, their attention instantly focused on her wellbeing. "I'm sorry I didn't tell you both about my . . . ah, good fortune. But I thought you must have known." She grimaced. "No, that is a lie; it won't do. I tried to keep it secret from everyone, though I don't really know how successful I was."

She levered herself up from the grass as she spoke, and rubbed at her left wrist with her right hand. Robal offered her an arm, but she waved him away.

With a wan smile set on her face she told them everything that had happened to her since she had sent them into Vindicare. A thick rage gripped Robal as Stella explained how Ma had betrayed her. "What was the price?" he growled. Stella suggested it might have been a misguided loyalty to the dead king. *There will have been a price*, the guardsman thought, but he kept his views to himself. He listened intently as she gave them the reasons for her belief that the corpse in the cabin was a Lord of Fear, a reduced but still potent remnant from the days when the Destroyer fled his ruin at Instruere. The priest asked questions incessantly, making it impossible for Robal to get any clear sense of what had happened. How many Lords of Fear accompanied the Destroyer back east after his defeat? How powerful were they?

"How about you let your sovereign tell her story, son," he barked in his best barracks-room voice.

For a wonder, Stella agreed with him. "You'll have plenty of time to hear the story behind the Lords of Fear," she told the priest. His response was a wide grin, which in Robal's view served to make him appear even more foolish than normal.

"I'm coming with you, then," the priest said, and Robal could have grabbed him by the throat, such was the complacency in his voice and manner.

"No decision has yet been made. Stella and I will talk about it and will convey our decision to you when we're ready to." His words didn't fool the priest, whose grin grew even wider.

An animal-like moan spun them around in the direction of the cabin. *Is the magician really dead? Has he come back to life?*

A broad-shouldered man staggered drunkenly onto the path. Robal went for his sword, only to realise it lay on the floor of the cabin, still covered in the magician's blood.

The man tripped over a tree root and went down on one knee. His teeth clacked together and he moaned again like a cow in distress. His struggle to regain his feet was painful to watch.

"He has lost his mind," said the priest, and took a step towards the path.

"Literally," Robal said. The back of the man's head had been laid open, the skull smashed and hanging, leaving visible a wet redness.

Stella put a knuckle in her mouth. "Do something," she pleaded with Robal.

"This was the priest's doing," said the guardsman. "Tell him to finish what he started."

"*Conal* did this?"

"Just before he ran the Lord of Fear through with my sword. Now turn away. Priest, go and fetch my sword. I have a mercy to perform."

Once before, a decade ago at the bitter end of the Border Wars, Robal had used his blade to end a wounded man's suffering. Sent east by a nervous Council concerned about the behaviour of the Piskasian army, he and another Instruian guardsman were ostensibly serving as mercenaries when the Hantils, tribesmen from Birinjh, invaded over the Armatura Mountains in search of grain. They had been driven back twice in the previous three years by a ruthless Piskasian force, but a prolonged drought in their homeland gave the tribesmen little choice but to sweep down on the rich cornfields of the Eastern Highlands. The fighting had been desperate, with no quarter given; and at the rump end of victory he and Peler were ambushed by a Hantil family unconnected with the fighting. Peler tried not to take any lives, but his caution lost him his own, hamstrung and then disembowelled by two boys who came upon him in stealth, and then fled in the direction of the mountains. By the time Robal fought off the mother and father his fellow Instruian was near death, begging for the only release Robal could offer him.

Affected by emotion, Robal's chest thrust had not been as steady as Peler needed. The harrowing few seconds that passed before Robal forced himself to take his friend's head dominated his dreams.

The image of Peler's anguished face, the sound of his screaming, even the involuntary twist of the blade in his hand as he scored a rib, came rolling back to Robal as he took the sword from the priest's hand and strode over to the suffering man. This time he did not allow sentiment to mar his stroke. He had learned his lesson. The hideously damaged brute died before he hit the ground.

Robal had cleaned and sheathed his blade by the time Stella and the priest turned back to him. He met their questioning faces with a short, professional nod, determined not to let them see how much the task had cost him.

Stella had other things on her mind. "Conal *slew* the Lord of Fear? *Conal* saved me?" She gazed at the moon-faced priest with surprise and something approaching admiration in her eyes.

Robal kept his features smooth, allowing none of his resentment to show. "Yes, your majesty, you were saved by the brave actions of a Halite priest." If that were not ironic enough to make his point, he would despair of her.

"Would someone care to explain how this might be?" Stella seemed unhappy; suspecting, perhaps, that she was being lied to.

The priest beamed his rude grin at her. "You'll have plenty of time to hear the story behind your rescue as we travel," he said.

We'll hear it many times, no doubt, Robal thought, not trusting himself to speak.

Of necessity the three travellers spent the night in the cabin. They were, after all, probably still being hunted by the greycloak Koinobia guards from Vindicare. Conal was surprised by how tidy the small house had been kept; cleanliness had associations with good morals as taught by the Koinobia, so, he reasoned, the reverse must also be true. The Archpriest always kept his study immaculate, a virtue any scholar could respect, though even he would have appreciated the domestic organisation evident here.

The priest twitched uneasily as he lay on the floor. The link between his fastidious Archpriest and the repulsive Lord of Fear was surely an inappropriate one; but, once made, the connection proved difficult to sever.

Conal had been given the task of disposing of the remains of the *Maghdi Dasht*. *An ignominious end to who knows how long a life of evil*, he cajoled himself into thinking as he swept the flakes of skin and bone into a pan. *Just a pile of ashes*. The lie almost worked, undone when he made his way down to the river and tipped out the pan, only for the breeze to blow the ashes back in his face. He choked and vomited for half an hour, until the guardsman had come looking for him. The stern-faced man brought him back to the cabin and gave him a cup of water.

Now he lay close to the place where Stella's blood had gathered. Robal had cleaned that, thank the Most High. The events of the day were murky at best; for some reason Conal could not remember anything clearly after stepping out of the boat on this side of the river. Robal had said something about him striking a man down—the one whom Robal had later killed; an action the priest considered distasteful, though necessary—and slaying the Lord of Fear. Impossible, of course. Who more than he, a student of the Falthan War, knew how difficult the *Maghdi Dasht* were to kill? Robal must be spinning a tale, lying to cover something up. But, if so, why could Conal not remember the events surrounding the Lord of Fear's death?

His thoughts turned to Stella. She was the true mystery. He had come to himself to find her hanging above him, while he knelt at her feet. Dead, bled out like a sheep or a cow, then alive again. Immortal, Robal had said. He desperately, so desperately, wanted not to believe it.

Despite all she had said to him, notwithstanding her friendly, open manner, she had kept her true secret hidden from him. He was her historian, her hope of avoiding the judgment of the Koinobia. How had she expected this evasion to serve her? Unless she had never intended for him to know.

Instead of maintaining his scholarly reserve, questioning all she said and putting her words to the test, he had fawned over her like an acolyte over his master. Had increasingly taken her word as truth. She had betrayed him. Made him into a fool.

No, it was important to be accurate. He had made himself into a fool.

Stella Pellwen, the Destroyer's Consort, was immortal. Now he knew the coin with which she had been paid for her treachery. Oh, and what coin it was! Never to die, to exist on and on, growing in wisdom and knowledge over the centuries, successive generations to enlighten: a prize to be favoured above all others. The thought of it made his chest ache with barely suppressed desire.

And when were you going to share your own little secret with Stella? said a voice in the back of his mind. A bitter voice, the unwelcome prompting of his conscience. He made himself face it. It was the key to his life, this constant attempt at honesty; a continual stripping away of the pride that accumulated around men with his talents.

His own little secret. How might the Destroyer's Consort react to learn that her travelling companion had been part of a Halite information-gathering team that had penetrated all the way to Andratan itself? They had spent a week in the fortress of their enemy, guests of a high-ranking Bhrudwan official whom they had convinced to extend them an invitation, believing them to be lawmakers from Bhu-bhu Nghosa. Andratan was an enormous place. He had not seen the Destroyer during his visit, spending the entire time dreading an encounter that never happened. The Halites were feted by their Archpriest on their return; Conal elevated along with the rest of them, becoming a senior figure in the Koinobia virtually overnight.

Not that you knew the Archpriest's plans for political control of Faltha. The voice again. How senior had he really been? Certainly not part of the inner circle that counted.

Yet in his hands he now held a secret that would admit him to any Halite circle he cared to join.

The priest, the guardsman and the queen left the cabin as early as possible the next morning, pausing only to take as much food as they could carry. Conal found himself tidying up after the other two; he was not normally the most tidy fellow and his own actions puzzled him, until he remembered his thoughts of the previous night. He immediately found himself in an impossible position: to continue cleaning in order to verify his own goodness, or to cease his tidying so as not to identify with the Lord of Fear—or the Archpriest. He cursed his foolish mind, but could not dismiss his feelings of discomfort. *Such are the problems facing a sophisticated man*, he reassured himself. *Or a half-insane fool*, whispered a small voice at the back of his mind.

As they closed the door of the cabin the attention of the three travellers was drawn to the nearby forest. Conal could hear moaning and crying, as though from someone in distress. In front of him Robal drew his sword, waved the others to stillness, and went forward to investigate. He returned, red-faced with anger and breathing heavily. "I should have let the brute suffer," he said, which was to Conal no explanation at all.

The guardsman led Conal and Stella to a small clearing in the forest a few hundred paces from the cabin. There stood a small enclosure, roofed with thatch and surrounded by thick stone walls, within which were imprisoned a number of people. Women, girls and boys, Conal noted with rising horror. No men visible through the grilled windows. The prisoners, if that was what they were, cried out anew on seeing the strangers approach.

The structure had a door made of iron bars, located on the far side from the cabin, secured by an enormous brass padlock. Robal sent Conal back to the cabin to search for a key. As the priest left the clearing he saw Robal lift a large block of stone and smash it against the lock in an attempt to break it open.

There was no key to be found in the cabin. Conal could have told Robal that if the guardsman had been prepared to listen. Conal had, after all, spent some time tidying there. Instead, he set himself to search the body of the man he had supposedly hit on the head with a tree branch, the man whom Robal had slain the previous day. It was a dreadful task; though the corpse did not yet smell he imagined he could sense the rottenness of decay, and flies were becoming interested in the horrible wound to the back of the man's head. The man needed burying, a task which ought to have fallen to him; but he'd never buried anyone before, had never seen a dead body until the night Dribna drowned in the Maremma. Conal hoped he'd not be asked. He searched hurriedly through the pockets of the tunic, eventually finding a small purse containing a key and a number of shiny coins. He suffered no pangs of conscience as he took the purse for himself.

Sensibly, the guardsman had given up bashing the lock by the time Conal returned. The mechanism was a little bent but essentially undamaged, and the key turned with ease. A click and the padlock fell away, the door swung open and more than twenty people walked slowly, hesitantly, out into the clearing.

Most of them, including all of the children, were near-naked and dirty; the remainder wore tattered and filthy garments. Some swung their heads from side to side as if scanning for danger, others collapsed to the ground and began to sob, and a few stood in the open, faces immobile, giving no impression they comprehended their surroundings. Three remained in the structure, standing with the same blank stare. Two more lay unmoving on the reed-covered floor, staring up at the iron bars below the thatch.

"What has happened to you?" Stella asked the prisoners. "Who has done this to you?"

"We aren't allowed to talk," said one of the older girls. Some of the others flinched as she spoke. "Have to keep quiet. If we talk they do us."

Conal saw Stella's face harden. "You can talk now," she said. "We have killed your captors. You are safe."

"Safe?" The girl spoke the word as if she had no idea of its meaning. "Show me their dead bodies. Show me where the ghost and his two boys lie. Dig them up and show them to me. When I see them dead, then I'll feel safe."

"*Two* boys?" Robal said quietly, flicking his sword out and assuming a fighter's stance. At this, the prisoners drew together, and a few of them ran for the safety of their prison.

The guardsman turned to Stella. "Do you remember two thugs?" His voice remained soft, but Conal could hear the doubt in his words.

The queen raised her chin as she answered. "You ask what I can remember? Have you ever died and come back to life again? Yesterday's events are a dream." She paused, then put a hand to her forehead. "Now I think on it, I can recall hearing conversations . . . there *were* two of them." Her head dropped. "Oh, Robal, I am sorry. I didn't want to think about what happened."

"Three chairs, three beds," Conal said. "Stella is not the only one to miss the obvious."

"So there is a second ruffian about." Robal scowled at the forest eaves. "We will talk later about yesterday."

"He won't be far away," said Stella. "He will have seen us leave—"

A bear-like roar rose up from somewhere behind them, in the direction of the cabin. The rest of the prisoners fled back into their cage as a broad-shouldered man lumbered into the clearing, sticks in both hands. "You killed Tunza!" he shouted. "You done in me da!" Without pause he threw himself at them, swinging the sticks as he came.

It was an execution. Conal had never seen one before; though they were infrequent in Instruere, most people had been to see at least one, to satisfy their curiosity if nothing more. The priest thought them morbid. Now, as Robal stepped smoothly forward and thrust his sword unerringly into the berserk man's chest, then jerked it out again, Conal realised that an execution cast a glamour all of its own. He watched the body continue forward, life already gone, its momentum sending it crashing against the wall of the cage, to fall on its back, eyes wide and staring. *I am alive*, he told the corpse in relief, *and you are dead. I am alive because I am good, and you have been punished because you are evil*. It felt almost as if he had borrowed life from the newly-dead man.

Just how evil the man and his brother had been began to emerge when the captives recovered enough to talk.

"Tunza and Ramzy would come and choose someone, do 'em and then kill 'em. Always over there, where we could see 'em." The speaker, a boy no older than twelve, cried as he talked and made no effort to clean the snot running from his nose. "Said we was rewards given 'em by their father for bein' good."

A little girl, surely six years old if not younger, said: "They catched us, they catched us!" It was all she could manage, and nothing anyone said to her could encourage her to say anything more.

"Ramzy done Faira yesterday," said the older girl who had first spoken. "She'd been here longer than anyone.

Months and months. Ramzy and Tunza both hated her, they said, because she had a harelip. Didn't stop Ramzy though." She shuddered and turned away from where the brute lay. "Took his time, then ran off when he heard shouting. We haven't seen anyone since, not even at sunset. They feed us at sunset, you see."

"Most High," Stella breathed, tears rolling down her cheeks. "How long has this been going on? Please, someone tell me it has not been happening for seventy years." Her face was white with shock.

Robal put an arm around her shaking frame, though his face held as little colour as hers. Conal wondered why he felt nothing as yet. *Because these unfortunates are of no account*, said the voice in the back of his mind. *Because you have a great deal yet to achieve, and will not allow yourself to be distracted by such things*. The words sounded reasonable, but something in his mind rebelled against them, recognising the horror they contained.

Conal listened with increasing detachment to the rest of the captives' story. The prisoners had been taken from the river, mostly, though some had been surprised in the fields, and dragged through the reeds and the forest to their prison. The deaths were irregular, sometimes with a week or more between visits from the brothers. Punishments for speaking or struggling were ruthless, and the two men had made it clear they could make death protracted or merciful depending on the prisoner's behaviour. The freed captives would have continued to volunteer information, but Stella put a stop to the flow of horrific description. Robal had by this time clapped his hands over his ears.

"We have to leave," Conal said into the silence

following the tales of torment. "My queen, you are being hunted by the Koinobia. If you wish to remain free, you cannot remain here. And I would like to find someone to treat my arm."

"The priest speaks sense," Robal rumbled. "And I do not want to stay in this clearing a moment longer."

"But we have people to care for," Stella said, anguish in her voice. "How can we leave them to survive in the wild? Look at them; some can barely stand."

"What do you propose we do?" The guardsman lifted her chin and looked down into her red-rimmed eyes. "March them back to Vindicare? Alert the authorities? You will be handing yourself to the priests. I will not let that happen, my dear." He dropped his hand. "Of course we will not abandon them. We will lead them north, away from the river and through the forest, until we find a village or a farmhouse. Then they will no longer be our problem. Will you agree to this?"

After a time, Stella gave him a clearly reluctant nod.

In the end three of the former prisoners did not complete the journey. One refused to come, spitting and fighting with teeth and fists and nails whenever anyone approached too closely. So they supplied her with some food and left her there. A second girl, terrified of the dark, ran off during the first night. And they woke to find a boy dead on the morning of the third day, the day they discovered a village. He had stopped breathing some time during the night. Robal could find no evidence of physical damage, and had no other explanation for his sudden death.

"We should have left them in the clearing," the guardsman said. "I fear by making them walk for days we have given them no chance to recover from their ordeal. We would have been better to seek out the nearest village ourselves and tell them what we discovered."

"I doubt they would have been able to care for themselves," Stella said. "How many would have remained alive by the time someone returned to help them? Assuming we were believed? And I think a few days on their feet in the warmth of the open air has helped them." She cast an eye over the group as they walked, saw the limping, the open sores, the glazed eyes, the weariness. "Well, a few of them, anyway."

Tell them the real reason. Her helping the Destroyer escape Instruere all those years ago, involuntary though it was, had led directly to the suffering of these innocents. *Directly.* It was her fault the Lord of Fear had survived, and in the intervening years she had not thought once about the fate of the *Maghdi Dasht. I thought they'd all died; I was sure of it. And now others pay the price for my assumption.* And a darker thought: *are there others out there? Other ghosts in the forest, haunting the eastward road, preying on passers-by?* She would make it a high priority when she returned to Instruere ... Except, of course, she was unlikely ever to return. Now the Koinobia had usurped the leadership, she would doubtless be declared an enemy. Her life would be forfeit; there would be a price on her head.

How have the Halites come to power so swiftly? She'd received no hint of it as queen, nor had Leith, despite those in the king's employ whose business it was to be aware of such things. *Complicity, that's the word underlying everything.* Alliances between the Instruian Guard and the Halites, forged in secret while the king lay dying. And that cursed Archpriest now probably the new ruler, though she had no doubt he claimed otherwise.

Stella sighed in relief when a small village came into view. The bedraggled procession of prisoners made their way along a brightly decorated main street, the village clearly in the throes of a festival of some kind. Stalls had been set up on both sides of the wide lane, banners flapped in the simoom wind, and children clapped their hands and laughed at the antics of performers.

The music ceased, children stilled and the villagers turned as one to face the group. A number of the freed captives cowered in the face of the silent attention.

"Milly! Milly!" a woman screeched, and came running out of the crowd. She stopped before one of the prisoners, a girl of perhaps fifteen years, one of those who had not spoken since her rescue. One of those, Stella thought, whom the torture had driven mad.

Milly—if it was she—shied away from the woman, who cried out in surprise. "Milly! It's me, your ma! What has happened to you?" She turned to Stella. "What happened to her?"

This was not going to be easy. Though Stella had determined not to talk about the worst abuses, any relatives of the prisoners would be shocked by even the least harrowing of the tales that would emerge.

The villagers gathered around, their festival forgotten, as Stella, assisted by Robal, explained about the brothers and the cage. There was anger at the words, which rose to fury, and some of the men decided then and there to mount an expedition to find the place, locate any other prisoners—or their graves—and bring any news they could back to the villages in the area. They rushed off to their homes, afire with plans to set out immediately.

Worst were the women who sought news of missing loved ones. "Have you seen my Sirla? We thought the river took her. Three years ago it was," one woman said.

"There must have been a wee boy, he'd be seven years old now, a little fellow with bright blue eyes and a smiling face," another woman said in tones so hopeful it almost broke Stella's heart to hear. "Please, is he there? Why didn't you bring him?"

Request after request, all but drowning her under the waves of raw emotion. The fear, the despair, the rekindled hope. *We've destroyed a village.*

In the end the travellers did not accept the perfunctory offers of hospitality advanced to them by some of the villagers, as much as they needed time to recover. Stella could feel the hostility their appearance had generated. A few, without lost children of their own, simply regretted the loss of their festival, of their fun or the income they were expecting: petty, selfish and not worth considering. But others were genuinely distressed, either because their lost child was not one of those returned, or—even worse, perhaps—because he or she was. Along with Milly, another prisoner, a young boy, was identified by frantic parents. Like Milly, the boy gave no indication of recognising his loved ones.

Stella watched as the village physic made a show of examining Conal's arm, partly because the woman could face no more of the horror that had been placed in her lap. "You've cracked it, all right," the plain-faced woman said, handling the limb as though it were a snake. "Not much to be done apart from keeping it still. Not much chance of that, if I know young men." She sighed. "Here's what will happen. I'll wrap your arm to your chest to keep it still. After a few days the pain will go away and it will start to itch. You won't be able to stand it, and you'll tell yourself your arm has healed quickly. You'll take the binding off, do something foolish and rebreak it, much worse this time. If you're lucky and it doesn't get infected, at the least it'll never set properly. You'll lose most of the use of it. So why don't we save the bother of binding it and just send you on your way?"

"No, no," Conal said, his face drawn with the pain. "I'll follow your advice—I'll not move it, nor will I unbind it before time."

"So they all say. Well, by the look of you you're not a woodsman or a farmer. Perhaps you've not the need for both arms. My husband has a saw; how about we take it off at the shoulder? Save you a deal of trouble later."

The priest's face took on a faintly pale cast. "Please, madam, just bind it as you said. I promise not to interfere with it before time."

Her point made, the physic immobilised his arm, taking longer than Stella thought she ought to. Avoiding the task of examining more of the prisoners.

"In a month or so seek out a doctor," the physic said. "Let him examine my work. If he says you can use your arm again, you may say my name in a blessing to Eternal Hal."

"That I will, lady; I am a—ow!"

Stella had nudged him in the back. "Sorry," she said, "but the physic has other patients to see to, many with needs greater than yours. And we must be leaving. We have a long way still to travel."

"I have payment," Conal said, drawing out the purse he'd taken. "How much do you require?"

"Nothing," the woman said, her severe face softening. "You have done a noble thing, bringing these children home, though I doubt many will thank you for it. Now, I have unpleasant things to do. Be careful with that arm of yours."

As soon as the physic had gone, Robal leaned close to Stella. "Sooner or later anger and suspicion will fall on us," he whispered to her, and she nodded agreement. They made an abrupt departure from the village after accepting offers of food and drink, but before the prisoners began to tell their tales. A few villagers marked their leaving with taunts and rude comments, but most bade them farewell.

"We are fortunate to escape before the worst of the story is told," Robal commented as they made their way northwards along a grassy lane. On either side tall poplars bent before the simoom.

"You could have defended us, I am sure," Stella said. "But I would rather avoid anything that imprints us on their memories more clearly than has been achieved already. The grey guards will certainly come through this village in search of us." They must have marked her escape to the far bank of the Aleinus.

"Well, then," Conal said, almost cheerfully. He seemed relatively unaffected by the tragedy of the prisoners. "Where do we go now?"

Robal growled, but Stella thought it a legitimate question. *I don't know,* she was tempted to say to the priest. *I have too many questions. I need to go somewhere that provides answers.*

"Somewhere the Koinobia cannot find me," she said after some thought. "Do either of you have any ideas?"

CHAPTER 17

THE LIMITS OF IMMORTALITY

IT HAD BEEN A FLIPPANT comment, Conal knew. Stella had not expected for a moment that either he or Robal would offer a serious suggestion. But the guardsman rumbled in his throat for a moment, then ventured his thoughts.

"I know a place beyond the reach of the priests and their interference," he said, casting a baleful glance at Conal as he spoke. "But the priest can't come. He stays here."

"Oh no," Conal said heatedly, rubbing at his arm. They turned from the lane onto a woodland path, walking under the spreading branches of large oaks. "No. The agreement specifies that I remain with Stella until she has told me her story. I cannot be discarded yet." The threat of being left behind lent him an inner strength he had not realised he owned; it seemed to pour into his body from the back of his head, along with a dozen other arguments as to why he should stay with them.

"Then Stella will remain in danger," the guardsman said. "I will not take a priest with me into . . . To safety," he finished lamely.

"Then I will not accompany you," Stella said, folding her arms and standing astride the path. "Conal is a danger to no one. He will give his word not to betray the location of this place to any priest or member of the Koinobia, and you will accept it. Then I will be in a position to evaluate your kind offer."

Robal squared up to her: a head and a half taller, weighing perhaps twice as much, but without the iron will to enforce his opinion.

Come, Robal, the queen will have her way. You are just posturing, wasting our time.

"Oh? And you are always transparent?" Robal snapped at him. Shocked, Conal realised he had spoken the words aloud. Not only was he losing control over his thoughts, his mouth also seemed to be falling outside his discipline.

"Come, you two, we remain in danger yet." Stella turned and resumed walking. "None of us will be immune from suffering should the Koinobia discover us. Give your word, Conal."

"I promise on my honour as a—on my honour," he amended, "never to reveal the location of the place to which Robal Anders takes us."

"Very well," Stella said patiently. "Now, Robal, tell him you accept."

"Tell him yourself," the man snarled. "Since it was you who decided his word was worth anything."

They came to the end of the woodland path, climbed a stile and crossed a main road. In the distance they heard a horse's hoofs beating the ground; they scrambled across the road, over a ditch and a second stile, and hid in the long grass of the field until the noise had faded to silence.

"I don't understand your resentment towards me,"

Conal said to the man kneeling beside him. *Yes, you do*, the voice in his head remarked. *Your kind has taken control in Faltha. Don't you think he is angered by that?* "But here's a question for you. A guard was executed in Instruere last year for killing his wife in a drunken rage. Do all guards kill their wives?"

"Of course not."

"So neither are all priests as you imagine. Let us concentrate our energy on getting the Destroyer's—on getting Stella to safety. If you are still not satisfied with my promises after that, then perhaps you can adopt your fellow guardsman's solution to rid himself of an inconvenient companion. Or you can show me that not all guards are alike. Agreed?"

"Very clever, wordsmith. But when you leave a man no choice but to do that which he mistrusts, you make an enemy. Be careful, priest. I'm watching you."

Conal stood, turned to Stella and dusted himself off. "And that is the best you are going to get from us," he said wryly.

"So I see." She sighed. "Very well, Robal, lead on."

The guardsman led them to Finar, a small town nestled into a hill overlooking the Aleinus River, which in this area, twenty or so leagues upriver of Vindicare, flowed from the northeast. While Stella and Conal hid in the fields beyond the houses, the guardsman took the coin Conal had found in the beast-man's purse and purchased further supplies.

"They have an eye open for us," Robal said when he returned. "I have purchased only half of what we need, for fear of being marked. The story of the ghost and his prisoners has arrived here before us; the town is full of talk. It seems that all the towns and villages in the area have lost children at unusually high rates over the last few years."

"And they suspected nothing?" Conal asked. "Organised no search?"

"All attributed to natural causes," the guardsman explained. "There are many ways a young person can be lost. Drowned, most of them were thought to be, or lost in the woods, taken by wild beasts. A few people thought it odd, apparently, but no one went further than suspecting the Wodrani craft plying the river. They were searched on occasion, but nothing was found."

"So many deaths to lay at the Destroyer's feet," Stella said quietly as they rose to follow the guardsman. "It seems our story still goes on. I had thought with Leith's death it was at an end."

"The Destroyer will answer for those deaths one day," Conal said.

"Oh yes?" Robal said over his shoulder. "How, exactly? If he is immortal, how can he ever be brought to account? What punishment suffices for what we saw, priest, when we cannot do the like to him?"

"But surely—"

"Enough! We are about to reach the river. I have hired a boat to take us to the southern side, from where we will travel by cart into the steppes of Austrau. The boatman must hear nothing of our true identities. We can carry on the debate once we reach the southern shore, should there be anything sensible left to say."

A tight-lipped glare reinforced the guardsman's words, and Conal had the good sense, or at least enough of an instinct for self-preservation, to remain silent.

Rain began to fall from a leaden sky as they were rowed across the grey Aleinus River. The boatman was a chatterbox, a cheerful, longfaced man enamoured of his own voice, and spoke to them of the Falthan War and the action his grandfather had seen at Aleinus Gates and parts further east. The three of them endured his wildly inaccurate tales, thankful that the self-absorbed monologue ensured the man asked them no awkward questions.

After an hour Conal found himself marvelling at the man's stamina: he rowed a heavy boat across the current without seeming to draw breath. The rain fell in sheets, muting the occasional clap of thunder and forcing Conal to help bail rainwater. Finally the man ran the boat aground on the muddy southern shore and assisted his passengers out, talking all the while.

"So my granda, he said the biggest battle was by Skull Rock, not at Vulture's Craw like the historians and the travelling players say. Reckoned had we lost at The Gap, there wouldn't have been enough army to resist the Destroyer at Vulture's Craw. Likely blessed Hal's sacrifice would have been meaningless. My granda fought with the Strauxmen at Skull Rock, but with the Fodhram at Vulture's Craw. Better chance of survival, see? And you'll have a better chance at survival, and protecting her majesty there, if you stay away from them greycloaks. Fare you well, then, and I'll be thankin' you for my payment. You can trust me, you can, not to say nothing to nobody."

Robal paused halfway through counting out the coin, as though his brain had finally caught up with the man's words. His head jerked up.

"Some of us," the boatman said with a deliberateness

lacking in his earlier speech, "have longer memories than others."

The two men stared at each other, then Robal nodded.

Stella, whose attention had been engaged in collecting and distributing their supplies, came over. "Is all well?" she asked.

"Yes, it is," Robal said, and shook the boatman's hand. "Fare well, friend, and with all good fortune."

"And you, sir," came the response.

"Would either of you care to explain that?" Stella asked as they climbed up the southern bank.

"No," said Robal and Conal together; they looked at each other in surprise, and both laughed.

The conversation turned the next day to the subject of death and punishment, prompted by Robal's question of the day before. The last of the coin Conal had appropriated had purchased a donkey and a small covered trap, and the three of them huddled together out of the thickly falling rain as Robal guided the stolid donkey down puddle-lined paths.

"Best way to break a drought," the guardsman said morosely.

"What's that?" Conal asked, picking at the strapping that held his broken arm to his chest.

"Plan some long-distance travel."

"Ah yes. I remember a storm—" He clamped his mouth shut, thinking better of mentioning anything about his previous travels.

"Yesterday you implied that the Destroyer cannot be punished for his evil," Stella said to Robal. "Does your argument depend on the assumption that death is the only punishment he deserves, or merely the worst that can be given?"

"Ah, you have thought about this," the guardsman said carefully. "I've had my mind filled with the back ways of this land. It's been a while since I travelled in this part of Austrau."

"Then let me answer," Stella continued. "I can think of many worse things than death. To be left alive when everyone you know and love passes on would be worse than death to me. Who knows what the Destroyer fears most? The loss of his power, perhaps. Or to be shown proof that his two-thousand-year rebellion was not justified. Whomever wishes to punish a powerful man must first find out what he fears."

"I would not fear being immortal," Conal said. "I cannot see what is to be feared about outliving one's friends."

Robal muttered something; Conal could guess what it was. "I have more friends than you might think," he said haughtily. "And to carry their memories into the next generation, and the next, and the next: would that not confer on them, through me, another kind of immortality?"

Robal snorted. "I've heard that argument spoken at funerals. But what does it matter to a dead man how long he is remembered? Death, priest, is the end. Present company excepted, of course," he said hastily.

"Why except me?" Stella said, eyebrows raised. "My problem is not that I return from death, but that I cannot seem to die. And don't think I haven't tried."

"Oh." Robal was clearly taken aback by this news.

"*Is* death the end?" Conal said, warming to the subject. This discussion was like those he had shared with other trainee priests. "You might just as well ask whether birth was the beginning. There is no answer from behind the blank walls either side of us. But the scrolls talk of worlds beyond the walls of time. Many of those who lived in Dona Mihst before the time of the Destroyer did not die, but were translated to be with the Most High."

"I'd heard that the words in question were added to later versions of the *Domaz Skreud*," Stella said. "The idea of translation was not found in the earliest writings of the First Men."

Conal felt his eyes widening. He should not be surprised she knew this, yet she had caught him off guard again. "Ah, yes, some do say that. I've not seen the scrolls first-hand, not that the originals exist now, anyway; short of journeying to Dhauria, it is not a judgment I could make. Still, death must surely bring more than oblivion."

"No more than the day is a brief awakening between two nights of sleep." Robal was proving an able debater, possessing a keener mind than Conal had suspected. "We look for stories that it is otherwise: wishful thinking promoted by old women at the bedsides of their husbands and children. I have looked into the faces of dying men and watched the light of life go out. It is like a flame extinguished. There is no candle lit anew somewhere else. It frightens me."

"But with some people the soul eventually dies, leaving the shell alive but uninhabited. Isn't there evidence of this among the living?" Conal used his neighbour as an example, describing how she had withdrawn into herself, becoming a drooling wreck looked after by her husband. "If the soul can die and leave the body, cannot the body die and leave the soul?"

Stella nodded. "A good argument, priest."

The guardsman cleared his throat. "What evidence do you have to justify your belief in a soul? Son, I've seen men suffer head wounds in battle. Damage to the brain always affects what you would call the soul. Good men change into something else. They become irritable, violent, sometimes murderous. If the soul is separate from the body, how can that happen?"

An image of old Thessana flashed through Conal's mind. One of the most acclaimed Halite scholars, he had collapsed in his room one day after complaining of a headache. The stroke wiped away all traces of the wise, urbane scholar, an exemplar to them all, leaving a man who died cursing and raving, his mind gone. In fairness he told Robal and Stella the story, eliciting nods from both.

"And we've all seen a more recent example of someone suffering a head wound," Stella said. "Though the damage could hardly have made him a worse person."

"But if we truly believed death was not the end," Robal pressed, "we would not fight so hard to stay alive. I say we know what death really means, but we try to avoid the knowledge. I am content to sleep at the end of a day well spent, and so shall I be content to die at the conclusion of a life of value."

"Really?" Stella asked him, her face softening.

The guardsman swallowed. "No," he said thickly. "But it gives me comfort if I don't think about it too deeply."

"How else do you comfort yourself?" she asked.

"Mind tricks. I tell myself that fearing death is futile. If I am alive, death is held at bay. If I am dead, I can no longer fear it. Why worry about what I cannot change?" He grimaced. "Doesn't stop me worrying."

"No offence intended, Stella," Conal ventured,

prompted by a voice in his head, "but given that you are immortal, how can you really understand the debate?"

Robal turned his head sharply, and Stella frowned for a moment. The guardsman made ready to speak, but she forestalled him.

"Don't make the mistake of confusing the gift of immortality conferred on the living with the hope of the soul's continuance after death," she said, an edge of warning in her voice. "Just because I am hard to kill doesn't mean I'm not afraid of dying."

Conal acknowledged the point with a nod.

Stella leaned towards him. "You really believe that to live forever would be a blessing, don't you," she said.

"Yes, I do." Conal had thought about this. "You have a duty to share your gift with the world. Think what an advantage we would have over the godless, the Bhrudwans and the *losian*, the rejected of the Most High who live in Faltha. With your blood, the First Men would live and the *losian* would die. They would not be able to assail us. The Koinobia could distribute your gift. You would be the hero of Faltha, the centre of the eighth scroll. Would that not be a vision worthy of achieving?"

Stella's glorious face had darkened to anger with his words, a terrible threat written there.

"I spoke not to offend," Conal said, unsure what he had said to invite her anger.

"Then you did not speak carefully enough, priest. Let me tell you something about immortality. We are some way short of this point in my story, but I see that unless you learn now you will not hear anything I say in future.

"The Destroyer took me for his consort, yes, it is true. He drew me through the Blue Fire, a sorcerous device that transported me across the world in an instant. I was an unwilling captive, duped by Deorc, his representative in Instruere. I cannot describe the terror the Destroyer inspires. His voice is able to strip a person bare, cleaving mind from body, leaving one exposed to his scrutiny. He is an expert at using torture and pain, and the fear of pain, to achieve his ends. He breaks everyone he meets. Priest, the reason I am immortal is that I defied him. He could not break me any other way."

She closed her eyes, remembering. "When the armies of Faltha and Bhrudwo closed for the first time at The Gap, I was at his side. He sought to display me, to use me to undermine the confidence of the Falthan army. Instead of cowering before him as he wished, I spat in his face. I would do it again. He struck me with his fist, breaking my head—the scars remain—and doing me grievous injury. I lost consciousness and only regained it weeks later.

"Immediately I felt different—I can barely remember what it was to feel as I did before he struck me. My skin burned and agonising pain ran through my veins. I was partially crippled all down one side. Eventually I learned that I had nearly died, and he had kept me alive only by infecting me with his own curse. I never asked him how he achieved it—I assume, I *hope* it was through the transfer of blood. He never referred to it again.

"I doubt I could convince you of the effect of all the years of pain. Have you known anyone who has died of a wasting disease? That is what it was like for me. The pain has eased only gradually over the decades, though perhaps I have grown accustomed to it. I would not have thought it possible. Everything I do is done through a haze, a barrier of hurt, which separates me from the world. Everlasting pain, Conal: is that something you wish to experience? Or to share with Faltha?"

The priest licked his lips. "Ask me again on my deathbed. Perhaps it will be more attractive then." An odd, disconnected part of him seemed pleased to hear she suffered. He flushed with embarrassment, as though she could read his thoughts.

She continued. "I have had years to think about this. Dear Leith's death made it all the more immediate. Don't you think he knew? Yet he chose to reject the gift. These were his words the only time we discussed the matter: 'Immortality is useful only if it continues a desirable state. I do not desire to prolong my life for the sort of price you pay daily.' I tell you honestly, the best thing of all would be for me not to have been born. Second-best would have been to die young, before events caught up with me. It follows that the absolute worst outcome for me is to live with this pain and fear forever. I am . . ." She broke. "I am no longer human."

Suddenly her body was taken by deep sobs, an anguish so intense Conal felt he was intruding on her nakedness. In an instant Robal had his arms around her. He flicked his eyes at Conal, indicating that he should take the donkey's reins.

"Death would be a release for me," she said, sobs still hiccoughing between her words. "I was terrified when the *Maghdi Dasht* took his knife to me, but I was so deeply glad I could finally lay down my many layers of pain and defeat." Her smile was a mask. "The priest rescued me; it seems the Most High has not finished with me yet. He knows I want . . . I just want to sleep. One night without pain. If I never wake up again, so much the better."

After that, there was nothing either man could say. Conal was not adept at social interaction, and he knew any offer of comfort, any attempt at empathy, would come across the wrong way somehow.

Yet the idea of immortality would not let him go. Yes, there were limits, he could see that now. The idea of never-ending pain did not appeal to him, but neither did the idea of never-ending darkness. And the days of godly men being translated to be with the Most High forever had ended with the Destroyer's rebellion, curse him. But perhaps a truly courageous man, one with a vision for Faltha, might overcome the limitations.

He fell asleep that night to the sound of the rain and the inner vision of the world's secrets falling into his hands. *All I need is time*, was his last thought. *Only time*.

The Central Plains of Faltha measured over three hundred leagues east to west from the Aleinus Gates to the Wodhaitic Sea, and two hundred leagues from the northern Remparer Mountains to the Veridian Borders in the south. In all that distance there were few places one could ascend to see the way the land lay. Robal led them to the summit of one such place, an unremarkable grass-covered mound surrounded on all sides by flat, featureless plains. The Steppes of Austrau, he called them, with something approaching reverence in his voice.

Conal could see little to be reverent about. Leagues of brown grass lay all around, no sign of human habitation save the narrow path they had been using, the occasional small stony stream running south to north. The constant, annoying susurration of the wind. None of the beauty Robal spoke of so fondly was evident from the little hill.

"The simoom, ulcers to his soul, is an ugly wind."

Conal tensed, then turned to identify the speaker, but no one was visible save Stella and Robal.

"Kilfor, you rascal, you took ten years off my life," Robal said, striding forwards. He reached down into the grass and hauled up a thin, smiling man of middle age. This curious specimen wore a wide moustache below beetling eyebrows; his weatherbeaten skin looked as though it had been soaked in brine for years. He had a red kerchief around his neck, while a small brown skullcap—from under which projected a shock of spiky black hair—a silver-threaded waistcoat, ragged breeches and thick leather wrappings above hard-wearing boots completed the ensemble.

"Happiness and luck to you, Robal, you crazy young maniac," the man said affectionately, cuffing the guardsman around the ears. "And these are your unfortunate friends?" He turned to them and bowed extravagantly. "Welcome to Chardzou, the dyspeptic heart of Austrau. I apologise for your guide. You both must have done something very bad in a previous life to have ended up with this useless man. His head is full of dung, you know."

"Robal," Stella said out of the corner of her mouth, "you didn't tell us you had arranged to meet a friend."

"Hah!" the strange man said. "He didn't know, that's why. Not that he would have remembered. Too many years down in that walled town by the coast, ulcers rot its soul. Soft living makes you blind, Robal. You walked right into that inn last night, sat down, tossed off your beer and never saw me. I am highly offended, friend. You are not the boy I knew."

"I thought I could smell alcohol on you," Stella said

primly. "You told us you would be in and out of the tavern as quickly as possible."

Robal spread his hands. "No self-respecting man from these parts would pass up the chance to cut the phlegm, begging your pardon." He peered at the stranger. "Kilfor, was that you under the wide-brimmed hat? The one who snored the whole time I was there?"

The man nodded, a broad smile plastered over his gnarled face, and patted the hat, attached by a clip to his belt.

"I am going deaf, if not blind," Robal went on. "Anyone in southern Austrau ought to recognise you from the sound of your snoring, since it is the only thing that outdoes the simoom. I have missed the place, I confess. Aspects of it, anyway."

"What is Chardzou?" Stella asked, genuine puzzlement in her voice.

"Ah now, Robal, will you not introduce me to this handsome young woman who, given her proximity to you, obviously lacks taste?" Kilfor hitched up his belt and ran a hand across his forehead in an impossibly comical imitation of a man seeking favour.

"No secrets?" Robal asked Stella.

"Well, maybe one. But you can introduce me accurately. Your . . . ah, friend may be more inclined to help if he knows whom he is helping."

"If you have a pretty face he will help you," said Robal. "Very well. Kilfor of Chardzou, be well met with Conal, one-time priest of the Halites but now on the run; and with Stella Pellwen, Queen of Faltha."

At the first name the man's brows lowered; but when Stella was introduced they flew up in shock. His hand froze in the act of shaking hers, and he sank to his knees.

"I . . . ah . . . pardon me, my queen, I . . . have been misled by your beauty." Conal watched as the man tried to recover his poise. "The last queen was an old woman, or at least so said Robal. You, now: no one could say that you were old."

Robal couldn't help laughing at his friend's discomposure. "Good try, Kilfor, but your charm has failed you today."

Stella smiled, pulling the man to his feet. "Actually, he has done remarkably well. Much better, in fact, than someone else I know, who tried to seduce his queen when first they met."

"Seduce? Oh, that is rich!" Kilfor laughed heartily, hands on hips. "Robal the playboy, unable to win the heart of a queen!"

"And who said he failed?" Stella said silkily. "Anyway, I am the previous queen; that is, I am Leith's consort. There is no new queen as far as I am aware. I appear to have aged well, if your flattering reaction is anything to go by. Now, if the introductions are over, can we not go to this Chardzou, so I might have time to think what to do next in safety?"

"She is too sharp for us country hicks," Robal said quietly to Kilfor as they made their way down the hill to their trap. "Best not to entangle yourself with her in a battle of words. I pitied her poor husband, actually."

"I heard that, guardsman." Stella's voice drifted back from a few paces ahead.

Behind them all, Conal smiled. It would take more than a few coarse jests to woo this woman. He would wait until the glib guardsman had made a complete fool of himself before making his own move. Whatever form that move finally took, he was now determined to win her heart.

Risible, said the small white voice at the back of his head.

Chardzou was a day's journey southeast of the hill. Finally, the trap pulled up at a clearing in the pampas grass that might equally have been sited anywhere else within a fifty-league radius. There, forming a rough circle, stood a few dozen ramshackle canvas structures, each anchored to its own wagon. "Blows here like forty thousand northmen with indigestion," Kilfor said by way of explanation. "Anything you build gets blown over a few times a year. Might as well build something easily replaceable. Besides, we move about. Can't live too long on one piece of land."

"I see," Stella said, though to Conal's ear she sounded uncertain.

"Kilfor, you crapulent boy!"

Startled, the travellers turned towards the source of the screeched greeting. There was no one to be seen outside the rents, though a partly shaded birdcage hanging from one of the wagons contained a large green-and-yellow parrot, busy ruffling its feathers. "Wipe your shoes before you come in!" the bird croaked at them.

Kilfor smiled, as did Robal. "Still haven't got rid of the old bird?" the guardsman said.

"He'd get rid of his father before getting rid of the bird," said an old stooped man, emerging from the tent beside the cage.

Robal rushed over to the man and gave him a hug.

"Sauxa! So good to see you again!" He paused to wipe a tear from his eye.

"Do I have a foster-son or do I have a girl?" The man kissed Robal on both cheeks. "It is good to see you again, Robal," he said gruffly, the released him. "Well, are you going to invite these children in, Kilfor, or shall we leave them outside to wither in the sun? Ulcers to your soul, what kind of host are you?"

Once inside, the autumn heat of the steppes faded quickly, and the cool ate in the jug the old man passed around was welcomed by them all. Conal took a look around the tent: far from the simple furnishings the plain exterior had led him to expect, the inside was adorned with rugs, tapestries, hangings and threads of every exotic colour and hue. Incense burned in a small brazier, enveloping them in a sweet-edged smell. Following the example of their host, they all sat cross-legged on the mat. Conal found the position extremely uncomfortable, and started fidgeting almost immediately.

Sauxa showed no obvious surprise when introduced to his guests. "We get all sorts here," he said dismissively, but Conal noticed him blow out a quick breath. For a time he avoided looking in the queen's direction.

"You will eat with us tonight," the old man said. "My son's a good cook."

"We don't want to be a burden," Robal said, evidently part of the courtesy.

Of course we will eat here, Conal thought. Was their host going to turn them out?

"No burden," Kilfor said, then lowered his voice. "The old man loves the noise his tongue makes. He'll talk your legs off and make them walk on their own if you let him."

"Speaking of legs," his father said loudly, "shake yours and go down to the river, you ill-mannered boy. We need more water."

In the end Kilfor took all three of his guests down to the river, an easy ten-minute walk that allowed them to ease the aches from their muscles. Down from the trap and amongst the shoulder-high grass, the world was reduced to the size of a tent. Only the cirrus-streaked sky stretched any distance.

Kilfor wielded a forked stick. "Snakes," he said. "It's a good idea to ride in a wagon. We have fifty types of snake here on the steppes. Vipers, whipsnakes, arrow snakes. Venomous, most of them. See the leather wrappings around my ankles? Thick enough to keep me safe. This stick will keep all but the worst of them away, but if you go walking on the steppes again, wrap your ankles in leather if you can get it, cloth if you can't—and don't go exploring in the long grass."

Conal picked his feet up off the ground as quickly as possible, as though walking on hot coals. He was somewhat mollified to see Stella adopt a similar ridiculous gait. Robal and Kilfor, at ease in this environment, refrained from passing comment, though an occasional smile twisted their lips. The priest wondered what would happen to Stella should she be bitten by a poisonous snake. *More to the point, what would happen to the snake?*

"Here's a beauty," Robal said, pointing to a dark, curled shape lying amongst rocks at the edge of the tallest grass. Doubled and tripled back on itself, the black-and-white serpent must have been ten feet long. It wore a white star above its eyes. "A young one. Adults get up to twice this size."

Conal edged to the far side of the path and feigned an interested look over at the monster.

"Good for the crops we grow," Kilfor said. "They eat the karakurt spider, deadliest thing I know. Paralyses its victims and lays its eggs in their mouths. The young feast on the tongue first, then work their way . . . No matter. No defence against something that can drop down your neck. We lose someone every now and again to the cursed spiders." He stood still for a moment, lost in thought.

Conal moved back to the centre of the path, equally distant from both walls of grass.

The river water was cold and pure, and the weary travellers soaked their limbs for a few minutes before returning to the camp.

"It's a beautiful landscape," Stella said to the old man.

"Beautiful?" Sauxa replied, his grin so wide Conal felt sure he could count every black tooth in the man's mouth. "The place is an abomination, a portal into the Destroyer's arse. One day I'm going to leave these fools and move back to the city. What's beautiful about wind that blows your treasures all the way to your neighbour? Or snakes that compete to see who gets to nibble on your leg? Did Kilfor tell you about the spiders? They paralyse their victims, then lay their eggs—"

"He told us," Stella said, laughing.

Kilfor leaned towards her. "My father has cursed the grasslands for fifty years, every year louder and longer than the last. He always reminisces about the few months he spent in Ehrenmal a while back; but the way my uncle tells it, he couldn't get back here fast enough. Now, he patient and listen to my father's stories. All you have to do is nod in the right places and he'll carry on all day. I have to go and cook the pilaf."

Rather than talking, the old man asked genuine questions about events in the wider world. They, in turn, asked him about life on the steppes. From time to time Kilfor would join them, inserting himself into the conversation with ease, then returning to his meal preparations.

After a while the most delicious aroma began to waft through the tent, making it difficult for Conal to concentrate on the discussion. He found himself half-asleep, as comfortable as the dull ache in his arm allowed him to be, his eyes resting on Stella's throat, watching it move as she spoke. The scar was faintly visible, but only to one who knew it had been a gaping wound through which her lifeblood had flowed.

Had she died and come back to life, or had her immortal blood kept her from dying? Was the answer merely semantics, as so many of his scholarly debates tended to be, or was there an important truth at stake? How could one find out? Would Stella herself know?

Her porcelain skin was so perfect. The scars from where the Destroyer had struck her had, after all these years, faded into virtual nothingness. How could such a beautiful vessel feel such pain? Such *alleged* pain. Had she really suffered, or was this a manifestation of the weaker sex? It was well known that men could bear much more pain than women. Had she sincerely overstated the price of immortality, or was she trying to keep it from others, to hoard it for herself?

A thousand questions. He put them aside when the meal was served: wheat grains mixed with carrots, and pieces of mutton dripping with fat. "You are a genius," he said to Kilfor.

The man smiled at him. "My father thinks so too. He praises my cooking to everyone he meets."

"Aye. Good for lining the stomach so one can drink the foul brew he makes," Sauxa said. "So bad it is that even the snakes won't bite anyone who's had more than a sip of it."

"Clean the dishes, boy!" the parrot squawked, sending Robal and Kilfor into paroxysms of laughter. Some joke from their shared childhood, no doubt.

Eventually the drink was passed around, a smooth but potent spirit, too strong for Conal's palate but remarked on favourably by Stella. "He'll make a good wife for someone," Sauxa said of his son.

"My fiancée will be pleased to hear it," Kilfor replied.

"His fiancée!" Sauxa exclaimed. "Travels around half of Faltha, does my boy, squeezing the rumps of the most beautiful women in the world, and he comes back here to marry a Chardzou. Can you believe that?"

"An Austapan, Papa, not a Chardzou. I'm not that inbred."

"Oh, an Austapan. Horseradish is no sweeter than beet-root, boy."

Robal choked on his drink, and Stella had to pat him vigorously on his back before he could take another breath. "His own wife was an Austapan," the guardsman said. "Sweetest woman you would ever meet."

"What happened to her?"

"Snake bite. Went down to the river—not this one, somewhere west of here—just as she had hundreds of times before, and stepped in a nest. Sauxa found her, cold and dead. He went and lived in Ehrenmal for a while after that, but the grasslands called him home."

"I was driven out of the city by a mob of jealous husbands," said the old man flatly. "If you can't tell the story right, don't tell it at all."

The evening drifted to a close, the simoom having abated, leaving them snug and warm in the strange tent. Conal felt a gentle contentment wrap itself around his heart. What would it be like to be part of a family such as this?

He lay awake long into the night, unable to answer his question.

CHAPTER 18

DECISIONS

STELLA AWOKE TO A BRIGHT morning and crushing pain. Outside, diffuse sunlight illuminated the open space where they had talked the previous evening, and a finger reached the rug on which she rested. No doubt the sun would have woken her had the pain not done so.

Her headache was severe; her eyes burned with it. She squeezed her lids closed, which served only to intensify the agony. Tears dripped down her cheeks, disappearing into the soft weave of her sleeping rug.

It hadn't been this bad for years. How had she put up with it, day after grinding day? A strange hollowness in her mind nagged at her like a missing tooth. It reminded her of something. She pursued the memory, clouded by pain and a rising fear: it reminded her of the months she had spent in the Destroyer's camp, when he drew on her strength with his magic. All those years ago, yet the memory remained fresh. He had set a hook in her, enabling him to draw on her at will, dampening her own volition, using her up as he fought the Falthans in the pursuit of his mindless revenge against the Most High. Every time he drew from her, the result was a painful emptiness that lasted for hours, sometimes days, accompanied by physical weakness.

Yet he had been merciful to her, after a fashion. She had been his unwilling accomplice in his headlong flight from Instruere amidst the ruin of his plans, after his defeat by Hal. He had retained barely enough sorcery to draw from his Lords of Fear, and with that strength had used them up one after the other, emptying them completely and discarding them as they made their escape over the city wall and across the river to safety. Yet he had never drawn on her so completely.

And now someone had drawn from her during the night. It was the only explanation for how she felt this morning. Then a more embarrassing possibility came to mind. The cognac Kilfor had shared with them had been near enough to raw spirit. *But I consumed only enough to be polite. Surely this is not a hangover?*

Stella grimaced at her own foolishness. She had still not shaken off the dread from her encounter with the Lord of Fear at Vindicare; no wonder she had allowed herself to be so easily frightened. And it had been years since she had last indulged in alcohol, though it didn't normally affect her so profoundly, and she couldn't remember having had more than a few sips last night. *Of course you don't. The more you drink, the less you remember.*

The tent spun around her and the light fractured into a thousand dagger-like prisms as she pushed herself into a sitting position. After a few minutes' panting the pain softened into an ache. It wasn't hard to imagine Kilfor brewing that ghastly liquor, his father at his shoulder offering genial and completely inappropriate advice. *You'll need more snake venom, boy, if you want it to have a kick. None of that Instruian stuff, mind. If it don't scald the skin off your throat it's nothing but lolly-water.* Stella found herself repressing a giggle, afraid to shake her head.

As the hollow thumping in her ears settled into the background, she began to hear voices coming from outside the tent.

". . . settle down here, or in one of the other communities. It would be the best thing for her." Stella struggled to place the speaker.

"For you, maybe. But you've never lived like a king." Definitely Robal, his tone defensive.

"And how can she live like a . . . like a queen now?" The first voice was Kilfor's. "She must make herself as ordinary as is possible if she's to survive."

"Come to the right place, then," said Sauxa.

"No one could call you ordinary, you old buffoon. She has to accept some change, at least until people have forgotten about her."

"That will take some time," Robal said.

"But what I don't understand is how she can look as . . . well, as young as she does. How long ago was the Falthan War? Forty years? She must have been twenty at the end of the war. That makes her . . . what? Sixty years old. She looks half that age."

"Don't know how you can tell, boy. I don't think you looked at her *face* once the entire evening."

"I have no doubt all women look impossibly young to you, old man."

"Seventy years, actually, since the Falthan War ended,"

Conal said, his cultured tones cutting across the banter as though it wasn't there. "If the records are correct, Stella Pellwen is in her eighty-eighth year."

Sauxa grunted, a distinctive sound. "Something not right about that. I know all that fancy living preserves a body, but this girl you've brought to my tent could pass for my granddaughter. If I had a granddaughter."

Stella could recognise a significant pause when she heard it. She barely had the energy to raise any anger at the fact that these men would discuss her affairs amongst themselves.

"I thought it was common knowledge that she made a deal with the Destroyer," Kilfor said. "Magical powers in exchange for the betrayal of her friends. Looks like immortality might be one of the benefits."

Stella gritted her teeth and staggered to the opening. When the world righted, she found herself staring down at the four men sitting at the points of a deep red rectangular rug. Conal was in the middle of saying something that sounded even more pompous than usual. All four heads turned towards her.

She opened her mouth to speak, and her stomach, still some distance behind events, finally rebelled. Her gorge rose and she barely managed to turn away before vomiting onto the grass.

I'm sorry, she tried to say, but the words were overwhelmed by a rising darkness. Her legs folded underneath her, she landed with a *huff* on the rug amidst the men, and the spinning world faded away.

"You are ill. Argue all you want, but you are not moving until we are satisfied you are well again."

Stella stared at her loyal guardsman, trying to assemble his blurred features into some sort of pattern. "I'm not ill," she said. "What is wrong with your ears? It's a hangover. I've had hangovers before, Robal."

"This is no hangover."

"Then what is it? The Chardzan physic could find nothing wrong."

"You muttered about poison while you were feverish. We all drank Kilfor's elixir and you were the only one to react like this." The guardsman lowered his voice and leaned over her, his mouth near her ear. "Did the priest come anywhere near your drink? Do you think he might have slipped something in your cup?"

"No!" Stella said sharply, pushing him away. "Robal, you had better overcome your dislike for Conal, otherwise harm will come of it. He's had plenty of opportunity to attempt to kill me, including once when, according to your testimony, all he had to do was *fail* to risk his life. And now he knows my so-called secret, why would he think poison would kill me anyway? Come, Robal, you are better than this. I got drunk and now I'm suffering for it. Nothing more sinister than that."

The guardsman shook his head. "I would have said you consumed less than any of us."

"As if that makes any difference. I've seen habitual drunkards throw back tankards of ale with little outward effect, and others fall prey to a glass of wine. Something in the brew didn't agree with me; I'm getting better, and it's time to move on."

"There is another kind of sickness women can suffer from . . ."

It took a moment for the meaning of his hesitant words

to sink in. "Are you trying to say that Conal and I—that we . . . well, are you?"

"You and the priest?" Robal laughed. "Hardly! No, I was thinking, ah . . ." He swallowed, obviously reluctant to voice his thoughts, picking his words with care. "I was thinking of the Lord of Fear, actually, or one of his sons. We don't know how long they held you before we . . . before the priest came to your rescue. Is it possible? Were you conscious at all times? Might one of them have attempted to acquire immortality . . . ah, another way?"

Stella shuddered, remembering her fear when the *Maghdi Dasht* approached her with his knife. "No," she said. "He was intent on my blood, nothing else, thanks be to the Most High. I have nothing else of worth to the likes of him."

"You are a prize, you know," the guardsman said, his eyes unfocused. "Clever, wise, beautiful, inheritor of an empire, possessed of immortality; if any man should lie with you . . ."

He flinched, as though realising he had spoken aloud; looked at her for a moment; then coloured, a raw redness rising from his neck to swamp his stricken face.

"Oh, my lady, I . . . I am a fool with nothing to offer save a brain too easily detachable from my mouth. Please forgive me." His body hunched slightly, as if expecting a blow, but he did not turn away from her.

A deep pain flooded through Stella, an agony totally unrelated to her illness. An agony of despair. Such a worthy man.

"My dear, I don't know what to say to you. Surely you have worked it out already? I don't know whether I would infect others with my curse by lying with them.

With Leith . . ." She choked back tears. "Leith died; shouldn't that have told you something? When we were young, before we fully understood all that immortality meant, Leith might have . . . but I loved him too much to take the risk. He understood; he remained faithful to the wreck he took as his wife. I heard the gossip. I knew that serving maids and highborn women alike offered themselves to him. They always used the same line, how he needed to have an heir. None of them understood that Faltha doesn't need a king, not in the long run. Leith saw himself as filling in until the Sixteen Kingdoms pulled themselves together after the war. The Falthan kings wouldn't have tolerated a dynasty in Instruere, we both knew that. So he turned them down—sometimes in my hearing, the brazen things. We would laugh about it, but it wounded me afresh every time."

She forced herself to look up into the guardsman's expressive, hurt-filled eyes.

"King Leith, he never touched you?" Robal whispered, obviously appalled for her. "You have remained . . . are still . . ."

"Yes," she said softly. "I have nothing to offer any good man. No empire, no wealth or dowry apart from a few polished stones, an intelligence marred by cynicism and anger, and such beauty as I have doomed to remain a reminder to any husband of his own mortality. An illusive, untouchable beauty, unsoftened by intimacy. Dear Robal, turn your thoughts towards someone worthy of you."

Brave words, but her heart bled. *So yet again am I punished. Oh, Most High, why do you hate me so?*

Conal approached them, a plate of stew in his hands. "My . . . Stella, Sauxa says you should try to eat." He glanced at her face and that of the guardsman. "Has he been upsetting you, my lady?"

"Yes," Robal said, just as she said, "No."

"It is no business of yours," Robal growled.

"Very well," said the priest, clearly offended. He placed the plate by her rug; the aroma was tempting.

"My thanks to you, and to Sauxa," she said. "I will attempt it in a moment. Now, tell me: when will we be ready to leave? And no nonsense about remaining here forever."

The priest cast an anxious glace at Robal, who returned it with a flat stare that fell just short of an outright threat.

"Stella, the others consider you too unwell to travel."

"I heard what they think before I was taken ill," she responded, raising her voice so everyone in the tent could hear. "Unfortunately, the men did not think to include me in the discussion. Therefore I see no need to include them in my decision."

"Which is?" Conal asked eagerly.

Stella looked more closely at him, trying to ascertain the source of his excitement. Had he overheard the conversation between herself and Robal? Surely he couldn't think that he . . . No, it must be excitement about resuming the journey. Stella knew the priest would not want to remain in this remote place, far from his scrolls and his books. So where did he want to be?

Wherever the subject of his life's work happens to be, that is where. The knowledge discomfited her as much now as it had when he first explained it to her.

"I'm going east," she said to them both. "East, to find some answers about myself. Come with me or not; it is your choice."

"How far east?" they both asked together.

"I am going to pay my old friend Phemanderac of Dhauria a visit." she said, not knowing she had decided this until the words left her mouth, but recognising their rightness as they did. "If he doesn't have the answers I need, only one other place remains."

Robal's features fell at her words; but, interestingly, a smile appeared on the priest's face. As though he knew exactly where she meant to go, and approved. Something within her began to cry a warning; or, perhaps, the cry had finally become audible.

The priest is not to be trusted.

Revulsion swept through Robal at her words. *How could she?* Nothing here was as it seemed. Stella had revealed far more than she suspected: not only did he know where her final destination was—if he was honest, he had guessed it some time ago—he now knew why she wished to travel there. Hers was a sad plight, desperately sad; he had indeed failed to think through the implications of her immortality. He loved her all the more for thinking of others, for not simply indulging her own appetites despite the awful consequences, especially when the likely outcome would end her own uniqueness. Instead, the despicable torture of the Destroyer and her own morality had condemned her to a lonely existence, isolation beyond his ability to imagine.

Only one person shared that lonely existence, and now Stella had announced she intended—no doubt had always intended—to travel in his direction. As much as he wanted for her to have happiness—to be honest, as much as he wished he could give happiness to her—Robal knew with a deep-bone certainty that she would not find happiness in the arms of another immortal. And not when that man was the Destroyer.

If he was right about her reasons for travelling east, she could not be trusted to act in Faltha's best interests. Far from it. He must be ever at the ready: should she give any sign of joining herself to their enemy, he would do anything necessary to prevent it.

His hand drifted towards his sword—hilt. *Anything.* He arrested the motion, then smiled encouragingly at Stella, his heart aching fit to break.

The five of them left the next morning, as soon as practicable after Sauxa and Kilfor had tasked others to take care of the possessions they could not carry with them. Robal shook his head as he loaded the last of their supplies in the back of the wagon. Yes, he was grateful that Kilfor and Sauxa were coming with them, at least to the edge of the desert: if anyone could see them safe to Desicca, the Deep Desert of Faltha, the two plainsmen could. But two more in their party was a further complication.

He climbed up into the tray of his own covered trap, shook the reins and eased back against the bags of vegetables as the donkey pricked up her ears and began her slow amble down the southern path and out of Chardzou. "Come on, Lindha, that's right, take your time," he cooed at her. No guardsman with any pride would choose a donkey unless there was no other burden-beast available, but Robal had become attached to the placid, even-tempered animal, to the point of giving it the name of his first—and extremely stubborn—ladylove.

At least someone in the party kept an even temper. He had tried broaching the issue of their destination again early this morning, managing only to raise Stella's anger to levels he had not seen before. *She doesn't know what to do*, he told himself, but the scenario played itself out in his mind with crushing inevitability. They would make the long journey to Bhrudwo, she would find some way to gain admittance to the Destroyer's presence, and Robal would never see her again.

It was as well he had not spoken his fear to her; she would likely have bawled him out more effectively than his old drill captain, if the way she had dealt with Conal was anything to judge by. The priest's only crime had been to suggest she did not look well enough to travel. After lashing him with her tongue, she had made him clear for her a space in the large wagon Sauxa and Kilfor had contributed to the expedition. He had completed the task as quickly as possible, then stayed out of sight until the last possible moment. Robal found himself wishing the priest had not reappeared.

Lindha kept up her steady pace all that day, and for a week thereafter. At the end of the sixth day, Sauxa halted in the midst of yet another featureless plain. "Here we will rest for a day," he announced, as though he were in charge of the enterprise.

"Rest?" Conal said to him as they climbed down from the wagon. "We've been travelling too slowly to need rest. Why not go faster?"

"We rest one day in seven," said Sauxa, holding up both hands. "Old plainsman tradition."

Beside him, his son snorted. "The old man makes up traditions to ease his haemorrhoids. Be a good idea to rest the animals, though."

"Lindha could keep going forever," Robal found

himself saying, slightly annoyed that he seemed to have
transferred his affection and allegiance from Stella to a
donkey. *Soft, that's what I am. Too long away from the
Pinion and my garrison.*

"May it be," Sauxa said, "but it would grind her down
in the end. She has a very long way to go, and you will be
thanking me for thinking of her before you are through.
Not all animals have hides as tough as mine."

"Or heads as thick," Kilfor retorted. "But, surprisingly,
the old man has come up with a good idea. There's no
hurry, is there?"

Both Conal and Robal raised their eyebrows at Stella,
who shrugged. Taking that for agreement, the guardsman
unhitched Lindha from her traces and set to rubbing her
down, thinking all the while about his colleagues in the Instruian Guard. Men he'd probably never see again; a career lost because of one impulsive moment.

"Ho, the camp!"

The hearty cry woke Stella, never an early riser, from a
disturbing dream, the fragments of which poured from her
memory like sand. She crawled from under the wagon,
rolling her blanket up behind her, and peered into the pale
morning sunlight.

A tall figure stood silhouetted twenty paces from the
wagon, arms spread wide. Robal and Kilfor strode towards him, bodies tensed for trouble. Conal came and sat
on his haunches next to where Stella knelt, still rubbing
sleep from her eyes.

"Anyone you know?" she heard her guardsman say to
Kilfor, and saw his barely perceptible headshake in reply.

"Probably just a traveller wishing to exchange greetings and news. Or a trader looking to sell his wares," Conal said, frowning at the man.

"I don't see a wagon," Stella said.

"What news?" the man said in a distinctive bass rumble. "Do you welcome strangers?"

"If they have food and tales to share, strangers are welcome to sit a while," Kilfor said. "We have finished breakfast, though enough remains, even after the attentions of my father, to feed a hungry man."

"And a hungry woman, I hope," Stella called. "Don't make him stand there."

The man followed Kilfor to the camp. As he moved from in front of the sun, Stella obtained her first look at him. His features bit into his face as though chiselled by a careless sculptor. Deep, wide-set brown eyes stared interestedly at the camp from below heavy brows; a narrow, aquiline nose surmounted a wide, full mouth and strong, stubbled jaw. An eyebrow quirked up as he noticed her regard, and he grinned a slightly lopsided grin at her. He was immensely tall, the tallest man she had ever seen, a hand or more taller than Phemanderac the Dhaurian. He eclipsed Robal by a full head. His clothes were of hoiled leather, a pleasing light brown, and, though travel-stained, were worn with a grace seldom seen outside of Instruere. A lightweight pack hung from his broad shoulders. She even noticed his long, slender fingers, which hovered near the hilt of a longsword.

"I am called Heredrew where I come from," he said.

"And where is that?" Robal appeared to have taken an instant dislike to the stranger, which was out of character for the guardsman. It came to Stella's mind that he had been somewhat on edge ever since they had left Chardzou.

"Haurn," the man said. "Tor Hailan, to be precise."

"Been there," Kilfor said, equally on edge. "Didn't like it; too cold."

Stella shook her head. What was wrong with the men? They were acting like dogs marking out territory.

"Your charms failed to impress the women, more like," Sauxa said.

"No women, you old fool," his son replied. "Tor Hailan was sacked by the Sna Vazthans over a hundred years ago. Manned now by warriors of Haurn against their return. And I mean *manned*. Is that what you are, friend Here-drew? A warrior of Haurn?"

The stranger surely could not fail to miss the hostility directed at him, but his smile never altered. "It is as you say," he said in a voice half rumble, half purr.

"And what brings you this way?" Robal asked, standing in front of him, arms folded.

"I'm searching for wisdom," he said.

Sauxa began to laugh, a dreadful braying noise that caused even Lindha to turn and regard him with gentle reproach. "Sorry, friend," he said, struggling to control himself. "But I was thinking just how far astray you are from your quest."

"Speak for yourself, old man," his son said.

"Oh, I am," Sauxa replied. "A man with more wisdom than I would not be travelling with puffadders like you two, who lack even the common politeness to invite a stranger to sit down for a meal. What is it, boys? Too tall for your taste? Afraid of being out-crafted by a Northman? To say I'm ashamed of you both would be to admit that sometimes I'm pleased with you, so I'll say nothing."

He extended a hand to the visitor. "Now, Heredrew, will you join us for a morning meal? I'm Sauxa; the boys can name themselves. The girl, she is one of my wives. Her father called her Bandicoot for some reason. Call her Bandy and she'll not take it askance."

"Be delighted to join you, Sauxa." The man stepped lightly past Robal and Kilfor; the latter busy turning a heated reply into a coughing fit.

Stella found herself struggling not to laugh. Time she put a lid on the old man, however, or next he'd be hinting at conjugal rights.

"I'm no wife of yours outside your dreams, old man. And Bandy isn't short for Bandicoot, as you well know. Come, Heredrew; share a meal with me and tell me of events in the north."

"I thank you, Bandy," he said solemnly, though with a glance at her that was far more knowing than she was comfortable with.

They sat opposite each other, the fire between them. Though the sun was now warming the air in preparation for its afternoon assault, the flames were welcome. Heredrew seemed to share her opinion, easing his long legs and shrugging off black leather boots. She tried not to stare at his feet.

"Had them made specially," he said. "The boots, not the feet." The grin again. He bit into a piece of bread from his own pack, then drew out another and offered it to her. "Hungry?"

She took it and ate. Though not truly hungry, she was taken by its sweetness. "Nice," she said.

"Now, Bandy. Ease my curiosity. You have the look of a northerner to me. Were you born around these parts?"

Damn that Sauxa. She hated having to invent and remember lies.

"I was indeed, Heredrew, in Chardzou; though I've lived much of my life in Instruere. My mother was from the north, she never said exactly where. Couldn't wait to leave it, apparently. One season on the steppes and she couldn't wait to leave here either. She dropped me and ran off to the next adventure."

"Call me Drew," he said. "Such an interesting story. Mine is tame in comparison. A life devoted to keeping the eastward watch on the new-built walls of Tor Hailan does nothing for the mind. My family petitioned the king for my release from my bond; normally a man such as myself has to serve until he reaches his fortieth year. I have two years to search the world for wisdom before I must present myself before the throne of Haurn and explain to them what I have learned."

"Where has your quest taken you?" Stella asked.

Conal sat down beside her. "Mind if I sit here, Bandy?" he said, and gave her a silly grin. She waved a terse permission.

"I didn't stay long in Haurn, as you can imagine. I went to Instruere and spent a month looking through whatever documents I could persuade the scholars and archivists to relinquish to the hands of an untutored northerner. They were actually surprised I could read them. I tried to set up an interview with the Falthan queen: it is said in the north that she is wise as well as compassionate. However, the king died while I waited for a reply, and the queen went missing immediately after. Killed by the Halites, everyone said."

"So we heard," Stella said, desperately hoping she was keeping her face smooth. "She missed the king's funeral."

"That's why everyone thought her dead. By all accounts she loved the king dearly. Instruere was an unpleasant place as the Koinobia struggled with the Council of Faltha for power, so I left and decided to take a risk in my search for answers."

Stella frowned. "A risk that brought you in this direction? You'll get hedge-wisdom here—grass-wisdom, actually—and while these people know how to live, we won't fill your head with thoughts profound enough to impress the King of Haurn."

"Well, as to that, I must confess I am here merely because here is between Instruere and my destination."

"Which is where? Where are you headed, Drew?"

"To the roots of the First Men, to find answers for my questions. Why would Sna Vaztha set out to conquer fellow Falthans? What happened to pit us one against the other? Only one place I can find answers to questions like that. I'm looking for Dona Mihst."

Stella felt her eyes widen involuntarily. Her hand went to her face and she nearly dropped her bread.

"It's a real place," Heredrew said confidently, apparently mistaking her surprise for disbelief. "The original place from where came the Four Houses of Faltha, the First Men who settled the Sixteen Kingdoms. Another reason I went first to Instruere is that in Haurn we have heard rumours that a scholar from Dona Mihst is— was—a friend of the Falthan king. I would very much like to have met this man of letters."

Kilfor and Robal sat down either side of the newcomer, in a clear attempt to intimidate him. Heredrew affected not to notice them.

Conal closed his mouth, which had been open for the last minute, and swallowed. "You seek Dona Mihst? That which is now called Dhauria?"

"I do, friend," Heredrew said evenly.

Robal and Kilfor signalled frantically to Conal to keep quiet. Stella could have told them not to waste their effort.

"Why, that is where we are travelling! I'm sure we'd welcome the company."

"You travel to Dona Mihst? Truly?" The man's face lit up in genuine pleasure. Beside him Robal held both hands to his forehead, while Kilfor did not trouble to conceal the anger clouding his features.

"Truly, Heredrew. Well, Sauxa and Kilfor will accompany us as far as the desert's edge, but the rest of us will cross the Deep Desert to Dhauria."

"For what purpose, may I ask?" Again the question was genuine, but Stella sensed the man was fencing with them. *He knows he is not going to be told the truth, and wonders how elaborate the lies will be. Very well, then.*

"I travel to Dhauria in search of answers," she said, an earnest intensity suffusing her tone. *Easy when you tell the truth.* "Answers about life and death, about the Most High and why he is so cruel."

She snapped her mouth shut. *Where did that come from? I was supposed to lie to him.* Robal shook his head in exasperation.

"Ah yes, being abandoned by your mother must leave you with many questions," said Heredrew, but his look said: *You and I both know I'm covering you. There's a story here and I want to hear it.* She smiled weakly. Things had come to a narrow pass when even the truth failed her. "And so good of your friends to accompany you. Your journey is much like mine, then."

With those words, or perhaps it was a matter of simple coincidence, something swirled at the back of her head.

The presence—*his* presence—which had remained dormant since her near-death at the hands of the Lord of Fear, surged into life. She had the sudden unsettling sensation that she was two or even three people overlaid one on the next, each with the same background, the same plans, the same destiny. She had felt something similar once before, on the docks at Vindicare.

"St—Bandy, are you all right?" Conal asked, reaching out a hand to her.

Stella shook her head, an action she instantly regretted.

"She's not well; something she drank. Perhaps we should excuse her."

Oh yes, Conal, thank you for your uncharacteristic thoughtfulness. She rose abruptly, which only accelerated the physical processes begun by the weird duplication in her head. Though she ran as quickly as she could, she barely made it behind the men's tent before she threw up her breakfast and much of last night's meal.

As the wagons rolled further south the few signs of human habitation faded to none. The last path turned to a rutted track and petered out at the edge of a field of wild wheat; beyond the field, the countryside grew progressively wilder. Flat prairie became rolling hill country, and the northern horizon expanded behind them until it seemed the travellers could see a hundred miles of golden haze.

It was discernibly drier here in the Edgelands. Stony streambeds held only a trickle of water, then none. The grasses clumped together in small brown huddles, narrow leaves and spikes closed against the bullying sun. A light dew would fall overnight, rising again as a thin mist in the hour after dawn. Every morning the sun arrived with more ferocity, relentlessly searching for hidden reservoirs of water. Unlike the travellers, the land had no wagons in which to hide, and was baked dry. Soil cracked, allowing the heat to penetrate the ground; the ends of the cracks flaked and crumbled, continuing the process by which soil turned to sand.

The donkey wilted noticeably. Robal rigged up a shade for her eyes, a clever combination of twine and canvas that kept the worst of the sun off her face. He noted with satisfaction that Kilfor and his father made a similar device for their pony. The guardsman considered making one for himself; he found he had to constantly shade his own eyes as they ground their way southwards towards the sun.

The man from Haurn walked beside Kilfor's wagon, showing no difficulty in keeping up. The more Robal thought about this, the more unlikely it seemed. This was a man from the cold northern climes, where snow covered the ground at least three months out of twelve. How, then, could he continue to match pace with beasts of burden in this arid environment? Yet there he strode, talking with Stella and Sauxa who rode on the wagon.

Robal could not pin down the source of his resentment towards Heredrew. The man behaved pleasantly, spoke with intelligence and good sense, and did more than his share of the work setting up and dismantling the camp, hunting for game and carrying water on the occasions they found a well. But he seemed too knowledgeable to be a first-time traveller, showing experience beyond his years. He behaved more like a Trader, one of those who chose the cover of merchanting to conduct spying missions for their sovereign. As a guard Robal had met a few of these people. King Leith's father had been a Trader, apparently, in the employ of the King of Firanes.

The guardsman would wait until Heredrew provided him with more substantial evidence. Should Robal voice his unease now, Stella would think him jealous; and to be fair, his feelings for her were confused and not to be relied upon. These feelings might well be influencing his view of this tall, handsome stranger who seemed so easily to captivate the Falthan queen.

Robal admired Stella greatly. Love was perhaps too strong a word, but to be near her was to experience the world a different way. In the past, he had listened with little tolerance to the romantic maunderings of his fellow guardsmen. He apologised to them in his mind. *Now I know what you were trying to say.* She knew of his feelings for her, but had not given any real indication whether she returned them. Certainly nothing a man could hold on to. A softening around the eyes, a gentle smile: these were things that could easily be misinterpreted.

As Conal the priest showed daily. The fool mooned over Stella, casting cow's-eyes at her whenever he thought she might be looking. He favoured her with his ill-informed, opinionated views about the world at every opportunity. All because she had thanked him for saving her life. He behaved exactly like a prickly desert plant: uncomfortable to be near, but with a small fall of rain would blossom into a gaudy flower until withered by the sun. It seemed only a matter of time before the priest proposed marriage to her.

Stella didn't seem to notice. She talked with him for some time each day, telling him more of her story—though not while Heredrew was nearby. She retained at least some sense. Robal listened whenever he could, whenever other duties did not demand his time—not that Conal performed any other duties.

You are a jealous idiot, he told himself.

The wagons crossed yet another broken ridge. The last of the spiny grasses were now behind them; they had completed the crossing of the Edgelands. Ahead lay Desicca, the Deep Desert.

A chaotic landscape spread before them. Huge untidy heaps of debris dotted a rubble-filled plain, sloping away into the distance where, at a much lower level than where they stood, a cliff rose cleanly into the clear sky. The plateau behind was broken by backlit rock towers, reminding Robal of Instruere viewed from the southern bank of the Aleinus River. Why, there was the Hall of Meeting, though obviously fallen victim to an earthquake; over there the Tower of Worship, leaning tipsily to one side. This wasn't how he had imagined the desert.

Travellers' tales spoke of enormous dune seas, slow-moving sand waves inexorably smothering villages and oases. Of sterile landscapes, of the complete absence of living things. But here, in a crevice, a small acacia thorn bush grew. It even showed a few tiny leaves, reflecting recent rain. The thorns had not protected the bush from grazing animals, however. Tracks went from bush to bush; though none of the animals were evident, the desert clearly harboured life.

Things are never as they seem, the desert seemed to be saying to him. *Something appears inhospitable, yet harbours life. Learn your lesson, put aside your prejudices.*

He could make an effort to accept the stranger from Haurn—Heredrew, call him by name—and even the pr—Conal. He would remain vigilant: the desert was a dangerous place, and only taught a lesson once. But for now he would extend his friendship to the others in the party.

First it was time to farewell Kilfor and Sauxa. The travellers continued a little way into the desert, reaching the partial shelter afforded by one of the debris mounds, then dismounted and made ready their goodbyes.

"Sauxa and I have been talking," Kilfor said as they gathered together.

"All you ever do," his father mumbled, but his heart wasn't in the insult. Kilfor ignored him.

"We wish to continue with you," he said in a rush. "I know it will put some pressure on the supplies, but we are confident we can bring down a gazelle or two to supplement the fare we provided you with. It's been a while since either of us left the steppes, and neither of us has been far into the desert. What it comes down to is this: we'd like to see Dhauria and the Vale of Youth with our own eyes. Call it a pilgrimage, whatever you like." He ran out of words, but the hopeful expression on his face remained.

His father maintained an air of studied indifference, but Robal knew better.

"Well . . ." Robal said, scratching his chin in an exaggerated fashion, as though on the cusp of a difficult decision. "It would be a sore trial on our already stretched patience. Stella, could you abide a few more days of coarse Austrau chatter?"

She pursed her lips. "Goodness me, how much more do you expect me to bear?"

"But how will the wagons travel across the desert? Surely the wheels will sink into the sand?" The priest had that superior look on his face as he asked the question, the one that made Robal's fists itch.

"Go and have a close look at the wheels, friend," Kilfor said quietly. "Wide-built rims, designed to travel in anything short of quicksand. And a desert doesn't have much sand, actually. Mostly rock and stones. We shouldn't have a problem unless we encounter a sandstorm."

"Ah, I . . . Forgive my ignorance," Conal said.

No one responded, no one said they forgave him, which pleased the guardsman. The silence stretched on.

"All right," Kilfor said with a false heaviness, his face a wide smile. "I'll just turn Bessa around and we'll make our lonely way back to Chardzou." He made to step forward, moving with overstated slowness.

"You're going to make us beg, you rogue." Robal went over and hugged Kilfor. "Stay with us as long as you wish." To his embarrassment he found tears forming in his eyes.

"Don't squeeze me so hard, you fool," Kilfor said. "You're a big man. I'll be no use to you broken."

They made camp under the cliff, and that night they set a large fire and drank some of Kilfor's cognac while watching the flickering shadows on the rocks behind them. Later they sang together, the droning songs of the southern plainsmen interspersed with the few lively ditties Robal knew without filthy words, and Heredrew taught them a resistance song of Tor Hailan. Stella had none of the cognac, Robal noted, but otherwise seemed to enjoy herself. *Not entirely a tragic figure, then.* He watched Heredrew capering to "I Met Her In The Alley" and the last of his doubts dissipated.

The following morning the travellers struck out towards Tammanoussa, the largest oasis east of Ghadir

Foum and the intersecting place of all important paths in this part of the Deep Desert. They crossed the Noussa Plateau in the furnace of midday—a mistake, Kilfor later admitted, as it took a great deal out of them. Only the desert lizards shared the plateau with the travellers, though a few birds hung in the thermals above, perhaps wondering when the foolish humans would collapse.

They rested in the heat of the second day, travelling only in the hours around dawn and dusk. Thus they found themselves approaching Tammanoussa as darkness spread across the desert, making setting up camp and gathering firewood difficult. Robal helped Sauxa unload the donkey and the pony. They hobbled the beasts with short ropes and left them to graze and drink at the large pool at the centre of the oasis.

Heredrew assisted Robal with some overdue repairs on the trap. A few of the metal rings through which were threaded the ropes holding the canvas to the tray had come loose; a couple could be fixed easily, but three needed new canvas sewn into the old. The northerner's long fingers proved nimble and dextrous as well as strong, forcing the large needle through two layers of canvas with ease, even in the poor light thrown by the fire.

"Interesting skills they teach in Tor Hailan," Robal remarked.

"Not a lot else to do while waiting for an invasion that will never happen," came the reply.

"Look, I apologise for mistrusting you. I'm a guard; it's in my nature and training to be suspicious of strangers."

"I understand," the tall man said, his voice as rich as syrup. "I, too, am a guard. Let us say no more about it."

They reached the far edge of the plateau late the next

day. Here the spine of central Faltha finally gave way, collapsing three thousand feet down to a vast white-sand sea studded with black debris cones. The effect was bizarre and unsettling. Heat shimmered across the horizon, hinting at true seas but offering nothing more substantial than a mirage.

The desert's second lesson. *If you see what you wish for, it is likely to be an illusion. Don't trust your senses*.

But what sort of teaching was that? It ran entirely in contrast to the first lesson. Perhaps that would be the third lesson: *There are no lessons to be learned from the desert*. To trust or not to trust. It seemed to have nothing to do with facts and everything to do with faith.

"Cast your eye along the ridge below us and out across the sands." Kilfor stood at his shoulder. "Perhaps a league or more out—look, can you see it? Watch closely."

Robal watched, and eventually his eyes picked up movement through the shimmering air. "What is it?"

"Could be a herd of gazelle, but we don't think so, not down there in that inferno. The old man says it's a camel train, heading our way. All we have to do is wait. By this time tomorrow, or even earlier, it will be upon us."

It seemed Stella couldn't wait. Early the next morning the travellers climbed down from the plateau into what Robal had always imagined desert to be. Heat so intense it stifled thought; sand hot enough to blister unprotected skin; and worse, a steady wind moving a man-high carpet of sand across their path from right to left. A profoundly inimical landscape. They ventured a little way into this harsh, unfriendly world, then halted.

"We won't survive a day of this," Kilfor said as they

gathered behind the wagons. "The sand will kill the animals, then us."

"Then we wait until the wind stops," said Stella. "It can't blow like this forever."

And if it does, only you will be here to see it cease, Robal thought.

At that moment shadows emerged through the sand haze: a camel, then another and another. The train had veered from the path to pass the wagons.

"A day and a half to Tammanoussa," Kilfor cried helpfully to the shrouded figure astride the lead camel.

Immediately the figure leapt from the beast and unwound the cloth wrapped around his face. The man was young, fair of face, and not at all the sort of weather-beaten fellow Robal would have expected in the desert. He looked more like a northman.

He spoke a few words in an unknown tongue, then called what sounded like a name. Another figure approached and unwound her face-covering.

"Tammanoussa?" she said, her eyes filled with hope. "The oasis is close by?"

"Indeed, yes," Kilfor reassured her. "We camped there the night before last. You are at the foot of the Noussa Plateau."

She turned and barked our instructions to those behind her, then addressed Kilfor. "We have an injured man who needs treatment. Are any of your party physicians?"

Robal's eyes narrowed: he had heard accents from all over Faltha, but not one like this.

"Alas, no. My father can do a little doctoring—"

Heredrew stepped forward, his height eliciting a start

from the woman. "I am a physician," he announced.
"Show me your wounded man."

Robal closed his eyes. This was too much: would their
companion next present himself as a swordmaster, a jeweller or a midwife?

Stella went with him. The two of them accompanied
the woman into the sand wind, vanishing from sight.
Robal checked on Lindha, ensuring the donkey did not
suffer too greatly in the annoying wind.

A woman's cry knifed through the desert air. Even before his conscious mind recognised it as Stella, Robal had
dropped the handful of oats he was feeding the donkey
and was rushing along the camel train towards her. His
mind filled with a dozen different developments, most involving Heredrew threatening his queen. *I should not
have let them out of my sight . . .*

He found her standing outside a covered wagon, her
face pressed into Heredrew's chest. Robal grabbed at her
shoulder. "What is it? What has he done?"

"Drew has done nothing," Stella said, turning her wet-
cheeked face towards him. "The man who is injured is the
man I wished to meet in Dhauria. He . . . he is near death."

Cursing himself for jumping to such a foolish conclusion, Robal pulled aside the cover and looked down upon
the ancient man lying there, then turned his head away.

"He was caught in a desert storm," Stella said.

"It happened a week since," the woman from the camel
train added. "We set out for Instruere six weeks ago, and
last week, while camping on the shores of Soba salt lake,
a courier stopped on his way east. 'The Falthan king is
dead,' he told us, and our master wept.

"Since then he has driven us by the force of his will. He

fears for the safety of the Falthan queen. We expected the king to live another year, at the least. So when the great sandstorm came he took a gamble and pushed on into it. We were eventually forced to take shelter, but when we counted ourselves we realised we had lost a man. My master went out into the storm to retrieve him. We found my master the next morning as you see him, on the threshold of death."

"Oh, Stella, I'm sorry," Robal said. His sympathy was the only thing he could offer. He held her hand as Heredrew stepped forward to examine the injured man.

His exposed skin had literally been sandblasted away. Worst were his eyes: what had once been clear orbs were now completely opaque. Robal could only imagine the agony the man must have suffered.

"Oh, Phemanderac," Stella said brokenly. "Look what Leith and I have done to you."

CHAPTER 19

THE VALE OF YOUTH

FEW OF THE TRAVELLERS slept that night. Stella was inconsolable in her grief. The others suggested she find a place to sleep, to relax until morning, telling her she could not help Phemanderac by staying awake, that there was nothing she could do. They meant well, but none of them understood.

Now Leith had gone, Phemanderac was the last left alive of those involved in the Falthan War, save herself. The last of the Company. The only one remaining to whom she could talk about her feelings, who would understand her troubles. Tender-hearted Phemanderac, who had loved Leith more than she herself had.

The gentle scholar would be approaching a hundred years of age, but had kept himself in relatively good health. Until now.

If he died, she would be alone.

So she stood by the wagon through the night, braving the relentless wind, feeling it pile sand up over her feet as she waited. Occasionally Heredrew would allow her in to check on his patient, to find there had been no change in his condition.

"He requires salves beyond my reach," Drew explained to her. "I am doing what I can for him, which is mostly easing his pain. I fear we will have to decide whether to take him east or west; and it is my opinion that he will not survive either journey. I am sorry to bear this news, as it is clear you know this man. But death would be a mercy."

"It would *not*," she said with all the ferocity she could muster. "You do not know him. I have seen him keep a hall filled with people silent for hours with his voice or his harp. He is one of the few men I know with the patience to make children laugh." Her voice steadied as she revived a long-forgotten memory. "He is a philosopher without peer; already they talk about him in the same breath as Hauthius and Pyrinius, the two greatest scholars since the Fall of the Vale. He is the link between Faltha and Dhauria, our best hope of understanding what really happened in the Falthan War. He is priceless, do you understand?"

Drew looked at her with a faintly amused expression, though his eyes burned bright. "Such passion! I am overmatched. And rare for a farmer's child from troublesome, rebellious southern Austrau to care so deeply for Falthan matters. There is more to you, Bandy, than you choose to reveal."

"This is not about me, not now. We might talk later of an exchange of secrets, warrior-physician of Haurn. In the meantime, heal my friend."

He nodded, acknowledging the point. Secrets kept might become secrets shared.

"There is one last measure I might try," he said, fingering a small pouch on his belt. "But it could as easily kill as cure. Ought I take the risk?"

"It is not my decision alone," Stella answered.

The woman from the camel train—Fenacia, she gave as her name—supplied him with the answer when Stella called her over. "Yes," she said. "None of us can bear looking at him like this. Supply him with some dignity, at least. Do what you can, physic."

The long night hours dragged their feet as they passed reluctantly by. Eventually, as the pre-dawn glow began to enliven the horizon, Stella felt a sudden wave of nausea wash over her. The hollowness in her head returned; before she could react, she found herself on her knees, retching weakly, her mind blanking into unconsciousness.

She emerged from the blackness to feel hands touch her, then arms pick her up. A familiar voice called for assistance. Someone dripped water into her mouth and then laid a cold cloth across her forehead.

"How is Phemanderac?" she asked weakly. "How is my friend? Why won't anyone tell me how he is?" The heads gathered around her all spoke at once, but her ears rang with a buzzing sound and she could understand none of them. "Tell me, please!" she cried, afraid that the hollowness she had sensed was Phemanderac's passing.

"He has . . . he has recovered," Fenacia said in a strange voice, motioning the others to silence. "He sits up in the wagon and asks after the man lost in the sandstorm."

"Recovered?" Stella said, bewildered. "But he was dying. He will be in extreme pain. May I see him?"

"Ah, lass, now there's the mystery," Sauxa said. "One of many this night."

Robal leaned over her, his soldier-smell reassuringly familiar. "Your friend is completely healed. There is no trace of the storm on his skin, and his eyes are clear. It is as though the injuries never happened. He does not understand what the fuss is about."

"There is a great deal you are not saying," Stella complained. "Where is Drew?"

"So to our second mystery," Robal said grimly. "It seems we may have been sharing the desert trail with a sorcerer. Fenacia here says she passed by the wagon and saw Phemanderac damaged and near death, then returned a few minutes later to find her master healed and you lying unmoving at the foot of the wagon. We have searched the camp for Heredrew, but he is not to be found. We can only assume he healed Phemanderac. Some of us suspect you happened across the miracle and, for some reason, he rendered you unconscious and made his escape."

"But . . . if he has such powers, why not remain to accept our thanks?" Kilfor said. "Why knock Ste—Bandy out? There is nothing criminal about sorcery."

"Ah, but there is," Stella said, as realisation swamped her in a bittersweet flood. "I recognise the signs. There is a kind of sorcery where the magician draws from others to effect his magic. It is a form of magic frowned upon in Faltha, if not exactly outlawed. I collapsed because Heredrew pulled strength from me in order to heal Phemanderac."

Conal nodded. "To steal from others, even to do good, is against the teachings of the Most High."

"Why did he not ask? I would have surrendered everything I have to save Phemanderac."

"Bandy, I must ask you this," said Fenacia. "What is our master to you, that you would show him such devotion? This is to us tonight's third and perhaps greatest mystery. None of us can remember having seen or heard of you before."

Weary, swamped by a welter of emotions and tired of the deception, she sat up and locked eyes with the Dhaurian woman. "I am Stella, the Falthan queen," she said. "Now take me to Phemanderac. I have questions to ask him."

A ripple of silence spread outwards from Stella.

"With respect, I once visited the court of the Falthan king," said one of the Dhaurians, an older man. "I sat beside Phemanderac on the High Table, and spoke with the king and queen. You do have her look about you, I'll grant you that. But she was much older than you, whoever you are."

Ah, this will prove difficult.

She cast her mind back. Phemanderac had once been a biennial visitor to Instruere, but as he grew older had appeared but four times in the last thirty years. This man was perhaps sixty, and his use of the word *once* suggested the visit was not recent. She pictured the evening Leith had received Phemanderac in the Hall of Meeting, a night of great ceremony, the scholar having attained the rank of *dominie*, the first in Dhauria for a generation. Thought hard. Yes, she was almost certain who this man was.

"You asked me a rather forward question, I believe," she said, looking straight at him and reading nervous corroboration in his eyes. "You wanted to know why I had served as the Destroyer's Consort. As I remember it, I never got to answer you, which was probably just as well for you. Your master explained matters to my satisfaction, if not to yours. I don't remember your name."

The man opened his mouth, then snapped it shut.

"I will say this, because others will think it," Fenacia said. "You look as though perhaps thirty summers have passed you by, no more. The Falthan queen is near as old as Phemanderac. How is this possible?"

"You of Dhauria live long lives. Is it unlikely that someone who spent years in the company of the world's most renowned sorcerers, people like Hal Mahnumsen, Deorc of Andratan and, yes, the Destroyer himself, might also be granted a long and hale life?"

The woman did not reply, but Stella knew her evasive answer had merely staved off further questions for a time. She stood, grasping the wide wheel of Kilfor's wagon for support, and set out in the direction of Phemanderac's cot, a procession of friends and onlookers in tow.

With a fluttering in her stomach she walked up to the wagon in which he lay and drew back the cover.

"Hello, Phemanderac," she said lightly.

His eyes widened slightly in his long, deeply lined face. "You look far better than anyone has a right to," he said.

"As do you, given what you've been through," she replied.

Then she could stand it no longer and threw herself into his bony arms, crying for all she was worth, as she never had since she was a little girl.

After the tears had ceased, Stella told Phemanderac her story, leaving nothing out. The old man, his long, horse-like face softened somewhat by his kindly eyes, smiled sadly at her when she had finished. The morning was well advanced, and preparations for a day's camp continued as they talked.

"Oh, my dear, you have suffered so," he said. "Pain and fear, such a combination to have been gnawing at your spirit all these years. I wondered about this the last few times I visited you. Dear Stella, will it embarrass you if I tell you I suspected something like this? More than suspected? Or if I ask why you did not trust me enough to share your secret earlier?"

"I trusted no one," she said, turning away from his steady regard. "It seemed my burden to carry."

"You told Leith, of course."

"Yes, of course. When he proposed his marriage arrangement to keep me safe from those who accused me of treachery, I told him everything I suspected at the time."

"When did you know you were immortal?"

"Phemanderac," she wailed, "how will I ever know? If the only proof I am *not* immortal is to die, then the only thing an absence of proof provides is evidence that I am not yet dead." She laughed weakly. "Does that make sense?"

"Better to say, as did Symarthia in her treatise on the Fountain of Youth, that immortality is at best a hope even for the immortal, and not verifiable fact."

"But I did think it likely I was immortal, even back then," Stella said. She assembled her thoughts with care; Phemanderac's logical mind would demand clarity. "I am almost certain he infected me with his blood. At least that is what the evidence suggests. The Destroyer often complained of the pain within him as a result of that one drink from the fountain. I suffered a similar pain when I awoke from the near-death from which he saved me."

"'He will be tormented for the rest of time by the power in his body,'" the scholar muttered. Seeing her puzzled look, he added, "From the *Domaz Skreud*, the Scroll of Doom that tells of the Destroyer's rebellion against the Most High."

"'Tormented for the rest of time' about sums it up," she said wearily. "I found myself linked to him in strange ways. I could sense his nearness, his moods, and when he suffered pain. Phemanderac, on occasion I still can."

His eyes widened at this, but he made no comment.

"I do remember what he said to me when I awoke. He and I, he claimed, were the only ones in the world with the gifts of Fire and Water. The Water of Eternal Life comes exclusively from the fountain in Dona Mihst. I can only have received the Water from him, from his blood. It makes sense."

"Indeed it does," he replied, sighing. "Let us follow the chain, so there can be no doubt. The Most High set the fountain in the Vale and told the First Men not to drink from it. A thousand years later Kannwar, later named the Destroyer, challenges the ban and drinks from the fountain. The Most High drives everyone from the Vale save the few who resisted Kannwar. He tells the First Men something of his purpose, saying: 'Do you not know that the very air of the Vale is laden with the spray of the fountain I set amongst you?' He explains the spray has preserved the First Men, granting them lives far longer than those who live in the outside world.

"Now, here is the truth I am reluctant to share with you, but share it I must. 'Your bodies cannot yet contain the undiluted Water of Life,' the Most High told the First Men. Symarthia and Hauthius both speculate on the meaning of the word *yet*. The Most High might have been using the fountain to condition the First Men. Perhaps in the future they might have been able to bear it. The Most High had a purpose for the First Men, interrupted by Kannwar's rebellion."

Stella nodded. "I own—owned—a copy of the *Domaz Skreud*. What you say conforms to my own thinking."

"Ah, then nothing I am saying is new to you. Good. The implication of the *Domaz Skreud* is that humans cannot bear immortality, not now, not yet. As the Destroyer himself showed. The Most High cursed him, saying: 'He will be tormented for the rest of time by the power in his body, a power he cannot control, a power that will destroy his spirit and his soul and his mind while preserving his body forever.' This has been confirmed by what you say of yourself and of the Destroyer. I am so sorry, Stella."

"But I have begun to bear it," Stella said. "It is now more an ache than an agony. And my scars have healed over the years. Remember when I returned from his thrall, how I could not uncurl my right hand? Apart from some stiffness, it now works nearly as well as my left. Might even the aches and stiffness disappear in time?"

"Alas, I will not be with you to see the truth or otherwise of that possibility."

His words reminded her how sick he'd been. How close to death. "I will leave you to sleep now," she said. "But I have been travelling for months because I wanted to talk with you about these things. Might we resume when you are rested?"

"I am an old man," he said. "It is well known that old men do not need sleep. However, perhaps it would be good to think for a time about what we have discussed."

He waved farewell to her, then beckoned her closer.

"Stella, I was sorry to hear of your loss," he said.

"*Our* loss," she corrected.

"Yes," he agreed. "Everyone's loss. I set out to visit him one last time, you know. But when I heard he had died, I began to worry about you. I thought perhaps you might find the political situation difficult to manoeuvre through, as it proved. I'm only sorry I didn't leave earlier."

"So am I, but who could have predicted he would die so soon? I am glad you are here now."

"As am I," he said. "Fenacia tells me I would have died if your travelling companion had not intervened. Where is he? I would like to thank him."

"I don't know. I will send him to you when he is found."

"Then we will talk more," he said. "Of yourself, and of our memories of Leith."

"Yes," she said, and left him to rest.

That afternoon Stella found herself caught up in other duties, including a discussion about what road the travellers should take. Robal argued that, as the main reason for travelling to Dhauria was now here with them, they should join with the camel train and head back west. Stella offered her opinion that Phemanderac would likely order the train to return to Dhauria. "Now that Leith is dead and I am deposed," she said, "there is little to draw him to Instruere."

"Might he be able to help you reclaim the Falthan throne?" the guardsman asked her.

"That throne is gone forever," she replied. "In any case, as I'm sure I have said, Leith never intended it to outlast him."

That night Robal took her aside and asked if she had seen anything of Heredrew. Only then did she remember her promise to Phemanderac.

"I know nothing more than you," she said testily. "Less, in fact, as I was unconscious at the time."

"And I was asleep. I am sorry, Stella, but I do not understand what the fellow stood to gain from befriending us, using sorcerous power to heal a man he'd never met, then leaving without stealing anything or killing anyone. Makes no sense to me. It's got my guardsman's nose twitching, it has."

Stella had not been able to spare much time to consider the mystery. "Since you show such interest in the man," she said, "I charge you to search out any information about him. Review with Kilfor and his father all your dealings with him. I must confess to feeling anger towards Heredrew. What he did, even if done in ignorance and given the good cause to which he applied my strength, is not easily forgiven. And, having drawn on me, he will now be somewhat aware of my—differences. Perhaps that frightened him away. Perhaps he guessed who I am."

Robal asked her a few more questions, then left to pursue the matter with his friends.

Stella was not able to rejoin Phemanderac until the next afternoon, after the scholar had made the expected decision to turn back to Dhauria.

The wind had abated enough for most of the sand carpet to be left undisturbed, so the journey was easier in that one respect. But the sun did not stint in its efforts to drink them dry.

Stella settled in beside the scholar as he sat in the back of his covered wagon.

"We were talking about the pain of immortality," she prompted him.

"I hadn't forgotten," he said. "I have been thinking about what you said. Your gradual recovery lends credence to Hauthius's 'Dosage' theory of immortality."

"There are theories? How many?"

"Three, in fact," Phemanderac said. "Shall I list them?"

Stella smiled: the young Phemanderac would have disgorged every detail with little regard for the interest level of his audience. "Please," she said.

"First is Symarthia's 'Indestructibility' theory. It is first because it is the earliest; Symarthia lived only a few hundred years after the rebellion. She maintained that the Destroyer simply cannot be killed, using as evidence the words of the Most High: 'He who drank of the fountain will surely now never die.' But we cannot tell from the text whether this prediction is an inevitable result of the Water of Life or merely a reflection of the Most High's knowledge of the future."

Stella told him of her experiments with starving, then described in more detail what the Lord of Fear had done to her in attempting to claim eternal life for himself.

"Hmmm. So your body is certainly more resistant to injury. Wounds heal more quickly, yet you can suffer gross trauma. To me this suggests you are not indestructible. Forgive me, Stella, but if I were to bind and burn you, then scatter your ashes to the world's four corners, how could your body, let alone your mind, retain any sense of immortality?"

She smiled. "Let us hope it does not come to that."

His eyes narrowed for a moment, then he continued. "So Hauthius's critique of Symarthia might well be

correct. He would be pleased to know that, the old rascal. His own 'Dosage' theory is the second major treatise on immortality. He took the position that the Water
of Life was an entirely natural phenomenon, albeit a
rare one, unaffected by magic. Given the fountain put
out a steady supply of water, it was possible for anyone
who partook directly of it, in defiance of the Most High,
to take any amount they chose. Following me?"

Stella nodded. The camel train, followed by Robal and
the others, wound its way along a well-used trail between
huge black mounds of rock. She tried to let her understanding follow Phemanderac's words in similar fashion.

"So, Hauthius argued, the man who took a larger quantity of the water would be more greatly affected than one
who took a little. This is supported by the words of the
Most High, who said that everyone living in the Vale
drank indirectly of the fountain, as its spray spread
through the air. Your tale of damage and gradual healing
offers further confirmation. You did not drink of the
source, instead receiving your dose, as it were, via a
second-hand source. Therefore it follows that you might—
might, I say—have received a lesser infection. One which
your body may be fighting. Perhaps you will overcome it
one day, and your blood will return to normal."

Her eyes wide open, she searched the scholar's face.
"Oh, Phemanderac, is it even possible?"

"I don't know, but it is at least cause for hope. And you
do look older than you did when you were infected. Perhaps eventually you will grow old and follow the path of
all men. Just more slowly than the rest of us."

"And the third theory? Does it offer even more hope?"

"Perhaps. It is Phemanderac's 'Theory of Limited Immortality'." He coughed modestly. "An outgrowth from Hauthius's work, actually. I argue that the soul or spirit of an immortal person may die, while the body lives on. It suggests immortality of the body only, you see. The immortal may choose to lay down her own life, letting it dry out like a desert stream, but life cannot be taken away from her. One's spirit will eventually weary of life, so in practice no one will live forever, even if Symarthia is correct and their body is indestructible."

"So, if you are right, I will one day succumb to weariness? Lie down and somehow stop living?"

"Fragile and of doubtful comfort, I'll admit; and not amenable to your evidence. Still, there is hope that your condition may not be permanent."

With that dubious thought reverberating in her brain, another day ended.

Over the next few days Stella and Phemanderac debated every angle of the subject. Robal came and joined them, crowding the undersized wagon, but the queen and the philosopher welcomed his commonsense views. Of Conal there was no sign, even though Stella sent for him, asking him to join their discussions.

Robal, in fact, offered the most hopeful and disturbing thought.

"Phemanderac," he asked early one red morning, after they had been on the trail only a short time, "does the Destroyer have any children? An heir, perhaps?"

"Children?" The lean man scratched at his chin with arthritic fingers. "No, none we know of, though it would prove difficult to track all possibilities."

"What I mean is, would the Destroyer have taken

lovers if he knew he might infect them with the immortality disease?"

Stella could not follow Robal's thinking, but Phemanderac's mouth made a wide "O" of astonishment. "You are suggesting a possible lack of immortal wives or heirs as proof that the Water of Life is not transmitted sexually?"

"Exactly. The man's been around for two thousand years, he must have built up a head of steam, if you know what I mean. Apologies, Stella."

His expression asked her permission to carry on. She motioned him to continue.

"Well," he said, "I'm guessing that immortality is a deal harder to transfer from one person to another than we have all been thinking. How long did the Destroyer work on Stella before she was healed of the injuries he gave her?"

She put a finger to her lip, worrying at a piece of loose skin. "A few weeks, maybe a month. But he turned to his blood as a last resort. At least, that's what I have always assumed."

"But how do you know? What if even blood-to-blood transfer is difficult? What if it took him repeated attempts? Maybe it was days or even weeks before you caught the cure, such as it was. Isn't it possible?"

Something Stella had long thought dead began to smoulder in her breast. *If Robal is right* . . .

"I thought you employed no philosophers in Instruere," Phemanderac said, his face split by a wide smile. "This man is a clear thinker. He serves you well!"

"Sometimes I can't think at all," Robal said, clearly pleased by the compliment. "But I lay awake last night working through the puzzle. Take the lack of immortals in

Bhrudwo to compete with the Destroyer for power and add it to the likely difficulty of transferring immortality even through blood, and I think the danger of anyone catching the curse from either immortal is very small. Meaning . . ." He smiled gently at Stella.

"Meaning," said Stella, her face draining of blood, "that I have spent the last seventy years in bondage to unnecessary fear. Meaning Leith died without . . . And I— oh, Robal!" And she turned to him and beat him on the chest with her fists.

"I know you meant it as a gift," she sobbed as the guardsman held her wrists. "But you have just made a desert of my virtue."

A desert indeed: a meaningless aridity, a self-imposed wasteland she had stumbled through all her adult life. Her only reward, if reward it had been, was a developing pride in her strength of self-denial. To watch others enjoying all the seasons of life had been a cruel torture, but one she had believed was necessary. A necessity in which she had involved her faithful Leith. To whom she could now offer no apology.

Phemanderac cleared his throat. "I must remind you both that this line of thinking—call it 'Robal's Theory of Transference' for now—has several unproven arguments," he said. "I can think of at least two alternative explanations for the Destroyer's lack of offspring. Three, actually. First, he might be above such things. It is not uncommon in Dhauria for leaders to turn their desires to energy they then use in the service of their fellows. Perhaps we are unusual in this." Phemanderac spoke quickly, unlike his normal measured tones, as though chasing his ideas out of his head. "This means immortality still may be transmitted by . . .

such contact. We cannot be sure. Second, the Destroyer may have insisted his partners ensure that they did not conceive. He may even have had them sterilised. Third, there might indeed be an army of immortals, or just a few, for all we know. Unlikely, yes, but I'm not sure anyone from Dhauria has thought to search."

Robal sighed. "So, the only way we can know for sure—"

"Is to ask him ourselves," Stella finished for him. "A course, as I know you are aware, I have already decided to pursue. You have simply given me more questions to ask him."

"Aye, I knew where you intended to go. I thought perhaps you were looking for an answer to your loneliness."

"So that is what was behind your odd behaviour," she said, her eyes softening. "I meant what I said. I'm not worth your attention."

The guardsman looked directly into her eyes with a gaze so intense she felt herself stir. "I have never thought that, Stella. And if there was a possibility that you might . . . that any of our ideas might have some currency, we should pursue this until we find out the answers."

"And if our pursuit takes us to Bhrudwo? To Andratan?"

"Then we will be careful, but we will go."

She found herself unable to hold back her tears. It seemed to her she cried enough to create an oasis in her own desert. An oasis that, after years of barrenness, might, perhaps, be something more than a mirage.

Conal clicked his tongue for the hundredth time. Reduced to driving a wagon through this hateful desert, a wagon pulled by a donkey, no less, and a stupid one at that. His pale skin burned and peeled no matter how many times he applied the stinking cream Kilfor had given him. He never got enough to eat or drink; his voice rasped from a parched throat. Not that he was given much chance to use it, except to chastise the stupid, *stupid* donkey. All this while others, less qualified than he, spent their days talking about the issues *he* had studied.

Stella had sent some Dhaurian lackey to ask him to join their discussion. Hadn't come herself. There was absolutely no reason for him to feel hurt. He'd declined the offer without thinking, without offering an explanation. Better no involvement at all than being treated as a thirteenth soldier.

Not since Dribna the guard had whacked the Wodrani boy over the head with his oar had Conal thought so little of their enterprise. A great deal had changed since he had been commanded to follow the Destroyer's Consort. Worryingly, the command had not come directly from the Archpriest; the assistant royal physician approached him in order that the Archpriest could truthfully deny the mission. So the physician had said. More than once since, Conal had doubted the wisdom of accepting the commission. The worst of his fears, greater than his dread of death, was that he would return to Instruere to find the Archpriest had not authorised his disappearance.

The scenario played out yet again in his mind. He returns with a tearful and repentant Destroyer's Consort, brings her into the Archpriest's study, trailed by an increasing number of awestruck Halites, and watches as Stella abases herself before his master. The Archpriest rises, then demands Conal explain his absence. He tries to speak, but his master begins the dreaded ritual: "By the authority of the Koinobia, and as the representative of the Most High in the world of men, I cast you from our fellowship. I bind your soul. I declare you *losian*, rejected of the Most High. Be now gone from our presence."

He is not allowed to return to his room; his notes and scrolls are lost forever. His desperate arguments and pleas for clemency are ignored. Everyone turns their face from his. As he stumbles from the study he sees the Archpriest reach down, take Stella's hand and pull her gently to her feet. "You are mine now, my dear," he says, but the voice is that of Robal the guardsman.

Conal opened his eyes and wiped the cold sweat from his brow. When had this happened, this darkening of the Archpriest in his mind? Had Stella so thoroughly subverted his allegiance?

A Dhaurian, a pretty young girl with her hair in three pigtails, jogged past the wagon, on her way to the rear of the train. A few minutes later she returned, settled to a walk, and turned her sun-dark face towards him. "Excuse me," she said, in a throat-wrenching accent. "I am looking for Cone the priest."

"Conal," he said. *The famous Cone, whose name shall be mispronounced throughout the world.*

"My apologies," she said, colouring. "The *dominie* has requested your presence."

"The who?" He knew his tone sounded abrupt, even rude, but the vision of his own humiliation was still too fresh in his mind to allow him to offer the required apology.

"Phemanderac the *dominie*," the girl repeated patiently.

"Oh. What does he want?"

"My lord, I do not know," she said, finally showing

some anger. "Come or do not come. His is the covered wagon near the head of the train." She made to leave.

"Wait," he said. "Tell him I cannot come, I am busy driving our wagon." A ridiculous excuse; he could easily ask Sauxa to look after the wagon. And he longed to be part of their discussions. But they had waited too long before asking him. It was, he assured himself, a matter of principle.

"Very well," said the girl, shaking her pigtails in disapproval. "I will tell him."

After she left him Conal stared out into the wilderness, his mind in free fall. So many religious metaphors came from the desert. Human rhetoric depended on expressing extremes, and the wasteland the camel train struggled through was certainly an extreme. An absence of water to bring life and to soften the hard edges of the land; speaking to Conal of a life lived outside the refreshing presence of the Most High. So few paths, so many opportunities to become lost, to die of thirst or to be burned up by the sun. Life was like that. One's whole future dependent on a simple choice, the significance of which was never obvious at the time. The desert was infertile, yielding nothing of value to humans; a metaphor, perhaps, for a life wasted on one's own selfish pursuits. A place where all the choices were hard, often made between one danger and another. A place to travel through, not to linger in. A place too vast for the human spirit to encompass. No wonder the First Men spoke of the desert with a combination of nervousness and respect.

A cruel place. How many steps to cross the desert? A thousand times a thousand? Place your feet on the trail nine hundred and ninety-nine times and no one praised you for it; they just expected you to keep going. But make one wrong step and the wilderness swallowed you up. There was no sense of balance, of fairness, here. The blazing sun did not ask you if you meant to become lost; the choking sand would not listen to your explanations for the choices you made.

"Friend Conal, would you spare me a moment?"

A tall, elderly man walked beside the wagon. A man with a long face, exquisitely ugly, sporting a nose that looked like it had been stung by a bee and sparse grey hair atop a misshapen crown. He wore a plain brown tunic and loose-fitting trousers, emphasising his gauntness.

The priest knew who this was, but said, "I'm sorry, you have the advantage of me."

The man began to breathe heavily as he tried to keep up with the wagon. "I am Phemanderac, a friend of Stella. She has asked me to speak to you, and encouraged me to give you a gift. Will you receive me?"

"Very well," Conal said, pulling the wagon aside from the train. Sauxa waved to him as the last wagon passed. Phemanderac waited for the dust to clear and then accepted a hand up to the tray.

The Dhaurian had what looked like a large scroll under his other arm. Placing it on the wagon beside him, he turned his disturbing gaze on the priest.

"What is it you wish to see me about?"

"Stella is very keen for you to read this history I have written. I, also, would appreciate the attention of a learned Instruian scholar." He indicated the scroll lying beside him, a faintly anxious expression on his face. "It is my only copy," he added.

"Very well," Conal said, trying not to feel flattered. He

couldn't pretend not to know of the Dhaurian's formidable reputation, though the official view of the Koinobia was that he was of no account. "I will care for it as though it were one of my own."

He chivvied the stupid donkey until it bore the wagon back to the rear of the train, then helped the aged scholar dismount. Kilfor, who was spending time with his father, took Phemanderac into his own wagon.

Conal drove on for a while after the strange Dhaurian left him, then found he could resist the scroll no longer. The author was a man who had witnessed with his own eyes many of the events of the Falthan War. For the knowledge contained within, surely the Archpriest could forgive Conal any indiscretion. He transferred the reins to his left hand, kept half an eye on the trail ahead, and began to unroll the scroll.

FLICTOPHILIA: THE LOVE OF WAR

Conal puzzled over the title for a moment. Perhaps the old man had brought with him the wrong scroll? He read on:

A History of the Falthan War
Phemanderac, dominie of Dhauria

The scroll itself was of the highest quality vellum, the calfskin a work of the most splendid craftsmanship in its own right. Of equal quality, the beautiful penmanship beguiled his eye.

To his chagrin, the rough trail frustrated his attempts to read the scroll. When he placed a hand on the calfskin to steady it, the stupid, *stupid* donkey baulked at his one-handedness on the reins. With two hands on the reins, the scroll kept rolling closed. The hours until the train halted for the night's camp were a severe torment.

As he dismounted from the wagon he was greatly tempted to give the donkey a kick. He restrained himself: the evil beast would probably give him better than it received.

It took another half-hour to get the campsite prepared. Sauxa and Kilfor assisted the priest after they finished setting up their own camp; Robal and Stella arrived a few minutes later, laughing together about some inanity. The guardsman made eyes at her; for a wonder, she didn't chastise him for it. Conal turned away, sickened, and busied himself with stirring the stew.

The evening meal could not pass quickly enough. *Let the others tidy up*. He took the scroll up into the wagon, lit the small oil lamp and opened the treasure.

Within minutes he was lost. Not because he failed to understand what he read, but because he understood it too well. The writer—surely not the juiceless old man who had brought him the scroll—knew human nature as no other he'd read. This was so much more than a history: indeed, it was not even presented in chronological order. Instead, it seemed to comprise a series of themes, each targeting a particular human trait, showing how the war might have been avoided or minimised had people behaved differently. The prose, the passion and the sheer force of the arguments all combined to capture him.

He read further down, coming across a map drawn in four colours. It was a detailed chart of Vulture's Craw, the last great battle of the Falthan War. Breathtaking in its simplicity. Conal rolled the scroll closed, his hands shaking.

I cannot surrender these ideas to the Archpriest. Their elegance would be despoiled by the man's intellectual clumsiness, their depth and power mined for political gain.

He had no way to verify the facts presented in this history. Many of them differed significantly from the Seven Scrolls of the Halites. Undoubtedly they would be suppressed by the Archpriest and his senior scholars: how could they possibly allow the whole foundation of their reaching to be challenged? Already, in the few sections he had read, the writer asserted that Leith made a decision at Aleinus Gates that cost nearly ten thousand lives, that the despised *losian* were absolutely essential to the victory at Skull Rock, and that soldiers of Straux committed atrocities on the bodies of dead Bhrudwan soldiers at the orders of their king. None of these events featured in the Halite scrolls.

The ideas contained in the document acted as water to his soul. He forgot about whatever mundane conversations Stella might be having with the Dhaurian philosopher. This, the scroll he held in his hands, could be the most important treatise he would ever read.

Conal the priest took a deep breath, checked that no stray dirt adhered to his hands, then unrolled the scroll and recommenced his reading.

The days ground into weeks, and every day Stella gave thanks that they had joined with the well-provisioned Dhaurian camel train. Two of the wells they had intended to use on the way east were dry, one having dried up in the month since the Dhaurians had passed this way travelling westwards. The Dhaurian chatelaine, Fenacia, managed the rationing of water very carefully; everyone felt thirsty, but none died. This was unusual: death attended even the most well-organised desert crossing, awaiting a single lapse in attentiveness.

There came a day when the sand gave way to thorn bushes and sickly scrub, then waving grasses. With surprising rapidity they left the desert behind, coming to a land of cooler breezes and running water.

In the late afternoon the camel train came to a halt, spreading to the left and to the right. Stella sat beside Robal as he gentled Lindha and the trapdown a moderate slope towards the head of the train. Behind them Stella could hear Conal muttering as he read Phemanderac's scroll.

"Why have we stopped?" Kilfor shouted as he drove his wagon up to theirs.

His father leaned over. "Because the Dhaurians have finally realised my son is a tick on their hide, sucking them dry. They will send him back across the desert minus his tongue, with his pony on his shoulders."

"Perhaps," said Stella, standing up in the tray. "But we have arrived."

Robal eased Lindha to a halt. He and Stella leaped from the wagon and ran forward like excited children.

"What's happened? Why have we stopped?" No one responded to the priest's plaintive voice.

"Ohhh," Stella breathed, unable to help herself.

She stood on the very edge of a chasm of stupefying depth, looking down into a deep, wide valley. Little fluffy clouds some distance below them indicated how high the cliff-top was; below the clouds—a long way below— wind-whipped whitecaps rippled across deep blue water. Her gaze was drawn to the opposite shore, a dark line suggesting a precipice of at least equal height, hazy in the remote distance. The water continued many leagues to her right, to the southwest, and in this direction the far cliff receded until it was barely visible. In the distance a bank of storm-clouds hung above a grey curtain of rain. But to her left spread the scene that had taken her breath.

There the cliffs narrowed somewhat. The sea washed up on a shore of pale sand, fronting a league or more of patchwork fields and forests, softened by a gentle golden mist. Behind this towered another cliff, forming the end of the valley, and at the place where the fertile fields met the rocky wall rose a city of red and white.

Dhauria. Which was once Dona Mihst, the Vale of Youth. The thousand-year cradle of the First Men, ended by the Destroyer's rebellion and the great flood unleashed by the Most High. The mother-city of the First Men, from whom Faltha had sprung. A shadow of its former glory, yet the shadow was still far greater than the sunshine of this present age.

Phemanderac smiled, a proud parent. "Welcome," he said.

COSMOGRAPHER

CHAPTER 20

THE DESERT CHILDREN

HEAT, THOUGH ON ITS OWN heat wouldn't be enough. Hunger, then. Yes, hunger would do it, but hunger was a lazy executioner and would take far too long, days perhaps, even weeks. Thirst would oblige him more quickly, but the death would still be an agonising, protracted one. For a time Captain Duon placed his hope in their pursuers catching them; though even then he would need to be fortunate to escape a prolonged death. The Marasmians had kept some of their captives alive night after night. There had been one in particular, a man—though in such extremity it had been difficult to tell—who had hooted and screamed his defiance for three consecutive nights. The Amaqi had found him on the fourth morning, lying in their path, the body of an owl stuffed in his mouth.

Perhaps expiring from thirst would be best, after all.

But Captain Duon's rational mind had no power in the desert. He shambled daughterback towards the bitter Skeleton Coast along with the meagre remnants of the mighty Amaqi army, all using their cloaks or other items of clothing to shield their faces from the worst of the sun.

Duon took his allotted sips from their rapidly dwindling store of water, as did everyone else. No food remained, but it hardly seemed to matter. The Amaqi knew they were being pursued; the Marasmians had not troubled to hide themselves since that dreadful first night after the Valley of the Damned—so the survivors now named it—but neither Duon nor anyone else chose to sit on the sand and await the creative hands of vengeance. Duon's clever mind told him the quickest way to die would be to refuse the water, that the slowest death was to continue as they were; but the desert took no account of clever thinking. It demanded you survive another moment, then another; it robbed you of the ability to plan, to think long-term.

A pity, then, that one could not die of shame. Though technically Captain Duon had not been in charge of the Amaqi army at the time the Marasmians ambushed them, the defeat was his responsibility. It had not been an honourable defeat; the name of Taleth Salmadi Duon would not be reported to the Emperor as that of a hero. No, he and the few hundred survivors of the great army of conquest had abandoned their fellows. Had run from the horror. When the Emperor heard of this humiliation, he might even order Duon's family executed.

If he heard of it. Someone would have to survive this flight from their tormentors, a possibility becoming increasingly unlikely. The Amaqi expedition would vanish in the desert, and no word of their passing would reach Talamaq and the royal ears.

We are being herded. The Marasmians wanted them to know this, to despair of life long before they lost it. There could be no other explanation for the constant taunting; the hourly discovery of artefacts from their captured comrades placed carefully in their path. Or sometimes bodies, their cruelly marred features inevitably recognised by at least one of the survivors. Bodies stripped of clothing and dignity, arranged obscenely in grotesque parodies of sexual congress.

Captain Duon knew exactly where the herders intended to drive their "cattle." He alone of the survivors had previously seen the bare ground where once had stood the city of Marasmos, an obscene reminder of the ruthlessness of an Amaqi emperor long past. There the remnants of the Amaqi army would be corralled, and the Marasmian goal of revenge would be consummated in slaughter. There Duon would find just reward for his cowardice at the cruel hand of some grinning savage.

To his mortification, Captain Duon did not even command the residue of the expedition. That honour had been taken by Dryman, a mere mid-ranking soldier, member of no Alliance. But, it seemed, a man of resource and persuasion. It was Dryman who kept everyone walking long after Duon would have surrendered. It was he who began to play tricks of his own: an attempt, Duon thought, to raise morale among the dispirited survivors.

During the second night Dryman had sent two soldiers ahead to disrupt the Marasmians' next attempt to intimidate them. Both returned midmorning, though one died a few hours later of a stomach wound sustained during the venture. The survivor reported a successful engagement, confirmed later in the day when the site was examined carefully and six dead Marasmian warriors were found. Emboldened, Dryman organised a raiding party that night, finding a dozen volunteers for what would be essentially a suicide mission. Many of the soldiers, despairing of their own lives, were keen to do something to silence their companions' constant shrieking and moaning that echoed about the hills during the cold nights. That the surprise attack failed was made clear later that evening when the volunteers added their screams to those who had been captured in the Valley of the Damned.

Dryman took himself off at nights. Duon watched him leave, suspicious of his fervid eyes and eager expression, resentful of the man's seemingly boundless energy. He returned before dawn, eyes feverish, but gave no clue as to where he'd been.

The Amaqi were encaged, and the cage was about to be lowered into the fire.

Torve maintained his Defiance, even though he could feel his strength leaving him. Each morning Lenares would come and watch, her once-pretty cheeks hollowing out by the day. They said little during the long hot marches, trying not to draw attention to themselves. Dryman had already intervened once when a couple of soldiers, half-crazed by thirst, had sought to reduce the number of survivors by two.

It seemed some of the survivors had adopted the belief that he and Lenares had led the expedition into the Marasmian ambush. Certainly none would credit their story, and after the third time his telling of their painful desert crossing was mocked Torve gave up. The soldiers needed to be angry at someone, and those most at fault for their predicament had been killed. He knew that further arguing would bring more unwelcome attention upon them, so he and Lenares each walked a solitary path, separated from the other survivors, and each other.

It hurt his newborn heart to watch Lenares suffer. She had already been near the end of her strength when the ambush took place; one night's sleep had not served to restore her. Whenever he caught sight of her she seemed on the edge of collapse. As usual, there was nothing he could do for her.

Just before dawn on the fifth morning Torve's chosen place of Defiance overlooked the steel-grey sea, and the end of everything seemed in sight. Lenares squatted a few paces away and watched with her usual frightening intensity that had disconcerted the Omeran until he became used to it. He finished his almost-dance to find his audience had grown: three small, curly-headed figures sat cross-legged on the sand, watching him with round eyes and absorbed faces.

"The desert children," Lenares said happily. "Just as you told me." So like her: she was more likely to be happy because Torve had been proved truthful than because the children might offer a chance of rescue.

First things first.

He beckoned the three children onto his circle; just as they had on the previous occasion, the children replicated his Defiance in movements so seamless as to be magical, inhuman. Lenares gasped; her numbers were telling her something, presumably.

If only he could communicate with the children. Were they aware of the Amaqis' desperate straits? Could they do anything to help? For that matter, how had they penetrated this far through the Marasmian perimeter?

Or were they Marasmian allies?

"Look, Torve," Lenares said. The youngest of the three children, a snub-nosed little boy of perhaps six years, took up a stick and spat on one end. Torve licked the inside of his cheeks: *saliva in the desert is a sign of wealth*, he thought. The boy extended his arm, then sketched a pace-wide square in the sand with the tip of the stick. Something in the flourish, perhaps, or in the boy's expectant look, suggested magic.

The Omeran expected a flash of light, a shimmering, a magical rustle of sound. Nothing. But when he looked closely he could see a small section of rocky plain within the square the boy had drawn, a slightly darker grey than the sand surrounding it. A picture of another place. The boy had opened a way between here and somewhere else.

The girl giggled and clapped her hands, then beckoned Torve and Lenares forward.

"Can we bring our friends?" Torve asked.

A furrow appeared in the centre of the girl's brow.

"Friends?" Torve repeated. "Over the hill there. May we bring them?"

Lenares' mouth described a perfect circle. Torve could only imagine what this door—this hole in the world—would be doing to her numerical perception. She wouldn't care, not now; her curiosity would overcome her fear, she would want to step through; Torve had no doubt he could do nothing to hold her back. Even as he thought it, she stepped forward and climbed through the hole as though leaving a room by a trapdoor.

With a strangled cry, Torve dived through after her.

A toe in the small of his back woke Duon from a restless slumber. "Get up quickly, boy," said a voice. "We have no time." Something in the tone jerked him awake and onto his feet before a clear thought had time to form.

It was Dryman, and for once the man showed concern on his face, even fear. "Forget your sword," he said. "Now, or you'll be left behind."

Duon grabbed at the sword-hilt as Dryman dragged him away from the still-sleeping camp. Figuring that the Marasmians could destroy them whenever they wanted, no guard had been set. What was the point? Dryman had argued. But now something had spooked him well and truly.

"*Run!*"

Oh yes, the man had been taken by fear.

Duon was well past running, but Dryman would not listen. The soldier half-dragged him away from the camp, over a dune and into the pale grey valley beyond. In the middle of the valley, on a patch of sand, lay a human-sized square of darkness, and as Duon panted down the sandy slope he watched one, two, three people climb into it and disappear. Two small figures remained.

"Our door to freedom," Dryman said, breathing hard.

"Freedom?" Captain Duon's head spun viciously; he was barely able to retain consciousness. His life crossed a boundary then, from the understandable to the surreal. *Finally*, said the voice in the back of his head. *Now, perhaps, we can achieve something.*

Duon groaned. He had forgotten his incipient madness, had not considered it as a means of escape from his situation. Might it not have been the kindest death of all, divorced from reality when the butcher's knives appeared in Marasmian hands?

Too late now. They were about to hide in a hole in the ground.

A shout from somewhere behind them. Dryman turned,

forcing Duon to follow. A score or more men sprinted down the slope behind them, some with spears in their hands. Dryman ducked as a spear hissed past, then pulled Duon forward.

They arrived at the dark squre at a dead run just as the last ankle disappeared. Dryman snatched at it, and with his other hand grabbed at Duon. Another spear flew low over their heads as the ground swallowed them.

Nothing could have prepared a disoriented Captain Duon for what happened next. He and Dryman tumbled *upwards* along a tube that looked like nothing so much as an enormous gullet. Blurred images of dunes to their left, of the sea to their right, smeared across his vision. Without warning they were ejected from the far end of the gullet, spewing out onto a rocky plain. Duon landed half on Dryman, half on a small child who snarled at him.

As he tried to get his breath back, he watched another child tap on the opening twice with a stick. The image of sand set in the stony desert floor seemed to solidify just as a Marasmian warrior approached the opening. The man's features registered first shock, then terror as it became apparent he was trapped between the doors.

Duon could still see into the gullet, but wished he could not. The passage contracted as it reverted to desert, slowly crushing the Marasmian in its grip of sand and stone. The young captain turned away a moment too late to avoid witnessing the man's features collapse in a welter of blood, his eyes popping out from his head. Had he and Dryman been but a little later . . .

"Who are these people?" Dryman said. Duon opened his eyes; the question was addressed to the Emperor's abandoned Omeran.

"I do not know," the slave replied. "I have met them before, but know little about them. They do not speak our tongue."

"I can see that," the soldier said impatiently, and turned to Duon. "They will take us somewhere else, then try to explain what they want with us. A service or reward of some kind, no doubt."

"What makes you think that?" Duon asked him. "And why did you save me?"

"I am something of a student of human nature," Dryman said. His back was to the Omeran, so he did not see—as the captain did—the astonishing effect his words had on the Emperor's pet. "They will want something in exchange for our freedom. And as for your presence here, how else did you think we were going to find our way through the desert?"

Behind Dryman the Omeran had fallen to his knees in something like shock, his mouth wide open, head shaking from side to side. The girl-cosmographer tried to pull him to his feet. Beyond them stood three children, talking urgently together in some foreign jabber. Too much was happening for Captain Duon to take in.

One of the children stepped forward. The tallest one, a boy, now with the stick in his hand. He pointed it at each of them in turn—the cosmographer, the Omeran, Dryman and the captain—and Duon found himself flinching away from it as though it were a poisonous snake. Then the child made a beckoning motion. *Follow us.*

Dryman shrugged, then began to walk towards the children. Duon followed: what other choice was there?

The remnants of the night seemed to last forever, slowly fading into dawn, a never-ending sequence of rock and sand in shades of grey. At one point they passed the Marasmian camp, just outside the ring of sentries. Duon saw the fires and the stakes and the squirming figures with the increasing detachment of the chronically exhausted. He sensed the presence in his head watching everything with an avid interest.

Some time later the cosmographer collapsed. Asleep, unconscious or dead, Duon could not tell and couldn't make himself care. Dead, it looked like, the way her head lolled in the Omeran's arms. The voice in his mind expressed regret, a sentiment Duon was too tired to share.

Lenares awoke to the sound of murmuring voices and a head-splitting ache in her temples. She probed her awareness as gingerly as a tongue exploring a rotted tooth, and was surprised to find that, even though she had been transported through space—and possibly through time—by some device, and had subsequently lost consciousness, she remained centred.

She was not sure how this was possible. Her spatial awareness, as Mahudia would have called it, retained its clarity. She could visualise exactly where she was on a map of Elamaq; the image of a circular map of bronze flashed through her mind, and she found she could locate her position on it also. Had the Daughter done something to her? Or did the map itself exercise some arcane power? It felt to her as though she emitted some unseen light in all directions, which returned to her complete with a numerical description of where it had been. It made Lenares feel as though she was the centre of the universe.

A new talent? A result of her close encounter with the hole in the world? An accidental overlay of numerical data? She would observe herself with care. She feared losing control of herself more than anything.

Torve and the soldier called Dryman were engaged in an intense conversation. Knees together, heads almost touching, they talked in undertones. Torve looked pale, his half-healed scars from the sun standing out on his cheeks as though they had been painted on chalk.

"She's awake," Dryman said, and the two men separated. "Remember what you've been told," the soldier cautioned Torve, to which the Omeran nodded unhappily.

Lenares glanced around her. She lay on a rectangular mat, woven from all manner of bright colours. Twenty-six different shades, her mind told her. She ignored it: the interminable calculating was becoming increasingly irrelevant. She did not know whether to be disturbed or comforted by this change. The mat lay in turn upon solid rock, a shining green marble polished, she guessed, by many generations of people and their rugs. A wall behind her was of the same rock, though much more angular; above her the rock extended in a small outcrop, to which a pale awning was attached, held outstretched by two gnarled poles set into cracks in the rock.

Apart from herself, Dryman and Torve were the only others in the alcove. *Three*, she told her mind, challenging herself to explain the significance of the number. *Numbers don't tell me everything*, she admitted to herself. *I know how many people are in this room, but not why Captain Duon is missing*.

As if summoned by her thoughts, the captain entered the alcove, carrying a large platter of food and a waterskin. Immediately every other thought was submerged by a rush of hunger and thirst.

"Just a little, Lenares," Torve cautioned, but his words made no headway against her body's desires. She heard his warning, would remember it after an afternoon of emptying her stomach amid virulent cramps, but at the time it didn't touch her. That night she ate and drank more carefully, having learned an important lesson about the limits of her self-control.

"What is this place?" she whispered to Torve after their evening meal, again served by Captain Duon, as if he were their servant and not their master. "Where are the children?"

"They are not here," Torve replied, his voice low, not so much a whisper as a melancholic rasp. "They have made camp some distance away, and are discussing what they should do with us."

"Why should they do anything with us?" Lenares asked. "Why not let us go on our way?" Not that she knew which way they ought to go.

"Because Captain Duon and . . . and Dryman are here with us. The desert people are afraid of them. Something is wrong in both of them, so the children say."

"Say? You understand them?"

"No, but they communicate their unease very clearly. When we first arrived they would not go near either man. I do not understand what Duon has done to earn such mistrust."

Lenares took a locust from the platter and dipped it in a sweet, sticky fluid. The taste burned itself on her tongue, drawing an astonishing wave of pleasure from her mouth that spread throughout her body.

"Wonderful, are they not," Torve whispered. She nodded, not trusting herself to speak.

"They are my ancestors," he said, and looked at her, a yearning in his eyes. He wanted her to understand something. "They are not Omeran; they are the people we Omerans changed from."

"How do you know this?" His words had triggered a cascade of images and numbers in her head.

"They know my Defiance," he said, "and have shown me from whence it sprang."

"They do look a little like you, though they are much more handsome." Belatedly she realised that her words might hurt him, so she softened them by extending her hand and taking his.

"What were you talking with Dryman about?" she enquired.

He jerked involuntarily, as though Lenares had tweaked a string tying him to something. "I cannot tell you," he whispered. "Please do not ask me about him."

"Why? Why can't I ask? What is wrong, Torve?"

"Please," he begged her. "If you press me, I must refuse you."

Lenares released his hand and sat back, surprised at the depth of hurt she felt at his words. What could be so secret that he must keep it from her? Her mind swirled with speculation; she could no more stop thinking about it than she could stop breathing. But underneath her mind's frantic activity lay a newly created hollow place, which, until his words, had been filled with love.

The only person without a wall erected to keep her out, the one man open to her scrutiny, a good man, not an animal as she once had thought, a man who loved her; but now with a secret. The knowledge that he could not share everything with her meant that, against her wishes, her mind shifted him from the category of one to the category of everyone. He was no longer special.

"I'm sorry," he said, and reached for her hand. She pulled away from him.

"Don't touch me!" she found herself saying, and the hollowness within her expanded with the words, a hole in her own world.

The next day the Desert Children, as Torve had taken to calling the tribe, came to visit them. For the occasion they hitched up the sides of the alcove, letting the sun warm the cold marble wall, so the Children could see their guests. *Their captives*, Lenares thought, though there was nothing to suggest they could not just walk away.

The Children formed a line, thirty or more strong, then all sat down on their haunches. The three Amaqi sat under the awning. Halfway between the two groups knelt Torve, waiting for whatever was to come. Lenares could see the similarity between him and the Children, could read it in the shape of their eyes, the set of the forehead, the width of the nose, though there were also differences. They had darker skin, finer features, more expressive movements. Indeed, everything they did was a dance. *They could well be his ancestors*.

Her mind drifted for a moment, imagining him finding kinship with the Children, deciding to stay with them, bidding her a sad farewell as she, Captain Duon and Dryman headed out into the desert. The thought drenched her in misery. *Why can't I let him have a secret?* She did not know the answer, but wished bitterly she did.

Two of the Children and an adult came forward and mimed horror at Dryman and Captain Duon. Torve did not understand, so she called out from where she sat.

He beckoned her forward. She knelt beside him and it felt so right it was all she could do to stop herself bursting into tears.

The mummers continued their display, and their actions were as clear as if they spoke in the Amaqi tongue. "They are frightened of Dryman and the captain," she said to Torve. "The two men are fruit that looks good on the outside but harbours worms within. They ask us whether these men belong to us and, if not, want to know if they can kill them."

A groan came from behind Lenares. "Why? What is wrong with me?" Captain Duon's questions sounded sincere, not an assertion of innocence. "Can they tell?"

"Better hope they can't," Dryman said, his voice as relaxed as it ever had been.

Torve tried to tell the Children that yes, the two men were known to them. After some confusion Lenares was satisfied the message had been understood.

After more graceful miming, Lenares reported: "The Children were willing to offer us shelter, but because the bad men are with us, they must take us to the borders of their lands and see us leave. They say that they nearly decided to kill us all, but the True Man—that's you, Torve—and the Woman who Sees—me—should be allowed to live. They say that, should we return without the bad men, they would welcome us into their clan and allow us to stay for a time. However, should they encounter the bad men ever again, they will kill them without discussion."

"If they could," Dryman muttered.

"Do they say what is wrong with the two men?" Torve asked.

"They do not know," said Lenares. "I think they might be like me. They sense much about a person from their smell, their . . . taste, but that's not what they mean. They can tell something is wrong, but not what."

"I have a question," Dryman said, raising his voice. "How have these Children survived for so long without being found by the Amaqi?"

The Children mimed at length. "The Amaqi cannot find their nose with their finger," Lenares said eventually, and Captain Duon barked a laugh. "This is the Children's land, bountiful and good, and the thick-heads—their name for us—can continue to live in the badlands."

"Do these Children know they are animals?" Lenares heard the perverse delight in the question, the desire to wound, but she asked it anyway.

To her surprise, the adult nodded. "Yes! They say they are like the deer and the monkeys and the water buffalo, all children of the . . . of the *giant*." Her voice tailed off as memories of her dream came crashing back into her mind.

"Oh," she said, images pounding her brain. "Oh, oh!"

"Lenares? What is wrong?" Torve hovered close, but she could not spare any of herself to formulate an answer. The memories came fast and hot, their power seizing her muscles and her mind.

The giant strides the land, scattering stones, creating the desert, the cradle of all life . . . the children of the giant gather at the waterhole and decided to search for their god . . . finding the giant, they transform him into their god by their worship . . . the children quarrel, killing each other, and refuse the god's help . . . he makes a daughter and a son out of a woman and a man, but still they refuse to listen . . . his Son and his Daughter betray the god and drive him out of the desert . . . his absence creates a hole in the world . . . the Son and the Daughter contend for control . . .

She did not realise she had acted out the powerful memories until she heard a rumbling chorus of agreement from the assembled Children. It took her some considerable time to explain to Torve what had happened.

Dryman growled audibly behind her. "From what source did this bastardised legend spring? Is this a belief of these animals here, or is it your own, cosmographer?"

Something about that last word, about the way Dryman said it, stroked a memory in Lenares' mind, but she did not have the leisure to pursue it.

"Neither," she snapped. "It is the truth." But, even as she said it she sensed the inadequacy of her assertion. *It is a truth*, her numbers told her. *You have the sum, but there are more than two factors, more than one way of arriving at the correct answer.* "It is true," she corrected herself.

And it is filled with information, with clues to what is happening in the world. Now all she needed was leisure to examine the memories Dryman's question had freed. Leisure, and the will to make her mind focus on anything but the frightening hollowness inside her, or the sudden overturning of her belief in one absolute truth. *More than one way to get a correct answer? Could a question have two true answers? Or more?* She felt . . . she felt as though she were a building cracking and breaking up in an earthquake. No, more like a building being destroyed and rebuilt.

Their time with the Desert Children could not be measured in hours or days. Here—wherever here was, exactly—the days seemed to pass differently; not so much at a different speed, Duon reflected, but without any speed at all. It was the difference between sitting on a camel and passing a man on the side of the road, and being that man and watching the camel pass. Like the man by the road, he seemed outside of events. Time passed, the sun rose and set, but without touching him.

Perhaps it was his preoccupation with propitiation. If the first time he had run from his command, abandoning his expedition to torture and death, had scarred him, his second enforced abandonment left him numb. For all his despair about his venal behaviour, he had not struggled when Dryman drew him away to the secret portal of the Desert Children. False, his despair had been, a façade intended to ease his own conscience.

He did not intend to make the same mistake again. This time he would not rely on a feeling to achieve redemption; he would serve those that remained. He carried water for them, tidied and prepared their dwelling, helped with the meal preparations and whatever else he could find to do. Guilt would not just be something he felt, it would become what he was.

But, he was forced to admit, a selfish motive lay even at the heart of this selfless behaviour. He needed a focus, anything, to stop himself going mad. Gradually Duon was being taken over by the voice in his head, the scornful voice that mocked his every effort to do the right thing. In his most lucid moments, he worried that he was breaking in two. Frighteningly, the voice in his head reassured him that he was not.

Duon tried talking to Dryman. The Children had identified both him and the soldier as "bad men," suggesting they could see his fractured mind. Perhaps Dryman suffered from something similar? But Dryman dashed this hopeful idea. "I am completely sound of mind," the soldier said in a tone of clipped assertion. "These desert anachronisms have labelled us, no doubt, because we ran from our army." He shrugged, as if such betrayal were of no account.

"How did you know about the existence of the portal in the desert?"

Something hard rose in the man's eyes. "I am not entirely talentless," he said. "You are trained to find new paths and explore them; I am trained to find a different kind of path and exploit it. Rather than subjecting me to interrogation, you would do better to ask yourself this: where will we go once these desert mice have done with us?"

"Will they let us go?"

"They will not be able to stop us."

"But they have magic. If a child is a sorcerer, what might their adults be capable of?"

"They have no reason to harm us. You fuss like an old woman. Are you sure the voice you say you're hearing isn't that of your mother?"

Duon gave up. "Keep your secrets, then. But I wish you had left me with the rest of the expedition."

"You are a fool," Dryman said, the last word overlaid exactly by the voice in Duon's head, a duet of condemnation. *Fool.*

The soldier continued his assault on Duon's illusions. "I take with me every tool I need. You are a tool. You are here because I need you to take me where I want to go. A man like you, Captain, cannot afford for a moment

to think he is in charge of his life. Others rule you and
they always will. Tie yourself in moral knots if you
must, but others are responsible for the direction you
have taken. How can a mere tool be held to account for
what skilled hands make it do?"

The man's words reverberated in Duon's skull. They
tempted him to surrender, to allow others to use him as
they would. Worse, they told him that he had already
done so by choosing to serve. He had made himself a
tool, a functionary with no responsibility.

He made his way back to the alcove, his mind a tangle
of severed threads. How quickly his life had been rendered meaningless, how cruelly his future had been taken
out of his hands. From the heady heights of favouritism
with a gracious, generous Emperor to the depths of his
discussion with the boorish Dryman.

You are layered in self-deception, said the voice in his
head, or perhaps it was his own thought. He was beginning to lose the ability to tell. *When the onion is fully
peeled, what will remain?*

Torve's secret tormented him like the sun. That was what
it was like: as though a second sun had been set in the
desert sky. It burned away at his Defiance. If it were possible for anything to undo thousands of years of breeding,
this was it. He could feel it draining him of integrity.

Worse, he could see its effect on Lenares. She knew he
was keeping something from her; he knew she would not
be able to bear it. He would lose her, had most likely already lost her, and his joy at discovering her unexpected
love had begun to evaporate.

Worst of all was what was to come. No one could save

him from it, not Captain Duon, not the Desert Children, not even Lenares. They would all suffer because of what Torve would be compelled to do.

They had already begun to suffer.

Next morning the Children assembled in front of the alcove, ready to see the Amaqi on their way. They asked Torve to remain, and indicated that Lenares could also stay, but of course such a thing had been rendered impossible. Torve could no more remain here, much as he wished to penetrate the mystery of their survival in the desert heart of Elamaq, than he could turn aside his heritage of obedience. He did not pass their invitation on to Lenares.

There seemed some unease amongst the Desert Children, a constant agitated turning of heads and movement of limbs, where in previous gatherings there had been calmness. A child came scampering towards the gathering, running almost on all fours, his face pale and cheeks streaked with tears. The Children listened as the child spoke, then a woman cried out and a man shouted in something between rage and agony. The man took a stride towards where Torve and the Amaqi sat, then visibly restrained himself. Two other Children, a man and a woman, walked after the crying child, who, after shaking his head a few times, relented and led them away in the direction Torve expected, back along the path the child had come from.

He knew what this was about. How could he not? It had stained his soul.

A few minutes later—they must have used their spit-and-stick sorcery—the Children returned, the woman holding something small and bloody in her arms. The dead child looked like a burst fruit. As she laid the body down on the stony ground between the two groups an absolute silence fell, interrupted only when one of the child's limbs flopped from its chest and dislodged a stone. An eerie moment, giving the impression, despite appearances, that the body was alive.

But it could not be. Not after what had been done to it.

Torve risked a glance at Dryman. The man regarded the scene before him with what looked like indifference, his arms folded, feet apart.

They watched as the Children argued amongst themselves. One of the youths was sent away, and returned with an armful of palm fronds. With these the Children honoured the dead girl—Torve knew the corpse for a girl, though its gender was no longer discernible—by layering them on the body. The Children came from the left and the right, each bearing a frond, and every one stared at the Amaqi after placing their offering on the child's remnants.

"Who did this?" Lenares whispered. But from the incredulous look on her face it was clear she guessed who had been involved.

The sun burned away in the sweating sky, towering above them in what seemed to Torve like judgment. The second sun, much closer and far more powerful, threatened to consume his soul.

The numbers crackled through Lenares' head like lightning; she had no way of stopping them. She wished she could hold them back, dam them like the Amaqi had done to the Marasmos River, withhold the knowledge they watered her with. If only there was some trick of forgetfulness she could play, a way of convincing her mind to ignore the numbers and concentrate only on what the others could see. A child, torn apart by some kind of wild animal.

The truth ... oh, it was the truth. A wild animal *had* torn the child apart. She could read it in her beloved's face, the face of an animal, a killer. He—it—knew. His face was frightened, appalled, but not surprised. And that Dryman, he had something to do with it too. There was a connection between them. But Lenares could not read the soldier; it was as though he wore a false face, a mask. She could not see his true face, it was hidden from her somehow. A mystery; perhaps the most important mystery of this journey filled with mysteries.

The Children, ancestors to the Omeran animal. How far had the Omerans fallen? How long ago had they lost their humanity?

The same three who had spoken to her at the previous meeting stepped forward. Their movements were not as composed as they had been; Lenares had trouble understanding them.

"One of you did this. He must step forward. We will kill him and let the rest of you leave. If he does not step forward, we will kill you all."

"They are bluffing," Dryman said when she relayed the message. "They cannot take human life. Not since they conspired with the Daughter and the Son to drive out the Father have they spilled human blood. They were appalled by what they did. Since then they have made a covenant with themselves not to interfere, which is how they survived. Until now."

"How do you know this?" Lenares asked him.

"Does it matter, witch-girl? Is what I say true?"

She nodded. *Or at least it is not false*. His words made her freshly aware of the growing gap between the two poles of her life, truth and falsehood, as though the twin rocks upon which she stood had suddenly begun to move apart, revealing a chasm between them.

Torve clearly wished to step forward, but his feet remained where they were. His body strained like a hound against an invisible leash. What could prevent him doing what he obviously wanted to do? She felt herself on the very edge of revelation.

The moment drew out, the two groups staring at each other over the small pile of palm leaves, until the Children began arguing with each other. While Lenares could not understand what was being said, the general flow of the argument was clear. To kill, in violation of their covenant, or to send their captives on their way? For a time the two factions seemed equally vehement, but gradually the man and woman—the child's parents—leading those seeking the deaths of the Amaqi gave way to the obligations of tradition. Dryman had been right.

"Come with us," the Children instructed Lenares, every trace of cordiality erased from their demeanour.

Torve drew alongside her. "Lenares," he began.

"Don't talk to me, don't touch me, don't look at me," she said, using the most menacing tone she could muster. "Don't think about me. You are a sick animal. Go away. I will not speak to you again."

She swung a fist and hit him, hard, on the side of the jaw. Two of her knuckles split but she didn't care about the pain. Welcomed it. He—it—went down to its haunches with a grunt of pain and surprise.

*   *   *

It took an hour for the dizziness to depart. He truly had not been anticipating her strike; he thought of his pretentious Defiances, in which he avoided every kick and punch any opponent threw at him. *One of the Children here could slay me with her fists. Lenares can send me to my knees. I am not worthy of being anyone's opponent.*

He recognised these thoughts for the despair they were, packaged them up and resolved to deal with them when next he had an opportunity to practise his Defiance. It seemed he would be fighting the whole world.

The Children of the Desert gathered around a flat patch of stony ground. One of the Children took a stick and spat on it and, as before, a rectangular hole opened at his bidding. Was the stick magical? Or the spit? And the portal, was it a permanent fixture or was it recreated wherever and whenever required?

So many things he wanted to know. He so desperately wanted to explore the kinship he felt with these people, to learn what he had lost, what they might be able to offer him. What they might be able to offer his race, all Omerans. More than anything he desired release from the cage he had been locked in. He was compelled to obey the voice of the Emperor by his upbringing, by his heredity; but obedience had lost him Lenares' regard, and would lose him so much more. Her death lay in his future; she would not be suffered to live.

Once she died he would earnestly wish his own death. Would beg his tormentor for it. But he would not be granted the release.

Through the portal they went, emerging at the edge of the Children's territory, he supposed. No. On the margin of a piece of broad, level ground, in the midst of which were propped a hundred statues or more.

Duon recognised what they were before anyone else. Even as the Children turned their backs on the Amaqi and filed back through the portal, he cried out in anguish and ran forward. Dryman followed him, a look of puzzlement on his face slowly replaced by one of comprehension.

Not statues, then.

There were twelve rows, roughly twelve people to a row; some with more, others less. About a hundred and fifty in total. Each one an Amaqi, mostly soldiers, but the occasional camp follower, all impaled on their own tripod of ash spears and covered with salt.

The pain must have been incredible. Many of them had expired, but a few still writhed on their improvised instruments of torture. While Dryman wandered up and down the rows, searching for survivors, Captain Duon stumbled over to a pile of discarded equipment, no doubt stripped from the soldiers, and was sick. After a while he took something from the pile—a sword—and walked amongst the tableau of dead and dying, cutting throats.

Me, it ought to have been me suffering here, Torve thought.

He would have welcomed it.

Thus the centuries-old crime was balanced, thus were the Marasmians avenged. The exhausted, depleted desert warriors watched the four surviving Amaqis weep and curse at the fate of their fellows, and judged the full cup of suffering finally drunk to the dregs. The Marasmians would not interfere, would not take the lives of those who remained; a full redress required that the tale be told throughout the world. Therefore a hundred of their fiercest warriors were detailed with the task of caring for these

Amaqis, ensuring they remained alive until they left Marasmian lands. They would watch over these four, now they were out of the hands of the desert demons; would protect them as best they could from every desert danger without revealing themselves. And when they returned from that task, they would join with their fellow Marasmians in raising the old city once again. Then, finally, Marasmian eyes would turn sonback, towards the headwaters of their sacred river, and the abomination there would be torn down.

That the city of the Amaqis would be destroyed as a result was, to their mind, an entirely beneficial side effect.

CHAPTER 21

NOMANSLAND

DUON LED THE SOLDIER, the cosmographer and the Omeran through a landscape every bit as jumbled and broken as the wasteland of his mind. In Punta province, the fatherback land of his birth, the hills were tame, ordered by rain and run-off. Not so here in the Had Hills to the fatherwards of Marasmos. Were it not for the winding path he had located and followed, he doubted they would have found their way through the hills. But finally, a month fatherwards of Marasmos, an arduous month, he had brought them through the hills to the fatherback edge of Nomansland, and to the edge of sanity.

Dryman had decided their direction, driving them fatherwards with the intensity of his will. A mystery, since the Amaqi expedition had been eviscerated, and the safety of Talamaq lay fatherbackwards. The soldier insisted they travel fatherwards, but would not offer any argument, and even Duon could not stand before him. It almost came to swordplay, there on the twice blood-hallowed site of old Marasmos, with the others watching silently, unable to comprehend what Dryman hoped to achieve. But after looking into Dryman's resolute eyes Duon decided not to press the issue.

So silent were the cosmographer and the Omeran during the interminable footsore weeks, for a time Duon thought they had lost the use of their voices. The dark-skinned man and the pale woman seemed to have put everything aside to focus on placing one foot in front of the other. Like him, they had been broken by the Valley of the Damned and the city of Marasmos. Certainly neither had been exactly sane even before the expedition had begun; now, Duon doubted whether they could be of any further use to anyone. Of course, he had the same doubts about himself.

Nevertheless Dryman drove them on, guarding the Omeran and the cosmographer as though they were the most important pair in the world. With Duon he was less careful, sending him on excursions to look for water, game or firewood. The captain knew he could escape at any time, but found himself bound to the others by cords of duty and guilt. As Dryman knew well.

Duon had seen disturbing signs on these journeys. Evidence that people lived in these barren coastal hills. More, a suspicion that someone shadowed them. The smell of smoke, the occasional footprint, a feeling between the shoulder blades that could neither be explained nor denied. A sense no professional explorer could afford to ignore. As though someone made sure they continued their journey away from Marasmian lands. Odd, then, that the travellers came in contact with no one as they made their way through the scrublands.

Though the true desert lurked inland, hinted at by a shimmering on the daughterward horizon, the coastal hills

were trial enough. It seldom rained in this broken country,
the regular sea fogs supplying the spindly trees and sparse,
spiky grasses with the water they needed. There was actually less potable water here; most of the deep wells were to
be found inland, where the meltwater from the alpine
heights emerged from a thousand-league journey sonwards.
None of the meltwater came this close to the coast, where
the few wells were small and brackish. They sufficed. Duon
felt, and Dryman agreed, that neither Lenares nor Torve
were in good enough condition to risk the desert.

While not exactly plentiful, food was relatively easy to
come by, reducing the need for water. In the second week
they came across a tangle of wild melons ripening nicely
amid a snarl of leafy vines lying on the sand. Dryman
bade them gather as many as they could carry, though this
cost them an unpleasant afternoon later in the week when
their improvised cloth bags were soaked by exploding
overripe fruit.

Dryman stood beside Duon and together they gazed
over Nomansland. The Had Hills had finally come to an
end, and now nothing but a long, gradual downward slope
separated them from the beginning of the badlands maze
that lay across their path.

"Ideally we should seek out and hire the Nehra to ensure our passage," Duon said.

"And how many lap-boxes of gold are we to offer
them?" Dryman's temper flared regularly; Duon tried not
to let it affect him.

"More than we have," he answered, spreading his
hands wide to indicate emptiness. The Nehra, the only
people who knew the twisted badlands everyone called
Nomansland, lived many leagues to the sonback. They

would guide people through the maze, but only for gold. They could charge what they pleased, as there was no way around Nomansland, which stretched across Elamaq from the sonwards coast to the mountainous daughterwards spine. Unguided venturers usually vanished without trace in the complex jumble of ridges, box canyons and dead-end valleys. There were no landmarks within Nomansland by which to orient oneself: all the summits were congruent, their tops flat, the valleys between them carved out of a relict plain by some ancient wandering river.

Those who survived here invariably claimed that routes would open and close like doors. A canyon could be entered, they said, and then surround a traveller on all four sides with steep talus slopes that collapsed on anyone foolish enough to try to climb them. Feeble excuses for those unable to navigate the badlands, most people thought. Not Duon. He had passed through Nomansland twice, both difficult traverses even when well equipped and with the help of their knowledgeable guides.

"Would they entertain a generous percentage of our wealth paid on our return fatherbackwards?"

"The Nehra would likely kill us for asking," Duon said. "What wealth could the four of us bring back, they would say." *So the man is motivated by riches. Thirty thousand of us might have wrested riches from the Nehra; four of us will earn only our deaths*.

"What wealth did the Emperor command you to seek, Captain?"

Duon hesitated before answering. As he was about to speak a low rumble came from somewhere to their left. Thunder, or something like it. Duon scanned the cloudless sky in vain.

"The earth is uneasy," Dryman said as Torve the Omeran reached the crest of the slope beside them, assisting the cosmographer. "I have felt small shakes over the last week." The soldier's eyes widened slightly, giving the impression he was making ready to do battle.

As they watched, a rolling curtain of dust approached them from the sonback. No, Duon corrected himself, his nervousness growing, *it is a wave. The ground heaves as though some burrowing animal approaches, throwing up sand . . .*

The wave arrived, a man-height distortion moving incredibly fast. With a heave it tossed them off their feet. Duon found himself dumped on his back amid a dustcloud. Something thumped across his legs, a body, the Omeran. A hiss and the sand came down on top of them, followed by a sudden silence.

The soldier came striding into Duon's field of vision, his teeth bared as though facing down an opponent. "Get up," he said unfeelingly. "We have a long way to go today."

What was Dryman? A mercenary seeking his fortune? A madman? Or a magician holding his three followers in thrall? What did he hope to achieve by continuing this hopeless venture? Mercenary, madman, magician: the possibilities rattled through Duon's head as he stood in obedience to the soldier's command.

The Omeran got to his feet and stumbled away, rubbing at his shins.

Another rumble, accompanied by an embarrassingly gentle shake, sat Duon on his rump. Dryman laughed, then hauled him to his feet. "The gods seek to unsettle us," the soldier said.

"The Emperor doesn't believe in the gods," Duon said automatically.

"Does he not? He ought to. He would, if he were here."

"Dryman, why are we throwing our lives away?"

"Ah, the worm has a voice." They walked towards the other two, who stood together, holding each other for support.

More than one voice, actually. The cause of my problems. "Why not return to Talamaq?" *One last try before we die.* "Surely the Emperor will raise another army? With you at its head, a guarantee of wealth and renown."

"Oh? Will I be as successful as the rich and famous Captain Duon?"

At this Duon snapped his mouth shut. In the back of his head, a light flashed white. *I keep telling you, you are a fool. Keep your mouth shut and I might just be able to guide you through this.*

Weary and soul-wounded, the captain offered no reply.

Misery wrapped itself around Lenares. She kept counting her steps, though she knew the total was more of an estimate than an accurate reflection of where she was. Just a reflexive habit. As were the steps themselves. She didn't need the numbers. Out here in Nomansland nothing seemed to have a point. She had lost the ability to tell what was most important, and the world around her had become nothing more than an endless numerical swirl of information.

She knew why. Her centre had changed. Instead of being tied to a place—Talamaq—she was now tied to a person. Torve. It had happened without her consent, something done by her subconscious mind in an attempt to . . .

what? Preserve herself? Hold onto love? Why had she
never centred on Mahudia, if the latter was the truth? It
angered her that her mind and body could so betray her.

And that was another thing. How could her numbers
mean anything if truth didn't stay still? A small part of her
was excited by what she was learning: in the face of love,
a love that could be both right and wrong, Lenares could
no longer settle for her former belief in the old binary of
absolute truth and falsehood. But the larger part of her was
adrift, floundering in a sea of meaninglessness. She wondered if she might be rejecting both centres, the old truth
of the Empire and the new truth of Torve's love.

*No, he rejected me. His is false centre. I cannot trust
him. Just as I cannot trust Talamaq and the Emperor.*

Whenever she thought on this, the image of the bronze
map shone in her mind. It had been centred on the house
of the gods, but she had the impression its centre could
move. Was the bronze map the truth, or merely a repre-
sentation of truth? The truth from one point of view? One
perspective? Lenares knew she was special, able to think
in ways no one else could, but even so this thinking taxed
her, pulling her mind in uncomfortable directions. The
problem rearranged itself in her head: her eyes beheld
truth, but she did not see everything. She saw from one
perspective only. The bronze map, though, was an attempt
to see everything. Even so, the view from above, from the
eye of the god, was still only a single perspective. Things
remained hidden even from the godlike gaze.

And now a word Mahudia had once taught her slipped
into her consciousness. *Omniscience.* The ability to know
everything. But such an ability must also involve the talent to see from *every* persepective *all at once.* Out of

every pair of eyes in the world at all times. Then, *if* that were not impossible enough, to make sense of what was being seen. And that did not include the things that no one could see.

The gods could not be omniscient. They just thought they were.

Most frightening of all, Lenares wondered what might happen to her if she did not soon discover something to centre her life around.

"Lenares?" Torve's gentle voice cut across her thinking.

She turned to him, angered; for a moment she had felt on the verge of some flowering of knowledge. "What?"

He flinched at her tone.

"Look at the mist," he said. "It doesn't feel right to me."

They had descended the slope and were now approaching the first of the badland canyons, a narrow opening between two ochre-stained stone ridges. Nevertheless, they could still see some way across the crazed jumble of ridges stretching into the distance; though their field of vision was shrinking. A strange pale mist began to rise from all about them, thicker in the distance, gossamer-thin nearby. The ridges vanished.

"Just what we need," Duon said from some distance in front of them, already little more than a grey outline.

The ground rumbled ominously below them.

Lenares glanced upwards to see the sky directly above her describing a blue oval, surrounded by mist. She turned: the path they had travelled was also obscured.

Her numbers screamed at her.

She grabbed Torve's hand. "It's *not right*. Look! The hole in the world hovers above us!"

From behind them came another rumble, and the earth cracked and heaved. A fifty-foot-high ridge reared up like a wave of the sea right across the path they had taken, rocks breaking like foam from its crest. The ground dropped away beneath them; for a moment Lenares thought they were about to be swallowed, but the whole valley floor fell sharply, perhaps one pace, possibly two, and the travellers landed together in a tangle of limbs.

Lenares dusted herself off, and reached again for Torve's hand. He might not be truth, he might not even be her centre, with his lies and deception, but he offered her comfort.

Around them boulders rattled as they rolled down uneasy slopes. The mist closed in; they could hear rather than see the rocks come to rest. Silence spread over Nomansland.

"The hole in the world is here," Lenares said. Something to focus on.

"I rather think we had worked that out," Duon said stiffly. Dryman grunted, stifling a laugh.

"Press on," the soldier said, but his next words were lost in a groan from somewhere in front of them. The valley floor jerked upwards twice as far as it had recently fallen. Lenares bit her tongue hard; the taste of blood blossomed in her mouth. She was sure she must have bruised Torve's fingers, but he did not let her go.

They entered a world of insanity. In Nomansland, with the hole in the world hovering directly above them, tracking them, all natural rules seemed to have been suspended. The land around them and the earth beneath their feet was in constant motion, and they made their way through it as though navigating across a choppy sea. They might enter a valley only to see it close behind them, might search for a way out and watch, bemused, as a wall collapsed, revealing an opening to another canyon.

Eventually it became clear to them that they were being shepherded. Some vast power opened and shut the valleys of Nomansland, forcing them to go where they were directed. Dryman resisted the unseen power at work. He turned them around, forced them to climb unstable mounds of rubble in an effort to retrace their steps. It did them no good. Within a short time all four of them were bruised, and fortunate not to have broken limbs. The soldier became more and more angry, enraged at powers beyond his control.

"It was not like this the last time I passed through," Dùon said.

"Oh? Don't you think you would have mentioned it to the Emperor if it had been?" Dryman roared. "Find me a path, explorer! Or you, cosmographer! What use are your number to me now?"

A new noise emerged from the general rumbles and groans. A moment later a hundred or more gazelles burst through a misty gap in the left-hand wall of the canyon and bore down upon them. The animals' eyes were orbs of pure fear; they leapt high in the air as though afraid to alight on the ground, willing themselves instead to fly.

The travellers threw themselves to the ground; it was all they could do. Even before they hit the dirt yet another jolt shook the canyon, accompanied by a growing roar. A wave of dust hissed over them. When Lenares raised her head, she saw the gap in the valley wall was filled in by an enormous landslip.

They could find no trace of the gazelles.

Night came, hours before Lenares expected it. She could not determine whether it was an unnatural darkness or her misjudgment of time; her numbers told her it was midafternoon, but she mistrusted the numbers. What did the truth matter? If it was dark, it might as well be night.

Dryman called a halt.

"We are trapped," he said in an angry voice. "We have been boxed in by this maze. Who is doing this? Why are they doing this?"

No one answered him. Lenares knew he wasn't really asking them. She suspected he knew the answers, or could at least guess at them. She, on the other hand, wanted to know who he was. Not a common soldier, for certain. She still could not discern his features clearly, as if he wore a disguise. A sorcerer? Lenares had never met a sorcerer. Did they have two faces? And why would a sorcerer pretend to be a soldier? She had almost worked it out some time back, but those thoughts were lost to her now.

The night that followed was far worse than the day. At least they were on their feet during the day, moving, ready to avoid whatever disaster rolled their way. The darkness hid the constant shifting and tossing of the land around them. Sleep was, of course, beyond them. They endured the darkness in a half-awake stupor, waiting for the next shake. Lenares found herself clinging to the ground as though she were about to be ripped away from it at any moment.

As dawn suffused the mist surrounding them, Torve surprised them by speaking. "If we are being treated like cattlebeasts," he said, "we are hardly likely to be slain before we have reached our destination."

The others thought about that for a moment.

"But how will we know when we reach wherever we are being taken to?" Lenares asked.

"When we are slaughtered," said Duon.

"And on such bravery and clear thinking is the Elamaq Empire founded," Dryman mocked.

"They are certainly not fattening their cattle before the slaughter," Torve said. "I lost the last of our food some time last night."

"I still have a little," Duon said. "Some figs, a few berries and a piece of melon from the last oasis."

"I'm sick of melon," Lenares said. Though they had given her stomach cramps, she'd eaten berries and figs throughout their journey over the Had Hills. She would eat them still, had there been any left, in preference to melons.

Dryman bared his teeth. "We have not been slaughtered yet," he said. "The gods make their mistake by not slaying us now. The cattle may yet escape their intended stockyard."

The days following rapidly disintegrated into surrealism. Along with the constant earthquakes and the ever-present mist came storms, floods, fires and plagues of animals and insects. At any time a storm might descend upon them, drenching them in torrential rain; the canyon would fill up, water would pour towards them, only to be swallowed by a trench opening propitiously at their feet. Or a cloud of hornets would materialise behind them when they sought to rest, forcing them to their feet, herding them on. Sheets of flame arose from fiercely hot rents in the earth, the heat pouring over them like a furnace, and were suddenly drowned by another flood, sending steam hundreds

of feet into the air. And at all times they were hedged
about by the mist, save a perfect circle above their heads,
within which could be seen the faint outlines of another
place entirely.

Lenares lost count of it all. She *lost count*.

And it didn't matter.

"Lenares, are you awake?"

"Yes," she whispered.

"I don't think we have much time left." Torve took a
deep breath. "I need to explain something to you."

She waited, the darkness obscuring his face and all the
clues her numbers required. She didn't need them: his face
was visible to her mind's eye.

"I am Omeran," he began unnecessarily. "We have survived because we are no threat to the Amaqi. Do you
know why they tolerate us?"

Lenares preferred to receive information directly, not in
this roundabout, rhetorical fashion. But it was Torve and he
clearly thought what he was saying to be important. "No,"
she said.

"Because we cannot disobey our masters. Lenares, this
is difficult. I am trying to tell you something, but I cannot
tell you directly. I have been commanded not to tell you.
That on its own might be clue enough."

"Why can't you disobey? Is there a magic spell at
work?" She didn't believe in magic spells, but then she
didn't believe in land that wouldn't stay still. The world
was not as she had thought it.

"No. Omerans were bred for obedience. Over thousands of years, Lenares, those who disobeyed were culled.
The Amaqi word. Killed, rather. Those who remained—

the obedient, the pliable—taught their sons and daughters to behave in kind in order to survive. It became a reflex, as important and as unconscious as breathing. Eventually we found we simply could not entertain the notion of disobedience. Could not even talk about it."

"But *you* can," she said.

"Yes; I am unusual, which is why I was given to the Emperor. Other Omerans have to give their obedience to anyone who demands it, while I am the Emperor's pet."

She bit her lip thoughtfully as they waited for the sound of a distant rockfall to fade away. "That is why you didn't become the slave of any expedition member who commanded you. It is why the Emperor could send you on this journey while he remained in his Palace."

Torve said nothing. She could hear his breathing, even and strong, close to her ear. Stones rattled somewhere in the darkness behind her. She could feel Torve's heat, and longed for him to take her in his arms.

But only if he is true.

Still Torve said nothing, as though encouraging Lenares to think about what he'd just told her. No, about what she'd just said.

"Did the Emperor send you on this expedition?"

"Yes," he said.

"Did he . . . did he remain behind?"

Silence; then, "I cannot say," he whispered. His voice left his mouth on a wave of warm air, arriving at her ear with reluctance.

"You cannot say more because your master commands you not to?"

"Yes." Fainter, as though forced through a rebellious throat.

"Well, Torve, you have set me a puzzle," she said briskly. "Did the Emperor command you before we left not to say whether he has stayed behind, or has he told you since? If so, how? Or can someone who stands in the place of the Emperor, someone like Captain Duon or Dryman, command you?"

"I take orders only from the Emperor himself," Torve said, then swallowed audibly.

"What would happen if you knowingly disobeyed your master?" she asked, a new realisation dawning on her.

"I don't know, Lenares," he said. "But if I told you what I want you to know, it would destroy me as a person. I don't think I could make my mouth say the words."

She reached out in the darkness and took his hand. "So that's why you said nothing to me. I thought you were keeping a secret. I thought you were no different to anyone else." She drew a deep, dust-laden breath. "Oh, Torve, I am sorry I doubted you. I truly did not understand. And please don't worry. When I solve your puzzle I will say nothing, and you will not have to find out what happens if you disobey your master. No matter that the Emperor is many weeks' journey from here; I respect your need to obey him."

"I am . . . you astonish me," he said.

She sensed him lean forward; she pulled him closer.

Seemingly without agreement or volition, and before either of them could find a reason to object, their mouths met in a kiss.

The next day was their last. Lenares sensed it, and from what the others said, they sensed it too.

The four travellers had learned to walk at a steady pace,

and to ignore the unnatural phenomena around, over and under them. Their knees ached with tension. Lenares found it impossible to relax completely when the earth boomed and shook and fire and water were likely to appear without warning.

Under a delicate overhanging arch they walked, between the gaping jaws of another valley. The arch collapsed behind them. A tremor shook the travellers from side to side. Down came a fall of rocks, shepherding them towards a small side canyon, the boulders halting short of the travellers, held back by an invisible barrier. They chose to try another canyon, which narrowed behind them, forcing them to run. Faster. The walls drew closer; Lenares brushed both sides of the canyon with her outstretched hands. A new urgency had possessed Nomansland. They emerged from the far end of the canyon like pips squeezed out of fruit.

"Oh no," Lenares moaned. "This is it. This is where we are being taken." *The slaughterhouse.*

This canyon was smooth-walled and perfectly circular, with a sandy floor: the heart of Nomansland. Behind them their entry sealed itself with a click. Above them hung the hole in the world, a perfect reflection of the canyon in which they stood. In the center of the canyon lay a small, jewel-like lake, perfectly still despite the roaring continuing in the canyons beyond.

Lenares' heart began to burn.

Around the lake stood three large rocks. Even before she drew closer, she knew what they were. The other three came up behind her.

"Stop!" she cried, in a voice so imperious the others halted in their tracks.

There is only one question to be answered. Is this the same room or is it merely a replica?

The answer was simple to find. Her own footprints in the sand, leading to one of the three seats.

No, there is another question. Can the Daughter rescue us from the Son? Can we do anything about the hole in the world?

"Lenares! This is the house of the gods!"

Yes, Torve, I know.

"How did we get here? How could we have travelled from Nomansland back to the Marasmos so quickly? Lenares?"

"I don't know, but nothing is stable here. Physical distance is distorted. And how do you know that the house of the gods was by the Marasmos valley? Might it not be somewhere else entirely, with many doors giving access?"

She scrambled up onto one of the other two seats, sat down and looked expectantly at the lake. The others were calling out to her, but she didn't bother with them. Couldn't. She had to know.

The seat of the missing god. The Father. The giant who became a god, the first of the Three. Surely if anyone could be granted absolute truth from an all-seeing perspective, it would be from this seat.

She waited, but the lake did not change, and the seat itself seemed dead.

A moment later Lenares realised the enormity of her mistake.

Above her, the hole in the world began to lower, rotating as it came down. A faint but shrill sound, like a keening coming from a far distance, emerged from the rapidly spinning hole. A lorn sound, the sound of a soul in torment, forever separated from life and love.

"Get out of the seat!" Torve cried. "Come down!"

Lenares could not move. The trap had been sprung. Megalomania was the bait, and she had taken it.

The sound began to rise in pitch and volume. Lenares wanted to clap her hands over her ears, but could not make her body obey her. The air around the canyon pulsed with power.

Down came the hole, until it touched the top of the circular canyon wall. The house of the gods now had a roof of sorts, a portal into another world, a world of anguish.

A hand touched her leg. Torve was trying to climb the seat, but the sheer intensity of the sound drove down on him, making it difficult for him to hold his position below her. Behind him Duon pushed, holding him up, while Dryman stood aside with his arms folded, as though observing an interesting experiment.

The canyon began to rotate. They were at the centre of a giant canister, spinning faster and faster. The centrifugal force knocked Dryman off his feet. He spun towards the wall, but one of the chairs got in his way. He smashed into it like a rag doll.

Then the hand of the god came for her.

She shrieked. The god did not have a body like that of a human; all Lenares could see of it were clawed fingers and, somewhere behind them, in the centre of the hole, two eyes filled with loathing.

The claws closed around her. The moment they touched her skin the spinning stopped. The hand pulled her, as well as all three chairs, those clinging to them and part of the valley floor, up into the hole.

Right into it.

Lenares felt herself enter the hole in the world, the destructive tear that had been devouring nodes and threads in the patterns of her numbers. She felt a ripple *change* her somehow as she was drawn into it. Her last terrified thought was that she had been swallowed by a giant. She waited to die.

All sound and vision vanished, replaced by a sense of falling. A moment later she thumped into something—a floor, the ground—and detritus from the room in the house of the gods crashed to earth all around her. As though an afterthought, after everything else had landed and the last sound ceased, something metallic smashed into her, driving all the breath out of her body.

She tried to breathe, tried, but nothing happened. Swirling lights exploded behind her eyes. She decided to stop fighting: immediately everything drained away, leaving a peaceful blackness like the tapestry velvet on the wall of the Emperor's Palace. She floated there a while, then that, too, passed and her awareness came to an end.

FISHERMAN

CHAPTER 22

SAROS RAKE

"TIME TO DO OUR SUMS." Noetos spoke with a degree of satisfaction. "Myself and the Seal—"

"Stop calling me that," Bregor said, to general laughter. Though the man's words were terse, the fisherman could see he enjoyed his newly achieved status as hero.

"Sorry, Bregor. Myself, the Hegeoman of Fossa . . ." He made swimming motions with his hands, prompting another burst of chuckling. "My sworn army . . ." Here he pointed at his miners, Dagla, Pril, Tumar and Gawl. "And these men and women from Makyra Bay."

The last named were a group of twelve, the most that Consina, the Hegeoma of Makyra Bay, could spare as payment for the debt she owed Noetos and his men. It had been more than he'd hoped for. More than he'd asked for, in fact, given the degree to which the fishing village would need to be rebuilt, and the threat of the Neherians returning with revenge on their minds.

"As for the first, the people I'll send north with you are no better with swords than they are with hammers," Consina had told him the day they'd left Makyra Bay.

"And as for the second, we'll take our chances. Nothing an extra dozen hands could do to help us should the Neherians come back. At least this time we'll be ready," she finished, referring to the watch she'd ordered set on the cliff-top above the village.

She had been right with her first comment, Noetos reflected; not that he'd seen them with hammers in their hands. Cyclamere would have said they used their swords like blunt instruments. Noetos had spent an hour drilling his army before the day's march, and another hour after they stopped for the night, and had learned that there was a limit to how much a person could achieve without natural talent. At the end of a week the best he could say about most of them was that they were less likely to hurt themselves wielding their weapons.

"I expect to meet up with the other miners from Eisarn Pit later today or tomorrow," he continued. "I don't know how many of them I can persuade to stay with us, but I will try." The alchemist, at least, would remain as close to the huanu stone as he could, Noetos would bet anything on that. "Even if only one or two choose to join us, we will have the numbers to bring down the Recruiters and free their captives." He wouldn't say their names, wouldn't even think them, until they were safe. *Don't tempt fate.*

Actually, his plan, such as it was, did not require more help than he already had. But extra bodies wouldn't hurt. It all depended on whether the Recruiters had gone inland or had taken the coast road through Kotzikas.

"Tell me," said Gawl, ever the provocateur. "Say we rescue your wife and son, but two've us're snuffed out. Is that fair trade? Or what if we lose four? What makes your missus 'n' sprong worth more 'n us?"

It's a fair question, Noetos told himself, trying to quell his rising anger. Gawl knew how to light his fuse. *An apt metaphor for a miner. Here's another: he'll chip away at me until he brings me down.*

It's a fair question, but there's no point in giving him a fair answer.

"Because you are a dead man," Noetos answered. "Or you would be by now—a week dead and rotting at the bottom of Eisarn Pit—if I had not intervened. So now what you and your companions are worth is up to me to decide."

"If we all ganged up on you—"

"But you won't." Noetos nodded his head to Dagla, Tumar and Pril, who were listening with interest. "Because your friends are finding they are enjoying being useful, and because, although none of them would say it to your face, they don't trust you, Gawl. You're on your own. Gang up on me by yourself and see what happens."

He turned to the others in his army. "Once I have my wife and son safely back with me, you will be free to go. I am asking no more of you than this."

"But, my lord," Dagla said, his reedy young voice rattling in his throat, "where are these Recruiters? How long is it gonna take t' find 'em?"

"It's only been a week since we left Makyra Bay. The Recruiters spent a night at Ydra, that we know, and continued north along the coast road. But unless they've covered their tracks well, or the citizens of Zagira, Progo and Cuku have been bribed or cowed into lying to us, it seems they no longer travel the coast road."

"So why don't we turn inland now? Pursue them hard instead of allowing them to get further away?" Bregor seemed to have developed a genuine interest in the rescue mission, though Noetos was not certain whether the Hegeoman yet believed in the Recruiters' ill intent.

"Because I want to be sure. Kotzikas is the largest of the coastal villages south of Raceme. If they stop anywhere on the road north, it will be there."

Gawl was about to carry the argument further, Noetos could read it on his face, when one of the Makyrans gave a shout. Over the nearest ridge came a slow procession: half a dozen mules, each heavily laden with what looked like supplies, led by the miners who had volunteered to warn the coastal villages about the Neherian fleet. They were followed by a score or more children, no doubt from Kotzikas, whooping and huzzahing like it was a summer holiday. *Which it most certainly is not*, Noetos thought. *They have just been warned of a Neherian invasion. Though it has in all likelihood been averted, they don't know that yet.*

"Glad to see you survived the Neherians," Seren said to him when the procession arrived. The Eisarn Pit nightshift overseer smiled. "We survived too, but we're not as famous as you and your army."

"Are they calling us an army?" Dagla asked, eyes wide.

"Yep," Papunas growled. "You lot, just learned to wipe yer bums and you're the heroes of the Fisher Coast. They want you to come down t' Kotzikas, y' know. They were happy to see us,"—just how happy could be gauged from his crooked smile—"but they'll be happier still to see you. Go down there and you c'n have anythin' you want. Although they think there's a hunnerd or more of you up here, so the stories go."

"How do they know?" Noetos asked bluntly.

"Someone from Makyra Bay took into her head t' put

out to sea. Well, she went north to Ydra, and took a boat from there, so's not to be seen by the salties. Good thinkin', that. Beat us to Kotzikas by a few hours, as it happens."

Ah, no wonder they're behaving like someone's given them a holiday, the fisherman thought. *I'd like to meet the woman who had the courage to brave the Neherian fleet.* He mentally saluted her. *Still, there are more important matters at hand.*

"Have the Recruiters been through Kotzikas?" he asked impatiently.

"Don't think so," said Seren. "At least, we heard nothing of them, and we did ask. There's no way travellers like them coulda been hidden."

"Oh, there is," Noetos said. "But, if my guess is right, I don't think they want to be hidden. I have been considering what they said to me when we fought in Fossa. I think they know about the huanu stone, and they want to lure me to a place away from villages, away from people, where they can take it from me."

Noetos noted Bregor's surprised grunt. *So the thought was slow coming to him also.*

"Makes sense, friend, doesn't it?"

The Hegeoman acted like a fish unsure of the hook. "I just don't see why officials of Andratan would behave like that. I've based my whole life on trust in authority. How could they operate with such disregard for their masters?"

"Ah, but are they? What if they are fulfilling Andratan's will? Do they want the huanu stone for themselves, or are they seeking a reward for safely delivering it into the hands of the Undying Man? Remember their official role: to find the precious things of the Fisher Coast and gather them up for Andratan to use." *To destroy.*

"I'm sorry, Fisher, your story fits every fact but one. What about the body of your daughter? You say she was killed by the Recruiters. Why did you leave her body in the Fisher House to rot?" Bregor flinched at the last word, sensing perhaps he'd gone too far.

"Hegeoman, I heard her die," Noetos rasped. "She pushed us out of the house with the power of her Voice."

"Even though you say she had no tongue."

"Even so! When I tried to return, the rear of the house collapsed in a rush of blue fire. I heard her scream. When I forced my way back inside I saw her on the floor, a knife in her back. I would have remained, would have cared for her body, but the Recruiters came at me with their swords, forcing me to flee. You know how many hours I was on the run that night, friend."

The last word twisted in the morning air.

Noetos continued, his face tight with anger. "I went back to Fisher House late that night, to find she had disappeared. Her body disposed of by the Recruiters. All I recovered was my sword. Be assured, Bregor, her whereabouts is a question I will ask of them. After I hear the answer from their dying tongues, my first task on returning to Fossa will be to find and bury her remains. My second, *friend*, will be to receive your apology."

Bregor bowed his head and closed his eyes, clearly unwilling to continue the argument further.

"Why do you find this so difficult?" Noetos pressed. "You were there at Nadoce Square when the Recruiters admitted what they'd done. Did you not believe them?"

"Fisher, you've said this before. I heard nothing that evening except you asking us for help. I suppose you are going to claim they used some sort of magic to keep their words from our ears?"

"Well, actually—"

"Oh my," said a familiar voice at precisely the wrong time. "Reasonable questions, fisherman, yes they are, if you expect people to risk their lives for you."

Noetos took a step towards the alchemist. Everyone around him took a step back. The children, suddenly aware of the increased tension, fell silent, except for one who began to cry.

Omiy held his ground. "So frightening, oh yes, this fisherman, such a temper, liable to explode at any moment. But I am not frightened, oh my, no. And why not? Because I deal with explosive alchemy every day of my life. The fuse is lit, but it is not too late for someone to pinch it. Like so. Tell me, yes tell me, how much further do you think the Recruiters have travelled in the time it has taken us to have this argument?"

Omiy actually smiled at him.

If this exasperating excuse for a man thought to escape his wrath by such a manoeuvre . . . But naturally he had, because he was right in what he said. What an extraordinary person. Of course, he would have to be. For such an eccentric man, survival in Eisarn Pit would depend on his earning the miners' respect.

Noetos ignored the pounding in his temple and smiled back. It was a feeble effort, that smile, but no other way to deal with the situation presented itself. The others would know he had nearly lost control of himself, but hopefully would also be reassured he could rein in his temper.

At least Bregor's voice was back to normal.

*   *   *

North of Kotzikas the land began to change. The last of the limestone ridges ended two days' walk from the village; sheep country replaced by alluvial plains and gently rolling hills upon which grain, oranges and olives were grown. Here the land became more important to the people of the Fisher Coast, and they turned their backs on the sea. The few coastal villages between Kotzikas and Raceme, a two-week journey to the north, were, according to the alchemist, small affairs and focused on farming.

Noetos and his followers crossed the Saar River, thereby leaving Palestra and entering Saros, and bore inland. There were no customs houses, no tolls; both countries were relatively new, part of the rubble left after the fall of Roudhos, and the former countrymen were reluctant to implement taxes on each other.

After surmounting a couple of low ridges, they came onto a wide plain, hedged at the far end by a cliff at least equal in height to the coastal cliffs around Fossa. This Noetos remembered as Saros Rake, the place from which his father had first shown him the sea. That exact spot was a few days' ride north, he guessed, but he was pleased to see his memory of the area bore some resemblance to reality. Saros Rake featured prominently in the plans he had laid.

The inland road between Tochar and Raceme had been built under the shadow of Saros Rake, on the far side of the Saar River from where Noetos and his army walked. Pril, one of his sworn men, had been born and raised on the Saar Plain and knew the less-travelled paths. Staying on the eastern side of the river would mean they were unlikely to be discovered by the Recruiters, Pril told them, but it would lengthen their journey and they would have to ford the river. There was no bridge, he said, south of Enrahl, where the road from Altima joined the road from Tochar to cross on an arched stone structure.

The next two days saw drizzle move in from the sea, sending a frisson of worry through the fisherman. This time of year a thick sea drizzle could last a week or more, totally unsuitable for his plans. But the morning of their third day on the Saar Plain dawned fine and the remaining clouds slowly lifted, allowing a gentle sun to counter the cool sea breeze.

By midday Noetos had had enough of being patient. He called Pril over.

"Where's the best place to cross the river?"

"Back a ways," the man said in a slow Sarosan drawl. "River's wide 'bout half a day's walk south. Folk can cross there 'n' barely get their feet wet." He seemed proud of his knowledge.

Noetos breathed deeply. "Pril, we need a crossing north of here. If we turn back now, we'll lose any advantage we might have gained over the Recruiters."

The man seemed unperturbed at the rebuke. "North a here? Well, we could try Cutter's Gap. A mite deeper there but it'ud make for a shorter crossin' if haste is drivin' you."

"Would everyone here be able to manage the crossing?" Noetos was not used to spelling out his intentions; his crew on the *Arathé* knew what he was going to ask before he asked it. Not so his sworn men, of whom Pril was definitely the worst.

"Naah," came the laconic reply. "We'd have tuh leave some a them on this here side."

"Well, that's no good," Noetos said patiently.

Omiy interrupted. "Pril, take us to the closest part of the river where I can cross, would you, yes?"

Pril's eyes widened. "Oh, beggin' my master's pardon, I see what y' want now. Sure, I c'n have yiz all at Chandlers Ferry afore sundown, if we hurry."

"A ferry? We won't have to ford the river after all?"

"Ah, nah, there use'ta be a ferry there, all broken now. A while back the river changed, dumpin' stone 'n' silt where the ferry use'ta cross. Put the ferryman—the chandler did it hisself—outa business. So the chandler, he did marry Sausin of Saar and moved t' town nigh six years ago now. Nuthin' left but a coupl'a broken-down buildin's 'n' an orchard goin' wild. Nice oranges, if ya get 'em afore th' wasps do."

"Yes, fine, enough about the wasps. No ferry, but a place to cross. It will get us to the Tochar road by tomorrow?"

"If we hurry," the man said, then pulled a floppy felt hat out of a pocket in his breeches and set it on his head. "Best we rattle our dags, eh?"

"Best we what?" Noetos asked Omiy when the man had made his way to the head of the procession.

"Oh my, Pril's family used to run sheep up on top of Saros Rake, yes. Best you don't ask him to give you a literal explanation." The alchemist thinned his lips in a rather prim fashion.

Alerted to the need for haste, the procession made good time northwards, stopping only briefly to purchase bread, fruit, cheese and a little dried meat from a local farmer. "Not much in the way of coins left," Papunas reported, waving a flat purse for all to judge.

"It's all right, I have plenty," Seren said. "We won't

starve as long as we don't make this army any larger'n it already is."

The Recruiters can't be far behind us. By this time tomorrow, we'll be lucky if the army isn't substantially smaller than it is now. Noetos tried not to feel guilt at the thought, and kept it to himself.

They forded the Saar River just before dark. Noetos argued for the crossing to be left until early the next morning, when they would be fresh, but Gawl pointed out that the water would be far colder in the morning. "Cold'll kill you more quickly than anything," he said.

"Not quicker'n a rock to the head," Noetos heard Dagla mutter. Gawl likely heard it, too, but if he did he kept his own counsel. *Be careful, boy. Gawl's looking for a fight; don't you give it to him. You're the best of them, and I don't want to lose you.*

The mules did not like the cold water one bit. Truth to be told, they hadn't liked much of the last week, pining for their southern hay and the quiet drudgery of the Palestran Line. The lead mule stamped her feet and refused to move, those behind her following suit. The men were forced to unbuckle their bags and sleeping rolls and attempt the crossing thus encumbered. Perhaps that, or general tiredness after many days on their feet—or a combination of both—explained what happened.

The Saar River was at this point a tangle of shoals and islands, interweaved by a braided flow of water slightly higher than normal due to recent rain. This meant that Noetos's army had to make crossings of six separate streams. The first three were achieved without incident, but at the commencement of the fourth ford the second man in the line, an older man from Makyra Bay, twisted his ankle on a stone. He immediately went down in the water with a splash, occasioning a few churlish barks of laughter. He must have hit his head on a hidden rock, because he did not resurface for some time; and when he did, he was already fifty paces downstream, face down in the rippling water, his pack beside him.

"Just one of you!" Noetos called, but his advice went unheard. Every man from Makyra Bay and most of the miners surged in the direction of their drowning comrade. It would have served as comedy had the results not been so catastrophic. Men fell over each other, cursing as they and their baggage found the cold, swift waters.

"Get to the banks!" Noetos shouted to the remainder. "Drop your gear, get downstream of them and fish them out when they come past!"

They found the body wedged between a rock and a tree stump about three hundred paces downstream. No one else was killed, but one of the miners suffered a broken wrist, and six bags were lost, including most of the bread, cheese and dried meat. A chastened and soaked group assembled around the fisherman, heads down.

"This is not good enough!" Noetos roared, and this time his anger was such that none dared speak. "In jest you have referred to yourselves as my army. I've seen you taking pride in what we did at Makyra Bay, how we beat off the Neherians and warned the coastal villages of the danger they faced. Where is that pride now? You are a rabble, not an army! From now on you are on a ship, and I am your captain. You do as I say or you are thrown overboard. You do not do what you think is right. You wait for orders. Orders that will come from me, or from Seren, Papunas or the Seal here. See the man lying there on the stones? You killed him by not listening to your commander. You are murderers. But this poor man is the last of your friends you will murder. Have I spoken clearly?"

All the while he spoke, Noetos felt himself drenched in shame, its coldness making him shiver. Their victory at Makyra Bay had been achieved by the initiative and heroism of people like Bregor and Dagla. He, Noetos, had been the one to rush off in disobedience to orders, even though they had been his own. *The speech of a hypocrite sounds bitter in one's ears*, he reflected.

The sun had set behind Saros Rake by the time he and his sorry army returned to the safety of the eastern shore, from where they had ventured less than half an hour earlier. The mules awaited them there, along with the wrangler and the alchemist who had been detailed to care for them. They made camp that night in the mouse-ridden ruins of the chandlery. Very little was said, and sleep—or at least the pretence of sleep—came swiftly.

Only one person spoke to Noetos that night. The Hegeoman made his bed next to the fisherman and, just before settling down to sleep, whispered: "You have not failed."

Noetos wished he could find a way to tell Bregor just how much those words meant to him.

As a gentle rosy dawn tinctured the plains, Noetos detailed two of the Makyra Bay men to take their dead townsman home, using one of the mules. The miner with the broken wrist had a bad night, but elected to stay with the army. No one spoke of the previous evening's events, presumably, Noetos suspected, in order not to invoke bad luck.

The remaining mules, of course, trotted happily across the Saar River just after dawn. This angered Noetos unreasonably, and it took him an hour to calm himself. He forced his mind to focus on the coming clash with the Recruiters.

An ambush is a chancy tactic, said Noetos's memory of Cyclamere. *It works best with numerical and technical superiority, and can be turned by a clever opponent.*

Technical superiority—the phrase gnawed away at the fisherman as they came to the Tochar road, a well-used gravel track running, as most Old Roudhos roads did, in a straight line, uncaring of mere topography. Technical superiority. Now he knew what the huanu stone could do he intended to exploit it, and hoped it might neutralise much of the Recruiters' sorcery. But there was something else . . .

They had reached the base of Saros Rake when it came to him. The steep slope looming above them reminded him of the walls of Eisarn Pit, in and under which the miners toiled day and night, using a combination of hard labour and alchemical explosions to free the ore from the grip of its enclosing strata . . .

"Omiy!" Noetos cried, startling those around him. "Alchemist!" He *tched* in annoyance. "Where is that man?"

"He stopped a while ago to help the wrangler with a loose pannier on one of the mules," Papunas said.

"Send someone to get him, would you?" *I am addleheaded. How could I not have thought of Omiy?*

"Yes, friend Noetos, you wished to speak to me, did you not?" Alone of them all, the alchemist seemed unaffected by yesterday's events. Noetos doubted anything would change his manner of address.

"I do. To be blunt, have you brought any of your alchemical devices and powders with you?"

The man frowned, as though witnessing some base indiscretion. "I am here, am I not? How could I be here without my equipment? Not all of it has survived the rigours of the journey, oh my no, I have lost a glass vial and water has dampened one of my packets of sulphur. Nevertheless, I present myself to you as an alchemist, with the tools of my trade at your service, yes indeed, such as they are. But, oh my, I thought we were intending to fight Recruiters, not play with chemicals. What do you want me to do—bring down this wall of rock?"

To his credit, the man had worked it out even before Noetos raised an eyebrow in the direction of Saros Rake.

"I was going to send a detachment of men up to the summit with instructions to find large boulders and ready them to be rolled down ahead of and behind our enemy," Noetos said. "I don't want to harm them, for fear of hurting their hostages. I intend to sow confusion among them, which we can rush in and take advantage of. But with you here, Omiy, that is not necessary, is it?"

Noetos sent the man with the broken wrist northwards on a mule, to look for any sign that the Recruiters had already passed this place. It seemed unlikely, given the rate the men had travelled northwards thus far, but not impossible. He'd tried to allow a margin for error in his own estimates, and for a quickening in the Recruiters' pace, but he hoped—depended upon, really—that they were still travelling slowly, trying to lure him north. Besides, sending the injured man north kept him out of trouble, and Noetos wanted to be responsible for as few deaths as possible.

Seren he sent southwards, saddling him with the more dangerous task of ascertaining how far behind them the Recruiters were, or if indeed they had chosen this road to travel northwards. It seemed the likeliest choice, especially if they sought to draw the huanu stone to them, but again there were no guarantees. Certainly Noetos wanted some word of their location before he went to the trouble of setting his trap.

Seren returned first. "They approach us at a leisurely pace," he said. "They will make camp tonight p'raps a league or two south of here. Can't imagine they'll make it this far. And no, b'fore you ask, they didn't see me."

The overseer's words set Noetos's stomach churning. Part of him wanted to abandon his elaborate plan and instead go charging down the road, his sword in his hand. He wiped sweat from his brow.

"Very well," he said. "Help yourself to what remains of our supplies. There's not much. Leave some for Mika, he might return this evening, though I doubt it. Meanwhile, Omiy and I have work to do. I will tell everyone else the plan tomorrow morning."

Noetos stood in the road, a solitary figure, as the Recruiters crested a gentle rise and came into view. Every muscle in his body tightened. *Doubt is the real enemy*, Cyclamere said, but the didactic memory did not continue. The fisherman knew the lesson, and so fixed on an image to stir his anger. Anger to smother the doubt.

Arathé on the floor. a knife in her back.

He had chosen his position with care, having identified a section of road that curved eastwards. The sun would be in their eyes, placing an element of uncertainty in their minds. They would know who he was, but not for sure. Not for a few moments yet.

He schooled himself to stillness. The first words would not be his. He tried not to strain his eyes, but he couldn't help counting. Nine. *Nine?* They had left Fossa as seven.

"Fisherman!" one of the men called to him. He held Anomer by the arm. "Isn't it a splendid morning to be out?"

They would be expecting him to respond, so he did not. All the old lessons were proving themselves. He'd mocked his tutors, doubted their wisdom. He blessed them now.

"It is a cool morning, but your tongue will not freeze if you use it," the Recruiter continued. "Why not use it to greet your son?" He thrust Anomer in front of him.

Noetos forbore checking his son for injuries, resisted looking at his face. He kept his eyes on the Recruiter who had spoken.

"Or perhaps your wife?" said a second man. "She would answer you; she's very friendly."

"Very," the first Recruiter agreed.

The Recruiters and their captives—and what looked like two young recruits, a boy and a girl—halted twenty paces from where Noetos stood.

"This conversation is lacking something, have you noticed?" said the man holding Anomer. "Our friend does not seem happy to see us. Which is strange, given how far he has come, how assiduously he has sought our company."

"We appear to be his only friends," the second Recruiter commented. "No wonder he has forgotten how to speak. Without his family, he has no one to speak to."

"We've been talking to your wife and son, fisherman," said a third Recruiter, his cowl down. This man's voice exhibited none of the hearty playfulness employed by his two fellows. "They have told us a great deal about you, about your past. From the scraps you allowed them to know, we have pieced together the shameful tapestry of your life. Scion of Roudhos, heir to the Fisher Coast. Coward. Your family is disappointed in you for keeping secrets. As you can imagine, they did not talk to us willingly at first. We had to do a little damage. Why not talk to us now and save us having to damage them further?"

Noetos did nothing more than shift his head slightly, so he could look directly at the speaker. Then he nodded.

"You are skilled with swords, you have magic by all accounts, and you outnumber Noetos. Why do you hesitate to attack him?"

The four Recruiters spun as one to face the speaker, Bregor, who stood at the head of Noetos's sworn men and half the Makyra Bay villagers, some fifty paces behind them. All had their swords drawn. Silence settled on the scene as the Recruiters considered this development.

"Good question, unless o' course they are afraid of the huanu stone."

In almost comical fashion the Recruiters swung around again. Behind Noetos, Papunas, the rest of the miners and the remaining villagers lined out across the road. All but Dagla had their weapons out; the young lad struggled to draw his sword from a reluctant scabbard. He gave up, bent and picked up a stone.

Noetos withdrew the carving of Arathé from its place on his belt.

A deadly quiet fell.

"Oh my," Noetos said, his voice loud, as it needed to be, echoing from Saros Rake to his right.

"In the name of Andratan—" one of the Recruiters began. Noetos never found out what the man was about to say, as at that moment the world exploded.

It was a much larger detonation than Noetos had expected. The air blurred with the force of it. Despite having braced himself when he signalled the alchemist, Noetos was knocked sideways by the blast; it lifted him from the road and hurled him onto the grass. All around him screams mixed with the thumps of rocks and pattering of stones. Noetos fought to regain his feet as a cloud of dust descended upon him. A deep rumble came from the direction of the nearby cliff.

The over-enthusiastic idiot had brought down Saros Rake upon them. His plan was breaking apart.

As the rumbling above him grew louder, Noetos ran through the dust in the direction of his wife and son. He stumbled over a body—not Anomer's but one of the young recruits, the girl, blood-spattered and broken. As he bent over her, his soldier's sense gave him the merest warning: the blade that might have taken his head instead caught him with the flat on his left shoulder. Still strong enough to score the leather jerkin he wore—courtesy of some nameless victim at Makyra Bay—and knock him off balance.

The follow-up stroke came with a speed Noetos would not have believed possible. A killing blow. The fisherman thrust up his left hand to intercept the stroke. The sword took his smallest finger at the first knuckle and cracked against the huanu stone. Noetos roared in anger and tried to pull his hand back, a reflex from the intense pain.

His hand would not move.

The swordsman, the Recruiter with his cowl thrown back, struggled to retrieve his sword. It was fixed to the huanu stone in Noetos's hand. The man's eyes grew wider as it became clear he was trapped. The stone in the fisherman's hand began to vibrate, to ... *draw*. Through the sword. It pulled something from the Recruiter, something he tried to resist, judging by the look of terror in his eyes.

"Let me go!" the man screeched, spittle flying.

"No," Noetos said.

Whatever the stone was doing to the Recruiter took less than a minute, perhaps twenty beats of the heart. In that time the sorcerer's face went from anger through shock to utter despair. He cast his head about, looking for help, but the dust haze obscured everything. The world condensed to two men on a country road. When the stone had accomplished its task it let the Recruiter go. The man slumped to the gravel, his sword clattering to the ground beside him.

"What happened?" Noetos asked hoarsely.

"It took my magic," the stunned man breathed.

"So, you are one of us now, courtesy of the stone you wanted to steal," Noetos said. "How does it feel?"

"Kill me," the man rasped, his eyes dead.

"That is a mercy I'll grant." Noetos put the carving of Arathé back in his belt, then positioned the tip of his sword in the correct place, between the ribs, and slid it home using his left hand to push, spattering drops of his own blood onto the man's robe. The Recruiter puffed out a single breath, the life leaving him as Noetos watched. He pulled the blade out and wiped it carefully on the dead man's cowl, then tore off a strip of the fabric to bind his damaged finger.

Revenge is a bitter drink, said Cyclamere.

You're wrong, old man. I've never tasted anything sweeter. Now be silent while I seek out more.

A further rumbling, then a loud crack. "Oh, oh my, get out of the way!" someone cried from high above them. Silence, then a roar that shook the earth.

Noetos wanted to remain where he was, intending to search for Anomer and Opuntia, but his feet had no intention of staying. He had gone perhaps fifty strides when Saros Rake came down behind him in a blast of air and rock.

This time the fisherman found shelter behind a large angular boulder that had no doubt arrived as a result of the first explosion. As he ducked behind the rock he saw that its edge had come to rest on the torso of a second Recruiter.

"You're not having much luck today," Noetos said to him, but the man's eyes were rolled up in his head. Unconscious.

Noetos raised his blade and, despite the growing pain in his left hand, made sure the Recruiter remained that way.

Sweeter still, he told the memory of his tutor.

After a while the grinding and crashing stopped, and Noetos emerged from behind the boulder to see the destruction Omiy had wrought. *At your behest*, he reminded himself, but he had not intended such a singularly catastrophic event. The dust from the second blast had settled somewhat, so he could see that the skyline had been forever altered. What had once been a steep slope of shale and broken rock, topped by a dark cliff-line, was now a hole torn from the escarpment's roots. Grass, bushes and even trees had come down in the massive landslide.

Here and there other people began to emerge from whatever boltholes they had sheltered in. They looked around, eyes dazed, mouths agape.

"Noetos! Over here!"

He ran in the direction of the shout, but it was not Anomer, just the third of the Recruiters, Ataphaxus, their leader, surrounded by Seren and his miners. A stand-off. Noetos wanted to ignore the summons. Let them deal with the man, while he went in search . . .

"Where is my son?"

The Recruiter's face set in a look of disdain. "Under the rubble. Who cares? This is about you, Roudhos, you and your stone. Give us the stone, surrender yourself to us, and we will allow everyone left alive here to go on their way."

"Us?" Noetos said. "You are mistaken; there is no longer any 'us'. Seren, take three of your men and bring back the bodies of the Recruiters. I want this man to re-assess the position from which he attempts to bargain. Don't worry, he won't try to escape, not with the huanu stone in my possession. We'll wait here for your return."

He sent as many as he could spare to begin the bleak task of searching through the debris. He desperately wanted to go with them, but wanted none of the Recruiters left alive.

By the time the miners returned, the last of the dust had settled. Still no sign of Anomer or Opuntia, and the fourth Recruiter and the remaining servant had not revealed themselves. Two of the returning miners carried between them the body of the first Recruiter Noetos had executed, while Seren bore a severed arm, which the miner eyed with revulsion.

"Had to cut it off, fisherman," he said in explanation. "The boulder was too heavy t' lift." The overseer threw the limb down at the feet of the Recruiter, whose face paled by the barest margin.

"So I can no longer bargain with you, Roudhos. No matter; there is still plenty to discuss."

"Call me that again and I will kill you," Noetos said.

"Fisherman, then. I merely intended to indicate that, with a word from Andratan, I could place you on the throne of a revived kingdom of Roudhos. Bring the arrogant Neherians down at a stroke, to place them under your feet. Does that appeal, fisherman?"

All around Noetos the miners stilled as the implications came home to them. Questions would follow, Noetos knew. Curse the man.

"Ignore him, boys. The man's a snake. He knows nothing of my past."

"Oh? Enough to know you would relish the chance to strike at Neherius."

"Who wouldn't?" one of the miners said, only to be shushed by his fellows.

"I would relish a meeting with my son or my wife far more," Noetos said. "Should either of them be harmed, my anger at Neherians will be as nothing to the rage I'll let loose on Andratan and its servants. Disarm him, Seren."

"I offer you this, then, in good faith," said the Recruiter as he gave up his sword. "Your Hegeoman and his men came upon us at the moment of chaos." He cast an awed glance up at the profile of Saros Rake. "After that I saw nothing of either prisoner. The rubble may have taken them, in which case I judge you to be responsible for their deaths for initiating such a foolish, indiscriminate ambush. Or they may lie to the south of us, having escaped the rock fall."

"Come with me, then, *prisoner*," Noetos snarled. "And if you think to escape, remember I subdued your fellows with sword and stone. I have no doubt I can do the same to you."

The Recruiter, cowl askew, stumbled forward at the point of Noetos's sword. The miners he sent in various directions, to search a second time for any sign of the living amongst the detritus spread over the Tochar road.

He found Opuntia dying in the arms of Bregor, some distance from the road, in a brake of thorn bushes.

"She was carved by one of the Recruiters," Bregor whispered, his eyes averted from the bright red blood staining her pale robe. "Just after your explosion. Before I could get to her."

"Opuntia, I—" Noetos began.

"Leave us be, fisherman," Bregor growled, his face misshapen with grief. "Let her pass in peace. She was always far more mine than yours."

"What?"

"She hates you, cretin. Hates your selfishness, your wickedness, your deception. Thanks to the Recruiters, she dies knowing she could have been a queen. Do you think she wants you here to witness her final humiliation?"

"I didn't mean . . ."

His explanation came to a halt. There had to be something he could say, some way of making her understand him, but her face was turned away from him, buried in the Hegeoman's shoulder. Noetos watched her chest rise and fall, slowly, shallowly, unevenly.

"Go and look for her son. Opuntia tells me he was alive

and unharmed, borne away by the Recruiter who cut her. Go. Leave her to someone who loved her."

Eyes blurring as if trying to erase the tableau before him, his heart clenched in the merciless fist of truth, Noetos could do nothing but obey.

"This is the sort of thing the King of Roudhos could have prevented," said Ataphaxus conversationally. "With my help—"

Noetos sunk a fist into the man's stomach. The Recruiter folded around the blow, then crashed to the ground, trying to catch his breath.

"You are to blame for this, not me," Noetos said, his voice rattling in a constricted throat. "We have nothing to talk about."

It took a series of gasping breath before the Recruiter was able to nod his head in agreement.

Noetos had used his right hand for the blow. He could feel nothing from his injured left hand. *Shock is an effective pain killer*.

As they reached the road, Noetos heard a rattling sigh, accompanied by a loud sob from the Hegeoman.

The fisherman's dream of a normal life, of a quiet existence, one far removed from the destiny to which he'd been raised and run from, had just died.

Anomer they found alive.

His son sat on rocks down by the Saar River, a few hundred paces from the road. The landslide had reached even here, flowing in a rush across the river, damming three channels, though water seeped through. Two bodies lay floating in the water behind the dam, and Anomer watched them spin slowly in the spiralling water.

Noetos climbed gingerly over the crumpled debris, signalled the Recruiter to stand where he could be seen, and sat himself down next to Anomer.

"Your mother is dead," he told his son.

The boy made no movement at the sound of his father's voice. "That's Cutalian, the servant of the Recruiters, floating in the water," he said in a voice so low Noetos had to struggle to hear it. "He told me I'd make a great sorcerer."

Noetos said nothing.

"And there's Jamik beside him. Such a gifted swordsman, and he was only thirteen. He always defeated me when we sparred. Why? Why did they have to die?"

My boy thinks he's dead, too, Noetos realised. *The shock has him. He sees himself lying face down in a river, or crushed under rock.*

"I saw Mother slain," his son said. "Bilitharn slid his long knife into her, right to the hilt. She didn't say anything, even when it came out with her blood on it. He went for me next, but Ataphaxus stopped him."

"So I should be thankful one member of my family remains alive?" Noetos said, unable to keep the pain from his voice.

"But Mother is dead," Anomer said, his own voice breaking. "Why did you interfere? They promised we would be unharmed if you surrendered to them. They would be restrained in their dealings with us, they said. Instead . . ." He indicated the bodies in the water pooling behind the landslide. "How many have died?"

Noetos grabbed his son's arm in what he hoped was a painful grip. "Have you forgotten your sister? Where was the Recruiters' restraint then? How could I leave you in their hands?"

"They were not all evil," Anomer said. "Ataphaxus protected me from Bilitharn."

"Are you asking me for mercy on his behalf?" Noetos jerked a thumb at the Recruiter. How could Anomer wish for such a thing? These were the men who had enslaved and used Arathé, who had killed Opuntia. The boy was not thinking clearly. Shock, no doubt. He did not answer Noetos's question.

Noetos himself was finding it difficult to think with any clarity. *Opuntia.* Her name clattered through his mind like a landslide. Her white face staring at the wreck of her daughter. *Clatter, clatter.* Her slim fingers unlacing his tunic. *Clatter.* Her voice, measured and precise, giving assent to his wedding vows. *Clatter.* The memories threatened to bury him. Yet her face was hazy in his mind's eye, as though obscured by dust.

Mercy? He owed the man Ataphaxus nothing. The Recruiters had destroyed his life. What he would do to the man was just.

He called for the others in a loud voice. Eventually the miners made their way down from the road and gathered around him.

"Oh dear, oh my," said a voice he did not want to hear. A man who could not be held responsible.

"Be silent, Omiy. You and I will talk later," the fisherman said. "I want a man to hold down each of this murderer's limbs. Hold him tight, because he will struggle."

Seren and Papunas took the man's arms, two other miners his legs.

"Attend," Noetos said, and drew out the huanu stone.

A terrible cry, almost too highly pitched for hearing,

emerged from the Recruiter's throat when he divined what was about to happen. His eyes bulged.

Noetos placed the carving on the man's chest. The hungry green stone drank the man's magical powers in an almost visible process. It was as though some vital essence was being pulled out of the man's skin, separated from his being, stripped like soil from a mountainside during an inexorable rain. Like the tide going out, never to return.

At the finish the man seemed smaller. Not someone to be feared.

"We'll let this one go," Noetos said as the miners allowed the Recruiter to his feet. "Go and find somewhere to die."

A moment later an urgent memory broke into Noetos's gelid thoughts. He called to Ataphaxus as the Recruiter made his way along the riverbank into the northern distance.

"Halt! Tell me of Arathé! What did you do with my daughter's body?"

The man looked over his shoulder, an expression of hatred and fear locked onto his face, then sprinted away in a furious flurry of arms and legs.

"Papunas, send a couple of miners after him. I must know the truth!"

"No, fisherman, or whoever you are," the overseer said. "Enough. We've paid for your help in delivering the Fisher Coast from the Neherian fleet. It is time t' give thought to the living, and let the dead rest."

"Aye, we have bodies to bury," Seren said. "And we are in desperate need of supplies. No more chasin', no more fightin'. You have questions to answer, and when we have heard the answers we will return to Eisarn."

"Fisherman, we owe you thanks for saving our village," said one of the men from Makyra Bay, the oldest of them.

"But we, also, must leave you now. We worry about what might happen to our people should the Neherians return."

Blow upon blow. Noetos turned to his sworn men. "I suppose you wish to be released?"

"Well, you did promise them, you did, yes," said the alchemist, when none of his men would speak. "It would make good sense for them to accompany the other miners. You have nothing to offer them beyond dreams of revenge, oh my, visions of destruction."

"Very well," Noetos said, enraged. "I will travel on alone."

Not that he had given any thought to where he might go; it seemed only that there were places pushing him away. First Fossa, then Neherius, now all of Old Roudhos.

Bregor stood on the top of the riverbank. "I'll think about staying with you, fisherman," he said, his voice tight with restraint. "I want answers. But first Anomer and I have a grave to dig. We will let you know when you may join us to bless her departure."

He had nothing to say to that.

A bitter drink . . .

"Be silent, Cyclamere," he said, and bowed his head.

When next he looked up, he was alone on the riverbank, apart from the two corpses in the water.

"Come then, friends, let's put you to bed," he said to them. "Unless there is someone here who thinks I'm not worthy to bury you?"

There was no answer among the silent stones of the riverbed, save the lapping of the ever-running water, like a thousand accusing tongues.

I killed them, he admitted, and his broad shoulders bowed under the weight of truth. *I killed them all.*

CHAPTER 23

RACEME HARBOUR

"WHERE'S GAWL?" Dagla asked.

Go away. Noetos turned over on his bed of straw on the chandlery floor. The morning had arrived far too soon.

"My lord, I ain't seen Gawl since last night. He might of run off. You want me to go look for him?"

It wasn't that he grieved for Opuntia, not really. He had loved her once, a young person's optimism; and, he believed, she had loved him. She'd said so. But he had lost her somewhere amid the children and the fishing and Old Fossa and the dishonesty and deception. He could never have told her about his father, his grandfather, about Roudhos. About how his grandfather lost a kingdom with one act of courageous stupidity. About how his family was murdered by Neherians to prevent Roudhos ever rising from the ashes. Had Noetos told Opuntia his secrets she would have—well, she would have got them all killed. So yes, he grieved, but mostly for his memory of her as she had been when he first met and deceived her. For what they had both lost.

"My lord?"

He had stood beside Anomer at her graveside as Bregor spoke of Opuntia in terms he could never have imagined. A completely different woman. There were some women, obviously, who were born to nobility. Something, ironically, the Hegeoman could supply, at least after a fashion, while the heir of Roudhos could not. He heard of her love of reading, her incisive mind, her generosity with her time, the hours she spent in Old Fossa helping young mothers. Things he had never seen.

Anomer spoke, then Noetos said something, he had no idea what, just words. It was too late for anything meaningful.

The three of them had scooped sand and soil over the shallow grave, then added rocks to deter scavengers. They had done this in complete silence. Then Noetos had taken his son and the Hegeoman aside and told them the whole bitter story.

"Please, my lord, d'ya want me to round up the others 'n' go lookin' for him?"

Another voice intruded. "Don't need to, Dagla. He's out with Papunas and a couple o' the others, shovellin' the dirt off the road."

Noetos turned over. "Seren," he said, "is Omiy about?"

The miner looked at him flatly. "He's hidin', fisherman. Like everyone, walkin' softly 'round you. We're all sorry you lost your wife, but to tell truth, we're all waiting for you to explode and take your sword t' someone."

"Yes, uh, I can understand that," Noetos said. "Would you go and get Omiy? Promise him I'll not touch my sword. I only want to ask some questions."

"I'll go," said Seren, "but I'll promise him no such thing."

The alchemist sat as far from Noetos as possible while still remaining under the chandlery roof. The late morning sun picked out gaps in the warped beams and slats above them, rendering the barn-like interior a headache-inducing combination of light and darkness. Seren made his way out, not without sending the alchemist a worried glance. Omiy shrugged his shoulders.

"I'm not a bully, Omiy," Noetos said. "Tell me what happened. I just want to understand."

The alchemist looked doubtful. "Oh my," he said. "I prepared the sulphur and the chenaile like I said I would, yes, yes. Calculated to perfection, I thought. Still think. You saw the pipe I used—very clever you said, did you not? Two chambers, chenaile separated from sulphur by a hollow wooden divider onto which I put acid, oh my, my own invention, always works, guaranteed never to fail. Genius was the word you used; tell me otherwise, stonebearer."

Noetos worked his way through this, then nodded. "I did say that."

"I know you told me to set my device off at the bottom of the slope, so you did, but that would not have given me enough protection from the blast, oh no. I know these things, I do, you should have trusted me; but no, you wanted to send your servant the alchemist into danger. Oh my, I don't want to die in one of my own explosions. Matter of pride, you see, yes; how will the name of Olifia the alchemist be revered among the nations if it was said of him that he perished by his own clumsy hand? Intolerable. So I took myself up the hill to the summit, I did. On your signal I dropped the pipe and took cover behind the crest of the cliff. The weakened wooden divider broke when the pipe hit the rocks a few paces below the summit, the acid entered the chambers, oh yes, and the device worked. Boom! Just as well I chose the summit for the site of the explosion, my friend, yes indeed. Imagine the chaos and death had I exploded it at the base of the hill. Might have brought down the whole cliff!"

"The cliff came down regardless," Noetos said.

Omiy looked shamefaced. "Ah yes, well, my mistake. More chalk and soapstone in Saros Rake than in Eisarn Pit. How was I to know it would shatter like that? You said to create a diversion, yes, you did. A diversion was created. I remain your servant, eager to please you."

Laid out like that, his explanation sounded reasonable. For a while after the explosion Noetos had suspected Omiy . . . but no. The alchemist had rejected the chance to steal the huanu stone back in Eisarn Pit. Had protected him and Bregor, in fact, from the other miners.

"Very well, there's nothing more to be said about it," Noetos pronounced. At this dismissal the alchemist leapt to his feet and rushed out the door. *That eager to escape my company. Am I really that fierce?* And the deeper question: *what have I made of myself?*

A faint noise distracted him from his musing. The metallic scrape of a blade as it was drawn from a scabbard, a noise his soldier's mind was attuned to. Before he had a moment to question its source he was on his feet, hand on his own sword-hilt.

Papunas walked through the open door of the chandlery, his sword in his hand. That was the moment Noetos should have attacked, when the overseer was framed by the door, but surprise and disbelief stole his awareness. By the time ten miners had filed in behind him, it was too late.

"We've come for answers to our questions, and for payment," Papunas said.

"Payment? And what payment do I receive for saving your countrymen?" Noetos asked bitterly.

"Y'get to live," Papunas said. But the look in the overseer's eyes told Noetos otherwise.

"Where is Seren? My sworn men?"

"Sent 'em off to escort the Makyra Bay lot back south. Told 'em it was your orders."

A lie. The villagers wouldn't need escorting. His men would not have taken orders from Papunas. They were too smart for that. Weren't they? *Oh, Alkuon.*

And where is Anomer?

That last question, at least, was answered swiftly.

"What is this?" his son asked, as another of the miners thrust him through the doorway, a hand clamped firmly on his shoulder. "Father, what is happening?"

"You are coinage," Noetos said, and launched himself at the miner holding his son. Six paces covered in an instant, fuelled by a rage finally let loose, a powerful overhand chop taking the miner's arm at the shoulder before the man could shield himself behind Anomer. A scream, the spurt of hot blood.

Noetos found his mind completely clear; he threw himself down and snatched the miner's sword from the floor. *It will cost me, but I must have it.* A sword struck at him, a clumsy blow that scored across his back, biting deep enough to draw blood, a fire of pain. Noetos twisted away from the miner who had made the blow, reached up, grabbed his son by the wrist and dragged him back into the centre of the room, handed him the miner's sword and stood there, panting.

Alkuon, the pain. He forced himself to speak.

"How much will the stone cost you?" he cried, barely making himself heard over the piteous screams of the miner trying to quench the flow of his lifeblood. "You've lost one man already. Come on, who will be next?"

This could go one of two ways . . .

With a shrill cry Papunas charged, followed by the others. Too tempting a prize to forsake now. He'd hoped to bleed their courage out. *No matter*.

Anomer and Noetos met them, swords raised, blocking the furious blows that fell on them. The fisherman tried a counterstroke, realising instantly that the wound on his back would not allow him to fully extend his sword arm. *Only one chance now*. He propelled himself into the nearest miner, careless of the man's sword, getting inside his reach, hitting him on the chin with the flat of his hand. Bones cracked. A swift sword thrust saw the man down.

Anomer!

No time to turn, he could not risk even a glance. He directed a vicious blow at one man's face, opening it; he turned his stroke into a defensive parry, barely avoiding a killing blow. The tip of an opponent's sword took Noetos in the thigh, penetrating two fingers'-width. The man's sword remained fixed in his flesh a moment too long. Noetos hammered him in the solar plexus with his elbow, then swept the blade across the man's neck before he began to double over. The miner raised a futile hand to his throat, trying to hold the wound closed, then slipped on his own blood, falling backwards to foul the legs of two miners behind him.

Too slow, too clumsy, any competent swordsman would have dispatched you before now. Cyclamere the critic. "I know," Noetos said as he stepped over his dying opponent and stabbed the two fallen miners through their throats, one, two; both lives ended by greed. "It's just as well they are not competent, then."

The fisherman eased himself backwards, gaining a moment's respite, his head twisting from side to side, searching for more opponents. His eyes fastened on Anomer. Six miners encircled his son, ready to strike. No other movement in the Chandlery.

"Give us the stone, fisherman, or we'll kill him," Papunas said.

"No, father!" Anomer shouted. "Trust me! Stay where you are!"

The words bit at him with all the force of a geas. Nevertheless, the fisherman shrugged them off, rejecting his son's sacrificial gesture, and launched himself towards the miners.

"Slow, slow, your limbs are as lead," Anomer said in a Voice as clear, as sharp-edged, as broken crystal. The power of the words washed over Noetos but could not take hold of him.

Sorcery.

"Heavy, your blades are heavy."

Six swordtips wavered; their owners grunted, struggling to keep them aloft. Noetos pulled himself up short of the miners.

Then his son, still crooning his words of beguilement, danced among them. *If I am a bludgeoner, this boy is an artist.* With his blade he drew a complex picture of death in the air, the lines of his sketch intersecting with tendons, muscles, flesh and bone. Not a wasted movement, not an errant brush-stroke; beautiful, horrifying perfection that ended when Anomer skewered Papunas through the throat, driving his blade into the door frame.

The miner spat blood over Anomer, then died.

Questions to be asked, but not yet.

Noetos checked each of the bodies for signs of life. Finding none, he took his son by the shoulder. "Retrieve your sword. We know nothing of the miners that remain. They might come for the stone as well."

Anomer made no move to take his sword, so Noetos pulled it from the door frame, letting the overseer's body slide down the blade and off the tip. His son was trying to wipe blood from his eyes. Not his own.

No, one of the miners *was* alive, the one whose face Noetos had slashed. His laborious breathing sucked through the hole in his cheek, through which teeth, bone and blood were visible. His eyes were clouded with pain.

"Answers," Noetos said to his son, looking to distract him from Papunas' blood.

He led Anomer over to where the suffering miner lay.

"We'll get help for you if you talk to us. Whose plan was this?"

A hiss of pain escaped the man's compressed lips, but no answer was forthcoming.

"I can make your death extremely painful," Noetos said. "Did Papunas put you up to this?"

"Answer the question," Anomer said in the shattered-crystal Voice. Though merely brushed with the edge of the compulsion, Noetos could feel the power in the words.

"No, not Papunas," the man said, his mouth springing open. The words were wet with blood. "Was Frina firs' suggested it. We worked on Papunas all the way north.

Didn't agree until day before yesterday." More sucking sounds as the miner sought breath.

"Was Omiy part of your plan? Seren? Gawl? My sworn men? Bregor?"

The lips clamped shut. Anomer repeated the question. Icy daggers pricked at Noetos's soul. *Such power*. Without the huanu stone he would not be able to resist it.

"No, none a them. Had ta keep it secret from Seren and from the Seal. Gawl laughed at us, told us you'd kill us all. Omiy was in for a while." The man stopped, panting, sucking. "Pulled out at the last minute. Wanted the stone for hisself. Promised not to tell you."

Damn. But at least his men had remained faithful. Even Gawl.

"What have you done with the others?" Anomer asked.

"Trussed 'em up. Couldn't have 'em tryin' t' warn you. Woulda used 'em as servants after. Frina's idea. Stupid." The man swallowed, then leaned forward and vomited clots of blood onto the floor. "Am I dying?" he asked them.

"No, you're dead," Noetos replied, and rammed his sword through the man's throat. His hands were shaking with anger; he could barely grip the sword's hilt to pull it free.

"He would have lived had he answered without compulsion," the fisherman explained to his son.

"All this death over a stone," Anomer said, his voice rough with shock and anguish. "The Recruiters told me of its value."

Noetos made to show him the huanu stone, then thought better of it. "Then they told you of its properties? How it negates magic? Anomer, for pity's sake, promise me you'll never touch it."

His son shuddered. "I don't want to see it as long as I live."

They found Omiy trying to loosen the rope binding Bregor and Noetos's sworn men. The alchemist squealed when he saw them and tried to run away. A word from Anomer slowed his progress, allowing Noetos—himself moving slower now because of his wound—to clap a hand on the man's shoulder.

"You sold us out."

"No, yes, yes, but I was wrong, I decided not to take the huanu stone after all."

"You decided not to share it with the others."

"Yes, no, yes, yes, you're hurting me. I'd rather you kept it than see it broken up amongst thugs, yes. They forced me to help them, they did."

"And the explosion? Was that part of the plan?"

Omiy cowered at the menace in the fisherman's voice.

"Yes, yes it was, part of *a* plan, but not part of *my* plan. I never intended the explosion to be so large, no, most certainly not. Someone tampered with the pipe, I'm certain of it, packed more chemicals in; there was less remaining in my pack than there ought to have been, I tell you the truth. Fools, they could have blown themselves up or poisoned themselves at the very least, yes; chenaile is a dangerous chemical. Perhaps they have poisoned themselves, ha! Dead now, they'll never know, oh my. They wanted to bring the hillside down on top of you, standing there as bait, and on the Recruiters, while we hid out of the way. Find the stone in the rubble afterwards."

"But how did they know of my father's plan?" Anomer said.

"Ow, the boy's voice, it nips at me. Unnecessary, tell him to stop." The alchemist pulled his head turtle-like into his neck. "I told them, silly, of course I did. When they suggested making the explosion larger I broke with them, yes I did. I want no interference with my craft, oh no. But I did not anticipate they would interfere anyway, woe to them. Someone could have been killed!"

"Someone *was* killed," Noetos said, and drew his sword. Omiy squeaked again.

Anomer reached out and placed a finger near the tip of the blade, steadying it. "No more slaughter," he said. "You had no good reason to kill the last of the miners in the chandlery, and none to kill this man either. Put your anger away and think of your remaining men."

Noetos grunted. Much as he didn't want to admit it, his son's words were wise. The tip of his blade made short work of the ropes.

"Did you know about this, Gawl?" he asked.

"Yeh, but I thought they wouldn't have the guts to go ahead with it. Didn't realise Papunas was involved, or I'd a spilled to you."

"Very well. We'll leave this place of death and travel north to Raceme. From there a boat can be hired to take Bregor back to Fossa. The Fossan folk—if any remain—need to know what has happened here. Anomer and I will go on, with any of my sworn men who wish to accompany us. There are questions I wish to ask the Keeper of Andratan."

"I'll come with ya," Dagla said eagerly. "I was sorry to've been caught. We c'd hear 'em plannin' to do you with their swords. I woulda helped, honest."

"I believe you would have, Dagla, and yes, you're welcome to accompany me. As are all of you, barring Omiy. The alchemist I bid return to Eisarn Pit. He should consider himself fortunate to retain his life."

Bregor dusted himself off. "And me? What if I have questions for the leader of Bhrudwo?"

"But . . . your wife. You can't abandon her, surely?"

"If I go back now, I'll never leave again. Whoever remains will want me to help rebuild, and how could I say no? But some things are more important than people. I believe she'd want to know the answers, too, especially since Opuntia lost her life. We both loved her, you know."

"Both? You mean . . . Hegeoman, I cannot believe this!" Noetos searched his heart for the rage that ought to have been there, but found nothing. An emptiness, maybe, and a great deal of shame. More shame than would be attached to Bregor's behaviour.

"The world is a larger place than you allow for," Bregor said. "I go north to find answers for all three of us."

"Our immediate destination has not changed," the fisherman decided. "We need to purchase supplies. Horses, too, if we can afford them. And one more unpleasant task remains. We must despoil the dead miners and take everything of value. We will not reach Andratan otherwise."

In the end, only Pril of Noetos's sworn men decided to accompany Omiy back to Eisarn Pit. The pull of family, he said, was stronger than any desire to get answers. Besides, he added with a shrug of his shoulders, he didn't really have any questions.

Seren agreed to stay with Noetos and the others. He was ashamed, he said, of how Papunas and his fellow miners had acted. He felt he owed Noetos something. For his part, Noetos was glad the man had made this decision.

The two men returning to Eisarn left that afternoon. Omiy asked for a mule, but Noetos refused. As an afterthought the fisherman confiscated Omiy's bagged and cloth-wrapped chemicals, with the view to selling them at the Raceme market.

"Oh, my," the alchemist moaned. "You'll get but a fraction of their value. The chenaile alone is worth more than a year's wages, so it is. Won't you reconsider?"

"Not after that revelation," Noetos said. "Now, be off with you. Pril, make sure the fool doesn't get into any mischief. He may have repented of his actions, but I no longer trust him."

"Aye," the morose lad said, and slouched off, the alchemist scuttling along beside him like a skittish spider.

They closed the door of the chandlery on the dead miners. The task of digging graves would have delayed them a day or more, and there were very few supplies remaining. "Traitors don't deserve a burial," Noetos said as he forced the rotted door into the frame.

"No," agreed Bregor. "They do not." He sighed. "I wonder, given everything that has happened here, how Andratan will view us?"

No one had an answer, but the question gave them something to think about.

Though they travelled north, away from the tropics, the weather grew warmer each day. Summer, in all its intensity, had overtaken them. Cloaks were stored in panniers, sleeves were removed from tunics, and even boots were dispensed with on occasion when gentle grasses flanked the road.

During the first two days Noetos suffered considerable discomfort. Neither of his wounds threatened his life, or even his long-term health: losing a finger was common-place among miners, Gawl told him. He'd get used to it, adapt. His back stung whenever he swung his arms, so while it healed Noetos adopted a stiff gait.

It was not until after they had crossed the bridge over the Saar River that Anomer began talking about his time as captive of the Recruiters. He had resisted them for a few days, he said, but much of what they endeavoured to instruct him made sense. "Particularly what they said about drawing on my Voice, of finding a harmony be-tween action and intent," the boy said excitedly.

"What do you mean?" Noetos asked. The seven of them wended their way down a narrow lane set between waist-high cornfields.

"They explained about the importance of intent, which comes before action. They teach that the Voice can affect the intent of weak minds, altering or at least limiting the action that follows. I used my Voice to slow the reactions of the miners in the chandlery. They didn't really want to be there, they doubted their ability to defeat you, so I grafted my words onto their doubts and fears. Then there is something Ataphaxus called the Wordweave. Apparently, someone strong in the Voice can say one thing but com-municate another. It has the same effect as what I accom-plished in the chandlery, except those affected don't realise it has been done to them. I have not yet mastered it." The words carried with them the faintest regret, as though his son wished his rescue had been delayed a few more days.

"You want to learn, don't you?"

"Well, of course."

"Despite the warning your sister gave her life to bring?" Noetos hardened his voice. "She told us that her Voice drew on the power of others. She said it damaged them."

Anomer had the grace to look embarrassed. "Yes, but father, what if the benefit to others outweighs the harm done? Wouldn't it be immoral not to learn the skill in case such a situation arose?"

For a blissful moment Noetos was back in Fisher House, arguing ethics with his son. "And who would be the judge, Anomer? Someone who stands to benefit from the use of such power?"

"Why not?" Bregor said from behind Noetos's left shoulder, shattering the illusion. "You decide when to use your sword, wounding someone to benefit someone else. How is this weapon of Anomer's any different?"

"Because it is unseen, and cannot be countered," Noetos said. "If I come at you with a sword, at least you can attempt to defend yourself, or run, or even try to talk your way out of danger. But what can you do if someone draws from your strength to use magic?"

"'Tis like the huanu stone," Seren said. "It draws magic from people; the fisherman's son draws strength from people by magic."

Noetos turned to the overseer and frowned. "Surely nothing like the stone!" As soon as he'd uttered the words he snapped his mouth shut. There was some kind of sense in what Seren had said; it would bear thinking about.

Anomer talked about his mother, of what she had told him during the days of their captivity: her love for the

Hegeoman and his wife; her sorrow at what Noetos had become. The Recruiters had asked them many questions about their lives, digging to discover as much as they could about Noetos and the huanu stone. Over a period of days Ataphaxus, the main questioner, put a number of facts together, eventually announcing he had solved the riddle posed by the talented fisherman.

"He said you were hiding in Fossa. That all you'd told us about your own parents was lies. I didn't believe them at first, but Mother did. She knew something about your stories didn't make sense. She was angry, father. I do believe that if you had rescued us on the day she learned who you really were, she would have taken to you with a sword."

"That is why I never told her," Noetos said. "The constant vision of her taking ship to Aneheri, marching into the Neherian court and announcing our claim to Old Roudhos. How long do you think we would have lived after that?"

"You should have told her," his son said. "It destroyed her, being shown she'd been taken for a fool all this time. Better still, with such a past you ought not to have married."

"You are right. Noetos said. "The cost, of course, would have been the non-existence of two pleasing children."

Anomer frowned. "Even so," he said eventually.

"And it is not as though your mother didn't have her own secrets, apparently," Noetos remarked. Even as he spoke he regretted the words. *Self-justification*.

"How do you know I don't have secrets of my own?" Anomer said.

"I know you're more sympathetic to the Recruiters and to Andratan than you're prepared to admit."

"That's not true! I saw what had been done to Arathé. How can you believe I would support a system that destroyed my sister?"

"Yet you see benefits in what the Recruiters bring, don't you, boy? You may travel north to understand, to learn, to perhaps effect improvement. I go to destroy." *To have my revenge.*

Bregor interrupted them. "You're sure the servant woman was your sister?"

"Without a single doubt." Anomer did not use his Voice, but the effect was the same.

"Ah," the Hegeoman breathed.

Noetos growled under his breath. *Finally he believes. After all my arguments, all the time we spent debating, he delivers the crowning insult.*

Five days after crossing the bridge over the Saar River, nine days in total north of the chandlery under Saros Rake, Noetos and his companions stood at the crest of a grassy hill and looked down on Raceme. Beyond the walled city the harbour glittered, though to the east a summer storm grumbled and complained, throwing the open sea into shadow.

"Big place, in't it," Dagla said.

A weight of memory settled on the fisherman's shoulders as he gazed at the familiar walls and towers of Raceme Oldtown. His eye was drawn above the cliffs, beyond the battlements, to the old Summer Palace, where he had spent so much of his childhood. The Palace seemed smaller than he remembered, a little more worn, grown old. As was the whole city; in the shadow of the approaching rain, Raceme lacked the sparkle he recalled. The town hunched over itself, as though ducking to avoid a beating.

Noetos set his feet on the first of the six flights of stone steps he knew so well. Hundreds of years old, each step had been worn smooth, dipping in the centre where most of the people had placed careless feet, like the fisherman did now. Each step seemed to take a season off his life; he knew how many were in each set, and worked out that, if it were true, he would arrive at the Suggate, the only way through Raceme's wall from the south, at about sixteen years of age.

He stepped off the last set and looked back. He'd left his companions well behind; simple proximity to this place had energised him. "Come on!" he called, ignoring the sharp looks this garnered from people using the stairs, and waved to Bregor and the others.

Easy, fisherman, he told himself. *Your wife died a week ago. This behaviour does not become you.*

He curled a lip. *None of my behaviour becomes me.*

Raceme had grown in the last twenty years. Houses had been built outside the walls, most constructed using timber as opposed to the whitewashed stone within the city proper. Conditions looked poorer here, certainly poorer than he remembered in Raceme itself. Perhaps the city had cleansed itself of its lower classes by forcing them beyond the wall; it was the sort of thing the councillors would do, conservatives that they were. Or had been.

A strange dualism settled on the fisherman. He had become two people: a boy, eager to explore, to seek out adventure, to learn, to whom everything was sharp-edged and filled with wonder; and at the same time a man, world-weary and with aching heart and blurry eyes. He was young and old, happy and sad, full and empty, home and in a strange place.

"Are we going in?" Anomer asked.

"Oh, of course," Noetos muttered, coming to himself. Or perhaps his two selves walked in step for a moment. "Bregor has the coin. The council will want payment before we can pass through Suggate and enter the city."

Anomer passed the message on, and before long Bregor was negotiating with city officials.

"Fifty? Fifty!" The Hegeoman's voice echoed in the narrow arch of the Suggate. "We wish only to visit, not to buy property!" Noetos craned his head forward, hoping Bregor would not make trouble.

"We ask for such a sum to ensure visitors to Raceme have sufficient means to afford the food and accommodation offered here." Noetos didn't need to see the official's face; he could imagine it from the words and the tone of voice.

"Taking fifty will ensure we no longer have the means!"

"Then, sir, you should enquire of lodings in the Shambles, through which you have but recently passed. I understand the epidemic of lice has all but abated, and as long as you are not frightened of roaches you should be able to get a decent night's sleep."

"But fifty is seven per person!"

"Aye, and that represents a thirty per cent discount."

"Tell him about the special citizen exemption," came a woman's voice from the back of the small toll booth set into the Suggate arch.

"Ah yes, the exemption. If you can induce a friend or

relative who lives in the city to accommodate you, we will waive the charge—as long as he or she presents him or herself here before you enter the city." The official sounded as though he was enjoying himself.

"That's stupid," Bregor complained. "How would my relative know I was here?"

"You could pay a fee of ten, go and find your relative, bring him or her to this window, and receive your discount then."

Noetos had endured enough. "Here's your fifty," he said, stepping forward and slapping the coins down on the stone sill. "And ten extra for your trouble. Good day."

"And a plesant day to you, sir, and I hope your bagman gets better soon," was the cheery response.

"Let's find an inn," Noetos suggested to his men once they and their mules were within the city. "I don't anticipate being here more than a day or two, but we do have to purchase supplies, so we cannot afford the best accommodation. I wonder if the Man-o'-War is still operating?"

"Likely," Tumar said. "Was last time I was here, anyway. Couple'a year ago."

A woman gave them directions, and within minutes they stood outside a three-storey whitewashed building with a green-tiled roof, a wooden sign in the shape of a jellyfish hanging above the orange door.

"My father knew the man who once owned this establishment," Noetos said to his son. Then, to them all: "Let's get settled in here. No funny business or drunken antics, lads; the militia here are very strict. You'll get a night in the stocks and we'll have to pay handsomely to have you released. Trust me, time in the stocks in a port city is not a pleasant experience. You don't know you're alive until you're being pelted with rotten fish guts. I'll sort out an arrangement with the innkeeper, though there shouldn't be too much trouble: the place looks half-empty."

The innkeeper was not the one his father had known. In fact, this innkeeper hadn't heard of his predecessor. He gave Noetos and his companions the entire second floor, which was accessed by a series of wide but rickety steps. Four large rooms would sleep them all in relative comfort.

"No wonder it was cheap," Bregor said. "It's built out over the stables." The stench was dreadful.

"It's only for a night'r two," Seren reminded him. "Not half as bad as Papunas' wind, rest his soul. Smells build up in a mine, this is nothing. No windows in mines." He opened the shutters, knocking a bird from its perch.

"Ah, salt air 'n' pigeon shit," Dagla said. "Perfect."

The seven men gathered in the private taproom on the third floor. The public bar down below had already become rather crowded, and prices for guests were slightly cheaper in the smaller, quieter room. A lone barmaid took their orders. While they waited for their wine and ale, they took their chairs and sat in a semicircle by the window, which framed a view of Raceme Oldtown, showing cobbled streets leading down to the port and the ocean beyond.

"Could get some rain," Seren said, easing off his boots.

"Nah, that storm's been out there fer ages," Gawl said. "A small one."

"We don't usually get to see storms unless they're right overhead, o'course," Dagla added.

Noetos looked closer at the masses of clouds billowing into the grey sky, then at the grey rain-curtains the clouds wore like skirts. Faint lightning flickered in the gathering gloom.

"The storm appears small because it is so far away," he said. "It is enormous, and it is coming this way. We will have wind and rain aplenty tonight."

Their drinks arrived, and for a time they dispensed with talk. Later, they spoke quietly of what direction they might take in their journey north, and whether it was better to go by land or sea. After some time the men took their meal in the taproom. Stew and turnips, the quantity and quality both impressive.

"Here!" Dagla cried, calling them over to the window. "In't that Omiy?"

"Looks like him," Seren muttered. "Turn around, you loose-head."

Gawl puckered his lips as if to whistle.

"Don't be a fool," Bregor said, raising his hand. "If it is him, he'll be looking for us. Let him go."

"'Tis him all right," Dagla said.

"Then keep back from the window until he's gone," said Noetos.

"Look at the storm now," Anomer breathed.

All eyes left the street and traced the ragged clouds up, up and further up. Much closer now, the true size of the storm was apparent. The westering sun painted the foremost clouds a pale yellow-tinged white, while those that followed took on various shades of darkness. At that moment a flickering tongue flashed across the sky; the ensuing thunderous boom took ten heartbeats to rattle the inn's shutters.

The barmaid came over to the window. "Storm's coming," she announced unnecessarily. "My job to shut the windows."

"It won't be here for a while yet," Noetos said

reasonably. "We'll close the shutters when we've finished—what are those?"

The fitful sun flicked a few stray rays across the sea at the base of the storm, illuminating a series of white sails scattered across the water, all filled with the wind bringing the following tempest.

"Fishing boats coming back to harbour," Anomer commented. "I hope they make it."

"No," Noetos said. "Not fishing boats. Oh, Alkuon, it's the Neherian fleet."

As the words left his mouth a bell began to toll, insistent, frantic. It was joined by another, and another.

People appeared at doors and windows; within minutes the same people left their homes, clutching whatever valuables they owned, and hurried up the streets towards Suggate and the hills. Others ran down the streets towards the port: eager sightseers, or determined men with weapons in their hands.

The fisherman pulled the shutters closed with a bang, then turned his stony face on the others.

"Come on, boys," he said, "gather your swords. We're needed down at the docks."

Gawl smirked at Dagla's pale face. "C'mon, lad, another chance for the Fisherman's army to make a name for itself."

"I feel sick," the boy complained.

Bregor groaned. "You'll have no need of a seal this time. Perhaps I should stay behind."

"But Raceme needs clear heads and intelligent minds," Noetos said. "Come on. If the Neherians take Raceme, there'll be no safe place for the heroes of Makyra Bay."

        *   *   *

Chaos ruled Raceme Harbour. A groyne of stone protected the inner waters from the worst of the waves; it was lined with people who, Noetos considered, had no business being there. The militia wasted no time with them, instead forming up along the top of the crenellated wall a hundred paces behind the docks. Noetos offered himself and his men to the young commander, who accepted with profuse thanks.

"My superior has gone to Tochar to be with his ailing father," the commander groaned. "I could do with his advice."

"We faced the Neherians at Makyra Bay and drove them off with the help of the villagers," Noetos told him. "Had I thought they'd try their luck further north I would have alerted the city authorities as soon as we arrived. I'm only sorry I didn't."

"You any good with that thing?" the commander asked Noetos, indicating his blade.

"Good enough, and so are my men."

"Very well. I'm sending a contingent of volunteers down to the docks. I'll make no secret of the fact that you'll likely end up as fodder for the Neherians unless you're more skilled than you look, old man. Up to you, but you can go with them if you wish. Now, I have men to deploy. Here's Captain Cohamma—do as he tells you. You're conscripted, the lot of you." He walked a couple of paces away, then turned back to them. "Oh, yes. Pay is five each per day. Make sure you're around to collect it."

Captain Cohamma turned out to be a capable, nononsense man in his fifties without a single tooth in his head. This made his instructions hard to follow.

"Gerron wiffit! Downa docks 'n' be reddy for me orders!"

Along with Noetos's army and the contingent of fifty militia, another twenty or so volunteers—many, by their expressions, regretting their impulsive bravado—lined up at the main dock.

The first of the Neherian boats came into view. As a lead craft it was surprisingly small, a dory with a single sail, reminiscent of Noetos's own boat. Behind it came the multiple-masted ships they had seen off Kymos and Makyra Bay, sails billowing like clouds, gaining on the lead boat.

Unless the small dory was not part of the Neherian fleet. A fisherman taken unawares by the storm, now fleeing the enemy fleet, trying desperately to make it to harbour . . .

"Father," Anomer said, his face drained of all colour. "Father, look. That is your old boat."

What?

The white dory breasted the swell in the manner he knew so well. Whitewash blackened by the scars wrought by fire. Single square-set sail cracking in the wind. Two figures wringing every last bit of speed from her, one young and broad-shouldered, one old and with a gut, both naked above the waist, their shouts audible as they passed the groyne to the cheers of the spectators there. And a third figure low in the stern, one hand on the tiller, the other hand bailing bilge water.

The first of the Neherian ships, a triple-masted carrack, bore down on the dory as though it were standing still.

"They won't be able to fit past the groyne!" one of the militiamen shouted.

But it seemed the Neherian captain had scant regard for his own vessel, driving it between the groyne and the city wall. A dozen spears were flung from the deck; a number of the spectators fell.

The younger of the two men sailing the dory—Mustar, Noetos could now see—shouted to the older, Sautea, who yelled something in response. They drew near the dock, a few hundred paces in front of the slowing carrack. Perhaps the Neherian captain had some sense after all. Behind the huge flagship, other Neherian vessels came into view. Someone threw a rope down to Mustar, whose muscles rippled as he drew it tight and secured it. Sautea clapped the boy on the shoulder, then extended a hand to the third figure.

The figure stood up, a woman. A woman who had guided Noetos's burned boat into Raceme Harbour on the wings of a storm, the wrath of Neherius behind her. Eyes glistening, she stared up at the spectators, obviously searching for someone, and Noetos's heart stilled as he recognised her.

Arathé!

extras

orbit

meet the author

Russell Kirkpatrick's love of literature and a chance en-counter with fantasy novels as a teenager opened up a vast number of possibilities to him. The idea that he could marry storytelling and mapmaking (his other passion) into one project grabbed him and wouldn't let go. He lives in New Zealand with his wife and two children. Find out more about Russell Kirkpatrick at www.russell kirkpatrick.com.

introducing

If you enjoyed **PATH OF REVENGE,**
look out for

DARK HEART

Book Two of the Broken Man Trilogy
by Russell Kirkpatrick

NOETOS THE FISHERMAN REACHED out a
trembling hand to his daughter. The daughter he had
thought dead.

At this moment nothing else mattered: not the threat to
Raceme, not the approaching Neherian fleet, not the coming storm. His fingers hovered above hers.

Don't touch her, part of his mind warned. He stiffened.
What about the huanu stone? The stone, of which he apparently had the largest piece known, stole magic from
whatever it touched. What would it do to Arathé, so
strong in the Voice magic?

You old fool, he chided himself, and blew out a relieved breath. *You left it in your room.*

You old fool, he chided himself. *You left it in your room.*

As his fingers touched hers he allowed himself to believe what his eyes told him. He knew of waking dreams, but had never experienced one: this must be what they felt like. The coarseness of her skin, calloused along her once-fine fingers; the unflattering weight of her, surprising despite his knowing how she had been mistreated by her supposed teachers. But, notwithstanding all this, warmth where he had expected the coldness of death. He had, after all, seen her with a knife buried in her back.

A waking dream or reality—which was it? After all that had happened to him and his family, could Noetos really argue there was a difference? As his mind wandered, the dream-like feeling intensified.

Of course he remembered Arathé couldn't talk, her tongue having been taken by the cruel masters of Andratan, along with so many other things. Yet, as he grasped her hand and pulled her up to the wharf, he could not stop himself asking the question.

"How?"

Arathé shrugged her shoulders in reply. As he watched, her eyes flicked left and right, as though looking for something or someone, widening when they rested a moment on her brother, Anomer, then flicking again, searching.

"Muhh?" she said, her tongueless mouth unable to shape the word. "Muh-huh?"

Noetos knew who Arathé was looking for.

"She . . . she . . ." He could barely bring himself to say it. "She is dead."

But it wasn't my fault, he wanted to add. He couldn't:

Arathé would know it for a lie. His foolish plan to rescue her mother and brother at Saros Rake had cost Opuntia her life. And, to be honest, he'd cared much more about his son's survival than that of his wife.

There. I've admitted it.

His daughter's sunken eyes widened slightly, then narrowed, as she stared into his eyes. Her hand, still clasping his, tightened around his fingers. A fraction of a second later she jerked him forward.

He tried to keep his balance, but as he stumbled past her she pushed him, hard. He overbalanced, then fell from the wharf and plunged into the water, narrowly missing his boat.

The Racemen kept their harbour dredged, artificially deep. Within seconds he was at the bottom, knees on the muddy sea floor.

Cast away, his mind screamed at him. *She cast me away.*

He could see only a few feet through the murk, and for a moment could make nothing of his surroundings. Dark hull shapes, grey clouds, the flickering silhouettes of fish. He would not drown, he told himself; he was the Fisher, a man comfortable in the water. It was only shock that pinned his arms to his side. Only shock. His daughter hated him. If his daughter hated him, he must truly have mishandled things. Opuntia's death—was Arathé blaming him? She could know nothing of the circumstances, yet she had already decided he was to blame, as though she had developed some kind of mind-reading ability.

She cast me away!

His limbs were heavy, so heavy. Nevertheless, he began to move them, sluggishly at first. He needed to explain things to her before Anomer and Bregor filled her ears with their view of events. Actually, he needed to breathe.

It's not all my fault!

Something snagged the collar of his tunic, pulling him back, and his head jerked forward. His mouth opened involuntarily and the last of his air bubbled from his lips.

"He's not dead," said someone.

"It'll take more than a dousing to kill this fool," said someone else.

"Fuhh, fuhh, fuhh'" a third voice repeated. It sounded distressed.

"He's all right, Arathé," said the first voice. "He's breathing."

Hardness under his back, water on his face, light in his eyes, the sounds of concern in his ears.

"We need to move him. The Neherians will be ashore in a moment, Alkuon curse them." The second voice was agitated. "Can't leave him for them, much as I'd like to."

"You grab his legs then," a new voice said. "I'll take his arms."

"No!" Noetos gasped, then coughed. The light coalesced into a ring of faces staring down at him. Arathé, Bregor, Anomer, Sautea, Mustar. "I can stand," he said. "Give me a moment."

He barely made it to his feet. Anomer placed a steadying hand on the small of his back. His son's wet clothes told Noetos who had pulled him from the water.

The fisherman glanced at Arathé. His daughter averted her face.

He wanted her to explain why she'd pushed him from

the wharf; he wanted to hear her say "Father, it was an accident," to tell him that really she loved him and understood he'd tried his best to save his family from the Recruiters. But another part of him admired her for not saying anything of the sort, for holding her silence. He knew her rejection of him, whatever the motivation, had some justification. His plan, however cruelly undermined by Omiy the alchemist, had been a poor one to start with.

Noetos looked out to sea. So much needed to be said, but they were out of time. The storm was upon them, white sails followed by swirling black clouds.